RENEGADE'S MAGIC

RENEGADE'S MAGIC

BOOK THREE OF
THE SOLDIER SON TRILOGY

ROBIN HOBB

An Imprint of HarperCollins*Publishers*

This book is a work of fiction. The characters, incidents, and dialogue are drawn from the author's imagination and are not to be construed as real. Any resemblance to actual events or persons, living or dead, is entirely coincidental.

Library of Congress Cataloging-in-Publication Data

Hobb, Robin.
  Renegade's magic / Robin Hobb.—1st ed.
    p. cm.—(The soldier son trilogy; bk. 3)
  ISBN 978-0-06-075764-9
  I. Title.
  PS3558.O33636R46 2008
  813'.54—dc22   2007029816

08 09 10 11 12   TD/RRD   10 9 8 7 6 5 4 3 2 1

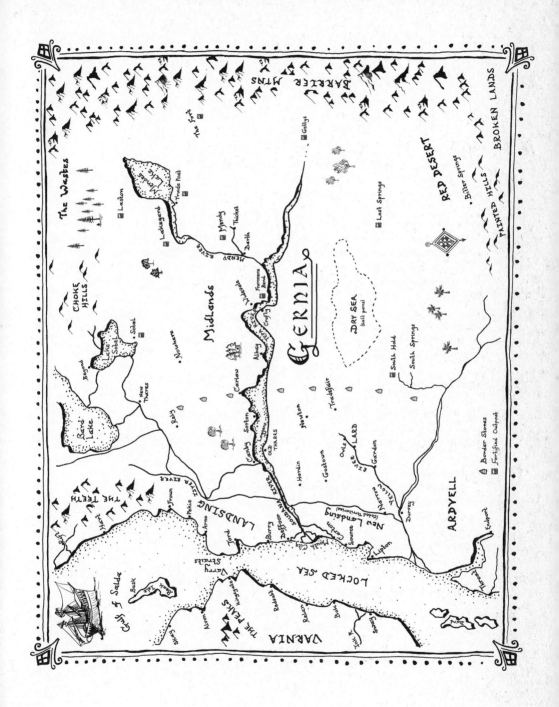

CONTENTS

CHAPTER ONE

SOLDIER'S END

I never spoke up for myself at my court-martial.

I stood in the box where they put me, and tried not to think of the agonizing bite of the leg irons around my calves. They were too small for a man of my flesh, and the cold iron bit deep into the meat of my legs, burning and numbing at the same time. At the moment, the pain mattered to me more than the outcome of the hearing. I already knew how it would end.

That pain is chiefly what I remember of my trial. It hazes my memories in red. A number of witnesses spoke against me. I recall their righteous voices as they detailed my crimes to the assembled judges. Rape. Murder. Necrophilia. Desecration of a graveyard. My outrage and horror at being accused of such things had been eroded by the utter hopelessness of my situation. Witness after witness spoke against me. Threads of rumor, hearsay from a dead man's lips, suspicions and circumstantial evidence were twisted together into a rope of evidence, stout enough to hang me.

I think I know why Spink never addressed any questions directly to me. Lieutenant Spinrek, my friend since our Cavalla

Academy days, was supposed to be defending me. I'd told him that I simply wanted to plead guilty and get it over with. That had angered him. Perhaps that was why he didn't ask me to testify on my own behalf. He didn't trust me to tell the truth and deny all the charges. He feared I'd take the easy way out.

I would have.

I didn't fear the hangman's gibbet. It would be a quick end to a life corrupted by a foreign magic. Walk up the steps, put my head into the noose, and step off into darkness. The weight of my falling body would probably have jerked my head right off. No dangle and strangle for me. Just a quick exit from an existence that was too tangled and spoiled to repair.

Whatever I might have said in my own defense would have made no difference. Wrongs had been done, ugly, evil things, and the citizens of Gettys were determined that someone had to pay for them. Gettys was a rough place to live, a settlement half military outpost and half penal colony on the easternmost boundary of the Kingdom of Gernia. Its citizens were no strangers to rape and murder. But the crimes I was accused of went beyond the spectrum of passion and violence into something darker, too dark even for Gettys to tolerate. Someone had to wear the villain's black cape and pay the toll for such transgressions, and who better than the solitary fat man who lived in the graveyard and was rumored to have doings with the Specks?

So I was convicted. The cavalla officers who sat in judgment on me sentenced me to hang, and I accepted that. I had shamed my regiment. At that moment, my execution seemed the simplest escape from a life that had become the antithesis of every dream I'd ever had. I'd die and be done with disappointment and failure. Hearing my sentence was almost a relief.

But the magic that had poisoned my life was not about to let me go so easily.

Killing me was not enough for my accusers. Evil would be punished with as cruel and vicious a vengeance as they could imagine. Darkness would be balanced with darkness. When the second half of my sentence was pronounced, horror froze me. Before I ascended the gallows to make that final drop, I'd receive one thousand lashes.

I will always recall that stunned moment. The sentence went beyond execution, beyond punishment, to total destruction. As it stripped the flesh from my bones, it would strip away all dignity as well. No man, no matter what his courage, could grit his teeth and keep silent through a thousand lashes. They would mock and jeer me as I shrieked and begged. I would go to my death hating them and myself.

I'd been born to be a soldier. As the second son of a nobleman, I had been decreed by the good god to be a soldier. Despite all that had befallen me, despite the foreign magic that had infected and poisoned me, despite my ejection from the King's Cavalla Academy, despite my father's disowning of me and the scorn of my fellows, I had done my best to serve my king as a soldier. This was what it had earned me. I would scream and weep and plead for mercy before folk who saw me only as a monster. The lash would strip my body naked of both clothing and flesh, exposing the sagging layers of fat that had been their first excuse to hate me. I would faint and be revived with a dash of vinegar on my back. I'd piss myself and dangle helplessly from my manacled wrists. I'd be a corpse long before they hanged my remains. They knew it and so did I.

Even my corrupted and maimed life seemed a better choice than that death. The magic had sought to take me from my own people and use me as a tool against them. I'd fought it. But that final night in my cell, I knew the magic of the Speck folk offered me my only opportunity to save myself. When the magic tore down the walls of my prison, I took the opportunity. I escaped.

But neither the magic nor the good folk of Gettys were done with me. I think the magic knew that I'd given only lip service to my surrender to it. But it demanded all of me, my entire life, with no ties left to bind me to this place and this people, and what I had never given willingly, it now took from me.

As I fled from the fort, I encountered a troop of returning cavalla soldiers. I knew it was not my bad luck that put Captain Thayer in charge of the troop. It was the magic that put me in the hands of the man whose dead wife I had apparently despoiled. It had ended predictably. The tired, frustrated men he led had rapidly degenerated into a mob. They had killed me in the streets, his soldiers holding me for him while he beat me to death. Justice and vengeance were sated on that dusty street in the small hours of the morning. Then, slaked with violence, they had dispersed to their homes and beds. They did not speak to one another of what they had done.

And in the hour before dawn broke over Gettys, a dead man fled the town.

CHAPTER TWO

FLIGHT

The huge hooves of my big horse made a steady drumming as we fled. As we passed the last outlying farms of the scattered town that surrounded the King's fort at Gettys, I glanced back over my shoulder. The town was silent and still. The flames on the burning walls of the prison had subsided, but a dark smear of smoke still smudged the graying sky. The men who had fought Epiny's sabotage all night would be trudging home to their beds now. I kept my gaze fixed on the road before me and rode grimly on. Gettys had never been my home, but it was hard to leave it.

Ahead of me, light began to spill over the mountaintops. The sun would soon be up. I had to reach the shelter of the forest before men began to stir. There would be some early risers today, people anxious to secure good vantage points to watch my flogging and execution. My mouth twisted, imagining their disappointment when they heard of my death.

The King's Road, that ambitious undertaking of King Troven of Gernia, unfurled before me, dusty, rutted, potholed, but arrow straight. I followed it. It led east, ever east. In the King's vision, it threaded through and over the Barrier Mountains and on, until it reached the far sea. In my king's dreams, the road would be a lifeline of trade for landlocked Gernia. In reality, his road ended only a few miles past Gettys, its growth foundered at the edge of the vale where the Specks' ancestor trees grew. For years, the indigenous Specks had used their magic to incite fear and desolation in the road workers and halt the road's march. The spell the Specks cast varied from a sharp terror that made men crawling cowards to a deep despair that sapped them of all will to work. Beyond the end of the road, the forest awaited me.

On the road ahead of me, I saw what I'd been dreading. A horseman was coming toward me at a weary walk. The rider sat tall in his saddle, and that as much as the brave green of his jacket labeled him a cavalla soldier. I wondered where he was coming from and why he rode alone and if I'd have to kill him. As I drew closer, the rakish angle of his hat and the bright yellow scarf at his throat betrayed what he was: one of our scouts. My heart lifted a trifle. There was a chance he'd know nothing about the charges against me and my trial. The scouts were often out for weeks at a time. He showed no interest in me as our horses approached one another, and as I passed him, he did not even lift a hand in greeting.

I felt a pang of sharp regret as I went by. But for the magic, that could have been me. I recognized Tiber from the Cavalla Academy, but he did not know me. The magic had changed me from the slim and fit cadet I'd been. The fat, disheveled trooper lolloping along on his ungainly mount was beneath the lieutenant's notice. At his current pace, it would be hours before he got to the town and heard that the mob had killed me in the streets. I wondered if he'd think he had seen a ghost.

Clove cantered laboriously on. The crossbred draft horse was no one's idea of a mount built for either speed or endurance. But he was big, and for a man of my height and bulk, he was the only possible steed that could carry me comfortably. It came to me that this would be the last time I'd ride him; I couldn't take him into the forest with me. Pain gouged me again; he'd be one more beloved thing that I'd have to leave behind. He was running heavily now, nearly spent by our mad flight from Gettys.

Well outside Gettys, a wagon trail diverged from the King's Road and led up to the cemetery. Clove slowed as we approached it, and I abruptly changed my plans. The cabin I had called home for the past year was up that trail. Was there anything left there that I'd want to carry forward into my new life? Spink had removed my soldier-son journal and taken it to his home. I was grateful for that. My journal held the full tale of how the magic had entered my life and slowly taken it away from me. There might still be letters in my cabin, papers that could connect me to a past and a family that I needed to abandon. I would let nothing tie me to either Lord Burvelle, neither my uncle nor my father. Let my death shame no one except myself.

Clove slipped into his ponderous trot as he labored up the hill. It had been only a couple of weeks since I'd last been here, but it felt like years. Grass was already sprouting on the many graves we had dug for the summer victims of the plague. The trench graves were still bare soil; they had been the last graves to be covered, when the plague was at its height and we grave diggers could no longer keep up with the steady influx of bodies. They would be the last scars to heal.

I pulled Clove in outside my cabin. I dismounted cautiously, but felt a mere twinge of pain. Only yesterday the leg irons had cut into my tendons; the magic was healing me at a prodigious rate. My horse blew at me, shuddered his coat, and then walked a few steps before dropping his head to graze. I hurried to my door. I'd quickly destroy any evidence of my former identity and then be on my way.

The window shutters were closed. I shut the door behind me as I stepped into the cabin. Then I recoiled in dismay as Kesey sat up in my bed. My fellow grave digger had been sleeping with a stocking cap on his bald head to keep the night chill away. He knuckled his eyes and gaped at me, his hanging jaw revealing gaps in his teeth. "Nevare?" he protested. "I thought you were going to—"

His words fumbled to a halt as he realized exactly how wrong it was for me to be standing in my cabin.

"Hang today," I finished the sentence for him. "Yes. A lot of people thought that."

He stared at me, puzzled, but continued to sit in the bed. I decided he was no threat to me. We'd been friends for most of a year before everything went wrong. I hoped he would not judge it his duty to interfere with my escape. Casually, I walked past him to the shelf where I'd kept my personal possessions. As Spink had promised, my soldier-son journal was gone. A wave of relief washed through me. Epiny and Spink would know best how to dispose of those incriminating and accusatory pages. I felt along the shelf to be sure that no letter or scrap of paper had been missed. No. But my sling was there, the leather straps wrapped around the cup. I put it in my pocket. It might be useful.

The disreputable long gun I'd been issued when I first arrived at Gettys still rested on its rack. The rattly weapon with the pitted barrel had never been reliable. Even if it had been sound, it would soon have been useless when I'd expended the small supply of powder and ball I had. Leave it. But my sword was another matter. The sheathed blade still hung from its hook. I was reaching for it when Kesey demanded, "What happened?"

"It's a long story. Are you sure you want to know?"

"Well, of course I do! I thought you were going to be lashed to pieces and then hanged today!"

I found myself grinning. "And you couldn't even get out of bed to come to my hanging. A fine friend you are!"

He smiled back uncertainly. It wasn't a pretty sight, but I welcomed it. "I didn't want to see it, Nevare. Couldn't face it. Bad enough that the new commander ordered me to live out here and keep an eye on the cemetery because you were in prison. Worse to watch a friend die, and know that I'd probably meet my own end out here. Every cemetery sentry we've ever had has met a bad end. But how'd you get out of it? I don't understand."

"I escaped, Kesey. Speck magic freed me. The roots of a tree tore the stone walls of my dungeon apart, and I crawled out through the opening. I nearly made it out of Gettys. I made it past the gates of the fort. I thought I was a free man. But then I met a troop of soldiers coming back from the road's end. And who should be in charge of them but Captain Thayer himself."

Kesey was spellbound, his eyes as round as bowls. "But it was his wife—" he began, and I nodded.

"They found Carsina's body in my bed. You know, if not for that, I think the judges might have realized there was very little to link me to Fala's death. But Carsina's body in my bed was just too much for them. I doubt that even one ever considered that I might have been trying to save her.

"You do know I didn't do any of those things, don't you, Kesey?"

The older man licked his lips. He looked uncertain. "I didn't want to believe any of that about you, Nevare. None of it fit with anything Ebrooks and I had ever seen of you. You were fat and a loner and hardly ever had a drink with us, and Ebrooks and I could see you were sliding toward the Speck way. You wouldn't have been the first to go native.

"But we never saw nothing mean in you. You weren't vicious. When you talked soldiering with us, seemed like you meant it. And no one ever worked harder out here than you did. But someone did those things, and there you were, right where they happened. Everybody else seemed so certain. They made me feel a fool for not believing you done it. And at the trial, when I tried to say that you'd always been a stand-up fellow to me, well, Ebrooks shoved me and told me to shut up. Told me I'd only get myself a beating trying to speak up for you, and do you no good at all. So, I kept quiet. I'm sorry, Nevare. You deserved better."

I gritted my teeth and then let my anger go with a sigh. "It's all right, Kesey. Ebrooks was right. You couldn't have helped me."

I reached for my sword. But as my hand came close to the hilt, I felt an odd tingling. It was an unpleasant warning, as if I'd just set my hand on a hive of bees and felt the buzzing of the warriors inside. I drew my hand back and wiped it roughly down the front of my shirt, puzzled.

"But you escaped, right? So me keeping quiet, it didn't do you no harm, right? And I'm not going to try to stop you now. I'm not even going to tell anyone that you come this way."

There was a note of fear in his voice that wrung my heart. I met his eyes. "I told you, Kesey. It's all right. And no one will be asking you if I came this way, because I met Captain Thayer and his men as I was leaving town. And they killed me."

He stared at me. "What? But you—"

I stepped forward quickly. He flinched from my touch, but I set my hand to his forehead as he cringed away. I put my heart in my words. I wanted to protect him, and this was the only way to do it. "You're having a dream, Kesey. It's just a dream. You'll hear about my death next time you go to town. Captain Thayer caught me escaping and beat me to death with his own hands. His wife is avenged. There were a dozen witnesses. It's over. Ebrooks was there. He might even tell you about it. He took my body and secretly buried it. He did the best by me he could. And you, you had a dream of me escaping. It comforted you. Because you knew that if you could have helped me, you would have. And you bear no guilt for my death. All of this was just a dream. You're asleep and dreaming."

As I'd been speaking, I'd gently pushed Kesey supine. His eyelids shut and his mouth sagged open. The deep breathing of sleep sighed from his lungs and in again. He slept. I heaved a sigh. He'd share the same false memories I'd left with the mob that had surrounded me. Even my best friend Spink would recall that I'd been beaten to death in the streets and he'd been powerless to stop it. Amzil, the only woman who'd ever looked past my fat and unlovely body to love me, would believe the same. They'd bear that tale home to my Cousin Epiny, and she would believe it. I hoped that they would not mourn me too sharply or for too long. I wondered briefly how they would break the news to my sister, and if my father would care when he heard it. Then I resolutely turned away from that life. It was gone, over, finished.

Once I'd been tall and strong and golden, a new noble's soldier son, with a future full of promise. It had all seemed so clearly mapped for me. I'd attend the Academy, enter the cavalla as an officer, distinguish myself in the King's service, marry the lovely Carsina, have a fulfilling career full of adventure and valor, and eventually retire to my brother's estate to live out my declining years. If only I'd never been infected with the Speck magic, it would all have come true.

Kesey snorted and rolled over. I sighed. I'd best be gone. As soon as the news of my death spread, someone would ride out to tell him. I didn't want to expend any more magic; I already felt the aching pangs of hunger that using magic brought on. As soon as I had the thought, my stomach growled furiously. I rummaged hastily through the food cupboard, but all the food looked unappetizing, dry and old. I longed for sweet berries warmed by the sun, earthy rich mushrooms, the spicy water plant leaves that Olikea had fed me the last time I'd seen her, and tender crisp roots. My mouth ran at the thought of such foods. Instead, I glumly took two rounds of hardtack from the shelf. I took a large bite and, still chewing the loathsome stuff, reached for my sword. It was time to be gone from here.

The sword burned me. It all but jumped from my hand when I let go of the hilt, as if magnetically repelled from me, and clattered to the floor. I choked on the mouthful of dry crumbs and sank to the floor, gasping and gripping the wrist of my offended hand. When I looked at my palm, it was as red as if I'd gripped a nettle. I shook my hand and wiped it against my trouser leg, trying to be free of the sensation. It didn't pass. The truth came to me.

I had given myself to the magic. Cold iron was mine no longer.

I stood slowly, backing away from my fallen sword and a truth I was reluctant to face. My heart was hammering in my chest. I'd go weaponless into the forest. Iron and the technology that it made possible was mine no longer. I shook my head like a dog shaking off water. I wouldn't think about it just now. I couldn't quite grasp all it would mean, and at that moment I didn't want to.

I gave a final glance around the cabin, realizing belatedly that I'd enjoyed living here, on my own, having things my own way. It was the only time in my life I'd had such freedom. I'd gone from my father's house straight to the Academy, and then returned to his domain. Only here had I ever lived as my own master. When I left here, I'd begin a life not as a free man, but as a servant to a foreign magic that I neither understood nor wanted.

But I'd still be alive. And the people I loved would go on with their lives. I'd had a glimpse, when the mob seized me, of a far worse future, a future in which Amzil's best hope was that the gang rape would leave her alive and Spink's that he would survive having his troops turn on him. My own death paled in comparison.

No. I'd made the best choice for all of us. Now it was up to me
to move on, keeping whatever shreds of my integrity remained. I
wished I wasn't going into my new life so empty-handed. I looked
longingly at my knife and my axe. No. Iron was not my friend
anymore. But my winter blanket, folded on the shelf, I would take.
One final glance around the cabin, and then I left, shutting the
door firmly behind me on Kesey's rattling snore.

As I came out Clove lifted his head and gave me a rebuking
stare. Why hadn't I freed him from his harness to graze? I glanced
at the sun. I'd leave him here, I decided. It was believable that if
the big horse had got loose in Gettys, he'd come back to his stall. I
couldn't take off his tack; someone would wonder who had done
that for him. I hoped whoever took him over would treat him
well. "Stay here, old chum. Kesey will look after you. Or someone
will." I gave him a pat on the shoulder and left him there.

I walked across the cemetery grounds that I knew so well. I
passed the butchered remains of my hedge. I shuddered as I recalled it as I'd last seen it, with the bodies jerking and twitching as
the rootlets thrust into them seeking nutrients and for a moment
I was plunged back into that torchlit night.

It was rare but not unknown for a person who died of Speck
plague to be a "walker." One of the doctors at Gettys believed that
such persons fell into a deep coma that mimicked death, to rouse
hours later for a final attempt at life. Few survived. The other doctor, an aficionado of the superstitions and psychic phenomena that
so fascinated our Queen, believed that such "walkers" were not
truly the folk who had died, but only bodies reanimated by magic
to bring messages to the living from the beyond. Having been a
"walker" myself, I had my own opinions. In my year at the King's
Cavalla Academy, I'd contracted the Speck plague just as my fellow cadets had. Once I'd "died," I'd found myself in the Specks'
spirit world. There I'd done battle with my "Speck self" and Tree
Woman, returning to life only after I had defeated them.

My erstwhile fiancée Carsina had also been a "walker." In my
final night as cemetery guard she had left her coffin and come
to beg my forgiveness before she could rest in death. I'd wanted to
save her. I'd left my cabin, intending to ride to town and get help.

Instead, I'd seen an unimaginable sight. Other plague victims had risen and sought out the trees I'd inadvertently planted. I'd known they were kaembra trees, the same sort of trees that the Specks claimed as their ancestor trees. I'd known that when I'd seen the poles leaf out. How could I not have realized the danger? Had the magic blinded me to it?

Each "walker" had sought out a tree, had sat down, backs to the trunks, and then cried out in agony as the hungry little trees had sent rootlets thrusting into flesh. I'd never forget what I'd seen that night. A boy had cried out wildly, his head and arms and legs jerking spasmodically as the tree claimed his flesh and bound his body tightly to its trunk. I'd been unable to do anything for him. But the worst had been the woman who cried out for help and held her hands out beseechingly. I had clasped those hands and tried with all my might to pull her back, not from death, but from an extended life that made no sense to a Gernian soul.

I'd failed.

I remembered well which tree had seized her so irrevocably, thrusting roots into her back, roots that would burst into a network of spreading filaments inside her, sucking into the young trees not just the nutrients in her body, but her spirit as well. That was how the Specks created their ancestor trees. Those the magic found worthy were rewarded with such trees.

As I passed the hacked stump of the woman's tree, I noticed that it had already sent up a questing new sprout. On the stump next to hers, a red-wattled croaker bird perched, watching me intently. It opened its wings and thrust its ugly head at me. Its wattles shook as it croaked accusingly at me. I shuddered. Croaker birds were the emblem of Orandula, the old god of death and of balances. I did not wish another encounter with him. As I fled from it, I realized that Clove was following me. Well, he'd soon turn back. I entered the forest and felt it take me in. It was like a curtain swishing closed behind me, signaling that the first act of my life was over.

This part of the forest was young, a regrowth after a fire. Occasionally, I passed a blackened stump overgrown with moss and ferns, or strode through the shade of a scorched giant who had survived that blaze. Bushes and wildflowers grew here in the sun-light that filtered down between the trees. Birds sang and darted from branch to branch in the early morning light. The sweet scents of the forest rose up to surround me. Tension drained from me. For a time I walked without thought, listening to Clove's hooves thud dully on the deep forest soil as he trailed after me.

It was a pleasant summer day. I passed two white butterflies dancing together above a small patch of wildflowers. Beyond them, I came to a mounded tangle of blackberry vines competing for light in a small clearing. I stopped and gathered a double hand-ful of the lush, black summer fruit. They burst in my fingers and stained my hands as I picked them. I filled my mouth with them, rejoicing in the sweetness that was both taste and aroma. I ground the tiny seeds between my back teeth, savoring them. Fruit such as this could take the edge off my hunger, but it could not satisfy me. No. As the magic had come to dominate my flesh and blood, I had learned to crave the foods that fed it. That was what I wanted now. I left the berry patch, hastening uphill.

The burned-over forest gave way to ancient forest with shocking suddenness. I paused at the edge, standing in the dap-pling sunlight among the younger trees, and looked into a dark cavern. The roof was a thick mass of intertwining branches. Ranks and columns of immense trunks marched off into the dimness. The dense overhead canopy absorbed and defeated the summer sunlight. There was very little underbrush. Thick moss floored the world, indented with a seemingly random pattern of animal trails.

I sighed and glanced back at the big horse. "This is where we part company, my friend," I told Clove. "Go back to the graveyard."

He regarded me with a mixture of curiosity and annoyance. "Go home," I told him. He flicked his ears and swished his badly bobbed tail. I sighed. Soon enough, he'd figure it out for himself. I turned and walked away from him.

He followed me for a short way. I didn't look back at him or speak to him. That was harder than I thought it would be. I tried not to listen for the dull thud of his hooves. He'd go back to where the grazing was good. Kesey would take him in and use him to pull the corpse cart. He'd be fine. Better off than me. At least he'd know what the world expected of him.

There were no human pathways in this part of the forest. I felt as if I walked through an alien abode, richly carpeted in thick green, beneath an elaborate ceiling of translucent green mosaic, all supported by towering columns of rich wood. I was a tiny figurine set down in a giant's home. I was too small to matter here; the quiet alone was enough to muffle me out of existence.

But as I hiked on, the quiet reinterpreted itself to me. The noises of men were not here, but it was not silent. I became more aware of the birds that flitted and sang challenges to one another over my head. I heard the sharp warning thud of its hind feet and the muffled scamper of a startled hare. A deer regarded me with wide eyes and spread ears as I passed its resting place. I heard its soft snuff as I passed it.

The day was warm and humid beneath the trees. I paused to unbutton my jacket and the top two buttons of my shirt. It was not too long before I was carrying my uniform jacket slung over my shoulder. Amzil had pieced the cavalla-green coat together for me from several old uniforms to fit my enlarged body. One of the tribulations of my magic-induced weight was that I was constantly uncomfortable in my clothing. Trousers had to be fastened under my gut rather than round my waist. Collars, cuffs, and sleeves chafed me. Socks stretched out and puddled around my ankles, and wore out swiftly at the heel from my excessive weight. Even boots and shoes were a difficulty. I'd gained size all over my body, even down to my feet. Right now, my clothing hung slightly loose on me. I'd used a lot of magic last night, and lost bulk proportionately. For a moment I considered disrobing and simply going naked as a Speck, but I had not left civilization quite that far behind.

My way led me ever upward, over the gently rising foothills. Ahead loomed the densely forested Barrier Mountains and the elusive Speck people who roamed them. I'd been told that the Specks had decided to retreat early to their winter grounds high in the mountains. I'd seek them there. They were not just my last possible refuge. That was also what the magic commanded me to do. I'd resisted it to no avail. Now I would go to it and try to discover what it wanted of me. Was there any way to satisfy it, any way to win free of it and resume a life of my own choosing? I doubted it, but I would find out.

The magic had infected me when I was fifteen. I had, I thought, been a good son, obedient, hardworking, courteous, and respectful. But my father, unbeknownst to me, had been looking for that spark of defiance, that insistence on following my own path that he believed was the hallmark of a good officer. He'd decided to place me in a position where ultimately I must rebel against the authority over me. He had given me over to a Kidona plainsman, a "respected enemy" from the days when the King's cavalla had battled the former occupants of the Midlands. He told me that Dewara would instruct me in Kidona survival and fighting tactics. Instead, he had terrorized me, starved me, notched my ear, and then, just when I'd found the will to defy both him and my father, endeavored to befriend me. I could never look back on those days without wondering what he had done to my thinking. Only recently had I begun to see the parallels between how Dewara had broken me and brought me into his world and the way the Academy harassed and overburdened the new cadets to press them into a military mold. At the end of my time with Dewara, he had tried to induct me into the Kidona magic. He had both succeeded and failed.

I had crossed into the Kidona spirit world to do battle with their ancient enemy. Instead, Tree Woman had captured me and claimed me. From that day forth, the magic had taken over my life. It had dragged, spurred, and coerced me to the frontier. In Gettys, I'd made one last attempt to claim my life as my own. I'd signed my enlistment papers as Nevare Burv, and taken up the only position the regiment offered, guarding the cemetery. Even so, I'd put my heart into my task, doing all I could to see that our dead were buried respectfully and left undisturbed. I'd begun to have a life again; Ebrooks and Kesey had become my friends, and Spink, my cousin's husband and my best friend from our Academy days, had renewed our friendship. Amzil had come to live in Gettys; I'd dared to hope she felt affection for me. I had begun to make something of myself, even believing I could provide a refuge for my sister from my father's tyranny.

That life did not serve the magic's purpose for me, and as Scout Hitch had once warned me, the magic would not tolerate anything that ran counter to its plan for me. It had destroyed Hitch's life to make him its servant. I knew I had to choose death or serve the magic. Before Hitch died, he'd confessed all to me. Under the magic's influence, he'd killed Fala, one of Sarla Moggam's working girls, and left the evidence that would implicate me. He'd done that, despite being my friend, despite being an otherwise upright man. I still could not imagine Hitch strangling poor Fala, let alone betraying me so treacherously. But he had.

I didn't want to discover what the magic could make me do if I continued to defy it.

CHAPTER THREE

LISANA

My path led me ever upward. Somewhere, I knew, the sun shone and the wind stirred lightly in a soft summer day. But here, beneath the trees, a soft green twilight reigned and the air was still. My footfalls were deadened by decades of leaf mold. Great trees, roots braced and humped against the rise of the hills, surrounded and shaded me, making the forest a many-pillared palace. Sweat ran down my face and my back. The calves of my legs ached from the steady climb.

And I was still hungry.

I'd had little to eat for the last ten days. My jail rations had been bread and water and a disgusting grayish pudding that was supposed to be porridge. Epiny had smuggled a tiny fruit tart to me, precious because it contained berries picked in this forest. When Tree Woman had sent her roots to break the walls of my cell, she had brought me the mushrooms that had given me strength for my magic. Those, and the hardtack and the handful of berries I'd picked in the morning, were all I'd had. Belatedly, I recalled that Amzil had told me she'd packed food in my panniers.

Well, that last act of affection was gone now, carried off by Clove with my saddle. Strange to tell, the loss of that food did not distress me. I was hungry for the foods that would feed my magic rather than the ones that sustained my flesh.

I had early realized that restricting my food and even fasting wrought little noticeable change in me. The only thing that consumed my fat was using the magic. In the last day and night, I'd used the magic more than I ever had before, and my appetite for the foods that would feed the magic now raged proportionately.

"I'm hungry," I said aloud to the forest. I half expected some sort of response: that mushrooms would spring up underfoot or a bush of berries would sprout nearby. But there was nothing. I heaved a sigh of disappointment, then paused and took a deeper lungful of air, breathing in through my nose. There. The faintest scent hung in the still forest air—I followed it, snuffing like a hound on a trail, and came to a bank of deep blue flowers nestled against the underside of a fallen log. I could not recall that Olikea had ever fed me anything like them, but the fragrance from them enflamed my appetite. I lowered myself to the forest floor to sit beside them. What was I doing, thinking of eating something I'd never even seen before? I could poison myself. I picked one, smelled it, and then tasted it. It was like eating perfume, and the flavor was too strong to be appetizing. I chose a leaf instead. It was fat-stemmed and fuzzy-edged. Cautiously, I put it to my tongue. There was a tang to the foliage that counteracted the sweetness of the flowers. I picked and ate a handful of the leaves, and then abruptly felt that although I was still hungry, I'd had enough of them. Was this the magic finally speaking clearly to me, as Tree Woman had told me it would? I couldn't decide if that were true or if I were deceiving myself. With a grunt, I heaved myself to my feet and walked on. I reached the rounded top of a hill and the walking became easier.

I found and ate a cluster of bright yellow mushrooms growing in the moss on top of a tree root. I came to a place where parasitic vines had attacked on older tree. The tree was losing its leaves and patches of its bark had fallen away, revealing the holes and tracks of insects intent on rendering it down into soil. But the vine that cloaked the dying tree was lush with thick foliage and large teardrop-shaped fruit, so purple they shone black in the filtered sunlight. Some of the fruit was so ripe that it had cracked and lightly fermented. Purple juice dripped from them. Bees and other insects hummed ecstatically round the vine, while over my head I could hear the competitive twittering of small birds. Some of the fruit had fallen to the forest floor. There was a busy trail of large black ants carrying off gobbets of pulp.

The other happy feasters convinced me that the fruit was edible. I picked one, sniffed it, and tried a small bite. It was so ripe that juice and soft flesh gushed into my mouth as my teeth pierced the skin. It was far sweeter than a sun-ripened plum, almost sickeningly so. Then the flavor of it flooded my mouth and I nearly swooned with delight. I discarded the large round seed and reached for another.

I don't know how many I ate. When I finally stopped, the skin of my belly was tight against the waistband of my trousers, and my arms were sticky to the elbow with juice. I wiped my mouth on the back of my hand and came back a little to myself. The pile of seeds at my feet numbered at least a score. Instead of feeling queasy, I felt only blissful satiation.

As I walked slowly away, I tingled with well-being. I became aware of the music of the forest, a symphony made by the subtle buzzing of insects, the calls of birds, the flutter of leaves in an unseen breeze overhead. Even my deadened footfalls were a part of the whole. It was not a symphony of sound alone. The scents of loam and moss, leaf and fruit, meshed with the sounds I heard, and the physical sensations of walking, of brushing past a low branch or sinking deep into moss. The muted colors in the gentled light were a part of it. It was all an amazing whole, an experience that involved me more completely than anything I'd ever felt in my life.

"I'm drunk," I said aloud, and even those words intertwined with the sudden spiraling fall of a leaf and the soft snag of a cobweb across my face at the same moment. "No. Not drunk. But intoxicated."

I liked speaking aloud in the forest, for it made me more intimately a part of it. I walked on, marveling at everything, and after a time, I began to sing wordlessly, letting my voice be guided by all my senses. I spread wide my arms, heedless that my coat fell to the forest floor. I walked away from it, singing with my whole heart, with every bit of breath I could draw into my lungs. I was transported with joy simply to be me traveling into the depths of the forest.

Simply to be who I was.

Who was I?

The question was like recalling a forgotten errand. I was someone, going somewhere, on my way to do something. My steps slowed, and for a long moment I was intrigued with the idea. I was centered and certain, confident of myself, but I could not quite define with a name who I was.

Nevare. Soldier's Boy. Like a slow waltz of two halves that have joined to be a whole and then spin apart again, I felt that sundering. And with Soldier's Boy's departure from my awareness, I suddenly felt the gap he left in me. I had been a whole creature, peacefully content in that wholeness. And now I was less than whole, and I thought I could understand how an amputee felt. My keen pleasure in the forest dwindled to my ordinary awareness of its pleasant smells and gentle light. The communion I had felt with it became a handful of threads rather than a complex network. I could not recall the song I had been singing. I'd lost track of my place in this world. I was diminished.

I blinked slowly and looked around me, gradually becoming aware that this part of the forest was familiar. If I climbed the ridge before me and veered to the east, I'd come to Tree Woman's stump. I suddenly knew that was the destination I'd been walking toward all day. *Home*, I thought, and that was like an echo of someone else's thought. Soldier's Boy considered her his home. I wasn't sure what Nevare considered her.

When I'd first encountered Tree Woman in Dewara's spirit world I saw a fat old woman with gray hair leaning up against a tree instead of the warrior-guardian I'd expected to battle. Challenging her would have gone against everything my father had ever taught his soldier son about chivalry. And so I had hesitated and spoken to her, and before I recognized her power, she had defeated me and made me hers.

I became her apprentice mage. And then her lover.

My heart remembered those days with her. My head did not. My head had gone to the Cavalla Academy, taken courses, made friends, and done all that a loyal soldier son should. And when the opportunity came for me to challenge Tree Woman as an adversary, I had not hesitated. I'd destroyed that other self who had been her acolyte, taking him back inside me. And then I'd done my best to kill her as well.

Yet at both those tasks, I'd failed. The Speck self I'd taken back inside me lurked there still, like a speckled trout in the deep shade under a grassy riverbank. From time to time I glimpsed him, but never could I seize and hold him. And the Tree Woman I'd slain? I'd only partially severed her trunk with a cavalla sword. That deed, impossible in what I considered the real world, had left its evidence here. Upon the ridge ahead of me was the stump of her tree. The rusting blade of my sword was still embedded in it. I'd toppled her. But I had not severed her trunk completely. The ruin of her tree sprawled on the mossy hillside, in the swathe of sunlight that now broke through the canopy of the forest there.

But she was not dead. From the fallen trunk, a new young tree was rising. And near her stump, I'd encountered her ghostly form. My adversary was still as alive as I was and the hidden Speck self inside me loved her still.

As Tree Woman, she was an enemy to my people. She was frank in her hope that something I would do would turn back the tide of "intruders" and send the Gernians away forever from the forest and mountain world of the Specks. At her behest, Speck plague had been spread throughout Gernia and still continued to afflict my country. Thousands had sickened and died. The King's great project, his road to the east, had come to a standstill. By all I had ever been taught, I should hate her as my enemy.

But I loved her. And I knew that I loved her with a fierce tenderness unlike anything I'd ever felt for any other woman. I had no conscious reason to feel that passion toward her, but feel it I did.

I toiled up the last steep stretch and reached the ridge. I hurried toward her, the anticipation of my hidden self rising with every step I took. But as I approached her stump, I halted, dismayed.

The stump of her tree had silvered and deadened. Even the unsevered piece that had bent with her falling trunk and kept the branches of it alive had gone gray and dull. I could not see her; I could not feel her. The young tree, a branch that had begun to grow upright after her trunk had fallen, still stood, but barely.

I waded through her fallen and dead branches to reach the supine trunk and the small tree that grew from it. When Tree Woman had crashed to the earth, her passing had torn a rent in the canopy overhead. Light poured down in straight yellow shafts, piercing the usual dimness of the forest and illuminating the small tree. When I fingered the little tree's green leaves, they were flaccid and limp. A few leaves at the ends of the branches had begun to brown at the edges. The little tree was dying. I put my hands on her trunk. My two hands could just span its diameter. Once before, in a dream, I had touched this little tree and felt how it surged with her life and being. Now I felt only dry, sun-warmed bark under my hands.

"Lisana," I prayed softly. I called her by her true name and held my breath waiting for some response. I felt nothing.

A wandering breeze ventured in through the hole in the forest's roof. It stirred my hair and made pollen dance in the shaft of light where I stood.

"Lisana, please," I begged. "What happened? Why is your tree dying?"

The answer came to me as clearly as if she had spoken. Last night, I'd been able to escape my cell because the roots of a tree had broken through the mortar and stones. As I'd climbed those roots to escape, I'd felt Lisana's presence there. Had the roots of her tree grown all that way, from here to Gettys, and then torn down the walls to free me? It was impossible.

All magic was impossible.

And all magic had a price. Only a few days ago, Epiny had stood here by Lisana's stump, and they had summoned me in a dream to join them. In hindsight, Lisana had been more ephemeral than usual. And more irritable. She'd been spiteful toward Epiny and merciless toward me. I tried to recall how her little tree

had looked then. The leaves had been drooping, but not alarm-
ingly so. It had been a hot day.

Even then, her roots must have been working their way,
through clay and sand, rock and soil, to reach Gettys and the
prison where I was held. Even then, she had been employing
all the magic at her command and all her physical resources to
reach me. I should have guessed that something of that sort was
happening when I could barely perceive her in my cell. Why had
she done it? Had the magic forced her to sacrifice her life to save
mine? Or had that offering been her own?

I pressed my brow against the slender trunk. I could not feel
her at all and suspected that the amount of life remaining in this
little tree was not enough to sustain her being. She was gone, and
it tormented me that I could remember we had shared a love but
could recall no specific memory, no detail of how it had begun.
I had dreamed of our trysts together, but like most dreams, I
awoke grasping only bright fragments of memory. Such gossamer
glimpses were too frail to survive harsh daylight. They did not feel
like true memories to me, yet the emotions I felt were unequivo-
cally mine. I closed my eyes and tried to will those memories to
the forefront of my mind. I wanted at least to recall the love we
had shared. It had cost her dearly.

In that focused contact, I felt a wisp of her being brush mine.
She was feeble, a moon waning away to nothing. She gestured
weakly at me, warning me back. Instead, I pressed closer. "Lisana?
Is there no way I can help you? Without your intervention, I
would have died."

Her bark was rough against my forehead. I clasped the trunk
of the small tree so tightly that it stung the palms of my hands.
Abruptly, her image came more clearly to me. "Go away, Soldier's
Boy! While you can. I gave my being to this tree. It consumed me
and became me. That does not mean I can control its appetite. All
things desire to live, and my tree desires life fiercely. Get away!"

"Lisana, please, I—" And then a red pain pierced my palm and
shot up into my wrist.

"Get back!" she shrieked at me, and with a sudden burst of
strength, she pushed me away.

I did not fall. The tree already gripped me too strongly for that. My forehead ripped free of the questing rootlets that had penetrated my brow. Blood ran bright red before my opened eyes. I bellowed in terror and with inhuman strength pulled my hands free. Dangling rootlets, red with my blood, pulled from my palms as I jerked my hands back. The tendrils dripped and twitched after me like hungrily seeking worms. I staggered back from the tree. With the back of my sleeve, I wiped blood away from my brow and eyes and then stared in horror at my wounded hands. Blood trickled from half a dozen holes in my flesh and dripped from my palms. As the drops fell to the forest floor, the moss at my feet hummocked and quivered. Tiny tree roots wormed up from the soil and moss, squirming toward the red drops that glistened like red berries. I pressed my bleeding palms to my shirtfront and staggered backward.

I felt dizzy with horror or perhaps blood loss. Lisana's tree had tried to eat me. My pierced hands ached all the way into my wrists. I wondered how deeply the roots had wormed into me, and then tried not to think of that as a wave of vertigo swept over me. I focused on taking another couple of steps backward. I felt sickened and weak; I wondered if the roots had done more to me than pierce my flesh and absorb my blood.

"Move back, Nevare. Keep moving. There. That's better."

Tree Woman was a misty embodiment of herself. I could see through her, but my sense of her was stronger. My head was still spinning, but I obeyed her, staggering away from the young tree.

"Sit down on the moss. Breathe. You'll feel better in a little while. Kaembra trees sometimes take live creatures as nourishment. When they do, they sedate them so they do not struggle. What you did was foolish. I warned you that the tree was desperate."

"Isn't the tree you? Why would you do this to me?" I felt woozy and betrayed.

"The tree is not me. I live within the tree's life, but I am not the tree and the tree is not me."

"It tried to eat me."

"It tried to live. All things try to live. And it will now. In a way, it is almost fitting. I took from it to rescue you. And it took from you to save itself."

"Then—you'll live now?" My mind seized on that most important fact.

She nodded. It was hard to see her against the bright sunlight, but I could still make out the sadness in her eyes that contradicted her soft smile. "I'll live, yes. For as long as the tree does. I spent a lot of what I had regained to reach for you in that cell. It will take me a long time to rebuild my reserves. But what you have given me today has restored me for now. I have the strength to reach for sunlight and water now. For now, I'll be fine."

"What is it, Lisana? What aren't you telling me?"

She laughed then, a sound I felt in my mind rather than heard. "Soldier's Boy, how can you know so many things and nothing at all? Why do you persist in being divided against yourself? How can you look at something and not see it? No one understands this about you. You use the magic with a reckless power that in all my time I have never witnessed. Yet when the truth is right before you, you cannot see it."

"What truth?"

"Nevare, go to the end of the ridge and look out toward your King's Road. Tell me where it will go as they push it onward. Then come back, and tell me if I will live."

The pain in my hands was already lessening. I wiped my sleeve over my forehead and felt the roughness of scabbing. The magic was again healing me with an unnatural swiftness. I was grateful, and also a bit surprised, not that the magic could heal me but at how easily I accepted it now.

I was full of trepidation as I walked to the end of the ridge. The soil there was stony, and as I approached the end, the trees became more stunted until I stood on an outthrust of stone where only brush grew. From that rocky crag I could look out over the valley below me. The vale cupped a lining of trees, but intruding into that green bowl, straight as an arrow, was the chaos of the King's Road. Like a pointing finger, it lanced into the forest. To either side of it, trees with yellowing leaves leaned drunkenly, their side roots cut by the road's progress. Smoke still rose from an equipment shed, or rather, from the ashes of one. Epiny had been thorough. She'd set off three explosions down there in an attempt to distract the town from my escape. Wagons and scrapers were a jumble of broken wood and wheels in one area under the scattered roof of a shed. Another collapsed building still smoldered and stank in the sweet summer air. And it looked to me as if she had exploded one culvert. The road had collapsed and the stream that had once been channeled under it now seethed through the rocks and muck. Men and teams were already at work there, digging the muck away and preparing to lay a new conduit for the stream. They'd have to repair that section of road before they could push the construction any deeper into the forest.

My delicately raised girl cousin had struck in a way that I, a trained soldier son, had never even imagined. And she had succeeded, at least for now, in halting the progress of the King's Road builders.

But as I was smiling at her success, my grin suddenly stiffened into a sort of rictus. This road, cutting through the mountains and to the sea beyond them, was my king's great project.

With that road, my king hoped to restore Gernia to greatness. And I looked on its delay and destruction with pleasure. Who was I?

I gazed down on the aborted road again. It pointed straight toward me. Well, not precisely straight. It would cross the valley and then climb the hill I was standing on . . . Slowly I turned my head to the left, to look back the way I had come. Tree Woman. Lisana. Her stump and fallen trunk were exactly in the path of the road. If the tree cutting continued, she would fall to the axe. I looked back at the road, cold flowing through my veins. At the end of the construction, two freshly fallen giants sprawled in a welter of broken limbs. They'd taken other, smaller trees down with them as they fell. From my vantage point, the new rent in the forest canopy looked like a disease eroding the green flesh of the living forest below me. And the gash was heading directly toward my lover's tree.

I watched the men toiling below. The sounds of their cursing and shouted commands could not reach me here. But I could smell the smoke of last night's fire and see the steady procession of wagons and teams and road crews as they toiled like ants mending a nest. How long would it take them to fix the broken culvert and patch the road? A few days, if they were industrious. How long to build new wagons and scrapers, how long to build new sheds? A few weeks at most. And then the work would press on. The magical fear that the Specks had created still oozed down from the forest to deter the workers and sap their wills. But, fool that I was, I'd given the commander the means to overcome even that. I'd been the one to suggest that men half drunk on liquor or drugged with laudanum would not feel the fear as keenly and could work despite it. I'd even heard that some of the penal workers now craved the intoxicants so much that they clamored to be on the work details at the road's end. The drugged and desensitized men would push the road on into the forest. I'd enabled that. It had almost earned me a promotion.

I recognized uncomfortably that my heart was turning more and more toward a forest way of thinking. The divide in me ran deep now. I was still a Gernian, but that was no longer sufficient reason to believe that the King's Road must be pushed through at all costs. I glanced back toward Tree Woman's stump. No. The cost to me alone was too high. It had to be stopped.

How?

I stood for a long time as the afternoon waned, watching the men and teams flailing away at their tasks. Even at this distance, I could see that the workers were impaired. No one moved briskly and mishaps abounded. A wagon trying to turn too tightly with a load of rock tipped over and dumped its cargo. An hour later, another wagon mired, and a third driver, trying to get past the mired wagon, drove his team into the ditch and overset his load there.

Yet for all that, the work was progressing. It might be tomorrow before they had replaced the culverts, and perhaps even another day before they had a drivable surface on the road there. But eventually, like patient insects, they would get it done. And then they would push on once more, cutting inexorably into the forest. Did it matter to me if they cut down her tree next week or three years from now? I needed to stop them.

Yet no matter how I racked my brain, I could not come up with a plan. I'd gone to the Colonel before the plague descended on us and begged him to stop the road. I'd explained to him that the kaembra trees were sacred to the Specks, and that if we cut them, we could expect an all-out war with the forest people. He'd dismissed me and my concerns. Silly superstitions, he'd told me. Once the trees were cut and the Specks discovered that no great calamity befell them, he believed they could more readily adapt to the civilization we offered them. Not even for an instant did he pause to wonder if there might be a grain of truth in what the Specks believed about their trees.

When I asked if the road could not go around the kaembra trees, he pointed out that engineers had mapped out the best route, and it went past Gettys and through the mountain pass that traders had once used. For years, the resources of Gernia had been committed to building the road on that route. An alternate path had once been considered, one that would have gone past Mendy and the Fort to cut through the Barrier Mountains there. But to redirect the road-building effort to that route would mean adding years to the King's project, not to mention absorbing the waste of all that had gone into pushing the road as far as Gettys and beyond it. No. Nothing so trivial as a stand of ancestral trees would halt the King of Gernia's grand vision.

The Colonel was dead now, a victim of the Speck plague. The Specks had struck back at the tree cutters in the only way they had. They'd done the Dust Dance for the visiting officials from Old Thares and the inspection team, and in the process had infected everyone with the plague. I'd warned him of that, too. If the Colonel had ever reconsidered my words, he'd taken all such thoughts to the grave with him. Even if I'd been able to go into Gettys and talk to the new commander, my words would make no impression on him. The two realities, Gernian and Speck, simply did not meet. The Colonel had not even been able to grasp that the Specks were at war with us. He had thought that because they came yearly to trade with us, we'd reached an accord of sorts, and that they would slowly adopt our ways. I knew better. Each year, in the course of that "trading" time, they attacked us, deliberately spreading Speck plague among us.

Our peoples couldn't even agree on what constituted a war.

I doubted the Specks knew of the magnitude of the blow they'd dealt us with the latest outbreak of plague. The Speck plague had struck down every visiting officer on the reviewing stand. General Brodg, our Commander in the East, had fallen, as well as his predecessor, the venerable General Prode. Those losses would echo throughout all of Gernia. And within the fort at Gettys most of our resident officers had fallen sick, drastically reducing the ratio of officers to enlisted men. The command at Gettys had been passed down three times in the space of a month. The man who had it now, Major Belford, had never commanded a post before. I wondered if the King would bother to replace him, and who would assume the position of Commander in the East. I wondered who would want it. Then I decided that such decisions no longer concerned me. I was a soldier no more. I wasn't even sure I was a Gernian.

A resolve formed in me slowly. I needed to stop the road, not just to preserve Tree Woman, but for the sake of both peoples. I needed to make building the road an impossible task so that King Troven would either give up the idea or completely reroute his road far to the north, through Mendy and the Fort. Once the King had diverted his energies to that route and pass, Gettys as a military encampment would lose much of its value. It might be abandoned altogether. And that might be the end of the clash between Gernians and Specks. Perhaps we could go back to peaceful and sporadic trading; or perhaps it would be even better if all interaction between my peoples ceased.

I felt like a curtain was rising in my mind. The time for trying to reason with either people was gone; it was time for me to simply destroy the road. It was a very rudimentary strategy, but I still felt a lift in my spirits to have devised it. I felt a bit foolish as well. Why had I not found this determination before now? The answer to that was easy. Even if I now knew what I wished to do, I had very few ideas of how to implement my plans. There was small sense in planning to do a task that seemed impossible. Impossible for any ordinary man with ordinary means. But I was no longer an ordinary man, was I? I'd given way to the magic and accepted this task. I, Nevare Burvelle, was going to destroy the King's Road.

It was why I'd been given the magic. Lisana and Jodoli, the Speck Great Man I'd met, had both insisted that my task was to turn back the intruders, the Gernians. They had told me that the magic had chosen me, had made me a Great One for that very task. The conclusion was inescapable. I was to use the magic to stop the road.

The only thing I still didn't know was how.

The magic had been growing in me, like a fungus overtaking a piece of fruit, since I was fifteen years old. For several years, it had skulked beneath my awareness. Only when I left home to go to the Academy had I become aware that something strange lurked within me. And only after I'd contracted Speck plague and survived it did the magic begin to change my body so radically. It had cloaked me in the fat that had made me an object of ridicule and disdain and hampered not just my physical life but my military career. Yet in all the years that it had possessed me and changed me, I'd only managed to use it for my own ends a few times. For the most part, it used me.

It had used me to spy on my people, to better understand "the intruders" and how they might be fought. It had used me to spread the Speck plague in our capital city and all through our Cavalla Academy, destroying a whole generation of young officers. It had used me again to know when best to strike in Gettys, so that the entire inspection team of officers and nobles from the West might be wiped out.

Every time I had managed to use the magic, even with the best of intentions, the magic had found a way to turn it back on me. Both Lisana and Scout Hitch had warned me against trying to use the magic for my own ends. About the only thing I'd learned about how the magic was actually wielded was that it flamed in response to my emotions. Logic could not wield it, nor could wishful thinking ignite it. It only boiled through my blood when my heart was completely involved. When I was angry or frightened or seething with hate, then the magic came to me without effort, and the urge to use it became well nigh irresistible. At any other time, attempting to bend it to my will was impossible. It bothered me, and not a little, that logic rather than emotion was prompting me to turn the magic against the road itself. Was not that a very Gernian reaction to a Speck problem? But perhaps that was why the magic had chosen me. Still, if I was going to use magic to stop the road being built, I would first have to find the heart to do it.

I turned my head and looked toward Lisana's stump. I thought of how I had nearly killed her, and what it had meant to me to discover that she was still alive. I thought of the sapling that had once been a branch, and how it rose from the fallen trunk of her tree. I'd seen that happen before. Nursery logs, they were called, when a row of branches on a fallen tree took to growing as if they were trees. But in Lisana's case, only one tree was rising from her fallen trunk. And if the road came through here, there would soon be none at all.

I held that thought as I walked down the hill toward the end of the road. It was steep going until I found the deer trail that cut across the face of the hill. I followed it down and the canopy of the forest closed over me once more, creating an early twilight. I walked in that gentle dimness, smelling the sweetness of the living earth. Life surrounded me. I had slowly come to understand that in my months of living by the eaves of the forest, but only today did the thought form itself clearly in my mind. All my life, I'd been accustomed to thinking of life as things that moved: rabbits, dogs, fish, other people. Life that mattered had been life like me, life that breathed and bled, life that ate and slept. I'd been aware of that other layer of life, of the still but living things that supported it all, but I'd thought of it as the lower layer, as the less important stratum of life.

Empty prairie was for plowing or grazing; land that was too poor for farming or cattle was wasteland. I'd never lived near a forest like this, but when I'd come to one, I'd understood why it existed. The trees were to be taken for lumber. The land had to be cleared to become useful. The idea that forest or prairie or even wasteland should be left as it was had never occurred to me. What good was land until it was tamed? What good was a piece of earth that did not grow wheat or fruit trees or grass for cattle? The value of every bit of land I'd ever trodden, I'd reckoned in terms of how it could benefit a man. Now I saw it with the eyes of a forest mage. Here life balanced as it had for hundreds, perhaps thousands of years. Sunlight and water were all that was required for the trees to grow. The trees made the food that fed not only whatever moving creatures might venture through this territory, but also became the food that replenished the soil when their leaves fell to rot back into earth. This working system was as refined and precise as any piece of clockwork ever engineered by man. It worked perfectly.

But the road would break the clockwork of the forest system just as surely as an axe blow could shatter a fine watch. I'd seen the damage from the ridge and I'd seen it up close when I'd visited the road's end. It wasn't just the trees they cut to make a clear path. It was how the road builders made all the same in their path. Every dip in the earth was filled level, every rise cut to grade. The different layers of rock and gravel that made up the roadbed were inimical to the flow of the forest life. The road was a barrier of deadness bisecting the forest heart.

The swath of death was wider than the road itself. Streams were diverted into culverts or blocked off. Brooks pooled and swamped land they had once drained and fed. The cut of the road severed roots beneath the earth, crippling the trees to either side of it. The construction slashed a great gash in the forest roof, admitting light where all had lived in gentle dimness for generations. The edges of the road were a crusty scab, and the road itself was like blood poisoning creeping up a man's veins toward his heart. Once the road had cut its way through the forest and across the mountains, the forest would never be the same. It would be an entity divided, and from that division, other roads and trails and byways would spread out into the forest as if the road had its own anti-life network of roots and tendrils.

Men would make more paths, with trails and byways branching out from them. Beneath that ever-spreading network of roads and paths and trails, nothing lived. Could death grow? I suddenly perceived that it could. Its spreading network could cut the living world into smaller and smaller sections, until no section was large enough to survive.

I'd reached the bottom of the hill. There was a stream there, and I paused to drink long of its cool, sweet water. The last time I'd been here, I'd come only in spirit, and Epiny had been with me. Epiny. For a moment, I thought of her, and for the moment, I was Nevare again. I hoped she would not mourn me too deeply or too long. I hoped her sorrow over my supposed death would not affect her pregnancy. And then I blinked, and those feelings and thoughts receded from the forefront of my mind. I became once more the forest mage, intent on my task.

I had to stop the road. I had to be ruthless. I had the power if first I could bring it up to strength.

It seemed weeks, no, months ago that I had hovered by this stream as a disembodied entity and Epiny had picked and sampled some of the scarlet drupes. In real time, it had been but a few days, and the heavily laden berry bush still offered me a plenitude of fruit. After I had slaked my thirst, I sat down beside it and method- ically began to strip it of berries. They were potent food for the magic, and as I ate them, I felt my reserves filling. I replenished the magic I had burned to escape the Gernian prison and the suste- nance that Lisana's tree had drawn from me. The wounds in my hands healed and the ache in the wrists quieted and then faded to nothing. I felt the sagging skin of my belly tighten as I consumed it. I filled myself with magic more than I did with food.

Large and heavy as I was, the magic lent me stealth. I moved through the woods with the same lumbering grace that bear and elk possess. In the lost sky above me, the sun was foundering to the west. The dimness in the forest deepened toward full darkness. I felt no weariness, even though I could not recall the last time I had slept a full and comfortable night. I was charged with both magic and purpose. Like a heavy shadow, I slipped through the forest toward the road's end.

I reached it as the crews were finishing their day's labor. Epiny's sabotage had been effective in its limited way. Today, the crews had not cut into any new trees or finished hauling away the bodies of the trees they had felled. Instead, all their time had been taken up with salvaging wagons and equipment and repairing the destroyed culverts to make the road passable once more. I stood in the gloomy shelter of the forest and watched them leave. Prisoners did the heavy labor of the road building, the backbreaking shovel, axe, and saw work. The prisoners had their overseers, and in turn, the overseers were backed up by the soldiers. Now, as the day ended, the last load of ragged, sweating prisoners shuffled to the remaining wagons. Some of the crew wore leg irons and were shackled into teams. Others enjoyed relative freedom in manacles. A manacled man can still use a shovel or an axe. Their chains clanked loudly as they climbed awkwardly into the heavy wagons that would carry them back to Gettys and their confinement for the night.

I waited until night was full before I moved. I ghosted along in the shelter of the trees, surveying the work that had been done today. I was not pleased to see that they had set a guard. Epiny's sabotage had alarmed them, I supposed. A lantern burned in one of the surviving equipment sheds. I slunk closer, and perceived that four men had been left on watch there. They sat sullenly around the tail of a wagon, their lantern in the middle of it, and passed round a bottle of rum. I did not envy them their lonely vigil. If I opened my awareness, I could feel the insistent itching of the fear, the prickling sensation that evil watched them and waited its opportunity to pick them off, one by one. Their loaded long guns leaned upright against the wagon's open bed, one beside each man. I frowned at that. Drunken fearful men would be quick to lunge for their weapons. The magic could heal me very quickly, but did not make me proof against instantaneous death.

I resolved I would give them no cause for alarm. Not yet.

I took in a deep breath of night and held it. I turned my eyes away from the yellow lantern light of the watchmen. I breathed out slowly, expelling the darkness I had held within me. The blackness of night hovered round me in a cloud. Cloaked in darkness, I stepped softly forward. Deep moss cushioned my footfalls as I moved away from the watchmen. Tree branches drew aside from me; bushes swayed from my path silently lest they betray me with a rustle. I had no light but I did not need it. I was a part of the forest around me and I came into full awareness of it.

For a brief time, it overwhelmed me. I became aware of the deep carpet of life that extended around me in all directions. I was a mote in that intertwining net of living things. Life extended deep beneath my feet in the rich earth with the questing roots and the burrowing worms and the scuttling beetles. Trees surrounded me and reached far above my head. Rabbits, deer, and foxes moved in the darkness just as I did, while overhead, birds both sleeping and wakeful perched on the branches.

As I began to comprehend that interconnectedness I became aware of a stabbing pain. I gritted my teeth against it and clutched at my belly, almost expecting to find a mortal wound there. But I was fine. It was not my body that hurt; the injury I sensed was to the larger organism through which I moved and in which I existed.

The road was the wound. It was a deep gash with a virulent infection, one that the forest could not heal by itself. The road builders had cut deep into the forest's green and living flesh, and filled that gap with gravel and sand and stone. Every time the forest tried to knit the wound closed with healing foliage, the road builders cut it back again. They were not like maggots in a wound, for maggots eat only dead flesh. These intruders maintained the slice of deadness they had placed in the forest, and cut back any attempt the forest made to heal itself. They had to go. Until the road builders were driven away, the forest could not heal.

It was a night of awakenings for me. I accepted that the forest was a living entity, almost godlike in its sprawling being. I accepted that if it was to survive, the intruders had to be banished. The road had already cut deep into the forest; the deeper it was pushed, the more the forest was divided from itself. If the road went all the way up into the mountains, the forest knew it was doomed.

But I still did not know what the magic wished me to do.

I drew back into myself, dizzied by my new awareness. It was hard to find my small human mind, and harder still to apply it to the task the magic had given me. Impatiently, I decided that there was no time to wait for the magic to discern the solution and convey it to me. The magic was so organic, so interwoven with the problem, that it could present no simple solution to it. And yet that, I felt sure, was what was needed. Something as direct and sudden as a hammer's blow. I suspected that the magic saw no solution, and that was why it had taken me. A very old strategic premise was that the best way to find an enemy's weakness was to become the enemy. The forest magic had passed beyond that; it had made the enemy one of its own, precisely for this reason. The hammer of Gernian logic and engineering would be wielded with the power the magic had given me.

I tried to find stillness within me, tried to feel the magic agree with that supposition. I felt nothing. But the logic of it was so clear that I brushed aside all doubt. This was why the magic had created me. In me, the power of the magic would be wielded with Gernian logic by a trained soldier. The time for subtlety was past. It was time for me to act.

I moved like darkness itself, flowing effortlessly, encountering no resistance. I paid no mind to the guards keeping their watch. They were irrelevant to me. I had seen what the magic had not perceived. Fear without foundation would sway men only to a point.

I would give their fear roots.

CHAPTER FOUR

MAGE WORK

At the edge of the road, I hesitated. Then I left life behind and stepped out into the silence of the soulless road. I felt I tore myself free of my roots to do so. With every step I took on the roadbed, I felt my awareness of the forest net of life stretch and tear. By the time I stood in the center of the road, I felt small and exposed. Overhead, there was no friendly canopy of leaves and branches, only a terrible rift that bared me to the endless night sky. I felt my Speck self retreat and Nevare came to the fore. I blinked my eyes as if I were waking from a dream. I looked around at all that must be done in the space of a night. Then I took a breath and began.

I felt like a commander on high ground, overlooking his massed forces just before the assault begins. I felt within myself for the magic. It was not an easy thing for me to do. I groped for something I could not feel or sense in any ordinary way. And once I thought I had found it, I had to find, not the will or the intellect, but the emotion to apply it.

It was harder than I'd expected it to be. I was, I discovered, tired of feeling. I'd had enough of hurt and betrayal and despair. I didn't want to open my heart to emotions strong enough to send the magic streaming through my blood. But I had promised. I closed my eyes for a moment and then opened them to the night. No color was left in the day, save what the pallid moon would wring from the landscape. The road all around me was a flat, gray stripe of desert . . . No, not desert. No matter how barren a desert might appear to be, it had structure and life and connections. This road had none of those things. Dry, forsaken, it had no life of its own and severed the connections in all the lives it divided. I had thought that when I toiled in the graveyard, I dealt in death. In reality, there I had been part of the turning cycle of life and death and life. Here was true death; here all life ceased.

Anger at what had been done warred with sorrow over the loss. With an effort of will, I turned my fury aside. Instead of hatred, I let my sorrow fill me. This dead stripe of earth had once been rich, seething with life in all its stages. I grieved for its bereavement. I let go of all self-restraint and became my grief.

Then I used the power of the magic guided by my Gernian logic.

Hitch had been right. I knew exactly what to do and I wanted to do it above all else. I lifted my arms and spread wide my hands, and then I lowered them, beckoning. I was confident of it. The magic had to come. Nonetheless, I felt a resistance from it, almost as if it questioned what I was doing. The magic was not accustomed to be used in such a way. What I contemplated was not the forest way nor the Speck way. But I knew what I was doing, and I was certain it would work. "It's a Gernian way," I said softly to the night wind. "A Gernian tactic to turn back the Gernians. Isn't that why you wanted me? To use me as a tool against my own kind? Then trust me to know how I am sharpest!"

The magic relented. I felt it well up from inside me and flow outward. It strengthened my arms and then filled my hands. They grew heavy with it. I kept them closed in fists, containing it until I was sure my focus was clear and my purpose strong. Then I opened my fingers and let the magic shoot forth.

I began where it was easiest. Water always summons life. Epiny had blown up the culvert and the pooling water had washed out part of the road and soaked even more. The work crews had gone far to repair it today, but the moist earth still beckoned. It was ready to receive what I had to give.

I reached to the smallest plants, the tiny single-leaved cresses, the strands of algae that waited in the stagnant ponds at the side of the road. Given time and no disturbances, they would, in the course of a month, repopulate the damp soil and the standing puddles. From the sun and the earth, they would draw sustenance in minute daily quantities. They would edge into the available space, slowly repopulating it as their resources allowed them.

I opened myself. I surrendered to them the energy that the magic had given to me. In a matter of moments, I fed them the resources it would have taken them a year to gather. And they re-sponded. Like an unfurling green carpet, the massed plants surged forward, enveloping the forsaken roadbed. They sank pale roots into the packed gravel, seeking the scant moisture of the settling dew, absorbing the dust of nutrients trapped among the pebbles. They were like new skin covering a gaping wound.

I choked the newly set culvert with greenery. I beckoned the lush, fat-stemmed, flat-leaved plants to fill it. I heard the rustle of their growth, and the muddy water that had flowed freely through it suddenly gagged, backed, and swelled. I waited. A crystalline trickle emerged from the filtering plant life and a pond began to back up on the high side of the road. By morning, I calculated, a new stream would be cutting its way across the road's surface. I turned away.

I strode down the road, naked to the moonlight and the dis-tant stars. I spoke to the trees that lined the road. I was as heartless as a herder culling cattle. Most of the trees that lined the road had had their side roots cut. They would linger for years, but they were already dying. To the weak, I commanded, "Let go your grip and fall!" The strong I bade, "Send out your roots. Buckle and break the road."

And as I strode along, I heard it happen behind me. I did not turn back to look at my destruction. I felt what happened. Dying trees crashed across the road. I felt the breeze they created as they fell, and bits of bark flew up and showered down again. Other trees stirred suddenly, and sent roots questing through packed earth and bedded gravel. They did not grow slowly seeking nourishment. They tunneled like gophers, thrusting and rucking the surface of the road like a crumpled rug. I walked toward the end of the King's Road and destruction followed me like a giant trampling the earth.

I drew abreast of the equipment shed where the guards kept their watch. They had heard the falling trees and the shifting earth of the buckling road. Long guns gripped in their hands, they had come to the open end of the shed. I saw them silhouetted against their fire. They could not see me. I was darkness against darkness, and their paltry light could not reach out to touch me.

They were shouting questions at one another. "What is it? What's happening?" But none of them were venturing out from the feeble shelter of the shed to see for themselves. I walked past them, the small sounds of my passage cloaked in the falling trees and shifting stone that followed me. I heard them arguing that someone should ride back to town and raise the alarm. No one wanted to go, and one man shrilly but sensibly demanded, "Alarm against who? Alarm against what? Trees falling? I'm not going out there."

I thought of bringing their shed down around their ears. I could do it. I could have commanded the trees to topple it with their roots. I did not. I told myself it was not because they were my erstwhile countrymen, but because it suited the purpose of the magic better to leave them alive and unscathed. Let them give witness tomorrow to how the forest itself had turned on the road and attacked it. I strode past them unseen, and in my wake the road surface burst upward with questing roots, only to be concealed moments later by falling trees. The terrified shouts of the guards were drowned in the groans and crashes of the falling timber. Their firelight and sounds faded behind me as I moved on.

I left the finished road behind, traveling over the roadbed that was still under construction. Here the soil had not been packed and the roadbed was not yet leveled. It was easier for the trees to hummock their roots across it. There were still plenty of dying trees lining the clearings. As each one fell, I felt slightly diminished. Did I have the right to tell them to surrender what remained of their lives? I steeled my heart and decided that I did. It was not the individual trees but the forest itself that I was trying to save. Yet the magic that made them topple was the most demanding of what I was doing, as if the magic itself were appalled by my ruthlessness. With a wave of my hand, I ordered a vine to crawl from the ditch and shroud the fallen tree in greenery. It did, sinking its roots into the fallen trunk and limbs and reaching up to unfurl leaves to sunlight that wasn't there. But I was. I fed them the energy that they needed, and felt the vines grow thick and tough as dried leather. Encouraged, I spoke to the brambles. It was harder to bring them forth; there was little in the soil to sustain them and they were reluctant, green troops quailing under fire. I gritted my teeth and by my will drove them out to where I needed them. The rising sun tomorrow would bake them brown. It would not matter. The thorny mat they left behind would be one more obstacle to the road builders. Cannon fodder, I thought, closed my heart to my doubts, and strode on.

My body diminished as I used the magic. My hated fat, the reservoir of my power, was dwindling away. It felt very strange. My trousers sagged on my hips. I could not hold them up; I needed my hands to do the summoning. Growling at the delay, I paused and tightened my belt. It pinched my loosened skin. I ignored it. I was nearly at the end of the road. I had to go on; I had to finish my barricade against the road builders. I summoned my will and my emotion once more, and threw wide the reserves I had stored. For a brief moment, the magic fought my will, and then the power came under my dominion again. The magic sang through my blood, intoxicating me with command. I brought the trees down more swiftly, laughed aloud as the road buckled in my wake. I spoke to the weeds and scrub brush that had survived in the ditches, and they burst into rampant growth, running up the banks and crawling across the road. My parade of destruction had become a charge. Nothing could stop me.

The end of the King's Road was a tangled darkness before me. I looked with the eyes of night and my heart sank at what I saw. The singing of the magic in my blood became a dirge. The loggers had brought down another kaembra tree. The massive trunk had been severed, and the fallen giant had crashed down onto the cleared apron that would eventually be part of the road.

I stood for a moment, my nearly depleted magic simmering in me, and stared at the tragedy. Until I had come east to Gettys, I had never imagined such trees existed. I had been raised in the Midlands, on the plains and plateaus where it might take a tree a score of years to increase its girth by an inch. We had ancient trees, but they were twisted, battered things with trunks as hard as metal.

The giants of the Speck forest still awed me. The fallen trunk that blocked my path was far too tall for me to climb over; I would have had better luck scaling the palisade that surrounded the fort at Gettys. I walked around its severed base, suddenly exhausted and staggering. While I had wielded the magic, I had not felt tired. Now my weariness hit me with full force.

Beneath my loosened clothing, my emptied skin sagged around me. The excess skin on my arms, legs, belly, and buttocks all but flapped around me as I walked. I groped at my body, finding the jut of a hipbone and the ripple of my ribs as if greeting old friends. The warning of Jodoli, a Great Man of the Specks far more experienced with magic than I was, came back to me.

"You can die from loss of magic, just as you can die from loss of blood. But it seldom happens to us without the mage knowing exactly what he is doing. It takes a great deal of will to burn every bit of magic out of yourself. A mage would have to push past pain and exhaustion to do it. Ordinarily, the mage would lose consciousness before he was completely dead. Then his feeder could revive him, if she were nearby. If not, the Great One might still perish."

I smiled grimly to myself as I tottered on toward the standing stump of the fallen tree. I had no feeder to come and tend me. Olikea, a woman of the Specks, had served for a time as my feeder. The last time I had seen Olikea we had quarreled because I had refused to turn against the Gernians and come live among the Specks. She had reviled me before she left; I'd been a great disappointment to her. She competed hard with her sister Firada,

Jodoli's feeder. I wondered, almost sadly, if I had ever been some-one that she cared about, or only a powerful but ignorant mage whom she could manipulate? The question should have meant more to me, but I was too tired to care anymore.

But I had done it. My blockade of the road builders would slow them for months. For a fleeting instant, pleasure warmed me as I thought how proud of me Epiny would be. But a chill thought followed it. Epiny would never know it was my work. She would hear of the dog's death I had died, and mourn me fiercely. If she heard of what had transpired at the road's end, she would put it down to Speck magic. I was dead to her. Dead to her, dead to Spink, dead to Amzil and her children. Dead to my sister, Yaril, as soon as word reached her. Dead to old Sergeant Duril, the mentor of my youth. My exuberance drained and darkness swirled around me. Dead to everyone I loved. Might as well really be dead.

I fell to my knees in my weariness. That was a mistake. The in-stant I settled into stillness, hunger woke in me and clawed at my guts and throat. It was beyond hunger pangs; it felt as if my guts were devouring themselves and I groaned with it. If Olikea were here, I thought hazily, she would bring me the berries and roots and leaves that sustained my magic. And afterward, she would have roused my passions and then sated them. Some desperate sentry in my brain realized that my thoughts were circling uselessly. The sky was graying. I'd spent the night as recklessly as I'd spent my magic. Daylight was coming. Time to flee.

It took me some little time to rise. I staggered on, my ears ringing. I felt as if I could hear a great crowd of people talking at a distance. There was that uneven rise and fall of vocalization, rather like water lapping against a shore. I lifted my eyes, but no one was there. Then my knees folded under me again. I had not gone even a dozen paces. I crumpled to the earth beside the massive stump of the fallen kaembra tree. I caught myself before I went facedown in the wood chips and sawdust that littered the forest floor. With a groan I twisted my body to lean my back against the stump. I had never felt such weariness and hunger, not even in my worst days of starvation in my father's house. "Am I dying?" I asked the implacable night.

"Probably not," a dusky voice behind me said. "But I am."

I did not turn my head or even start. Despite my own distress, I felt shamed to have forgotten that others suffered more keenly than I did. "I'm sorry," I said to the tree. "I'm sorry. I tried, but I was too late to save you. I should have tried harder."

"You said you would speak to them!" he cried out. "You said you would do your best to put an end to this." His outrage and pain rang, not in my ears, but in my heart.

I closed my eyes to sense him better. "I thought you would be dead," I said thoughtlessly. My own deep weariness and stabbing hunger eroded my manners. My magic was at its lowest ebb. I could barely sense the old Speck in the tree. Once his hair had been dark, but now it was long and gray, with the streaks of white barely showing against it. His pale blue eyes were almost white, and his speckled markings had faded against his skin to a dapple of freckles. He'd been old when he went into his tree, I suddenly knew. Once he had been fat, a Great One, a forest mage like myself, but now he was bleeding to death. As his magic ran out of his tree, his flesh hung flaccid around him. I stared at him, wondering if that was how I looked, and if our fates would be the same.

"I *am* dead," he told me bitterly. "Swift or slow as the end may come, it certainly comes now. They cut me with cold iron, with many, many blows of cold, sharp iron."

I shuddered, imagining the pain. Could it have been worse than a thousand lashes? He had been unable to flee his fate as I had done. His life had depended on me, and my paltry efforts to save him had failed.

"I'm sorry," I said with great sincerity. "I did try. I was too late for you. But what I have done tonight should frighten the road builders. If they find the courage to try again, I have created a chaos they will not quickly undo. Even if they start tomorrow, it will be months before they undo my destruction. Winter is coming and work will stop when the snow flies. I have bought us some time in which we can seek a permanent solution."

"Months," he said with scorn. "Part of a year? What is that to me? Nothing, now! I am dead, Jhernian. My death will be a slow fading to you, but I will be gone before the spring comes. And to me, it will seem but a wink of the eye. Once we have our trees, we do not count time in hours or days or even seasons as you do. I am dead. But while there is still enough of me left to speak, I will tell you again. Delaying them is not enough. You must drive these intruders out, so that they never come back. Kill them all, if you must. For years now we have refrained from that, but perhaps it is the only thing that will stop them. Kill them all. A delay? What good does that do? You have been just like any other Jhernian, bidding living things die to please your ends, and then claiming you have benefited us all! What a fool you have been, throwing magic like dust, wasting a hoard such as has not been seen for many years!"

I had scarcely the strength to answer him, but so stung was I that I rallied what little remained to me. "As the magic wished me to do, I have done."

He laughed bitterly. "I did not feel the magic speak at your act. Instead, I witnessed you bending your will to force trees to their deaths, to push plants to spread where they cannot sustain themselves, to push life just as unnaturally as the intruders have pushed death. Any of us could have told you that it would not work. Tomorrow, half your magic will be undone by the rising sun as the plants wither and fade. What a waste!"

I felt childish and everything seemed unfair. The magic had never told me clearly what it wanted of me. The ancestor trees had never offered me advice. "I did not know I could seek your advice," I said stiffly. I was so tired. It was hard to make the words form in my mind.

"Why do you think we exist, if not to answer questions and give advice? What other value could the ancestor trees have? A silly, selfish continuation of life and pride? No. We exist to guide the People. We exist to protect the People."

"And the People are failing to protect you." I felt a deep sadness and shame.

"The magic is given to you to protect us. Use it as you are supposed to use it, and we will not fall."

"But—the magic showed me the forest, alive and complete. The road is the death that cuts through it. If I can remove the death, if I can stitch the halves of the forest back together—"

"You are like a little child, who sees the nut but does not comprehend that it came from a tree, let alone that it holds another tree. Look larger. See it all."

He lifted me or perhaps he released me to rise. What he showed me is hard to put into words. I saw the forest again, as the magic had shown it to me, as a perfectly balanced dance of lives. And the road still intruded into it, a skewer of death. But the forest elder lifted me higher still, and I saw the road not as a single stripe of death, but as a feeler reaching out from a foreign organism. The road was to that system, not a stripe of death but a root, securing it in new soil. And just as I had imagined the pathways and byways that would spread out from it as small rootlets, so they were. And if I followed that root back to its source, I saw the Kingdom of Gernia, growing and spreading just as organically as a vine crawling up a tree. The vine that used a tree to reach the sunlight did not intend evil to the tree; it was incidental that it sucked all life from the tree as it climbed and spread, shading the tree's leaves with its own tendrils and foliage. The roads fed Gernia, and were focused only on sustaining their own organism. For Gernia to live, the road must grow. It could not survive without its growing, spreading roots. My civilization and the forest were two organisms, competing for resources. One would shade out the other.

Then, just as quickly as I had risen over all, I was in my own flesh again, leaning against the severed tree, bereft of strength and hope.

Defeat soured even my brief memory of the triumph I'd felt. I spoke softly. "Magic can't change it, Tree Man. It isn't the road or the fortification at Gettys. It isn't even the people who have come here. It's so big, it can't be stopped. You know that even if I could kill all the intruders, I would not. But if I did, if we killed every last man, woman, and child in Gettys, it would be only like clipping off the end of a tree's branch. Other branches grow. Next summer would see more people here, and the road building would start again. For the Gernians to come here is as inevitable as water flowing downhill. Now that some have come, others will follow, seeking land to farm or routes to trade and wealth. Killing them will not stop them from coming or building this road."

I drew a breath. It took so much effort. I thought again of the vine, climbing and choking and overshadowing the tree. "I see only one possible path. What we must do is find a way to persuade the intruders to take their road elsewhere. Show them a route that does not come through the groves of the ancestor trees. Then both our peoples can live alongside one another in peace."

It was getting harder and harder to organize my thoughts. Speaking seemed a great effort. My words were slurring, but I couldn't find the energy to sit up and speak clearly. I closed my eyes. A final thought jabbed at me and I made a vast effort to voice it. "If I can stop the road builders, if I can divert them, cannot you send up a new sprout and live? Tree Woman has."

"Lisana's trunk was not completely severed. Although her crown and trunk fell, enough of a connection was left that her leaves could go on making food and one of her branches was positioned well to become a new sapling. But I am cut off short, and have no leaves left. Even if I could, I would have to send up a sapling from my roots, beginning as no more than a sprout. I would be greatly diminished for scores of years."

"But you would be alive. You would not be lost to us."

He was silent.

All my exhilaration at spending my magic was suddenly gone. We had come full circle back to my great failure. Everyone insisted that the magic had given me the task of making all the Gernians leave and putting an end to their road building. It was impossible. I'd told them that, endlessly, but no one listened. Even the tree elders know that the intruders could not be stopped. Not even with magic.

I managed to lift my hand and placed it against his bark. Something was very wrong with me. I could not feel my legs and my vision suddenly faded. Had I closed my eyes? I could not tell. I forced out sluggish words. "I have used too much magic. I do not have a feeder to revive me. If you wish, take whatever nourishment you can from my body. Use me up. Perhaps you can live that way. Perhaps someone else will find a way to stop the road and let the Gernians and Specks live in peace. It is beyond me."

Silence greeted my offer. Perhaps I had offended him. As strength fled my body, I decided it no longer mattered. I pushed my fingers into a fissure in his bark; my hand would stay in place even if I lost consciousness. My whole body was clamoring for sustenance and rest. I suspected it was too late. I'd passed the redemption point. "Use me up," I offered him again and let go.

"You have no feeder? You are a Great One and no one attends you? This is intolerable!" His words reached me from a great distance. I sensed he felt insulted more on his own behalf than concerned for me. "This is not how a Great One dies, untended and treeless. What have the People come to, to allow such a thing to happen?"

My hearing was fading. I was distant from his dismay and alarm. I wondered, dispassionately, what the penal workers would think when they found my deflated body here. It would certainly be a mystery for them. A great mystery.

Everything stopped.

CHAPTER FIVE

THE OTHER SIDE

L isana," I said.

She did not hear me. I saw her more clearly than I had in many days; she was as she had been in my dreams when I was at the Cavalla Academy in Old Thares. The Tree Woman was sitting with her back to her tree trunk. Her glossy hair was tangled on the bark. She was naked, a fleshy woman of indeterminate years. The day's early sunlight dappled her flesh as it streamed through the canopy foliage, and I could not tell the real dappling of her skin from that which the sunlight created. Her eyelids were half closed, her breathing heavy and slow. I smiled down at her, my gaze fondly tracing the lines of her plump lips, the small furrow in her brow that deepened when she was annoyed at me. I came closer to her and whispered by her ear, "Lisana! I'm here."

Her eyes opened slowly, sleepily, without alarm. The little line on her forehead deepened in puzzlement. Her eyes moved past me and looked through me. Her rounded shoulder twitched in a small shrug. She started to close her eyes again.

"Lisana!" I said more urgently.

She caught her breath, sat up, and looked around. "Soldier's Boy?" she asked in confusion.

"Yes. I've come back to you. I've done my best to stop the road building. I failed. But I'm finished. Finished with all of it. So here I am, come to be with you."

She scanned the forest all around her twice before her eyes settled on me. Then she reached out a plump hand to me. Her fingers passed through me, a sensation rather like sparkling wine spilling on my flesh. Tears welled in her eyes. "Oh, no. No! What has happened? This cannot be. This cannot be!"

"It's all right," I reassured her. "I used up all the magic in me to try to stop the road. My body is dying, but I'm here with you. So that's not so bad, is it? I'm content."

"Soldier's Boy, no! No, it's not bad, it's terrible. You are a Great One! The magic made you a Great One. And now you are dying, treeless and untended. You are already fading from my eyes. And soon you will be gone, gone forever."

"I know. But once that body is gone, I will be here with you. And I do not think that is a bad thing."

"No. No, you fool! You are vanishing. You have no tree. And you have fallen—" She closed her eyes for a moment, and when she did, tears spilled from them. She opened them wide and her gaze was full of anguish. "You have fallen far from any sapling. You are untended and unprepared and still divided against yourself. Oh, Soldier's Boy, how did this happen? You will fade away. And when you do, I will never see you again. Never."

The wind blew softly through me. I felt oddly diminished. "I didn't know that," I said lamely. Stupidly. "I'm sorry." As I apologized to her, a flicker of panic raced through me and then faded away. There wasn't enough life left in me to panic. I'd made a mistake and I was dying. Apparently not even a Speck afterlife was available to me. I'd simply stop being. Apparently, I hadn't died correctly. Oops.

I knew I should be devastated. An emotion washed through me, too pale for me to recognize. "I'm sorry," I said again, as much to myself as to her.

She stretched her arms wide and gathered into her bosom what was left of me. I felt her embrace only as a faint warmth. It was not even a skin-to-skin sensation, but was perhaps my memory of warmth. My awareness was trickling away. Soon there would not even be enough left to be concerned. I'd be nothing. No. Nothing would be me. That was a better way to express it. I vaguely remembered how I would have smiled.

The water was sweet. Not just sweet as fresh water is sweet, but sweet as in flavored with honey or nectar. I choked on the gush of it into my mouth, coughed and felt the coolness spatter down my chest. Then I drew a breath through my nose, closed my lips around the mouth of the water skin, and sucked it in. I drank in long gulping drafts, pulling in as much liquid as my mouth would hold, swallowing it down and then sucking in more. I sucked the water skin flat. Nonetheless, I kept my mouth firmly clamped to it, sucking fruitlessly at it. Someone pinched my nose shut, and when I had to open my mouth to breathe, the water skin was snatched away. I moaned a protest.

Another one was offered to me. This one was even better; it was not just sweet water. The liquid was thicker. Meat and salt and garlic were blended in a thick broth with other flavors I did not know. I didn't really care. I sucked it down.

The disorganized sounds around me suddenly evolved into language. "Be careful. Don't let him have that much that fast." A man's voice.

"Would *you* like to be his feeder, Jodoli?" That was a voice I recognized. Olikea sounded just as angry as she had been when last we parted. She was a powerful woman, as tall as I was and well muscled. Her anger was not a thing to dismiss. I suddenly felt exposed. I tried to draw my arms and legs up to protect myself, but felt them only twitch in response to me.

"Look. He's trying to move!" Jodoli sounded both surprised and relieved.

Olikea muttered some sour response. I did not make out her words, but someone else did. A woman spoke. I did not know her voice.

"Well, that is what it means to be a feeder of a Great One. If you did not wish to have the work of it, you should not have taken it on, little sister. It is not a task to take up lightly. Nor should it be seized merely as an opportunity to advance yourself. If you are weary of the honor of tending to him, say so plainly. I am sure there are other women of our kin who would be glad to take him on. And they, perhaps, would not have let him fall into such a state. What if he had died? Think of the shame you would have brought down on our kin-clan! Such a thing has never befallen one of our Great Ones."

"Jodoli has extended himself into such a state! I have heard you complain of it. He often tells the story of nearly dying from using too much magic."

Olikea's sister stiffened with fury. I became aware I'd opened my eyes to slits. I recognized her. Oh. Yes. Firada looked very like her younger sister, yet their features bore very different expressions at that moment. Firada's hazel eyes were narrowed with displeasure. She had crossed her arms over her chest and stared at her younger sister contemptuously.

Olikea was crouched over me. She held an empty leather skin in her hands and her lips were drawn tight with fury. Her eyes were green. She had a dark streak from her brow to the tip of her nose and the speckles on her face were more generous than her sister's. On the rest of her body, her specks were a dappling that became streaks on her ribs and legs, almost like the striping on a cat. The striping was repeated in her hair. I had thought she was about my age but now she seemed younger. Her skin blushed a hot pink today around her dapples. She wore the most clothing I'd ever seen her don. It consisted of a leather belt slung on her hips, with several pouches attached to it, and some loops that held simple tools. Although it was decorated with beads, feathers, and small charms made from fired pottery or beaten copper, its function was to allow her to carry her supplies with ease rather than to cover her body.

Jodoli stood well back from both of the sisters. My fellow Great Man and sometime rival was not nearly as large as I was, but his size would have turned heads in any Gernian setting. He wore his black hair in plaits. His blue eyes were surprising in the dark mask of pigment on his face. "Stop your quarreling. He's awake. He needs food now, if he can stomach it."

"Likari! Give me that basket of berries and then go and get more. Don't stand about staring. Be useful."

For the first time, I noticed a small boy just behind Olikea. He had green eyes like hers and the same stripe down his nose. Probably their younger brother. In response to her words, he jerked as if poked with a stick. He thrust a heavily laden basket at her. The moment she took it, he turned and scampered off. His reddened bare buttocks were dappled like a horse's; I almost smiled to see him run.

But Olikea's scowl bored into me. "Well, Soldier's Boy. Are you going to eat, or just stare about you like a frog on a lily leaf?"

"I'll eat," I said. Her offer of food drove all else from my mind. I would do nothing to offend her, lest she change her mind about feeding me.

Slowly it broke through my foggy brain that I was going to live. I felt a pang of regret at that, strange to say. I had not planned to die nor especially enjoyed the prospect, but it had been invitingly simple. All my worries would have been over: no more wondering if I was doing the right thing. Now I was back in a world where people had expectations of me.

I reclined in a natural shelter formed by a vine that had climbed up a sagging branch of a great tree. Its drapery made a thicker shade for me in the muted light of the forest. The moss beneath me was deep and soft. I suspected that Jodoli had used his magic to form such a comfortable couch for me. In the same moment that I knew I should thank him, Olikea dropped the basket of berries beside me. My attention was riveted upon it. It took all the strength I had to command my wasted hand and arm to move. The emptied flesh hung from my bones in a flaccid curtain of skin. I dug a handful of berries from the basket, heedless of how I crushed the ripe fruit and shoved them into my mouth. The flavor blossomed in my mouth, life-giving, sweet, tangy, redolent of flowers. I chewed it twice, swallowed, licked the dripping juice from my hand and scooped up another handful. I pushed them into my mouth, as much as my mouth could hold. I chewed with my lips pursed tight, afraid some morsel would escape them.

Around me, a storm raged. Jodoli and Firada scolded Olikea and she responded angrily. I had not an instant's attention for it until the basket was emptied of berries. It was not a small basket. It should have filled me, but with every bit of replenished energy, my body only grew stronger in clamoring for more. I wanted to demand more, but some underlying craftiness told me that if I angered Olikea, she might not help me. I forced myself to hear what she was saying.

" . . . in the light where the Great One's tree had fallen. As a result, I am burned. Even Likari was burned, though the little wretch did almost nothing to help me. It will be days before I can move without pain, or even sleep comfortably!"

Jodoli looked embarrassed for me. Firada had pursed her lips in the Speck gesture of denial and looked stubbornly righteous. "What did you think it meant to be the feeder of a Great One? Did you think all you had to do was bring him food and then bask in his reflected status? If that was all there was to it, a Great One would not need a feeder. All the People would simply feed him. No. A Great One needs a feeder precisely because he will not fix his mind on the ordinary concerns of life. He will listen to the magic instead. Managing the ordinary part of his life is your task. You are supposed to seek out the proper foods for him and be sure he has them in full variety. You are supposed to keep the nits out of his hair, and aid him in his washing so that his skin stays healthy. When he dream-walks, you should stand watch over his body until his soul comes back to it. And you are supposed to see that his line continues. That is what it means to be the feeder of a Great One. You seized that duty for yourself as soon as you discovered him. Do not pretend he chose you. You found him; he did not come seeking you. If you are tired of the duty, then say so and set it aside. He is not uncomely, even for a plain-skin. And all have heard of the gifts he gave you! There are other women who would gladly take up the tasks of being his feeder, in the sole hope of getting his child. You have not even been successful at that, have you?"

My gaze traveled to Olikea's face. Firada's words were like rainfall on dry ground. They pattered against my senses and only

slowly soaked into my brain. The Gernian in me pushed his way
to the front of my mind, commanding me to pay attention to what
was going on. Olikea had rescued me. I'd lain where I'd fallen, in
the sunlight. She'd been burned when she had to emerge from the
forest to drag me back into its shelter. Speck skin was notoriously
sensitive to light and heat. She'd risked herself. For me.

And she wasn't sure I was worth it. Nevare the Gernian was
inclined to bow his head to that and watch her walk away, without
too many regrets. I had once believed that Olikea was genuinely
infatuated with me, to the point of feeling guilty that her feelings
were so much deeper than my own. To hear that Firada believed
Olikea cared for me only as a way to gain power put everything
in a very different light. I was not a prize bull to be groomed and
exhibited as a possession. I still had my pride.

But the Speck part of me perceived things from a very different angle. A Great Man not only needed a feeder, he was entitled
to one. I was a Great Man of the Specks, and Olikea's kin-clan
should have felt honored that I had chosen to live among them.
For Olikea to decide that she did not relish her duty was a grave
insult to me as well as a threat to my well-being. Anger upwelled
in me, an anger founded deep in a Speck awareness of the affront
to me. Was I not a Great One? Had not I given up everything to
become a vessel for the magic? What right had she to begrudge
me the assistance that most would have found an honor?

A peculiar tingling ran over me from head to foot, not unlike
the pins-and-needles sensation of a limb that has been still too
long. From somewhere in me, Soldier's Boy summoned strength
and sat me up. My Speck self, so long subjugated by my Gernian
identity, looked around with disdain. Then, as if he were pulling
off a sweaty shirt, he peeled himself free of me. In that instant,
he separated us and I, Nevare the Gernian, abruptly became a
bystander observing my own life. He looked down at his wasted
body, at the empty folds of skin where once a wealth of magic
had been stored. I felt his disgust with me. Nevare had wasted
his magic, wasted it in a temporary solution that saved no one
and nothing. He lifted the empty ripples of belly skin and then
let them fall with a small groan of dismay. All the magic he had

stolen from the Plainsfolk at the Dancing Spindle, all the magic he had acquired since then and painstakingly hoarded, gone! All of it foolishly squandered in a vain show of power. A fortune had been traded for trinkets. He lifted the folds of his depleted belly and then let them fall again. Tears of rage stung his eyes, followed by a flush of shame. He had been immense with magic, full of power, and stupidity had wasted it all. He gritted his teeth at his diminished status. He looked like a starved man, a weakling who could not even provide for himself, let alone shelter his kin-clan. That wastrel Nevare knew nothing of being a Great Man, nothing of magic. He had not even chosen his feeder well, but had simply accepted the first woman who offered herself. That, at least, could be quickly mended. He lifted his eyes to stare sternly at Olikea.

"You are not my feeder."

Olikea, Jodoli, and Firada were staring at him in amazement, the sort of amazement that would be roused by a stone speaking. Olikea's mouth opened in shock and a parade of emotions passed over her face. Insult, shock, regret, and anger all vied to dominate her features.

As Nevare, I watched the drama unfold before me as an audience rather than a participant. I could hear and see, but I could not speak or control the body I inhabited. I was aware of his thoughts. Could I influence them? I could not find in myself the ambition to try. My Speck self's devastation at how I had wasted our magic drained me of purpose. Let him deal with the unreasonable demands of the magic and see if he could do any better!

I watched with sour amusement as Olikea tried to master her face. She strained to look concerned rather than insulted. Olikea had never heard this man speak to her in such tones before. It angered her, but she tried for a calm voice. "But, Soldier's Boy, you are weak. You need—"

"I need food!" he snapped. "Not useless talk and whining complaints. Food. A true feeder would have seen to my needs first and saved rebukes and complaints for later." Within the wasted body, I moved like a shadow behind Soldier's Boy. My Speck self submerged me in his interpretation of the world. I surrendered and became still. Olikea glanced sideways at her sister and Jodoli.

She hated being humiliated before them. She squared her shoulders and tried a firm and motherly approach. "You are hungry and weak. Look at what you have done to yourself. Now is no time to be difficult, Soldier's Boy. Stop saying silly things and let me tend to you. You are not yourself right now."

I smiled in harmony with Soldier's Boy. She had no idea how correct she was.

At that moment, I became aware of a scent on the air, the smell of something essential. He turned toward it, forgetting Olikea. The small sunburned boy was returning with a basket full of berries. He was hurrying, his round cheeks joggling as he trotted up to me. "I've brought you the berries," he called as he hastened up. His eyes met mine. I think he suddenly realized that it was unexpected for me to be awake. His blue eyes reflected a child's horror at how wasted my body was. Then, as quickly, horror was replaced with sympathy. He thrust the basket at me. "Eat them! Eat them quickly!" In his haste, the basket tipped and a few berries bounded out of it to rest on the moss like scattered jewels.

"Clumsy boy! Give those to me! They are for the Great One," Olikea told him sharply.

The youngster simultaneously cringed and pushed the basket toward her. As Olikea dropped her hand to take the basket, Jodoli looked away; Firada scowled. "No," Soldier's Boy said firmly.

"But you must eat these, Soldier's Boy." Olikea's manner had changed in an instant. From being stern with the boy she went to cajoling me. "They are what you need to regain your strength. Once you have strength back, we can begin to replenish your magic. But first, you must eat these."

The smell of the berries reached his nostrils, piquant and tempting. He shivered with want. He clasped his hands together to keep from snatching at them. "No. I take nothing from you. The boy brought the gift to me. Let him present it to me. The honor of serving a Great Man is his."

Nevare would have blushed to say such words. Nevare would never have claimed such importance for himself. But this was not Nevare, no matter how I might think of him in terms of "I" and "me." This was someone else, and I was only his silent shadow.

Olikea caught her breath. Her eyes narrowed and I thought she would challenge his words. Instead, she stood abruptly, turned on her heel and stalked away. Jodoli and Firada stared after her, but the boy's full attention was on me. Awed by the honor, he dropped to his knees, the basket cradled in both his hands, and then walked on his knees toward me. The closer he came, the more compelling the smell of the food became. Soldier's Boy did not take the basket from him, but dipped both hands in to fill them with berries and then raised the cupped berries to his mouth. In a very short time, the basket was empty. As Soldier's Boy heaved a sigh of satisfaction, the boy's face shone. He leapt to his feet, then seemed to recall he was in my presence and dropped back to his knees. On his knees, he again backed away from the forest mage and then once more rocketed onto his feet. "I know where there are yellow mushrooms," he exclaimed, and before Soldier's Boy could respond, he spun about and dashed off.

My Speck self looked around. I had expected to find myself in a Speck village, but there were no shelters, no cook fires, nothing to indicate that we were anywhere except in the wild heart of the mountain forest. "Where is everyone?" I heard Soldier's Boy ask, and realized the stupidity of his question. He took a breath. "Jodoli. How did I come to be here?"

Jodoli looked uncomfortable but spoke bluntly. "You overspent your magic and fell, dying, near the end of the intruders' road. One of the ancestor trees was shamed to see a Great Man perish so, untended and without a tree to take him in. He used what life was left to him to start the whispering. And Lisana, your sponsor, added her strength to make it a command. I was summoned, as was Olikea. Firada came with me to tend me. And Olikea brought Likari to run and fetch for her.

"It was Olikea's duty to bring you back into the shade, for you had fallen in full sunlight. She and Likari were burned bringing you to safety, for even depleted, you were a heavy load for them to shift, and there was no time for them to weave shade-cloaks for themselves. Once you were beneath the shelter of the trees, Firada was able to help them. We brought you here, well away from the brightness. And Olikea set about doing what she could to revive you. I am surprised that you are restored even this much. Never have I seen a Great One so depleted."

"It was a foolish waste," Soldier's Boy growled. He leaned back on the moss and looked up at the fragments of sky that showed through the dense canopy overhead. "All that magic consumed by futility. What I did may delay their cutting of the trees, but it will not stop it. And while it may frighten them or puzzle them, I fear that it will only set their minds to working on how they can overcome it rather than make them give up their plan. I know the task of ridding our land of the intruders is mine; but I do not know how I am to accomplish it. That still eludes me."

"The magic does not give a man a task unless there is a way to do it," Jodoli said comfortingly. The words had the rhythm of an old saw.

"Perhaps. But always I have been told that when you are on the right path, the magic lights the way and makes all clear. That has not happened with me, Jodoli. I am blind in the darkness, feeling my way through a task that does not seem to have a solution." It was strange to hear my voice without consciously deciding to speak. Very strange, and a tingle of dread ran along my nerves.

Jodoli looked acutely uncomfortable that Soldier's Boy had confided his deficiency to him. I knew that Great Men seldom became close friends; they might be allies or more likely rivals. Power was to be shepherded for one's own use, for the good of one's kin-clan. To admit to him that all my vast magic had been spent to no avail embarrassed Jodoli on my behalf. Soldier's Boy knew there was no point in withholding that information from him. Perhaps he had some inkling of a solution to our woes.

But if he had or did, he did not share it then. "In time, the magic will reveal your task, I am sure," he said. He gave a sideways glance at Firada, and for the first time I noticed how shocked she was. The Great Ones did not admit ignorance, I suddenly knew. That Soldier's Boy had done so frightened her; the Specks looked to their Great Ones for leadership and guidance. Was not the magic of the forest in them, showing them what they must do? For me to admit that I felt no such inspiration from the magic frightened her. What if not even the magic could halt the flow of the intruders? What if even the Great Ones of the Specks could not save them? I regretted my words.

"I am sure it will. I am only tired and discouraged, and thus spoke as I did."

"Of course. Eat and restore yourself and all will be well."

Soldier's Boy shook my head ruefully. "It will be days before I have restored even a third of my bulk, and months before I can amass that much magic again. It was a terrible waste."

"Why did you do it?" Jodoli asked.

Soldier's Boy shook his head mutely. It was already a mistake to have confided in Jodoli as much as he had. If he told Firada and Jodoli that the ignorant Gernian part of him had done it, it would only confuse them. Possibly it would turn them against him. He could not let that happen. I was beginning to suspect that if he were to accomplish his task, it would require all the support he could muster. And all the strength.

A wave of hunger washed through him again, and he was suddenly aware of a terrible thirst. "Is there more water?" he asked.

"In that skin there, perhaps," Jodoli said stiffly. He gestured at it, but did not move to pass it to me. I sensed another misstep on Soldier's Boy's part. Jodoli was not his feeder, to see to his basic needs. Firada stood motionless at his side, well aware that it was not her place to offer him anything. He heaved our body to a sitting position and managed to reach the water skin. It was not full but there was some in it. He drank it down and then asked plaintively, "Where is that boy? What is his name again?"

"Likari," Firada said. "My nephew's name is Likari."

The water had helped but it was still difficult to keep his thoughts fixed on anything but his hunger. "Your nephew. I thought perhaps he was a younger brother."

"No. He is my nephew. Olikea's son."

I tried to keep the dismay from my face. "I did not know she was *married*." I had to slip into Gernian to find the word I needed.

Firada looked puzzled. There was no such concept in Speck society. Nevare's guilt for sharing sex with a married woman had briefly spilled over into my Speck self. "What is this 'married'?" Firada asked. She spoke the word as if it might indicate a disease.

"A word from another place and time," Soldier's Boy said airily. I sensed his discomfort that I'd been able to influence his thoughts and words. "It means that she is devoted to a man. Dedicated enough to bear his child."

Firada wrinkled her brow. "I do not remember who fathered Likari. Olikea probably knows. She was barely a woman when she decided to have him, and quickly wearied of caring for him. She only pays attention to him when he can be useful to her."

Nevare's outrage at such a thing collided with Soldier's Boy's sense that it did not matter that much. The child belonged to his kin-clan. He would be cared for even if his own mother did not assume a major role in his life. It took a few moments for my inner turmoil to subside. Had Soldier's Boy felt the same frustration that I now felt when Nevare had been in charge of my life? I suspected it was so. The Gernian part of me was suspended now, able to think and judge but not to take action. I now knew I could influence Soldier's Boy's thoughts, but not control his actions. The best I could do was make that other self thoughtful and force him to compare the two different worlds that had created this duality.

He had been silent too long. Both Firada and Jodoli were looking at him oddly. "I suppose that I acted hastily in sending Olikea away. Perhaps the boy will tend me now until I can select someone who is better qualified."

Jodoli glanced aside from me and puffed out his lips in the Speck gesture for "no." Still not looking at me, he suggested, "Perhaps you are braver than I would be, taking on such a young feeder who is untrained. He will know some of the foods you must have, and Likari is clever enough to quickly learn his duties. But there will be some ways in which your comforts will be lacking. Unless you seek comfort of a different sort."

His words were oblique but I took his meaning. Nevare was affronted. Soldier's Boy answered bluntly. "I have sent Olikea away. If she does not care for this child, why would I give her another one? And depleted as I am, I think it will be some time before I desire a woman. Chiefly what I need now is food, drink, and rest. The first two the boy can provide for me, and the last I will take on my own."

"But you cannot rest. Not yet." Jodoli was emphatic.

"Why not?"

"Because it is time to journey. Our kin-clan was well on our way up into the mountains when the summons reached me that we must return to save you. It is the time of the traveling. You cannot linger here. The snows will catch you long before you reach the Wintering Place if you do."

Firada spoke up, stating plainly what Jodoli had skirted. "It is only by Jodoli's magic that you are alive. He used much of his reserves to bring us here to you swiftly. But for his intervention, you would still be baking in the sun while Olikea and Likari journeyed back to the Vale of the Ancestor Trees."

"I owe a debt of food and thanks to Jodoli." Soldier's Boy acknowledged the obligation.

Firada pursed her lips in disapproval. "And with such a young and inexperienced feeder, I do not see how you are going to pay it. Likari will be strained to provide enough for you. He is a good boy, but young. How will he gather enough to pay back to Jodoli what was spent on your behalf?"

Jodoli looked aside. It was beneath a Great Man to fuss over such trifles. If he had demanded to be paid back, it might seem that he was not powerful enough to shrug off such an expenditure of magic. But it was the duty of his feeder to keep track of such things and be sure that other folk not only recognized their debts to the Great One in their midst but paid back such debts with appropriate foods. Firada stood her ground squarely, even though it was awkward for her to confront a Great One in such a way. The foolish expenditure of my magic had cost me much in status as well as power. My size had been sufficient reason for folk to respect me. Diminishing and stupidly endangering myself had undermined my standing with Olikea's kin-clan. My position, I suddenly saw, was precarious. The kin-clan already had a Great One. Supporting him and gathering the foods requisite to keep his power fed was already their burden. Having seen my poor judgment, they might think supporting a second Great One a poor bargain.

Soldier's Boy drew in breath, well aware that puffing his lungs with air was a poor substitute for a good show of fat. I probably looked ridiculous, a bony man covered in sagging skin trying to invoke the dignity and power of a properly fed Great One. Nevertheless, he maintained his bluff.

"It will be paid back. Be assured of that. I am not a man to be chary of paying his debts. It will be paid back, and when I regain my size, if Jodoli is ever in need in any way, he will know that he can count on me to return the favor."

That raised her brows. Great Ones were usually rivals and often bitter ones. To offer a favor and possibly an alliance was unheard of among the Specks. I could almost see her weighing the benefits. What power could be controlled by one kin-clan that supported an alliance of two Great Ones? Had such a thing ever been?

She turned to look at Jodoli. Something passed between them in that long look. Jodoli inclined his head slowly toward me. "I will take you at your word. You need not trouble to pay back what I expended just yet. For now, Likari will have to do his utmost to keep you fed enough to travel swiftly. After you reach the Wintering Place will be soon enough for you to redeem your debts to us."

His use of the plural did not escape me. A wash of weariness swept over me suddenly. If my body could not have food immediately, it demanded sleep. If it could not replenish flesh, then it would rest until it could. Where was that boy? He'd spoken of yellow mushrooms. My mouth ran at the thought of them. It was difficult for Soldier's Boy to rein his thoughts back to the matter at hand.

"Debts? Then you will accept my offer of aid, I believe."

He nodded gravely. "I had not considered it before now, but perhaps it is the only thing that would work. An alliance of Great Ones might convince Kinrove that he can no longer act alone. He must talk to us of his plans, and he must hear us when we speak. He may be the largest of us, and perhaps his dance has kept the intruders away for all these years. But he must be made to see that the power of such magic is fading, and the cost to the People is high—some say too high to be borne. Two winters ago, I spoke of this to him. He laughed at me. Last winter I again raised my concerns. He would not hear me. He said that I should be ashamed to criticize his dance when I had done nothing to protect the Vale of the Ancestor Trees. As our kin-clan summers closest to the Vale, he said I should consider it my duty to be more watchful. Yet is it a matter of being watchful? I do not think so! And while our kin-group may have the summering grounds closest to the Vale of the Ancestor Trees, the trees house the ancestors of us all! Yet he behaved as if he had taken on a duty that I should have borne alone, as if I should consider myself and our kin-clan in debt to his! For a dance that has not ever made the intruders draw back, and has scarcely kept them at bay!"

His words were important. Soldier's Boy knew that. And yet weariness struggled to close his eyes. He could stay awake only by thinking of the mushrooms the boy had promised me. With a sudden pang, he recalled the heaped baskets of food that Olikea had used to bring me, and how skillfully she had prepared and balanced the feasts. Perhaps he had been too hasty and too proud when he had dismissed her. He suddenly wished he could call her back even as he gritted my back teeth together at the thought. No. He'd lost standing enough. He would not risk looking as if he could not make up my mind.

He looked around anxiously. Hunger was making him frantic. He could no longer focus on anything Jodoli was saying. To his great relief, I saw Likari toiling through the trees. The basket was so heavily laden that he was carrying it in his arms instead of by the handle. Soldier's Boy sat up taller and tried to see what he was bringing.

The boy's eyes were bright and he began shouting long before he reached us. "I'm sorry I was so long, Great One. On my way to the mushrooms, I found a patch of clingfruit, so I brought those as well. There were many of them, the red growing right alongside the yellow ones. And I brought all the mushrooms, from both sides of the trees. I know you are hungry, so I hurried. Did I do well?"

His sun-flushed face had gone even redder with his exertion, so that his specks were almost eclipsed in it. Soldier's Boy smiled and nodded, reaching eagerly for the basket. He was suddenly so famished that he could not speak. Likari knelt as he lowered the basket. He began to take the food out of it but Soldier's Boy could not wait. He reached in and took handfuls of the clingfruit. I was not familiar with it, and the gelid feel of it was shocking. "Watch out for the pits!" the boy exclaimed as Soldier's Boy put one in my mouth. He nodded, already immersed in the soft pulp and sweet tang.

But Firada scowled and said, "Is that how you address a Great One, Likari! With no title, no bow of the head? Do you presume to tell him how he should eat his food? What sort of a feeder are you? Oh, this boy is much too young! He will bring shame on our kin-clan. Someone else must be found for this task."

The boy shrank in on himself, crestfallen. He looked up at Soldier's Boy with wide eyes. They looked hazel now. His specks were shaped like teardrops and dappled his face almost evenly except for the streak down his nose. The rest of his little body was more striped than spotted. The backs of his hands and the tops of his feet were a solid, sooty black. It reminded me of a horse's markings. Soldier's Boy spat out a rough pit. As he lifted another fruit from the basket, the boy's eyes suddenly swam with tears. I couldn't stand it. I pushed at Soldier's Boy's thoughts.

"He has brought me food, and given it to me quickly. That, right now, is my chief requirement in a feeder. I am sure Likari and I will get along well enough for now, and perhaps even better as we get to know each other."

The boy's face brightened as if he'd been given a handful of gold coins. He peered up at his aunt through his lashes and struggled not to grin. He was trying to be respectful of her. Good. Soldier's Boy pulled the basket closer. The clingfruit was wonderful but he suddenly wanted the mushrooms. He dumped the basket out on the clean moss beside me. The food made a substantial heap. He grinned at it and picked up a cluster of mushrooms.

"Can you find me more food while I eat this?"

Likari glanced at Firada. Conscientiously, he made a grave bow. "Certainly, Great One. As you wish, Great One. I will see what I can find."

Firada had looked disapproving when I had praised the boy. Now, at this sign of deference from him, she relented. She spoke briskly. "Go to the bend of the stream where the three big rocks are. Dig in the sandy spot there. You may find blue mollusks. They are excellent for rebuilding a Great One's strength. On the muddy bank, you will find fat grass growing. It will not be sweet anymore; spring is long gone. But the roots will be thick and nourishing. Fetch those as well. See that you wash them well before you bring them to him. When a Great One is as famished as this one is, he is sometimes too hasty in his eating. He may take in dirt or bones if the food is not prepared correctly before it is offered. And dirt and bones may clog his bowels or put him into a fever."

"Yes, Aunt." He looked at the ground. "Thus did I fear that he would swallow the pit of the fruit as well." When Firada looked grim at this bit of cheek, he added quickly, "But I should have phrased my caution more respectfully. Thank you for your instruction, and for sharing your gathering places with me. Well do I know that often such places are guarded secrets."

Firada was mollified. She sounded almost motherly as she said, "I wish you to do well at this, if you must attempt it, Likari." Then, in a sharper voice, she added, "But you must not linger here talking while your Great One waits for food. Go. Hurry. Be back before he has finished what you have brought him!"

The boy nodded violently and scuttled away. Soldier's Boy was only peripherally aware of his leaving, for the food still claimed most of his attention. I think Jodoli understood this. He waited until the mushrooms were gone and most of the clingfruit before he spoke again. "It is good that your feeder found mushrooms for you. They will help, and if he can find the blue mollusks, that will be even better. You will need your strength tonight if we are to travel swiftly."

My mouth was full of fruit. Soldier's Boy could not speak, so he raised my eyebrows at him.

"We cannot linger here. We must travel tonight. I spent magic to quick-walk here and to bring Firada, Likari, and Olikea with me, all in a single night! Tonight, we must begin our journey back. We will not make it with as much haste. Still, the season is too late for you and your feeder to travel in an ordinary fashion. You will have to spend magic to quick-walk yourself and Likari to the Wintering Place."

Questions popped into my mind. Why were we going up into the mountains as winter was coming on? Surely it would make more sense to winter in the foothills than to travel to where the cold would be most extreme and the snow deepest? I was not sure Soldier's Boy knew how to quick-walk, let alone how to take someone with him when he did it. Quick-walking was a Speck magic, a way to traverse a long distance very swiftly. Soldier's Boy shared my doubts. He hastily crammed the last of the clingfruit into my mouth. As he chewed them, I felt suddenly steadier, more anchored in the world and in the day. He swallowed gratefully, but before he could ask Jodoli any questions, Firada asked one of her own.

"What of Olikea?" she asked gravely. "Will you quick-walk her back to the People?"

I saw Jodoli's hesitation. "I wished to be full of magic when I spoke to Kinrove. I have already spent more than I intended in coming here and bringing all of you with me. Nevare intends to pay us back, but—"

Before he could say anything more, Soldier's Boy interrupted. "Olikea came here on my behalf. And I suspect that she did not come willingly. I feel a debt to her. I will quick-walk her back." He did not wish to be any deeper in Jodoli's debt.

He looked doubtful. "Will you be strong enough to quick-walk yourself, Olikea, and Likari?"

"If I am not tonight, then I will have to stay here and rest and eat and try again."

Olikea had not gone far. I suspected that she had lingered quite close by, listening to the conversation and watching how I interacted with her son. Now she emerged from behind one of the immense trees. She strolled toward us in a desultory way, but the glances she gave me were still full of both anger and injured pride. She would not look at me directly but instead addressed Jodoli. "I would prefer that you were the one to quick-walk me back to the People. Once we are there, I will bring food to you to pay you back. Or I will go now, to find food so that you will be strong when we travel tonight."

A spark kindled in Firada's eyes at her sister's words. She moved, placing her body as a barrier between Olikea and Jodoli.

She narrowed her eyes and her voice sounded like an angry cat's snarl as she said, "I know what you are trying to do. It will not work! You angered your own Great One and he has rejected you. Do not think you can ingratiate yourself with mine! Jodoli has been mine since he passed through his trial! I have fed him, I have groomed him, and countless times I have rescued him from his own foolishness. Now that he stands ready to make challenge to Kinrove, do you think you will come wheedling with sweet words and tasty tidbits to steal him from me? No. Step back from him, sister. You had your chance and you wasted it. You will not take mine from me."

I stared in horrified fascination as Firada set her weight as if she were a man preparing for a wrestling match. Her knees were flexed slightly, her arms held away from her body, ready to grip her opponent if Olikea decided to charge. She gave her head a toss and a shake to clear her streaky hair from her face. I blinked my eyes and saw her as Soldier's Boy did. My Gernian manners had kept me from staring frankly at their near nakedness. Now with admiration I noted the muscles beneath the ample weight that Firada carried. She was formidable. Her younger sister was taller, and in no way dainty, but if I had been placing a wager I would have bet on Firada to win.

I am not certain that Olikea had been challenging her sister over Jodoli. She looked a trifle surprised and daunted at Firada's angry defense of her territory. Her mouth worked and then she puffed her lips disparagingly. "I do not want him. I want only to be conveyed back to the People. That is all. Everywhere and always, Firada, you think other women want what you have. You are foolish. You value him too much. He has been slow to grow, placid, almost stupid in how he lets you herd him about and pasture him as if he were a Gernian's sheep. You may keep him, and we shall see how much good comes to you from him."

She shook her hair back, lifted her chin in defiance, and turned her back on both of them. Jodoli, I noted, showed little interest in the exchange. I wondered if he were truly as passive as Olikea named him, or if it was beneath the interest of a Great One to take affront at such an exchange. Firada bared her teeth at

her sister. It could have been amusement or satisfaction at having
vanquished a potential rival. I had no time to ponder it further,
for Olikea strode up to me and stood over me in a manner that
was almost threatening. I had never had the experience of looking up at a naked woman who was bristling with fury. It was both
daunting and strangely arousing.

"You are right. It was your foolishness that demanded I come
here. You owe me transport back to the People."

Soldier's Boy said nothing. I was inclined to be a gentleman
and see that she was safely returned to her family. But the Great
Man was a bit weary of her exploitation and demands. She still
seethed before me. He compromised and spoke firmly. "If you
wish me to quick-walk you back to the People, I will need the
strength to do so. I will attempt it if you aid Likari in finding food
for me today. That seems fair to me."

He would have been wiser not to add the last comment. It was
like spark to powder. She exploded with righteous indignation.
"Fair? Fair? You know nothing of fair. For months, I have brought
you food, taught you even what foods you should be eating. I have
lain with you for your comfort and release. I have nagged you, to
no avail, to allow me to feed and tend you as a Great Man should
be attended. I have struggled to make you behave as you should
and to teach you your duties to the People. And what has been
my thanks from you? Have I been lifted in honor by my people?
No! Have you done great deeds for them? No! Instead, you have
spoken of the intruders as 'my people' and said that there is nothing that will turn them back! Treachery and ingratitude. That is
what I have received from you! Insults and disobedience! How is
one to be the feeder of such an insufferable Great One? And now
look at you! All the work I did for you is wasted. You are thin as a
starving man, thin as a man no one respects, thin as a man cursed
by the forest, thin as a man too stupid to find food for himself.
You will do no great deeds. It will take months, perhaps a year or
more, before you become as fat as you were. And every day that
you struggle to regain the power you wasted, Jodoli will eat and
hoard his strength and grow. You will never be greater than he is.
And when all the kin-clans gather at the Wintering Place, you

will be mocked, and the people who bring you will be mocked. All my work, all my fetching and gathering and tending of you, you have wasted. What good did it do me? What good did it do any of my kin-clan?"

It was like watching a geyser erupt. Every time I thought she would pause for thought, she only gulped down a deep breath and blasted me again. Jodoli and Firada were mute witnesses, horrified in that fascinated way of people who watch an unthinkable event take place. I think Soldier's Boy took it calmly only because within myself I was so divided as to how to react. The Gernian wished to acknowledge that she had not received what she had expected. The Great Man resented the burden of abuse.

Soldier's Boy crossed my arms over my chest, only too aware of how the skin hung limp and empty on my forearms and breast. Even my fingers looked odd to me, their plumpness lost. I shared his sudden wave of mourning for all my hoarded magic lost. Olikea was right. I looked like a man without power, unhonored and thin. I would be mocked at the gathering of the kin-clans. Disappointment flooded me and it turned into anger. He pointed a finger at her. "Olikea," he said into her tirade. I do not think he used any magic, but she was silenced as suddenly as if he had.

"If you wish me to quick-walk you back to the People tonight, go find food for me now. Otherwise, I will be too weak. If you do not wish to help feed me, that is fine. Beg passage of Jodoli. But those are your only two options. Choose, and do it quietly."

She narrowed her eyes and their green made it a cat's stare. "Perhaps I have choices you know nothing about, Jhernian!" She turned on her heel and strode off into the forest. I stared after her, wondering how I could ever have imagined that she felt love or even affection toward me. It had been a transaction. Sex and food given to me in the expectation that I would acquire status and power, and that she would share in those things.

Firada puffed breath out of her pursed lips, dismissing Olikea's show disdainfully. "She has no other options. She will return, with sweet food and sweet words, to wriggle into your favor again. My little sister has always been thus. My father spoiled her after my mother was taken."

Jodoli came and ponderously lowered his bulk beside me. Soldier's Boy suppressed a wave of envy. Jodoli looked very fine, his skin smooth and oiled, his belly sleek and rounded as a gorged forest cat. His hair was glossy, sleeked back from his face and then braided into a fat tail. I looked away from him, unable to bear the sharp contrast with my saggy skin and protruding bones. "We must speak, Nevare, of Olikea's accusations. I know you have been a divided man, unwilling to concede that the intruders must be killed or driven back. But now that they have cast you out, perhaps you will feel differently about them. Perhaps you will admit that they do not belong here."

Soldier's Boy rubbed my hands together, looking at my fingers. A divided man. Little did he know how accurately he spoke. "How do you know they cast me out?" he asked Jodoli.

"The magic whispered it to me. You would not come to the forest of your free will, so it had to turn your people against you. Now they have disowned you. When you say 'my people' today, to whom do you refer?"

It was not a question just for Soldier's Boy, a Great Man of the Specks. It was for Nevare to answer as well. Soldier's Boy spoke for both of us.

"I do not think I will say 'my people' for a very long time."

CHAPTER SIX

CONFRONTATIONS

As Nevare, I did little the rest of that day. I retreated to the back of my mind and became an onlooker in my life. Soldier's Boy ate the food that Likari brought him, drank deeply of clean water, and then slept. He woke to the wonderful aroma of hot food. Olikea brought it. A hastily woven net held leaf-wrapped packets the size of my fist and roasted tubers. The packets held chunks of fish cooked with a sour root. The leaves that held them were edible and added their own piquant touch of flavor. He ate the food and commented on it favorably. That was the only conversation between them. Neither apologized or explained where the situation now stood. It seemed far simpler a resolution than could ever have occurred between Gernians.

When Likari brought food, he ate that as well. I do not think that pleased Olikea but she didn't talk about it. Instead, she took a wooden comb from her shoulder pouch and painstakingly combed out my hair. She spent far longer on the task than it deserved; I had never realized how good such a simple thing could feel. I do not think Firada approved of Soldier's Boy's easy acceptance of Olikea's return. She announced that she was taking Jodoli down to the stream to wash him and to rest there. She stalked away and he stolidly followed her, a placid bullock of a man.

Olikea ignored their leaving. Likari had gone off to look for more mushrooms. She continued to work her comb through my hair. There wasn't much of it. I had given up keeping it in a cavalla soldier's short cut some time ago, but there was still not enough to plait or dress in any fashion. Still, it felt good, and the Great Man allowed her gentle touch and his full belly to lull him. He fell asleep.

Strange to say, I did not sleep. I remained awake and aware of all the sensations a man may feel with his eyes closed. I wondered if this was how it had been for my Speck self in the days when I had been so firmly in charge of my life—or thought I had been. In a way, it was pleasant. I felt that I had let go of the reins; surely no one could hold me responsible now for the chaos that my life had become. The early afternoon was warm, summer stealing one of autumn's days, but here, deep in the shade of the forest, there was a pleasant chill that tickled the surface of my skin. If I lay very still, my body warmth lingered around me, but the slightest breeze stole it away. It did not much bother me. The moss I rested on was deep and my body had warmed it. I was comfortable. I was naked, I realized belatedly. Olikea must have taken my clothing when she rescued me. She had never approved of how much clothing I wore. Her discarding it struck me as foolish. Naked, others would more quickly see how wasted and thin I was. However strange my clothing might have seemed, at least it might have kept some of the disdain and mockery at bay. Among the Specks, few things were more pitied and despised than a skinny man. What kind of a fool could not provide for himself, or earn enough regard from his fellows to have them help him in a time of injury or sickness? I looked such a fool right now. Well, Soldier's Boy was in command of the body now; he would have to deal with it. I let my mind drift to more pleasant thoughts.

I heard birdsong, the sound of the breeze in the needled trees, and the very light rattle of falling leaves whenever a gust of breeze was strong enough to dislodge them. I could hear them cascading down, ricocheting through the twigs and branches until they finally reached the forest floor. The Speck were right. Summer was over, autumn was strong, and winter would be on its heels. Real cold would descend, followed by the snows and harsh winds of winter. Last winter I'd had a snug little cabin to shelter me. This winter I would face that weather with not even the clothes on my back. A tide of dread started to rise in me, but again I turned it back with the simple demurral: it was not my problem. Specks seemed to have survived well through the ages. Whatever their tactic was, even if it was simply the stoic endurance of cold and privation, Soldier's Boy would learn it and last the winter.

A bird sang again, loudly, a warning, and then I heard the crack of its wings as it took hasty flight. A moment later I heard something heavy settle into the branches overhead. A shower of broken twigs rattled against my face, followed by the slower fall of leaves. I looked up in annoyance. A huge croaker bird had settled in the tree above me. I grimaced in distaste. Fleshy orange-red wattles hung about his beak, reminding me both of dangling meat and cancerous growths. His feathers rattled when he shook them and it seemed as if I could smell the stench of carrion on them. His long black toes gripped the branch tightly as he leaned down to peer at me. His eyes were very bright.

"Nevare! You owe me a death."

The croaked words shot ice down my spine. I arced as if I'd been hit by an arrow, and then peered up at the creature in the branches overhead. He was no longer a bird. He wasn't a man, either. Orandula, the god of balances, teetered on the branch over my head. His long black feet gripped the branch with horny toenails. His nose was a carrion bird's hooked beak, and the red wattles dangled from his throat now. His hair was a thicket of unruly feathers, and feathers cloaked his body and dangled from his arms. Unchanged were his piercing bird-bright eyes. He cocked his head and stared down at me. He smiled, his beak stretching horribly as he did so. As I stared, fixed with terror, his little black tongue came out of his mouth, dabbing at the edges of his beak, and then retreated again.

It wasn't real. It was too horrible to be real. Every prayer I knew to the good god bubbled to the top of my mind. I tried to form the words, but Soldier's Boy slept on, his mouth closed, oblivious to my terror. I tried to close my eyes, to block out the sight of the old god, to make him a dream. I could not. My eyes were not open. I did not know how I was seeing him. I struggled desperately to lift an arm and put it across my eyes, but my body did not belong to Nevare. Soldier's Boy slumbered on. I could not look away from the old god's piercing gaze. It was horrid to experience such terror, and to feel at the same time the slow and steady breathing of deep sleep and the calm heartbeat of a man contentedly at rest. Soldier's Boy could sleep but Nevare could not flee from the god in the tree above me. A whimper tried to escape me; it could not. I tried to look away; I could not.

"Why do they always do that?" Orandula asked rhetorically. "Why do men think that if they cannot see a thing, it goes away or stops existing? I should think any sane creature would want to keep its eyes fixed on something as dangerous as me!" He opened his arm-wings and rattled the pinions at me menacingly, and the whimper inside me tried to be a scream. His smile grew broader. "Yet, without exception, when I pay a visit such as this, men try to avert their eyes from me. It's useless, Nevare. Look on me. You are mine, you know. Neither your good god nor your forest magic will dispute my claim. You took that which was intended for me. Your life is forfeit. You owe me a death in payment. Look at me, Nevare Burvelle!" When he commanded me to look on him, a strange thing happened. A chill calm welled up in me, just like the cool air over the water within a deep well. I recognized something in him, or perhaps something in my situation. Inevitability. I still feared him with a heart-stopping intensity but I knew I could not escape him. Struggle was pointless. The calm of despair filled me. I could look on the god I had cheated. I found a voice to speak to him, one that did not use my lips or tongue or lungs. I met his gaze, even though it was like pressing my palm against the tip of a sword.

"A death? You demand a death? You had a hundred deaths, a glut of deaths. How many did I bury at the end of the summer?

Strong soldiers, little children. Strangers. Enemies of mine. Friends. Buel Hitch. Carsina." My voice broke on the name of my former fiancée.

Orandula laughed like a crow cawing. "You tell me what I took, not what you gave me. You gave me nothing! You stole from me, Nevare Burvelle."

"All I did was free a suffering bird from its impalement on a sacrificial carousel. I lifted it from the hook and released it. How is that so great a trespass that I must pay for it with my life? Or my death."

"You wronged me, man. The bird was mine, both its life and its death. Who were you to say it should not suffer? Who were you to pick it free and put life back into it and let it fly away?"

"I put life back into it?"

"Hah!" His exclamation was a harsh croak. "There speaks a man! First you will pretend you did not know how grave a thing you did. Then you will deny you did it. Then you will say—"

"It's not fair!"

"Of course. Exactly that. And then finally, each and every one will claim—"

If I had had lungs, I would have drawn a breath. I invoked the strength of the words with the full force of my fear. "I am a follower of the good god. I was dedicated to him as a soldier son when I was born, and I was raised in his teachings. You have no power over me!" The last I uttered with conviction. Or attempted to. My words were drowned in the caws of his laughter.

"Oh, yes, the final denial. I can't be your god; you already have a god. You keep him in your pouch and let him out on occasions such as this. Calling on your good god is so much more effective than, say, pissing yourself in terror. Or at least it has a bit more dignity." He spread his tail feathers and leaned back, rocking so hard with laughter that the big branch shook. I looked up at him, unable to avert my eyes. He took his time getting his hilarity under control. Finally, he stopped laughing, and wiped his feathered arm across his eyes. He leaned forward, turning his bird's head sideways to look at me more closely. "Call him," he suggested to me. "Shout for the good god to come and rescue you. I want to

see what happens. Go ahead. Yell for help, man. It's the only thing
you haven't done yet."

I couldn't do it. I wanted to. I wanted desperately to be able to
cry out to some benign presence that would sweep in and rescue
me. It wasn't a lack of faith in the good god's existence. I think I
feared to call on my god lest he come to me, and find me lacking and unworthy. I knew in my heart, as most men do, that I'd
never really given myself fully to his service. I do not speak of the
way that a priest resigns his life to the service of a god, but rather
to how a man suspends his own judgment and desires and relies
on what he has been told the good god desires of him. Always,
I had held back from that commitment. I had always believed, I
discovered, that when I was an old man I could become devout
and make up for my heedless youth. Age would be a good time
to practice self-discipline and charity and patience. When I was
old, I would give generous alms and spend hours in meditation
while watching the sweet smoke of my daily offerings rise to the
good god. When I was old, and my blood no longer bubbled with
ambition and lust and wild curiosity, then I could settle down and
be content in my good god.

Foolishly, I had believed that I would always have the opportunity to be a better man, later. Obviously, a man's life could end
at any time. A fall down the stairs, a chill or a fever, a stray bullet;
youth was no armor against such fates. A man could lose his life
by accident, at any moment. Some part of me, perhaps, had known
that, but I'd never believed it at a gut level.

And I'd certainly never considered that at any moment, an old
god could materialize and demand my life of me.

I didn't merit the good god's intervention and, worse, I feared
his judgment. The old gods, I knew, had been able to plunge men
into endless torment or perpetual labor, and often did solely for
their own amusement. Such anguish on a whim suddenly seemed
preferable to facing a just banishment.

My cry of supplication died in me unuttered. I looked up at
Orandula, the old god of balances, and felt myself quiver with
resignation and then grow still. The feathers on his head quirked
up in surprise.

"What? No shrieks for rescue? No pleas for mercy? Eh. Not very amusing for me. You're a bad bargain, Nevare. Looks like half of you is the most I can get, and it isn't even the interesting half. Yet, being as I am the god of balances, something in that appeals to me."

"Do what you will to me!" I hissed at him, weary already of teetering on that brink.

He fluttered his feathers up, gaining almost a third in size as he did so. "Oh, I shall," he muttered as he eased them down. He leisurely groomed two wing plumes, pulling them through his beak and then settling them into order. For a moment, he seemed to have forgotten me. Then he pierced me with his stare again. "At my leisure. When I decide to take what you owe me, then I'll come for it, and you'll pay me."

"Which do I owe you?" I was suddenly moved to ask him. "My death? Or my life?"

He yawned, his pointed tongue wagging in his mouth as he did so. "Whichever I please, of course. I am the god of balances, you know. I can choose from either end of the scales." He cocked a head at me. "Tell me, Nevare. Which do you think an old god such as me would find most pleasing? To demand your death of you? Or insist that you pay me with your life?"

I didn't know the answer and I didn't wish to give him any ideas. My fears toiled and rumbled inside me. Which did I most fear? What did he mean when he said those words? That he would kill me and I'd become nothing? Or that he'd take me in death and keep me as his plaything? What if he demanded my life from me, and I became a puppet of the old god? All paths seemed dark. I stared up at him hopelessly.

He fluttered his feathers again, then suddenly opened his wings. He lifted from the branch as effortlessly as if he weighed nothing. Then he was gone. Literally gone. I didn't see him fly away. Only the swaying of the relieved branch testified that he had been there.

"Do not wake him!"

Olikea's warning hissed at Likari did precisely what she had told the boy not to do. Soldier's Son stirred, grunted, and opened his eyes. He drew a deeper breath, and then rubbed his face. "Water," he requested, and both his feeders reached for the water skin that lay beside him. Olikea was a shade faster and a bit stronger. She had her hands on it first, with the better grip, and snatched it from Likari. The boy's eyes widened with disappointment and outrage.

"But I was the one who went and refilled it!" he protested.

"He needs help to drink from it. You don't know how. You'll get it all over him."

They sounded for the all the world like squabbling siblings rather than a mother and her son. Soldier's Boy ignored both of them, but took the water skin away from Olikea to drink from it. He nearly drained it before he handed it back to the boy with a nod of thanks. He yawned and then carefully stretched, noting with displeasure how the limp skin dangled from his arms. He lowered them back to his side. "I feel better. But I need to eat more before we quick-walk tonight. I would like cooked food to warm me; the world will cool as night comes on."

He groaned as he sat up, but it was the groan of a man who has eaten well, slept heavily, and looked forward to doing the same again. How could he be so unaware of all that had befallen me while he slept? Did he even sense that I still existed within him? How could he have been so blithely unaware of Orandula's visit to me and how it had terrified me? Yet so he seemed. How had it been for him, submerged within me for the better part of a year? I recalled the moments when he had broken through and into my awareness, and the times when he had forced me to take actions. What had it taken, there at the Dancing Spindle, for him to push me aside while he first stole and then destroyed the magic of the Plainspeople? Had it been a burst of passion, or had he simply gathered his strength and waited for a moment when he desired to use it? I needed to learn how he had manipulated me and to discover why he was now ascendant over me if I were to survive and ever recapture control of the life we shared. I was not certain that I wished to be the one in command of our life, but I did know that I was reluctant to cede full control to my Speck self. I refused the notion that I might never again control my own body.

The strangeness of the situation suspended my judgment of it. The terror I should have felt hovered, unacknowledged.

Likari had anticipated Soldier's Boy's appetite. In his basket, there were several fat roots from a water plant and two bright yellow fish that were just now gasping their last breaths. The boy presented the basket expectantly. Soldier's Boy nodded at it, pleased, but Olikea scowled.

"I will cook these things for you. The boy does not know how."

Likari opened his mouth to protest, and then shut it with a snap. Evidently his mother had spoken true. Nonetheless, his lower jaw and lip quivered with disappointment. Soldier's Son looked at him dispassionately, but I felt for the boy. "Give him something!" I urged my other self. "At least acknowledge what he has done for you."

I could sense his awareness of me, just as I had once been the one to feel his hidden influences on my thoughts and actions. He scowled to himself and then looked at the boy again. His shoulders had fallen and he was withdrawing. Soldier's Son lifted the water skin. "My young feeder will fill this again for me. The cool water was very good to have when I awoke."

The boy halted. My words transformed him. He lifted his head, squared his shoulders, and his eyes sparkled as he smiled up at me. "I am honored to serve you, Great One," he replied, taking the water skin. The words were a standard courtesy among the Speck when they addressed a Great One, but the boy uttered them with absolute sincerity.

Olikea folded her lips tightly, and then briskly added, "Bring firewood, too, when you come back with the water. And see that it is dry, so that it will burn hot to cook the fish quickly."

If she meant her words to sting, she failed. The boy scarcely noticed that she was giving the command. He bobbed acquiescence and raced off to his task.

Soldier's Boy watched Olikea as she scoured the area for kindling and twigs to get the fire started. She pushed the newly fallen leaves away to bare a place on the forest's mossy floor, and then peeled the moss away to reveal damp black earth. There she arranged her kindling. She untied one of the pouches from her belt and took out her fire-making supplies. When she did so, I felt a tingly itch spread over my skin. Soldier's Boy shifted uncomfortably. Idly, I noted that the steel she used to strike sparks from the flint was of Gernian make. She had set to one side a handful of sulfur matches. For all her professed hatred of the intruders, she did not despise the technology and conveniences they had brought. I smiled cynically but Solder's Boy's lips did not move. He seemed to be thinking something else, wondering how many other Specks now carried steel so casually, even knowing the iron in it was dangerous to magic. He ignored my thoughts. Was I a small voice in the back of his mind, a vague sensation of unease, or nothing at all to him? All I could do was wonder.

Olikea built the fire efficiently. I considered her as she moved about the area, gathering twigs to feed the tiny flame, stooping down to blow on the fire, and then as she began to cut up the roots and clean the fish from Likari's basket. I could not compare her to Gernian women at all, I realized. She moved with ease and confidence, as completely unaware of her nudity as Soldier's Boy was. That was odd to consider. He felt no surge of lust for her. Perhaps it was that I'd spent so much of his magic he felt as if he could barely stand, let alone mate with a woman. I stood at the edge of his flowing thoughts; he was not thinking of sex, but of the food she was preparing. He was gauging how much he could rebuild his strength by nightfall and how much of his magic he would have to burn to quick-walk all three of them back to the People.

Quick-walk. One could travel that way, seeming to stride along at an ordinary pace, but covering the ground much more swiftly. A mage could carry others along with him, one or two or even three if he was powerfully fat with magic. But it took an effort to get the magic started, and stamina to sustain it. It would not be easy for him, and he was reluctant to burn what little reserves he had restored. Nevertheless, he would have to do it. He had said that he would, in front of Jodoli. A Great Man never backed away from a feat of magic he claimed he would do. He would lose all status with the People if he did.

Likari came back with an armful of firewood. Olikea thanked him brusquely and sent him for more water. I suspected she was trying to keep him at a distance from Soldier's Boy while she carried out the more obvious tasks of a feeder. She seemed to feel my gaze on her and turned to look at me. As our eyes met, I felt as if she could still see me, the Gernian, buried inside Soldier's Boy. Did she notice that he had changed in his demeanor toward her? She dropped her eyes and appraised me as if she were looking at a horse she might buy. Then she shook her head.

"Fish and roots will help but what you need is grease if we are to rebuild you quickly. Likari will not find that in this part of the forest at this time of year. Even if he could, he is too small to kill anything. Once we have rejoined the People, you will have to do the hunter's dance for us, and summon a bear before it goes to its winter rest. Slabs of bear meat thick with fat will build you quickly. I will cook it with mushrooms and leeks and red salt. It will take time, Nevare, but I will restore you to your power."

Her mere description of the food made my mouth run with saliva. She was right. The body craved fat. The fish and roots suddenly seemed meager and unsatisfying. Soldier's Boy sat up and rubbed the loose folds of his belly. Moving slowly and cautiously, he got to his feet. The whole body felt peculiar. It was strange to be so light. I had built muscle to carry the fat that was now gone. My skin sagged all around me, wrinkling in unexpected places. He held my arms out from my body, looked down on my wasted form, and shook my head in disgust. He'd have to begin all over again.

"I can restore you," Olikea promised me as if she'd heard his thoughts. "I can be a very good feeder to you."

"If I allow it," he reminded her.

"What choice do you have?" she asked me reasonably. "Likari cannot even cook for you. He certainly cannot give you children to help care for you when you are old. You are angry with me now. I was angry with you before. Perhaps I am still angry with you, but I am smart enough to know this: anger will not get me what I want, so I will set it aside. Anger will not get you what you want and need. You should be wise enough to set it aside and let things go back to the way they were. The People will have enough reasons to mock you and doubt you. Do not give them any more by having a mere boy tending you. Let me be by your side when we return. I can explain that you spent all your magic in making a great tangle of forest that will protect our ancestor trees through the winter. I can make them see you as a hero who spent all he had in an effort to protect that which is most important to all of us, rather than as a fool who depleted himself yet found no glory or power in doing it."

I was beginning to perceive the Specks in an entirely different way. I'd always been told they were childlike and naïve, a primitive folk with simple ways, and so I had treated Olikea. I'd imagined she was passionately in love with me, and actually flogged myself with guilt over taking advantage of the infatuated young maiden. Plying me with food and sex had been her tactic to win me, and to enjoy the effects of bringing a man of power and girth into her kin-clan. She competed with her sister far more savagely than I'd ever striven to outdo either of my brothers. But, far from being enthralled by me, she had seen me as a tool for her ambition and used me accordingly. She spoke now, not out of love or affection, but only to point out that anger was keeping both of us from what we wanted. Even our potential children were not the fruit of our affections for each other, but my insurance against feeble old age. She was hard, hard as whipcord, hard as tempered steel, and Soldier's Boy had known that about her all the time. He finally smiled at her.

"I can set my anger aside, Olikea. But it does not mean that I set aside my memory of what caused my anger. It is very clear to both of us how my power may benefit you. Less clear to me is why I need you, or indeed why your kin-clan is the only one I should consider for my own. While you cook for me, perhaps you could explain to me why you are the best choice to be my feeder, and why your kin-clan, folk who already have a Great One in their midst, would be my best home among the People. There are kin-clans that have no Great Ones, where a feeder would have all the gathering skills of a kin-clan to aid her in caring for me. Why should I choose you?"

She narrowed her eyes and folded her lips. She had wrapped the fish and roots in well-moistened leaves and put them to steam

in her fire. She poked vindictively at them with her cooking stick;
I was sure she would rather have jabbed me with it. Soldier's Boy
watched her coolly, and I could feel him speculating on which
would win out, her anger or her ambition. She kept her gaze on
her cooking and spoke to the fire.

"You know that I can prepare food well, and that I gather
food efficiently. You know that my son, Likari, is an energetic
gatherer. Name me as your feeder, and I will put him in your service as well. You will have the benefit of two of us bringing you
food and seeing to your needs. And I will continue to give you
pleasure and seek to become pregnant with your child. That is not
an easy task, you know. It is hard to catch the seed of a Great Man
and harder still to carry his child to term. Few of the Great have
children of their own. But I already have a son that I can put in
service to you.

"If you wish to have two of us serving you, before you have
become fat and worthy again, then this is the only way it can be
so. If you choose Likari over me, then I will have nothing more
to do with either of you. And if you choose to leave my kin-clan
when we reach the Wintering Place to find a feeder among some
other clan, well, I will see to it that all hear of how faithless you
are, how clumsy with your magic, and how you wasted a wealth
of it to very little success. Do you think that every woman wants
to be a feeder? You will find, perhaps, that there are not that many
of us willing to give up our lives to serve one such as you."

Soldier's Boy had let her have her say without interruption.
When he held his silence after she had finished, she glanced up at
him once, her annoyance plain. He made her wait, but I noticed
she did not prod him. Finally he said, "I do not like your threats,
Olikea. And I believe that yes, actually there will be many women
at the Wintering Place who would want to become my feeder and
share in my glory and power, without making threats or sour faces
at me. You still have not given me a powerful reason to choose
your kin-clan. Do Jodoli and Firada support the notion of another
Great Man sustained by your kin-clan?"

She didn't answer directly, but the way she lowered her head
and scowled told me much. At that very moment we heard their

voices through the trees, and in a moment more they came into sight. Jodoli looked clean and well rested. His hair was freshly plaited, and his skin had been rubbed with fragrant oil. "Like a piece of prize livestock," the Nevare portion of me thought wryly, but I felt Soldier's Boy keen jealousy cut through me. In contrast to Jodoli, he felt grubby, unkempt, and skinny. He glanced at Olikea; she likewise burned with frustration. She spoke louder than necessary.

"The boy has done well at finding food for me to prepare for you. After you have eaten, I think I will help you bathe. And then perhaps you should sleep again."

Jodoli gave a huge, contented yawn. "That sounds a good plan, Nevare, if we are to quick-walk tonight. Ah. That food smells good."

A remarkable thing happened. Firada bristled at his compliment to Olikea. Olikea looked at her sister and said almost sharply, "I have prepared all this for Nevare. He will need his strength." Then, with a sideways glance at me, she added to Jodoli, "But perhaps we can spare enough for you to have a taste."

"We will share it with Jodoli and Firada," Soldier's Boy suddenly decreed. "I owe them thanks for bringing you here. Sharing food to replace the magic the Jodoli spent on me is called for, I think."

He took command of the situation that easily, and presided over the meal that ensued. I was pleased that he did not forget Likari. The boy had made trip after trip at Olikea's request, bringing firewood, cooking water, the wide flat leaves of a water plant to wrap the fish, and so on. He sat at a respectful distance from the adults, looking as if he could barely keep his eyes open, but eyeing the food all the same. Soldier's Boy's announcement that he would share food had brought out hospitality in Jodoli as well. He asked Firada what supplies she had brought with her. She had meal cakes seasoned with a peppery herb and little balls made of suet, dried berries, and honey. These were combined with the food Olikea had prepared to make a delicious and generous meal for all of us. Likari seemed very conscious of the honor of being given Great Man's food to eat. He ate it slowly, in tiny nibbles that reminded me of my days locked in my room under my father's jurisdiction, and he seemed to savor each morsel as carefully as I had then.

There was little talk. Jodoli and Soldier's Boy concentrated on their food as only Great Ones know how to do, while Firada and Olikea regarded one another in wary rivalry. Soldier's Boy did more than eat; he considered each mouthful as he chewed it, enjoying flavor and texture, but also calculating how much of it his body could store for later use as magic and how much he must keep ready for the simple business of living. He was not pleased with his results. What he ate today he would almost certainly have to use tonight to quick-walk them back to the People. He couldn't begin to rebuild his resources until they reached the Wintering Place. The fat and easy days of summer were past; he wondered if the People would be generous with their winter supplies when it came to feeding an unproven Great One.

After the meal, Jodoli announced that he planned to visit the Vale of the Ancestor Trees until the cool of the evening. "Magic is always easier when the sun no longer beats down on us," he observed, and I knew it was so without knowing how I knew it. "We will meet again at the Wintering Place?" he asked me, and Soldier's Boy nodded gravely and thanked him once more for his aid. I watched them depart, Jodoli moving unhurriedly while Firada gently chivied him along.

Olikea was as good as her word. She even made a show of helping Soldier's Boy to stand and then guiding him down to the stream's edge. Likari came with us, and she put him to work, bringing fine sand to scrub my feet and handfuls of horsetail ferns to scrub my back. Nevare would have felt embarrassed to have a young boy and a lovely woman wash his body while he sat idly in the shallows and let them. Soldier's Boy not only allowed it, he accepted it as his due.

Olikea tsked over the sagging folds of skin, but served me well. I had never known that having someone scrub my feet and then massage them could feel so delightful. I think she realized that she nearly paralyzed me with pleasure, for after I was washed, she had me rest on the clean moss beside the stream while she rubbed my back, my shoulders, my hands, and my neck. It felt so good

Soldier's Boy did not want to fall asleep and miss the sensations, but of course he did.

I slept when Soldier's Boy did that time. The physical weariness and needs of the body were his to bear, but I think there is a soul weariness that one can feel, and I felt it. Less than two days had passed since my life had profoundly changed. I'd been a condemned man escaping execution one night, and a mage who had spent all his magic the next. Those were two giant strides away from the boy who had been a second son, raised to be a cavalla soldier. I think my awareness needed to retreat, and it did.

When next I noticed the world, I was looking up through Soldier's Boy's blinking eyes at the interlacing tree branches overhead. The leaves were shivering, rustling so hard against one another that many of those loosened by autumn's bite were breaking loose from their weakened grips on twigs and falling. A few falling leaves became a flurry of yellow and orange, and then a blizzard. I stared up at them, befuddled. The sound of their falling was unearthly; there was a rhythm to the trembling of the leaves that sounded like people whispering in the distance, a rhythm that had nothing to do with the wind.

There was no wind.

And the voices were there, whispering.

There were dozens of voices, all whispering. Soldier's Boy strained to pick out a single thread of sound.

"Lisana says—"

"Tell him, tell him to come now!"

"Hurry. She's mad with grief, she's threatening—"

"Fire fears no magic. Hurry."

"Soldier's Boy, Nevare, tell him, wake him, tell him to hurry—"

The air was thick with falling leaves. The rustling whispering filled the air. Soldier's Boy rolled to his belly and scrabbled to his feet. He swayed and then steadied himself against the trunk of a nearby tree. His stirring had awakened Olikea. She had been sleeping against his back. He spoke to her. "I have to go to Lisana right now. She's in danger. The mad Gernian woman is threatening her."

CHAPTER SEVEN

EPINY'S ULTIMATUM

Soldier's Boy led the way. Olikea followed unwillingly and Likari, laden with the supplies, trailed after them. "What does she need of you?" Olikea had demanded angrily as she sat up.

"She's in danger," Soldier's Boy replied. "I have to help her."

He did not wait for her to respond to that, but set off immediately. He was stiff and his body seemed unfamiliar after so many months as a very fat man. He ached, but he forced his legs to bend and he hurried. The trees whispered to him, urging him on in a flurry of leaves and a susurrus of voices.

"He'll be too late—"

"All of us, not just Lisana—"

"—her own fault for dividing him—"

"Why didn't the fear stop her? How did she get that far?"

"Stolen magic. She burns with it."

"Drop a branch on her. It might kill her."

Sweat broke out on Soldier's Boy's back and trickled over his body, finding new wrinkles to settle in and new places to chafe. He labored on. His body was lighter and his muscles strong, but every part of him felt strained and old and creaky. His heart flopped wildly in his chest. His half-digested meal seemed to slosh inside him miserably. Nonetheless, he forced himself to hurry.

Behind him, Olikea kept up a string of reminders and warnings that made it hard for him to listen to the whispering. She did not seem to hear it, or perhaps she just dismissed it as wind in the trees. "You are being foolish. Why do you need to go to Lisana? What can she need from you? You will use up all your strength, and then what will happen to us tonight? Must we spend another full day here while you rest and eat before we can rejoin the people? Most of the kin-clans have already reached their winter settlements and will soon go on to the trading beaches. I want to be with them when they reach the Trading Place. Always, there is much talk, feasting, dancing, music, and trade when all the kin-clans come together for the winter. We will want to enjoy it, not arrive there exhausted. And I do not wish to first show you there as a skeletal man with no energy. As it is, we must spend a few days at my lodge before we go on to the Trading Place. I must prepare you so that you command respect. Nevare! You are not listening to me! Slow down."

Despite his weakened condition, she was having a hard time keeping up with him. I realized he was doing a quick-walk, making the distance between himself and Lisana contract. He was not using a great deal of magic, but it made the trees blur slightly and the ground seemed less solid under his feet. Olikea and Likari were pulled along in his wake. When he caught the first whiff of smoke, he suddenly redoubled his efforts, consuming the magic as if he had infinite reserves. In two strides, we stood beside Tree Woman's stump.

Epiny had heaped leaves, some dry and some freshly fallen, in a large mound against the stump. My cousin stood, her teeth bared with satisfaction, watching thick white smoke rising from the tiny fire she had kindled at the base of Lisana's stump. She had a ready supply of dry branches next to her, to feed the fire once she had it established.

Epiny herself looked a fright. Her hair was pulling out of braids that looked as if they'd been plaited days ago. She wore a shapeless green dress, cut to allow for her growing pregnancy, and round her middle, above her growing belly, a battered leather belt with tool loops on it. A canteen hung from one side of it. She'd snagged her dress on something; there was a long rent in the skirt, and it was obvious she'd simply let it drag behind her as she trekked through the forest to get here. Brambles and dead leaves clung to it like a dirty train. She'd unbuttoned the cuffs of her sleeves and turned them up to bare her forearms. Her face gleamed with sweat, and the throat and back of her dress were damp with it. Her hands were smudged with dirt and soot from her fire-making efforts. As I approached, she drew the back of her forearm across her brow, wiping sweat and leaving a streak of dirt in its wake. An open leather pack rested on the earth behind her. Despite her disheveled appearance, she seemed to seethe with energy.

"Burn!" she cried in a low, mad voice. She gritted her teeth and I heard them grind together. "Burn, you cheat, you whore of magic. Burn, and be dead forever. As dead as Nevare. I *did* what you asked! I did all you asked; you promised you'd save him if I did! But you didn't! You let Nevare die! You lying, cheating bitch!" The words poured out of her like thick acid. She stooped awkwardly over her belly to snatch up an armload of the firewood and flung it onto the smoldering leaves. They compacted under the weight of the fuel. For a moment, I thought she had smothered the fire. Then the smoke thickened and a tiny tongue of flame wavered up among the heaped wood. It licked the bark of Lisana's tree stump longingly.

And all the while, Lisana herself manifested as a fat old woman with gray-streaked hair standing with her back against her stump and her arms spread protectively behind her. Her incorporeal presence could do nothing. Her bare feet and her long dress of bark fabric and moss lace dangled down into the lapping flames. I do not think she felt the fire but she still screamed as the flames ran up the trunk.

It had been weeks since it had last rained. The forest was dry. I suddenly understood what the whispered words had meant. Fire fears no magic. Tiny sparks whirled aloft on an updraft of heat, floating on bits of blackened leaves. It was not just Lisana that was in danger. If this fire spread, it could engulf the entire mountainside and the Vale of the Ancestor Trees below.

Soldier's Boy had my memories. He knew her name and our language. "Epiny! Stop! Stop that! You'll kill us all." He rushed forward and kicked barefoot at the fire. He scattered it, letting air into the smoldering mass, and the flames gushed up, crackling like laughter. Epiny, startled, made no move to stop him. She stared at him, her mouth hanging open.

"Put it out, put it out!" Lisana shrieked.

I do not think Olikea and Likari heard her, but they recognized the danger all the same. Heedless of burns, Soldier's Boy was stamping at the edges of the burning fire. Olikea had taken the food pouch from her belt and was using it to beat the flames down. But it was Likari who unshouldered the heavy water skin he had been carrying. Opening it, he squeezed the bag, directing the stream into the heart of the fire. Epiny had retreated when the three had rushed up on her. Now she stood transfixed, watching as they tore her fire apart and poured water onto it and then stamped and smothered the remaining flames. In a few moments, the danger was past. Olikea was near sobbing with terror, but Likari was capering with joy. Soldier's Boy sank down. He saw another glowing ember, and lifted a handful of the wet leaves and quenched it. All three of them were streaked with smoke and soot.

"I told you!" Lisana shouted angrily at Epiny. "I told you I'd kept my word. Even if I hadn't, the magic would have. The magic doesn't lie and cheat. There, you see him? You see? Nevare is alive. What you bargained for, you got. Nevare lives!"

Soldier's Boy turned toward her. Epiny stared at him. Her eyes ran over his dwindled body, but I think his nakedness was just as shocking to her. To her, he was a piebald thing, tanned face and hands, skin pale white and sagging where it was not sunburned scarlet. She blushed, then deliberately fixed her eyes on my face. I burned with shame but Soldier's Boy scarcely noticed his nakedness before her. With great hesitancy Epiny asked, "Nevare? Can that be you?"

"It's me," he lied. And for the first time, I fully realized my position. This other entity was controlling my body. Completely. Using it as he willed without regard for me at all. I flung myself against his walls, and battled hard to take back control of my body. I could feel his contempt for Epiny, and recalled that she had been instrumental in defeating him the first time we had battled. He looked at her and saw his old enemy, come back to give him more trouble. I saw my cousin, ravaged by grief, dirty, tired, thirsty, and miles from where she should be. She was heavy with her first pregnancy, and I knew that it was a difficult one. She should have been home, safe in her house, with Spink and Amzil and Amzil's children. I thought I had arranged all that. When I'd changed the memory of every witness to the mob, when I'd sent Spink and Amzil home relatively unscathed, I thought I'd bought that for her. I knew that if I'd tried to stay, if I'd even planned to make some sort of a return to the people I knew and loved, the magic would have found a way to take them all away from me.

Two nights ago, it had nearly done it. If I hadn't surrendered to it, if I hadn't used it and allowed it to make me its own, Amzil would have been gang-raped on the streets of Gettys. Spink, I knew, would have died fighting to save her and to protect me from the mob. What would have become of Epiny, her unborn child, and Amzil's little children then? Unchanging grief for Epiny, loss and poverty for Amzil's children. That was why I'd made that sacrifice. Everything I'd done, I'd done to save them.

Yet here she was, wild-eyed and disheveled, miles from home in a hostile forest. And a man wearing my flesh was pretending to be me. She goggled at me, trying to make sense of what she was seeing. "You're naked," she pointed out in distress. "And you're . . . you're not fat anymore. What happened to you? How could that happen in one night? How can you be alive? Spink and Amzil saw you killed. Spink saw you beaten to death on the streets, by his own fellows, his own regiment. Do you know what that's done to him? Do you know how that's made him hate everything he was once so proud of? Amzil saw the end of everything that she had just begun to hope for. But here you are. Alive. I don't understand, Nevare! I don't understand anything!"

She took two hesitant steps toward me. Had I opened my arms, she would have rushed into them. But Soldier's Boy did not. He stood before her, naked and unlovely, my arms folded across my chest, and asked her solemnly, "Why did you come here? What do you want?"

"Why did I—what? I came to avenge you, you great idiot! To make her suffer for your death as we were all suffering. I came to make her sorry for betraying you, to punish the magic for not keeping its word! And what do I want? I want my life back! I want my husband to see me when he looks at me instead of looking through me. I want Amzil to stop scowling and snapping at the children. I want her to stop weeping at night. I want my baby to be born healthy and happy, not into a house where daily we endure floods of desolation or tides of panic. That's what I want. That's what I came for. I knew I wouldn't get it, but I thought I could at least kill one of those who had taken it from me."

I felt as if I were dying. I threw myself against Soldier's Boy's awareness, trying to break through. I wanted to take her in my arms and comfort her; I wanted something for Epiny. It seemed that everything I'd thought I'd purchased for her by turning my back on Gettys was hollow and sordid by the light of day. I hadn't solved anything when I'd given way to the magic. I'd only left them to muddle through grief burdened by guilt that none of them deserved.

"I won't let you kill her." He spoke flatly to Epiny. "You should just go home. Pretend you never saw me here. Accept that I'm dead. Then leave Gettys. Go back west where you and your kind belong." He lifted his eyes to Lisana as he spoke, but I had the oddest sensation that he could not see her. The strangest part was that I felt Lisana definitely could see *me*. I stared through his eyes at her, begging her for some kind of mercy, for some splinter of kindness for my cousin. What had she ever done to them save try to protect me and stand by me? Why did she have to suffer so for the magic?

Lisana spoke softly to Epiny. "As you see, Jhernian, I spoke truth to you. The magic keeps its word. Nevare isn't dead."

Epiny swung her head back to look at me. Her lips were parted and she swayed slightly. The whites showed all around her eyes. I'd once seen a horse that had been ridden near to death. She reminded me of that poor beast, as if she stayed on her feet more by sheer willpower than by physical strength. She stared at me for a long time, then looked back at Lisana. Her voice was flat. "Don't try to deceive me. That's not Nevare. I know Nevare and that's not him. You forget that the magic touches me? You forget that I can look at his aura and see that something is very wrong? You can't cheat me again, Tree Woman. I intend to kill you or die trying." She stooped down. For the first time, I saw the small hatchet she had used to cut her firewood. Against Tree Woman's thick stump, it looked ridiculous, a child's toy. But it was a toy made of iron. Its presence burned against my skin. When Epiny raised it over her head, her teeth bared in a grimace of hatred, Soldier's Boy acted, springing between her and the stump and catching her falling wrist. He squeezed hard and the hatchet fell from her grip. He caught her other wrist when she tried to rake his eyes with her nails. Despite his wasted condition, he held her easily. Epiny snarled and shrieked at him wordlessly. She kicked out at him; he accepted the blows.

"Her mind is gone," Olikea opined. She sounded appalled, as if Epiny's loss of dignity were shameful to her as well. "It would be a kindness to kill her." She spoke in Speck, her words directed to Soldier's Boy. The lack of malice in her voice chilled me. She meant it. She thought Soldier's Boy should put Epiny down as one would a diseased dog. She ventured closer to pick up the hatchet. I feared she would do the deed herself, just sink the shining blade into Epiny's spine.

"No!" I bellowed. "Lisana, help me! Please! Don't let Epiny be killed! It will be too much for me to bear!"

I made no sound. I had no command of lips or lungs or tongue. I spoke not in words, but in a flow of thought that dismissed the need for words, just as Epiny and Lisana spoke to one another. They were the words of my heart, voiceless in the world. All I could do was to plead and threaten. I was helpless to stop what was happening. My hands held my cousin helpless and waiting to be slaughtered.

Lisana looked at the scene before her. Epiny's struggles against Soldier's Boy had become increasingly feeble. His big hand trapped her thin wrists. She all but dangled in his grip. Behind Epiny's back, Olikea had raised the hatchet. Likari watched the drama with the rapt attention of a small boy staring at the unintelligible behavior of adults. The hatchet began to fall.

"Epiny!" I cried out mutely. A stray beam of sunlight moved on the blade as it traveled.

My impotent threats had not moved Lisana. Soldier's Boy looked at her stump; again, I had the feeling that I was seeing Lisana in a different way from him.

"If I help kill my own cousin, I'll go mad! My hatred for him will be unending. Can Soldier's Boy serve the magic while a madman gibbers in the back of his mind?"

When Tree Woman slowly shook her head at me, my heart sank. She spoke.

"Stop."

Now that I knew what such magic cost, I saw the effort go out of her. Tree Woman's presence dwindled when she spoke, but for me, it had the desired effect. Olikea's resolve failed. She lost her grip on the hatchet. It tumbled to the ground behind Epiny. Soldier's Boy did not release his grip on my cousin, but he set her back on her feet. She twisted one wrist free and folded that arm across her belly, in a gesture that was both supportive and protective. When he released her other wrist, she staggered a few steps away from him and then burst into tears. With both arms, she cradled her pregnancy. She didn't look at him, but past him at Tree Woman's stump. "Why?" she demanded of Lisana. "Why did you do this to Nevare? Why my cousin, why me? We were innocent of any crime against your people. Why did you reach all those miles to take him hostage to this fate? Why?"

Lisana stiffened. Her presence wavered for a moment, then seemed to grow stronger as she gathered her reserves and retorted, "Blame the Kidona, not me! He is the one who took your cousin and tried to make him a warrior to use against me. I, I was the one who had mercy. I could have just stripped his soul from his body and he would have died in all worlds. If I had not thought to offer him to the magic, he would have been dead all these years. The magic chose to keep him. Not I. I didn't know its reasons. But the magic chose him and now it has taken him. You'd best accept that, Jhernian woman. Just as he must accept and become whole to the magic. Nothing is going to change it. What the magic takes, it keeps." Perhaps only I could hear the old resignation in her words. She, too, had been chosen and kept by the magic. She, too, had never lived the life she had imagined for herself.

"Please," I thought to Lisana, hoping she still had some influence with Soldier's Boy. "Please. Let me talk to Epiny. Let me send her home. Let me have that small comfort before I must bend to the magic's will."

Soldier's Boy was staring intently at the stump. "Lisana?" he asked. There was a world of longing in his voice. He ignored the sobbing woman, and Olikea scowling in puzzlement at them. He stepped up to the stump and put his hands on it. "Lisana?" he said again. He glanced back at Epiny angrily. I felt the indignation in his heart that the Gernian woman could obviously see and speak to his beloved when all he could behold was the stump of her fallen tree.

Lisana sighed heavily. "I'm a fool," she said. "I know I'll regret this. Speak to her, then. I'll help you."

I had hoped she would do something to Soldier's Boy, to give me control once more of the body. Either she could not, or she did not trust me that far. I felt the most peculiar sensation, a cold peeling as if I were being skinned away from my life. A moment later, I could see Lisana much more distinctly, and I once more had the disembodied sensation I'd felt when she'd called me from my cell. Speaking to Epiny had been my errand then. Now I looked at my cousin and suddenly didn't know what to say to her. I could see Soldier's Boy as Epiny saw him. It was a shock. He wore my naked, sunburned body differently. I would never have stood in that posture; I would never have been so completely unselfconscious of my nakedness before my cousin. Yet, with the fat stripped from my flesh, I saw my face almost as it had been when I had set out for the Academy. Despite the sagging of the emptied jowls, I looked more youthful than I had in the last year. My blond hair was an untidy tousle but with a sickening wrench I could recall that I had been a handsome young man once. The sudden mourning I felt for that lost attractiveness shocked me with its intensity. I had never thought myself vain, but I had enjoyed being a man that girls smiled at. It was a distorted glimpse of the tall, golden cadet that I'd been. It was like a knife in my heart.

Epiny had lifted her eyes to Lisana, and when her gaze fell on my ephemeral self, she gasped. She lifted a seeking hand toward me, as if she would strive to touch me. "Nevare?" she asked.

Soldier's Boy glared at her and then leaned close to the tree stump. "Lisana?" he pleaded. We all ignored him.

I found my words. I suddenly knew that only the truth could satisfy her, and I gave it to her. "Epiny. Epiny, my dear. Yes, it's me. I'm here. I'm sorry. I did what I had to do. I used the magic to make Spink and Amzil believe I was dead. I made the entire mob in the street there believe that they'd achieved their goal and beaten me to death. Then I left. It was the only way for me to escape cleanly, the only way to break my life off from yours."

"But—" Her eyes were wide with shock. She looked from me to Soldier's Boy in my body and back again.

I spoke hastily, talking through her attempted interruption. I knew Epiny well. Once she started talking, I'd never get a word in edgeways. "The magic wouldn't let me stay. Don't you see? It boxed me in and gave me no choice. If I'd tried to stay, the mob would have beaten me to death. Amzil might have survived being raped by them, but I doubt it. And we both know that Spink would have forced them to kill him, too, before he would submit to simply witnessing something like that. The magic wanted to make it impossible for me to go back to Gettys, to force me to flee to the forest and do its will. The magic won."

Epiny was panting, both from the warmth of the day and her exertions. Her shoulders rose and fell with it. As I'd spoken, fresh tears had begun to stream down her dirty face. I thought they were for me. They were not.

"We both know that Spink would never have allowed them to beat you to death without throwing himself into the fray. It runs counter to all that he is. And yet, Nevare, you have left him believing that somehow he allowed it to happen and emerged from it with only a few bruises. Amzil must believe that as well; she insists that he sacrificed you to save her. They are both miserable. Last night, for the first time, Spink decided that he needed Gettys Tonic. Rum and laudanum. It let him sleep, but when he awoke, he looked no better. So he took a half dose and went off to his duties. He left in a haze. Amzil dosed both herself and the children into oblivion; they were still sleeping when I left. I do not know what is to become of any of them.

"Spink resisted both the gloom and the terror of the magic for so long. Now that he has crumbled twice, I fear his walls are breached. I do not think—"

Her words ran out as if her private fear were too terrible to utter aloud. She gave a half sob and, before I could speak, asked me angrily, "Do not you see, Nevare? What you have chosen for all of us saves none of us! The magic will still destroy us; it will just take longer to do it." She swung her gaze to Lisana. "And so I will say it again. The 'bargain' you offered me was a cheat and a sham. I did as you asked, I did as the magic asked, and in return, all will be taken from me."

"I do not control the magic," Lisana replied stiffly. "It does as befits the People." Her words were cold but I suspected that she had been moved by what Epiny had said.

"Can you see her? Can you speak to her?" Soldier's Boy asked wildly.

Epiny glared at him. "She's right there. Cannot you see her?"

Lisana answered her question. "As I told you. I cannot control the will of the magic. Soldier's Boy does not see me, and I can speak only to the facet of him that is Nevare. Perhaps it is our punishment for failure. Perhaps it is simply the effect of dividing the soul. One half often acquires an ability at the expense of the other half." She hesitated and added in a low voice, "I never foresaw that he would remain divided this long. Whole, I think he would succeed."

"I cannot see her. I cannot hear her. I cannot touch her." The frustration in Soldier's Boy's voice was apparent. Olikea, behind him, looked affronted.

I knew what it was, without understanding it. "I kept that part. I kept the part that lets me see and speak with Tree Woman in this world. Because—" I fumbled toward knowledge and guessed, "Because that part had always belonged mostly to me. When Soldier's Boy was with you, he was in your world. I had to reach to speak to you from mine."

"Do you think so?" Lisana asked me, and it was a genuine question.

Epiny sank down exhausted on the moss. She pushed her tumbled hair back from her sweaty face. "What does it matter? It's all destroyed. There is nothing in this life left for any of us. It does not matter who you love, Nevare, in what world. Neither you nor the one who wears your body will have joy and peace. And I must go home to the slow destruction of mine."

"Epiny." I spoke quickly, before I could change my mind, before Lisana could silence me. "Go home to Spink. Tell him the truth. That I used magic on him. That he did nothing cowardly. I used him to get Amzil safely away."

"And of course he will believe me," Epiny replied, sarcasm cutting through the grief in her voice. "He will not think me mad, oh no."

"He will believe you if you give him proof." I racked my brain for an instant. "Tell him to go to the graveyard and talk to Kesey. Ask Kesey if he had a strange dream the morning I died. Ask Kesey if my sword was on the floor when he woke. If he tells the truth, Spink will have his proof." I hesitated. "And if you must, tell him to ask Scout Tiber. He had a glimpse of me as I fled that morning. I'd just as soon he wasn't reminded of it, but if Spink doubts still, have him ask Tiber."

Epiny was still breathing hard, her shoulders rising and falling with it. "And Amzil," she demanded. "What about Amzil?"

"I think it is better that she continues to believe that I am dead."

"Why?" she demanded.

I hesitated. My reason sounded vain, even to myself. "Because she is a stubborn woman. I think she might attempt to come after me and rescue me, if she thought I had given up everything to save her. If she knew how I loved her, she might risk herself."

Epiny rubbed her hands over her eyes. The soot and tears combined to smear a mask across her face. "Perhaps I know her better than you, in some ways. She is also a pragmatic woman. She puts her children first in her life."

She paused, and I bowed my head. She had said enough. I understood. Then she added, "But I think it would mean a great deal to her to know that she had been loved that way by a man, at least once in her life."

I thought about that. I thought about how much Amzil's whispered words in Gettys the night she had helped me escape meant to me. Epiny was right. It was good to know such things, even if they could have no consummation.

"You may tell her also, then," I conceded. "And you can tell her that I loved her. Love her still, even though I must leave her."

Epiny gave a strangled laugh. "I not only 'may,' I can, and therefore I shall, Nevare. I have not forgotten how shamed and foolish I felt to discover how long you and Spink had kept a secret from me. I will not do that to Amzil!"

"I'm sorry," I said, and meant it.

She glanced away from me to Soldier's Boy. He was glaring, a flat-eyed intimidating stare. He wanted to blame someone for his inability to see Tree Woman but could not decide whom. It startled me to realize that my face could look so mean. The expression deepened the lines in his face; that made me wonder if it was a look I had often worn without being aware of it. Epiny looked from him to Lisana. "Does he know what's going on? That you're letting me talk to the real Nevare?"

"He has never been stupid," Lisana said, with some pride in her voice. "But like Nevare, he has suffered from being incomplete. That can happen when a soul is divided; part becomes impulsive, and the other half indecisive. Half can be given to dramatic shows while the other half expresses next to no emotion at all. One acts without thinking; the other thinks without acting."

Epiny looked from one to the other of us. "That makes sense," she said calmly.

Soldier's Boy spoke. "I know what is happening here. I do not know why she is permitting it. Make the most of it, Gernian woman. It will not happen again." He crossed his arms over his chest.

"What are you waiting for? We've put out the fire. You should kill that woman and leave. Look at her. She's sickly. She looks like a string with a knot tied in it; how can any woman that skinny be pregnant? Do it and be done with it, Soldier's Boy. You are wasting strength that you will need if you are to quick-walk us to the People tonight." Olikea spoke in Speck. I do not think Epiny understood her words but her disdain was unmistakable. Epiny smoothed her hair back from her face and turned aside from Olikea without making any response or even seeming to notice her. I wondered if Olikea even recognized that Gernian snub.

"He is right," Lisana said. "Your time is short. Nevare, you begged this from me. You said you could send her home. Speak whatever final words you have to say to her, and then you must be on your way."

"Send me home!" Epiny said, sparks of anger kindling in her sunken eyes. "Send me home? Am I a dog then, to be told, 'Get home!' and I obediently trot along?"

"No!" I said hastily. "No. That's not it at all. Epiny, you have to listen to me now. You can do no good here. Go home to Spink and Amzil and her children. Do what you can for them, comfort them with the truth, if you think it will be comfort, and above all, have a care for yourself and your baby. Do whatever you can for my little sister. Yaril is beyond my reach now."

"What? What are you going to do? And why are you speaking to me like this, instead of— Why does he have your body?"

"I don't really know. I think that his part of me is the stronger half now, and so he gets his way. I am where he was after I first defeated him."

Lisana was nodding silently.

"Nevare, you must try to be stronger! You must fight him and take control of your body again. Come back to Gettys. Look at you. You've lost the fat. You could be a real soldier now."

"Epiny, think! I could also be hanged for escaping from my cell, once they realized that they hadn't killed me the first time. There is nothing left for me back in Gettys."

"He cannot prevail against Soldier's Boy," Lisana said quietly. "His time is past. He had his chance and he failed. His solutions have not solved anything. It is time for him to let go, to become a part of Soldier's Boy and time for Soldier's Boy to try his way. They need to unite their strengths."

Epiny's face changed. Her expression hardened and something very like hatred shone in her eyes. "I will not let you destroy him," she said. "He will fight you and I will fight you. We are stronger than you know. He will take back his body, and he will come back to us. I know he will."

Lisana shook her head. She spoke calmly, patiently. "No. He will not. You would be wiser to listen to him. Go home. Take care of what is yours. When your child is born, leave this place and go back to your own lands."

Epiny stared at Lisana levelly. "I won't give up on Nevare. If you want me to leave, you will have to give me back my cousin."

Lisana didn't smile or snarl. Her face was impassive. "I believe that when they are one, they will succeed where both failed before. I believe that then he will accept whatever magical task he must do, and that when he does it, the intruders will leave our land. What I am offering you is a chance to save yourself and your child. Go now, before you are driven out. I do not know how the magic will rid our lands of the intruders, but I do not think it will be gentle. Gentleness and persuasion have been tried without success. The time for that is past."

"I won't give up on Nevare," Epiny repeated. She said it as if perhaps Lisana had not heard her or had not been paying attention. "I don't believe he will give up. He will keep trying, and when he is strong enough, he will take back his life from Soldier's Boy, and he will come back to us."

I tried to think of some response.

She smiled at me and added, "And if he does not, then come next summer, when the days are long and hot and the forest is dry,

I will burn it. All of it." She was suddenly calm. She folded her hands together and held them in front of her. She did not look at me at all. Her face and hands were dirty, her dress smudged and torn, and her hair was falling down all around her face. But it was as if all her sorrow and pain had drained out of her, as if nothing was left but the determination; she was like a shining steel blade drawn from its worn scabbard.

"This is the gratitude of a Jhernian," Lisana observed coldly. "The magic kept its word to you. I have shown you your cousin, alive as promised, and even interceded that you might say farewell to him. I have offered you a chance to escape to the west with your baby. And in return, you threaten to destroy us."

I knew that Soldier's Boy could not hear Lisana's words, and yet he seemed to reply to them. "I will kill her now," Soldier's Boy announced, and Olikea, grim-faced, nodded.

Epiny probably did not understand the words he spoke in Speck, but she recognized the threat. It did not move her. "You can kill me," Epiny said. "I doubt it would be difficult for you." She lifted her chin, as if baring her throat to him. Her eyes remained locked with Lisana's. Epiny didn't say anything else. Yet danger hovered in the air, unspoken and all the more worrisome that it was undefined.

"Kill her," Olikea said quietly. There was fear and desire in her voice. "Use this." She drew a knife from a sheath on her belt and offered it to him. It had a glittering black blade, obsidian. A memory stirred. It was as sharp as a razor, a knife fit for a mage who must not touch iron.

Soldier's Boy took it from her, then looked about helplessly, as if seeking guidance. He could not hear Lisana. He could not seek her guidance and Epiny's fearless acceptance of her position clearly bothered him. I saw him decide there was something he didn't know. I wondered if there were, or if Epiny was bluffing. I longed to ask her and knew I could not even look as if I wondered. I tried for a small smile to match hers. I probably failed.

Soldier's Boy decided. He struck with the knife.

I felt his decision a split moment before he acted. Two things happened in the next instant. I stopped him. I didn't know how I did it, but I stopped him in midlunge. It startled him, and worse, it burned more of his small reserve of magic. I'd actually used his magic against him, to prevent him injuring Epiny. I was as surprised as he was.

And Epiny, despite her ungainly pregnancy, ducked down abruptly and then lunged toward the hatchet that Olikea had dropped. She hit the ground harder than she had planned; I heard her grunt of pain. But she came up gripping the hatchet, her teeth bared in triumph. "Let's see what happens when you get hit with cold iron!" she threatened him, and she threw it, as hard as she could, at Soldier's Boy's head. It made a nasty solid noise as the butt of it hit his forehead. He dropped. I do not know if it was the force of the impact or the iron hitting his body, but he shuddered, twitched, and his eyes rolled back in his head. Likari's mouth hung open in an O of shock. Olikea screamed like a scalded cat and rushed Epiny.

And I watched, helpless. Not only was I disembodied, but the only body I could have hoped to affect was unconscious. Olikea was taller than Epiny, heavier, accustomed to more physical activity and unencumbered by clothes or pregnancy. She flung herself on Epiny as a cat leaps on prey. Epiny dodged to one side but still went down beneath her onslaught. Both women were shrieking, the most unhallowed sound that I had ever heard. Epiny used language I would not have suspected her of knowing, and fought with a strength and ferocity that astounded me. She fought to defend her unborn child as much as herself. Olikea was on top but Epiny writhed in her grip to face her and drew first blood, raking her nails down Olikea's face and breast. For all that Epiny's clothing encumbered her, it also protected her from casual damage, and when Epiny rolled to one side, drew her leg up and then managed to kick Olikea in the belly, her boots became a definite advantage.

As Olikea gasped, Epiny crawled frantically away. I thought she was trying to escape, but as Olikea recovered and went after Epiny, my cousin once more snatched up the fallen hatchet. Olikea, thinking herself threatened, grabbed the flint knife that still rested in Soldier's Boy's slack hand. But Epiny did not come at her; instead, she pressed the blade of her weapon to Soldier's Boy's throat. "Back off!" she snarled. "Back off, or neither of us gets him. He'll be dead." They did not share a language, but the threat was as obvious as the blade held to his throat.

In that moment, I suddenly realized that it was me they were fighting over. I was astounded.

Olikea froze. Epiny remained as she was, crouching over Soldier's Boy, the cold iron of the hatchet not quite touching his throat. She looked feral and predatory, hunkered over my body. Then she caught her breath, gave a small grunt of pain, and put her hand on her belly and rubbed it softly, almost reassuringly.

"You won't kill him," Olikea asserted after a moment. "He is your cousin."

Epiny stared at her and then looked at me. I translated for her. "She says you won't kill me because I'm your cousin."

"No," Epiny retorted bluntly. "Right now he isn't. My cousin is over there." With her empty hand, she pointed to my disembodied essence hovering near Lisana. "This, this *creature* in his body is something that Tree Woman and the magic made. It might have been part of my cousin once, but she twisted it into something completely foreign to what Nevare is. And rather than see that creature masquerading as Nevare, I will kill him. Without compunction. I will not let this beast pretend he is Nevare Burvelle."

I watched Olikea listen to the flood of foreign words. None of them were needed; she knew all she needed to know by the blade that hovered over my throat.

Lisana spoke. "Soldier's Boy is as much your cousin as Nevare Burvelle is. When he came to me, sent by that old Kidona to be his warrior-champion, I captured him and divided his soul. Deny it as you wish, but Soldier's Boy is not a separate creature from your cousin. Both parts of him are needed to be a whole. You cannot cast him out of the body. Kill him, and you kill your cousin, the Nevare you know, just as surely. Have you the will to kill Nevare to keep Soldier's Boy from using the body?"

Olikea could not hear Lisana's words. She had risen and was slowly circling Epiny, her knife low and ready. "Now what will you do, you skinny Jhernian wretch? Kill him and I'll kill you. I'm bigger than you, and stronger. You know I'll win. How long can you crouch over him, threatening him? What will you do when he wakes up?"

"I don't know," Epiny replied, but she answered Lisana, not Olikea. "It seems we are at an impasse." After a moment, she added, "If my cousin Nevare is never to regain his body and his life, and I am to be attacked and killed anyway, then neither of us has anything to lose if I kill him now. Do you agree with that?"

I was silent, considering the question. I didn't know what would become of me if Epiny killed my body. Did I care? Just the fact that I had no immediate answer to that question made me mute. For most of my life, I'd had goals that had driven me. What did I have now? Perhaps, like Epiny, I'd reached a dead end. Briefly, my cousin's gaze met mine. I saw love in her eyes, but also resolution and resignation.

It did not look good for my body. Slowly I nodded at her. She shifted her gaze to Lisana. "You see?"

Lisana was quiet for a time. Then she asked abruptly, "What do you want, Jhernian? What will it take to make you leave this place and never return?"

Epiny was silent for a moment. I could see her hand trembling. I think the hatchet was getting heavy in her grip. "I assume you mean without killing him," she said after a pause.

"Yes." Lisana bit off the word.

"Talk to ME!" Olikea abruptly demanded. "I am the one who is here. I am the one who can kill you!" She made a menacing motion with her knife.

"Shut up!" Epiny barked at her, and touched the hatchet blade to Soldier's Boy's throat. He made a small sound in his throat. Olikea took a step back, glowering at her.

"She's dangerous, Epiny. Be very careful. She'll kill you if she can."

"I know that," Epiny said hoarsely. "I may have to kill your body." Tears filled her eyes and spilled but only anger showed on her face. "How can it be any worse, Nevare? Shall I go down whimpering and begging for mercy? I doubt any would be shown.

If I must lose it all, then at least I'll extract a price from them. They'll know I was here; I won't be stepped on like an ant."

The desperate courage in her words moved me. "You should have been your father's soldier son," I told her quietly.

"He's waking up!" Likari cried aloud. I'd almost forgotten the boy was there. He'd hovered at the outskirts, watching everything but saying and doing little. Now he pointed at my body. My eyelids fluttered and Soldier's Boy's hands twitched against the mossy ground.

Epiny might not have understood Likari's words, but the tone alerted her. She lowered the hatchet until its blade rested against Soldier's Boy's throat. He made an incoherent sound. I did not know if he protested the bite of the sharp edge or the burn of cold iron against his throat. Epiny leaned forward over him, so close that all he could see was her face. I watched his eyes blink bewilderedly and then focus on her. She spoke in a low growl.

"Don't move. Listen to me. Tell that woman with the knife and the boy with the water skin to go away. Tell them that you don't want them to hurt me. Send them down to wait by the stream. Tell them to stay there until you come to them. Say only those words. I will know what you say. If you say any more than that, or any less than that, I'll kill you. Do you understand me?"

He licked his lips and rolled his eyes to look at Olikea. Epiny didn't hesitate. She pressed the blade more firmly to his throat. Distantly, I felt it slice my skin and, more intensely, I felt the hot/cold kiss of iron against my flesh. It made my magic bleed, and that was more painful than the fine cut it scored on my skin. "Please, don't!" Soldier's Boy croaked. Epiny eased up but didn't move the blade.

"Tell them," she said quietly.

"Olikea. Likari. Go down the ridge to the stream. Wait for me there. Don't do anything else right now, just wait down there until I come."

Epiny's glance flickered to me. I confirmed that she'd been obeyed. "He did as you told him. He's ordered them to go down to the stream and wait."

Olikea looked rebellious. Likari wriggled in an agony of in-decision, torn between curiosity and obedience. "Shall I leave you here, at her mercy?" Olikea began in protest, but Soldier's Boy broke in on her words with, "Go. Just go now, or she'll kill me. I can manage this situation better if you are not here, Olikea. Go down to the stream. Wait for me there."

"Oh, you look so much in control of the situation!" Olikea snarled. She glared at Epiny and kept the obsidian blade at the ready as she backed away. "Someday, Jhernian woman. Someday it will be just you and me." Then she turned angrily on Likari. "Why are you still standing there? He told us to go wait by the stream. And that is what we must do."

"He told her to go away, and she and the boy are leaving," I hastily interpreted before Epiny could look at me. I wanted her to keep her wary gaze on Olikea. "But she threatened that someday she'd get back at you."

"That's fine," Epiny said almost absently. There was strain in her voice. She kept her gaze fixed on Olikea and Likari, watching them until they were out of sight. Crouching over me, pressing the knife to my throat, was uncomfortable for her. Her pregnant belly got in her way. I could see that it was hard for her to remain still, the hatchet blade pressed lightly to my throat, and all her weight on her bent knees.

"And now what?" Lisana asked in a low voice. "What will you do now? Do you think this is over? That Soldier's Boy will let you just walk away after you have threatened the forest?"

Epiny blew the hair away from her eyes and then looked up at Lisana. "And do you think it's a good idea to ask me that question while I'm in this position? The simplest way for me to resolve it would be to cut his throat and go my way. By the time they realize he's not coming, I'll be long gone."

"Do you think the forest would allow you to escape that eas-ily?" Lisana countered.

Epiny sighed. "No. I don't think the forest or the magic will allow any of us to escape. It wants the impossible. It wants to re-verse the flow of the years; it wants to go back to when Gernians came here only to trade for furs and then to leave. It won't happen. It can't happen. And as long as the magic demands that, there will never be a resolution. Not for any of us."

I looked from Epiny's bowed head to the sweat drops rolling slowly down my own face and then up at Lisana. Epiny was right. As the thought came to me, I felt as if my existence wavered. The magic was weakening. Lisana was weary and there was little magic left in my own body for me to draw on.

"Epiny! I'm fading. I'm sorry. I did what I thought was wise, but it helped no one. Not even me. Farewell. I loved all of you the best that I could. Get away if you can. Get all of you away."

Suddenly I was in my body, looking up at Epiny. I think she saw me in Soldier's Boy's eyes, because she said softly, "You stopped him from killing me. Remember that you could do that. Believe you'll eventually find that strength again, that you'll master him again. Until then, I'm sorry, Nevare. I'm sure you'd do the same thing in my place. And you know, you really deserve this."

She lifted the hatchet from my throat, but before I could stir, she reversed her grip on it. The blunt end of it hit me squarely between the eyes, and I knew nothing more.

CHAPTER EIGHT

QUICK-WALK

When I became aware again, Epiny was gone. I didn't immediately realize that. With Soldier's Boy, I felt woozy and disoriented and unable to focus my eyes. My gut heaved with nausea. Being struck on the head hard enough to cause unconsciousness is never a joke, and my body had endured two such assaults in rapid succession. I could barely breathe past the thickness in my mouth, and I could not stir my limbs. I felt Soldier's Boy's frustration as he used yet more of his rapidly dwindling magic to speed the body's healing. Even so, we lay motionless and queasy for a good hour before he felt well enough to sit up.

That was when he discovered that Epiny had taken a few precautions before she left. The leather strap of her bag was tied securely in my mouth as a gag, and strips torn from the draggled hem of her dress were knotted about my wrists and ankles. Soldier's Boy rolled onto his side and began working against his bonds. Tree Woman spoke to me as he did so.

"Your cousin is more resourceful than I thought. Truly, she would have made a better servant to the magic."

Little as I wanted to serve the magic, the comparison still
stung. "Maybe if my self hadn't been divided, I would have been
a better tool for the magic. Or a better soldier."

"That's likely," she admitted easily. Soldier's Boy didn't hear
her. He wasn't looking at her tree stump, so I couldn't see her.
But I could imagine her gentle, rueful smile. I hated what she
had done to me. I hated how the magic had twisted my life away
from my boyish dreams of a glorious career of a cavalla officer, of
a gentle well-bred wife and a home of my own. I'd forfeited it all
when I'd battled Lisana and lost. She had been the engineer of my
downfall. Yet I still felt tenderness toward Lisana, my Tree Woman.
It was no longer based entirely on Soldier's Boy's love for her. I
sensed in her a kindred spirit, someone who had come unwilling
to the magic's service but, like me, saw a need for it.

"So. What will happen now?"

She sighed, light as wind in the leaves. "Eventually, Olikea or
Likari will come back and help you. Or you'll wriggle free on
your own. And then you must eat heartily, and quick-walk to join
the People at the Wintering Place."

"I didn't mean it that way. I meant, what will become of
Epiny and Spink? What will happen to them?"

She sighed again. "Let go of that life, Nevare. Embrace the
one you are in now. Join the sundered halves of your soul and
become one."

That hadn't been what I was asking her. "Will you try to harm
Epiny?" I asked her directly.

"Hmf. Did she try to harm me? A few more minutes of that
fire, and we would not be having this conversation now. I've told
you before, I cannot control the magic or what it does." A pause.
Then her voice was gentler. "But for whatever peace it gives you,
I'll tell you that I will not be attempting any revenge on her." She
made an odd sound that might almost have been a laugh. "The
less I have to do with your cousin, the better for both of us, I
think."

"Thank you."

Olikea did not come to find me. Jodoli did, stumping up the
ridge with a scolding Firada in his wake. He, too, had heard the

summons of the whispering leaves, but he had been farther away and Firada had not wanted him to quick-walk them to Lisana, thinking it better that Soldier's Boy handle whatever the difficulty was with the Gernian madwoman on his own. Firada was not pleased with Jodoli consuming energy to rescue me yet again. She grumbled about it the whole time that he was untying me.

"What happened here?" Jodoli asked as soon as the gag was removed from my mouth.

"Nevare's cousin Epiny attacked Lisana. But do not concern yourself with it. The threat has been dealt with. I'm sorry that I used more of your time."

"You call this dealing with a threat?" Firada asked tartly. "We find you bound and gagged, and your feeders nowhere in sight!"

"I sent them away, to keep them safe. It is dealt with. Let it go."

He spoke in a commanding way that I expected her to find offensive. Instead she just puffed her cheeks and then settled in abrupt silence. Soldier's Boy turned to Jodoli. His face was equally disapproving, but I suspected that some sign from him had quieted Firada.

"Jodoli, I thank you for coming yet again to my aid. Please, do not delay your journey to rejoin the People any longer. I will need another day here to gather strength before I am able to do any magic. But do not linger here on my account."

"We have no intention of doing so," Firada responded quickly.

Jodoli's words were more measured. "Indeed, we must depart tonight. But I wanted to let you know that I went to look at what you did to the intruders' road. I think you bought us a season of respite, and perhaps more. It is not a permanent solution. None-theless, I do not think you used your magic in vain. Firada is cor-rect that I must rejoin our kin-clan tonight; they are unprotected when I am not with them. I hope you will hurry to rejoin us as quickly as you can." He glanced about, his eyes lingering on Tree Woman's scorched trunk.

Soldier's Boy got slowly to his feet. His head still pounded with pain, and hunger squeezed him again. All the magic he'd acquired, he'd used in healing the worst of his injury. He sighed. "I go to regain my feeders. We will see you soon, at the Wintering Place. Travel well."

"At the Wintering Place," Jodoli confirmed. He reached out and took Firada's hand. They walked away. I did not "see" the quick-walk magic, but in less than two blinks of my eye, they had vanished from my sight. When they were gone, Soldier's Boy turned back to Lisana's stump.

He walked over to it, knelt in the deep moss, and gravely examined the damage. There was not much; the fire had licked the outer bark, scorching it but had not penetrated it. He nodded, satisfied. He gripped the hilt of the rusty cavalla sword that was still thrust deep into the stump. Heedless of the unpleasant buzzing that the proximity of the metal blade woke in his hands, he tried to work it loose. To no avail. A nasty recognition stirred in my own thoughts. As a mage, I'd now experienced how unpleasant the touch of iron felt. Yet Lisana had never once reproached me for the blade I'd felled her with and then left sticking in her trunk. I felt shamed.

But Soldier's Boy continued unaware of my thoughts or feelings. He pushed through growing underbrush to reach the young tree that reared up from Lisana's fallen trunk. He set his hands to its smooth bark and leaned his head back to smile up at its branches. "We must thank our luck that she did not know this is where you are truly most vulnerable. This little one would not have survived such a scorching as your trunk took. Look how she seeks the sun. Look how straight she stands." He leaned forward, to rest his brow briefly against the young tree's bark. "I really, really miss your guidance," he said softly.

Behind us, Lisana spoke. "I miss you, too, Soldier's Boy."

I knew he could not hear her. She knew it, too, and I heard the isolation in her voice, that her words to him must go unheard. It was for her rather than for him that I said, "She misses you, too."

Soldier's Boy caught a breath. "Tell her that I love her still. Tell her I miss her every day. There is not a moment that goes by when I do not remember all that she taught me. I will be true to what she taught me when I go to the Wintering Place. This I promise. Tell her that. Please, tell her that for me!"

He was looking at her little tree. I wanted him to turn and look at the cut trunk, where Lisana still manifested most strongly for me. But it was not easy to make him hear me, and I did not want to waste the effort. "She hears you when you speak. She cannot make you hear her replies, but what you say aloud, she hears."

Again, he halted, turning his head like a dog that hears a far-off whistle. Then he slowly reached out to the little tree and drew a finger down its trunk. "I'm glad you can hear me," he said softly. "I'm glad we at least have that."

I heard Lisana sob. I wished I could have met her eyes. "She's by the stump," I said, but my strength was fading.

Lisana spoke to me again. "Please. Tell him to walk down the line of my fallen trunk. Near the end, another small tree has begun. Tell him that it is for him, when the time comes. I'm preparing a tree for him. Please tell him."

"Look for another little tree, near the end of her fallen trunk," I said. I pushed the words as hard as I could. But he did not hear me. After a pause, he spoke aloud to her. "I'm tired, Lisana. Tired and hungry and empty of magic. I need to find sustenance. And as soon as I can, I must leave for the Wintering Place. I haven't forgotten what you told me. Believe me. What you taught me, I will live." He was very still, as if listening for me or for Lisana, but after a time he closed his eyes, puffed his cheeks, and turned away from the little tree.

He started to follow the fading trail that led back down the ridge and eventually into a valley where a small stream flowed. Weariness dragged at us. He muttered as we walked, and after a time, I realized he was speaking to me. I listened more closely to his rambling words. "You used it all. Did you hate us that much or were you just stupid? I saved that magic, hoarded it all thinking that I might get one chance. And now it's all gone. Gone. You always complained to everyone who would listen that I'd stolen your beautiful wonderful future. Is that why you destroyed mine? Was it vengeance? Or stupidity?"

I had no way of responding. I was little more than a spark inside him now, clinging desperately to my self-awareness. The idea of letting go came to me. I shook myself free of it. What would happen to me if I did? Would I cease to be entirely, or would all my ideas, thoughts, and knowledge suddenly be merged with Soldier's Boy? Would he consume me as I had tried to consume him? If he integrated me into his being, would I have any awareness of it? Would I live on only as odd bits of dreams that sometimes haunted the Speck mage I would become?

The thought of merging my awareness with Soldier's Boy and becoming merely a part of him held no appeal for me. Instead it filled me with loathing, and I struggled against it. "I am Nevare Burvelle," I told myself. "Soldier son of a new noble lord. Destined to be a cavalla officer, to serve my king with courage, to distinguish myself on a field of battle. I will prevail. I will keep faith with Epiny and I will prevail." I would not become a set of disconnected memories inside some hulking forest mage. I would not.

And so I wearily clung to my identity and did little more than that for the next two days. I was an observer as Soldier's Boy hiked wearily down to the stream. He found Likari dozing on the shady bank while Olikea scavenged in the shallows for a grayish-brown leggy creature that looked more like an insect than a fish to me. As she caught each one, she popped its head off with her thumbnail and then added it to the catch heaped on a lily leaf on the stream bank. The animals were small; two would fill her palm. She already had a small fire burning. As Soldier's Boy approached, he greeted her with "It is good that you are already finding food for me."

She didn't look up from her hunting. "I already know what you are going to say. That you have used up what magic you had, and we must stay another night here. Did you kill her?"

"No. I let her go. She is no threat to us. And you are right that we must stay here, not one night, but three. I have decided that before I travel, I will rebuild some of my reserves. I will not be the Great Man I was when we rejoin the People, but I will not be this skeleton, either. I will eat for three days. And then we will quick-walk to the people."

"By then almost everyone will have returned to the Wintering Place! The best trading will be done, and all that will be left there are the things that are not quite perfect or have no newness to them!"

"There will be other trading days in years to come. You will have to miss this one."

Olikea filled her cheeks and then puffed the air out explosively. She had caught two more of the creatures, and she flung them down on those already heaped on the stream bank so hard that I heard the crack of their small shells as they hit. She was not pleased, and I was dimly surprised by how easily Soldier's Boy dismissed her feelings on the matter.

She looked at him at last and surprise almost overcame her sullen glance. "What happened to your forehead?"

"Never mind that," he said brusquely. "We need food. Busy yourself with that." With his foot, he stirred the sleeping Likari. "Up, boy. Gather food. Lots of it. I need to fill myself."

Likari sat up, blinking, and knuckled his eyes. "What sort of food, Great One?"

"Any food that you can get in quantity. Go now."

The boy scuttled off. Olikea spoke from behind me. "Do not blame him if he cannot find much that is good. The time for the best harvesting is past. That is why we go to the Wintering Place."

"I know that." Soldier's Boy turned and walked to the stream's edge, upstream of Olikea. With a grunt and a sigh, he hunkered down and then sat on the ground. He reached over, pulled up a handful of water-grass, rinsed the muddy roots off in the flowing stream and then peeled the slimy outer skin off them. He bit off the thick white roots and, as he chewed them, uprooted another handful of the stuff. The flavor was vaguely like onions.

By the time Likari returned with an armload of shriveled plums, Soldier's Boy had cleared a substantial patch of water-grass. He ate as methodically as a grazing cow. Olikea was busy with her own task; she had steamed the leggy creatures in layers of leaves and was now stripping them of legs and carapaces. The curl of meat from each one was scarcely the size of my little finger, but they smelled wonderful.

They ate together, with Soldier's Boy taking the lion's share
of the food. The plums had dried in the sun's heat; their flesh was
thick and chewy and sweet, and contrasted pleasantly with the
little crustaceans. When the food was gone, Soldier's Boy commanded them both to find more, and then lay down to sleep.
When they woke him, they had roasted a pile of yellow roots that
had little flavor other than starch, and a porcupine was cooking on
the fire. Likari had killed the creature with a club. Divested of its
fur and quills, it showed a thick layer of fat. "You can see the kind
of weather that soon will come!" Olikea warned him.

"Let me worry about such things." Soldier's Boy dismissed
her.

Night was deepening when that meal was gone. They slept in
a huddle, Olikea against his belly and Likari cuddled against his
back. Soldier's Boy used a tiny bit of magic to hummock the moss
into a nest around them while Likari had gathered armloads of
fallen leaves to cover them. Over the leaves, he spread the winter
blanket from my cemetery hut, even though both Olikea and
Likari complained that it smelled odd. He had discovered that
they had disposed of the clothing he had worn when they found
him. Olikea had cut the shining brass buttons from his uniform
and kept them, but the rest of it was gone, dropped somewhere
in the forest when they were moving him. So all that he carried
forward from my life was a winter blanket and a handful of buttons. It seemed fitting.

As they settled together in their bed with Olikea's warm back
to his chest and her firm buttocks resting on his thighs, Soldier's Boy
felt an insistent stirring of lust for the woman, but set it firmly aside.
Later, after he had regained some of his flesh, he could enjoy her.
For now, he must not expend any effort save to gather and eat food.
As for Olikea, she showed no such interest in him at all, and Likari
seemed blissfully unaware of any tension between the adults.

For the next two days, that was the pattern. As long as there
was enough light to see, Olikea and Likari gathered food and Soldier's Boy consumed it. They moved twice, following the stream,
as Soldier's Boy systematically harvested and ate every edible item
that it could provide for him.

There was a freeze on the third night. There had been twinges of frost before, enough to hasten the turning of the leaves, but that night, the cold reached beneath the forest eaves. Despite the mossy nest and deep blanket of leaves, they all shivered through the night. Soldier's Boy awoke aching, and Olikea and Likari were both grumpy. In response to Olikea's complaints, Soldier's Boy told her, "We will travel tonight. I have regained enough reserves that we will go swiftly. For now, go about your gathering. I will return shortly."

"Where are you going?"

"I go to the road's end. I will not stay there long; have food ready for me when I return."

"This is a foolish risk you take. There will be workers there; they may attack you."

"They will not see me," Soldier's Boy said firmly. And with that as his farewell, he set out.

As Soldier's Boy had recovered his reserves and strength, so had I. He was still not as immense as he had been, but he had regained flesh and energy. He moved purposefully through the forest. The fallen leaves carpeted the moss. They rustled as he strode through them. As he approached the road's end, Soldier's Boy slowed and went more cautiously. For a large man, he moved very quietly, and he paused often to listen.

He heard only birdcalls and, once, the thump and rustle of a disturbed rabbit. Emboldened, he ventured closer to what had been the road. Stillness reigned.

By this hour of the day, workers should have arrived, but there were no signs of them. He moved cautiously along the edge of the road. The greenery I had sent out across it had browned, but the vines and crawling brambles had survived and looked undisturbed. Where I had sent plants to block the culverts, swamps had formed on either side of the road. Insects buzzed and hummed near them.

He came to the shed where the men had been keeping watch that night. It was deserted. He walked through it and found the dice still out on the rough table just as the men had abandoned them. No one had been back here since that night.

"Perhaps it was not a total waste of magic," he conceded reluctantly. "It looks as if the intruders are discouraged. I do not think they will come back before spring."

He had turned back into the forest before I realized that he had deliberately spoken to me.

"I thought I was doing what the magic wanted me to do." I could not decide if I wanted to apologize to him or not. It seemed strange to apologize to myself, and even more so to have to apologize for an action I'd been pushed into taking. I wasn't even certain that he was aware of what I'd tried to say to him. I thought of the times when I'd thought I'd felt Soldier's Boy stir inside me, the moments when my thoughts had seemed more Speckish than Gernian. Always, I'd felt that he deliberately concealed himself from me. Now I wondered if he had tried to share his views, only to feel as smothered as I did.

He spoke again, almost grudgingly, as if reluctant to acknowledge me. "The magic was mine, not yours to spend. And the magic speaks to me, not you. You should not have tampered with it."

He seemed to resent me as much as I did him. It scarcely seemed fair. He was the one who had invaded my life. I reined in my resentment and asked my most pressing question.

"Do you know what the magic wants you to do?"

He grinned hard. I sensed him weighing whether or not to reply. When he did, I felt it was because he could not resist the urge to brag. "Several times, I have acted on what the magic wished me to do."

"When? What did you do?"

"You don't remember the Dancing Spindle?"

"Of course I do." At the Dancing Spindle, actions I had taken had ended the Spindle's dance forever, and dispersed the magic of the Plainspeople. I knew now that Soldier's Boy had taken into himself as much of their magic as he could hold and had hoarded it. "But what else? When else did you obey the magic?"

His grin grew wider. "You don't know, do you? That amuses me. Because at the time, I thought I felt you resisting me. And even now, I do not think I would be wise to tell you the things the magic prompted me to do. There were small things that I did, things that made no sense to me. But I did them. And I kept them from you, lest you try to undo them. You thought you had pushed me down; you thought you had absorbed me and made me a part of you. But I won then. And I've won now, Gernian. I will prevail."

I nearly warned him not to be too certain of that. Then I decided not to provoke him to keep his guard up against me. He spoke no more to me but found and followed the stream to rejoin Likari and Olikea. She was sitting close by the fire, her arms wrapped around her naked body. The day had warmed, but not much.

"Finding food would keep you warmer," he told her. "This is the last day we shall spend here. We'll eat, and then sleep until nightfall."

"There isn't much left to find here!" Olikea protested, but just then Likari made a lie of her words.

He ran up to me, proudly displaying six silver fish hung from a willow wand through their gills. "I caught them all myself!" he exclaimed. His hands and forearms were bright red from exposure to the icy waters.

"Wonderful!" Soldier's Boy praised him and rumpled the boy's hair. The child wriggled like a happy puppy. Olikea took the fish with a sour expression on her face and went to work cleaning them of guts and scales. Soldier's Boy went back to the stream and began eating water-grass stems. He would have preferred to eat the foods richest in magic potential, but lacking those, he would fill my belly with anything that was edible.

When Olikea returned from her gathering, a hastily woven carry sack held big mushrooms and a quantity of prickly cones. She gave the cones to Likari, and he pounded them on a rock by the stream to shake loose the fat seeds inside them. The mushrooms were thick and dense, with ranks of tubes rather than gills on the undersides of their orange caps. Olikea cut them into fat slices to toast over the fire with the fish.

After everyone had eaten, they all arranged themselves in the moss-and-leaves nest to sleep for the rest of the day. I felt no need for such rest. Instead, trapped behind the darkness of Soldier Boy's closed eyes, my thoughts chased their own tails in endless circles. What had he done for the magic that I hadn't even known about, and when had he done it? In dread, I thought of the times I had awakened from sleep-walking to find myself outside my cabin. Had it happened then? Or had it occurred when I was home in Widevale, or even while I was still at the Academy? I recalled how the Speck dancers had come to Old Thares with the traveling carnival. When I had seen them, I had lifted my hand and given them the sign to release the dreaded Speck plague on our capital city. Yes. I could see now that that had been the work of Soldier's Boy. But what else had he done that I'd scarcely been aware of? Had he influenced my thoughts about my father? Had he precipitated my quarrel with Carsina?

When I decided that wondering about it was futile, my thoughts turned to Epiny, Spink, and Amzil. I wondered if Epiny had reached her home safely, and if she had been able to convince both Spink and Amzil that I was still alive and that they had not failed me. I wondered about the rest of Gettys as well. I was fairly certain that my death would be dismissed easily. I doubted that there would be any serious inquiry into it. Gettys was a town composed of soldiers, penal workers, and former penal workers and their families. The Speck magic flooded the town with alternating tides of fear and despair. It was a place where violence and crime were as common as the dust blowing through the streets. A man beaten to death by a mob would only briefly shock the inhabitants, and no one else would ever know of it. I imagined that the official report, if there were one, would say that a condemned prisoner, Nevare Burv, had been shot to death while attempting to escape.

The knowledge that I was actually the son of Lord Burvelle of the East would have died with Colonel Haren. I was fairly certain that he would not have confided it to anyone else. So there would be no formal notification of my father. I wondered how Spink and Epiny would explain my death to my sister, and if she would pass the news on to my father and Sergeant Duril, my old mentor. I hoped that Yaril would have the strength of will to keep the news to herself. My father had disowned me; to hear that I had died while escaping a death sentence would only vindicate his poor opinion of me. As for Sergeant Duril, he knew how easy it was for soldiers to lose contact with families and friends. Let me simply fade out of his life and his memories, without any knowledge of my shame. I didn't want the old soldier to think that somehow his teaching had failed me or that I had turned my back on all I had learned from him. Let me be forgotten by them.

And what did I hope for myself? Hope. It seemed a bitter word now. What hope could I have, imprisoned in my own flesh and about to be borne off to the Speck Wintering Place? I had no idea where that was, nor could I begin to guess what Soldier's Boy planned for the future. Obviously he was committed to the magic. He would do whatever he thought he must to drive the Gernians back west into our own lands. How far would he go?

I'd heard rumors of another Speck Great Man, the most powerful one of all. I racked my memory for his name and then had it. Kinrove. Olikea had mentioned him as someone she hoped I would surpass; I imagined that she hoped Soldier's Boy would supplant him as the most powerful Great One. Lisana had mentioned him in another way, as had Jodoli. Kinrove was the source of the dance, whatever that was. For years, he had maintained a magic with it, a magic that was supposed to hold the intruders at bay, maybe even drive the Gernians away completely. But it had not, and now the younger men were becoming restless, and talking of bringing war to the Gernians in a way they would understand. No, I corrected myself. In a way "we" would understand. I was still a Gernian, wasn't I?

It was hard to pin down what I was anymore. I could not even decide whether to think of myself as "I" or "he."

My other self was a frightening mystery to me. I didn't know what he had already done in obedience to the magic or what he was capable of doing. Well, that wasn't exactly true, I abruptly realized. He had been capable of turning the Speck plague loose on the Gernian capital city. He'd deliberately infected my fellow cadets of the King's Cavalla Academy, successfully wiping out half of a future generation of officers. If he could do that, what would he not do? Was this ruthless creature truly a part of myself, an aspect of Nevare Burvelle that Tree Woman had peeled away and infected with the magic? If he had stayed a part of me, would I have been capable of such deadly, traitorous acts? Or would the self that I was now have ameliorated him, balanced his warlike nature with more ethics and philosophy? Was he a better soldier than I was in that he was burdened only with loyalty to "his" people and cause?

Was he the sort of soldier my father had wished me to be?

Such thoughts were not cheering, especially confined as I was to the sleeping body of my enemy. For a short time, I tried to pretend that I had options. I'd stopped him from killing Epiny, hadn't I? That meant I had some control over him. And I'd been successful in making him hear my thoughts. Did that mean I could influence him? Or, as Epiny had believed, eventually master him again?

I tried to feel my body as I had once felt it, to be aware of tickling leaves against my skin, of Olikea's hair tangled across my face, of the ball of warmth that was Likari curled against my back. I could sense those things, but when I tried to move a hand or lift my foot, nothing happened. My only achievement in that long afternoon of their nap was to focus my attention on Olikea's hair on my face. It tickled. It itched. I wanted to move my face away from it. It annoyed me. I nattered and nagged at the sleeping Soldier's Boy with such thoughts until, with a grunt and a sigh, he lifted a hand to brush her hair away from his face. I had done it!

Or had he, of his own will, simply moved an annoyance away? I had no way of knowing.

As night descended, they stirred, first the boy, and then Soldier's Boy and Olikea. They had little to do to prepare to travel. Olikea and Likari had left the migrating People in a hurry, rushing to rescue me. She had her hip belt of tools and pouches. The boy filled his water skin for us. We had my winter blanket from my hut. Olikea had saved some cooked fish and water-grass roots in a carry-net. Soldier's Boy yawned, stretched, and rubbed his face, scratching irritably at his unshaven cheeks. Then he told them, "It's time to go. Come with me."

He took the boy's hand, but seemed to judge that Olikea could follow on her own. I wondered how he determined who would quick-walk with him. How did he extend the magic to include them? How did he do the magic at all? I sensed nothing, only his desire to travel swiftly now. Perhaps that was all it took. For a time, they walked in what seemed a very ordinary fashion, threading their way quietly through the dusky forest. They came to a faint path through the trees, and Soldier's Boy grunted and nodded as if pleased at finding something.

After that, we traveled swiftly. His pace didn't quicken. It seemed to me that he walked as he had before, and the sensations I experienced with him were little different from any walk I'd ever taken. Occasionally I felt a dizzying lurch, or stumbled as if the path had suddenly risen under my feet. That was disconcerting. The trees and brush did not rush past us, yet it took only three steps to climb a steep hill, half a dozen to follow a long ridge, and then in a few strides we dipped down into a valley, crossed a river, and climbed the opposite side. After that, our path led us ever upward. Despite the deepening night, we walked in a brief gray twilight that extended only a few steps ahead of us.

We climbed the flank of a mountain, traversing the steep side, followed a pass, and then crossed yet another mountainside. And always we went higher.

As we climbed, the night grew colder around us. The others hugged themselves and their breath showed white in the moonlight. We were above the tree line now. The ground was hard and cold underfoot. I winced for my unshod feet tramping along such harsh terrain but Soldier's Boy appeared not to notice.

We came to the mouth of a pass. To either side of us, towering mountains gave us no other option. There was a campsite at the mouth of the pass, an area where many small fires had burned. There was plenty of evidence that a large group or several large groups of people had passed through the area recently. "Are we stopping here until tomorrow?" Olikea asked.

Soldier's Boy simply walked on. We followed the pass as it wound its way between two steep-sided mountains. The air was dry and cold and we were soon glad that Likari had filled the water skin. As we trekked on, I became aware of how Soldier's Boy used the magic in a steady stream. Olikea and Likari kept pace with him. I could sense their weariness. The magic might mean that they covered ground much faster, but hours of walking in the cold at a swift and steady pace were telling on them. "How much farther are we going tonight?" Olikea almost wailed at one point.

"We'll stop and rest at dawn," Soldier's Boy deigned to tell her.

"But we've passed the best stopping place," she complained. "I did not prepare for Stone Passage. I thought I would have a chance to gather firewood and more food before we entered it."

"Wherever we are at dawn is where we will rest," he said, ending the discussion.

Soldier's Boy pushed ruthlessly on. Scowling, Olikea began to salvage items left behind by other migrants. She darted from side to side, picking up ends of torches and bits of firewood that had not completely burned to ash. Soldier's Boy appeared not to notice, but slowed the pace slightly. When Likari began to lag behind, he gruffly ordered the child to keep up. I felt pity for the boy; he could not have been more than six or seven, and to compel him on this forced march on such a long, cold night seemed cruel to me. If Soldier's Boy thought about it at all, I could not sense it. The pass grew narrower and narrower and the mountains ever steeper and more sheer. It seemed to me that this path might simply come to a dead end, but they all pushed on as if following a familiar way.

By the time dawn began to gray the sky, it was only a stripe of light over our heads. The way we traversed was more like a cavern with a crack in the roof than a pass. I had never even imagined such a place. The filtered light showed me that many folk had passed this way and recently. To either side of us was the detritus of a busy trail: discarded rags, a frayed basket, scraps of food waste, and other litter. Olikea seized the basket and put her wood into it without losing the pace. The light grew stronger, but still Soldier's Boy walked on. Jodoli had been correct when he said that the magic was harder to summon in the light of day than at night. Soldier's Boy began to weary and to feel queasy from the way the landscape lurched and jumped as he passed it. Quite abruptly, he came to a halt. "We'll rest here," he announced.

"Here?" Likari asked in surprise. "This isn't a stopping place."

"It is now," Soldier's Boy replied grumpily. Olikea didn't say anything. At a gesture from Soldier's Boy, the water skin was passed around. Olikea dumped her trove of salvaged fuel on the ground in a heap. She stared pointedly at Soldier's Boy. He puffed his cheeks in refusal.

"Making fire uses too much magic. You light it."

For an instant, her lip curled up to bare her teeth. Then she turned her back on him, took out a Gernian-made flint-and-steel set, and set to work. Soldier's Boy gritted his teeth to the unpleasant buzz of the exposed metal. She used part of the basket as tinder to catch the sparks, and the charred wood caught swiftly. It was not a large fire, but it pushed back the shadows and offered a little warmth. They shared the food Olikea had brought. On this rocky trail, there was no moss for Soldier's Boy to command and no leaves to blanket them. Soldier's Boy chose a spot along the edge of the trail wall and lay down. The ground was hard and cold. Olikea circled him, looking unhappy, and then took her place at his side. Likari lay along his back. The one blanket did not cover all their bodies. The dwindling warmth from the dying fire was almost meaningless in such a cold and stony place.

"I'm cold," the boy whimpered once. Soldier's Boy made no response but I felt him release some of his stored magic. My body warmed, and the two of them pressed closer. After a short time, I heard the boy sigh heavily and felt him go lax.

Olikea had put her back to my belly. She pressed in closer against me and yawned. Silence fell and I thought she slept. Then she asked, "Do you have a plan? For when we get to the Wintering Place?"

Soldier's Boy was quiet for a long time, but I knew he did not sleep. With him, I stared wearily at the stony walls of the chasm. When he blinked, I felt the grittiness of his eyelids. The magic was like a small campfire burning in him, consuming the reserves he'd gathered. When he spoke to the dimness, I wondered if Olikea were still awake. "I'll have to wait until I'm there. I've never been there before, you know."

"But you know the way. How?" Olikea suddenly seemed uncertain.

"Lisana. Lisana shared many of her memories with me. She made this journey scores of times, first as a young girl and then as a Great One. I rely on her memories."

They were quiet again and I felt Olikea relaxing against the warmth of his body. His arms were around her, holding her close to me. I felt sorry for her. Behind Soldier's Boy's closed eyelids, he was thinking of Lisana. My thoughts drifted toward Amzil. If only she were the woman in my arms now. Olikea exploded that fantasy.

She spoke softly. "You are not one of us. To some, that will be a problem. They may even be angry that you have come there."

"I know. It will not make my task easier."

"You will have to prove yourself to them before they will accept you as part of our kin-clan, let alone as a Great One."

"I was thinking of that."

She drew a deeper breath and let it out slowly, a prelude to sleep. "How long will it take us to reach the Wintering Place?"

"We could be there tomorrow. But I do not wish to move that swiftly and arrive there depleted of power. We will move more slowly and stop sooner."

"That makes sense," she agreed, and then said, "I need to sleep now."

"Yes," Soldier's Boy agreed. But it was some time before he closed his eyes. I sensed he was weighing his options and planning a strategy. But I could not find a way into those thoughts and suspected he deliberately kept them from me.

CHAPTER NINE

JOURNEY IN DARKNESS

I became an observer of my own life. Soldier's Boy was the first to waken. I'd been awake for hours, alone in his darkened skull and feeling oddly helpless. I knew that he was planning something, something that would affect both of us forever, but had no idea what it was or how I could influence him. I'd again attempted to move the body, to "sleep-walk" it while he was unconscious and succeeded not at all. All I could do was to wait.

He stretched slowly, mindful of the two sleepers who flanked him. Awkwardly, he disengaged his body from theirs. They both burrowed into the warm space he left, now sharing the blanket more comfortably. He walked a short distance away from them before he relieved himself. Overhead, a narrow stripe of blue sky showed. I tried to decide if the mountains were leaning closer to one another overhead, or if distance only made it seem that way.

When he went back to Olikea and Likari, the two had cuddled
together. In the semidarkness, Olikea embraced her son, and both
their faces looked peaceful. I wondered who the boy's father was
and where he was. Soldier's Boy understood far more of Speck
customs than I did. I found my answer in his mind. Only rarely
did Specks select a mate and remain with one person for life. The
kin-clan was the family who would raise the children born to
the women. Usually, mates came from outside the kin-clan, and
often the journey to the Wintering Place or the Trading Place was
when young women met males from other clans for those liaisons.
It was not necessary for a boy to know who his father was, though
they usually did. Often fathers had little to do with sons until they
were old enough to be taught the hunting rites. Then a boy might
choose to leave his kin-clan to join that of his father, or he might
decide to remain with his mother's people. Women almost never
left their kin-clans. It was not the Speck way.

"It's time to travel again," Soldier's Boy said. His voice
sounded odd.

Olikea stirred, and beside her, Likari grumbled, stretched, and
then recurled in a tighter ball. He scowled in his sleep. Olikea
opened her eyes and then sighed. "It's not night yet."

"No. It's not. But I wish to travel now. The nights grow colder.
I don't want to be caught here when winter bites hard."

"Now he worries about it," she muttered to herself, and then
seized Likari's shoulder and shook it. "Wake up. It's time to travel
again."

We did not quick-walk. The light from above reached down
to us. It was the strangest natural setting that I had ever experienced. What had seemed like a pass between two mountains had
narrowed to a crevasse. We walked in the bottom of it, looking up
at a sky that seemed to grow more distant with every step of our
journey. The sides of the rift were slaty, the rock layered at an angle
to the floor. Rubble that had tumbled down into the rift over the
years floored it, but a well-trodden path threaded through it. Moss
and little plants grew in the cracks of the walls.

By late afternoon, the crack that showed the sky had narrowed
to a distant band of deep blue. We came to a place where water

trickled down the stony walls. It pooled into a chiseled basin, overflowed it, and ran alongside our path for some distance before it vanished into a crack. We refilled the water skin there and everyone drank of the sweet, very cold water. Plants grew along the stream, but not luxuriantly. It was evident that they had recently been picked down to the roots. Olikea muttered angrily that nothing had been left; tradition demanded that some leaves must always be left for whoever came behind. Soldier's Boy, his stomach grumbling loudly, lowered himself to his knees. He put his hands in the cold water, touching the matted roots of the plants lightly.

I felt the magic flare up in him and then ebb. Then he took his hands away and slowly stood up. He shook icy water from his hands. For a distance of six feet or so, the plants had pushed forth new foliage. Olikea exclaimed with delight and hurriedly began to harvest the fat leaves.

"Remember to leave some," Soldier's Boy cautioned her.

"Of course."

They nibbled on the leaves as they walked. The food was not enough to satisfy Soldier Boy's hunger, but it kept him from focusing on it. They did not talk much. The crack of light above us continued to narrow. The cold was a constant, and I think they all suffered from it, but no one spoke of it. It was simply a condition they had to endure

My eyes had adjusted to the dimness. As she had the day before, Olikea began to gather the stub ends of torches and bits of firewood. Soldier's Boy said nothing about this but kept the pace slower so that she could manage it without being left behind. We came to another trickling wall stream. This time the catch basin was obviously man-made. It was the size of a bathtub, and the sides were furry with a pale moss. The water that overflowed it ran off into the dimness in a groove that had probably been originally cut by people and smoothed by the passage of the water. Again Likari filled his water skin and we all drank. "We should have brought torches," Olikea fretted as we left the water.

In a very short time, I saw why. The crack overhead that had admitted a bit of indirect light vanished. I looked up. I could not tell if it was overgrown with foliage or if the rock had actually closed up above us. I suddenly felt a squirm of great uneasiness. I did not want to go any deeper into this crack that had now become a cavern. If Soldier's Boy or any of the others shared my discomfort, they gave no sign of it. I felt Soldier's Boy kindle the magic within him to make a stingy pool of light around us. We walked on, Likari and Olikea close beside him.

At first I assumed that the darkness was temporary. I kept hoping that the overhead crack would reappear. It did not. The stream that paralleled our path added an element of sound and humidity to our passage. The cold became danker, with an organic smell of water and plant life. Our luminescence briefly touched white mosses and clinging lichen on the walls. When Olikea saw a cluster of pale yellow mushrooms leaning out from a mossy crevice, she crowed with satisfaction and hastily harvested them. She shared them out and we ate them as we walked. I felt Soldier's Boy heightened awareness of the cavern after he had eaten them. His energy seemed renewed and the light that he gave off became more certain. Both Olikea and Likari seemed renewed by the mushrooms as well, and for a time we traveled more swiftly.

Occasionally I heard splashes from the stream, as if small startled frogs or fishes were taking alarm at our light. The sheen on the rocky wall on that side of the cave showed more water sliding down to feed the stream. It flowed merrily beside us, and this, more than any sensation of descending, told me that our trail was leading us downward.

When Soldier's Boy finally decided to stop, the others were footsore, cold, and weary. Olikea seemed grateful that he had chosen a regular stopping site. Here the cavern widened out substantially and there was a large blackened fire circle. Olikea was able to salvage quite a bit of partially burned wood. While she kindled it, Likari went off to investigate an odd structure built into the stream. He came back with three pale fish. "There wasn't much in the trap. These ones were barely big enough to get caught in it."

"Usually, it teems with fish and there is plenty and to spare." Olikea shot Soldier's Boy a meaningful glance.

"We are the last, most likely, to make the passage this year. When we come in the wake of so many people, it is not surprising that others have harvested and hunted before us. Three fish are enough for us, for tonight."

"Enough?" she asked him, shocked.

"None of us will starve," he clarified.

"But you will not look like a Great One when we arrive."

"That is my concern, not yours," he rebuked her.

"It is not my concern if others mock me that I have tended my Great One so poorly that he looks like a rack of bones? Not my concern if we reach the Wintering Place and you have not even enough magic to kindle a fire for yourself? I shall be completely humiliated, and you will be mocked and disregarded. This does not concern you?"

"Other things concern me more," he told her. Then he turned away from her in a way that suggested the conversation was over. Muttering, she went about the task of preparing the fish for cooking. Likari wandered at the edges of the firelight, exploring the abandoned trash. He came back to his mother's fire with a tattered piece of fabric. "Can we make shoes from this?" he asked her, and they were soon both involved in that task.

Soldier's Boy walked away from them. His personal light went with him. He walked toward the wall of the cavern. There the ceiling dropped low, but he ducked down and walked hunched for a time. The dim circle of light around us showed me little more than the stony floor in front of his feet. His back began to ache and I wondered where he was going and why. When the ceiling of the cavern retreated, he straightened up and stood tall again. He closed his eyes, then breathed out hard, and suddenly light burst into being all around me. It was no longer his personal light that shone. We were in a different chamber, separate from the long rift we had been following. The cavern we were in was as large as a ballroom, and everywhere I looked, the walls sparked with crystals. Somehow Soldier's Boy had woken light from them, and it illuminated the cave.

The crystals glittered brightly as he drew closer to them. They were wet and gleaming and appeared to be growing from the walls of the cavern. Some were quite large, their facets easy to see and other were tiny, little more than a sparkle against the cavern's dark wall. Soldier's Boy seemed to consider them for a long time;

then he chose a protruding crystal structure and broke it from the wall. I was surprised at how easily it came away, and also at how sharp it was. Blood stung and dripped from his fingers as he carried it away from the wall and back to the center of this cavern.

There was a pool there, as dark as the crystals were brilliant. Soldier's Boy lowered himself down to sit beside it. He dipped his fingers in it and they came up inky with a thick, slimy liquid. He nodded to himself. Then he began to systematically prick himself with the point of the crystal and then dab some of the noxious liquid onto each tiny cut. The cuts stung, but the slime itself did not add to the pain. In fact, it seemed to seal each tiny wound as he dabbed it on.

He worked systematically, doing both his arms from the shoulders down and then the backs of his hands. He was working on his left leg, jabbing and dabbing, when I became aware that a new light had joined us in the cavern. It was yellow and flickering. Olikea had wedged two burned torch ends together to make one that was barely long enough for her to hold without scorching her hand. As she drew near to us, she exclaimed in sudden pain and then dropped it. She no longer needed it. The light of the crystals glittered all around us still.

"I didn't know where you had gone. It worried me. Then I saw the light coming from here. What are you doing?" she demanded.

"What you suggested. Becoming a Speck, so the People will accept me," he replied.

"This is only done to babies," she pointed out to him. "During their first passage."

"I am not a child, but this is my first passage. And so I have determined that it will be done to me, even if I must do it myself."

That silenced her. For a time, she stood watching him prick my flesh with the broken crystal and then dab the wound with the black slime. Her feet were wrapped now in clumsy shoes made from the old fabric that Likari had found. Her failing torch added a flickering yellow to the light around us and was reflected in the glittering crystals that surrounded us. As it began to die away, Olikea asked quietly, "Do you want me to do your back?"

"Yes."

"Do you . . . how do you wish it to be? Like a cat? Like a deer? Rippled like a fish?"

"You may decide," he said, and then bowed his head forward on his chest to present his full back to her. She took the broken crystal from him. She worked swiftly as if this were something she had done before. She made a series of punctures, then daubed them all with a handful of the thick, soft muck. The pain seemed more intense when someone else did the jabbing.

I heard a sound behind us and became aware that Likari had joined us. "The fish is cooked. I took it away from the fire," he said. Uncertainty filled his voice.

"This won't take long. You may eat your share," Olikea told him. But the boy didn't leave. Instead he hunkered down carefully on the shard-strewn floor and watched.

When Soldier's Boy's back was finished, Olikea had him stand, and did his buttocks and the backs of his legs. Then she came around in front of him and regarded him critically. "You haven't done your face yet."

"Leave it as it is," he said quietly.

"But—"

"Leave it. I am of the People, but I do not wish any of them to ever forget that I came to them from outside the People. Leave my face as it is."

She puffed her cheeks, her disapproval very evident. Then she handed him back the crystal. "The food will be cold, and our fire dying," she observed, and turned and left him there.

He stood by the muck-filled pond, turning the crystal slowly in his hands. He remembered something then, something of mine. When I was just a boy and Sergeant Duril was training me to be a soldier, he always carried a sling and a pouch of small rocks. Whenever he caught me unwary, I could expect the thud of a rock against my ribs or back or even my head. "And you're dead," he'd always tell me afterward. "Because you weren't paying attention."

After a time, I'd begun to save the different rocks he used to "kill" me. I'd had a box full of them before I'd left home.

He held up the crystal for Likari to see. "I want to keep this. Do you have room in your pouch for it?"

"I can put it with your sling."

There was a small surprise. "You have my sling."

"I found it in your old clothes. I thought you might want it again."

"You were right. Good boy. Put the crystal with it."

The boy nodded, pleased at the praise, and reached to take it from me. "Careful. It's sharp," Soldier's Boy warned him, and he took it gingerly. He stowed it away in one of the pouches on his belt, and then looked up, a serious question in his eyes. "Let's go eat," Soldier's Boy told him, forestalling it, and led the way back to the dwindling fire and the food.

The fish was very good, but there wasn't enough of it. I could feel that Soldier's Boy had used too much magic making light and warmth. He was wearied. At this stopping place, there were alcoves hollowed into the lower walls of the chamber. He chose a large one and clambered into it, and was unsurprised when Olikea and then Likari joined him there. The moisture in the air made the chill more noticeable, as if the cold were settling on us like dew. Our combined body heat warmed the alcove, but the single blanket did little to confine our warmth. It leaked away and cold crept in. He decided that he could not afford to use any more magic that night; we'd simply have to get by.

Soldier's Boy fell asleep. I did not. I hovered inside him in the darkness and pondered everything I'd witnessed. I am not a fool. I immediately connected the many tiny injuries he'd dealt himself and the inky slime he'd rubbed into them to the dapples on any Speck's skin. Was it some sort of a tattoo that they inflicted even on the smallest child? Olikea's specks had never seemed like tattoos to me. They'd even seemed to have a slightly different texture from the rest of her skin. I'd always assumed that all Speck babies were born with, well, specks on them. Was it possible that the Specks were not Specks when they were born?

Because I was aware, I think I was more conscious of Soldier's Boy's rising temperature. His flesh flushed warm and the tiny stinging wounds that he had dealt himself began to itch. He muttered in his sleep and shifted uncomfortably. Without waking, he scratched first one arm and then the other. He shifted again, causing the others to murmur in protest, and then dropped into a deeper sleep. Almost as soon as he did, I felt his fever rise higher.

He was ill. Very ill. He'd sickened my body and I was trapped inside it, voiceless and helpless. Every place where the crystal had pierced his skin now itched abominably, far worse than any insect bite or sting that I'd ever endured. When he sleepily scratched at the sores, I could feel how puffy and swollen each one was. I felt something pop like a blister and then the wetness of blood or pus on my skin. I longed to get up and go to the water, to wash myself and clean the injuries, but I could not rouse him at all.

He was deep into dreams now, and as his fever climbed, his dreams became brighter and sharper edged and harder to ignore. He dreamed of a forest that was impossibly green, and a wind that swept through it like the waves on an ocean, and somehow there were ships on those waves, ships with brightly colored sails that floated and spun through the forest treetops. It was a bizarre dream of bright colors and giddy shapes, and it completely fascinated me. I wondered if my rationality would give way to his fever.

Then I felt him leave the body.

It was a strange sensation. For a moment, I felt I was alone in the fever-racked shell. Desperately I reached out to try to regain control of my physical being. Then, as if the current of a river had seized me, I felt myself pulled away from my body and out into an otherness. It was like being dropped down a shaft. I felt shapeless and unanchored; then I became aware of the part of me that was Soldier's Boy and held tight to him. It was like gripping the mane of a runaway horse.

He was dream-walking. I knew that right away, but it was as unlike my experience of dream-walking as a rushing river is unlike a quiet pool. It was a wandering fever dream, energized by the heat that tormented his body. He snapped from one awareness to the next, without pause or purpose, like a captured fish darting about in a bucket of water. We brushed wildly against Olikea's dreams, a memory of shared lust, and then rushed toward Lisana. He beat furiously about her, like a bird trying to break through a window, but could not sense, as I did, how she reached toward him, trying to catch and hold the connection. She gave a lonely cry as he darted away again.

I was disconcerted that the next dreamer I glimpsed was my father. Why would Soldier's Boy seek him out, I wondered, and then knew that he was Soldier's Boy's father just as much as he was mine. My father was sleeping the shallow sleep of an old man. The Speck plague and his stroke had aged him beyond his years. He dreamed of being clad once more in brave green and leading a flanking movement that would close off the enemy's retreat. In his dream, he battled Plainsmen who rode leggy white horses and brandished battle-axes at him, but I saw him as an ailing old man, his age-dappled hands twitching against the blankets of his bed. We burst into his dream, and I rode by his side, as brave as he was, astride Sirlofty once again. My father looked over at me, and for one wild instant, he was glad and proud of me. I knew then I had broken into a cherished dream, one in which I had fulfilled all his plans for me. But just as my heart warmed toward him, I grew fat, bursting my buttons and spilling out of my shirt, my flesh obscenely pale and jiggling.

"Why, Nevare? Why? You were supposed to be me, all over again! Why couldn't you be a good soldier for me? If I was only allowed one son to follow after me, why couldn't you have fulfilled the task? Why? Why?"

The old man's muffled dream shouts woke him, and he broke free of our dream touch. For a second, I saw his room at Widevale, glimpsed the fireplace and his bedstead and a bedside tray laden with all sorts of medicine bottles and thick heavy spoons.

"Yaril! Yaril, where are you? Have you abandoned me, too? Yaril!" He shouted for my sister like a frightened baby calling for his nursemaid. We left him there, sitting up in his bed and calling. It tore at my heart and that surprised me. I'd been able to be angry with my father, even hate him so long as he seemed like a man and my equal. To see him frail and afraid stole my anger from me. Guilt racked me suddenly, that I'd caused him so much pain and then left him alone. For that moment, it mattered not at all that he'd disowned me and cast me out. When I had been a child, I had always felt protected by his sternness. Now he wailed for the sole child fate had left him, alone and forlorn, sonless in a world that valued only sons.

Even as my awareness reached toward him, longing to protect him from the doom he had brought down on himself, Soldier's Boy swept on, snatching me away from him. I caught glimpses of other people's dreams, splashes of color against the fantastic canvas of Soldier's Boy's own dreaming mind. I could not focus on any one sensation: it was like trying to read the riffled pages of a book. I saw a word here, a paragraph there. He had no memories of his own; the connections that called him were mine. Trist dreamed of a girl in a yellow velvet dress. Gord was not asleep. He looked up from the thick book he was studying, startled, saying, "Nevare?"

Sergeant Duril was sleeping the sleep of exhaustion, dreamless. No images floated in his mind, only the gratitude that for a time, his aching body could be still, his painful back flat on his mattress. My presence in his mind was like a drop of oil falling on a calm pool. "Watch your back, boy," he muttered, and sighed heavily. Soldier's Boy swept on.

I do not think he was aware of his burning body, but I was. Someone trickled cool water past his lips. His mouth moved ineffectually. I sensed how tight and hot his skin felt. Distance and fever distorted Olikea's words. They seemed sharp, yet I could hardly hear them. "He makes a fever journey," I thought I heard her say, and Likari piped up with a question that ended in the word "name."

Olikea's response faded in and out of my hearing. "Not a baby," she said disdainfully, but I wasn't sure I had heard her correctly. My attention was caught by a fantastic landscape. Never had I seen colors so intense. Very large objects came into my view, things so big that I could not see what they were until we had swept past them. Then I wondered if the butterfly had seemed so large because we were close to it, or if it truly had been so immense that it covered half the sky and it seemed small only as we retreated from it.

"Fever dream," I told myself, but it was hard to believe that it was only a dream and that I had not been transported into some other world.

Then, most tantalizing of all, we crashed into Epiny's dream. Her dream was sweet and simple; she was sitting by the fireside in the sitting room in her father's house in Old Thares. Next to her was a beautiful carved wooden cradle mounted on a rocking stand. A curtain of fine lace, all worked with pink rosebuds, draped the cradle. She sat next to it, reading a book and gently rocking the cradle. She looked up as I crashed into the room.

"Nevare? What have you done to yourself?"

I looked down. I was immensely fat again, and mottled with specks. I wore a garment like a wide belt, and from it hung a number of pouches. My neck was ringed with necklaces of leather strung through beads of polished stone. My wrists were likewise decorated. Soldier's Boy opened his mouth to speak. With frantic energy, I fought him for control of the mouth and words. Here, I suddenly discovered, we were much more equally matched. I could not force out the words I wanted to say, but neither could he. We stood before Epiny, two battling spirits in one body, voiceless as the mouth worked and only nonsense sounds came out.

Epiny's image of herself suddenly brightened and firmed, as if she had come closer to me without moving. "Nevare. You are here, aren't you? This is that 'dream-walking' you wrote about in your journal! Why have you come to me? Is there something important I must know? Are you in danger? Are you hurt? Where are you, Nevare? What do you need of me?"

Epiny in the flesh could be overwhelming. Epiny on this dream plane exceeded that. As she focused herself on me, she seemed to grow larger. The room disappeared; only the cradle remained at her side, and despite her frantic questions, she continued to rock it in a calm and calming manner. I thought I finally understood what the "aura" she told me about was. Epiny radiated her self like a fire radiates heat. In this place, nothing was concealed. Her intensity, her curiosity, her burning sense of justice, and her equally hot indignation at injustice; it all flowed out of her, a corona of Epiny-ness. It was humbling to stand there and feel the waves of her love for me beat against me.

I wanted so badly to stay and speak with her. Soldier's Boy's desire to stay mute and flee was equally strong. Caught in that tug-of-war, we were a silent presence full of conflict.

"If you cannot speak to me here, at least hear what news I have. It may comfort you to know that both Spink and Amzil believed me when I told them that you lived. It was such a re-lief to them. Neither had wanted to admit to the other that the memories of that night were truncated and contradictory. Still, there have been repercussions. Spink can go about his daily tasks, knowing that he did not fail you. But it has still changed his heart toward the men he rode with that night. He cannot abide the sight of them. He knows how capable of evil they are. He avoids Captain Thayer, Carsina's husband, but the man knows that Spink despises him. I fear he will take umbrage against Spink someday. I fear for him, Nevare. He cannot hide what he knows about those men; it shows in his face and his eyes whenever we encounter any of them. And they, I think they feel they must be rid of him; perhaps it is the only way in which they will be able to forget that night. They believe they beat you to death, or at the least, witnessed their comrades doing so. But their memories are not clear on exactly how it happened. So when Spink looks at them with disgust, well, I do not think they know what to believe about themselves.

"And Amzil does not make it better. I do not know what you said to her that night, but it has made her fearless. And when I gave her your message, that you loved her but had to leave her, it hardened something in her. Now she is worse than fearless when-ever she encounters one of those men. She torments them. When she sees one of them on the streets or in the mercantile, she does not turn her eyes away or avoid him. Instead, she stalks him like a cat, meeting his gaze, walking up on him and staring him straight in the face. They flinch from her, Nevare. They look away, they try to avoid her, but she is making them hate her. The one who tried to stand up to her, who would not leave the store when she glared at him? When he looked at her with disdain, she returned his gaze and said aloud, loud enough for other customers to hear her,

'Perhaps he has forgotten what happened the night a mob beat the grave digger to death. I have not. You think you know what I am; I've heard you call me the Dead Town Whore. But I *know* what you are. I remember every detail. And I would far rather be a whore than a sniveling coward.' He fled from her then, convinced that what she recalls is what others recall of him as well.

"Winter will close around us soon, Nevare, and winter is not a good season here in Gettys. It is a time when every injury festers, and the cold and the dark promise to hide every evil thing that is done. I am afraid. I bar the door at night, and Spink sleeps with his pistol cocked and ready on the bedside table. He has talked of resigning his commission; he no longer wishes to serve with these men. I think that if winter were not so close, he would do it, and we would flee, for the sake of the baby. Such cowardice would scald him and leave a scar that would never heal. Yet, when spring comes, if nothing has improved here, what else can he do? Better that he take us away from here than that he is shot in the back and I am left at the mercy of these wolves. So he has told me himself."

Her words cut me like razors. I had thought I had been saving them all when I cut myself adrift. Instead I had not only plunged them into danger and torment, but then abandoned them all to take care of themselves. I did not deceive myself that I could have been of great use to them, but it seemed cowardly that I was not there at all. Most troubling to me was Amzil's anger and the behavior it prompted. I could not blame her for it. How must it be for her, to see walking on the streets the men who would have raped her, even to death? I wished she would flee to a safer place, but not if it meant leaving Epiny pregnant and without the comfort of another woman near. It was all too horrible to contemplate. I tried to reach my hands toward Epiny, but they were not mine to control, not even in a dream. I focused all my will on trying to say even one word to her.

That was a mistake. For while I devoted my strength to that, Soldier's Boy tore us free of Epiny's dream and fled with me. I looked back as we took flight, and saw Epiny looking up after us. She dwindled in the distance until she was gone.

"They should just go away." Soldier's Boy was speaking to me, but the words echoed and I knew that in the other world, he raved in his fever. If I reached, I could be aware of that body, burning inside and yet shivering with cold in the dank cave. I heard people whispering. Perhaps it was Olikea and Likari. Their voices sounded wavery and frightening.

"A death. Or a life. Which do you owe me, Nevare? Which will you give me, Nevare?"

An immense croaker bird confronted us. The carrion bird was black and white, with brilliant red wattles around his beak. The wattles were thick and fat and somehow disgusting and threatening at the same time. He opened his beak wide and I saw how strangely his tongue was fastened into it, and how sharp his tongue looked.

"I am not Nevare! I am Soldier's Boy of the People. I owe you nothing."

The bird opened his beak wide with amusement. He rattled his wing plumes, resettling them, and a sickening wave of carrion stench wafted against me. "Neither debts nor names are so easily shed, Nevare. You are who you are and you owe me what you owe me. Denying it does not change it."

"Nevare is not my name."

Could a bird grin? "Nevare is a soldier's boy, a soldier's son. The name that you use was given to you only because you are Nevare, and the son of a soldier. And a soldier son. And that is as true as that you owe me a death. Or a life. However you wish to name it, it is what you owe to me."

"I owe you nothing!" Soldier's Boy shouted at him and his words echoed in a distant cave. He was braver than I was. His hands darted out to seize two great handfuls of the croaker bird's plumage. He gripped the bird and shook him, shouting, "I owe you nothing! Not a life, not a death! I owe you nothing!"

Far away, someone shrieked and then the croaker bird took flight, laughing like a mad thing.

Cold water splashed Soldier's Boy's face. It was a shock, and with a shudder he opened our shared eyes. He blinked, trying to focus, and lifted a shaky hand to wipe at his eyes. Olikea was angrily untangling her hair from his fingers. A water skin on the ground beside him gurgled out its contents. It took a moment for him to make sense of it, and then the unjustness of it broke his heart. "You threw water on me," he wailed accusingly, and he sounded like a weepy child. His voice shook with weakness.

"You ripped out my hair when I was trying to give you a drink! And if you think you owe me nothing, then consider that I owe you less than nothing!"

I could barely make out her features. The fire had subsided to a dim red glow. The body was cold and ached badly. Olikea looked tired and haggard. I became aware that strands of her hair were still tangled in my fingers. I'd ripped them out of her head. "I'm sorry," I said, aghast, and then was shocked when the words actually came out of my mouth.

"Olikea!" I began, but abruptly lost the power to speak. I could feel Soldier's Boy's anger at me thrumming through his body. He was weak and ill and tired. His strength was barely enough to confine me. I stopped struggling against him. I was listening to Olikea's words.

"We are out of food, and there is scarcely any firewood to be found. We must go on to the Wintering Place. Can you walk?"

It was hard for him even to think about it, his head ached so. "I can't quick-walk. Give me water."

She picked up the slack water skin and held it for him. He drank, and was surprised at how thirsty he was. It cleared the thickness from his mouth and throat. He felt more alive. "You are right," he said when she took the water away. "We need to move on from here. Even if I cannot quick-walk, we should try to move on."

She nodded grimly.

Likari suddenly loomed up out of the darkness behind her. He carried an armful of salvaged wood. "It's hard to find anything in the dark—is he awake now? Are you better?" He leaned unpleasantly close. Soldier's Boy involuntarily drew back from the boy's looming face and closed his eyes. "Did you find a name? When babies make this journey, it is often their naming journey. Did you find your name?"

"Nevare," he croaked out, then angrily shook his head. Once. Shaking his head made the world spin. He lifted his hands to his face. The skin of it was hot and dry and tight. He rubbed his eyes; they were crusty.

"Nevare is the name you had before," Olikea observed tartly. "And I do not think you were wise to do this. We are ill prepared to spend time here waiting for you to recover."

"I am not interested in whether you think I am wise or not." He placed his hands flat on the cavern floor. He turned onto his belly, got his knees under him, and finally tottered to his feet. He tried not to let her see the effort it cost him, but when she took his arm and put it across her shoulders, he didn't have the will to resist her.

"Likari, bring our things and whatever you have scavenged that might be useful." Olikea sounded skeptical that we would get far but eager to try. Plainly she wished to be out of the dank cave. She and the boy had to be at least as hungry as Soldier's Boy but neither complained.

"I do not have the strength to make a light for you," Soldier's Boy grudgingly admitted. "We will have to travel in the dark."

"There will be light enough for us to make our way, once we are away from the fire," Olikea asserted.

That puzzled me, but Soldier's Boy seemed to accept her statement. Likari had gone to fill the water skin and retrieve our blanket. He returned with it slung over his shoulder. He had also bundled together the bits of firewood he had scavenged and tied them with a leather thong so that he could carry them easily. He came to Soldier's Boy's other side and took his hand. Without ceremony, he set my hand to his shoulder, as if confident he could take some of my weight. With no more ado, we set forth.

The dim red glow of the fire quickly faded behind us and we walked forward in darkness. Soldier's Boy was content to let Olikea lead him, and she seemed confident of the way. So many others had trodden this path for so many years that it was flat and smooth. Soldier's Boy did not think of such things. He focused simply on moving his body along. Fever ran over his skin like licking flames. The places where he had pierced his skin with the crystal itched. He scratched the scabs off and fluid leaked from the swollen cuts. He decided that he had been foolish to use the crystal, yet in the same thought, doggedly determined that his act and the pain and fever that followed it were necessary. His joints ached, and his head pounded with pain. The desire to lie down and sleep soon became a pressing need, one that was even stronger than the hunger that assailed him. Yet both had to be ignored as he pressed on toward his journey's end. All thought became a narrow focus on walking. Ghost light crawled and danced at the edges of his fevered vision. He squeezed his eyes shut, opened them, and then blinked again, but could not banish the dots of sickly luminescence. He tottered on.

Gradually I became aware that the ghostly light was not an illusion. It occurred in patches and in tiny moving dots. It was a pale, creamy green and sometimes a white-blue. The blue lights were the ones that moved. When one hummed up to us, hovered near my face, and then flittered away, I recognized that it was some sort of underground lightning bug. That knowledge helped me to resolve what I was seeing. The greenish patches became a glow-ing slime or moss on the cavern walls. The blue insects frequented such patches, eating or drinking perhaps, and adding their light to it until they were sated enough to take flight again. The softly lit patches of gentle green seemed to occur at almost regular in-tervals. I decided that whatever it was, moss or plant or slime, the Specks had deliberately marked their trail with it as a dim light to show the way for travelers. I admired their innovation at using such a natural material even as I wondered at their lack of plan-ning in other regards. I thought of my own beloved cavalla, and knew that if this were a path we used frequently, there would have been caches of firewood and food. I wondered if the Specks did not care for one another in that way or if they had simply never thought of such things.

I became aware of something far more important to me. In his weariness and pain, Soldier's Boy was focusing all of his resources on staying upright and walking.

He was not guarding against me.

My first impulse was to attempt a coup against my oppressor and regain control of the body. Luckily, I swiftly realized that it would leave me in the position he was now occupying: feverish, full of pain, and battling hunger. But if I remained quiescent for now, it might be that he would lose even more of his wariness of me, and that when next he slept, I could at least dream-walk on my own. And so I curled small within the prison of my own body and awaited my opportunity.

CHAPTER TEN

DREAM-WALKER

Soldier's Boy did not last long. I do not know how far we had traveled in the darkness before he gave a sudden groan and sank down. Both Olikea and Likari did what they could to ease him gently to the stony floor of the cavern. Once there, he curled into a large miserable ball. For a time, it seemed all he could do was breathe. His eyes were closed tight.

Olikea speaking to Likari and the soft sounds they made were my only clues to what was transpiring. The boy set a small fire and Olikea kindled it. The tiny warmth was more a taunt than a comfort. They tucked the blanket around him.

"Drink. Open your mouth. Your body burns with fever. You must drink."

Soldier's Boy obeyed her. The liquid in his mouth and running down his dry throat was a comfort, but the small amount that splashed him seemed horribly cold. Olikea wet her hands and wiped them over his eyes, rubbing gently at his sticky eyelids. Soldier's Boy turned away from her ministrations but nevertheless felt the comfort of them. He sighed once, heavily, and then sank into a very deep sleep.

I worried at how racked with fever my body was. That it weakened him and distracted him was an advantage to me, but I did not want to regain command of a body that was hopelessly crippled or dying. I was tempted to try to ask Olikea for more water. I was certain it would be good for me, but decided that such a bold act might call Soldier's Boy's attention to me. I would attempt a dream-walk first.

I felt almost a thief as I did so. His bodily resources were low. Consuming what little of his magic remained seemed a cruel trick. Even so, I gathered my strength and ventured out.

It is difficult to describe that experience. I had dream-walked before, but not deliberately and often at someone else's summoning. It was the first time I had attempted to master the magic in such a way, and I soon discovered that I faced a challenge. While Olikea and Soldier's Boy had tottered along, the sun had risen and the day begun. All the people I had hoped to visit via their dreams were up and about their lives. I could find them easily enough; it was not a distance I traversed. The thought of a beloved friend seemed to bring me to them, but their conscious minds were busy with other things and refused to see me.

Just as I had not been able to gain a real link with Gord the night before, so it was today with Spink and Epiny and Amzil. I was like a little buzzing fly. I could hover round their thoughts but not penetrate them. Their experience of their waking world was too strong to permit me entrance. Frustrated at trying to contact those three, I tried to think whom else I might find dozing. Yaril came to mind, and before I could decide if it were a wise course or not, I found myself inside her bedchamber at Widevale. She was napping after a hectic morning. I ventured into a dream that seemed not restful at all, for it was cluttered with things that she must do. Shimmering folds of a pale blue fabric vied with supervising the day's washing. Something about cattle was troubling her, but most pressing of all was an image of Caulder Stiet staring at her as hopefully as an urchin staring at a store window full of sweets.

"Tell him no," I suggested immediately. "Tell him to go away."

"He's not that bad," she said wearily. "He can be as demanding as a child, it's true. But he is also so desperate that someone see him as manly and competent that I can steer him simply by suggesting things he must do for me to praise him in those lights. It is his uncle who wearies me the most. Rocks, rocks, rocks. They are all that man can think about. He pesters the help and asks a thousand questions a day, yet seems strangely secretive as to what it is that he is seeking. And he is most presumptuous. Yesterday, I discovered he had taken workers from repairing the drive and had them digging holes along the riverbank and bringing him buckets of rocks taken from the holes. As if he has the right to give orders on our land simply because I am betrothed to his nephew! Oh, how that man maddens me!"

I said nothing though I felt great concern. I could almost feel the press of her words, the tremendous need she had to speak of her problems to someone.

"Duril brought the problem to me because he says the work on the drive must be finished before winter, or erosion will have its way with the carriageway. So I went to Father, and he told me that women who worried about such things were usually much older and uglier than I was, and had no prospects. So I had to go to Caulder and fret and fuss about the road and how bumpy it made my carriage rides, until he went to his uncle and said that he thought it best if they did not take Duril's workforce off his project before it was finished. And his uncle said he would only need the workers for a few more days and then they could go back to working on the driveway. As if he had the right to decide what is most important for the estate!

"I am beginning to hate that man. He is insidious, Nevare, absolutely insidious. He manipulates Caulder with such ease, and flatters Father into thinking that Professor Stiet is a very wise man, and someone to trust. I think not. I think he sees Caulder's marriage to me as an opportunity for him to come into a nice lifestyle. It seems that every time I think I have control of my own life or at least some control, someone comes along to muck it up! If his uncle would only go away, I am perfectly confident that I could manage Caulder to my satisfaction. And to his, I might add. He asks little of me. All I have to do is be pretty and tell him flattering things about himself. But his uncle! I am convinced that the man plans that after I am wed to Caulder, he will settle in here and run things to his liking.

"It makes me furious, Nevare. Furious. At you. Because it is entirely your fault that this has fallen on me. I should not be dealing with any of this. If you had not let Father chase you away, if you had sent for me or come back, then, then—"

"Then everything would be all right?" I asked her gently.

"No," she said grudgingly. "But at least I would not be alone. Nevare, it meant so much to me to hear that you are alive. I was so shocked when your note fell out of Carsina's letter, and then I had to laugh at what a reversal that was. How many times did a note for her come concealed in a letter to me? And what an amazing twist of fate that she would be in Gettys and would renew her friendship with you, even to helping you conceal a letter to me. I wrote back to her immediately, thanking her and reminding her of our wonderful days before we so stupidly ended our friendship over a man! What fools we were! Though, in my heart, I still have not forgiven her for her ill-treatment of you, even if I was a party to it. I've told myself that if you have forgiven her enough to entrust her with a letter to me, then I have little reason to hold a grudge. It was such a relief to know you were alive, and that you had actually become a soldier, as you always dreamed you'd be. I long to tell Father, but I have not yet. I dream that someday you will come riding back up to the door, tall and brave in your uniform, to show him that he completely misjudged you. Oh, I miss you so much! When can you come home for a visit?"

I cursed myself for how unthinkingly I had wandered into her dream. She was not aware that she was asleep and dreaming me there, nor had she realized, as Epiny had immediately, that I had intruded into her dream in a very magical way. Epiny had been prepared to understand what was happening by reading my soldier-son journal. Yaril had only the most basic idea of what had befallen me. And with a lurch, I suddenly realized that, when the days were counted up, I had "died" less than ten days ago. Neither news of my shameful conviction for rape, murder, and unnatural acts nor news that I had been killed trying to escape would have reached her yet. The last word she would have had from me was the note I had hidden inside a letter I'd blackmailed Carsina into sending her. She had no idea that Carsina was dead of the plague, let alone that I'd been found guilty of taking liberties with her dead body. Had anyone written anything to her since I'd sent her that note? Had there been time for Spink or Epiny to send her a letter about what had become of me? I wished I'd asked Epiny, but I hadn't, and she hadn't mentioned it to me. A colder thought came to me. Yaril had replied to Carsina's letter. Would Carsina's husband think that he must respond to that note, to let his wife's correspondent know of her sad end? I felt sickened at the thought of how he would paint me for her. I had to prepare her in case the worst happened.

"Yaril. You're asleep and dreaming. You know I'm not really here. But this is more than an idle dream. I'm using magic to travel to your dreams and talk to you. What I am telling you is real. I'm alive, but I can't come to you or send for you. And for now, you must not speak a word about me to Father. Or anyone else."

"What?" A frown wrinkled her brow. The room suddenly wavered around us. Streaks of light broke through my image of it, as if someone had suddenly opened a curtain a crack. Or fluttered her eyelashes as she dreamed. My words had been too sudden, too startling. I was waking her up.

"Yaril! Don't wake up yet. Please. Keep your eyes closed. Stay calm and listen to me. You might receive word that I've disgraced myself, that I died for vicious crimes I'd committed. You might get a letter from Carsina's husband. Don't believe anything he says about me. It's not true. I'm still alive. And eventually I'll find a way to come home to you someday. Yaril? Yaril!"

The world disappeared around me, washed away in a sudden flood of light. I'd wakened her. And I had no way of knowing how much credence she'd give to the dream or even how much she would remember on awakening.

"Yaril?" I asked desperately of the empty light. There was no reply. Doubtless her waking thoughts filled her mind and excluded any touch I might make upon her senses. I hoped I had not given her too great a fright. Would she dismiss my visit as a bizarrely vivid dream?

I had nowhere to retreat from the light and it seemed painful to me. Magic, I reminded myself, worked best in the night. It was time to go back to my body.

I had used Soldier's Boy's magic; he would know that when he awakened, and I suspected he'd keep a tighter watch on me after this. I'd had one opportunity to use the power of dream-walking and I'd made a mare's nest of it. I could feel my flesh pulling me back toward it and I let myself be drawn back into my body. Soldier's Boy slumbered on, his eyes closed. I used my ears and nose to deduce what was happening around me. I could smell smoke and hear the tiny crackling of a small fire nearby. Olikea and Likari were speaking softly to each other. Some distance ahead of us on our path, there was another fish trap in the cavern stream. The traps were woven like a basket and set in the stream's current. Fish could swim in, but finding a way out was more difficult, especially for large fish. There might be fish in it. They were both desperately hungry. They debated softly as to whether one of them should travel ahead to check the trap and then return with fish from it, and then argued as to which of them should go. It was a wearying thing to listen to, a battle between hunger and fear of the darkness.

At the last it was decided that Olikea would go. She warned Likari not to stray too far from me, and to be sure to feed the fire, but only slowly. She would be relying on its light to find us again.

"Give him water if he asks for it, and do not leave him."

"What else should I do for him?"

"There is nothing you can do for him except to stay near him and give him water when he thirsts. He chose this journey of his own will; he knew what the crystal and the black water would do to him. I do not think he gave any thought as to how it might affect us. But this is what it is to be the feeder of a Great One, Likari. Great Ones do not think of their feeders, but feeders must think only of the Great Ones we serve."

With that last admonition, she turned and left the little boy sitting beside the tiny fire in the immense darkness. After a short time, he drew close and sat with his back braced against mine, a faithful little guardian. I was impressed with both his obedience and his courage, and touched by his loyalty. He was such a young child to be left alone in the dark, charged to take care of a sick man.

Soldier's Boy slumbered on in his aching fever-sleep. The not-silence of the cavern settled around us. The little fire made the tiny noises of flames devouring wood. I could hear, if I strained, the distant rush of the stream in its stone channel, and the occasional buzz of one of the lightning bugs as it whispered past us. Likari gave a shiver, sighed, and settled closer against me. His breathing deepened and steadied, and then became the openmouthed snore of a small boy. Tedium set in.

It seemed all my frustrated mind could do was chew over past events and rebuke myself with my foolish mistakes. I tried to make plans for the future and could not. There was too much I didn't know. Even if I could seize control of the body right now, it was too sickly for me to go back the way I had come. Go back to what? I asked myself dully.

When I had left Gettys, I had said that I was giving myself up to the magic and would do its will. I thought I had, when I'd attempted to block the road builders from cutting any more of the ancestor trees. Now, bereft of any other distraction, I began to wonder why Soldier's Boy had been hoarding the magic and what he had hoped to do with it. Plainly my squandering of it had set back his plan. But what had that plan been?

Did he truly know a way to send all the Gernians fleeing from the Barrier Mountains and the adjoining lands? What could he bring down on us that would be so terrible that the military and the settlers would withdraw and the King give up his cherished road? How ruthless was he?

With a lurch, I knew the answer to that. More ruthless than I was. He'd taken my ruthlessness. That was frightening.

I tried to recall who I had been before Tree Woman and the magic had divided me. What would I have considered too extreme a solution to the clash between the Gernians and the Specks? It was hard to think in those terms. His loyalty to the Specks seemed absolute. With such loyalty as his sole criterion, could anything be too extreme? I made my heart cold and stopped thinking of the Gernians as my people; stopped thinking of them as people at all. If they were vermin, how would I drive them away?

The answer came to me, instantly and clearly. The fear and the disease that the Specs had already unleashed on them were merely discouragement. If I were Soldier's Boy, and I wished to destroy Gettys and make it uninhabitable, I would set fire to it. In winter, when the inhabitants had no place to take refuge. Drive them out of their homes and then pick them off. For an aching instant, I could picture Amzil and her children fleeing through snow, Epiny heavily pregnant or carrying a newborn. They could not outrun an arrow. If the Specs struck with stealth, late at night, they could pick off the fleeing victims at their leisure.

The moment the plan came into my mind, I shuddered away from it. I locked my thoughts tight, praying he had not sensed them. I was already traitor to one folk, showing the Gernians how to drug themselves against the Speck magic to cut down the trees. I would not betray both of them to each other.

I did not think it likely Soldier's Boy would come up with such a plan. He was more Speck than Gernian. The Speck did not winter near Gettys. It was possible, I hoped, that they did not see constructed shelter in the same way that I did. To discover what he might be planning, I would have to think as he would. I would have to become him. That thought would have made me grin, if I'd had a mouth to call my own. I'd have to become myself to understand myself.

Slowly the truth of that sank into me. Perhaps it was my only strategy. To stop Soldier's Boy from doing whatever he was planning to do, I'd have to merge with him. I'd have to become him, force him to share my sensibilities, make him see that he could not destroy my people without destroying a part of himself.

The moment I realized the fullness of what I was considering, I rejected it. This scrap of "self" was all that was left of me. If I surrendered it to him, if I lost my self-awareness to become part of him, how could I know if I influenced him or not? I suspected it was an irrevocable act. I feared that in the final analysis, he remained stronger than I was. I'd vanish into him. And I'd never know if I'd saved the people I loved or not.

I determined that I would surrender and become a part of him only if there were no other options. Until then, I would fight to take back the life that was mine.

Likari's snoring had ceased. He pressed closer to me and spoke very quietly. "I'm cold. And I'm tired of the dark. How long has she been gone? What if something happens to her?" He shivered suddenly and something like a sob shook him. "I'm scared," he said, even more quietly.

I had not thought he could press closer, but he plastered himself against me. I could feel his heart race and heard his breath quicken as he peopled the darkness around us with every bogey-tale creature that his young imagination could summon. I wondered what night terrors inhabited the dark corners of a Speck's mind. I could recall, only too well, how I had been able to bring myself to the shaking edge of terror simply by staring up into the darkness of my room and letting my imagination run wild.

When I was very small, I would let the terror progress to the point at which I would shriek from the nursery for my mother or nurse to come running to rescue me from my self-induced panic. The terror was almost worth the coddling and the warmed mug of milk.

By the time my father took over my upbringing I was too big to shriek from my nursery. I would on occasion flee my bed to seek out the nanny I shared with my sisters. But I did that only once after my father had declared himself in charge of me. I was tapping anxiously at the nanny's bedchamber door when my father caught me. To this day, I do not know what alerted him. He was still dressed in his smoking jacket and trousers. In one hand, he carried a book, his finger trapped to mark his place. He looked down at me severely and demanded, "What are you doing out of your bed?"

"I thought I saw something. In the curtains by my window."

"You did, did you? Well, what was it?" His tone was brisk and severe.

I stood up a little straighter in my nightshirt, my bare feet cold on the floor. "I don't know, sir."

"And why is that, Nevare?"

"I was afraid to look, sir." I looked down at my bare feet, shamed. I doubted that my father had ever been afraid of anything.

"I see. Well, it is what you will go and do now."

I glanced hopefully up at him. "Will you come with me?"

"No. Of course not. You are to be a soldier, Nevare. A soldier does not retreat from what he imagines might be an enemy. In an uncertain situation, a soldier gathers information and, if the information is sufficiently important, he reports it to command. Imagine what would happen if a sentry came back to his commander and said, 'I left my post because I thought I saw something. Would you come back with me and see what it was?' What would happen, Nevare?"

"I don't know, sir."

"Well, but think. What would you do, were you the commander? Would you leave your post to go see what had frightened your sentry?"

I answered truthfully with a sinking heart. "No, sir. I would tell my sentry to go back and find out what it was. Because that is his task. My task is to command."

"Exactly. Go back to your room, Nevare. Face your fear. If there is something in your room that requires action from me, come to me and I will help you."

"But—"

"Go, son. Face your fear like a real soldier."

He stood there while I turned and walked away from him. Only a few months ago, my room had been close to the nursery and to my sisters' nanny. My new room seemed very far from those safe and familiar places. The hall that led to my bedchamber seemed long and very dim. The wick in the lamp on the wall bracket had been turned low for the night. My heart hammered when I reached my own door. I had slammed it shut behind me when I fled so that whatever monster was lurking there could not follow me. I slowly turned the knob. The door swung into the darkness.

I stood in the hall, peering into my room. It was dark. I could see the rumpled white sheet on my bed. As my eyes adjusted, I saw more detail. The bedclothes hung to the floor, and anything could be concealed behind them and under my bed. The only other pieces of furniture in my room were a desk and chair. It was possible something lurked in the chair alcove under the desk. As I watched, the long curtains stirred. The window was open, as it was every night, that I might enjoy the benefits of healthful fresh air. It might be only the wind. But it might not.

I wished I had a weapon of some sort. But my wooden practice sword and stave were both inside the wardrobe and that was on the other side of the room. I'd have to face my fears unarmed.

To an adult, the situation might have seemed laughable, but I was a victim of my own imagination. I had no idea what might be lurking in those slowly stirring curtains. Even if it was the wind now, could the being previously hiding behind them now be concealed under my bed? My heart was thundering in my ears at the thought; I'd have to get down on my hands and knees to look under the bed. Once I'd lifted the bedclothes, anything that was under there would most likely spring for my face. It would scratch out my eyes. I was certain of it.

I didn't want to look. I thought of racing across the room and jumping up on my bed and simply forcing myself to stay there. Perhaps there was nothing at all under my bed. Perhaps I was being foolish. I could stay awake all night. If anything did emerge to attack me, I could shout for help then. I didn't have to confront it now.

Except that I did. My father had ordered me to do so. It was what a soldier would do. And I was a second son, born to be a soldier. I could be nothing else. And I could do no less than my duty.

But it did not mean that I had to be a fool in doing it.

I slipped quietly away from my room and hurried through the deserted corridors down to a parlor. My home was quiet and almost unfamiliar at that late hour. There was no bustle of servants, no opening and closing of doors or snatches of voices. I heard only the padding of my own bare feet and my panting breath. When I entered the parlor, it was deserted, lit only by the dying flames in the fireplace. Spooky. I went to the rack of fire irons and selected the poker. It was heavy, much heavier than my practice sword. I hefted it in both my hands and decided it would have to do.

It was awkward to carry it back to my room. The end of it seemed magnetically drawn to the floor, but I gritted my teeth, gripped it firmly with both hands, and marched back to my room with it.

The door was ajar as I had left it. I did not give myself time to think or hesitate. I charged into the room, dropped to one knee, and swept the heavy poker under my bed. It encountered no resistance. Emboldened, I used the log hook to flip up the bedclothes. Poker at the ready, I ducked down for a quick glance. The dim light from the hallway showed me nothing was there.

I staggered back to my feet, the heavy poker at the ready, and stalked over to the blowing curtains. Again, I swung the heavy poker, hooking the thick fabric and pulling it out from the wall. Nothing there.

But my imagination had already discerned my diabolic opponent's likely strategy. The creature would be in my wardrobe by now. Heart hammering, I gripped the poker in one hand and with the other jerked the wardrobe door open. I gave an incoherent gasp of terror as the motion caused the clothing inside it to stir. Then I struck, jabbing the poker so firmly into the closet that the heavy tip of it struck and scored the wooden backing.

A shadow loomed suddenly over me from behind. I spun, my poker at the ready. My father caught the end of it in a firm grasp and, with a quick twist, disarmed me. I stood, looking up at him in dread.

He smiled down on me. "Well, what is your report, soldier?"

"There's nothing there, sir." My voice shook. I'd made a fool of myself before my father. He'd seen how scared I was.

He nodded at me. "I agree. Nothing to be frightened of. And I'm proud of you, son. Very proud. If there had been anything there for you to fear, you would have vanquished it. And now you know that you can face what scares you. You don't have to run wailing for your mother or nanny or even me. You're a brave boy, Nevare. Someday you'll make a fine soldier."

He leaned the heavy poker against the wall near the head of my bed. "I think I'll just leave that here for the night. In case you should think you need it again. Now. Into bed with you and go to sleep. We've a busy day tomorrow."

I climbed up onto my bed, and he spread over me the covers that I'd half dragged onto the floor. He leaned down and set his palm on my brow for a moment. "Good night, son," he'd said, and then gone out of the room, leaving the door ajar so that a slice of dim light fell on my trusty poker.

The memory had come back to me in a wild rush, triggered by the boy's trembling body pressed up against my back. It was a child's memory and now, as a man, I reordered it. My father had waited and watched to see what I would do. He hadn't interfered, but he had been watching over me. And he'd been proud of me, his soldier son. Proud of my courage, and he'd told me so. I don't remember how many nights the poker had remained in my room by my bed. But I don't recall that I ever felt a night terror after that.

Whatever might have happened in the years that followed, regardless of how we had parted, my father had given me something then. Given me something far more important than if he had carried me back to my bed and checked my room for imaginary threats himself. When had I lost that father?

When had he lost his soldier son?

I tried to lift my hand. I could not. Soldier's Boy's control of the body was complete. I could not even open my eyes. Instead, I poked at his awareness. It burned low. He was physically exhausted from battling his self-induced fever. It took all the focus I could muster to break through his stupor. I offered him my memory of my father and my current awareness of Likari's fear. He received it but did not rouse from his torpor.

"Do something." I pushed at him relentlessly. "Do something for the boy. Now."

"Go away. Let me rest."

I would not. I was a thorn in his legging, a pebble in his bed. He finally gave in.

"Water?" he croaked. "Likari?"

"I'm here," the boy instantly replied in a shaky voice. "I have the water skin."

"Help me drink."

The darkness pressed close around us. Likari fed the fire a small bit of wood, and as a flame licked at it, he used the brief bit of light to offer me water. He was not adept at it. The skin fountained water, and wet my chin and chest before Soldier's Boy was able to catch it in my mouth. Then it was wonderful, cool and sweet and soothing. He had not realized how thirsty he was. Likari stoppered the skin. Soldier's Boy rubbed his hand over my wet chin and scrubbed at my crusty eyes with it. Even the dim light of the fire seemed too bright for his fever-stricken eyes.

"Where's Olikea?" Soldier's Boy asked Likari.

"She went ahead, to see if there was any fish caught in the next fish trap." The boy hesitated and then added, "She's been gone a long time."

"I'm sure she'll be back soon." It was hard to talk. Soldier's Boy's head hurt so badly. To press my ideas on Soldier's Boy, I had to share his sensations. I steeled my will and pushed at him. He spoke grudgingly. The act took effort and hurt his head. "But you've stayed here by my side in the darkness. To watch over me."

"Yes."

"Thank you for the water, Likari. It's good to know you are here."

The boy had stopped shaking. His voice was steady when he said, "Olikea said it was part of being a feeder. I'm proud to be a feeder for you, Nevare."

"I'm glad you are here," and for that brief instant, I was truly
the one who spoke. Soldier's Boy was sinking back into his stupor. His weariness dragged at me. I'd tangled my awareness too
completely with his, and now as he sank into sleep, I went with
him. But dimly I was aware that the boy resettled against my back,
and that he trembled no longer. I let myself sink into the darkness
with Soldier's Boy.

CHAPTER ELEVEN

THE WINTERING PLACE

The aroma of cooking fish coaxed me slowly out of a very deep sleep.

I came out of it clutching a peculiar dream. I'd been sitting in my father's study. He was in a dressing gown and slippers, seated in a cushioned chair in front of an autumn fire. His hair was neatly combed, but in a way that made me think he had not done it himself. There were slippers on his feet; it was the guise of a man who had not been outside the house in days. On a table near his elbow was a bowl of late apples; their fragrance had perfumed the room. My father's face was bowed into his hands, and he was weeping. His hair had gone gray and the hands that covered his face were ropy with tendons. He seemed to have aged a decade in the single year I'd been gone.

He spoke to me without looking at me. His voice sounded odd, the words badly formed. "Why, Nevare? Why did you hate me so? I loved you. Fate made you the only son I could truly claim as my own, the only one who would follow in my footsteps as a soldier and a cavalla officer. You alone could have won glory for our name. But you threw it all away. You shamed me and you shamed yourself. Why? Why did you destroy yourself? Was it to spite me? Was it because you hated everything I was? What did I do wrong? How did I fail to inspire you? Was I such a poor father to you? Why, Nevare? Why?"

The questions were like a driving rain, relentless and chilling. They soaked me with guilt and confusion. He was so miserable. So hurt and vulnerable, so profoundly hopeless in his sorrow.

"I did everything I could think of to make you want to change, Nevare. Nothing moved you. Even when I took your name and home from you, you never once said that you wanted to try again. You never once said you were sorry for what you had done! You never came back. Did you hate me so badly? Why, son? Why couldn't you just be what you were born to be? Why couldn't you have taken what I'd earned for you, and enjoyed it?"

In that dream, I was mute. I was not even sure I was really there. Perhaps I watched him through a window. Perhaps the window was in my mind.

I woke confused. The fragrance of apples had changed to the aroma of fish, and I was cold, not warmed by a fire. My father would not weep for me; he had driven me away. I rubbed at my sticky eyes. My head still hurt, but not as badly as it had. I was hungry and very, very thirsty. I opened my eyes. Olikea had returned. She'd built up the fire. On stones beside the coals, two fine fat fish were baking. Food. Light. A bit of warmth. All good things.

But as I took a deep breath and tried to sit up, I realized what else had changed. My fever was gone. The sores still itched abominably, and when I scratched, one loose scab peeled away under my nails. But my fever was gone. I sighed heavily. "Is there water?" I heard myself ask hoarsely.

"You're awake! Oh, good. Likari, bring water."

The boy was no longer sleeping against my back, I realized. He came into the light, bringing the water skin with him. "I kept watch while you slept," he told me proudly.

I smiled. But when I tried to thank him, I abruptly became aware that I was not the one in charge of the body. Soldier's Boy smiled at him with my mouth and felt kindly toward the boy, but he did not utter the words of thanks that I would have said. Instead he nodded at him and took the water skin from his hands and drank heavily of the cold, sweet water.

I pulled my awareness apart from his. As I did so, I felt that he knew I had separated from him again. His smile widened. Because, for a time, I had merged with him and had not fought him. I had not even been aware that I existed separately from him for those minutes. "I'm feeling stronger," he said aloud, and I cringed, thinking that he aimed the words as much at me as he spoke them toward Olikea and Likari.

I held back from him, silent and observant, as Olikea finished cooking the fish and portioned it out. They all ate greedily, scarcely letting the fish cool before gulping it down. When it was gone, Olikea proudly produced a double handful of a viscous-skinned fungus. It wasn't shaped like a mushroom, but instead had a fingered structure. In the barely flickering firelight, they looked yellow. The appearance repulsed me but Soldier's Boy took a deep breath of their enticing odor.

"Mage's honey," Olikea named it proudly. "Very nourishing to the magic. Never before have I seen it growing in such quantity. It was on the wooden lip of the spill for the fish trap, all growing in a fringe. This will replenish your strength and put you on your feet."

Both Likari and Olikea were still hungry, yet neither of them showed any desire to share this food. Instead they watched intently as Soldier's Boy picked up one of the gelatinous structures and set it on my tongue. My physical reaction to it was immediate. I felt a shiver run over my whole body; my skin stood up in gooseflesh and the hair rose on my head and on the backs of my arms. An instant later, I actually tasted the mage's honey. It was named for its color, not its flavor. The taste was not unpleasant, but it was not memorable either, offering only a faintly musky flavor. As Soldier's Boy chewed it, it had the texture of an overcooked jelly. It was not appetizing. But when he swallowed it, the shiver that I had experienced on my skin was repeated, but as a quivering throughout my entire body. The sensation was so intense that I was not sure he enjoyed it. Yet he picked up another of the fungi and put it on my tongue.

The sensations were sharper and more prolonged with each one. At the fifth one, I thought I heard Olikea mutter, "See how he glows with power now!" but I did not pay much attention to her, so completely did the sensations absorb me.

When every bit of it was gone, I sat shivering. My senses were painfully alert to every sort of stimulus, but my awareness of touch was overwhelming. It seemed to extend beyond my skin like a cat's quivering whiskers. I noticed the movement of air currents in the cavern, felt the striations in the rock beneath me, and even sensed the disturbance of the air caused by an insect flying past me. As I sat there, the acuity of my senses only increased. I could see in the darkness with a clarity of vision that surpassed my ordinary sight in daylight. At the same time, a restless energy crawled through me and over my skin, demanding that I be up and doing something, anything. Soldier's Boy rose abruptly. "It is time to travel," he announced, and my own words sounded like trumpets in my ears, not just when he uttered them, but when their previously faint echoes returned to me.

"Fill up the water skin, roll the blanket, and gather our things," Olikea urged Likari in an excited voice. "We will quick-walk now, I'll wager."

So charged with energy was he that it was difficult to wait for them. I think Olikea sensed his restlessness, for she caught at my arm as I rose and clung to it, bidding Likari, "Come, come quickly, and take his other hand."

The boy came at a run and seized my free hand as if his life depended on it. Perhaps it did. The magic rippled through me like fire in my veins.

In four steps we burst forth from the dark and dank cavern into daylight and a brisk wind. The day was heavily overcast with fat gray clouds, but the light was still shocking. Soldier's Boy halted, dazzled, and only when both Olikea and Likari tugged hard at my hands before stopping did I realize the momentum we had had.

When Soldier's Boy glanced back, I could see the opening of the cavern we had left as a tall crack in a jagged rock face. We stood on a beaten pathway on a hillside covered in tall, yellowed grass and fading gorse. Ahead of us, the trail wended its way down into a sheltered valley thick with evergreens. In half a dozen places, plumes of smoke drifted up past the treetops, only to be quickly swept away by the fresh breeze. A swift-flowing river from the mountains behind us divided the valley; even at this distance, I could hear the river's voice, deep and greedy. It ran a steep course downhill, and stones moved with it, grinding and grumbling. Its waters were white with rock dust. It cut through the valley like a cleaver. In the distance, the sun was coming up over a sparkling bay at the river's mouth. I had never seen such a dazzling vista. "Is that the ocean?" Soldier's Boy asked dazedly. I shared his question, wondering if I were beholding the final destination of the King's Road.

Olikea glanced at the distant water and shrugged. "It is a great water. No one has ever gone around it, though if you travel north far enough, it is said there are islands one can visit. They are cold and rocky places, good for birds and seals that eat fish, but not a place for the People. This valley is the best place for us. It has always been our Wintering Place."

"Why?"

"By now the leaves will have fallen in the forest on the other side of the mountains. There will be no shelter from that light, or the deep cold. Here, the trees never lose their needles; it is always dim and gentle beneath their canopy. Snow falls in the valley here perhaps one year in five, and when it does come, it does not linger. It rains here, sometimes a great deal, but rain is kinder than snow and freezing, I think. In both late autumn and early spring, fish are thick in the river, and deer in the woods. In winter, we can live in plenty here."

"Why don't you stay here year-round?"

She looked at Soldier's Boy as if he were daft. "The ancestor trees are not here, nor will they grow here, even when we have planted seedlings here. And in the summers, this is a place of fog and rains and floods. Sometimes people have tried to stay here, thinking they were too old to make the journey or that they would prefer to summer here. They do not prosper; sometimes they do not survive."

Soldier's Boy had bowed his head. Her words tickled at his mind, waking memories that Lisana had shared. He lifted his head and looked out over the valley. Then he pointed and said, "There. Those rising columns of smoke over there. That is our village, isn't it?"

His eyesight was as shockingly keen as his sense of touch. His gaze picked out glimpses of mossy roofs and then small figures moving nearby. The thick foliage of the prevalent evergreen trees obscured most of the village scene. I could not tell how large a settlement it was. As he watched, a flock of croaker birds rose suddenly from their perches in the trees. They circled once over the village and then flew toward us, cawing loudly.

"Yes. And from the amount of smoke, most of our kin-clan have already returned there. I thought they would still be at the gathering place at the river's mouth, trading." She shook her head in disappointment. "We are too late. All our folk have gone to the Trading Place and returned already. What a shame! All the others will have new jewelry and winter robes, but I shall have to make do with what I have left from last year."

"I did not think you cared for robes and pretty clothes." Soldier's Boy gestured at her near nakedness.

"In the Summer Place, there is no need to be hampered by such things. But now?" She wrapped her arms around herself and shivered. "One must be warm. And if a woman is prosperous, she chooses to be warm in beautiful garments."

"We have missed the trading time?" Likari asked dolefully. The distress on his small face was heartbreaking.

"There may be a few of the clans gathered there still. But the best of the trading will be done. Look at the valley and see the rising smoke. The People have returned to their traditional spaces for the winter. Trading is over." Olikea pronounced the words like a doom.

Likari's face fell and he sank into a morose silence.

Soldier's Boy was perhaps trying to be practical when he reminded them, "We have nothing to trade anyway. We would have gone that extra distance only to be taunted by the pretty things we could not obtain."

Olikea gave him a sideways glance. "*You* have nothing to trade. I had plenty in my pack; I gave it to my father to carry it here for me, when I was called away to care for you. I had my trading all planned. Last year, the Spolsin kin-clan had lovely sealskin capes to trade. Warm, sleek spotted fur that sheds water! That was what I meant to get for myself at the trading time. Now I shall have to do with my old wolfskin coat. I hope the mites have not got into it over the summer! Last year, maggots devored Firada's sealskin boots; she would have been barefoot for the winter, had not Jodoli traded magic for her to have new boots of elk hide with fox trim." There was no mistaking the envy in her voice. Obviously her sister had the better bargain in a Great Man.

"And did you think of what I would wear, when you discarded my old clothing?"

She looked at him in consternation. "Better to go naked than to wear those disgusting Gernian rags. It would shame me to have you go about the People in such garb! I would beg my father's old clothes from him first!"

Soldier's Boy grimaced and I felt the tingling in his blood grow dim. The cold wind chilled him. He'd shut the magic down. I had a glimpse of his thoughts. He was conserving the magic, saving up every bit of it that he could hoard.

My arm itched. Soldier's Boy scratched it, glancing down at it as he did so. I was horrified at what I saw, but Soldier's Boy looked at Olikea and changed the subject, asking, "How do I look? Did the pattern stay in place? I like my arms. I am glad I did not scratch them too much and spoil them."

I could sense his satisfaction and pride, but I felt only horror and dismay. The result of wounding himself with the crystal and the slime was now clear. My skin bore a pattern of blotchy scars from the injuries and the subsequent infections. I was a Speck.

I had never suspected that Speck children were born with unblemished skin. I had thought the dapples that marked their people were inherent to their race, a defining difference that set them apart from both the Gernians and the Plainspeople. To discover that it was a deliberate marking, a cultural rather than a biological difference, disturbed me. Soldier's Boy had irrevocably marked my body in a way that proclaimed I was no longer Gernian. The fat had been an extreme enough departure from my image of myself. This was worse. Even if by some miracle I discovered a way to regain control of my body and return to my previous level of fitness, my skin would be forever scarred with the dapples of a Speck. I felt helplessly suspended as I watched my own life drift even further from my reach. Soldier's Boy's satisfaction was, I suspected, twofold. He had marked himself as a Speck, to further his own cause. And by doing so he had dealt me a crippling blow, claiming the body even more as his own. I suspected he could feel my despair and rejoiced in it.

Olikea looked at his face critically. Then she walked slowly around him as if he were a horse at the fair and she were considering buying him. When she came back to face him, her eyes were approving. "I have marked babes before; Likari is my work, and you can see that I patterned him tightly, so that when he grew, his pattern would still be attractive. With you, it was more difficult, for you are a man grown, and yet you have lost so much fat that your skin was slack. Even now, it is possible that when you are full again, your pattern will not be entirely pleasing. But I do not think it is likely. Your back is dappled like a brook trout, but I looked to the mountain cat for your shoulders. I wish you had let me mark your face. Even so, it looks very good. You have the camouflage of both hunter and prey, a very strong marking. That they have turned out so well is very auspicious."

She smiled as she spoke, well pleased with her work. But then the pleasure faded from her face and she folded her lips. "But it is a shame that you must show yourself so to our kin-clan, let alone to Kinrove at the winter gathering. Nevare, we must fatten you as quickly as possible. That is all there is to it."

"Such is my intent also," Soldier's Boy replied. I was unsurprised to hear him say so, and yet my spirits sank again.

"Shall we go on to the village, then? If you quick-walk us, we can be there in just a few moments." She frowned, squinting.

"I wish to be out of the light. Even at this time of year, when the clouds are thick as good furs, the light still dizzies me."

Soldier's Boy was silent. Plainly he was thinking, but his thoughts were inaccessible to me, and I lacked the spirit to pry my way into them. When he spoke aloud, it sounded as if he had reached a hard decision. "I will send you on soon. But I cannot show myself to the People this way."

"This way?" Olikea asked, puzzled.

"Thin. Poor. With my markings barely healed. This is not how I wish them to see me, not how I wish them to think of me." Distress was suddenly evident in his voice. "If I present myself to them like this, I will never attain the standing I must have. They won't listen to me at all."

"And so I have warned you, over and over! But you would not listen to me!"

Olikea sounded both satisfied and angry at having her opinion so completely vindicated. But I felt they were talking at cross-purposes. Olikea was thinking of status and honors and gifts. I could not discern Soldier's Boy's thoughts clearly, but I suspected he was thinking of strategy. His next words chilled me, for they were words I had often heard from my father's lips.

"If I wish to command, I must appear to be in command already when I am first seen. Even if I must delay my arrival at the village. When we get there, I must be well fed. All of us must appear prosperous. If I go to our kin-clan now, they will see me as a needy beggar and an embarrassment to them."

"But what can we do about that?"

"Not go," he said abruptly. "Not go until I am ready. Not go until you are ready."

"Until *I* am ready? I am ready now. I am more than ready to seek my lodge and be comfortable again. My father will have food, and he will share with me. There is much to do to prepare my lodge for the winter. I must take down my sleeping skins and shake them out, and air my winter furs." She looked at me suddenly in a very odd way. "As I am your feeder, I suppose you will live with me now." She ran her eyes over me as if I were a large piece of furniture that might not fit in her parlor.

"Does Likari live with you?" Soldier's Boy asked her.

"Sometimes. As much as a child lives with one person. He seems to prefer my aunt's lodge to mine, and often he is at my father's or with Firada. He is a child. He lives where he pleases. No one denies a child a meal and a place by the fire."

"Of course," I replied, but I sensed that Soldier's Boy was as surprised as I was. And as oddly pleased. It seemed a wonderful idea to me, that a child could choose where he lived and no one would think of turning him out. That a child could expect food and a warm place to sleep from anyone in his village. Amzil's children came to my mind; well, such had they found at Spink's home.

"I am his feeder, too!" the boy suddenly but stoutly insisted. "I will live where the Great One does."

"Do you think I will put up with having both of you underfoot?" she demanded. "I will have work enough to take care of him!"

"I will not be underfoot. And I will be taking care of him, too. Did not I stay and guard him while you went to get the fish? Have not I brought food often, and carried the water and the blanket all this way? It is my place and I will have it."

"Very well," she conceded, but not graciously. "My lodge will be small for the three of us, but I am sure that somehow we will manage."

"If need be, I will build it bigger," Soldier's Boy suddenly asserted. "But I shall not go to it today. You will, Olikea. Go home, to your lodge, and find your trade goods. Then set out for the trading meet right away."

"But—but the best of the trading is done. And the walk to my lodge will take me half the day, and then there will be two, perhaps three more days to walk to the Trading Place. Everyone will be gone. And what will you be doing?" This last she asked suspiciously, as if she expected him to somehow trick her.

"I will keep the boy with me. And we will also be journeying toward that place, to meet you there. So when you set out, bring extra sleeping skins for us. Winter comes on quickly. I do not wish to sleep cold."

"Your plans make no sense to me. I am weary of journeying, and you have no supplies. Let us go to my lodge now, and have a good rest and a hot meal. Then, when you are recovered a bit, you can quick-walk us to the Trading Place." She ran her hand over her head and then glanced up at the overcast sky, obviously bothered by the light and impatient to be on her way.

He considered. I think he was tempted by the idea of a hot meal and a restful night in a warm place. But then he shook his head. It was a Gernian gesture, I suddenly realized. He was incorporating more of me into himself. I wondered fearfully if that meant I was losing myself to him. He spoke.

"No. I will not show myself to our kin-clan again until I can do so with pride. I am determined that when next Jodoli sees me, I will have put on flesh and appear as a prosperous man."

"And how will you do this?" Olikea demanded. "What will the others think of me, returning without you?"

"I am not entirely sure. But it is not for you to worry about. If anyone asks about me, tell them that I sent you on ahead. For now, think only that you will be getting what you want, time at the trading fair. Go on, go now. Likari and I will find you there."

"There will be many questions for me when I arrive at my home village without either of you!"

"Just smile and promise them a surprise. Tell them the boy is safe with me. And then start off for the Trading Place. Four days hence, we will find you there."

"Four days?"

"You said you might need to sleep. You will arrive before we do. Brag of the Great Man you have found. Trade with abandon, as if you have no need to strike the best bargain, as if you know you have untold wealth."

Her brow had furrowed and her eyes shifted with uncertainty. She wanted to go to her home, she wanted to rest and then to journey to the Trading Place for the last days of trading. But curiosity was biting her like an insatiable flea. "What are you planning?" she demanded.

"I am planning to arrive at the Trading Place four days hence and impress everyone. Including you."

"But if I go and I brag of you and trade my goods recklessly, and you do not come, I shall look a fool!"

"But if you do, and I do arrive, then you shall be celebrated and honored as a woman of great foresight."

She was silent, staring at him.

"I know it's a gamble, Olikea. Only you can decide if you will wager or not."

A moment longer she stood, debating, and then she turned on her heel and walked away toward her village. We watched her go. Soldier's Boy then glanced down, to find Likari looking up at him uncertainly. Olikea had departed without even a farewell to the boy, let alone a list of cautions for taking care of him. I thought of how wary Amzil had been about letting me take care of her youngsters for even a few minutes. Yet plainly Olikea regarded Likari as an independent entity, one capable of making his own decisions or objections to the decisions of others. I was not sure that I approved, but the system seemed to work for this boy.

Had Soldier's Boy heard the echoes of my thoughts? He met Likari's gaze. "Do you wish to go with me? Or to return to the village with your mother?"

He drew himself up. "I am your feeder. You have said I will go with you. So I shall."

"Very well." Soldier's Boy sent a final glance after Olikea. The sun shone on her skin. She was as unconcerned as a lioness as she strode down the trail toward the villages. As he watched, she entered the shelter of the trees and was lost to sight.

"What do you mean to do?"

"I intend to hunt. You will help me. And I intend to eat. A lot. Then when I have grown as fat as I can in four days, we shall quick-walk to the Trading Place. And there I shall trade."

He cocked his head at me. "What will you trade?"

"I'm not entirely sure yet. What is considered valuable?"

He furrowed his brow. His eyes were very serious as he pondered my question. "Tobacco. Tobacco is always good. And furs. Pretty things. Things that are good to eat. Knives."

"I think I should have asked your mother before she left."

"Probably. Why do you call Olikea my mother so much?"

"Well. It is what she is, isn't it?"

"I suppose. But it sounds odd to me." He glanced about and said anxiously, "We should go beneath the trees. I start to burn."

"I feel it, too, especially in my markings." All my skin had become more sensitive to light, but my new specks were noticeably sore, even from this brief exposure to sunlight. Soldier's Boy began to walk slowly down the path that Olikea had taken and Likari fell into step beside me. His small dark head bobbed as he walked. "How is Olikea usually named to you?"

"Olikea."

"You do not call her 'Mother' ever?"

This seemed to puzzle him. "A 'mother' is what she is, not who she is," he said after a time.

"I see," Soldier's Boy replied and I thought I did.

The wind rose, sweeping down on us. He looked back the way we had come. High above the cavern from which we had emerged the peaks already boasted snow. He felt a pang of guilt. "You must be cold. I should have sent you with Olikea."

"Winter is coming. It's right to be cold in winter. The wind will be less keen once we are in the shelter of the trees."

"Then let's hurry," Soldier's Boy suggested, for the keenness of the wind stung his bare skin almost as much as the light had. Likari might be philosophical about being cold because it was winter, but he saw no reason to be cold if he didn't have to be.

Even when we reached the shelter of the trees, he was cold, and I was suddenly skeptical about Soldier's Boy's decision. He had nothing from his previous life save his blanket. The boy carried a small amount of gear: a water skin, the fire-making supplies, and a knife and a few other basics in his pouch. But he himself was nearly as resourceless as a child newly born to the world. I thought how they had abandoned my worn clothing and suddenly mourned those meager possessions as if they were squandered treasure. Cold and hunger pressed us, extending their claws even into my awareness. What was he thinking? Why hadn't he followed Olikea to her house? We could have been warm and fed by now. Likari seemed to share none of my doubts but toiled along at Soldier's Boy's heels, patient as a dog.

This was a different sort of forest from the one on the other side of the mountains. It was greener and lusher. Most of the trees were needled evergreens, and ferns were thick in the mossy shade. I was suddenly grateful for the dimness they provided. Huckleberry bushes mocked me with their past-season greenery. The forest here smelled different, wetter and greener, than the woods on the far side of the mountains. The signs of human habitation were plainer here. The path we followed was well trodden and at intervals lesser paths separated themselves like tributaries branching out of a river. Fat gray squirrels seemed plentiful. One stopped halfway up a tree trunk to scold us, jerking his tail at us and angrily denouncing our presence in his forest. If we'd had my sling, we'd have had squirrel stew very shortly. Perhaps some trickle of that thought reached Soldier's Boy, for he hesitated and almost I thought his hand went to a pocket that wasn't there. Then he shook his head and walked on. He had something else on his mind. But what could be more pressing than a need for food? I knew he was hungry. It ate at him as it had once eaten at me. But whatever was driving him now had sharper teeth. I tried to sense what it was, but felt that he shielded it from me.

We had walked for perhaps an hour when Soldier's Boy halted and stood, staring about himself like a hound trying to pick up a lost scent. There was no pathway, but after staring around and noting several of the larger trees, he gave a sharp nod to himself and left the trail we had been following. Likari glanced at the worn trail that led toward his home village, gave a small sigh, and followed him.

Soldier's Boy did not move with certainty. He paused often, and once we backtracked and then went on in a slightly different direction. When we came to a lively stream that crossed our path, he smiled. They both stooped to drink the icy water.

Likari wiped the back of his hand across his mouth. "Where are we going?"

I was surprised when Soldier's Boy answered him. "To Lisana's old house. It's hard for me to find the way; much has changed since she actually walked these hills. Saplings have become mighty trees. The old paths have been devoured by the moss and ferns, and new ones have been trodden. It is confusing to me."

"The old Great One, Lisana? She is a tree now?"

"But she wasn't always a tree. Many years ago, she lived close by here. She told me about her house here. She spoke to me, very strongly, in my earliest dream visions. And later, she was my mentor and instructor." And lover, he might have added, but he did not.

"Do you think her lodge will still be there, after all these years?"

"Probably not. But we shall see."

I ventured closer to Soldier's Boy's thoughts and aligned myself with him. I could not tell if he was aware of me or not. I tried to be very still and unobtrusive. I felt like a small boy trying to peer over his father's shoulder while he was writing a letter.

He had Lisana's memories and consulted them like a map. The path to her home had wound past a rise, and then between two immense trees. Only one of them was still standing. The other was an empty stump, like a rotted-out tooth sticking out of the forest floor. Soldier's Boy walked between them and then paused, thinking. Uphill, he decided, because he remembered that she had enjoyed a good view of the valley.

She had stopped living in the village when she became a Great One. Too many unfulfilled dreams resided there. The man she had loved had not wished to be the feeder of the Great One, to live always in the shadow of her power. She had no desire to see his children scamper past her door each day. She had never truly taken a feeder. There had been villagers who served her, and all her kin-clan had been proud to have produced a Great One. She lacked for nothing; they saw to that. Food, jewelry, furs to sleep under, music to lull her to sleep, perfumes to stimulate her thoughts—she had but to express a wish for something and it was provided to her. In return, she served her people well and faithfully.

She lacked for nothing. Nothing except the simple life that she had once believed she would have. Nothing except a man who had turned away from her when power touched and then filled her.

A tremendous sympathy for her flooded and filled me. I had thought we were so different, but peering through Soldier's Boy's mind and sharing her memories, I suddenly found many places where our experiences touched.

Her home had been stoutly built of cedar logs. The roofs of such houses were sharply peaked and the eaves reached almost to the ground. Roofed with logs and thatched with moss, it had been, and as the years passed, ferns and mushrooms had grown on the roof and sprouted from the moss chinking. She had encouraged the growth. Her house was alive, an incarnation of the forest from which she drew her power. It had been fitting.

He passed it twice. I saw it before he did. I tugged, stamped, and poked at his awareness until he finally turned back. He was looking for her house as she remembered it, roomy yet snug, and with a well-trodden path leading up to it. It was long gone. I recognized the overgrown green mound as what remained of it.

In this rainy forest region, the folk built houses of cedar for a good reason. In favorable conditions, cedar doesn't rot. In adverse conditions, it rots very slowly. Lisana's house had been well built, of thick logs sealed with boiled pitch. Even so, time and the elements had had their way. Years ago, the front wall had boasted two window openings and a door. Trailing vines had overgrown them in a curtain of roots and tendrils, and eventually, moss had filled in the gaps. Soldier's Boy found the door by touch, thrusting against the greened walls until he reached a place that gave to his push.

Likari watched him in silence as he thrust his arm in elbow deep and then tore away at the wall of foliage. It was not easy work: the roots were tough and woody, and the moss was thick, but eventually he had torn out a hole big enough to look through. He peered into darkness that smelled of damp and rich rot. Likari, near naked, had begun to shiver.

"Build a fire for us while I do this," Soldier's Boy suggested. Likari gave a relieved nod and ran off to collect twigs and dry debris.

Soldier's Boy cleared the doorway and ventured inside. He blinked, letting his eyes adjust. The walls and roof had held, but the forest had still invaded. Cascades of pale roots had penetrated and actually strengthened the walls. More groping white roots dangled from the ceiling. The earth floor was damp underfoot. He could make out vague shapes that had been her possessions. There, against the wall, that would have been a chest of cedar-wood and that collapsed huddle of moss and mildew was where her bed had been. He found one of the windows and began to clear it to let more light in. The central hearth of careful dry-stone work had survived, but the smoke hole above it was blocked. The afternoon was advancing. He looked out of the low door. Likari had kindled a small fire and was perched on the rolled blanket beside it.

"Come in here! You see that? Climb up there and open it up for us. Once that's done, we can bring the fire inside. We'll be a little more comfortable tonight."

The boy peered into the darkened lodge. He wrinkled his nose in distaste for the damp smell and the busy beetles and pale roots that dangled down from the ceiling. "Could not you just speak to the forest and bid it give us shelter for the night?"

It was presumptuous but Soldier's Boy chose not to take offense. "I could. But that would use magic. And I need to build my magic, not spend it. So, tonight, we will stay in here."

I sensed that he had other reasons, and most of them were that his beloved had once lived here. He looked around a chamber that a Gernian would have considered a root cellar and saw a cozy home, lit by a warm hearth and filled with the comforts that befitted a Great One. His secondhand recollections startled me. He recalled copper cooking pots and green glass bowls, hair combs of ivory and silver pins for her hair. Yet his memories of her wealth were tinged with sadness. Perhaps only he knew how lonely she had been. Did he think that somehow he could retro-actively amend that by residing here?

While Likari tugged and pulled diligently at the shrubs, roots, and moss blocking the smoke hole, Soldier's Boy moved purpose-fully about the room. She had had no heir to inherit her wealth, not even a favorite feeder to claim three cherished possessions. So, as was their custom when dealing with folk who were full of magic, her home had become taboo once she had died. Magic had a price and left a residue, the Speck believed. This chamber remained as it was the day she last left it. Lisana had died on the far side of the mountains. She had known she was dying, and had stayed behind to be near the tree she had chosen. Her youngest brother and three of her feeders had stayed with her, loyal to the end, to prop her failing body against the tree and guard it until the tree could send its seeking roots tendriling into her body to absorb both the nutrients of her corpse and all that remained of her person.

These things he knew almost as clearly as if they had happened to him. These were the memories Lisana had given him. And so he went to where a shelf had been, and groped on the floor amid the wreckage of the long-ago rotted plank. From its debris, he lifted a soapstone lamp. He went outside and scrubbed it with fallen needles beneath a cedar tree. He would get oil for it when he went to the Trading Place. He held it in his hands, feeling it warm beneath his touch. She had liked to sit outside in the mild evenings of early autumn with its soft glow lighting the night.

He looked up at the sky through the lacy fronds of the cedar trees. The light was going fast. If they were going to eat tonight, he had to hunt now. He clenched his teeth. Now that he had found the house, he didn't want to leave it. He longed to lovingly restore it to what it had been, to see the log walls lit by dancing firelight, to recline on the bed where she had slept, to drink from the cups she had used. He ached for her with a depth of feeling that bordered on obsession. He was sick with his loneliness and love, and I pitied him.

Yet for all that, he disciplined himself, as my father had taught him when he was the same boy I was. He looked up to young Likari, who was still dispiritedly dragging roots and moss and vines out of the smoke hole. "Do you still have my sling?"

Likari grinned. "I saved it for you." He fumbled in a pouch at his belt and then tossed down the flap of leather with the long thongs wrapped around it. Soldier's Boy caught it neatly. He turned to leave.

"Do you wish me to hunt for you?"

Soldier's Boy was almost startled. He hadn't even considered it. He made a quick decision. "No. Thank you: finish clearing the smoke hole. Then clean the hearth inside and bring the fire into the house. Gather some firewood for the night. I'll see what I can get for us to eat."

The boy stood in a half crouch over the chimney, staring at him. He made no reply. Soldier's Boy turned and walked away from the house reluctantly. He didn't want the boy to tidy the hearth. He wanted to do it himself, to be sure that every stone was put back as it had been when Lisana lived there. He hadn't gone a dozen strides when the boy called after him, "Great One, this is a bad-luck place! Please! Don't leave me here alone!"

Soldier's Boy halted and turned, surprised. "Why is it a bad-luck place?"

"A Great One lived here, and now she is gone. We should not be here. To come here uninvited is the worst sort of luck. It does not matter that she has been gone for a long time. The bad luck is still here." His voice quavered on the last words. He pinched his mouth shut to keep his lip from trembling.

Soldier's Boy stood still, listening to chill wind in hemlock and cedar needles. Then he said, "I was invited. And you are my feeder. It isn't bad luck for me to be here, or for you."

The boy didn't reply. I looked at him through Soldier's Boy's eyes and thought how young he really was. Soldier's Boy didn't give it another thought. The light was going fast now. This time of day animals would be on the move, but it would not last long. I might pity Likari, left alone with his fears, but Soldier's Boy simply assumed he would cope with them.

His hunting luck was good. I could feel him draw on my skill and experience with the sling when he used it. It felt odd, almost as if he were bleeding me for sustenance. At the same time, he could not open that link and take from me without leaving his own thoughts vulnerable to my spying. I caught a glimpse of his plan. He would stay here, in Lisana's house, and eat all he could for four days before making a quick-walk to the Trading Place. He hoped he could regain enough of his weight to be impressive to the folk gathered there. There was something else, too, something he guarded more closely. I could not see it, but knew he antici-pated it with excitement but also with a strange regret.

This was a different forest he moved through, as different as the forest on the other side of the mountain had been from my prairie home. That was a revelation to me. I had thought that all forests would be, well, forests. To discover that they differed as much as one city does from another was almost shocking. On this side of the mountains, evergreens predominated, cedar and spruce for the most part. Their fallen needles carpeted the earth and I tasted their resinous scent with every breath. I passed anthills that were waist high; at first glance they seemed to be merely heaps of rust-brown needles. Ferns were also plentiful, and mushrooms in astonishing variety. He recognized some as energizing for his magic and picked and ate them. Soldier's Boy recognized them from Lisana's memories. My reluctance to trust such a secondhand memory swayed him not at all from eating every last one of them. And when he had finished, the subtle humming of the magic in my blood rose. He walked on with a satisfied smile. He liked being able to take care of himself, I realized.

The first hare he saw escaped him because he had foolishly not thought to gather stones for ammunition before he set out. He sought out a stream, and again I felt him pilfering my memories to select stones of the right size and heft for the sling. I resented that. He had his own secrets that he kept from me. Why should I share the skills I'd worked so hard to perfect? I clenched my mind shut to him.

He paused a few moments by the stream to drink, and then to make several practice shots with the sling. He was not very good at first. He selected a tree trunk as his target. The first stone went wide, the second grazed the bark, and the third did not leave the sling at all but fell at his feet. I felt his frustration, and felt, too, the hunger that gnawed at him. He needed what I knew.

I gave in, reasoning that if he did not eat, my body would suffer. When he reached again for my memories, I actively offered to him what he needed to know, not just how to stand and when to release the stone, but also the "feel" of the sling itself. The next two stones he launched each hit the tree trunk with a solid and satisfying "thwack!" He grinned, replenished his ammunition, and stalked on, suddenly a predator in these woods.

He killed the next hare he saw with a single stone and lifted the limp carcass with satisfaction. It was a big one, and fat for winter. Satisfied, he headed back toward the cabin. They would have fresh meat tonight. It wouldn't be enough to sate him; he felt as if he could eat four more just like it. But it would calm the hunger enough to let him sleep. Tomorrow he would send the boy out to forage as well. Tomorrow, he promised his growling belly, would be a day of plenty. For tonight, the single fat rabbit would have to do. He hurried through the gathering gloom.

He smelled the smoke through the trees, and then saw flickering light through the cabin's window. Winter, with short days and long nights, was venturing closer with every day. He felt a lurch of fear as he considered how poorly equipped he was to face the turn of the seasons, but then gritted his teeth. He had four days. Four days to fatten himself, to find trade goods and trade them. He needed winter clothing and a steady supply of food from a loyal kin-clan. But he wouldn't get those things by going to the Trading Place looking like a skinny old beggar. "Power comes most easily to the man who appears powerful," he said aloud. I felt a lurch of dismay. Another of my father's teachings. Would all the harsh wisdom he had passed on to me in the hopes of making me a better officer now be turned against Gernia and my king? Traitor, I suddenly thought. Renegade.

I was suddenly glad I was dead to my world. I wished with deep passion that Epiny didn't know I was still alive, that no one did. I had the sudden sick conviction that all I'd ever learned was going to be used against my own people. Coward that I was, I did not want anyone to know that I was the one responsible. If I had had my own heart any longer, it would have felt heavy. As things stood, I had to endure Soldier's Boy's satisfaction as he strode up to the house.

A croaker bird abruptly appeared, probably drawn by the smell of the dead hare. Cawing loudly, he swooped in to settle on the main roof beam of the little house. He perched there, looking down on the scene with bright and greedy eyes.

Likari was crouched in front of the cabin by the small fire he'd kindled earlier. He looked miserable and alone, and at the sound of Soldier's Boy's approach, he looked up fearfully, the whites showing all around his eyes.

"What are you doing out here?" Soldier's Boy asked him severely.

Likari squirmed. "Waiting for you."

"Then it has nothing to do with being afraid of bad luck? With doubting what I told you was true?"

The small boy looked down at his bare feet as he crouched by the fire. Did Soldier's Boy feel pity for him? His tone was gentler as he asked, "Did you do all I asked? Is there water and firewood? Did you clean the hearth stones of moss and earth?"

"Yes, Great One. I did everything that you told me to do."

"Well. We are in luck. My hunting went well, and I have a nice hare for us to eat tonight. Do you know how to skin a hare and make it ready for the pot?"

The boy hesitated. "I've seen Firada do it. I could try."

"Another time, perhaps. I'll show you how it's done tonight." Privately he thought that he didn't want any of the meat wasted by a clumsy skinning job.

"We don't have a pot to cook it in."

"You're right. Perhaps. Come inside with me. Let's see what we do have."

Lisana's memories told him that she had had a stewing pot of fired clay. It had been a favorite of hers, glazed a creamy white on the inside and adorned with black frogs against a dark blue background on the outside. It had been just the right size for cooking. He went to the place where she had kept it. Beneath a rumpled carpet of thick moss, his seeking fingers found only fragments of fired pottery. He pulled one from beneath the moss and wiped it clean. Half of a leaping frog remained on the shard. Next to it, a greenish half-moon of badly corroded copper was all that remained of a once-gleaming pot.

It saddened him unreasonably. What had he expected? How many generations ago had Lisana lived here? It was irrational of him to hope that her possessions had endured. I was surprised to find that her cabin and its contents had survived at all. How could he be so disappointed that a fired pot had not lasted?

As he crouched outside alongside the boy and they gutted and skinned the hare for roasting, the answer came to me. He carried Lisana's memories and the grief he felt now over the destroyed pot was as much her grief as his. It had been a cherished possession, and somehow it had been important to her that it still existed. As if, I slowly reasoned, the survival of her possessions was the continuation of her life.

As the thought came to me, I could suddenly experience Soldier's Boy's emotions as he felt them. As if I were a traced overlay of a sketch, I came into synchronization with him. For a fractional moment, I was Soldier's Boy. If I had relaxed, I would have merged with him, would have dissolved like salt stirred in water. For one paralyzed moment, I felt lured by that. In the next instant, I leapt like a hooked fish and tore myself free of him. I retreated from him, heedless of fleeing into darkness. I sank myself deep, beyond his reach, beyond Lisana's memories. Or so I tried. I could not quite escape the sound of his voice.

He smiled slowly and spoke softly. "Eventually I will win."

"Win what?" Likari asked him.

"Everything," Soldier's Boy replied. "Everything."

CHAPTER TWELVE

TRADE GOODS

Unwillingly, I was drawn back to watch them. The boy ate one hindquarter of the hare and Soldier's Boy devoured the rest. He gnawed even the gristle off the ends of the bones, and the smaller bones he ground between his teeth and swallowed.

I felt almost like myself as he scraped the small hide and pegged it out to dry. He'd hunted, fed himself, and now had the simple chores of a man responsible for himself. Scraping the hide put me in mind of how I had done such tasks for Amzil, and how that simple life had once beckoned me. I suddenly missed them just as much as Soldier's Boy missed Lisana. I wondered if he could feel my emotions as I did his, if he could understand that I loved Amzil as he loved his tree woman.

Beside me, Likari watched me work on the hide in awe.

"I never saw a Great One do work before," he said innocently. "Jodoli does nothing for himself. He does not even pick a berry or wash his own body. Firada does it all. But you hunt and cook and scrape the skin."

Soldier's Boy smiled at the lad's amazement. "There are many things I can do. It is good for a man to know how to do things for himself."

"But you have magic in you. If you have magic, you don't have to do hard work. I wish I had magic."

"Magic can be hard work in itself, Likari. But work, even hard work, can give a man pleasure if he does it willingly and well."

That, I thought to myself, smacked of Sergeant Duril. I wondered if that old Gernian value was one that the Specks shared with us, or if Soldier's Boy was more Gernian than he knew.

The meat was gone but the smell of it lingered sweetly in the air. The fire burned well on the cleaned hearth, and the smoke found the smoke hole effortlessly. Likari had done his tasks well. Soldier's Boy mused on the hearthstones. Lisana had chosen them as much for their beauty as their imperviousness to heat. They were all the same deep green, smoothed by the valley's river and hardened by her ancient fires. Looking down at them, Soldier's Boy could pretend her lodge was as tidy and cozy as it had been when she was alive.

He looked at the Speck boy staring so intently into the flames. Likari crouched close to the comfort of the fire, obviously still uneasy at being inside the Great One's old lodge. The boy seemed to feel his gaze. He glanced up fearfully and looked back at the fire. Soldier's Boy frowned, and then looked around the room, trying to see it as the boy might. The pale roots that hung down or roped over the walls reminded him of the hare's bared entrails. Or perhaps of dangling snakes. The interior of the lodge was damp and musty. Beetles and insects were much in evidence.

"Where will we sleep?" Likari asked.

Soldier's Boy glanced over his shoulder. For an instant, he saw with Lisana's eyes. There was a wooden bedstead, stoutly built to be a Great One's resting place. It was lush with furs, heaped with woolen trade blankets, a warm and comfortable retreat at day's end. Then he blinked and there was only a rumpled carpet of moss and ancient debris on the floor. Soldier's Boy stood up. An emotion rose in him, filling his chest and dimming his sight with tears.

Then he extended his hands toward the collapsed bed and dangling roots.

I had done magic: I thought I knew how it felt. But I had wielded the magic in much the same way that Soldier's Boy had used my sling, without skill or efficiency. I had flung magic ruthlessly, profligately. The way Soldier's Boy used it reminded me of my mother's deft hands when she embroidered; stitch, stitch, stitch, stitch, stitch, and a green leaf appeared on a linen handkerchief. She never wasted a moment or an inch of floss. Soldier's Boy used the magic in that way, with precision and economy. He gave no general command. Instead, he gestured at first this rootlet and then that hummock of moss. The root stirred, squirmed, and then braided itself neatly with three other roots before twisting upward and tucking itself back into the decaying roof beams. The moss clump crept over a fragment of old wood, devoured it, and then joined itself to a fellow hummock of moss. Root after root, moss clump after moss clump followed the examples of the others. I recognized what he was doing. He was drawing on my knowledge of engineering and structure. The dangling mat of roots over the old bed became ropes that wove themselves through the roof beams, reinforcing them. The moss devoured what little remained of Lisana's old bed and bedding and fashioned itself into a plump green pallet.

Likari's hushed voice came from behind me. "I thought you were saving your magic."

Soldier's Boy gave his head a shake as if awakening. "I didn't use that much," he said, almost apologizing to himself.

"Will we sleep there?" the boy asked.

"Yes," Soldier's Boy said decisively. "Where's the blanket?"

"Outside." When Soldier's Boy turned to look at him, the boy was staring stubbornly at his feet.

"What is it?"

"I don't want to sleep in here," Likari admitted in a hoarse whisper.

"But I do," Soldier's Boy said firmly. "So we shall. Bring my blanket here."

"Yes, Great One," he replied in a subdued voice. He went outside.

Soldier's Boy gave a great sigh, perhaps of resignation. Then he walked slowly around the inside of the lodge, studying the walls and ceiling and the framing of the windows. The rolled-hide window covers that had once existed to be pegged in place against winter's chill were long gone. I wondered why he was bothering about window coverings when there was an obvious bulge in one of the walls. Would this lodge stand for another winter? I felt he pushed the question at me. I tried to ignore him, but the engineer in me could not stand the unstable wall. I focused on it until he shared my impression of it. He nodded gravely, perhaps to me, and then with studied flicks of his fingers, he reinforced it with roots. The logs were too soft to be pulled back into alignment, but he could stabilize them. Dangling roots wove themselves into networks and attached themselves to the ceiling and the walls. The limber webbing strengthened the existing structure. By the time Likari returned with my old blanket, the ceiling of Lisana's lodge was reinforced and tidied. Likari glanced about in surprise, then smiled gratefully at the change. The light from the hearth fire now lit the room evenly. I had not realized how intimidating the fingery shadows of the roots had been until they were gone.

Soldier's Boy took the old blanket from Likari and shook it vigorously. The wind of its passage fanned the fire and dust hung thick in the air afterward. Soldier's Boy regarded it sternly. "Tomorrow," he announced, "you will wash the blanket and hang it near the fire to dry. For tonight, shall we sleep on it or under it?"

"Under it," the boy replied decisively. Then he added carefully, "At least, you will. It is not a very large blanket. I wish there were more."

"We will get more when we go to trade. Lisana used to have many thick rugs and colorful blankets." Soldier's Boy spoke the words as if they were a spell. I suddenly knew that he said them out loud simply because he missed her so badly. Talking about her made her seem more present, even if his only audience was a small, sleepy boy.

He spread the blanket on the bed of moss. Then he moved slowly around the room, carefully recalling it as it once had been. Likari remained by the hearth fire, sucking on a bone and regarding him curiously.

Moss and mildew covered the cedar chest that he tried to drag closer to the firelight. It fell into splintered fragments when he tried to open it. He pushed aside the white webbed remnants of the lid. Insects had long ago loosened the lush fur from the hides. Even the leather was holed and green. Woven woolen blankets had been devoured by moths into threads and rags, the bright colors lost to decay. Their hearts had rotted into a solid, smelly mass. With a grunt of disgust, he dropped the corner he had tried to lift and wiped his hands on the floor.

"You can go to sleep if you want to," he told the watching boy. Likari was happy to scurry to the moss bed and crawl under the blanket. But he didn't go to sleep. He regarded me with bright, curious eyes as Soldier's Boy prowled the room, unearthing more remnants of Lisana's possessions.

A heavy copper bowl had gone green and black with verdigris; the pattern hammered into it had been lost forever. The few wooden artifacts that had not vanished were riddled with wormholes or spongy with age. The more decayed bits of Lisana's life that he uncovered, the more sad and rotten the derelict lodge seemed. He could not pretend she had been here just yesterday. Decades, if not generations, had passed.

Resignation and sorrow rose in him like a tide; I could not tell how much of the emotion was his and how much belonged to Lisana's shade. He put more wood on the fire. In that circle of light, he set out the few possessions he had salvaged as if he were arranging a memorial to her. Two glass bowls. The soapstone lamp. A tiny jade spoon for cosmetics. He put them in a row. It reminded me horribly of how we had set out the plague bodies to await burial.

And all the while, he kept glancing back toward Likari as if waiting for something. Gradually the boy's eyes sagged shut. Slowly his breathing deepened and steadied. Soldier's Boy unearthed an ivory comb. He took it back to the fire's light and spent a ridiculous amount of time cleaning it. When he was finished, he looked again at the lad.

"Likari?" he asked softly.

The boy didn't stir. Satisfied that he was well and truly asleep, Soldier's Boy gave a small sigh. He took a brand from the fire and went quietly to the far end of the lodge.

I thought at first that he was reliving Lisana's secretiveness as he slowly walked his fingers along the moss and root tendrils that coated the log wall. The pegs that had secured the hollow piece had long ago rotted away. The roots that had penetrated it held the concealed lid shut more securely than the pegs ever had. He pulled and tugged them away carefully, but the lid still came to pieces as he opened the hiding place. I knew then it was not secrecy but reverence that had made him wait for privacy.

This had been Lisana's secret. He lifted away the broken pieces of wood and revealed a hollowed space. Within it rested all that remained of her most treasured possessions. Here she had concealed her secret indulgences, the ornaments and jewelry that would have been appropriate to a woman of her people but not necessary to a Great One. They were, I realized, the trappings of her banished dream. For Lisana, it was not a cavalla saber or a set of spurs or a soldier-son journal. Soldier's Boy drew from the niche a dozen heavy silver wrist bangles, gone black with tarnish, and then four wide torcs, three of silver and one of beaten gold. There were striated ivory bracelets made from some creature's tusks and large hair ornaments of jade, hematite, and a blue stone that I didn't know. The seams of the leather pouches beneath them had given way. He had to lift them carefully, cupping them to keep the contents from spilling out. These he carried one by one to the fire's light. Woven gut strands were weakened or gone, but the polished beads remained, ivory, amber, jade, and pearl. Trip after trip he made from the cache to the hearth, setting out a king's ransom of jewelry and carved ornaments. Layer after hoarded layer he took from the wall. I caught glimpses of Lisana's memories of them. There were small trinkets, a bone fish and a jade leaf, that had been gifts from her father when she was a little girl. Some of the others were ornaments she had acquired by trading when she was a young woman seeking to draw a certain young man's eyes to her. But most of it was the loot she had effortlessly gained as a Great One, gifts and offerings and treasures from a grateful kin-clan.

When he had emptied her hiding place, he sat for a long time by the fire, wistfully sorting through the trove. Long he held in his hand a fist-sized ivory carving of a fat dimpled baby. It came to me that it was a fertility charm, and that Lisana had made efforts not to be so alone in her life. Those efforts had availed her nothing. Great Ones, I suddenly knew, had few offspring, and all such were highly valued by the People. I saw Olikea's frequent bedding of me in a different light and felt both naive and foolish that I had ever thought she was attracted to me for myself. In my mind, I reviewed her dalliance with me. She had never deceived me. I had supplied the context for our sex, to make myself believe her interest in me was as romantic as it was carnal. It hadn't been then and it wasn't now. She had expected me to wield power she would share. And she had hoped to be the mother of a rare and valued asset to her kin-clan—the child of a Great One.

I felt a rush of shame and resentment. My deception of myself was my own fault, but it was easier to be angry with Olikea than to admit that to myself. I stoked my resentment with the idea that she had dared to think of my child as if it would be a valuable piece of livestock. I resolved to have nothing more to do with her.

Then I realized it was no longer my decision to make. I opened myself to Soldier's Boy's thoughts, and found that he was giving no consideration to Olikea at all. He accepted all she had done, all she had offered me, all she had hoped to profit as natural and normal. Of course she would want a Great One's child. Producing such a baby would have benefited both of them in terms of the regard of their kin-clan. Of course Olikea would have fed and pampered and bedded me. It was what a Great One's feeders did.

Even Lisana's feeders?

No. She'd had no long-term feeders. She hadn't wanted that sort of relationship.

And later, when she had tried for a child?

His thoughts darted away from my touch like a fish darting away from a flung stone. Ah. That question stung, did it? Interesting.

He sat by the fire, looking at Lisana's impressive collection. I could feel both Lisana's sentiment about it and Soldier's Boy's more pragmatic evaluation of what rested there. Before him, if he could find the will to use it, lay the instrument of his rise to power. There was wealth enough there to command instant respect from the People, whether he wore it, traded it, or distributed it as largesse. Here was the foundation of his plan, if he dared to seize it and use it as his own.

But that, of course, was the sticking point. It was not his. It had been Lisana's; it was Lisana's still, in his mind, as she lived in his heart. Just looking at it made him feel closer to her. She had treasured these things; it seemed heartless and mercenary of him to raid her cache and then think only of what her treasures could buy for him.

I felt him yearn toward her. He picked up a large jade pendant in the shape of a lily leaf and held the cool stone against his cheek. Slowly it warmed, just as it had warmed against her breast when she had worn it. He opened his heart and reached wildly toward her, but it was a hopeless reaching. Ever since I had defeated him in that other world, ever since his topknot had been torn free of his skull, he had not been able to see or hear or touch Lisana. I had taken his anchor in that world and now it belonged to me. He had glimpsed her in the times I had contacted her, but only through the filter of my awareness. That was not what he longed for. He wanted to live alongside her in that other world as he had when he was her apprentice—her apprentice and eventually her lover.

His mind turned rawly to those memories. He had come into awareness of his own existence slowly, like an opening blossom. Just as I had grown and learned under Sergeant Duril's tutelage in those years, so he had learned from his mentor. She was the guardian of the path that led to the spirit world. She stood the watch and kept away those who did not belong. It was tedious work and she could never completely relax her vigilance. There was always a part of her that remained on her sentry duty even at their most tender moments. It had been his first lesson in how demanding the magic could be; it took from a Great One whatever it and the People needed. A Great One might have magic, but it was not without cost.

Grief and weariness suddenly washed over him in a double wave. The nagging hunger that was his constant companion gave up and was still. His body wanted only rest. He walked ponderously to the moss bed, in the heavy stride of a man accustomed to his bulk. At the side of the bed, he lifted briefly the slack folds of his belly flesh.

"You wasted my wealth, Nevare." It felt peculiar to have him address me so deliberately. "Now must I disperse Lisana's treasure to try to regain my standing. You are so Gernian in your arrogance and wastefulness. But now you must live within me, and I shall teach you how a Great Man of the People conducts himself."

He groaned softly as he lowered himself down to the bed. The night was growing cooler, and the wind pushed damp air in the windows and door. As Likari had observed, the blanket was not large enough to cover both of them. He curled himself around the sleeping boy, lifting the edge of the blanket to take small shelter beneath it. He sighed and then trickled out magic. The moss stirred softly and then grew around him and the boy, cupping them and then creeping around their bodies as if he were a fallen log. Slowly his body warmed them. He slipped into a deep sleep.

I did not.

I held myself, small and silent in a dark corner of his mind. I waited. I had not liked it that he addressed me by name. I knew we were both more aware of the other than we ever had been, and slowly we were becoming more accessible to each other. I felt exposed. I waited for his mind to dim into sleep. I thought he might dream, but he did not. Perhaps he was too weary.

I let the night deepen to full dark before I dared stir. Then, almost as if I had my own body, I stretched my being. Gently I peeled my awareness away from his and wondered if he would awaken to that loss.

He slept on.

Dream-walking was still a new skill to me. When I ventured out in search of Epiny, it was like riffling the pages in not just a thick book but in all the books in some grand library. I did not feel that I moved geographically but through some other nameless spatial layer. I had to focus not only on where Epiny might be but also on how her dream had felt to me the last time we had touched. I finally discovered an anchor in her silly silver whistle. I thought of it, how it shone, the otter's shape, and finally its shrill annoying blast. As Scout Buel Hitch had once described it, so it was. As if I walked into another room, I entered Epiny's dream.

Perhaps she would have called it a nightmare. We were in a small curtained alcove just off a grand ballroom. I could hear the music and catch glimpses of the lovely dresses and gaily slippered feet of the dancers and their finely attired partners as they whirled past a crack in the curtains. I could smell hundreds of fine beeswax tapers burning as well as catch the aroma of rich roast meat, freshly baked bread, and the waft of fine wine. Through the music, I could hear the tinkle of silverware and glasses and cheery laughter as the richly dressed aristocrats dined. All were enjoying the jovial festivities.

But in her dream, Epiny was a tiring maid. Pregnant and heavy in a worn gray dress, she was hastily pinning up hair disheveled by a lively dance or mending a slipper whose tie had been torn, or primping a bit more powder onto a haughty young girl's graceful neck. Her dream, I quickly saw, was all about waiting and working in the dim shadows while others danced and laughed and enjoyed themselves in the splendor of Old Thares. She was weary. Her back ached and her feet were swollen but no one seemed to care for the discomfort of her advanced pregnancy. The merry dance went on without her.

"Do you wish that you could go home?" I asked her softly.

"Home?" She smiled bitterly. "This isn't home, Nevare. Do you wish you could go back to your old dreams?"

She gestured at me, and I looked down at myself. I was slim and dapper in my green cavalla cadet uniform with the gleaming brass buttons. My black boots shone with a high gloss. I looked as if I had come as a guest to dance at her dream ball. I felt oddly embarrassed.

Epiny's spirit was strong and her mind quick. As soon as she realized that we were in a dream together, she took control of it. The music softened and the chattering women in the alcove vanished. Only Epiny and I remained. She sat down gratefully on a hassock that hadn't been there a moment ago. "So," she said into the quiet, "you've come to let me know you're alive and well. When will you come home?"

"I am alive. And well, in a way. But I don't think I'll be coming home anytime soon, if ever. Soldier's Boy still has control of my body. He has made me a Speck, complete with dapples. And we are staying in Lisana's old lodge. He has unearthed a cache of her jewelry. He has a plan to make himself a powerful man among the Specks. After that, I don't know exactly what he intends, but I know he still thinks all Gernians should be driven far from the Barrier Mountains. There is little I can do about whatever he plans. I have to keep my guard up just to retain my own awareness. I am still Nevare, and I don't want to let go of that self. But I'm not sure how long I can hold out against him."

It was strange. I hadn't planned to say those things to her, or realized how worried I was that Soldier's Boy would absorb me. "Is that why you've come to me? To ask my help?" She almost sounded hopeful.

I was startled. "Do you know a way to help me?"

The brightness of her face dimmed. "No. But I was hoping you were going to ask something that would make me feel useful. Something that would make a difference." She looked up at me. "Why else would you come to me in my dreams like this?"

Why had I come? I spoke honestly, wondering if it would be my last chance to speak to her. "I came for comfort, I think. To find someone who cared about Nevare."

The light not only came back to her face; it warmed and gentled her features. "Nevare, I thank you for coming, then. I am that. I do care about you, and if you take comfort in hearing me say it, then I am comforted that I can say it." She looked, for a moment, as young as she had been in Old Thares. I realized then how much her harsh life at the frontier outpost was aging her. Her features were sharper, her skin more weathered. She had never been a fleshy person, but now it seemed that the resources of her body had dwindled away from her arms and legs and face and into her burgeoning pregnancy. Compared to the women of the Specks, she was a stick figure. In a Speck gathering, she would have been pitied and Spink disdained for his failure to keep the woman he had impregnated plump and gleaming through her pregnancy.

"You are so thin," I said without thinking.

She laughed and placed her hands on her rounded belly. "Thin?"

"That is the baby. I am speaking of you, Epiny. Your fingers are like little twigs."

Concern flitted through her eyes. "My stomach is still un-settled by my pregnancy. Everyone has told me, over and over, that my morning sickness will soon be over. But it just goes on." She shook her head at me. "But I am tired to death of talking about myself. Whenever I see another woman, it seems all she wants to do is advise me or commiserate with me."

"Even Amzil?" I asked her, smiling.

She did not smile in return. "I am concerned for Amzil," she said softly.

"Is she sick?"

"Would that it were something as simple as that! She is bitter beyond telling, Nevare. She had a glimpse of a dream, and then it was gone before she could put her hands on it. And she blames ev-eryone and everything for her unhappiness: the town, the cavalla, the soldiers on the street, the officers and their wives, the towns-men. I think she even blames Spink and me to some degree."

"With time, it will pass," I said, with no confidence I spoke truth. There had been time, but each time I thought of the life I would never share with her, the pain was still as sharp. It had not passed for me.

"I wonder if she will allow it to pass? She seems to treasure her pain. She swings from holding her children and weeping over them, saying they are the only love she will ever know, to snapping at them impatiently or to simply staring past them, her needle-work neglected in her lap." She halted the tumbling flow of her words and then said hastily, "I do not mean to speak against her or to gossip. There are times, of course, when she is just Amzil, and she works very hard to keep the house tidy and the meals prepared. But I fear for her."

"Fear for her? Why?"

"Oh. It is the same thing I told you about before. Whenever she sees one of the men who . . . who accosted her that night, or who looked on and did nothing, she will not look aside, but stares at them as if her eyes could burn holes in them. Or she asks them, with acid courtesy, how they are doing that morning and bids them 'good day' in a tone that plainly says she hopes they have anything but a good day. Some of them are cowed by such behavior. But there are a few who regard her with hatred that she knows their shame and fears them not. They cannot clearly recall what happened that night. Neither can Amzil nor Spink. There is a gray time in their minds, and I know that Amzil and Spink are tormented by what might have happened in those moments. Spink would like to think he behaved honorably and with courage. But he simply cannot remember. Amzil would like to think that she fought off her attackers, but she has nightmares in which she goes limp with terror and cannot even cry out and the men do foul things to her before you can intervene. I cannot think what those men imagine to fill in those missing hours. It eats at them like a canker, I think. Amzil has led them to believe that she does recall what happened, and she flaunts that in front of them and treats them with fearless disdain."

"One of them will kill her," I said dully. "Simply to put an end to that reminder. Simply to be sure that no witness remains."

"So I fear," Epiny said and sighed.

"Every time I have tried to use the magic to my own good, it has cut me. Cut me and burned those I hold most dear."

"I fear that is true."

"And I fear that there is only worse to come, Epiny. The Specks' anger against the Gernians grows. The young men, I am told, are restless and want to do worse than the magic already does."

She gave a small, bitter laugh. "What worse could there be?"

"I don't know. And that is what I fear. Soldier's Boy has access to my memories. I fear he will turn what I know against Gettys.

Epiny, there must be some way to resolve this. Some way to make the Gernians leave our lands and stop cutting our ancestor trees."

For a moment, Epiny just looked at me silently. Then she cocked her head, leaned closer to me, and said, "Nevare?" in a cautious voice.

"What?"

She reached across to me and set her hand on mine. "You are Nevare?"

"Of course I am. Why? What?"

"You said 'our lands' and 'our ancestor trees' as if you were a Speck."

I sighed. "Did I? I share Soldier's Boy's thoughts so much. And sometimes, what he thinks makes a lot of sense to me. It's not comfortable to see both sides so clearly, Epiny. I can never retreat to feeling right or justified about anything. The Gernians are wrong to cut the trees without taking the Specks' beliefs into consideration. The Specks are wrong to sow disease and deluge the Gernians with misery."

"But we committed the first wrong. We came into their land and took it from them."

"They took it from the Kidona."

"What?"

"They took those lands from the Kidona. Took the lands and forced a settled folk to become nomads. And then did all they could to destroy the magic of the Kidona and deny them access to the spirit world."

"What?"

I shook my head. "It's that—no matter how far you go back, someone took the land from someone else. I don't think anything can be solved by trying to work out who stole it first. The solution is in the future, Epiny, not the past."

I'm not sure that she even heard me. "There must be a way to make us stop cutting the trees. There has to be someone who can stop the road. Someone who would listen to what you've learned, to what we know now. Someone who would believe us and have the power to act on it."

I shook my head. "It will never be that simple, Epiny. We're talking about the movement of people here. You can't just say 'stop' to progress."

"The Queen could." A strange light had come into her eyes. "Why did I never think of it before? The Queen is fascinated with all things mystical and magical. Before I 'ruined' myself, I was a guest at her séances; it was probably due to her séances that I became so vulnerable to magic. If I wrote to her, reminding her of who I was, if I told her what we've discovered about the Specks and the trees . . ."

I snorted. "That silly woman, with her superstitions and mystic circles and séances? No one takes her seriously."

Epiny laughed, and it was a hearty laugh. "Oh, Nevare, listen to yourself! You are caught up in a web of magic, and yet still disdain the Queen for believing in it!"

I had to laugh with her. "My father left a deep imprint on me. Even when I know he taught me incorrectly, I still have all those old reflexes. Even so, my comment stands, Epiny. You and I may know that her studies are not foolishness. But enlisting her as our ally wouldn't work. She's powerful, but most of her nobles still regard her fascination with mysticism as, well, a foolish quirk. No one would believe what you wrote to her. And we have no proof, short of bringing her out here and letting her break a proper Gettys Sweat."

That brought a muted laugh from Epiny, but the thoughtfulness didn't leave her face. "I could send her your soldier-son journal. That would convince her. And where she took it from there would be—"

"No!" I was adamant. "Epiny, in the good god's name, don't make what has befallen me any worse. You'd ruin the Burvelle name with that book. I was far too frank, much too honest. I wish I'd never kept that journal."

"It's safe with me," she said quietly. "You can trust that I won't do anything dangerous with it. Don't you think I know what it would do to the Burvelle name? After all, once that was my name, too." She was silent for a time and then asked, "Would you want me to send it to my father, to keep it under lock and key? He would, if I asked him to."

"And never read it?"

She hesitated. "I would ask him not to. But it would be very hard for him. He'd want to know why I had it and how I'd come by it, and all sorts of things that I'd have a hard time explaining. But, yes, I think he'd be honorable about leaving it unread, if that was what I stipulated. It's a book that should be preserved. And it would be safer in the Burvelle library than in the back of my cupboard."

I scarcely heard her words. My mind was busy with another thought. "What have you told your father about me?"

She bit her lower lip. "Nothing. And that pains me, Nevare, but there it is. I cannot think what I could tell him. Or your sister, or your father. Or your poor old sergeant teacher. And so I've kept silent, and now that winter is closing in, no one will expect to hear anything from us until spring. I pity your little sister, left in an agony of waiting and wondering. But I just couldn't think what to write to her. Do you think that is awfully wicked of me?"

"No worse than what I've done." I felt something, a tugging, a weakening in me. I felt a peculiar recognition. Soldier's Boy slept restlessly. He might even now be waking up.

"You're fading," she said mournfully. "Come to me again tomorrow night, Nevare. We must be able to find some solution to this. You cannot simply vanish into him!"

"I don't know if I can come again."

But before I had even finished my words, I was gone from her dream. I felt the pull of Soldier's Boy's awareness stirring. With every passing day, we became linked more tightly. Now it seemed that when he was wakeful, there was not enough left of my awareness for me to dream-walk. For a moment, I felt my dream superimposed on his. "Lisana," he groaned, but he dreamed only. Not even in his dreams could he reach her.

He shifted in the moss bed. The only part of him that felt warm was where Likari slept against him. In his sleep, Soldier's Boy scowled and then used a bit of magic. It warmed both of

them, settling over them like a good bear rug. He sank into sleep.
I waited then, waited until his breathing was once more deep and
steady. I was tempting my luck and I knew it, trying to slip away
from him twice in one night. But my concern for Amzil was such
that I felt I had to risk it. This time, when I tugged at his magic,
pulling free what I needed, he stirred slightly and scowled. I dared
take only a little. Now or never, I challenged myself, and fled with
it, arrowing straight to Amzil. Finding her was effortless; I had
only to think of the sole kiss we had ever shared, and I was with
her, holding her, tasting her mouth, smelling her skin. I found her,
and for one wildly joyous instant, I broke into her dream. "Amzil!"
I cried and reached to pull her into my eager embrace.

"No!" she shrieked. She sat up in her bed and I felt her fight
wildly to break from her sleep. "No more dreams of you. You're
gone, and I'm here, and I have to live with that. No more foolish dreams. No more foolish dreams." She sobbed on those final
words, and then leaned her head on her arms. She sat in her bed
and wept. I hovered near her, but found a wall so tight and so
strong that I sensed she had been building it for a long time.

"Amzil, please. Please let me into your dreams," I begged her.
But even as I spoke, I felt the magic dwindle away. My vision of
her faded. Suddenly I was back in my body, trapped like a fly in
an overturned glass, alone with the rest of the night to ponder
my fate.

CHAPTER THIRTEEN

HOARDING

Soldier's Boy arose the next morning before Likari did. He brimmed with sudden purpose, as if the night's sleep had infused him with life and meaning. Moving quietly, he went to an unused corner of the lodge where a bench had once stood. The moss had eaten it. He peeled back a thick layer of it to bare the splintery fragments of the old bench. Then, making many trips, he transferred Lisana's treasure to this new hiding place. When he was finished, he rolled the moss layer over it again. Only keen eyes looking for such a hidden cache would have noticed it.

He left the lodge and walked down a short slope to where he had remembered a stream. It was still there, but it had changed. Once it had run swift and clear. Now it meandered widely over an area thick with reeds and ferns. With his hands he scooped a deeper place, let the silt swirl and clear, and then cupped handfuls of water to drink and then rub over his face. He shook his hands clear of the cold, shining drops and then turned and looked up the rise to Lisana's lodge. For a time, he was silent. Then he spoke aloud.

"There is a lot to do in a very little time. Winter approaches. I will need a stout door, window coverings, a firewood supply, oil for her lamp, bedding, clothing for myself, and a store of food. Yet the key to all those things, Nevare, is not the hard work that you immediately think about. No. The key to those things is that I must eat and grow as fat as I can, and I have only a few days in which to do it. And only one small boy to help me provide for myself. We're going to winter here rather than at the kin-clan's village. That will not please Olikea, I think, but I do not care. She thinks only to use me as her key to power and status in her kin-clan. Her ambition is too small. I will not be the Great One of her kin-clan. I will be the Great One of the People, the Great One of all the Great Ones. But before I confront Kinrove, I must look like a man full of power and capable of wielding it."

I do not know which was more startling, to have him address me so plainly or to have him make me a party to his plans. Did he think I would help him? Or did he think me incapable of opposing him? Either way, I might well prove him wrong. But for now, he exuded an air of well-being that was at odds with the burning hunger that seethed through him. He drew in a deep breath.

"Likari! Awaken. I have chores for you!"

It took a moment or two before the small boy stood in the doorway. He looked around for Soldier's Boy, rubbing his eyes sleepily.

"Two tasks for the day. Gather enough wood for three nights. No, four. When we come back, we will not want to have to do that task before we sleep. And when that is done, find food. Any and every sort of thing that you can gather that a man can eat. Fish, meat, roots, berries, greens, nuts, fruit of any kind. If you see it and you know it can be eaten, gather it and bring it back to the lodge."

"Yes, Great One." The boy managed to utter the words before he was ambushed by an enormous yawn. He knuckled his eyes again and then without another murmur went off down the faded path in a purposeful trot.

Where there is water there is almost always food. It may not be food of a sort that one regards with relish, but it can be eaten.

Soldier's Boy ate it. He found a grass with a fat, oniony bulb on the end and pulled and ate them by the dozen. I was heartily sick of the flavor before he was; or perhaps he no longer cared what anything tasted like. He was bent on quantity, not quality, in his consumption. He moved upstream and found ragged and yellowing water lily leaves decaying on top of a small pond. Snails clung to them. He popped them loose of the vegetation and ate them, crunching down shells and all. I would have felt nauseated if the stomach were my property, but my squeamishness meant nothing to him.

Uphill of the stream a tangle of wild roses in a dappled patch of sunlight were heavy with yellow and red rosehips. These at least were tangy and sweet. Some were as big as the end of my thumb, with a thick layer of soft flesh over the packet of somewhat fuzzy seeds in the middle. I would have eaten only the flesh, but he put them into his mouth by the handful and ground up seeds, pulp, and all before he swallowed. When the patch had been stripped of fruit, he moved on.

So the morning passed. He knew the foods of the forest and moved like a grazing animal. By midmorning, I found myself wondering why man had ever stopped being a forager and hunter and become a farmer. Without any previous investment of toil, there was abundance here. Only when he had wearied of fruit, roots, and vegetation did he return to the stream bank. He drank heavily of the cold, fresh water, and then judiciously gathered a handful of likely stones.

For the next two hours, he employed the sling. He brought down a squirrel, and then two rabbits. He also found a bee tree, the inhabitants moving more slowly in the cool weather, yet still quick to buzz and swarm when he deliberately thudded a stone against the hollow trunk. Mentally he marked its location, and I knew he would return after a few freezes had subdued the swarm for him.

The squirrel and rabbit carcasses he carried in his hands hampered any further hunting or gathering, so he returned to the lodge. Before he settled down to gut and skin them, he saw ample evidence that Likari had been busy. There was a clumsily woven but effective bag made from vine. The boy had lined it with big leaves and used it to bring home a trove of gleaming-shelled nuts, superficially similar to the chestnuts I had enjoyed at the carnival in Old Thares. Four fish hung from a piece of hooked willow threaded through their gills. He had also gathered wild parsnip and garlic and a tuber that was yellow inside when I snapped one in half. I immediately envisioned a savory stew, and shared Soldier's Boy's regret that we had no suitable cooking pot.

He skinned the rabbits and squirrels, pegged out the hides, and inspected the hare skin from the day before. He took it from its pegs, kneaded it between his hands to take some of the stiffness from it and then staked it out again. As he stretched the hide he realized he was lucky that no scavengers had come to carry it off in the night. Would he be so lucky again?

He hung the fish and the fresh meat higher in the crook of a tree, and then urinated at the base of it, a clear sign to any other forest residents that he was claiming ownership of the area. He fed the hearth fire a few sticks of wood to keep the coals alive. Feeding a fire was much easier than starting one again. Then he returned to his foraging.

He filled his belly that afternoon, but did not stop eating. Everything that was edible, he ate. Mushrooms in a clump grow-ing in the shade, and then young fat bracket fungi that grew like shelves on the stumps of dying trees he ate. He found fallen cones and sat on the ground amid the prickly things to shake out the plump seeds and eat them. He ate them, and continued to eat, past sufficiency to repleteness and on. The man stuffed himself and took satisfaction in the distending of his belly.

Thrice, he found foods that he knew would amplify his magic. The first was a sort of giant celery. It stung and then numbed his mouth as he ate it, but that did not deter him. Usually, a Great One ate this mixed in with other foods to mask its bitterness, but he had no time for such niceties now. He ate until his gorge rose in protest at the bitterness, and then moved on, but made a note to remember where it grew. Later, he would return to harvest the fat white roots.

He pulled down from a tree trunk a half-dead vine that had climbed up it to reach the sun's light. The vine was stiff, the leaves gone brown and curling, but seed heads remained where the flowers had once been. Those were his prize. He ate them, cracking the seeds between his teeth and spitting out the shells. Their flavor was rich and brown and sweet. Colors seemed brighter after he had consumed them and the scents of the forest stronger. Indeed, he followed his nose to his next treasure, a windfall of ripened fruit. The tree had shed most of it. It was dark purple with a stone like a plum, but a flavor that was very different. Those on the ground were half fermented. Wasps, bees, and a few late butterflies clustered on the ones that had split open. A few fruit had landed well and were sound if withered at the stem end. These Soldier's Boy ate with delight, and then he shook the tree to bring down a hail of fresh ones. When he had eaten as many as he could stomach at that time, he gathered an armful more and carried them home cradled against him.

He walked slowly back to the lodge as the sun crept down the sky. The sun would set to the west, behind the mountains. He knew that once the peaks had devoured the orb, night would sweep in like a curtain falling. Yet he did not hurry. He hoarded the food inside him and the magic it nourished. He felt full and almost sleepy. He decided that when he reached the lodge, he would nap, then rise, cook all the meat and fish, and feast again.

The boy was already there. He had more fish with him, not strung on a stick, but an armful of them. They weren't gleaming, speckled trout such as he'd left that morning. These fish—five big ones—were so heavy that his back bent back and his stomach jutted with the strain of holding them. They were not as pretty as trout. Their skins were tattered, their blunt noses buffeted. Teeth showed in their long snouts. "They come each year," he told me. "Waves of them, coming up the river, fighting their way against the water. And then they get tired, and they go in the shallows. They are very easy to catch there. Many of them die and rot on the banks of the river. Gulls and eagles come to get them. These ones had come far upstream, into the shade of the forest. I got them easily. There were many more. Shall I bring more tomorrow?"

"I think we shall both go tomorrow," Soldier's Boy told him happily. It was all coming back to him, along with Lisana's

anticipation and keen pleasure in this season. The season of the
fish runs was a time of plentiful food for everyone. There would
be fish to bake in the fire, fish for soup, and lots of fish to smoke
in strips for winter food. Fish to dry and grind into fish meal that
could be stored in pots and would last until spring. He felt a surge
of the purest, childlike contentment in the world, a feeling that
had eluded me so long that I almost didn't recognize it.

"Tonight, we feast!" he told the boy. "And tomorrow, we fish,
and we feast again!"

"This is a very good time," the boy replied. He stuck out his
little belly. "I shall grow fat as a waddling bear."

Soldier's Boy ran a critical eye over the child. He was thin
right now, unacceptably thin for the feeder of a Great One. "Yes,
you shall! I want you to eat well, and oil your hair and skin with
the fat from our catches. I want you to show everyone at the Trading Place that we are prosperous and cherished by the magic."

Likari grinned. "I think I can manage that."

"Good!" Soldier's Boy's enthusiasm was genuine. "Build up
the fire and prepare the coals for cooking. Tonight, we feast!"

While the boy did that, he planned to rest. But as he turned
to enter the lodge, an unexpected guest arrived. He came down
through the tree cover in a clattering of black and white feathers. The croaker bird landed heavily on the ground and waddled
toward them, both cautious and curious.

The boy paid no attention to the scavenger bird, merely
giving the creature a glance, and then went back to loading up
his arms with firewood. Such birds were common visitors to
any camp or village. They preferred dead meat, and the longer
it had been dead, the more they relished it. But they would eat
almost anything that humans did not. For one to arrive at the
lodge, attracted by the smell of the rabbits or fish, was scarcely
surprising.

But Soldier's Boy stared at it with a mixture of resentment and
hostility. When the bird's gaze met his, I felt a shiver go through
him. Something more than a carrion bird looked at him out of
those eyes. "Go away," Soldier's Boy said in a low voice. "You have
no call upon me. I owe you nothing."

Can a bird smile? This one bobbed his head, reminding me of a man convulsed with laughter. He opened his beak wide. Perhaps he just tasted the air, but perhaps he mocked Soldier's Boy. The bright red interior of his mouth flashed like a beacon.

"Nothing, Nevare? You owe me a death. Or a life. However you prefer to see it." He lifted a clawed foot and swiped at his beak. "Which do you think is the better offering to a god you have offended? A death? Or a life?"

Orandula's voice, deep and rich with an undercurrent of mockery, rang clear inside my head. I heard it. I knew that Soldier's Boy heard it, too. This, at least, was a dread we shared. Fear drove his defiance more than courage.

"I don't serve you. You are not my god. And I owe you nothing."

The bird hopped closer, just two hops, in that effortless way of moving that only birds can do. He cocked his head and regarded me closely. "An amusing concept, that. The idea that men can choose which gods have power over them. Do you think that if you choose not to believe in me, I have no power over you? Do you think you can choose to have debts or not to have them?"

Soldier's Boy strode suddenly forward. He picked up one of Likari's fish and held it out to the bird. "Here. This is dead, and it's much bigger than the bird that was freed from your sacrifice. Take it and be gone." He flung it disdainfully at the god-bird's feet. The croaker bird fluffed his feathers and hopped back from the dead thing. Soldier's Boy stood, his body stiff with fear and anger. The bird looked at the dead fish. Hop, hop. Turned his head to point an eye down at it. Then darted his beak down to rip a shred of it free.

"Fresh. But still good. I'll take it. But you know, it does not discharge your debt. This is not a death or a life. It's only a fish. And you have not yet answered my question." He stabbed his beak down again, tore off another scrap of flesh and, with a quick jerk-toss of his head, caught it in his mouth and swallowed it. "Which would you rather owe me, little Great Man? A life or a death?"

"I owe you nothing!" Soldier's Boy repeated angrily. "I took nothing from you."

"You were there. The bird was released from me."

"That wasn't me!" Soldier's Boy exploded. I do not think he was even aware of how Likari was regarding him. At the edge of Soldier's Boy's field of vision, the boy crouched in the door and regarded him with wide eyes as the Great Man continued his debate with a carrion bird. The boy stepped back inside the door, as if frightened.

The bird didn't even seem to be looking at Soldier's Boy as he bent his head and busily tore another strip of flesh from the fish. He'd bared the gut sack. He plunged his beak in and probed busily before coming up with a dark string of gut. He snapped it up with relish. "Not you, eh? Then who, Great Man? Who freed the sacrifice?"

"Nevare did it! Nevare Burvelle."

The bird opened his beak, and squawked a wild laughter from his wide red mouth. His wings stuck out to the side and he bounced as he squawked. Perhaps, to someone else, it would have sounded only like a croaker bird croaking. When he finally finished, he stabbed and tore another piece of fish free. Then he looked at Soldier's Boy with one bright eye and asked, "Aren't you Nevare Burvelle?"

"No."

The bird cocked his head the other way.

"Nevare. Speak up for yourself. Don't you owe me a sacrifice, to replace the one you took?"

Miraculously and suddenly, the body and the voice were mine. Shock tingled all through my skin. I swallowed and drew a deep, freeing breath.

"Answer me, Nevare," the bird-god commanded.

"I serve the good god. Not you. And I didn't mean to have anything to do with you. All I did was free a bird," I said. My heart soared. Despite the threat to me, I had the body again. I clenched and unclenched my hands, marveling that I could.

"Serve who you like," the bird replied callously. "It does nothing about the debt you owe me. Do you really think that serving one god will protect you from the demands of another? Do you honestly believe that we derive our powers because you believe in us? What sort of an impotent god would that be? 'Believe in me so I can be a god!' Is that what gods should say to men? How about, 'Believe it or not, I can control your world'?" He turned his head and looked at me out of the other eye.

As swiftly as my control of the body had come, it went. Soldier's Boy gave a sudden gasp as if he had been holding his breath.

"What do you want from me?" he demanded of the god in a low growl. I felt the anger that seethed through him, that for even a moment, his control had been lost.

"Oh, this is tedious," the bird replied. He put his head down and for some moments worried flesh from the fish carcass, snapping it up in lumps. He was silent for so long that I thought he had gone back to being a bird rather than a god. Then he spoke again. "There is nothing amusing in having to repeat myself. For the last time, Nevare Burvelle and whoever else is sharing that skin you walk in: you owe me. This is your last chance to amuse me by taking the choice into your own hands. What will you give me? A death or a life?"

Soldier's Boy stared, transfixed, at the croaker and I shared his gaze. I had no answer and I dreaded that Soldier's Boy might speak for me.

We were saved or perhaps condemned in the next moment. Likari spoke from the door of the lodge. "Great One, the fire is ready for cooking." His voice shook slightly.

Soldier's Boy made no response.

And in the next instant, Likari darted at Orandula, waving a stick of firewood at the bird-god and shouting, "Go on! Shoo! Stop stealing our fish, you old robber bird!"

To my surprise, the croaker bird snatched up the fish and took flight. He lifted his wings wide and flapped them heavily, scarcely keeping ahead of the small boy pursuing him with the stick. It would have been laughable, if the bird had been only a bird.

Once the bird had gained a safe perch, he set the fish down on the branch and put one possessive foot firmly on top of it. He crouched low over it, peering down at the boy with his wings half opened. "The boy!" he croaked. "Yes, the boy. You could give

him to me to discharge the debt. What do you say, Nevare, not-
Nevare? Which do I get? His life? Or his death?"

Horror chilled me and my other self seemed likewise shocked
to stillness. And again Likari reacted before either of us, sending
the piece of firewood spinning up. It clacked loudly against the
bird's perch. "Go away!" he shouted at it. "You are bothering the
Great Man and I am his feeder! Go away!"

"My turn to choose!" the bird cawed. Then he caught the fish
up in his beak. He lifted off the branch, made one swooping pass
through our midst, causing Likari to duck like a mouse before an
owl's dive, and then, beating his wings swiftly, the bird vanished
into the darkening forest.

"There. I scared him away!" Likari announced. He spoke with
a boy's bravado, but his voice shook slightly.

Soldier's Boy was hoarse as he asked, "Frightened of a bird,
Likari?"

"No. But I could tell you did not like him. And I thought to
myself, 'It is my duty as a feeder to make sure that no one and
nothing disturbs the Great Man.' And so I came to chase him off
for you. And to tell you that the coals are ready for cooking the
meat."

"You are a very fine feeder indeed," Soldier's Boy told him,
and the sincerity in his voice could not be mistaken. "And I thank
you for driving the bird away. He was bothering me."

The boy's chest swelled. "If he returns, I shall kill him for you.
But for now, we should cook our food. The coals are ready."

"Then let us cook," Soldier's Boy agreed. I thought perhaps
he would tell Likari more or at least warn the boy to be wary of
croaker birds, but he did not. He helped the boy carry the meat
and fish into the lodge. They cooked the meat on spits over the
fire and baked the fish on the hearthstones beside it. They cracked
and ate nuts companionably while the cooking meat filled the
lodge with wonderful smells. They both ate heavily, with Likari
trying to defer to Soldier's Boy and Soldier's Boy insisting that
the lad should eat heartily and "get a belly to be proud of." He
set an example for the boy, stuffing himself until I was amazed he
could force another bite down. They ate the meat right down to

the bones. These the boy carried a short distance from the lodge and dumped. Afterward, they both walked down to the stream and washed before Likari filled up their water skin again.

The night was deep and cool around them. Through the thick evergreen canopy, a few stars were visible. The light that spilled from the lodge's windows and door barely reached to the stream. They walked back carefully in the gloom. "I need to build a door for the lodge. And get some coverings for the windows before the winter rains come in earnest."

"Tomorrow?" the boy asked in dismay.

"Oh, no. Tomorrow is for fishing. And eating. There will be no other chores but those until we go to join Olikea at the Trading Place. Making the lodge ready for winter can wait until we come back." I caught a faint thought from the edge of his mind. If he were successful, if he impressed them sufficiently, he wouldn't have to bother with such things. Other people would feel honored to worry about them for him.

They walked companionably back to the lodge, threading their way through darkness to golden light. Around them, the night sounds of insects, small and large frogs, and crickets orchestrated a curtain of sound around them. The sounds meant that all was well: only a sudden cessation of them would speak of danger and small things gone into hiding. Soldier's Boy and Likari both knew that; they were steeped in such knowledge, as comfortable as any animal in the forest that night. It bothered me that Soldier's Boy could so seemingly put the threat to Likari out of his mind.

Thinking about it would not make the threat any less.

I felt that thought pushed at me from him and grudgingly accepted it. He didn't like it that Orandula had threatened the boy. He was simply more capable of setting such a threat aside until a time when he could do something about it. All my worry had never solved anything.

They went to bed and the boy soon fell asleep against Soldier's Boy's back. It was not as chill tonight, but the mosquitoes hummed with an energy that promised rain before morning. The boy went right to sleep, but Soldier's Boy lay still and silent. After a time, I sensed him sinking down into something that was not sleep. It was similar to a state I recalled from the days when my father had starved me. His body temperature dropped, his heartbeat slowed. I could feel something happening but I couldn't tell what it was. After a few moments, stung by curiosity, I pushed at his dimmed awareness. "What are you doing?" I demanded.

His response was slow and guarded. "Storing magic."

"You're making yourself fat again."

"That would be how you would see it. I would see it as marshaling my reserves. Wasn't that a concept you learned in the Academy? To prepare your reserves so that you would be ready for any contingency?"

His response silenced me. I drew back from him. He didn't care. He'd set a reaction into motion; I could feel every bit of the food he'd eaten today being stored away inside him. I had thought it would take him a long time to become fat again, but now I saw that he was willfully working toward that goal. I could feel the slackened folds of his flesh refilling. He'd sunk back into a stillness deeper than sleep, a state of complete rest that freed his body to concentrate on conserving all the food he had taken in.

His body. My body? No, at this point, it was definitely his body, functioning as he prompted it to do. I thought of using his suspension to try to slip away in a dream-walk. But I could not think of where I would go or what I would accomplish by doing it. If he ever became aware of my excursions, I feared he would find a way to cage me more firmly. So, regretfully, I decided that I would not waste my opportunities in casual walks. I would go out only when I had a destination and specific information to convey. The moment I decided that, I felt lonelier but I knew it was my wisest course of action.

Some time in the night, he passed into a true sleep, and I with him. In the morning, he rose again, refreshed and well pleased with himself. He ran his hands over his belly and thighs, rejoicing to find that the skin had tightened as it filled again. He had not been awake long before Likari came staggering and yawning from bed to join him. Soldier's Boy ran a critical eye over the lad.

"You're growing, so it is hard to put flesh on you. But today we will try. Come. Show me your fish stream."

He followed the boy some distance from the lodge, to where a swift-flowing stream cut its way through the forest. The shady banks of the watercourse were steep. At first Soldier's Boy could not see any fish; then his eyes adjusted, and he saw that there were plenty of them. Most of them hung finning in the water beneath the undercut banks of the stream.

Likari had dropped to his belly. Like a lizard, he wriggled up to the stream's edge and lay there, being careful not to cast a shadow or make any sound that might alarm the fish below. Then, in a single movement, he thrust his arm into the stream, scooped it under a fish and flung it flopping onto the bank beside him. The creature looked to be the veteran of a long and difficult journey. His skin hung in tatters, and some predator had taken a bite out of his back. But he still flopped mightily and could have managed to throw himself back into the stream if Soldier's Boy had not picked him up by the tail and slammed his head firmly against a nearby tree trunk. By the time that swiftly brutal execution had been done, there was another fish flopping on the bank. It received the same treatment as its fellow.

So the morning went, save for an interval when Soldier's Boy left Likari to slay his own fish. He moved well back from the stream and gathered wood and twigs. He was stingy with the magic; it took him three tries before he called up a spark large enough to kindle the dry wood. Once it was going, he fed it until it was a useful size. Soon there were fish cooking over it.

All day long, the man and boy caught, killed, and ate fish. It seemed a monotonous meal to me, but I sensed that Soldier's Boy was not interested in taste right now. He enjoyed what he ate, but not in the sensuous way that I had employed his keen senses. He was too focused on consuming quantity to pause for long considerations of flavor and tenderness and the note of smoke that the fire put into the fresh fish.

When evening began to fall, they still had more fish than they'd been able to eat. They walked home slowly, carrying the surplus catch. Some they cooked and ate that night. Soldier's Boy put a sturdy green branch through the gill slits of the others and hung them up in a row suspended over the hearth fire in the lodge. Before they went to sleep, he had Likari gather green alder branches. These they heaped over the diminished fire, making a fine smoke that flowed up and past the fish. Then they went to bed.

This was the pattern of the next two days. Soldier's Boy's belly and thighs and arms filled out at a rate I would have thought impossible if I had not witnessed it. Even Likari managed to gain a small paunch, though the little boy was far too active to flesh out quickly.

On the morning of the fourth day, when Likari awoke, he found Soldier's Boy already standing outside the lodge, contemplating the new day.

"Come," he said. "It's time for us to go to the Trading Place."

CHAPTER FOURTEEN

THE TRADING PLACE

Soldier's Boy had regained a good deal of his weight. He was still not the magnificent Great Man he had been, but his size was respectable. The height I had inherited from my father benefited him there. He was a head taller than most of the Specks I had encountered. The height coupled with his newly recovered weight made him appear bigger than he was. Yet his satisfaction was tempered with regret as he spread the blanket out on the earth inside the lodge and began to load Lisana's treasure onto it. Weight alone would not win him the standing he needed. He'd have to make sacrifices. Likari watched him as he lifted each prize from its concealment under the moss and put it gently on the blanket. When he was finished, he carefully rolled the blanket in such a way that the jewelry and other treasures were securely trapped inside it. He picked it up and heaved himself to his feet with a sigh. "It's time to go. Are you ready?"

"Where did you get all those beautiful things?"

"They used to belong to Lisana."

The boy looked extremely uncertain. "It's dangerous to touch things that once belonged to a Great One."

"Unless you are the rightful heir to them. Lisana left these things to me. They are mine now, to do with as I wish. To use as I judge best to use them."

The boy stared up at him silently. Soldier's Boy said nothing more to him about it. I was once again struck by the differences in how I would have regarded a six-year-old boy and how Soldier's Boy treated Likari. He did not make allowances for the boy's youth or small size or lesser strength. He did not condescendingly explain his answers to the boy's childish questions. He simply gave him tasks, and expected that the boy would do his best to meet the requirements. When he failed due to size or age or strength, he did not rebuke him, but merely accepted that the boy would have to grow into them. It was a very different concept of childhood. I wondered if I would have been happier to have been a Speck child.

I had little time to ponder the question. Soldier's Boy took Likari's hand. "Are you ready?" he asked the child, and without waiting for an answer, he set off.

I was beginning to become familiar with his magic. I comprehended more of the quick-walk than I had before. He drew on Lisana's memories of the journey to the Trading Place. He thought of the passage there, and in his mind he ran quickly through every impression of the journey that she could recall, in order. A man can think of the journey to a place much more swiftly than his legs can carry him. We traveled at a speed somewhere between the two, not as fast as his mind nor as slow as his legs. Every time he blinked, I saw a different section of our journey before us.

And when he stopped after what seemed no more than a pleasant walk, we looked out on a wide vista of shale beach. Beyond it, huge waves crashed against the shore, and beyond them was a limitless expanse of water. It was hard for me to comprehend. The water stretched as far as the horizon, a deep blue touched with tips of white. Light bounced from the water up into my eyes. And

the sound of the waves crashing on the beach! It filled my ears so
that I felt I could hear nothing else. The smell was as engulfing.
Its salty musk spoke more of life than even the forest scents had.
I had heard tales of the ocean before, but they had not prepared
me for this. I could have gazed on it for hours, trying to grasp the
immensity of it. No matter how long I live, I do not think I will
ever forget that moment. Many small boats were pulled up on the
shore. Ships of a type I'd never seen before rode at anchor on the
distant slow swell. Some flew banners, but I didn't recognize any
of them. Truly, I stood facing the shores of a different world. Was
this what good King Troven dreamed of? Bringing his road here
to join Gernia to these trading vessels?

Soldier's Boy was undazzled by any of it. "I came too far!"
he muttered to himself, and then turned round. Behind us, on a
gentle rise beyond the shale beach, was a market town such as I
had never seen. I'd expected that the Trading Place would be some
sort of crossroads or temporary encampment of several tribes of
people. Instead, I looked on a gathering of folk that was easily
the equal of the Dark Evening carnival in Old Thares. All sorts of
structures—some tentlike, some built of stone, and others hastily
constructed of driftwood—formed a long line that paralleled the
beachfront. People in all manner of dress and undress wandered
the market contentedly. Smoke rose from cooking fires, and despite the sound of the surf at my back, I heard sheep bleating,
musical instruments playing, and above it all, the clattering of a
thousand tongues. I stared, as astonished by this sight as I had been
by the ocean. If this was the ebb of the trading time, what had it
been at its fullness?

Beside Soldier's Boy, Likari put his hands over the top of his
head. He crouched down, squinting his eyes. "Too much sun, too
much sun!" he wailed.

In the same moment, Soldier's Boy became aware of an itching, burning sensation on his shoulders and the top of his head.
Stooping, he seized Likari's hand. Before the boy could even stand,
he was dragged back what seemed like two steps. When next my
eyes focused, we were standing in the shelter of an evergreen
forest. Peering through the trees, I could see the Trading Place.

A long gentle slope of open land led down to it. All around us were the remains of temporary shelters and old campfires. I knew without even thinking about it that this was the area where the Specks customarily camped when they came to trade. It was deserted. The ashes in the fire pits had been rained on. "There you are!" Olikea's voice came from behind him. Soldier's Boy turned around. Behind him was a temporary shelter of woven screens. Olikea emerged from the doorway, looking annoyed with him. Despite her grim expression, I felt his mouth go slack at the sight of her. Never had I seen her arrayed as she was now.

She had dressed herself against the chill wind. I had seen her naked a thousand times; why did covering her body suddenly make her so alluring? Why did it suddenly awaken my own awareness that I was all but naked? She wore what would have been a simple dress on a Gernian woman. It was blue and came down to her ankles. She had paired it with a red apron with white ruffles and embroidered cherries on it. The long sleeves of her dress were full, and the lace cuffs drooped around her hands. On her head, she wore a yellow bonnet elaborately decorated with lace, ribbons, and feathers. Her long hair spilled from under it and poured down her back and around her shoulders. A red silk scarf was loosely wrapped around her throat. As I stared at her, she took little black fingerless mitts from an embroidered green silk bag and drew them onto her hands. "I have been waiting here for you since last night."

On a Gernian woman, the mixed bits of wardrobe would have been laughable. On this wild Speck woman, they seemed an elaborate costume worthy of a barbarian queen. Necklace upon necklace of glass and ceramic beads circled her neck. Her left arm was heavy with bracelets of beads and bangles of silver and copper from her wrist to her elbow. Her face was painted with cosmetics in an elaborate parody of a Gernian woman.

"Why are you dressed like that?" Soldier's Boy managed to ask.

"I came to trade. If I do not show what I have to trade, other women will not want it." She gestured at herself. "These things from the Gernians, we are the only folk who have them to trade. If I wear them as if I intend to keep them for myself, others will offer a better price to persuade me to part with them. Besides, I like how they cover me from the sun." She lifted a pink frilled parasol and carefully popped it open. Likari yelped with surprise and delight.

"You are beautiful," Soldier's Boy said, and I was surprised at how heartfelt his words were.

"Yes," she agreed. "And I am glad to see that you have managed to refill your skin a bit. You are not as magnificent as you were, but at least you will not shame me."

"Have you been down to the Trading Place already?" he asked her, ignoring her chide.

"Luckily for you, I have." She gestured at her shelter. "Likari, there are garments for both of you in there. Bring them out."

The boy gave a squeak of anticipation and scuttled into the shelter. In a moment, he emerged. An immense fold of striped cloth filled his arms. He brought it to me and then shook out a long tunic of rabbit skin. He tugged it on over his head and gave a sigh of relief. I chided myself for not realizing how chilled he had been. "Do I have shoes?" he asked anxiously.

"You will not really need them until the snow falls." She dismissed his concern. "Well?" She turned her attention to me. "Get dressed so we can go to trade. Only beggars come to the trading fair ungarbed as if it were summer. A Great One should be wearing furs and necklaces. But at least you shall not look as if you are completely unrespected."

Soldier's Boy shook out the garment. It was made of wool or something very like it, with alternating stripes of blue, brown, and red. There was little shape to it; when he held it up, it looked like a large rectangle of fabric, with a hole for my head and two more for my arms. "Put it on, put it on!" Olikea urged me, and then impatiently helped pull it over my head. It was large and came all the way to my feet. It left my arms bare. I had not realized how chill the day was until my flesh was shielded from it. "The stripes make you look very fat," Olikea said with great approval. "And see, it is loose. Plenty of room for you to grow big again. When it is tight on your belly, you will look magnificent. But for now it makes you look like a man of substance."

Likari had vanished into her shelter again. He emerged with two wide-brimmed hats woven from bark strips and a fat pot of something greasy and dark red. It wasn't food. As Soldier's Boy watched, the lad dipped two fingers into the pot, scooping up some of the stuff and then busily smeared it down one of his arms. It went on thick and brownish-red, like a good coat of paint. "This will keep the sun from scorching me," he said with relief.

"Do not forget to coat the tops of your feet," Olikea warned us.

Soldier's Boy was expecting to put on his own paint, but Olikea motioned impatiently for him to sit down. She stripped off her gloves, pushed back her lacy cuffs, and then applied the paint to me with a practiced hand. She did not merely smear it on as Likari had. She worked carefully and skillfully, swiftly marking swirls and stars into the thickly applied pigment. When she was finished, the decorative markings went from my shoulders to my wrist. "There," she said, obviously pleased with her work. "Now you are fit to be seen. I have spoken of you, as you bade me. I said I would bring you soon to trade, so folk will be watching for you to come. A pity that you have nothing of worth to trade. You shall be little better than a beggar at the Place."

"But he is rich!" Likari exclaimed. "He has brought the wealth of three kin-clans rolled up in the blanket. Beads and jewels and ornaments such as I have never seen!"

"What! Let me see!" Astonishment and avarice warred in her eyes.

He had not planned to unveil his wealth until he was at the Trading Place. Soldier's Boy had thought that a sudden show of it would stun my beholders. As he slowly unrolled the blanket to display row after row of dazzling treasure, Olikea nearly fainted with ecstasy. "Where did you get it?" she demanded to know.

"From my mentor. Lisana taught me in the other place. She made me her heir. This is her wealth, rightfully come to me."

"Lisana's hoard!" Olikea exclaimed. "I'd heard tales of it. Some said that she never had it, others that she found a way to take it into death with her. Most believe it was stolen from her lodge by an honorless one, and that the thief took it to her death with her when she drowned trying to cross a river to escape the bad luck such treasure brings."

"I told you it was bad luck!" Likari shrilled excitedly.

"Not if it is truly his. Oh, this, this piece is beyond value. You must not trade this; you will never get the likes of it again. And this, no, this is not for trade. I will wear this, and all will envy that I am your feeder. And these, oh, such ivory! These you must wear yourself."

Soldier's Boy felt a sudden pang of something. Jealousy from Lisana's shade? Anger that Olikea would flaunt what Lisana could no longer wear? He held my face slack against it, pondering, and did not resist as Olikea lifted his hand, and slid heavy bangles of gold, ivory, silver, and inscribed horn over my wrist. The weight felt peculiar to me: no Gernian man would have adorned himself this way.

She was not finished. She exclaimed in dismay that so many of the necklaces had come unstrung. "We shall not even show these things. People will try to trade for them a bead, two beads at a time, giving up nothing but trinkets in return. No, these we will save for another time, when they will fetch what they are truly worth. This winter, I will restring them for you."

When she came to the fertility figurine, she gave a gasp. She touched the ivory baby with one fingertip, as if expecting it to stir to sudden life. After a long moment, she took a deep shuddering breath. "This is the stuff of legend. With this, I think, we will make you a Great One to stand among the greatest of Great Ones." Her voice shook and her face had paled around her markings. She took the scarf she had been wearing around her neck and carefully wrapped the baby in it as if it were a bunting and set it aside. She looked up at Soldier's Boy, gave him a smile like the sun rising, and then went back to her sorting.

She crouched over the blanket of treasures like a greedy magpie thinking of snatching up shiny things. I felt Soldier's Boy's resentment of her mercenary attitude even as he gritted his teeth and accepted her expertise. Keeping these things would not bring Lisana back, nor would it save her tree. If parting with the treasure was what he must do to gain power among the People, then that was what he would do.

So he held his tongue as she decked him with ornamentation. She adorned herself and even the boy. She had woven bags with her that she had used to transport her trading goods to the fair. Now she sorted his wealth into them, some to keep, others to repair, some to trade easily and some to reserve for those capable of being provoked to bid against each other. The ivory child went gently into the most ornamented bag, and she surrounded it with the most valuable of the treasures. She hummed and chuckled as she did so, obviously well satisfied that her Great One was already profiting her.

She had him sit while she combed and dressed his hair with a sweet-smelling oil. She changed the order of the bracelets on his arm so that they would contrast better with one another. She gave the boy a few of the flawed or cracked beads so that he might do some of his own trading. Finally she pronounced herself satisfied and they set off for the Trading Place.

The shady hat and the paint worked well enough. The light was still a bit unpleasant but not overwhelming. The wide-brimmed hat sheltered his face and eyes. Likari wanted to run ahead and she did not forbid it, nor tell him when or where he must find them again. Again, I marveled at the difference in how the People treated their children. She assumed he'd have the sense to come back after he'd traded his beads away, and left the work of finding us to him. As Soldier's Boy's glance took in the size of the fair and the milling folk that populated it, I had doubts about her wisdom. Her next words shocked me.

"A pity that we have missed the peak of the trading. There were twice the tents and booths here two weeks ago, I have heard. Most of the Sea Folk and the Coastal Ones have already departed. They wished to be home before the storms of autumn grow strong."

"Twice as many people?"

"Of course. As summer ends, the winds bring the traders from the south. For a short time, their ships can anchor and their small boats come ashore. But soon the storms of winter will scour these beaches. Before that happens, both ships and traders will be gone from here. The Trading Place will be deserted until next autumn."

She paused and looked at him severely. "Because you have de-layed us we will have only a few days to do our trading. The most unique goods are probably long gone. But some say these are the best days to trade. People are more desperate to make a bargain. Or so I have heard. We shall see."

Throughout the morning and into the afternoon, Olikea proved her value a dozen times over. She was a shrewd trader, moving easily from aggressive to reluctant as needed to strike the best bargain. At first, Soldier's Boy tried to ask questions or even make offers, but a sharp sign from Olikea warned him to keep silent. I soon realized that his silence was not a mark of his sub-servience to her; rather it announced that he was too important to be involved in these trivial details of trade. Briefly, he chafed over letting her make the bargains, but soon came to see it was to his advantage to give way to her. She made ridiculous offers, argued persuasively, appeared uninterested in counteroffers, and then, with a smile, would be securing their latest bargain.

She was sage in how much of his wealth she showed, and to whom. I noted that she used up the lesser pieces first, acquir-ing for Soldier's Boy a warm wolf fur cape and boots soled with walrus hide and woolen felted socks to go inside them. These he donned immediately and quickly enjoyed the benefits of being warm. She bargained on, acquiring tall fur hats for both of them, woolen mittens, and for him, a second long wool tunic, black with white spirals embroidered into it.

Once I was properly and grandly attired, she became more selective, both in what she chose to buy and what she would offer for it and even with whom she would trade. She struck a haughty air, and we strolled at a pace designed as much to display me as to give her the opportunity to make a leisurely examination of the vendors' wares. It made Soldier's Boy smile at the same time that he realized that Olikea was more valuable to him than he had given her credit for. She understood the finer points of establish-ing their status here.

Soldier's Boy was focused on the trading but the market held my attention. I'd never seen such a place. Obviously this location had been occupied and used as a market for decades, perhaps hundreds of years. Yet there was a strange air of temporariness to it, as if it might vanish in the wink of an eye. Cobbled-together booths full of wares often butted up against small stone cottages where the traders slept and cooked their meals. A number of these cottages stood empty now, but the litter of recent habitation still surrounded them. They were mute witness to Olikea's assertion that the market town had been larger only a week ago.

And larger still decades ago. The remnants of other cottages, entire streets of them, remained as walls of rubble open to the sky. I suspected that there had once been a permanent settlement here rather than this annual trade rendezvous. What had become of it? That was a question that only I pondered.

Olikea and Soldier's Boy were too caught up in their trading. Olikea revealed that she wore not one but three Gernian dresses, one over the other. She stripped them off as she traded them away. Her trading partners seemed avid for all her Gernian goods and there was much evidence that other Specks before her had also trafficked well in such items. I felt consternation at seeing such an abundance of Gernian hats, ribbons, boots, paper, and parasols. From trinkets and tokens to fine jewelry and leather goods, I saw it all.

Above all, the great quantity of Gernian tobacco—stacked bales of it—astonished me. Despite the restrictions on trading it with the Specks, the exchange was obviously flourishing. Toiling men were transporting the bales down to the small boats, which were then carrying it out to the anchored vessels. Pale men with red or golden beards and shaven heads stood guard over the merchandise, and turned deaf ears to other traders trying to buy a share of it. It was also for sale in smaller quantities in market stalls run by Specks. There were pipes on the premises for those who could not wait to consume their purchases. I was astonished at the effect the mild weed seemed to have on the Specks who were buying and smoking it. Outside the stall, half a dozen near-naked beggars pleaded for a single draw from a pipe or even the charred bits of cinder from the pipes' bowls. They seemed heedless of how the sun burned and blistered their bare flesh. They had traded all they possessed for tobacco and now begged for it. It was pathetic and horrifying. Olikea gave them a furious glance and then swept past the tobacco stalls, forcing Soldier's Boy to hasten his stride to keep up with her.

"They barter goods to buy poison. They are fools," she pronounced when Soldier's Boy asked her why she hurried on so rapidly. "They shame their kin-clans and they shame the People. It is fine to trade in such stuff; the sea traders are very anxious to buy it from us. But why we sell poison to our own folk, I do not know." Then, as if he had expressed an interest in it, she added, "And all know it is toxic for Great Ones. Do not even think of trying it!"

We came to a sector of the market that was surrounded by a zone of empty stalls. The demarcation was very clear. The five or six market stalls ahead of us were set apart. Olikea suddenly took my hand. "We do not go that way, Great One. Come. Let us go down this row next."

"But why? Why are those stalls so isolated?" All manner of possible reasons flashed through my mind. Disease. Foreigners. Unclean or blasphemous items.

Olikea spoke softly. "They are worse than the tobacco mongers. They trade in iron. They do not care what it does to the magic. They say that iron will come inevitably; that it will rule us, for our magic has not succeeded in sending iron back to where it came from. Our Great Ones do not like it. They forbade it. But these traders are young or are from other places, and do not respect our ways. Once they had discovered that a Great One might forbid it, but that the magic could not expel them . . . well. Few here respect them. But in truth, many are hungry for the tools that do not break and stay sharp. There are many who own them, without speaking about them. Our Great Ones mostly ignore it."

I thought of the little flint and steel that I knew she carried for fire-starting, and a small knife of hers that I'd once glimpsed. Soldier's Boy said nothing of those but did tell her, "I wish to go there. I want to see what they have."

"This is not wise, Nevare. It may sicken you or weaken your magic, just when you are recovering it."

"I will go there and see what they have. I think it is important for me to know this."

"As you will," she growled. She let go of my arm. Soldier's Boy had gone half a dozen steps before she grudgingly fell in behind me. He glanced back at her. A number of other folks at the market had turned their heads and were watching me. Several spoke to their neighbors and other heads turned. One stall owner suddenly covered his wares with a blanket. Another closed the shutters on his enclosed stall. Stubbornly Soldier's Boy walked on.

He felt the iron before I saw it. It was like the buzzing of a nearby hive of bees. He felt the same sense of danger, and as the buzzing grew stronger, Soldier's Boy had to resist the urge to brush at my skin. He stayed to the center of the street and looked at the stalls. The merchandise confirmed Soldier's Boy's suspicions.

Gernian trade items. It was all from Gernia.

We passed a stall where a Speck was selling Gernian tools and implements of iron. Knives, hammers, pliers, scissors, and needles had attracted an eager crowd of buyers. The presence of the metal became a hot itchy rash spreading over my skin. Soldier's Boy forced himself to go on. I knew what Soldier's Boy was looking for now. Guns. And powder. It was forbidden to sell them to the Specks, but like the tobacco trade, there were many traders who sidestepped the prohibition for the high profits.

The next booth held edged tools, mostly axes. There was a large crosscut saw on display at the back of the booth, and a sturdy wooden barrel held a long measure of heavy iron chain. And along the side of the booth, there was a long rack of swords. There were all manner of them, most of them spotted with rust. Few were anything a gentleman would care to own. At the sight of them a sudden wave of vertigo made him stagger a step side-ways. Around me, the other buyers were stopping to stare at us. Several turned their heads aside and hurried away from this part of the market, as if shamed to have been seen here by a Great One. The iron pressed on my magic like hands around my throat. Soldier's Boy gasped for breath.

Olikea noticed my discomfort. "I warned you. You should not be here." She took my arm again, turned me around, and hurried me along. Soldier's Boy felt grateful for her guidance. His thoughts were so addled I wasn't sure he could have left on his own. "They should not sell such things where a Great One might pass," she huffed. My consternation at seeing so many Gernian goods became anger and then felt like betrayal. If the Specks hated us so, and resented what we were doing to their forests, how could they so cheerfully profit from our contact? Soldier's Boy's contradictory thought pushed back at me. "Why do we hate you? Look at what you do to us. You will kill our ancient trees, poison our young men, and kill our magic. Do you wonder that you must leave?"

When we had left the ironmongers behind, Soldier's Boy could breathe again, although he felt a bit shaky. Olikea had me sit down on a low wall. She hurried away and soon came back with a large mug full of a cool, sweet fruit juice. As he drank it, I looked around at the market with new eyes. There was ample evidence that this pattern of trade with Gernians was not new. I saw scraps of Gernian cloth woven into the headdress of a tall, pale man. A woman's apron, much mended, had become a cloak for a small Speck child who darted through the teeming throng of traders. From what I knew of history, we had traded for years with the Specks long before King Troven had established a military outpost at Gettys. Had they previously refused our iron? I didn't know.

When she was certain I had recovered, Olikea took me from stall to stall, acquiring necessities as she traded away Lisana's treasures. I ceased to pay attention. It was too painful for me to watch Lisana's possessions treated as mere commodities. Let Soldier's Boy deal with those feelings. Instead, I let my mind become caught up in the pageantry of the place. It put the Dark Evening carnival in Old Thares to shame. There were musicians and jugglers at one intersection, and hot food booths were sprinkled throughout the marketplace. I counted three races of men that I had never encountered before. One booth was run by tall, well-muscled folk, both the women and men, with freckled skin and hair that ranged from orange to straw yellow. Olikea had no success at their booth. She greatly desired the glittering crystal beads and figurines they offered, but they had no interest in her goods. Only tobacco would they have. All of them smoked pipes and their booth breathed the fumes of the aromatic herb out into the fresh sea air.

Olikea stalked away from there, affronted, and Soldier's Boy followed like a docile ox. We did not stop at the next two stalls. "They are the Shell Folk. They have nothing we need. Only those from across the salt water want their strings of purple shells. We have no use for them."

At the ivory stall, we stopped, but not for ivory. Olikea traded for two small kegs of lamp oil, and arranged that we would claim them later.

Three stalls away, six tiny men traded exclusively in items woven of grass. They had mats and hassocks, shoes, cloaks, and hammocks, all woven from the same peculiar blue-green reeds. Olikea had no interest in their goods and strolled past where, I confess, I would have lingered to stare. Every one of the little men was heavily bearded and yet was no taller than Likari. I wondered where they had come from but knew I would never get to ask that question, for Soldier's Boy did not share my curiosity.

Olikea stopped at the next stall. A smith there displayed his works of tin and copper, brass and bronze. He had spearheads and hammers, arrowheads and blades of all sorts and lengths. While Olikea studied the knives, Soldier's Boy picked up a strange arrow. Behind its sharp tip it widened to a sort of basket-cage before fastening to the shaft. The smith left his assistant helping Olikea and came to Soldier's Boy. He spoke Speck badly. "For fire. You wrap the gara so, in a rag." The smith picked up a smelly, resinous block. It dripped, barely a solid. "Then you put it in the basket. Set fire to it before you shoot it. Whatever it hits will burst into flames!" He threw his callused hands wide, simulating the explosion of flammable stuff. The smith seemed quite enamored of his invention, and shook his head in disappointment when Soldier's Boy turned aside without making an offer.

Olikea traded away an ivory bracelet for a large brass knife in a sheath ornamented with mother-of-pearl and amber. The handle of the knife was made of a dark hardwood. I questioned the value of such a knife as tool or weapon, for I doubted that it would hold an edge. That did not seem to be Olikea's concern. It came with a very long belt of white leather. This she fastened carefully about Soldier's Boy's middle so that the strap rode atop his belly and emphasized the swell of it. The knife, nearly as long as my forearm, hung grandly at his hip. Olikea grinned her satisfaction and then hurried us away from the smith's tent.

Women laughed and chattered, men with bangles in their ears and braids down their backs stalked past us, and small children in all manner of garb raced from stall to stall. The atmosphere reminded me of a carnival.

A bronze-skinned woman in a long red tunic accosted us. She carried a tray of small glasses filled with exotic liquors in bright colors. I smelled anise, mint, and juniper, but more penetrating by far was the scent of strong alcohol. Olikea waved her grandly aside. I wondered if the woman's skin coloring was natural or a cosmetic. I looked at the backs of my now-dappled hands and wondered why that should matter. I myself was now buried deeply within dapples and fat and overshadowed by my other self. How could I ever again expect to tell anything about another person by looking at her body?

I was pondering this when I abruptly realized I had retreated into a literally "senseless" state. I was no longer hearing, seeing, or smelling the market. I had become an entity of pure thought, a being wrapped in a body but deprived of its apparatus. I was suddenly drowning, smothered by flesh. My awareness leapt and struggled like a stranded fish, and then abruptly meshed with Soldier's Boy again. I felt air on my skin and I longed to take deep gasping breaths of the cool stuff. A thousand scents—smoke, spices, sweat, cooking fish—rode the air. I devoured the sensory information. I could see and I joyously beheld the moving crowd of brightly clad folk, the noon light glittering on the bright and glistening sea, and even the shell-strewn path we followed. I was like a prisoner granted a glimpse of the outside world again.

I suddenly perceived that was exactly what I was. I was trapped in a body that was no longer mine, and only by sharing Soldier's Boy's awareness could I sense anything.

I feared I was losing myself in him. I should tear myself away, I thought, but could not bear the sensation of solitary confinement in his body. With a sinking heart, I knew I was becoming resigned to my subordinate existence. I was losing the will to fight him.

I looked through his eyes in a daze of despair, looked out at his world as a passenger looks out of the window of a carriage. I could not control where I was carried nor what I saw. I became passive with hopelessness.

We passed the deserted husks of two stalls. At the third, Olikea stopped.

Waist-high stone walls defined the space. It was a generous area, the size of a cottage. Long poles of bleached white driftwood supported a brightly colored awning. The tasseled edges hung down, flapping in the ocean breeze. Soldier's Boy had to stoop to enter. "Let me be the speaker here," Olikea warned him in an undertone.

"I shall speak whenever I decide to," he rejoined gruffly. He looked about at the displayed merchandise, his fascination tinged with horror that gave way to dim recognition. Here were the tools and pharmacopoeias of the shaman's trade. Bundles of feathers, strings of teeth, and dried herbs on the stalk swung in the open breeze, suspended from the poles. Cleft crystals sparkled and chimes tinkled. Nameless bits of dried animal organs occupied a row of fat ocher pots. Tightly stoppered glass vials of oil jostled against polished stones in an array of colors and sizes.

A plank shelf held a succession of copper bowls brimming with trade items. The first held necklaces made from snake vertebrae. Olikea lifted one and the strand moved sinuously. She gave a small shudder and dropped it back in the bowl.

The next bowl held an assortment of shriveled mushroom caps. "For dream-walking," she noted aloud, proud of her knowledge.

Tightly crinkled green-black dried leaves filled the next copper bowl. They looked like leather to me, like dried lizard skin. Olikea started to stir them with a finger, then paused uncertainly, her hand hovering over the bowl.

"Dried seaweed. To strengthen the blood of a Great One after the exertions of his magic." The woman's voice was as desiccated as her wares. She came tottering out of a curtained nook at the back of her stall.

She was a Speck, but so old that her dappling had faded to a faint watermark on her skin. Her hair was very white and so thin that I could see her pink scalp through the tendrils of it. Age had spotted her scalp and her dark eyes were filmy. Both her ears were pierced with many holes, and in them she wore small earrings of jade and pearl. With both hands she grasped the broad head of a white walking stick. It looked like it had been fashioned from one bone, but I could not think what animal would have bones of that size.

The old woman peered at Olikea, paying no attention to me. "You do not need to be here," she announced. "Your sister has already purchased all that is necessary for the Great One of your kin-clan. Unless, perhaps, he has fallen ill?"

"I have not recently seen my sister or Jodoli," Olikea replied stiffly. "I am not here on her behalf. You might notice, Moma, that I have a Great One of my own to tend now. Or has age so darkened your eyes that you cannot perceive even one of such glorious girth?"

Olikea stepped to one side as if she had been concealing me behind her. It was a laughable charade, like hiding a horse behind a cat. But Moma obediently lifted her hands as if suddenly astonished. Olikea caught the old woman's cane before it toppled. Moma seized it back from her and stabbed the cane in the ground at my feet. "He is magnificent! But I do not know him! What kin-clan have you robbed? Who now weeps and gnashes their teeth that he has been lured away? Or have you taken a new loyalty to his kin-clan, Olikea?"

"I? Never. I know to whom I was born. Indeed, Moma, I have stolen him. I took him from the foolish Jhernians, who did not even know his worth."

"No! Is such a thing possible?" The old woman teetered forward a few steps. With one veiny hand, she patted the swell of my belly as if I were a large and friendly dog. I thought she was astonished that a Gernian could become a Great One. But then she said, "They did not know his power, even when he carries it in such glory? How can this be?"

Olikea pursed her lips sagely. "I think they are blinded by all the iron they use. Even on a Great One, iron, iron, iron. Iron in knots on his chest, and on a great buckle he wore at his waist!"

"No!" Moma was scandalized. "I am shocked that he was not stunted by such treatment."

Again Olikea pursed her lips in the Speck gesture of denial. "I fear he was, mother of many. Great as he is, still I must wonder what he could have been if he had not been mistreated and near starved of his proper foods."

"Tormented with iron and starved," Moma lamented for me. "Then you have been his savior, Olikea?"

Olikea spread her hands and bowed her head modestly. "What else was I to do, Moma? If I had not gone to him, I fear he would have perished."

"Such a waste that would have been! And at a time when the People have more need of our Great Ones than ever."

So far Soldier's Boy had remained silent. I sensed his approval of Olikea's words.

Moma set one of her wrinkled hands atop the other and rubbed the back of it. "So, then, you who have never before had the care of a Great One have come to trade with me. There is much you will need for him, so much. I fear you may not have enough to barter. Yet I shall do the best I can to see you have at least some basic supplies for him. It is the least I can do after all he has suffered."

"You are kindhearted, Moma, very kind indeed," Olikea replied in a rather brittle voice. "But I think I have brought enough trade goods to provide well for my Great One. If your prices are fair, that is."

The old woman's eyes retreated into pits of wrinkles when she narrowed them. "The best goods, fairly priced, are still expensive, girl. Winter comes. It is easy to find the berries, the nuts and herbs, the gall of a squirrel when the world is green and growing. But in winter, those things are gone and feeders must turn to the wise provider who has harvested and stored such things. Who is that provider? Why, only Moma! Only she has what the Great Ones need to dream-walk, to hear music in the wind, to quick-walk tirelessly, to see with the hawk's eye, to walk the hidden paths."

"Varka has a stall of herbs also." Even to my ears, Olikea's interruption sounded impertinent and challenging. It seemed unwise. What was she thinking?

Moma took offense, as I had expected her to. "Oh, yes, he has a market stall. And he will sell to you, cheaper than I will, if what you want are moldy herbs and berries dried away to sour pits! Do you think to drive a hard bargain with me, little Olikea? Beware. All know that there are never enough quality supplies to see all of the People's Great Ones through the winter. Those with foolish feeders must do without.

"I do not need to sell my goods right now. And if you will not meet my price, I shall not. I will keep them and I will wait. Before winter is gone, Kinrove's feeders will seek me out, to buy all I have and at a good price, too. And they speak to me always with respect."

"Oh, respectful tongues are fine," Olikea conceded in a tone that said otherwise. "But only if those tongues speak of the very finest trade goods. I shall not disappoint you in what I offer, Moma, but do not think me a foolish little girl. I know what things are worth."

With the back of her hand, Olikea pushed aside the bowl of seaweed. In its place she set out the dark blue leather pouch and made a ceremony of opening it while Moma pretended disinterest. Her failing eyesight betrayed her, for she craned her neck to see as she leaned closer to the plank shelf. She was tellingly silent as Olikea lifted the treasures from the bag and arranged them carefully on the plank. She did not hurry. Earrings went with their matching necklaces and bracelets. Figurines were carefully spaced. These were Lisana's finest treasures. I had never seen them in strong, clear daylight. Despite their years, they shone, glittered, and gleamed. Earrings of carved ivory vied with those of hammered silver, figures of jade and amber flanked soapstone statues, bracelets of linked gold spiraled temptingly on the plank.

I wondered why she displayed it all. Surely we would not trade all of our best items for dried leaves and shriveled mushrooms. A rising tide of dismay tightened my throat; Soldier's Boy shared my extreme reluctance to see Lisana's treasure frittered away. Yet Moma stood with bated breath as Olikea opened the bag wider and peered within. Then Olikea dipped her whole hand into the bag. Gently, as if lifting a living creature, she raised the scarf-wrapped object. She held it in her palm and deftly opened the wrappings to reveal the ivory child cradled there.

Moma gasped in awe and one of her hands lifted. The reaching fingers reminded me of a hawk's greedy talons. They were stretched toward the sleeping baby, the fertility charm that had failed Lisana but remained her greatest treasure. Horror rose in me.

"No!" I exclaimed, and in that same instant, the word emerged from Soldier's Boy's throat. For that moment, we were fused, a single united entity. I was shocked at how wonderful it felt. I was full of power and whole. This was what I could have been, had the Tree Woman never divided me. I felt a flash of anger at all the ways my life had gone wrong. This was what I should have been!

But the emotion and the thought were not solely mine. They stank of Soldier's Boy and I tore myself free of him. I would not become a minor part of some Speck shaman, some forest mage. I was still Nevare, Nevare Burvelle, and I did not intend to surrender that. As if from a distance, I heard Olikea respond to me. She gave a silvery laugh. "Oh, no, of course not! This is not for trade. I know what your hopes are, Great One! We could not part with this, not until it has done its work for us."

And before Moma's reaching fingers could touch the figurine, Olikea had flipped the scarf back over it. As quickly as she had displayed it, she lowered it back into the open sack. Then she patted my arm as if I required calming and reassurance.

Moma held out an entreating hand. "Wait. Do not be hasty. For that one item, I will give you a winter's worth of magical provisions. A *generous* winter's worth."

Olikea laughed again, but this time I heard not the tinkle of silver but the clang of steel. In disbelief she asked, "Is a Great One's babe not worth more than a winter's worth of herbs?"

"Two winters," Moma offered and then recklessly changed it to "Five winters."

"Not for ten winters. Not for barter at any price," Olikea replied coldly. Then she stood a moment, tapping her lips as if considering something. "I am young. I have many bearing years ahead of me, and as I have already borne a child, I know I need not fear I am barren. So, perhaps . . . To a very trustworthy woman, a woman of good standing, I might lend this charm. For only a season, of course, just long enough for her womb to catch a babe. Then I must have it back."

I sensed an invisible bargain was being struck. Difficult as it was, both Soldier's Boy and I held ourselves still. Moma's breathing was loud, an echo of the endless rush of the waves against the shore.

"How came you to have it?" she suddenly demanded. "The Ivory Child passed out of all knowing more than two generations ago."

"That does not matter," Olikea informed her. "It has been kept well, in secret, and used wisely. Now it is my turn."

"It is a very desirable thing," Moma told her. "Some would kill to possess that. You should be careful, very careful, of showing it here in the Trading Place."

"I think you give me wise counsel, Moma. I will be more cautious. I will not show it again." Her sudden show of respect and deference to Moma's wisdom surprised me. Olikea paused significantly and then added, "And if one comes to me, quietly, wishing to talk of borrowing it, then I will know that she knows only because you have judged her a worthy and trustworthy woman. For only to you have I shown this. She would be in both our debts, such a woman."

Moma smiled. It came over her wrinkled face slowly but it was a wide smile. For such an old woman, her teeth were very good. "That she would," she agreed, pleased and thoughtful. "That she would."

Something seemed to have been settled between the two women, something I did not grasp. They were both very pleased with themselves, as if they had reached an important accord. After that exchange, they traded, but in an oddly congenial manner. I sensed that Moma gave us very good value and she insisted on choosing for Olikea the largest dried mushrooms and the preserved herbs with the best color. She carefully folded our purchases into little packets made from woven reeds. The packets filled a substantial net bag. Some of Lisana's jewelry she took in exchange, but the most of it Olikea returned to the pouch. At the last, however, Olikea held out a pair of large silver hoop earrings rimmed with drops of amber.

"Always you have been so kind to me," Olikea told her. "Ever since I was a little girl, you always had a kind word for me. Please accept these as a gift, as a sign of our friendship. I know it would please my Great One if you wore them as a sign of the warmth he feels toward you."

Olikea held them out in her palm, not to Moma but to me. Subtly she jostled her hip against mine. Soldier's Boy took her hint. He lifted the earrings from her hands. Holding them delicately, so they dangled appealingly, he offered them to Moma. "I would be very pleased to see you wearing these."

She lifted one hand from her cane. Her fingers were like a careful bird's beak as she plucked the proffered earrings from his fingers. She did not hesitate. "Help me, please," she begged Olikea in a hushed voice, and the young woman obliged. The silver and amber earrings dwarfed all the ones the old woman already wore. They glittered in the sunlight. Moma gave her head a slight shake and the earrings swung against her neck. "All will notice these," she said with quiet satisfaction.

"That they will, and by them know how kindly you have treated this Great One and how highly he regards you."

Moma nodded her head low to me and then reminded Olikea, "But you have not told me his name."

"He has two, and both lie oddly on my tongue. The first is Soldier's Boy. The second is Nevare Burvelle."

"I fear these are not lucky names," Moma replied with concern.

"I am one who believes that a man makes his own luck. I do not fear my name," Soldier's Boy said aloud.

"Wisely spoken," Olikea observed, but her quick glance entreated silence from him. "And now we must go," she continued to Moma.

"Will you journey back to your kin-clan tonight? Or stay another night near the Trading Place?"

Olikea appeared thoughtful. "I think we shall spend another night here, if only to enjoy the foods of the market, and to look at the beach and the water when the evening light is kinder to us." She paused and added significantly, "I think we will take our evening meal there, if anyone cares to seek us out."

Moma gave a happy sigh. "I think that is wise. Good evening to you, then."

And yes, as we departed, it was evening. We had passed the whole day in our trading and Soldier's Boy was suddenly both very weary and ravenously hungry. My feet hurt and my leg muscles ached from walking on the sandy paths. I felt a pang of dismay at how much farther we must walk and how long I must wait either to eat or rest. Soldier's Boy had a more direct solution.

"I am going to go sit on the rocks and soak my feet in the seawater pools," he announced. "Find Likari. Have him bring me food there. Hot food, and wine of the forest to drink. Do not be long."

I saw a ripple of surprise pass over Olikea's face. It occurred to me that she did not comprehend completely that Soldier's Boy was the one she must deal with now, and that the compliant Nevare Burvelle was beyond her reach. She licked her lips, thought for only an instant, and then replied. "Yes. That is good. We will attend you shortly." She took a short breath and then added cautiously, "If anyone seeks to speak to you, you should tell them that they must wait until your feeder has fed you."

"Of course," he replied, as if he had never considered otherwise. And then they parted, with Olikea hurrying toward the food booths and vendors and Soldier's Boy leaving the path to walk toward the beckoning sea.

CHAPTER FIFTEEN

THE INVITATION

He crossed a gray sandy beach to an outcropping of darker stone. There he moved unerringly to a place where the rounded stones were interspersed with tide pools. The thin sun of autumn had not much warmed the water, but cold as it was, I am sure it was still much warmer than the waves that crashed and rolled against the outer beach.

He sat down heavily on a throne of stone and grunted as he tugged off his new boots and peeled down the woolen socks. My feet had never seemed so far away from my body as they did when he bent over his huge belly to reach them. He had to hold his breath, for the action pinched his lungs. He tossed both boots and socks casually to one side and then sat up with a groan. He took a long breath and then slowly lowered his feet into the water.

His foot basin was a tidal pool, fringed with dark seaweed and mysterious with foreign life. As his feet entered, the flowers on the bottom of the pool abruptly closed and retreated to their roots. I had never seen such a thing happen and was startled, but Soldier's

Boy only laughed with pleasure and lowered his feet into the icy water. The cold was a shock and he gasped and lifted his feet, but then dipped them in again and then out. After several such treatments, the water did not seem so cold, and he lowered his feet to soak them. He sat staring out over the moving water. Then he spoke aloud. "We could be very powerful."

I became small and still, a rabbit crouching in the underbrush, pretending to be invisible.

"If you joined with me willingly now, I do not think there is anyone who could stand against us. Know that if you do not willingly join me, eventually you will still become a part of me. Bit by bit, I expect you shall erode and dissolve into my awareness. What will you be a year from now, or five, Nevare? A discontented memory in the back of my mind? A small touch of bitterness when I look at my children? A pool of loneliness when something reminds me of your sister or your friends? What will you have gained? Nothing. So come. Be a part of me now."

"No." I thought the word at him fiercely.

"As you will," he replied without rancor. He turned his head and looked back toward the market stalls. He widened his nostrils and took a deep appreciative breath of the salty air and of the mouthwatering food smells that rode on it. His mouth ran with anticipation and he gave himself over to thinking of roast pork so tender it would fall from the skewer, of crisply browned fowl cooked with sea salt and stuffed with onion bulbs, of apple-bread thick with nuts and dripping melted butter. He sighed happily, enjoying the anticipation, relishing even his hunger. Soon he would eat. He would eat with great pleasure, savoring every bite, knowing as he enjoyed the taste and the aroma that it was contributing to his power, to his well-being, to his reserves of strength. He contemplated the coming meal with a simple and joyous satisfaction that I don't think I'd ever taken in any experience. I knew a moment of greenest envy, and then my small emotion was washed away in his leap of pleasure.

His wait was over. Down the beach, leaping impatiently ahead and then doubling back, came Likari. He capered like a dog enjoying a long-promised walk. His trading must have gone well.

He wore a peculiar cap, red and white striped, with a long tail. At the end of it was a set of bells that jingled as he pranced. Behind him came two young men. Between them they bore a long plank as if it were a stretcher for an injured man. Upon it were bowls and cups and covered plates. At the sight, Soldier's Boy swallowed and then could not help but smile. Behind the food bearers, walking more decorously than Likari, came Olikea. She had sold off her Gernian dresses, and wore now a long loose robe of bright scarlet, gathered with a sturdy leather belt. The belt was studded with silver, and at every stride, black boots trimmed with silver flashed into view. Behind her came three servants bearing her day's purchases. Soldier's Boy watched with pleasure as the parade drew nearer.

He was not alone in his anticipation. Great gray gulls, on seeing the approaching food, circled overhead, tipping their wings to hover over it. Their raucous cries filled the air overhead. One, bolder than the rest, swooped in to try to steal from the feast bowls, but Olikea gave a shout and sent him fleeing.

Likari spotted him and ran ahead, full of smiles. He reached Soldier's Boy, dropped down to the ground beside him, and breathlessly said, "We bring you a feast, Great One!"

The boy had not overstated it. By the time the men carrying the stretcher of food reached them, Likari had set up stones to support it. The men carefully lowered their burden and then stood back from it. Olikea had arrived by then. She paid them off and dismissed them with a flourish, telling them to return later to retrieve their master's dishes and cutlery. The other serving men set down their burdens. Olikea dismissed them as well, telling them to come back later to assist us in carrying our purchases back to our camp and to bring a beast to pack the kegs of oil. Only one she kept, telling him to keep the gulls from troubling us as we ate. As the rest trudged off down the beach, Olikea sat down gracefully beside our makeshift table. Soldier's Boy had eyes only for the steaming vessels of food and the tall glass flask of deep red wine, but my mind was chasing itself in circles. I had always thought that beyond the mountains, our king would find only primitive tribes to trade with. But here we were sitting down to a rustic picnic served on glass and ceramic dishes brought to us by servants of some master who operated a food booth. I felt anger at myself that I had so misread the Specks and their trading partners. The culture and civilization on this side of the mountains might be vastly different from Gernia, but I was coming to see that it was no less sophisticated and organized. I'd been blinded, I decided, by my attitudes about technology. These people who walked naked in the forest and lived so simply by summer enjoyed all the trappings of a different sort of civilization in winter. Obviously these people had followed a different path, but my assumptions that they were lesser, that they were simple primitive folk in desperate need of Gernian civilizing, reflected only my own ignorance.

My musings did not distract Soldier's Boy from his meal. Rather, it was the other way. As the covers were lifted from the dishes and the aromas wafted up, his anticipation welled up and drowned me. My thoughts were tossed and turned in his sensory enjoyment of the meal, and at last I surrendered all thought and simply let myself focus on the experience.

It had been so long since I had eaten without guilt. Before the magic had infected me, at the Academy, food had simply been sustenance. Most of it had been simple and honestly prepared, good in its own way, but certainly no one had taken care to make it enjoyable. At its worst, it had been bland and edible. At its best, it had been tasty. Before that, at my home and at my uncle's home, there had been well-prepared meals, and I recalled hazily that I had enjoyed them, and had even looked forward to some favorite dishes.

But never had I sat down to a sumptuously prepared meal, a meal tailored especially for me, and immersed all my senses in it as Soldier's Boy did now. I did not know the names of the dishes, and many of the ingredients I could not identify. That did not matter. To begin, there was a flesh dish, bite-sized chunks of meat cooked in a ruddy sauce. This was ladled up and served over a steamed black grain. The grain was chewy and added a nutty flavor to the dish. It was presented to Soldier's Boy with golden sliced fruit swimming in its own juices and sprinkled generously with little pink berries that I did not know. The fruit was sweet, the berries sour, and the syrup that surrounded them was touched with mint. A large glass goblet of what he thought of as forest wine was poured to accompany it.

And that was only the first course.

Some dishes I knew. The fragrant freshly baked barley bread, the thick pea soup, a whole roasted fowl stuffed with the onions that he had scented earlier, a rich yet simple cake baked from sugar, eggs, and a golden flour, sliced apples baked with spices and sweetened with wild honey, and little speckled hard-boiled quails' eggs. Likari shelled these for him, dipping each one in a sprinkling of spices before passing them to me. They were heaven, each a small package of piquant flavor.

Soldier's Boy groaned with delight, loosened the white belt, and waited while the final dish was prepared for him. He had eaten without thought, without concern for what that much food might do to him or what others might think of his appetite or his greed. Yet it did not feel like gluttony to me. He had eaten as a child eats, with pleasure in the textures and the tastes of the food.

I envied him so much I hated him.

By the time they were finishing their meal, the sun was sliding down behind the mountains. The water had crept closer to the shore and was lapping at the rocks. The lower tide pools were already covered, and it seemed that with every breaking wave, the ocean crept closer to us. I'd read of tides, but never really seen one turn before. The oncoming water, venturing so steadily closer, filled me with a strange uneasiness. How far would it come? Soldier's Boy did not share my worry. Olikea was ignoring the advancing water, scanning the beach behind us. Likari, sated long before Soldier's Boy was, had left the table and was frolicking at the water's edge. As each wave came toward him, he would race along its white foam edge, splashing in it.

Soldier's Boy surveyed the emptied plates and flasks with satisfaction. Then he gave a great yawn. "It is nearly time to go," he told her. "The tide is coming in."

"Let us linger just a little— Oh! Here they come!" The sudden smile of anticipation that lit her face puzzled me. Soldier's

Boy's gaze followed hers. Someone, or several someones, were approaching us carrying lanterns. The lights bobbed and swayed as they came nearer. I thought it would be the servants come to reclaim their master's serving plates and vessels. Olikea reached up and smoothed her hair and sat up a bit straighter. I recognized the grooming of a woman who expects important visitors. I wondered if Soldier's Boy did.

As the lanterns drew closer, I could see that they were carried on poles. Two boys held them aloft, and walked to either side of a plump young woman. A boy in his early teens walked behind her, carrying a wooden box. We watched them come, and as they drew nearer, Olikea frowned. "She's little more than a child," she said, displeased. As they got closer, she added quietly, "This is not what I expected. Let me be the one to speak to her."

Soldier's Boy made no response to that. Neither of them stood, but Likari came hurrying back to us to gaze curiously at the approaching procession. I think that Soldier's Boy shared with me the deep comfort of a very full belly. He was thinking more of a good sleep than he was of anything else. He continued to watch the emissaries as they approached but did not stand or call out a welcome. Olikea, too, waited in silence.

"Who are they?" Likari demanded.

"Hush. They come from Kinrove, unless I am mistaken. Likari, say nothing to them. Only I am to speak." Her wine cup still held a few swallows of wine. She lifted it in one hand and leaned across the "table" to ask me, "Are you full, Great One? Are you well fed?"

"I am that."

"Then I think we are finished with our trading here. Tomorrow we will journey home to my lodge. All that will make you comfortable awaits you there." She spoke these words in a clear and carrying voice that was certain to reach the ears of the approaching people. She glanced at them and then put her gaze back on me as if they were of no concern to her at all.

They stopped a short distance away. The girl cleared her throat and then called out, "Olikea. Feeder of the Jhernian Great One! We come as messengers and gift bringers, but we do not wish to interrupt a meal. May we approach?"

Olikea took a small sip from her wine cup and appeared to consider the request seriously. Then she replied, "My Great One says that he is sated. I suppose you may approach."

The lantern bearers advanced, and when they were close to our impromptu table, they halted and wedged their poles into the rock. The light from the lanterns swayed and leapt over us. Wickerwork enclosed the lanterns and cast strange shadows over us. The plump girl approached. She was dressed all in white, and her robe and shoes were immaculate. Her smooth black hair was drawn back from her face and held in place with several dozen ivory pins. She was a Speck, but the uneven lighting from the swaying lamps made it hard to see her markings. She lifted her hands and splayed them on her breast, revealing over a dozen sparkling-stoned rings on her fingers. She nodded her head in a formal greeting to us, fluttered her hands in the Speck gesture of subservience, and then spoke. "Word has reached Kinrove that there is a new Great One at the Trading Place, a man never before seen, and from a people long judged to be our enemy. This is a surprise to all of us. This has filled the Greatest of Great Ones with a desire to meet him. And so I am sent to offer the new Great One an invitation to visit the camp of Kinrove and his feeders tonight, to accept his hospitality and to exchange what news there may be. His feeder is invited also, of course. The feeders of Kinrove send to her these gifts that she may be pleased with them and persuade her Great One to come with us tonight."

The girl made a gesture and the young man came forward. As he came into the light, I saw that he was round-faced and heavy-bellied. His legs and arms looked soft and rounded rather than muscled like a man's. He approached Olikea, and then sank slowly down before her. Olikea said nothing. The boy made an elaborate show of opening the chest. Once it was open, the woman approached. She lifted out a lacy veil edged with tiny chiming bells. She displayed it to Olikea, shook it to make the bells ring, and then folded it and offered it to her. Olikea accepted it gravely but still said nothing.

Again the girl reached into the chest. She brought out simple wrist bangles. At first glance I thought they were metal, but they clacked softly against one another as the girl displayed them. They were wood, then, but made from a wood so black that it resembled stone. There were six of them, and again the girl offered them to Olikea. Olikea held out her arms and sat without comment as the woman slid three bracelets onto each of her wrists.

The final treasure to be displayed was wrapped in a very finely woven mesh of reeds. The girl lifted it from the box, drew a small bronze knife from a sheath at her hip, and cut the mesh away. A tantalizing aroma rose from it. Soldier's Boy could smell almonds, ginger, honey, and rum. Or something very like rum. The girl offered the cake to Olikea, saying, "These are baked once a year and mellowed with liquor for a year. They are special, cooked only for Kinrove's enjoyment. He sends one to the new Great One and his feeder as a welcome gift."

The cake that Olikea received was the size of a dinner plate and flat like a griddle cake. With her eyes on the girl, Olikea broke the dark brown confection into two pieces. She presented one to me, and then sat back in her place. She took a bite of the dark rich cake, chewed and swallowed it slowly, and then took another, and finally a third. After she had swallowed her third bite, she looked at me and said quietly, "I judge it safe to eat and flavorful, Great One. Perhaps it will bring you some small enjoyment."

No change of expression passed over his face. He lifted the aromatic cake and took a bite. As he chewed, a symphony of flavors spread out on his tongue and filled his nostrils. In my whole life, I had never tasted anything as delicious as that cake. Sweet mingled with spice and tamed the heady taste of the liqueur that had mellowed it. The almonds had been ground to powder to produce such a fine texture. It literally seemed to melt away on my tongue. After I swallowed, the taste of it lingered, not just on my tongue but as a perfume in my nostrils. It was delectable.

Olikea was waiting. After she saw Soldier's Boy swallow, she asked with feigned anxiety, "Was it acceptable, Great One? I hope it did not offend you."

He did not respond immediately. When he spoke, it seemed he had considered his words well. "I am sure Kinrove enjoys such things and expected that I would like them as well. It was a kind gesture of him."

This faint praise seemed to rattle the girl. She had been watching their expressions closely. I think she had expected them to praise the cake rapturously and was puzzled that they had not. So was I. It seemed an ungracious way to receive a gift. I was embarrassed at his churlishness, but Olikea seemed to expect it. She turned back to the girl and said, "My Great One is not offended by this token. He understands that it was sent as a sign of friendship."

The girl and the boy exchanged glances. The lantern bearers shifted their feet and then stood silently. I listened to the rising evening wind. It stirred the loose sand of the beach. Behind us, the swelling tide was venturing closer. From the direction of the Trading Place, I saw other lanterns approaching. Those, I surmised, would be the ones coming to clear away our plank table and the bearers who would carry our purchases for us.

It seemed to me that the silence stretched too long before the girl spoke. "Would you care to accompany us to the camping place of Kinrove? He has many rich and wonderful foods to share, and offers you a place to soak in hot water, scented oils and men skilled in applying them, and soft beds with warm blankets for the night."

Olikea was still. Then she turned to me, leaned closer, and asked softly, "Would the Great One be pleased by any of these things?"

Soldier's Boy considered. To all outward appearances, he was calm, but I felt the quick energy that swirled through him. "I can accommodate Kinrove," he said at last, as if he were granting the man a favor rather than accepting a graciously tendered invitation.

Again the young envoys exchanged looks. After a moment, the girl turned back to us. "We will return to him, then, to let him know you will be coming. We will leave a lantern bearer with you, to guide you to us at your leisure."

"As you wish," Olikea said. As if they were already gone, she turned her face away from them to look only at me. After a moment, she lifted her cup and drained off the rest of the wine. She appeared to be steeling herself to something.

Kinrove's envoys retreated a short distance, briefly whispered together, and then departed. A single lantern bearer was left behind. He waited respectfully out of earshot.

"Shall we go to the camp of the Great One?" Likari finally asked them when he could no longer stand their continued silence.

"Hush, foolish one!" Then Olikea spoke on in a lowered voice, "Of course we will! This is a great opportunity. Do you know how long Jodoli waited before Kinrove sent for him? Over three years! And Nevare has been invited on the first day of his first visit to the Trading Place. That is unprecedented."

The boy leapt up and kicked his feet in the air. "Then let us go!"

The scowl Olikea gave him would have curdled milk. "Sit down!" she hissed at him. "And do not move or speak again without my leave, or you shall be left here for the night to wait for us to return. This is not a time to appear foolish or eager. We must not be incautious. Kinrove is a man to fear. What he wants, he takes. Do not forget that. We have no cause to love or trust him. And he has begun his courtship of Nevare's friendship with a veiled insult. Nevare is a Great One, Likari. Yet Kinrove sends messengers who are barely more than children, not even his lesser feeders, to give us this invitation. And they speak of Kinrove as the Greatest of the Great Ones, as if all must acknowledge that without discussion. All this he does to assert that he is above Nevare."

Likari had sunk down onto his heels. He looked from me to his mother and scowled. "But all say Kinrove is the largest Great One who lives, perhaps the largest Great One who has ever lived. All respect him and acknowledge his power."

"But that may soon change!" Olikea insisted, and she smiled. She looked, for that moment, like a woman who contemplated vengeance. "Look at Nevare. He eats without effort, for pleasure, not even forcing himself. And he grows quickly. Think how short a time it has been since his skin hung slack on him and he was almost too weak to move. Look how much of his weight he has already recovered. The magic has blessed this one. Already he is greater than many of the Great Ones from the other kin-clans.

Surely you have seen how Jodoli looks at him, knowing well he will be supplanted by Nevare in less than a year. If our kin-clan turns to him, if he is fed on the best foods, on the foods that nourish his magic, I think that in less than two years he can equal Kinrove, and perhaps surpass him.

"So we do not go to Kinrove now, shaking our fingers in humility and groveling to him. No. We go to let him see that he has a rival, and to demand his respect from the very beginning. Nevare must bear himself as a contender if he is to be seen as one He cannot be seen as desiring too much what Kinrove offers him. He must accept it as if it is natural and perhaps less than what he expected."

"But—but the food, and the steaming waters and the oil rubs and soft beds!" The boy spoke in a longing whisper and his mouth hung half ajar with wanting.

"We will go. We will enjoy those things, but we will not appear surprised by them or appear to enjoy them too much," Soldier's Boy directed him.

Olikea suddenly looked a bit less pleased. "I am not sure we should take him with us. The boy is too young for such things. And there are dangers in Kinrove's camp, sights that I do not think he should see. Perhaps it would be best if he remained here. When the servants come to clear the dishes—"

"Likari will go with us. And he will be seen as one of my feeders, and treated as one of my feeders, with honor and respect."

"What will they think of you, having a youngster in such an important position?" Olikea objected.

"They will think," Soldier's Boy replied heavily, "that I am a Great One who does things differently. One who has a different vision and would lead the People in a new direction. Now is not too soon for them to become accustomed to that idea."

The tone he used effectively put an end to the conversation. Olikea sat back slightly and considered me as if she had never seen me before. Perhaps, I thought to myself, perhaps she knows now that it is not Nevare she speaks to, no matter how she names him.

The table servants reached us. We rose then, but slowly, stretching and telling one another what an excellent meal we had enjoyed.

Olikea was very particular as she spoke to the servants who would carry our possessions. They had brought a beast of burden as she had charged them. It was a strange animal to my eyes, dun colored, with toes rather than hooves, a skinny body compared to a horse, a drooping sad face and long flopping ears. I heard her call it a quaya. When she was satisfied as to how they had loaded our possessions, she left them and walked ahead to our lantern bearer.

"You may guide us now," she told him.

He gave us an uncertain look, as if he could not decide whether to be haughty or humble. When I got closer to him, I realized that although he was as tall as a grown man, he was still a youth. Soldier's Boy frowned. Olikea was right. There was a slight insult in that they had not sent any full-fledged adult with the invitation.

Our bearers had brought their own lanterns, so Olikea deigned that Kinrove's lantern carrier would walk well ahead of us. I think it was so that she could converse freely without worrying that he would eavesdrop.

He set an easy pace, perhaps because he was accustomed to the unhurried gait of a Great One. We followed, and once we had left the loose sand of the beach we struck a surprisingly good track. It was level and wide enough for a cart, let alone pedestrians.

"Are not you going to thank me?" Olikea asked after we had gone some small ways. Likari had fallen behind, fascinated with the quaya and its handler, so they had a small measure of privacy.

Her tone had made it plain that he owed her thanks for some special feat of cleverness. "For what would I be thanking you?" Soldier's Boy demanded.

"For making Kinrove take notice of you so swiftly."

Soldier's Boy felt a prickle of surprise. "It was my intent that he notice me. For that reason only, I came here to trade."

"And not because you might find yourself shivering in the cold as soon as the rains of winter began, of course!" Then she dropped her sarcasm and said, "No matter what you brought to trade, Kinrove would have remained aloof to you. No. It was not what we traded with or what we bought, but what we refused to trade that brought this swift invitation to meet him."

He did not need to think long. "The Ivory Babe. The fertility charm."

Olikea smiled smugly in the darkness. "Kinrove has six feeders. Six. But of them, there is only one who has been with him since the beginning of his days as a Great Man. It has taken her much work to remain his favorite and to keep his attentions to herself. But Galea grows older, and she has never borne him a child. She knows that if she does not soon produce the baby that he desires, he will turn to another feeder, to see if she cannot serve him better. She grows desperate with her need to become pregnant in order to keep his favor."

Soldier's Boy slowly processed this thought. "So we are invited tonight not because Kinrove wishes to meet me but so that his feeder can find a way to persuade you to give her the Ivory Child."

"So she thinks!" Olikea exclaimed happily.

"I do not wish to part with that item," he told her firmly. "It means much to me."

She turned to look at him in the dim and shifting light cast by the lantern bearer. Soldier's Boy glanced at her and away. "It would please you if I bore you a child?" she asked. Her delight was evident in her voice.

Soldier's Boy was startled and spoke perhaps more harshly than he intended. "It would *not* please me to trade away something that Lisana treasured as much as she treasured the Ivory Child. It was important to her. I would keep it to honor her memory."

Olikea took half a dozen more strides in silence and then said with sharp bitterness, "It would serve you better if you learned to value the efforts of a woman who is here rather than preferring your memories of someone who is a tree now."

I heard the hurt behind her harsh words. Soldier's Boy heard only the disrespect to Lisana and the other tree elders.

"I suppose you must strive to be important now," he said sharply. "For you know you will never earn a tree for yourself."

"And you think that you will?" she retorted angrily. "Remember, at the end, a Great One is at the mercy of his feeders. Perhaps you should seek to build a bond and some loyalty, so that when your time comes, there will be someone to take your body to a sapling and fasten it correctly and watch over you until the tree welcomes you."

That was as savage a threat as any Speck could ever offer to a Great One. I felt his shock that she would dare say such a thing reverberate through our shared soul. I would have, I think, sought to mollify the woman, as much for the deep injury she obviously felt as for my own future well-being. But Soldier's Boy said only, "You are not my only feeder, Olikea."

They both fell silent. Darkness was closing in around us now, making it difficult to see the terrain we crossed. We followed the beach, but our path gradually led us farther and farther away from it until the crash of the incoming waves was a muted whisper. Our trail took us up a gentle rise through an open field, and still not a word was spoken between the two.

So it was that they were at odds as we approached Kinrove's encampment. I had pictured a campsite with tents and cook fires. When we crested the small hill, what we looked down on was far more like the temporary encampments that a military force on the move might set up. It was a small town of folk, with a perimeter marked by torches and straight streets between the sturdy pavilions. It was also, I perceived, a substantial walk away, and even though our journey would be downhill, the darkness was deepening every moment and my legs were already weary from the long day of standing and walking. I could feel Soldier's Boy's displeasure at the situation. A sound like distant music, oddly muffled, reached us.

A few more steps, and the sensation was not mere displeasure. A sudden wave of dizziness swept over him, followed by the clench of nausea. He groaned suddenly and halted, swaying. Strange to say, the lantern bearer leading us had already stopped. Even as Soldier's Boy took long, deep breaths to counteract his queasiness, the man lifted his lantern and waved it in three slow arcs over his head. Then he grounded it again and waited. The vertigo swirled Soldier's Boy around again and then, just as suddenly as it had come, it was gone. Soldier's Boy took a deep gasping breath of relief and next to me Olikea did the same. As he recovered, a question came to me, one that I thought desperately important. I pushed it strongly at Soldier's Boy. "He guards his boundaries. Why? What does he fear?"

I could not tell if I'd reached him or not. He made no response to me.

For the first time, our lantern bearer spoke directly to us.

"Kinrove's guardians will admit us now. Kinrove, Greatest of the Great Ones, will quick-walk all of us to his pavilion."

CHAPTER SIXTEEN

KINROVE

I had no more time to ponder who or what Kinrove guarded against. To be presented with the idea that he was powerful enough to quick-walk our entire party down to him from such a distance was unnerving. But the lantern bearer said only, "Walk with me," and stepped out. We followed, and the night blurred around us. In a single step, we stood before a grand pavilion. That show of raw power was nearly lost on me as I looked about at the display of might that greeted us. Ranks of torches illuminated Kinrove's pavilion and the open space that surrounded it. The music I had heard in the distance now sounded all around us. A fine dust hung in the air, the smell of burning tobacco was thick, and everywhere crowds of folk churned past us. The sudden assault on all my senses overwhelmed me for a few moments as I struggled to make sense of the scene around me.

Substantial timbers supported the pavilion's leather walls. The walls were painted in ocher, red, and black in designs that were strange to my Gernian self yet familiar to Soldier's Boy's eyes. The music came from half a dozen musicians on an elevated stage. They blew horns and pounded drums, but there was no melody to their music, only rhythm. And the churning folk that had at first so confused me were actually a train of dancers, each one touching the shoulder of the one before him, and dancing in an endless chain that encircled not just Kinrove's pavilion but wove a serpentine path through the smaller tents of the encampment. Many of the dancers carried short-stemmed pipes with fat wooden bowls. Soldier's Boy blinked as the dance wove past him.

The dancers were all manner of folk, men and women, young and old, some brightly dressed in rich clothes and others looking worn and ragged. Women and girls predominated. Their bare feet had pounded the hard earth to loose dust. They did not dance lightly: every footstep landed with a thud. Their feet kept time with the rhythm of the music and stirred the dust that hung in the air all around us. Some looked fresh but most of them were worn thin as sticks.

Their faces were what arrested me. I did not know the theme of their dance, but they all wore expressions of fear. The whites of their rolling eyes showed, as did their bared teeth. Some wept, or had wept. The dust clung to the wet tracks down their cheeks. They did not sing, but there was moaning and sighing, a dismal counterpoint to the endless drumming and the blatting of the horns. When they drew on their pipes, they took deep breaths and then expelled the smoke in streams from their nostrils. None of them took any notice of us. They danced on, an endless chain of misery and rhythm.

We stood for what seemed a long time watching them pass. Likari appeared at my side and leaned close against me, obviously both dazzled and frightened. Olikea's face was pale; she reached out and seized her son by the shoulder and abruptly pulled him closer to her, as if danger threatened him. Soldier's Boy patted Likari absently and looked round for the lantern bearer who had guided us here. He had vanished, leaving Soldier's Boy, Olikea, Likari, and the bearers with their quaya standing in the midst of this organized chaos. We waited, inundated with noise and dust, long enough that Soldier's Boy began to seethe at the slight. Just as he turned to Olikea to complain of it, the door hanging of the pavilion was whisked aside and the plump young woman who had earlier visited us emerged.

"So you have come!" she declared as if mildly surprised. "Welcome to Kinrove's kin-clan and our Trading Place encampment. I will have someone guide your bearers to a place where your goods can be stored while you visit us. Kinrove bids me invite you to enter his pavilion and find refreshment there."

With this, she swept her hand toward the opened flap of the tent. Soldier's Boy nodded curtly to her and stepped up onto the wooden platform that floored the pavilion. He had to stoop to enter it. Olikea and Likari followed him. As soon as the heavy leather flap dropped down behind us, the sounds of the music and dancers outside were muted. I had not realized how much of an irritant it was until I was relieved of it.

The leather walls enclosed a substantial chamber. It was warm, almost too warm, and stuffy from the number of people it held. In a strange way, it reminded me of Colonel Haren's rooms at Gettys. It gave me the same strange sensation of having been transported to another place and time far from the forests and meadows and beach.

The floors were covered with reed carpets woven with designs that echoed the painting on the outside of the pavilion. Strips of bark fabric decorated with feathers and multicolored glass teardrops hung down from the shadowed ceiling. Suspended glass lanterns lit the room and drove the shadows back into the tapestry-draped corners. A long table burdened with food ran the full length of one side wall. There were several thronelike chairs in the room, all well cushioned and obviously designed to accommodate the weight and girth of a Great One. I was surprised to see that Jodoli occupied one of them, and a young but very heavy woman sat in another, smoking an elaborately carved ivory pipe. When she noticed me looking at her, she parted her lips and expelled a disdainful stream of smoke at me.

On the side of the tent opposite the food table, servants were pouring large jugs of steaming hot water into an immense copper bathtub. The water was scented and the rising steam perfumed the air. Other serving folk were coming and going, bringing in smoking platters of freshly cooked food and removing empty tureens or replenishing wineglasses.

But all of this coming and going of people bringing hot water and fresh food or removing dishes or refilling wineglasses was only the busy framework around the central spectacle. On a raised dais in the very center of the tent, Kinrove reclined in a cushioned hammock. The man was immense. Flesh was heaped upon flesh in rolls until the skeletal structure that had once defined him as a man was buried and muted. His body literally overspilled him; his belly sat in his lap and his head and chin were sunken in the roundness of his shoulders. A loose green robe covered him but did nothing to disguise his bulk; rather, it emphasized it. Broad stripes of gold outlined the contours of his body and repeated them. Among Gernian folk, such a man would have been an object of both ridicule and fascination. I had seen a man half his size displayed as a "fat man" in a Gernian carnival tent. He had been mocked and stared at. Here, Kinrove was an object of awe bordering on worship.

The man ruled the room. The gaze he turned on us was piercing, and there was power rather than indolence in the hand that lifted and beckoned us closer. His gesture was oddly graceful. He wore his flesh as another man might have worn a wealth of jewelry or the badges of his military rank. He used his size to command. The whole purpose of the pavilion was to center our focus on the sheer body size he had attained and it worked very well indeed. I was stunned by him. Feeders came and went around him, bringing food and drink, carrying off dishes, wiping his hands with moist cloths, massaging his feet and legs. A special stand at his elbow held several elaborate pipes and heavy glass canisters of tobacco. All the faces of those serving him showed deference, even affection. I saw no sign of resentment or anything less than devotion.

With a small jolt, I recognized the attitude that was displayed. When I was a small boy, my family had gone to visit the estate of another new noble family. They had lived up the river from us, a two-day journey, and I recalled how sternly my father had admonished me that Lord Skert was to be treated with great respect, for he had made many sacrifices for his king. I had expected to see some mighty muscled giant of a man, with a big beard and a booming voice. Instead, we were introduced to a man whose legs no longer worked. He was pushed from room to room in a wheeled chair, and burn scars had smoothed and twisted the side of his face and neck. Despite his scars and his disability, he had the bearing of a soldier. In the few days of our visit, I had come to see that he wore those scars as if they were medals he had earned. He was not shamed or humiliated by them; they were a part of his service record and he displayed them as such.

So did Kinrove. The size of his body obviously hampered him. Despite the scented oils being rubbed into his feet and calves, his legs looked painful, dusky, and swollen.

When he saw us, he moved his hand slightly, opening his palm to bid us enter. He inclined his head very slightly to the left. Again, I was struck by the grace of these small movements. There was an economy of motion to them that seemed full of beauty. "So. Here you are! I have heard of your coming among us, Soldier's Boy, trained by Lisana." He paused, cocked his head slightly, and said slyly, "And I give welcome also to Nevare of the Plain-skins."

Before I could respond to that strange greeting, he turned his attention back to the larger gathering and spoke loudly for their benefit. He had to pause between phrases. Even the effort of speaking taxed his wind. "You are not unknown to us. Jodoli has told us of how Olikea found you and rescued you. He has also"—and here his smile grew very wide—"told us of your first contest of might with him! It was a good tale." He chuckled, and all around the room, his merriment was echoed in rippling laughter.

He took another breath. "So I am pleased that you accepted my invitation." A breath. "It pleases me to confer with the Great Ones of the People from time to time, to hear from them how our war goes, to accept their thanks and to direct them as to how their efforts might best aid me." A breath. "Jodoli had told me that you were a very substantial man, before you burned much magic in a . . . shall we say 'inexperienced' rather than 'vain' attempt to stop the Jhernians?"

I felt the flush of hot blood that darkened Soldier's Boy's face. *You did this; you brought this shame on me!* He thrust the fierce thought at me, but to Kinrove he smiled and said, "I do not think my effort vain if it protected our ancestor trees for another season. I will do whatever I must to keep them safe until a final solution can be found."

"So you would do what you must to drive the invaders from our land. Good. The magic asks much of us, and much especially of your kin-clan this year. I summoned Jodoli here, as the Great Man of your kin-clan, to speak to him of the magic's need for more dancers. Imagine my surprise when he told me that his kin-clan had not one, but two Great Men now. Of course as soon as I heard that, I knew I must send for you. Such a strange thing to my eyes you are, a Great Man who grew up among the intruders. Jodoli thinks you are the key to the final solution. So the magic told him, in a dream, he says. And so the magic has whispered to me also. What do you say to that, Nevare of the Plain-skins? Do you know a way that we have not yet tried, Soldier's Boy? Do you know a way to drive the Jhernians from our borders and restore peace and prosperity to our folk? Perhaps with a new dance that has not yet been danced?"

He had paused often to breathe as he spoke to me. His frequent pauses made it hard for me to decide if he had finished speaking. His question sounded dangerous to me. Twice he had referred to me by both names. Inside Soldier's Boy, I huddled small. I did not like this Speck Great One addressing me directly. He saw too clearly.

Kinrove smiled. He did not move, but I felt that he leaned closer, and that he could see, not just Soldier's Boy, but me, Nevare, hidden inside him. He held out two fingers toward us, like open scissors, and then closed them together. The gesture seemed fraught with magic. "A joining makes a path," he said, and I felt threatened. His eyes peered more sharply. "A man cannot dance if his left foot tries to go one way and his right another. The dance happens when a man is in harmony with himself."

"I know a way to drive the Jhernians away!"

Her voice cracked on the words, but it was emotion that made it do so. The young female Great One ensconced in a chair across from Jodoli spoke. She stood, spreading her arms wide. When she did so, the bright yellow and black robe that she wore billowed out around her, amplifying her considerable girth. I was sure it was a contrived gesture to make her seem larger than she was. I was grateful that she had attracted attention away from me, even though I felt Soldier's Boy's annoyance that she had interrupted the challenge between Kinrove and himself. Beside me, Olikea released a pent breath. I wondered if she was relieved or annoyed.

The female Great One drew a deep breath. She folded her arms at her elbows, bringing her hands in to touch her ample bosom. The bright fabric billowed again as she bade him, "Speak to me, Kinrove! Or rather, listen! I know a way, and I have come here to speak to you of it! You were reluctant to allow me to come in, and since I have arrived, you have given me no chance to be heard. You fritter away our time with food and pleasures and trivial gossip. You make me wait as if I am of no consequence at all, even though I have told you I bring the words of not just my kin-clan, but the dissatisfied of many kin-clans. Then *he* appears"—and she waved a disdainful hand at me—"and you forget entirely that I am here. Why do you trouble with him when I am here? He is of the Plain-skins. He is the enemy. Someone has marked him as if he were of the People, but how can he be? Vermin beget vermin, not stags. If you wish to show us something of your power tonight, do so by killing him. Be rid of him, Kinrove. He but does what Jhernians have always done; they come, they take what is ours and use it to evil ends. He has usurped our magic and done us no good with it. Begin to find your ultimate solution by killing him and then finish it by listening to me!"

She looked directly at me then, and I felt, as Soldier's Boy did, the buffet of her power. He'd had sufficient warning to set my muscles and not stagger back from the blow, but her intent was clear. She'd meant to at least knock him down and humiliate him in front of the others if not do physical damage. I think it was the first time I'd met the eyes of another human being and actually felt the hate emanate from them.

"Stop!" When Kinrove spoke that word, I felt what the soldiers in Gettys had felt the night I had stopped them before they

killed me. It was a word of command backed by more magic than
Soldier's Boy could resist. I hadn't realized that Soldier's Boy had
mustered his magic to use against the girl. Perhaps he had done it
more intuitively or instinctively than as a planned reaction. But in
that moment, he dropped his guard just as a numbed hand releases
a weapon. Across from me, the girl spasmed as if doused with cold
water. I saw her take a deep, quivering breath. Then she retreated
a step, with her two feeders coming swiftly to help her take her
seat again. I could see that she was shivering and angry. Her teeth
were bared in her fury, or perhaps clenched to keep them from
chattering. I looked at her and thought that I would not have
chosen to make an enemy of her.

Soldier's Boy found his voice and spoke more boldly than I
would have under the circumstances. "I did not come here to be
insulted and attacked." He gestured to Likari and Olikea to follow
him and turned toward the door.

Behind us, I heard a flurry of steps and then frantic whispering. We were nearly at the tent flap when Kinrove spoke behind
me. "This is not the meeting I intended, Nevare of the Plain-skins.
Turn back, Soldier's Boy. Let us welcome you, and let us speak
together."

Soldier's Boy turned very slowly. It did not escape him that
a feeder, older and more gloriously robed than the others, stood
at Kinrove's side. Galea, without a doubt. She clasped her hands
before her, looking both anxious and hopeful. Soldier's Boy
spoke.

"I am not 'Nevare of the Plain-skins.' I am not completely
Nevare, though I will answer to that name. Soldier's Boy is an
awkward name, for it names me as belonging to the Gernians.
But I am of the People. I bear the marks of one of the People. I
was accepted by the elders and instructed by Lisana. I have left the
folk that I was born to, left the lands where I grew, and traveled far
to come to you. If you do not wish to accept me, then speak to
the magic that summoned me. Say to the magic that made me a
Great One that you are wiser than it is, and would have me leave."
Slowly he crossed his arms over his chest and then stood silently
confronting Kinrove as if daring him to commit that blasphemy.

Kinrove's face flushed, and next to me, I heard Likari give a small whimper of fear. Soldier's Boy stood firm and Olikea stood tall beside him. Whatever their earlier quarrel had been, they now stood united. The movement in the room had stilled. Outside the tent, the music thumped and squawked and the endless line of dancers shuffled on. It was a sound as eternal as the waves rushing against the beaches. I recognized it for magic and felt the drag of it against my senses. I wished it would stop so I could think more clearly.

I think Kinrove must have given her some sign, for Galea suddenly left his side and came bustling toward us. "Come, this is a poor way for us to begin. See, Nevare of the People, the bath that Kinrove ordered prepared for you awaits you now. And there is food and drink, freshly made, with which all of you can be refreshed. After you have relaxed a while we will all think more clearly and can begin to know one another. Come. Come."

These last words she spoke not to us, but to a gaggle of young assistants that she beckoned forward. They moved cautiously as if they feared they were throwing themselves into a fray, but Galea's face grew stern at their hesitation, and they suddenly came forward in a rush of brightly colored robes and reaching hands.

For the next few moments, I was almost glad it was Soldier's Boy who was wearing my body rather than me. At first he stood stern, arms crossed still. Then, as if he were offering them an honor, he slowly opened his arms and held them out from his side. Olikea did the same and Likari copied her. Kinrove's servants disrobed them, removing their garments respectfully. Two scuttled up behind me with a throne, so that Soldier's Boy might be seated while they drew off my boots and socks. Off to one side, the slighted and insulted young woman sulked, her angry magic virtually glowering around her. Her feeders, two men, whispered and patted at her, trying to soothe her. No one else seemed to pay attention to her at all. All around us, the previous bustle and noise of the pavilion had suddenly resumed, as if some dangerous crisis had passed, as perhaps it had. The three of us were escorted to our bath.

There was a feel of ritual to it that perhaps put the others at ease, but to me it was a bizarre experience. I'd never shared a bath with anyone, let alone a woman and small boy, nor been attended throughout it by people who thought it their duty to scrub and rinse my back, to be sure that my feet were clean even between my toes, let alone support me while I lay back so that yet another attendant could massage a fragrant soap through my hair and then rinse it out. Olikea supervised all these attentions in a very possessive way, and Likari soon joined in, warning them sternly not to get soap into my eyes and to be very gentle where my feet and legs were scratched from my barefoot days in the forest. After Soldier's Boy had clambered from the tub and was being toweled dry, Olikea and Likari received similar attention. Olikea maintained a dignity that said such was only her rightful due, but Likari wriggled like a happy puppy and exclaimed over the wonderful smells of the soaps and oils.

Galea's assistants quickly surrounded me. It alarmed me and I tried to warn Soldier's Boy to be on his guard against treachery. He either ignored or did not heed me as he relaxed in their hands. Three women were drying him carefully, lifting the folds of flesh to be sure that no moisture was trapped anywhere, while others were combing out my hair and dressing it with a fragrant oil. My feet were massaged and anointed, the many small scratches and abrasions on my calves were tended, and then two young women smoothed a buttery unguent onto them. My nails were carefully and gently trimmed and cleaned. Soft slippers were brought for my feet, and my own robe restored to me. A smoking table was set up near my chair, and an array of tobacco of various shades of brown displayed for my choice. Olikea shook her head firmly and motioned them all away, much to the amusement of Kinrove's feeders. "I do not allow him to have that," she said firmly, and while some of Kinrove's assistants nodded their approval, others rolled their eyes at Soldier's Boy in mock sympathy. Clearly my feeder managed my health with a strict hand.

Throughout all these attentions, the business of the pavilion had gone on about us. A number of emissaries had come and gone, and strain as he might, Soldier's Boy had been unable to hear much of what had transpired. Some seemed intent only on buying the goodwill of the Great Man; these ones brought tribute in the form of all sorts of food and rich goods. One, an older woman, had come seeking some sort of a boon from him. It was solemnly refused her, and she left weeping and angry, escorted from the pavilion by several of Kinrove's feeders. At this turn of affairs, the young female Great One looked more displeased and sullen than ever. She watched with great disapproval as Soldier's Boy was dried and tended. Her scowl was dark and threatening. And always, always, the endless drumming and thumping of the music and dancers went on like the beating of a giant heart. I longed for it to cease, for quiet to flood in and soothe me.

But that was not to be. No one else at the gathering seemed to pay the constant noise any mind. Once Soldier's Boy was dressed and ensconced on a throne again, Kinrove deigned to notice him once more. He made a signal to his feeders, and Soldier's Boy was lifted, throne and all, and carried within a comfortable speaking distance. Jodoli and the young Great One were also lifted and brought forward, but I noticed that our chairs were arranged so that Jodoli was between her and me, and she was at a slightly greater distance from Kinrove's elevated dais than either of us. Cushions were placed at my feet and Olikea and Likari made themselves comfortable there. Other people carried in tables already laden with food, plates, wine, and glasses, and these were placed in easy proximity to our chairs. It was all done swiftly and graciously, yet his hospitality did not extend to permitting his guests onto his dais. He kept his vantage: to look at him Soldier's Boy had to tilt my head. The message was not subtle at all: he regarded himself as Greatest of the Great Ones and asserted his right to lord it over other Great Ones.

But the aroma of the food mollified the resentment and wariness Soldier's Boy felt. I was shocked at how his hunger roared back to life at the sight of it. The quality of the food offered to us from Kinrove's table made our earlier feast seem a crude meal indeed. The style of preparation and the spices used were foreign to me, as was the way the dishes were presented, but I could not quibble with the result. The flavors brought back rich memories to Soldier's Boy of when Lisana had been alive and had dined as grandly as this every day. This lavishing of attention and catering to needs were how the Specks rewarded their Great Ones. For some years Kinrove had been the Greatest of the Great, but Jodoli and every other Great One anticipated that as they grew in size and mightiness, their kin-clans would pay this sort of homage to them. To sample this lifestyle now was a foretaste of what might come. Likari's beaming little face betrayed that he was very much enjoying himself. Olikea looked around with greedy eyes, storing up her memories of this wonderful night. This was what she aspired to; she would live as Galea did, waited on hand and foot and accorded all the respect due to the favored feeder of a Great One.

There was little conversation; talking would have interfered with the eating. Olikea asserted her right to be the one to serve food to Soldier's Boy, and this she did so assiduously that my mouth was scarcely ever empty. Firada was there to tend to Jodoli's needs. She appeared to compete with her younger sister to be even more attentive to Jodoli than Olikea was to me. A moment later, I realized there *was* competition there, not for the food but for how much of it each of us could consume. Soldier's Boy was sated and more than sated, but Olikea kept pressing him to eat, enticing him to try a bite of this or to have just one more mouthful of that. Behavior that had been shameful at my brother's wedding less than two years ago was now hailed as the height of manners. Not only did Soldier's Boy honor Kinrove with enjoyment of his food, he achieved status for himself as he continued to eat long after Jodoli had turned his face away from Firada's entreaties.

The only competition was the young female Great One who had earlier expressed the desire to kill me. Between bites, Soldier's Boy watched her from the corner of my eye and tried to overhear the few words that were spoken by her. I gleaned that her name was Dasie and that her people lived to the north of my Specks. Soldier's Boy searched the recollections Lisana had shared with him. In summer, the two kin-clans had little to do with each other. It was only in winter when they came to the coast and shared the same hunting grounds under the eaves of the evergreen forest that the kin-clans crossed paths. But they shared with our kin-clan what we shared with every Speck kin-clan: the Valley of the Ancestor Trees. Their Great Ones were entombed there, living in the kaembra trees just as ours were. The two trees that had been the first to fall had been their eldest elders. My kin-clan mourned them as a loss to the People, but Dasie and her kin-clan mourned them as murdered relatives. It did not matter that the people embodied in the trees had died generations ago; if anything, it made their lingering awareness and wisdom all the more precious. The Gernians had destroyed their deepest link to their past. Their hatred burned hot. And so she watched as Soldier's Boy ate, and I watched her. Her primary feeders were two men, one about my age and the other a man of about forty years. They conferred with each other as they fed her, and several times Soldier's Boy caught the younger man staring at him with extreme dislike.

This was not at all the initial meeting that I had expected with Kinrove, and I wondered again what his strategy was in inviting us here. That his feeder hoped to win the use of the fertility image I understood. But looking at the man and feeling the sense of command that he exuded, I doubted that was the whole of why we had been summoned. The tension between him and Dasie was palpable. Why was she here? What did she hope to gain? I suspected that Kinrove played a deeper political game than we knew. It worried me.

I began to wish that Soldier's Boy had not eaten earlier. My belly was uncomfortably distended now. He no longer ate with pleasure. Instead, he watched Dasie and matched her bite for bite. She was slowing; her feeders bent over her, urging her to continue eating. She accepted another bite.

It was only then that I became aware of Olikea's role. She was showing a substantial portion of food each time she held it to Soldier's Boy's mouth, but a good part of it she was palming, making it appear that he was eating a lot more than he actually was. A flush of anger and frustration passed over Dasie's face, and she abruptly turned away from her feeders. Olikea made a mime of feeding him not just one, but two more mouthfuls of food before she warned Soldier's Boy, loud enough to be overheard, "I think you should stop for now, Great One. Later, I promise you, I will find more food for you."

We had won. Soldier's Boy breathed a soft sigh of relief. His gut ached, but as he looked slowly from Dasie's sulky countenance to a chastened Jodoli, he knew it had been worth it. He had established himself in the order. He lifted his gaze to Kinrove. His feeder was starting a pipe for him. The Great Man gave no sign he was aware of what had just happened, but Soldier's Boy was smugly certain that he was. Kinrove spoke.

"We have eaten together, and I trust you took pleasure in my food. Now let us speak to one another, for I would hear what is happening with the People, both far and near. Jodoli has told me of the kin-clan you share, Nevare. His words have saddened me. It is a great loss for us to know that yet more of our ancestor trees have fallen. And yet I savor my triumph as well. Many have spoken against my dance, saying that it costs our people too much. But what cost is too high to pay for keeping our ancestor trees? If the dance stops and the Jhernians flood forward with their iron blades to fell our ancestral groves, what good does it do that we are still alive here?" His hands moved as he asked each question. They spoke as eloquently as his words. "Does the leaf outlive the branch? The dance continues to protect our forest. Without it, I believe that all our ancestors would have been slaughtered by now. Without my dance, by now the Jhernians would be standing right here, and our magic would be lost. The People would be ended. But my great dance makes the fear that holds them at bay. My great dance sends weariness and despair rolling down on them. Against my dance, they have not prevailed and they will not prevail. Only my dance has saved us."

He smiled down on us, as if inviting us to agree with him. Jodoli nodded slowly, but Dasie only looked at him with narrowed eyes. Soldier's Boy was very still, waiting and watching. I noticed what he apparently did not; Olikea looked at Kinrove with stark horror. Kinrove looked at Soldier's Boy, still smiling with his lips, but his eyes were waiting for his response and weighing his value as he did so.

Soldier's Boy finally spoke. "The intruders are still there, Great One Kinrove. They still intend to cut the trees and to build a road that will bring them to our winter grounds. The Trading Place is full of their goods, and iron is traded without regard for the well-being of our magic. Our own people bring the most dangerous parts of the intruders among us. Simply holding them back will not prevail. I do not speak against your dance, but I do not think it is enough to save us."

Next to me, Olikea jumped as Dasie suddenly spoke. "The intruder at least speaks the truth! The dance isn't enough, Kinrove! The dance is not enough to protect us! And at the same time, the dance is too much. It is too much of a price for the People to pay. You sit on your throne and call yourself the Greatest of the Great! You smile and say you have saved us, that our trees still stand, as if we should forget the ones who have fallen. As if we should forget those who dance and dance and dance to work your magic. Six years ago, before the magic touched me and I became a Great One, do you know what I was, Kinrove? I was a child weeping for my kin-clan. For that was the year that you sent the magic on us, sent it on your own people, to command those that it touched to come and be part of your dance. Sixteen of my kin-clan came to answer your call. Sixteen: two old men, nine young women, four young men, and one boy. That boy was my brother, just a year older than I was."

She paused as if waiting for him to deny it. Kinrove just looked down at her quietly. His words, when they came, were without mercy. "Every kin-clan has sent dancers. Your kin-clan has not contributed in any greater way than any other. We must have dancers for the dance."

"How many of those taken from my clan six years ago still live? How many still dance for you?" She paused, but did not really give him a chance to respond. Soldier's Boy was listening intently. I shared his focus; I sensed we were close to the heart of a mystery. Olikea had been standing behind him, her hands resting possessively on his shoulders. At Dasie's words, her fingers had slowly closed until she gripped his robe with knotted fists. He could hear her tension in her breathing and feel it in her stance. What was this?

"I will tell you, Kinrove. For before I came into your grand pavilion this evening, I stood and watched your dancers pass. I watched them make three circuits. I studied each face as each one passed. I saw no joy in any of them. Only fear. Or despair. Many wore the look of one who knows that death is soon to come. A few hate you, Kinrove. Did you know that? Do you ever go outside and look at the faces of those you have called to dance? Have you forgotten that once your dancers were the People?"

The pavilion had grown quiet. Serving folk still moved, but they had slowed, as if they lingered to hear an answer. The importance of her question sang silently in the air around us. The drumming and horns and the endless shuffling of the dancers seemed to grow louder in that stillness.

Kinrove's answer was not as strong as it could have been. "The magic calls the dancers. I but send it out. Every year, in rotation, it goes to a different kin-clan. It goes forth and it summons, and some answer that summons. I cannot control who is called. I do only what is needed. And those who are called and come here to dance, dance for all of us. It is not a shameful calling. When they die, they are buried with respect. Their lives have served us all well."

"They have not had lives!" Dasie asserted in response. "Especially not those who answer the call when they are little more than children. Their lives stop on the day they come to you. What do they do from that day hence, Great One? Do they laugh or take mates? Do they have children or hunt or talk around the fire in the evening with their neighbors? Do they have any life of their own? NO! They dance. Endlessly. They dance until they drop, and then they are dragged away from the chain for a brief rest, fed the herbs and foods that will fill their bodies with energy again, and then they are taken back to the dance. They dance until they are mindless, nothing more than bodies in motion, like spindles weaving your dance of magic. And then they die. Why are their deaths so unimportant to you? Why are their deaths worth so much less than the death of a person who left his body a hundred years ago?"

I felt the same shiver that ran up Soldier's Boy's back. I knew what the magic's call to me had done to my life. I thought of all the dancers I had glimpsed so briefly on my way into the pavilion.

I tried to imagine what it would be like to serve the magic in an endless dance. I knew how the magic had commanded me. I'd seen what it had done to Hitch. But what if it had demanded of me that I dance, endlessly, in a circle? What if I'd known that the dance would be the final sum of all my life? What would it be to rise daily from brief rest, knowing that all that day I would dance until weariness dropped me? Was the fear they had worn on their faces real? Did they dance in terror or black despair as a way to generate the waves of magic that rolled over the King's Road and through Gettys? I could not imagine such an existence, nor the leader who would condemn his people to live it. Even the prisoners who labored on the King's Road always knew there was eventually an end to their task. Some died before they reached that end, true, but those deaths were not inevitable. Many reached their freedom and even realized the King's promise of land and a home of their own. Kinrove's dancers were expected to dance their lives away, in the name of keeping the ancestral forest safe. And apparently he saw no eventual end to the dance, no final solution. To keep the intruders at bay, the dance would have to go on forever.

It appalled me. I was shocked that any leader could use his people so. I tried to break into Soldier's Boy's thoughts: "And I'm not the only one who thinks it's monstrous. Look at Dasie, Soldier's Boy. She and others like her are why Kinrove has a magical barrier around his encampment. He may call himself Greatest of the Great, but not all believe he should wear that title." As before, I received no acknowledgment from the other half of myself. I retired to seethe quietly to myself.

At last Kinrove spoke. "I do not undervalue my dancers, Dasie. Without them, I could not weave the magic that protects us all. I spend them only because I must, just as I spend myself. They and I are part of a greater magic, one that you do not comprehend. You ask if their lives are not worth as much as those of our elders. No. They are not. Each elder in a tree was a Great One in his time, chosen not by man but by the magic. And in the years they have existed since then, they have acquired ever more knowledge. They hold our past for us and guide us toward a future. Those who must die to protect them should feel honored to do so. They are honored by us while they live and dance. We give to each the best care we can—"

"Except to give them back their lives!" Dasie cut in angrily. I could feel her anger. I do not know if she meant to expend magic, but she did. The fury rolled off her in waves; Soldier's Boy felt it as a surge of unfriendly warmth against my skin. Her feeders were leaning forward, whispering to her urgently, but she paid them no mind. "For years you have used them, Kinrove. Used them, and claimed the magic they made as your own. You have styled your-self the 'Greatest of the Great' on the heaps of their bones. You say you do it to save us from the Jhernians. But you take from us more than we can replace. Yearly the dancers die, and we do not bear enough children to replace them. You are dancing your own people to death in the name of saving them."

Kinrove looked aggrieved and angered. "You criticize what I do, Dasie. You tell me to do it differently. But you, what do you do to protect your people and our ancestor trees? You want to end my dance, but what will replace it? You have been a Great One less than a hand of years, but you will tell us what we must do to drive the intruders back?"

She was not daunted. She took a step toward him. "I will tell you what you must do to keep from killing our own people! Let them live in their homes, find mates, and have children. If after I have been a Great One for twenty years, I forget that, as you seem to have done, then I hope some youngster will come before me and remind me of it. What good is it to save the trees of our ances-tors if they have no descendants left to honor them and seek their wisdom? And as to the intruders, yes, I have an answer to that. We must kill them. Kill them, and kill any who come after them, and keep killing them until no more of them come."

"You are a child." Kinrove said the belittling words flatly, but in a tone that made them more statement than insult. "You cannot recall what has gone before, because you were not born then. We tried to use the magic against the intruders, to take it right to their homes. Their iron confounds us. Within their village, our magic is weak. Our mages struggle to wake a spark from wood, cannot bid the earth comfort us, cannot even warm our own bodies. The only magic we have found that will work within their walls is the Dust Dance. And no one knows why it works when all other magic fails. By itself, it is not enough. It kills them, but they only call for more of their brethren from the west. Before you were a Great One, when first they threatened our forest of ancients, we tried to fight them as we have seen others fight. We rose against them and went to battle, protected by the magic of the Great Ones who came with us. But they fired their guns at us, and the iron passed through our magic and then our flesh, tearing as it went, flesh and bone and organ. The Great Ones who had thought to protect our warriors died that day. Many of our young men died. So many. A generation, Dasie. Shall we speak of how many children were not born because there were not men to father them? You say that over the years my dance has devoured the People. And what you say is true. But what my dance has devoured over all the years we have danced it is still less than the number of warriors who fell in that day."

Dasie opened her mouth to speak, but a sharp gesture from Kinrove cut off her words. I do not know if he used magic or merely the force of his personality to silence her. There was power in this man, in every nod of his head or flick of his fingers. Great power. I felt there was something more there, something I was missing, but his words caught me up and distracted me.

"I was there, Dasie. I saw them fall, my father and my two elder brothers among them. I was not a Great Man then, though I had begun to grow fat with magic. No one else had noticed it in me, and I scarcely dared to believe it myself. But what I saw that day taught me the one thing that I still know is true. We cannot take the magic as a weapon and use it within their walls. The iron thwarts us. But the magic can be our wall that holds back the swelling tide of the intruders and keeps us safe. And as soon as I was large enough to implement such a plan, I did so. And because I did so, you were able to grow up, in relative peace, in our own forest and mountains. You say you want to bring war to the intruders and death? Dasie, I am your war!"

His voice shook with passion. I was shocked when Kinrove's eyes left her and came to rest on me. "Have you nothing to say to this, Soldier's Boy–Nevare?"

There was a long moment of silence. I felt Soldier's Boy draw his courage together. Then his cold words stunned me. "Kinrove, I think that Dasie is right. Indeed, you have worked a great magic, and it has held them at bay for years. All of the People should feel gratitude to you for that. But the wall has begun to crumble. And I will tell you a fearsome thing, Kinrove. The intruders do not understand that we are at war with them. They do not even recognize the magic of the Dust Dance, let alone the power of the magic that sends fear and sadness down upon them. I have walked among them as one of them. Do you want to know what they believe? They think we are simple, primitive people, living like beasts in the forest. They pity us and they despise us. They think they will help us to become like them, and that we will be grateful for that. They believe we long to be just like them, and they are very willing to help us forget how to be the People and become just like them.

"They believe that eventually they will cut our trees and build their road and that we will forget what it is to be the People. They say that they will trade with us, and come to this land to trade with the folk from across the salt water. Our Trading Place would become theirs. A city of intruders would rise here. They would come here, with their iron and tobacco, and in a generation or two, we would no longer be the People. You have slowed their advance, Kinrove, but you have not stopped them. The dance has done all it can. Now it is time to fight them in a way they understand."

The Great Man looked incredulous. His clenched hands rose over his head. They fell as he thundered at us, "You have no memories! You do not recall the last time we stood to fight them, how many of our people died in that single day! If we do as she suggests, it will not take long for all the People to be dead, and no one will be left to guard our trees or mourn when they fall! That is not the answer I expected from you, Soldier's Boy–Nevare! Do you seek still to shirk your task? Do you think

I have not taken the herbs that bring the magic's true dreams to me? I know who you are! I know what you are! Why do you not do your duty and obey the magic? You are the one who was supposed to drive the intruders from our lands forever. All the Great Ones know this! Jodoli knows this, and I know he has spoken to you about it. I even know that you have told him that you do not know what the magic wants you to do! If we pressed Dasie, perhaps even she would admit that the magic has whispered to her that one is coming who will drive the intruders from our lands."

He turned his head so abruptly that the blame he had been heaping on me appeared to belong to Dasie. If he had thought to see her quail, he was doomed to disappointment. She struck her breast with her open hand.

"Me, Great Kinrove. Not him. I am what the magic wants, and my way will clear the land of the intruders and restore the dancers to their families. I know this is so. He is not your answer; he is just in the way, confusing us. But as you seem charmed by him, pay attention to what he says. He says I am right. So will you listen to me? Will you help me to make the plans that will free us of the intruders forever?"

Kinrove flicked his hand at her, dismissing her. "I have listened to you tonight. All I have heard, Dasie, is the utterance of an unproven youngster seeking to make herself important. You wanted so desperately to speak to me, and finally I gave way and let you in. But you have not listened yourself, to anything that has been said. You just want to make this gathering listen to your ideas. We have listened. Now you should leave." His extended palm pushed toward the entry of his tent, as if he were literally pushing her out of the door. His tone was adamant and his words final.

"I feared that you would say that," she said, but her tone sounded as if she had not feared any such thing, but had hoped for it. "I do not willingly do this, Kinrove. I know it will sow discord among us. But you have to be shown that your ways no longer work. You have to be shown that I know how to remove the intruders from our land. And it begins by showing you what they would do if ever they reached this far. It starts now!"

I do not know how the signal was passed. Perhaps it was a magic that I did not know, a near instantaneous dream-walk into someone else's mind. Perhaps she had simply timed her speech and brought events to this pass just as she wished them to happen. In any case, I felt it and I saw Kinrove's eyes widen as the shock of it passed through him. The magical barriers that had guarded his encampment fell away in tatters. I felt them tear and give way, cloven by iron blades.

CHAPTER SEVENTEEN

TREACHERY

Soldier's Boy could read the magic as clearly as if he were witnessing the events with my eyes. Blades, iron blades, had cut and torn the magical barrier around Kinrove's encampment. Like knives through silk, they had shorn his protection away. Iron was moving toward the pavilion at a deadly pace. Soldier's Boy already felt it burning against him. Kinrove looked about in consternation. "We are under attack!" he announced to his people. "Arm yourselves!"

But he was already too late.

Through that barrier had swarmed Dasie's followers. They came at a run. She could not quick-walk them all; she was not that strong. And those that were bearing iron, her magic could not move at all. But she did not need many of them. Half a dozen armed warriors suddenly strode into the pavilion. They moved like hunting cats through the chaos. Their copper-bladed weapons caught the light and flashed as each took up his position.

Her strategy was well planned, and her warriors knew their roles perfectly. They rushed in, and in an instant, each Great One was being menaced with a blade. Feeders and servers shouted and shrieked in horror. Folk attempted to flee in all directions. Tables were overturned, dishes and food went flying, and Kinrove's own guards were hampered by the panicked mob as they struggled to reach his side. "Take her prisoner!" Kinrove shouted at them, even as he struggled to master the man and the blade that threatened him. A young man with a gleaming copper blade sprang at Soldier's Boy. Olikea and Likari pressed close to me, and in a matter of moments, Soldier's Boy had summoned his magic to protect them.

I saw the warrior menacing us react. He gripped his sword more tightly and leaned on it, as if hoping that the magic that held him back would give way for just an instant. Soldier's Boy's heart was pounding with effort. We both knew that if his shield of magic gave way, that sword would sink straight into his chest. Including Likari and Olikea in his sheltered space demanded a great deal of effort. I could feel the magic being consumed as his effort burned it away. He spared a quick glance for Kinrove.

With a greater reservoir of magic at his command, Kinrove was almost in control of the situation. With a pointing finger and a clenched-fist gesture, he'd forced his attacker to his knees. The man, his eyes dazed, seemed intent on trying to plunge his blade into the wooden floor of the pavilion. Soldier's Boy shifted his gaze sideways. Jodoli and Firada were safe but under siege as we were. For her part, Dasie was using her strength to keep Kinrove's warriors at a distance from her. Sweat stood out on her face. Four men, each bearing a large flint blade, had surrounded her. They pressed toward her but could not reach her. Her feeders had drawn knives of their own. They were back-to-back, outside her circle of safety and unhampered by it. Kinrove's guard had chosen not to close with them. I read in that their inexperience. For too long, they had counted on the Great One's magic to protect them all.

"Come take this man prisoner! Leave her for me to deal with!" Kinrove commanded them. His attacker had succeeded in wedging his blade into the floor. With an addled expression, he was trying to shove the blade still deeper. Kinrove's guards looked relieved to be given a simpler target. They moved to close in around the man, and I dreaded that at any moment I'd see him slain. Kinrove turned his eyes toward Dasie. She met his gaze. Slowly he lifted both his hands, open palms toward her, and then began to bring them together as if he were squeezing something. I heard her make a strangled sound, as if she expended great effort. His moving hands slowed and then halted. Without touching, they struggled against one another.

Despite the threat that menaced us, Soldier's Boy's eyes were drawn to watching her. Dasie trembled suddenly and I thought all her defenses would give way. Then she suddenly took a deep breath, threw back her head, and gave a wild cry as if she had thrown all her resources into one blow. Kinrove flinched, shook his head wildly, and then hung his head, panting. His hands fell to his side. One of Dasie's feeders laughed aloud, a hoarse triumphant sound.

Before Kinrove could recover, I heard a sound I'd never expected to hear in Speck territory. I knew well the clatter of hooves. I put the pieces together quickly. Dasie's reinforcements had arrived. The force that she could not quick-walk down to Kinrove's encampment had just charged into Kinrove's encampment on horseback. And they bore iron, lots of iron. Soldier's Boy could feel it.

We heard wild cries of confusion outside, shouts of angry men and shrieks of terror. The flap of the pavilion was torn loose and six armed Specks raced in. Each bore one long sword and carried a second, shorter blade of iron. The motley collection of armor they wore would have been laughable, if not for the impact of the iron. The shock of the metal near stunned Soldier's Boy. He felt as if the air in the place had been torn asunder by an explosion. A man with an iron sword swiftly replaced the fellow who had threatened us with a copper one, and handed his extra blade to the first man. He waved the weapon at us and I felt Soldier's Boy's magic shield literally fall to threads. In that instant, I expected to die, but the warrior merely rested the tip of the blade against my breast. That was enough. Just the presence of the metal made it hard for Soldier's Boy to breathe.

The presence of iron in the room disrupted all magic. The balance of power in the pavilion shifted until a blade was menacing every Great One in the pavilion except Dasie, while four were pointed at Kinrove. Dasie's two feeders still flanked her, flourishing bronze blades. They quickly moved her and her chair as far as they could from the iron without taking her out of the pavilion. Her brow was furrowed and her breathing seemed labored, but undoubtedly she was in a better situation than the rest of the Great Ones.

Kinrove was pale and his lips puffed in and out with every breath he took. Not one but the tips of four iron blades touched his flesh. It was quickly apparent to me that all of his feeders and other hangers-on were accustomed to relying on his magic for defense. They gawked, stupefied, as if expecting that at any moment Kinrove would seize control of the situation. But, confronted with the iron blades that could end all his magic as well as his life and physically unable to defend his own person, he could barely sit up and was gasping in shock at his own predicament. His eyes darted wildly, taking in the situation, but he gave no orders. Perhaps he had no breath to spare.

Outside, the wild clatter of hooves continued as more and more horsemen arrived. More stunning than the sound of horses being drawn to a halt outside the pavilion was the event that followed it. The music, the ever-present din that had pressed against my ears and body since we arrived at the encampment, rattled to a halt and then ceased. There were shouts of confusion outside and cries of fear and anger. Suddenly the tent flap was torn away and one of Dasie's lieutenants shouted to her, "We have halted the dance, Great One! We are already in the process of finding those stolen from our kin-clan. Are you in command inside the pavilion?"

"I am!" Dasie called back to him. "Proceed as we planned. Fight only if anyone resists you. Even then, refrain from killing if it is possible. Enough of the People have already been killed for this dance. I do not wish the blood of my own people to be on my hands."

As the young man strode away, Dasie spoke to those of us still inside. Her voice shook at first, but as she went on, she seemed to gain strength. "As you have heard, I do not wish to harm anyone. All I want, at this moment, is to free those stolen from their lives to dance for Kinrove. If everyone does as we say, all will go well. None of the People will be injured. Resist, and Kinrove may die. I do not want to be pushed to that extreme! So, all of you, please move over and stand near the tables of food. Go now. Go. Yes, I mean all of you, feeders included. Your Great Ones will have to manage for themselves for a short time."

I watched her through Soldier's Boy's eyes. I could see that the iron bothered her; it bothered Soldier's Boy even more, for the heavy blade hovered not a handspan from his heart and the man who held it was flinty-eyed and smiling. Yet, "Go. Obey her," he told Olikea, and when Likari clung to him, whimpering, he shook the boy free and said harshly, "Take him with you." Olikea seized her son by the shoulder and steered him away. The boy looked back over his shoulder, agony in his eyes. Soldier's Boy couldn't as much as nod to the boy. The presence of the iron was a crawling sensation, as if stinging ants swarmed over his entire body.

I assessed our chances. "If he lunges at you, move to the right, drop to the ground, and roll. It may buy you a few moments. He doesn't hold that weapon as if he knows how to use it."

I offered him the thoughts and felt his irritated response: "I see no advantage to being stabbed while rolling about on the ground as opposed to sitting in a chair. Be quiet. Don't distract me now." He was focusing every bit of his self-discipline to remain still and not react to the stinging of the iron. He had begun to sweat. He'd used magic to defend himself and already his body was clamoring for food to replenish it. He pushed his hunger aside.

I took his advice, mostly because I had no other ideas to offer. Dasie had risen from her throne. She stalked the room, her feeders to either side of her. She took short, savage puffs from a pipe, and puffed the smoke from her lips in explosive little bursts. I think she listened, as I did, to the confusion of sounds from outside. There were shouts of joy and also wild weeping and a clamor of questions as her men sorted through the dancers looking for their stolen loved ones. She walked over to me and stood behind the shoulder of the man who held the sword. Her eyes were not kind. Earlier she had urged Kinrove to kill me. I had no reason to think she had changed her mind. She had said she did not wish to shed blood. I wondered if her forbearance would extend to not shedding *my* blood.

Kinrove suddenly spoke. His hands were still and his words seemed to lack power. "You. You are not of Dasie's kin-clan. You are Clam Grounds clan. Why are you here, obeying her orders?"

He asked his question of the young man who menaced him with a sword. I could not see the warrior's face but his voice was steady and calm as he replied, "I am here to fetch my sisters home to our kin-clan. I would follow any Great One who offered me the opportunity to do that."

Dasie abruptly turned aside from me and strode up to Kinrove, stopping well away from the iron. "I have tried to tell you and you would not listen. Do you think it is only my kin-clan who are heartsick for their stolen ones? No. Our weariness of your futile magic extends through many kin-clans. When we leave, our relatives go with us. I do not think you will have enough dancers left to protect your pavilion, let alone work your great magic. If you are wise, after we depart, you will let the others go back to their homes. Perhaps with that act you can buy yourself some goodwill from those your magic has so long betrayed. Perhaps once you have freed those you enslaved, you will no longer need to use the magic of the People to shield yourself from the People's anger."

"I, a betrayer? What of yourself, Dasie? Do not you and your magic belong to your kin-clan? Yet here you are, with a mongrel horde of followers, rising up against the People. By what authority do you do this? Your kin-clan gave birth to you. They have poured their resources into making you great. You should care first for their interests rather than making this grand grab for power you are not capable of wielding."

She laughed. "You think that is what this is about, Kinrove? You think that I seek to tear you from your dais and take your place? I care nothing for the power you wield. I do not want to be what you are. My care is for the People, and not just the folk of my own kin-clan, but all who have been forced into slavery by your dance."

"Again, you fool, it is not I who have called them to dance but the magic! Will you defy the magic?"

"I will defy *your* magic! Each one of the folk that I rescue will be given a little necklace of iron chain to wear. You will not be able to summon them back! Show him, Tread."

At her command, one of the warriors menacing Kinrove lowered his sword. With his free hand, he pulled the collar of his leather shirt open to reveal the little iron chain he wore around his neck. "Your magic cannot command me, Kinrove," he said quietly.

Kinrove's eyes seemed to bulge from their sockets and his face grew red. "You, a Great One of the People, will pollute us with iron? Do you know what you do, bringing that foul metal among us? Do you know how you will cripple your own magic as well as all magic to follow you?"

Dasie lifted her arms and slid back the sleeves of her robe to expose her pale arms. The folds of flesh on her arms hung slack and empty. "I know what iron costs me! For the past month, I've lived with iron! I've known its burn every day. And I know what magic costs. I've consumed nearly all I had simply to come here and take back from you what belongs to every member of the People. If you manage to kill me before I depart here, it will still have been worth it, Kinrove. I would not mind dying if my kin-clan remember me as the Great One who chose to use her magic to free them from you! Even if I had to use iron to do it."

"You think you've freed our people?" Kinrove dragged himself upright, closer to the menacing blades. He drew in a deep breath with difficulty. I think only his anger gave him the strength to go on. Before my very eyes, he seemed to be diminishing. "You are selfish and stupid, then. You've killed our people. You disrupted the dance. Without the onslaught of the magic, the intruders will find their wills again. Do you think they will wait until spring to attack our trees, to come into our forest to try to find us and destroy us? No. By this time tomorrow, their iron will be biting into our trees. Our ancestors will be falling, and the invasion of our forest will have begun!"

"The winter will hold them at bay!" Dasie asserted. "That is why I chose to act now. The cold and the snows will immobilize them. We have time, not much time, but some. Time to rally ourselves, time to take up arms and move against them in a way they will understand. How many years have our people danced, and danced in vain? The intruders haven't left. And they won't, Kinrove, not while all we do is dance fear and discouragement at them. The fear and discouragement, they have lived with and battled. It has not made them leave. They will leave only when they know that if they stay, they will die. That is the dance they will understand."

Kinrove's voice thickened, and I was surprised to see the glitter of tears in his eyes. "You have killed us all, Dasie. You do not know the Jhernians. They are like stinging ants or angry wasps. You can kill one or you can kill a dozen. You can kill a hundred. But so long as the hive exists, more will come. And they will be angry. I sent them a magic they did not understand, and for years that held them back. If you go to kill them with weapons, yes, that will be a war they will understand. And it is a war they are very, very good at waging."

Dasie scarcely seemed to be paying attention to him. I think the demands of her body had temporarily overwhelmed her. I could not even imagine how much magic she had burned to accomplish this. I do know that Soldier's Boy watched her with avid envy as she walked over to the food tables. She took food from the dishes there and ate, without discrimination or grace, but with only the drive to replenish herself. It reminded me of a horse drinking after a long day's ride. She made a brusque gesture at one of her feeders, and he quickly filled a pipe for her. He held it for her, and from time to time she took it from him, pulling long draws from the pipe in between mouthfuls of food. For a time, an odd silence held in the pavilion. From outside the pavilion, we could hear chaotic voices, shouted commands, and occasional cries of joy.

Soldier's Boy kept as still as a small animal hiding in deep grass. He glanced over at Jodoli. Sweat was running down the sides of his face and he looked ill. His eyes were glassy and his mouth hung open. He looked back at Kinrove, who was weeping openly now.

Dasie turned away from the table at last. She looked around at us all. In her two hands, she held a round of dark brown bread. "What should I do with you?" she asked Kinrove. "I do not wish to kill you. I think that if you will agree to leave off this mad dance, you could still be of great use to your kin-clan. And even more use to me, if you would help me. But I don't know if I can trust you. I thought of making you swallow a little pellet of iron, or shooting some into your body. I've heard that can destroy a Great One's magic completely. I don't wish to do that to you. Or to Jodoli. But I have to be sure that neither of you are plotting against me behind my back. If you will not help me, I at least need to know that you will not hinder me."

"You have destroyed my dance." Kinrove drew a deep, shuddering breath. "My dance is broken. I will need whatever magic I can rebuild to save my own kin-clan. You have condemned the People. I will not have the power to save them. But I will do what I can to keep at least my kin-clan safe." He struggled for another breath. Almost reflexively, he glanced toward his feeder, Galea. She stood, hands clasped before her, her face tensed in an agony of fear for him. He took another breath. "Dasie, I will not hinder you," he said quietly. "I will not permit any of my kin-clan to hinder you. By the magic, I swear this."

"Put your swords away," she said quietly to the men who surrounded him, and they sheathed their weapons. She glanced at Galea. "You may tend to your Great One," she told her, and the woman snatched a bowl of food from the table and raced to his side. Other feeders followed her, surrounding Kinrove, wiping the sweat from his brow with cool, damp cloths, offering water, wine, and delicacies, and all the while exclaiming with dismay at how his magic had been drained by the iron.

Dasie had turned her attention to Jodoli. "And you?" she asked him severely. "Will you try to stop me from what I must do?"

Jodoli was not without his pride nor did he lack intelligence. His head had sunk forward onto his chest. Sweat ran freely down the sides of his face and his robe was drenched with it. He rolled his head back on his shoulders and looked up at her as she stood over him. His eyes were horribly bloodshot. "Can you believe," he wheezed out, "anything a man says when a sword is at his chest?"

She stared at him. Then she made a curt gesture, and her warrior moved the tip of his blade away from Jodoli's chest. Jodoli's breathing eased but he still said nothing to her.

Dasie did not have the stomach for it. She gestured angrily at the feeders and servers who huddled still along the wall. "Come to him! Bring him water and food." Then she turned back to Jodoli. "I ask you, by the magic, to tell me the truth; do you intend to hinder me in any way?"

"What could I do to stop you?" he demanded of her. "I have seen far more of the Jhernians than you have. Like Kinrove, I think what you do is madness. You will stir up the hornets' nest and all of us will be stung. I think I will do what Kinrove does; I will do all I can to protect my own kin-clan, and hope that the rest of the People can care for themselves."

Despite being at her mercy, he spoke to her as if she were a small, selfish child. His disdain was not lost on her. "When I have driven the intruders away," she said to him through gritted teeth, "then I will send for you. And you will come to me and thank me and beg me to forgive you for how wrong you were. I think you may be surprised, when I put out the call for warriors ready to defend our lands, how many of your folk will answer that call. Many of us are sick and weary with waiting and waiting and waiting for someone to drive them away."

I thought he would be wise and keep silent. Firada was at his side now. She held a cup to his lips and Soldier's Boy watched enviously as he drank deeply. When he lifted his face from the cup, he drew three deep breaths. Dasie had started to turn away when he spoke to her. "They have always come to our lands, Dasie. The intruders are not newcomers here. Go to the elders if you do not believe me. Dream-walk to the oldest of your kin-clan and ask. Always they came, at high summer, to trade with us. In times past, before they built their Gettys Fort, we let them come into the mountains and some even journeyed as far as the Trading Place. How else do you think they came to know of it? It was only when they tried to build their road through our Vale of Ancestors that we had to stop them. If you kill the intruders, even if you kill every one of them at Gettys Fort, do you truly believe no more will come? Can you be so childish, so simple as to believe that killing them will drive them away forever?"

Anger froze her face into a grimace. She leaned forward to glare down at him. "I *will* kill as many as I *can* kill. And if more come, then I will fight them, and I will kill them. And if others come behind them, then I will kill those others. How many can there be? Eventually, they will stop coming. Or I will have killed them all." She lifted her gaze from Jodoli and turned it on me. "It isn't that hard to kill them. I'll show you. I'll start with this one."

She stalked toward me like a heavy-bodied cat intent on prey. The iron sword pointed at my chest still held Soldier's Boy immobile, not with its threat so much as by virtue of the metal. Sweat ran in trickles down my back and side. He felt light-headed, dizzy, and nauseous, and yet Soldier's Boy focused on marshaling his magic against the iron. His reserves were dwindling dangerously. Both Olikea and Likari had ventured out from the line of servers and feeders still herded up against the wall. Olikea looked both angry and frightened. As Dasie strode toward me, Likari broke away from his mother with a shout and ran to stand between the advancing mage and me. He looked at the iron sword, sensing the terrible toll it was taking on me, and then spun back to face the oncoming woman, panting with terror.

She scarcely spared him a glance. "Out of my way, boy."

"No. Stop! He is our Great One! I am his feeder. I cannot allow you to kill him. You will have to kill me first!"

He didn't speak it as a threat, but merely as a statement of what all knew to be true. Any feeder would lay down his life to protect his Great One.

She stopped. "Step away from him, lad. He has deceived you. He is not of the People and he doesn't deserve your loyalty, let alone your death."

"You are wrong." Soldier's Boy panted out the words.

"Be silent!"

He ignored her command. "Kill me, and you go against the very magic that made you what you are." He did not speak the words smoothly, but gasped them out, a few at a time. I could taste blood at the back of his throat. He could not resist the iron much longer. "You throw aside a tool, a weapon, crafted by the magic. If you kill me and then go to do battle with the intruders, you will lead your warriors to slaughter. They will fall, by the dozens, by the hundreds. The intruders will be angered against you, and they will bring thousands against you. Without Kinrove's dance to hold them back, they will flood up like water rising from an angry river and fill your forest with death."

"Be silent!"

"You threaten us with iron! Where did you learn that? Do you think they will not shoot iron into *your* body and destroy your magic? Do you think that the People will survive when the Plainsfolk did not? The intruders defeated the Plainspeople with iron and with bullets, and if you wage war in the same way they did, then you will meet the same fate."

Her fury built with every word he gasped out. She swelled like an angry cat as she stood before us. She seemed to be groping for words or perhaps for the surge of will to murder him.

He spoke quietly, a whisper now, fading with his strength. "But I know how to drive the intruders back. That's why the magic made me. It takes a stag to know how to defeat another stag in a battle of clashing antlers. No matter how brave or strong, a seal cannot fight that way." He drew a breath and swallowed with effort. "I know how to turn their own ways against them. Kinrove's dance cannot stop them." He paused, drew breath. "You cannot kill enough of them to stop them." He panted, drew a deep breath. The world was black around the edges. "But I know how. Don't kill the only Great One who knows—" His words spiraled away and his head wobbled on his neck. Blackness closed in around us. I could not see, and the sounds I heard came from far away. My hands and feet tingled and were gone. Soldier's Boy was unconscious, and I was cut adrift from my body's information in a floating blackness.

That shrill keening was probably Likari. A woman was shouting, and possibly it was Olikea, but it might have been Dasie ordering Soldier's Boy to tell whatever secret he knew. I could still feel the iron; it was dangerously close to us. I wanted to flee this body, go to Lisana for help, dream-walk to Epiny, do something, but both his magic and his physical strength were so depleted that I was trapped there. Trapped and aware, while he was blissfully unconscious of the imminent death that hovered. I waited, torn between anticipation and dread, for the iron blade to rush into my chest. I didn't want death; but in the moments before he had collapsed, Soldier's Boy had threatened me with the only thing that seemed worse right now: complete dishonor. He had offered to become a traitor for Dasie, to turn my knowledge of my own people against them.

Time changes when one is deprived of one's senses, but not one's consciousness. I felt as if I spent years in that hellish sus-pension, torn between hoping he'd die and fearing he'd live and condemn me to be a traitor. Hours passed, or perhaps days. In a desperate bid for my honor, I tried to take my body back, but had no idea of how to do so. I could not feel my hands, my feet, could not open my eyes. I could not feel my heart beating or time my own breathing. A terrible thought came to me; perhaps he *had* died, but not taken me with him. Perhaps his part of my mind was gone and my body already stilled and starting to stiffen, and I'd been left behind in the unlife that wasn't a death, either. If I'd had a mouth or lungs, I would have screamed. Instead, I did something that surprised me; I prayed.

Not to the good god, but to the god of death and the god of balances. I prayed to the god who had demanded of me either a death or a life. "Come and take me now!" I begged him. "Take this, death or life as it may be, and be satisfied. I give it to you freely."

There was no response, and in my boundless darkness, I won-dered if I had just committed a blasphemy against the good god, and if this was what it meant to be godless.

How much time I passed in that state, I will never know. I do know that, before Soldier's Boy awoke again, I sensed him there with me. He coalesced around me, and for one brief moment, I thought I'd be able to take him into myself and become whole again, on my terms. I was very still, afraid that if I roused him in any way, he would resist the process. Slowly I began to sense my body again. My head ached and whirled. I could see nothing and sound was just a formless roar around me, like the surf I had listened to earlier that day. My hands and feet tingled strangely. I felt my fingers twitch against the fabric of my robe, and that rasp of flesh against thread was, after my deprivation, the most heady sensation I'd ever felt. I pressed my hand against the weave, treasuring the contact, but in that moment, Soldier's Boy became aware of me. By a means I could not sense, he wrested control away from me.

"You have no right!" I railed at him as we floated together as prisoners within the body. "I was born to this body and it belongs to me! You would use it to turn me into a traitor to my own people. How can you do that? I do not understand you. How can you be so dishonorable, so false?"

His response shocked me. "Do you think that I don't recall my boyhood in the Midlands? Do you think I was not born into this body as surely as you were? You cannot think I came suddenly into being when Lisana made me hers? No. I was always a part of you. She peeled that part of me free of you, and gave me my own life, my own will, my own experiences, my own separate education. But she did not create me from nothing. Do you think I don't recall Father and his 'discipline' and endless requirements? Locked from the instant I drew breath into being his 'soldier son,' separated from all else so that he might convince me it was the only thing I could be. How could anyone forget that? How do you manage to forget it? Why are you still his puppet, still the obedient little soldier that your people made you be? You say you do not understand me, because I look at what was done to me and resent it. I cannot understand you, because it seems all you long for is to return to that servitude. You would be the game piece of a king who has never seen your face, no matter what injustice or abomination you must commit in his name."

For a moment, I was speechless, shocked at the bitterness and anger in his voice. Stunned, too, that he could accuse me of longing to be a puppet and a tool of tyranny. A moment later I marshaled my own indignation. "What of you? How are you different?

If Dasie takes you at your word, you will be killing people who only ever offered you kindness. How can Spink or Epiny deserve your anger? How can the prisoners deserve to be attacked by you and driven back west? What righteousness is there in that?"

"The Specks were here first! And their forest stood long before your fort. This land is theirs. The intruders must be driven out. I but side with the people who were here first."

"Then perhaps I should side with the Kidona. Did not they have the foothills before the Specks ever ventured down into them? Were not the Specks the 'intruders' then into the Kidona lands? How far back shall we go, Soldier's Boy, to decide who is right here?"

"He's waking up. Quick, water, but not too much!"

The voice was Olikea's, right by my ear. I was suddenly aware that I was lying on my back, and my head was cradled in the softness of her lap. I could feel her warmth, and smell the good smell of her body. A moment later, my head was lifted and I felt liquid lap against my lips. Soldier's Boy parted them, and moisture came into my mouth, and with it, sweetness. My body became a single surge of hunger, of thirst. Mindless, Soldier's Boy sucked at the liquid and a moment later recognized it as fruit juice. He drained the cup, gasped, and then forced a word from my lips. "More."

"Slowly. Go slowly." Those words were to me. Then, "Refill the cup. Quickly!" That command was given to someone else, probably Likari. He'd opened my eyes, but shapes and colors seemed to whirl and blend rather than resolve themselves into sensible images. He closed them again. The cup came back, and with it my sense of smell. It was a thick apple juice, spiced and warmed, and this time he drank it more slowly. It helped but my whole body was still in distress. Things simply felt wrong inside me, far beyond the horrible hunger that chewed at me. I'd come as close to dying as a man could and still step back from the brink, I decided.

"Can he speak yet?" The voice that demanded an answer to that question belonged to Dasie.

"You nearly killed him. Can you expect him to speak so soon after such damage? Look at him! The skin hangs from the bones of his face. It will take me weeks to rebuild him to where he can eat with pleasure, let alone wield any power."

Soldier's Boy coughed and then cleared his throat. It took all his will to drag in his breath, and something more than mere will-power to send it out as words. "I can speak." He opened his eyes again. Light and darkness swam and mingled, shadows formed and suddenly Dasie's face was looming over his. He shut his eyes and turned away from her, sickened by the memory of iron.

"You said the magic made you for a reason. That because you have been one of the intruders, you know how to drive the intruders out. You said it was not by Kinrove's dance, nor by my fighting a war as they fight them. But what else is there? Tell me, now, unless it was all just a trick to keep me from killing you."

The liquid Soldier's Boy had swallowed seemed to have fled my mouth. Likari hastened back with another cup. I could smell it and Soldier's Boy could not keep my eyes from being drawn to it. But Dasie's outstretched palm denied the boy access to me. Soldier's Boy could not think of anything at that moment except the cup of lifesaving moisture, just out of reach.

"Speak!" she commanded Soldier's Boy and I felt a feeble spark of his temper.

He tried to clear his throat and could not. He rasped out the words "If . . . a trick . . . stupid to . . . abandon now."

Anger flared in her eyes. She had pushed him too far. "Then I'll just kill you now."

He coughed. His throat was thick, as if he'd been ill for weeks. "That's your . . . answer for everything. Kill it. Better kill me then. You don't have patience. For strategy."

"What strategy?"

He shook his head. He could barely lift his hand but he pointed a trembling finger at the cup Likari held. His lips remained closed.

Dasie gave a snort of disdain. "Very well. Your 'strategy' seems to be that you will keep silent until I allow you food and drink. I shall. Because I know that at any time I need to do so I can kill you. You will keep. Right now, I have other things to attend to."

She straightened up and looked around. In that moment, she looked to me more like an officer assessing a situation than a Speck mage. She spoke to her feeders. "Bring me fresh food and drink. I have need of it. Necessary as the iron is, it still leaches strength from me to be around it. Have all of the swords put safely away, except for two. I wish a man with a sword to remain here, at an appropriate distance from Kinrove. He should be aware of the iron while taking no harm from it. The same for Intruder Mage here. He"—and she gestured toward Jodoli—"may leave as soon as his feeders have him ready to travel. I go now to speak to all the dancers. Those of our kin-clan will travel to our winter grounds with us. Others who have saviors among our warriors may go with them. But I want everyone enslaved by the magic and forced to dance to know that they are now free, and that if they require help to return to their own kin-clans, we will give it."

Olikea held a piece of soft bread to my mouth. It had been dipped in oil and honey. As Soldier's Boy chewed, my body rejoiced at the sweetness. Strength from it came into me.

A young warrior had been standing by one of her feeders as Dasie spoke, obviously waiting to report to her. The moment her words paused, he made an obeisance to her and then said, "Great One, we have already given that news to every dancer. We have told them they are free to go, and that if they need help, we will give it. But some of them—"

"Some of them will stay with me. And dance again. Because they have felt what they are doing and know what they are doing is within the design of the magic."

The interrupted warrior made another brief obeisance. "Even so, Great One," he said in confirmation of Kinrove's words.

"You have twisted their minds!" Dasie accused him.

"The magic has spoken to them," Kinrove countered. He still rested on his dais. Several of his feeders stood near him, offering food and drink. He handed a cup back to one of them, drew a shuddering breath, and spoke. "The dance is the work of the magic, Dasie. How can you think it comes from me? The magic has always spoken to me in dance, that is true. When I was younger and less filled with the magic, I danced myself, danced until my feet bled, because that was when the magic spoke most clearly to me." He accepted a cup from one of his feeders, drained it, and handed it back. He spoke more strongly. "To each of us, the magic comes in its own way. My dance is not something I created to enslave our people. The magic gave me the dance as a way to hold the intruders at bay. And it has worked."

"The dance must not be stopped." I had not known that Soldier's Boy was going to speak. I was as startled as Dasie was. Firada had Jodoli on his feet and they had begun to help him out of the pavilion. At my words, he froze and looked at me strangely. I gave an emptied cup back to Olikea. Likari was trying to hand me a piece of fruit. Soldier's Boy made a small gesture with my hand, bidding him wait. He drew a deep breath and tried to put strength into his words. "The dance protects us. That shield must not be dropped now. It will take time for me to prepare my war."

Even that brief run of words had tired Soldier's Boy. Olikea handed him a cool glass; it was not water, but a very pale golden wine. He drank from it and felt some energy come back. I alone knew of Soldier's Boy's hidden flash of anger at what Dasie had done to him. She had drained him of the magic he had so painstakingly built up. Drained it to no good ends when it was what they all would need most in the weeks to come! But he let nothing of that show on his face as he gave the glass back to Olikea. All eyes were still on him. He knew the power of his silence and was not quick to end it, despite the anger kindling in Dasie's eyes. He tipped the glass again, draining the last of it, and handed it back to Olikea. "I need meat," he said quietly. "And the mushrooms that have the orange circles inside the stems. And dried cirras berries. Fresh would be better, but I do not think anyone will have those."

"I will get them," Olikea replied in a low voice, and rose from her place beside him.

"You seek to rebuild your magic reserves," Dasie accused him.

"As should you. As should Kinrove and Jodoli. It will take all the magic that we can muster if we are to prevail against the intruders. But the first magic that we will require is that Kinrove reconstructs his dance. The intruders are resilient beyond your imagining. Even a day or so without fear and sadness, and they will rekindle their ambitions to cut the trees and build their road. The magic I did before I left there will occupy them for a time. And the winter snows will slow them. But I know them, Dasie. Without fear and sadness to weigh them down, they will push onward, in any weather, to achieve their aims. You need Kinrove's magic to keep them corralled like herd beasts. It will be greatly to our advantage if they are huddled within their town and fort when we move against them."

"No!" I shouted within him. I could feel his thoughts forming. Something Epiny had said long ago drifted through his thoughts. "Fire fears no magic." He smiled. "No!" I cried out again, but it was not my voice he heard.

"Like corralled beasts," Dasie said slowly. She licked her lips as if she were thinking of a favorite food. She took a slow breath. "You do have a strategy. Don't you?"

He let the smile reach his lips and widen. "I do," he confirmed. The memory of the coppersmith's tent drifted through his mind. "But you will need me for it to work. And I will need my magic. Even more, you will need what I have that is not magic. You will need the knowledge I have that can work in places where iron makes magic fail."

She was silent for a time. Her feeders, her warriors waited on her words. Inside Soldier's Boy, my agony burned me. *Traitor, traitor, traitor. Kill him now*, I begged her. *Do not listen to him. Just kill him and let it be done.*

"You shall have it. For now. You shall have your magic, and I will have my iron always near you, at the ready. If I think you have lied to me, at any time, I can kill you. Remember that." She glanced at her own feeders. "Bring his feeders food. Whatever he wishes." Her gaze moved to Kinrove. "You. I will leave with you whatever dancers wish to remain. Use them as they wish to be used. But any who wish to leave, I will allow to leave. I go to speak to them now. When I return, we will take counsel together, we three." She smiled. "The intruders will be banished from our lands. Or they will die."

CHAPTER EIGHTEEN

BOXED

Dasie kept her word. I had expected that she would quickly depart Kinrove's encampment after she had freed the dancers. I still believe that was her original plan, but discovering Soldier's Boy had changed it. She stayed, and she schemed with us for the next ten days, as both Soldier's Boy and Kinrove grew fat again.

It was alarming to me how quickly Soldier's Boy regained both his girth and his magic at Kinrove's table. I do not think he could have fattened his body so quickly on any other foods. Kinrove's phalanx of feeders gathered, cooked, and served the foods that were most powerful for our magic. Soldier's Boy ate almost constantly. That he did so with evident enjoyment, even relish, only made me angrier at him. He consumed the food of the Specks that would most quickly restore his magic, and all the while, he plotted with Dasie against my own people.

Kinrove, poor man, had become a guest at his own table. Dasie had broken his power. Despite how quickly he regained most of his flesh, Dasie dominated him, not just by iron but with her unpredictability. In bringing iron swords into his encampment and attacking other Great Ones, she had done the unthinkable. All feared her. Kinrove's extended kin-clan kept their distance from the Great Man's pavilion, I think out of fear of what Dasie might do to Kinrove if they appeared to threaten her. His kin-clan provided for us, food and drink and tobacco, and his feeders served us, but Dasie was the commander of our days, not Kinrove. Dasie had a proprietary air toward not only Kinrove's feeders and possessions but toward the Great Man himself. She did not say that she intended to use the Great Man's powers for her own ends, but she did not need to. Her cavalier attitude said it all.

Yet Kinrove had his own small triumphs and seemed to relish them. As he had predicted to Dasie, some of his dancers stayed. The majority left. They rested, ate, and regained the strength to travel, and then, over several days, they departed from his encampment to seek the winter grounds of their own kin-clans. A good part of Dasie's force departed with them, to help them journey home. Some of their guides were brothers or daughters or other kin, who had joined forces with Dasie as a way to bring the stolen relatives home. Others had no relatives among the rescuers, but left on their own or in small groups.

Olikea took Soldier's Boy on a brief walk in the fresh air on the morning after Dasie's attack. I watched some of the dancers depart. Most were thin, a few emaciated. The faces were lined, their eyes haunted as if they had just wakened from a terrible dream and were not yet free of its grip. I'd seen expressions like those before, on the faces of the penal workers forced to endure the terrors of the forest on a daily basis. I recalled my own experience of "breaking a Gettys Sweat." They had danced to send that paralyzing terror and draining sadness down to Gettys. It had been horrible for us to experience it, but for it to come to us, these dancers had had to experience it first. I wondered that Kinrove and his magic could demand that of anyone he cared about.

Stranger still to contemplate were the dancers who stayed. I caught only a glimpse of them. They were a small group compared to the throng who had danced before, perhaps no more than three dozen. They hunkered together around the dais where their drummers had set the rhythm, and Kinrove's own feeders brought them food and drink. Other feeders massaged their legs with oil and rubbed their backs. The eyes of those dancers were haunted but also determined. They reminded me of elite troops, taking a rest before joining the next bloody battle. They fought the intruders, at great cost to themselves, but it was a cost they paid willingly.

Someone had to pay the costs to win a war, he thought to himself. He turned to Olikea. "I have an errand for Likari. An important errand. You must give him whatever of Lisana's treasure you think he will need. Send him back, quickly, to the coppersmith's tent. I only hope he has not left the Trading Place yet. Likari must purchase for me as many of the basket arrows as the smith has to sell. And the resin, the stuff the smith said to put inside the baskets. Send him quickly, within the hour. Tell him that when I need them, I'll ask for them."

"What for?" Olikea demanded, but Soldier's Boy only replied, "Do as I ask, but tell no one else." He left her to find and send the boy, and returned alone to Kinrove's tables. His words had filled me with dread, but not even I could pry from his mind what his complete plan was.

Before that day was out, I heard first a single drum thumping, and then others taking up the tempo. The horns joined in, and even through the thick leather walls of Kinrove's pavilion I heard the thudding of their bare feet on the dust as they pounded out the magic that held Gettys in thrall.

Dasie heard it, too. She was at table with us, eating as heartily as any of us. She had, I noted, grown rounder of face since first I had seen her. Her iron bearers, three warriors with swords, were seldom far from us, but did not come close enough for the iron to be painful. One stood by the door flap of the pavilion. As long as he was there, no Great One dared approach it without Dasie's express permission. Two more stood against the wall of the pavilion, stationed where Dasie could always see them and they could watch her. At any sign of danger to her, all knew, their orders were to attack and slay both Kinrove and me. She lifted her head when the drums first sounded, and held still as the beat grew stronger. After the dancers had begun their circuit, she heaved a great sigh and motioned to one of Kinrove's feeders to put more meat onto her platter.

"No one can save a man from himself. Or a woman," she said wearily.

Kinrove set down his cup. "Those men and women are saving us," he said. There was a touch of defiance in his voice.

"They have protected you for years," Soldier's Boy agreed, to Dasie's annoyance. Then he added, "But their protection of you is not complete, and the intruders have found a way to defeat it. They drug their slaves so that their senses are dulled to the magic you send. That is how they were able to push past the magic and into the forest to cut more ancestor trees this summer. They will use those slaves far more ruthlessly than Kinrove drives his dancers. Unless we stop them before spring frees the forest from snow, they will cut deeply into our ancestral groves this coming summer." In his mind's eye, I knew he saw Lisana's little tree. How vulnerable she was, compared to the forest giants. Her tree's grip on the forest floor was tentative; it still fed mostly through the root structure of her old tree. He had to protect her.

I shared that goal with him but, unlike Soldier's Boy, I was not willing to sacrifice every soul in Gettys, and any who might come after them, to guarantee Lisana's safety. I wondered if Dasie was, and resolved that at some point I would find out.

Dasie set her own cup down with a thud. "Unless we stop them? Did you not say to me that you would stop them? But your words were an empty lie, weren't they? You don't know how to stop them. But I do. With iron. With the same iron they have turned against us. Iron is the answer." She looked around, smiling at the shocked silence that her words had wrought. "Oh, yes." She nodded to their horror. "Iron. Pistols and long guns. I have traded for some, and I will acquire others. I have a plan. It will require the cooperation of all the kin-clans. All the furs the People take this winter will be traded only for guns. There is one among the intruders, a traitor to them, who will make this trade with us. And when we have the guns, we will turn them on the intruders. They will know what it is to fall when iron balls rip through their flesh. If our magic cannot bring them down, then we will turn on them the very weapons they have used against us. What do you think of that, Intruder Mage?"

Soldier's Boy set down his mug with a great thump, as if to outdo Dasie's gesture. "I think you are a fool," he said deliberately. "You have accused me of mouthing empty lies. Now I accuse you of saying stupid things. Bring iron among the People, and we will not be the People anymore! Bring iron, and we will not need to fear that the intruders will kill our ancestor trees. We will do it ourselves as we walk among them. Bring iron into our villages, and do you think any children will grow to be Great Ones again? Do as you suggest, and we will not have to worry about the intruders anymore. We will have become the intruders, and we will kill ourselves."

Dasie's face had reddened as he spoke. By the time he finished, her mouth was pinched white in the middle of her face, but the rest of it was scarlet, save for the dark specks that patterned it. She gripped her glass so tightly I thought it would shatter in her hand. I think it had been a long time since anyone had spoken so harshly to her, let alone told her she was stupid. She had probably thought that no one would dare to speak to her so. I wondered if we would survive Soldier's Boy's rudeness. Olikea stood with her breath bated. Likari was frozen in the act of offering more food. I think their thoughts were as mine. But Soldier's Boy seemed strangely still when I touched his mind, as if he were playing a game and awaiting his opponent's next move.

For a moment, she was so enraged she could say nothing. When she finally found words, they were the dare of an angered child. "If you think you can offer a better plan, then you should do it now, Intruder Mage! And if you cannot, then I think you should be the first of the intruders to die! I will not wait and wait for you to speak the wisdom you claim to have. Out with it! What is your great magic that you will loose on them?"

Soldier's Boy remained strangely calm. At a gesture from him, Likari set down the platter of meat that he had been offering to him. Soldier's Boy leaned close to the lad. "Bring to me now what you bought for me at the market." As he ran off to obey, Soldier's Boy drew himself up straight, as if to be sure that all eyes were on him. When he spoke, his voice was soft. I knew the trick. The others leaned toward him silently, straining to hear what he would say.

"I know the start of it will please you, Dasie. For it begins with killing. It must," he said. His voice was so gentle, it almost hid the razor's edge of his words.

"No!" I shouted inside him. I suddenly knew what was coming. Why had Epiny ever spoken such prophetic words? He paid me no heed.

"It begins with killing," he repeated. "But not with magic. No. And not with iron. Our magic will not work in their fort. And whatever iron we might use against them, they would use triple that against us. And with experience, which we do not have. We must use a force that fears neither magic nor iron." He looked around at his audience, as if to be sure he had them. With exquisite timing, Likari had arrived. His arms were filled by a doeskin-wrapped bundle. Soldier's Boy let the boy continue to hold it as he folded back a corner of it and drew out one of the basket arrows. He held it up. "We will use fire. We cage it in this arrow. And we will use ice. We will attack them in the winter, with the fire that their iron cannot stop. And the fire will expose them to the cold that iron cannot fight. Magic will take us there, and magic will bear us away.

"But that will only be the beginning."

He had them now. He smiled at them as he gave the arrow back to Likari. He saw there were only a dozen in the boy's bundle, but kept his disappointment from showing as he turned back to his audience.

"Kinrove has always been right about one thing. Killing alone will not drive them away. And you have been right about another thing, Dasie. We must bring war to them in terms they understand." He smiled, first at the one Great One and then at the other, and I admired how he drew them closer with his acknowledgment of them. "The intruders must know, without mistake, that the deaths come from us. And we must not kill ALL of them. Some few must be allowed to survive. Perhaps only one, if he is the right one. Someone of rank, of power, among them."

Outrage returned to Dasie's face. He ignored it. "That one becomes our messenger. We send him back to his king, with our ultimatum. A treaty. We offer not to kill them if they abide by the rules we give them."

"And what rules would those be?" Dasie demanded.

"That," Soldier's Boy said quietly, "we will determine. Certainly one rule would be that no one might cut any tree that we say must be protected. But it might be better, perhaps, to say that they may not even venture into those parts of the forest."

"And they will leave their wooden fort forever and never come back!" Dasie added with satisfaction.

Soldier's Boy shrugged slightly. "We could say such a thing to them. But if we did, it would make them less likely to abide by our treaty. And it might foster discontent among the People."

"Discontent? To know that we were finally safe from the intruders? To know that our lives could resume peace and order?"

Soldier's Boy smiled unpleasantly. "To know that the trade goods that so profit us each autumn would no longer flow through our hands." He reached out casually and set his hand on the back of Olikea's neck, as if in a caress. "Let alone to bedeck ourselves." About Olikea's neck were several strands of bright glass beads that I had given her. Strange, I thought, that Soldier's Boy noticed her ornaments when I myself scarcely gave them a second glance.

Dasie refuted him with disdain. "We had trade with the West long before we had Gettys like a scab on the land. Long before they tried to cut a way into our forest, we had trade."

"And we welcomed it!" Soldier's Boy agreed affably. "But after we massacre every Gernian and tell them they must never build a home near Gettys again, nor enter our forest, how many traders do you think will come to us? What do we have that they must get from us and only us? For what will they risk their lives?"

Dasie was silent and sullen, pondering this. Then she burst out with "They have nothing that we need! Nothing. Better to drive them from the land and make ourselves free of their evil and greed."

"It is true that they have nothing that *we* need." Soldier's Boy put the slightest emphasis on the word. "I am sure that no one here carries a flint-and-steel for fire-making. No one here has tools of iron in his home lodge. A few wear beads and gewgaws, garments or fabrics from the west. But you are right, Dasie. We do not *need* them for ourselves. All the garments that my feeder brought with her to the Trading Place she quickly traded away to those other traders who came from across the salt water. They seemed to think they *needed* what she had brought. She made many excellent trades with them, for things that she thought that she needed. But I am sure you are right. Once we have left behind the trade goods of the intruders, we will find other trade goods, of our own making, and trade just as profitably as ever with those who come from across the salt water. They will not ask us, 'Where is the bright cloth that we came so far to obtain?' Doubtless they will be happy to trade only for furs."

Silence did not follow his words. Dasie was still, but whispered words ran like mice along the edges of the room. Hands furtively touched earrings or fabric skirts. No one dared to raise a voice to tell Dasie she was wrong, but that torrent of whispering told her what everyone knew she didn't want to hear. Trade with the intruders was essential if the People wished to continue trading with those who came from across the sea. Game meats and hides, leather and furs, lovely objects carved from wood would buy them some things, but the traders from beyond the salt water were most eager for the trade goods from the west.

Soldier's Boy delivered the killing blow. "I am sure that few among us would miss tobacco. And we will find other things to trade with the other folk who come to the Trading Place. When they discover we no longer have tobacco from Gernia, they will not sail away in disappointment; we will find something else they desire." He spoke in an offhand voice, as if this would be the simplest thing in the world to do.

Dasie's scowl deepened. One of the feeders had placed a stack of crisply browned cakes at her elbow. She seized one and bit into it as if biting off the head of an enemy. When she had finished chewing and swallowed, she demanded, "What are you suggesting, then? Why bother to attack them if we are not going to drive them away forever?"

I felt the muscles in Soldier's Boy's face twitch but he didn't smile. "We attack them and kill enough of them to let them know

that we could have killed them all. And we attack them in an organized way that makes them think that we are like them."

"Like them?" Dasie was getting offended again.

"Like them enough that they can understand us. Right now,
they treat us as we treat rabbits."

Dasie made a sound in her throat. Yet another simile she didn't
appreciate.

Soldier's Boy spoke on implacably. "We do not think that we
should go to the Great One of the rabbits and ask his permission
to hunt his people. We do not say to ourselves, 'There are the
lodges of the rabbit folk. I will stand here and call to them before
I walk among them, so they know I come peacefully.' No. When
we want meat, we hunt the rabbits and kill them and eat them.
If we wish to walk past the burrow of a rabbit, we do. If we wish
to build a lodge where the rabbit burrow is, we do not ask the
rabbit's permission or expect him to take offense if we do so. We
do not care if he takes offense. Let him go somewhere else, we
think. And we do as we please with the place where he was."

"But they are just rabbits," Dasie said.

"Until you see a rabbit with a sword. Until rabbits come in
the night to burn down the lodge you have built. Until the Great
One of the rabbits stands before you and says, 'You will respect my
people and the territory of my people now.'"

Dasie was still frowning. I suspected that Soldier's Boy had
chosen a poor technique for presenting his idea. "Rabbits do not
have Great Ones," she pointed out ponderously. "They have no
magic. They do not follow a leader and take a common action.
They cannot make fires, or talk to us and demand our respect."
She spoke scornfully as if pointing this out to a slow child.

Soldier's Boy let half a dozen heartbeats pass. Then he said,
very softly, "And that is exactly what the intruders say of us. That
we have no rulers, and our magic is not real. That we have no
potent weapons, nor the will to use them. They do not imagine
that we will ever demand that they respect our territories, because
they do not think that we have territory."

"Then they are stupid!" Dasie declared with great confidence
in her opinion.

Soldier's Boy gave a small sigh. I think he wished that he could agree with her. Instead, he said, "They are not stupid. They are, in fact, very clever in a way that goes in a different direction from what we think of as clever. While our young men go forth to hunt, to build lodges, to begin their lives, their young men are sent to a place where they spend all their time learning how to make all of the world their territory."

Dasie narrowed her eyes. Obviously, she didn't believe him.

"I have been there," Soldier's Boy said into the skeptical silence. "I learned there what they teach their warriors. And I learned how it could be turned against them."

Cold fury welled in me. Would he turn what he had learned at the Academy against us? Two, I thought, could play at this game. I hardened my heart to his treachery and listened to every word he uttered.

"They do not respect a people who do not live in a fixed place. They do not respect a people who follow their own wills instead of living by the commands of a single ruler. They will not treat with us or believe that we claim the territory we claim until we convince them that they have been deceived, that we are, in fact, very much like them."

Dasie shook her head. "I will not waste time with these deceptions. I wish simply to go down to them and kill them. Slaughter them all."

"If all we do is slaughter them, then more will simply come after them." He held up a pleading hand to halt her objection. "First, of course, will come the slaughter. But in the wake of that, the few who survive must be told that we have a 'king' of our own. Or a 'queen.' They must believe that there is one person who can speak for us. And with that one person, they will make a treaty, like the treaty they made with the far queen who defeated them. Boundaries will be set, new boundaries that fence them out of our lands. And rules of trade."

"Rules of trade?" Dasie was listening to him now.

"To make them greedy," Soldier's Boy said. "And to assure us of the tobacco we need for the trade. With only one intruder will we trade. That one we will make wealthy. It will be in his best interests to remain the only one we trade with. We will choose someone strong, someone who will hold the others at bay for us, and will obey our rules for the sake of keeping a monopoly on trade with us. Greed will protect us better than fear." He paused and smiled at her grim face.

"But first, there must be fear."

She slowly returned his smile. "I think I begin to understand. Their weakness becomes our strength. Their greed will be the leash that holds them back. It is, I think, a good idea. Together we will plan this." Her smile grew colder, wider. "And the first part we will plan is the slaughter."

Soldier's Boy gestured to Likari and the boy filled his plate. Olikea appeared with a flagon of beer. He scarcely noticed that they tended him. I was a mote of despair, suspended inside him. He had considered his plan well. If he could carry it out, I judged that it would work. He ate some of the meat and then said to Dasie, "The massacre is actually our simplest task. The intruders have long ago lost all wariness of us. They deem us no more threat than the mice that scamper through the stable, and pay as little attention to us. Kinrove's dancers will strive to keep them demoralized and fearful. It is a pity that more of them did not stay to create a stronger magic"—and he paused delicately—"but Kinrove will have to make do with those he has. In the days and nights before our attack, we will have him increase the power of his magic; when we attack, the intruders will already be exhausted and dispirited. They will almost welcome our killing them." He smiled and drank.

It was too much for me. I gathered all my awareness and fury, sharpened it into a point, and with all my strength, tried to unseat Soldier's Boy from my body. I know he felt my attack, for he choked briefly on his beer. He set his mug down firmly on the tabletop. He spoke internally, to me only.

"Your time is past. I do what I must. In the long run, it is for the best, for both peoples. There will be a slaughter, yes, but after that, the war will be over. Better one massacre than year after year of eroding one another. I have weighed this long, Nevare. I think it is a decision that even Father would understand. And I cannot permit you to interfere. If you will not willingly join me, then I must at least keep you from hindering me."

He boxed me.

That is how I thought of it then and how I recall it now. Imagine being imprisoned in a box with no light, yet no dark, no sound, no sensation against your skin, no body, nothing except your own presence. I'd experienced it once before, briefly, when he had been unconscious. The experience had not prepared me to endure it again; rather, it had only increased my dread. At first I did not believe what he had done. I held myself in stillness, waiting for the absence of all things to pass. Surely there would come some glimmer of light, or dimming of shadow, some whisper of sound, some whiff of scent. How long could he completely suppress half of himself?

That brought an unpleasant thought to me. Had I ever done this to him? When I thought I had absorbed him and integrated him back into myself, had he hung in this senseless internal dungeon? I did not think so, I decided. This, I felt, was a very deliberate act on his part. He sought to render me harmless. Down here I could not distract him. Did he suspect that I'd slipped away from him before and dream-walked on my own? Was that what he feared? He should. Because if ever I was in a position to do so again, I would immediately get to Epiny to warn her of the impending attack on Gettys.

Time, as I have mentioned before, is a slippery thing in such a place. Are hours moments or moments hours? I had no way of knowing. When my first period of internal ranting and shrieking passed, I tried to calm myself. The measuring of passing time seemed to me to be of the utmost importance, and I tried to give myself that comfort in any number of ways. Counting only led to despair. The mind counts faster than the lips, and even when I deliberately slowed my count, I realized that reciting an eternity of numbers only deepened my hopelessness.

It was the most solitary of solitary confinements that could exist. Men went mad from isolation; I knew that. Despite the suffocating lack of otherness that surrounded me, I held grimly to my sanity. He could not, I told myself, suppress me forever. He needed me. I was part of him, as surely as he was part of me. And a time would come when I could slip free of him and dream-walk to warn Epiny. Unless the time for such a warning had passed all usefulness. I veered away from that thought. I would not think what I would do if I emerged from this only to find Gettys destroyed and everyone I cared for slaughtered.

I found other ways to anchor myself in time. I recited poetry I'd memorized for various tutors. I worked math problems in my head. I designed, in excruciating detail, the inn I would have built at Dead Town if I'd stayed there with Amzil. I walked through every step of it, sparing myself nothing. I forced myself to raze old buildings. Mentally, I moved the old lumber out of the way, one load at a time. With a shovel and a pick, using string and sticks, I leveled a building site. I built myself a crude wheelbarrow and with it hauled gravel for a sturdy foundation. I mentally computed the number of cubic feet of gravel my foundation would require, estimated the size of a barrow I could push, and relentlessly forced myself to imagine each trip, down to the shoveling in of each load, the pushing of the barrow, the dumping of it, and even how I would spread it with my shovel. Such was my obsession, and my effort to stay anchored in the world.

And when my inn was built, I thought of how I would bring Amzil and the children there and surprise them with a snug, clean home of their own. I'm afraid I imagined an entire life there with her, gaining her trust, building our love, watching her children grow, adding our own to the brood. It was mawkish, a schoolboy fancy that I embroidered over and over, yet when all other diversions failed, I could taunt myself with thinking of her and pretending a life of shared love.

Not all the time, of course. No one could have lingered in that endless emptiness and stayed completely rational. There were times when I railed and threatened, times when I prayed, times when I cursed every god I could name. I would have wept if I'd had eyes to weep, I would have taken my own life if it had been within my power to do so. I tried every way that there was for a man to escape himself, but in the end, I was all that there was, and so I had to come back to myself.

I plotted a hundred revenges. I shouted to his unlistening ears that I would surrender myself if only he would allow me to stop existing in this vacuum. I found a deep faith in the good god and lost it again. I sang inane songs and made up new verses for them.

I did all those things not for a hundred years, but for a hundred centuries. I became certain that Soldier's Boy had died long ago, but that somehow I continued to exist among his slowly decaying bones. I lived in a place beyond despair. I became stillness.

I do not know if it was because I stopped trying to exist or because he forgot to fear me. Tiny bits of sensory information began to drift down to me. It did not happen often; I could not conceive what "often" would mean anymore. A sour taste. A brief scent of wood smoke. Likari's giggle. Pain from a cut finger. Each tiny bit of sensation was something to be pondered. I did not rise to them like a fish snapping at bait. I was too worn down for that. I let them drift down to me, where I considered them without haste.

One brick at a time, a wall can rise. One small experience at a time, life and awareness came back to me. I felt like a toad emerging from hibernation, or a pinched limb slowly tingling back to life. A conversation was falling all around me in disconnected bits.

"The horses are essential."

"Then they'll have to learn, won't they?"

"Find a way to carry fire, then. Clay pots nested inside of one another, perhaps. And carry the oil separately. That would be less showy than torches."

For the first time, I caught a soft mumble that could have been another voice. I savored it. Soldier's Boy spoke again.

"No. Find someone else to do that. These men must remain here. They have to concentrate on what they are doing."

"I know it's heavier. Aim it higher than the target you want it to hit. But be careful. It must hit the wall high, not arch over it. We don't have many. We will give three to each of our four best archers."

"Drill is essential. It's boring, but it's essential. If we attack as you suggest, then the intruders will still see us as a disorganized horde. Ranks and precision will convince them that they have finally incurred the wrath of the Great Queen of the Specks, and that she has sent her army against them."

I did not open my eyes. I had no eyes. I became aware of Soldier's Boy rubbing his eyes, and when he was finished and opened them again, an immense vista of detail unrolled in front of me. Color and shape and shadow. I could not at first interpret it all. There was so much, it was overwhelming, painfully so. Was this what it was like the first time a newborn child beheld the world? I held myself back from it, keeping my distance as if it were a fire that might burn me with its intensity. Very, very gradually the scene resolved itself around me.

I was indoors, in a place I didn't recall. It was a comfortable place. There were woven rugs on the floor, wall hangings, and comfortable furnishings. I sat in a sturdy chair with cushioned arms and a well-padded seat, comfortably close to an open hearth. Near my elbow was a laden table. An open bottle of wine was flanked by a steaming roast with near-bloody slices of meat coiling from the side of it. Roasted round onions were cozy with thick, bright orange baked roots. A loaf of dark bread had been cut into thick slabs and a pot of golden honey rested beside it with a large spoon sticking out of it.

Soldier's Boy had been outside. Had he been reviewing the troops? Mud crusted my boots. Someone crouched before me, taking them off my feet, his head bowed to his task. One of the feeders who assisted Olikea with my care, I suddenly knew. His name was Sempayli, and he had come to my service from another kin-clan because he wanted to serve the Great Ones who would strike back at the intruders. A number of men and a few women had come to me that way. Dasie had been right about that. There was a deep discontent stirring among the Specks. Things were changing too quickly for the older folk, and the younger folk felt affronted by the intruders' assumptions. Many felt it was time to strike back, and hard.

All that information poured into me in an overwhelming flood. I could scarcely digest it, but there was no respite. Life was happening all around me, unpausing and constant. All I could do was try to catch up. Soldier's Boy drank red wine from a crystal glass, and for a long moment, the twin sensations of taste and smell ruled me. Heavenly, heavenly wine.

Across from me, Dasie was enthroned in a similar chair. Her feeder was kindling a pipe for her. The Great One had grown. Her belly and thighs and bosom were burgeoning curves that spoke of her wealth and comfort. That realization came to me so naturally that I did not at first recognize it as a Speck interpretation. My mind fluttered round it like a moth around a flame. They saw the lean, muscled folk of Gettys as the result of hardship and unnatural strife. Such bodies were the result of people who lived against the world rather than with it. They did not relax and accept the bounty the world offered them. They did not recline with one another in the evenings, making music or having soft talk. They constrained their deprived bodies with restrictive clothing and tight belts and snug shoes, and punished themselves with endless activity. They forced themselves to go out in the harsh sunlight and the cruel cold, as senselessly as if they were animals rather than humans. They seemed to rejoice in the harshness of life, restricting themselves from the enjoyment of food, sex, and plenty.

As if in reaction to the stinginess they inflicted on their bodies, they demanded largesse everywhere else. A trail through the forest created itself as folk traveled from here to there. A trail was as big as it needed to be for the traffic on it. Only the intruders would think that they needed to enlarge a trail with axes and shovels and wagons. Only the intruders would build a crust of dwellings over the lands so that they could winter in a place where the snow fell thickly and cold was a crushing blow. Only the intruders would rip all plants and trees from a space and then open the skin of the earth and force new plants to grow in precise rows, all the same. The Specks would never understand a folk who chose hardship over comfort, who insisted on tearing a life from the land rather than one flowing over the world and accepting its plenty.

It was like seeing a stranger across a crowded room and actually "seeing" him before recognizing him as an old friend. All that I accepted about my own people, all our values and customs, were, for that moment, peculiar and harsh and irrational. If a man had enough to eat and plenty besides, why should he not be fat with enjoyment of his life? If he did not have to work so hard that life leaned the flesh from his bones and put muscles on his limbs, why should he not have a softer belly and a rounder face? If one had the good fortune to be treated well by life, why should it not be reflected in an easier body?

For that skewed moment, I saw the Gernians as a nation of folk who sought difficulty and strife for themselves. They built roads to enrich themselves, to be sure, but did they ever enjoy the riches they accrued? No. It appeared suddenly that riches only became the foundation for seeking ever more difficult tasks, and often on the backs of those that life had not favored. I suddenly recalled the road workers, those poor souls forced to labor on the King's Road both as penance for their crimes in Old Thares and as payment for the land they would receive when they'd worked off their sentences. The Specks, I suddenly knew, regarded them with bottomless pity and horror. This was the only life those poor beings would ever know, and the intruders condemned them to live it in privation and want, knowing only work and discomfort. Viewed like that, what we did was monstrous. The Specks had no way of understanding that we considered it justice that our king punished them for crimes they had committed and a special mercy that he offered them a reward for that labor. A false reward, I thought sourly, remembering Amzil's tenuous existence.

I came out of that reverie to awareness of myself as Nevare. I felt as if I'd been fished from the depths of a cold dark pond and revived. For a time all I could do was hover behind Soldier's Boy's eyes and revel in my own existence. Gradually I found my footing in time and place as well as in my self. Time had passed. I struggled to learn how much.

I was in Lisana's old lodge, but it had been refurbished with Speck luxury. The rugs underfoot and the hangings on the wall were trade items, as were the gleaming copper pots and heavy china dishes and crystal glasses. The bed in the corner of the room was a welter of thick furs and wool blankets. The garments that Soldier's Boy wore now had been tailored to his ease, and were all in shades of forest greens and browns. His wrists were heavy with gold bracelets; I felt the weight of earrings dangling from my pierced earlobes. His increased girth and Dasie's were marks of their standing among the Specks. Their feeders had feeders of their own now. The People held them in high esteem and their lifestyle reflected it.

I felt in vain for the vibration of iron anywhere in the room. If Dasie felt the need to threaten him anymore, it was not with iron. Their postures bespoke two warlords taking counsel together rather than a dictator and her hostage. My mind groped back to the words I had awakened to. The Great Queen of the Specks? I considered her through Soldier's Boy's eyes. Yes. And he was her warlord. So they were beginning to consider themselves.

The double irony was not lost on me. To save the Specks, they were becoming a mirror of the intruders they sought to drive away. Dasie with her weapons of iron, and Soldier's Boy with his army in training. Did they think they could ever step back from those things, once they had used them?

The other prong of irony was as sharp as any iron blade as it stabbed me. Here it was, the golden future I'd been promised as a child. I was living it. I was the leader of a military force, serving a queen, with the wealth appropriate to my station and a lovely woman at my beck and call. Olikea had just come into view. She did not carry the dishes of food, but with her hand gestured to those she wished cleared away and where the fresh ones should be placed. I suspected she had chosen my wardrobe, for her own mirrored it, rich browns and delicate greens. She resembled Firada even more now, for her body had filled out to rounder, gentler curves. The feeder of a Great One reflected his status with her own. My gracious lady, and at her heels, the son of the household: Likari in a green tunic and leggings with soft brown boots on his feet. His glossy hair had been bound back with ties and beads of green, and his smooth cheeks were round with shining health. Soldier's Boy's eyes strayed to the boy and I knew his fondness and pride. Then his attention darted back to his conversation with Dasie. She was protesting.

"I listen to my warriors. They are still mine, you know. You train them, but it is to me that they bring their concerns. They are tired of rising early and standing in lines, bored with all these practices at moving together, at the same speed, doing the same thing. How does this help us to defeat the intruders? Will they stand still while we walk in lines across the field to attack them? Are they so stupid? Is that how they fought their wars?"

"Actually," Soldier's Boy confirmed for her, "they do. But no, we will not march on Gettys in formation. Eventually, though, when we show ourselves to the Gernians, they must see not a Speck raiding party but the Speck army. I've told you this before, Dasie, over and over. We have to become an enemy they can recognize. When the time comes, the warriors must dress alike and move in unison, controlled by one commander. That is power that the intruders will recognize. Only then will they respect us."

"So you keep saying. But I do not like that we become, every day, more and more like the people we wish to drive away. You say our warriors must run faster, be harder of muscle and keener of eye when they use their bows. My people say to me, 'we are strong enough, hardened enough to fish, to gather, to hunt. Why does he push us so?' What am I to answer them?"

"You should answer them that, for now, they must do more. They must be harder and more ready than the warriors we will face. The hunt does not demand as much of a man as standing battle does. During a hunt, a man can rest or he can say, 'It is too much work for that much meat. I will hunt something smaller,' and let the prey run away from him. But in battle, the man who turns away becomes the prey. No one can stop because his arms are weary or his legs shake with strain. It stops only when your enemy is dead and you are still alive.

"It is good to say, we are brave and strong, but I have lived among the intruders. And those we will face will be brave and strong and well trained and desperate. I hope to take them by surprise and lay waste to them all before they can react. But I cannot promise you that. Once roused, they will be quick to organize themselves. They will not flee before our advance but will stand firm, for they will know they have nowhere to flee. They will shoot at us in volleys, for the men who are reloading their weapons will trust their comrades to protect them while they do so. That is the strength of an army, that the strength of your comrade's arm protects his fellow as well as himself. And they are experienced. They will know, when we attack, that if they do not fight back strongly enough we will slaughter them all. They will fight like only the cornered fight—to the death and beyond. Even when they know that victory is irretrievably gone, they will stand and fight."

"You speak of extremes. The warriors are ready to fight as hard as we must fight to win," Dasie asserted.

"Are the warriors ready to die to protect their comrades, in the hope that their fellows will win?" Soldier's Boy asked her quietly.

She was startled. "But you say that our plan is good. That Kinrove's dance will have demoralized the protectors of Gettys, that we will fall on them when they are full of sleep and confused. You have said we will slaughter them." She paused, her anger and indignation building. "You promised this!" she accused him.

"And we will." He replied calmly. "But some of us will die. This we have to admit, going into this battle. Some of us will die." He paused, waiting for some sign that she accepted this. Her face remained stony. He sighed and went on, "And when a warrior is injured, or when he sees his brother fall, dying, he cannot *then* decide that the price is too high to pay. Each of them must go into this battle thinking that if he must die for us to win it, then he will. It is the only way. This is what I am trying to teach them. Not just how to quickly be where I tell them to be, not just how to obey an order without conferring with one another or arguing. I must build them into a group that has a focus and a goal, a goal that is more important to each of them than his own life. We will not have more than one chance to do this well. The first time we attack them, we must wipe them out. It is our only hope."

Dasie lowered her chin to her chest, thinking. Her eyes were closed to slits as she stared into the fire. At last she said in a soft, sad voice, "This is worse than Kinrove's dance. In the dance, they gave up their own lives to protect us. But now you tell them they must kill, and yet must still give up their own lives. I thought to save my people from such things. You are telling me I have only plunged us even deeper into it."

"And I have more to say." Soldier's Boy shifted slightly in his seat. "You will not like to hear it. But I know it is true. We need to support Kinrove in his dance. He has complained to me weekly that he does not have enough dancers for the magic to work well. He is bitter, saying that you broke his magic for the sake of your personal feelings, and now that you require it to work, you demand more of him than he can do. He says he needs more dancers, if he is to send fear and sadness not just to the edges of the forest, but deep into Gettys. And that is where we need it to be." He paused and then looked at the fire as he said quietly, "We must allow him to summon more dancers."

She looked at him incredulously. "Can you say this to me? When only three months ago, I took iron into his encampment to free the dancers? Don't you understand at all why I did that? His dance was destroying us; the price he demanded to hold the intruders at bay was too high. It had torn the fabric of our families, and our kin-clans. I stopped the dance so that the People could go back to living as they used to live. What is the point of what I did if now I say to my people, 'You must not only submit to being summoned to the dance, to dance until you die, but you must be willing to take death to the intruders and perhaps die there as well.' Where is the peace and tranquility and return to the old ways that I promised them?"

I scarcely heard his response. Three months ago? My eternity of isolation had only been three months? Listening to them, I had feared I eavesdropped on an ongoing war council. I now knew, with a surge of hope, that Gettys had not yet been attacked. There was still time to stop this. How to stop it, I was not yet certain. But I had time, if only a small amount.

Soldier's Boy was talking to her, low and earnest. "Before our people can go back to being what they were, to living as they have always lived, we must free ourselves of the threat from the intruders. So, yes, we must change, for this small time, yes, we must subject the People to these things. In order to save them."

"In order to save them, I must permit Kinrove to work a summoning on our own people? I must let him turn the magic on the People again?"

"Yes." Soldier's Boy spoke heavily and with regret.

"You are certain that this is your counsel to me?"

I thought I heard a trap in her words. Either Soldier's Boy did not or he was past caring. "Yes."

"Then so be it." She heaved herself out of her chair and stood. The scarlet and blue robes that she wore fell into heavy folds around her. Her feeders came immediately to stand at her side, ready to assist her should she require it. "Bring my wraps," she told them. "And have my bearers ready my litter. We quick-walk back to my lodge tonight." She turned back to Soldier's Boy and grumbled, "It makes no sense that you insist on living here. It is a hardship on everyone that you are so far from every winter village."

"Yet here I must be. And many of my kin-clan have seen fit to come and join me here."

"Yes. I have seen that. A second little village of your kin-clan grows outside your door. And it is good that they are here. That way, when the summoning falls on them, you will see it."

I shared Soldier's Boy confusion and foreboding. "Falls on them?"

"Of course. I shall tell Kinrove he may resume his summoning. And your kin-clan was next in line to be summoned. Do not you recall? That was why he had invited your kin-clan's other Great One to his encampment near the Trading Place. He made that small concession. Before he sent each summoning, he told the Great One of the kin-clan that he would be doing so. That was why Jodoli was there. He agreed to it, as he had been forced to agree to it before. And now, it seems, you have agreed to the same thing."

Soldier's Boy was silent. I sensed his reluctance. He did not want the summoning to fall on his kin-clan. He dreaded that Kinrove would take the men he had so painstakingly trained for battle and use them instead for his dance. But having said that Kinrove must have the dancers for the attack to succeed, he had no way to refuse it. How could he say the sacrifice of his kin-clan was too sharp, but that others must pay it? He chewed at his lower lip and then gave a fierce shake of his head. "Very well, then. Let Kinrove send a summoning. It must be done. Those who dance are warriors of another kind. And the sooner the threat is removed, the sooner all warriors can put down their arms or cease their dancing."

"As you wish," she said, as if she were conceding something to him. Her feeders were all around her now, swathing her in woolen wraps and a heavy fur cloak. I heard men's voices outside the lodge, and suddenly the door opened, admitting a blast of wind and driven rain.

Soldier's Boy gave an exclamation of dismay. Dasie laughed. "It's only rain, Great One. If you do as you propose, we will face snow and the great cold of the winter in the west lands."

"I will face it when I must," he retorted. "I do not need it blowing into my lodge right now. Soon enough I must endure it, and then I will."

"That you will," she replied. She pulled a heavy hood up over her hair. One of her feeders was immediately there, tugging it forward and securing it around her face. Dasie had grown in girth and importance. I had not recalled her having so many attendants at Kinrove's pavilion. She strode toward the open door. The moment she was through it, Soldier's Boy made an exasperated gesture and a young man rushed to close it behind her. A woman piled more wood on the fire to replace the warmth that had been lost from the lodge.

"Do you think that was wise?" a shaky voice asked beside him. Soldier's Boy turned to look at Olikea. She was offering him a mug of a steaming liquid. Her eyes were very large. Her lower lip trembled; then she firmed it into a pinched line. He took the mug from her.

"What choice did I have?" he muttered unhappily. "We must endure what we must endure. It is not forever." Then, "Have you seen a summoning before? Tell me of it."

Olikea looked grave. She spoke carefully, more carefully than she had ever spoken to me. Plainly her relationship with Soldier's Boy was far different from how she had near-dominated Nevare. "I wish you had asked me what a summoning was like before you told Dasie they must be resumed. I would have urged you to try anything else before letting Kinrove call dancers from our kin-clan again."

"Just tell me how a summoning comes," he responded irritably. His anger covered a lurking fear that she was right. Small and silent, I rejoiced in my ability to once more read what he felt and know what he knew. Tiny as a sucking tick, and as secret, I clung to his mind.

Olikea spoke slowly and with reluctance. "The summoning has been a part of my life for as long as I can recall. Kinrove rotated them among the kin-clans. There are twelve kin-clans, so with good fortune, the summoning only fell on us once every eight years or so. He tried not to summon more than once a year, or so he said, but it is more often than that. He had to keep enough dancers, and—" She hesitated and then said bitterly, "And when people danced themselves to death, they had to be replaced."

"What happens in a summoning?" he asked her uneasily.

She looked away from him. "No one knows just when it will come. The magic comes over everyone. It is like feeling sleepy or hungry. It comes and it plucks at you, asking you if you want to join the dance. It asks everyone. Some can say no. Last time, I said no. Part of me wanted to go, but a greater part did not. I do not know why I was able to say no to the dance, but I could." She fell silent, staring into the flames of the fire. Her eyes narrowed and her voice went flat. "My mother could not. She left us and went to Kinrove's dance."

"Just like that? Just left?"

"Yes." She sat down in Dasie's empty chair. Her eyes had gone distant, and despite the warmth of the fire, her skin stood up in bumps on her arms. She rubbed at herself as if she were cold. "It was a summer night when the summoning came. It was—oh. I think it was eight years ago. My family was gathered around the fire. Our mother had been singing us a story-song, one that both Firada and I loved to hear, about a silly girl shaking a nut tree. In the middle of the song, the summoning came. We all felt it. It was like a chill up my back, or the crawling when your skin wishes you to scratch it, or perhaps thirst. One of those feelings that comes from the body, not the mind. My mother just stood up and began to dance. Then she danced away, down the path into the night. We watched her, and then I felt it coming over me. And

I was just a little girl, and all I could do was stay near my father, saying, 'No, no, I don't want to dance, I won't go.' It took all I had within me to say I would not go. That summoning lasted a full night. It was like watching the wind tear leaves from a tree. The magic blew through our kin-clan, and some held tight, but others were torn away from it. And off they went. We called after them, begging them to come back, but none of them did. A little boy, no more than two, toddled after his mother, screaming. She didn't even look back. I don't think she heard him, or remembered that he existed."

"And did you, did you ever see your mother again?" I knew he didn't want to ask the question, and knew also that he felt he must.

Olikea snorted. "What good would it do?" She leaned toward the fire and pushed in a piece of firewood that was on the edge. Then she spoke quietly, as if confessing something foolish she had done. "I did see her, once.

"Wherever Kinrove goes, his dancers go with him, always dancing. It was during the autumn moving time, when all of us use the hidden way to come back to the ocean side of the mountains. Kinrove's folk passed our kin-clan, and with them went his dancers. All were forced to give way to him. He called himself the Greatest of the Great, and before Dasie threatened him with iron, he could do as he wished. So all stepped aside for his kin-clan and his dancers to pass. And I sat and I watched, and I saw my mother. It was terrible. She danced fear, and it was all over her, like a stink clinging to a rotten fish. Her hair hung in mats and her body had gone to bones, but she still danced. Not for much longer, I do not believe, but that afternoon at least, she still danced. She danced past Firada and me, and never once let her eyes linger on us. She did not know us or remember us. She had become her dancing. She was like the road slaves that the intruders use to build their road, but at least they know they are slaves. She did not have even that."

I felt Soldier's Boy try to dismiss it, but there, at least, some of my sensibilities prevailed. He said quietly, "I am sad to know that you lost your mother that way."

"It was hard," Olikea admitted with a sigh. "Firada and I were both young still, with much to learn about being women of the People. The rest of our kin-clan took care of us; a child is always welcome at anyone's hearth. But it was not the same. I listened to other mothers teach their daughters, telling stories of when they themselves were young. Firada and I lost all those stories when our mother danced away." She paused. "I used to hate Kinrove. I did not think that anyone, not even a Great One, should have so much power over us. That day when Dasie held a sword to him and forced him to free the dancers, I hated her. Not because she did it, but because she did it too late for my mother and me."

Did Soldier's Boy wonder the same thing that I did? Why, if they had hated a Great One like Kinrove, had both Firada and Olikea sought out such men to become their feeders? She seemed to hear my unvoiced question.

"When I took you in and began to tend you, I thought that I would create a Great One of my own, one far greater than Kinrove. One greater than Jodoli, for Firada, I saw, did not have the same ambition that I did. I thought you would be the one to surpass Kinrove and become the Greatest of the Great. I believed you would find a way to drive the intruders away forever, and end Kinrove's dance." She hesitated, and then said quietly, "Before I met you I even dreamed it. I thought the magic sent me that dream, and when I first sought you out, I believed it was because the magic told me to do so."

She left the chair and came to sink down to sit on a cushion near Soldier's Boy's chair. She leaned her head against my thigh. Soldier's Boy stroked her hair. I wondered what had passed between them in the months that I had been gone. Olikea seemed milder and more tractable.

"What do you believe now?" he asked her gently.

She sighed. "I still believe the magic sent me to you. But I have come to see it differently. I believe that I am caught in the magic just as you are. It cares nothing for my ambitions. I will tend and serve you and you will tend and serve the magic."

"I have said that Kinrove should send a summoning."

"I heard you say it."

"It will fall on our own kin-clan."

"I know that also."

He didn't ask her what she thought of that or felt about it. That would have been a Gernian question. He waited for what she might decide to tell him. She sighed heavily. "I like what your power has brought me. I fear the summoning. But I know it has never taken a feeder, so I am safe. I do not want to see any of our kin-clan summoned. I do not like that you call for it. But it was the year for our kin-clan to endure the summoning. I think that, even if you had never existed, it would have come to this. So I do not blame you for it. But I feel a secret shame. I wonder if I am able to face the summoning because the magic has given me so much through you that I no longer care what it might take from someone else."

I am not certain what Soldier's Boy felt about her thoughts, but I had a definite twinge of uneasiness as I wondered what my presence here had done. I suddenly saw my coming as the trigger for a long chain of events, with distant results that I'd never be able to imagine, let alone compute. Was that what magic was? I wondered. Something that happened by such a convoluted chain of events that no human could have predicted it from the initial event? Was that the force that we called "magic"? The question twisted in my mind. Strike a steel against flint, and the first time a spark jumps, it seems like magic. But when the spark jumps every time, we add it to the list of things we can force the world to do. It became our science, our technology. A spark put to gunpowder would explode it. A lever could always levitate more than I could lift. But magic, I thought slowly, magic worked only when it suited magic to work. Like a badly trained dog or a strong-willed horse, it obeyed only when it wished to. Perhaps it rewarded only those who obeyed it. For some reason, that idea frightened me.

A stronger question rose in me. I wanted to push it at Soldier's Boy but refrained. If he knew I was aware and stirring again, I suspected he would box me in once more. At the mere thought of that, cowardice overwhelmed me. I kept my question to myself. Had Lisana had a clear image of what would happen when she claimed me for the magic? Had the magic taken me and given me to her to train? Or had she taken me, thinking she could train me for the magic? I suddenly wanted a clear answer to that question. My mind whirled with questions. What had first put me in the path of the magic? Dewara. But my father would never have known Dewara if he had not shot him with an iron ball and destroyed his magic. Had that event also been the will of the Specks' magic? Was I merely a link in a chain of events so intricate that no one recalled the beginning of it or foresaw the end? If that was true, where had it actually begun? Would it ever end?

Whilst I had been pondering, Soldier's Boy's life had gone on. Evening had descended, and the household was preparing itself for rest. The dishes had been cleared away. His feeders had brought him a long robe, a sort of nightshirt, and his body had been soothed with scented oils and then wiped clean. His bed was prepared for him. Where once only Olikea had tended him and Likari had aided her, now a full dozen serving folk came and went at their various tasks. Olikea presided over them and left no doubt as to her primacy. Likari mostly made a show of tending him; he was more pet than feeder, but no one seemed to resent that. The Great One obviously enjoyed the boy's company, and the affection between them was mutual.

The bustle of the evening preparations faded. Soldier's Boy was comfortably propped in his bed. Likari slept on a pallet at the foot of it and Olikea shared Soldier's Boy's bed, sleeping warm against his back. The lanterns in Lisana's lodge had been blown out; the only light came from the fire in the central hearth. A feeder minding the fire and keeping it burning well through the night was a silhouette against it. Several others settled on pallets at the other end of the room. Outside the lodge, all was quiet. There was the sweep of wind, and the uneven pattering of rain that fell more from swaying branches than from the distant skies above. The central hearth kept the damp and the cold of the winter night at bay. All in all, it was the most comfortable night that I think I'd ever witnessed Soldier's Boy enjoy in my body. His belly was full, he was warm, and danger was far away, on the other side of the mountains. I had expected him to settle in and slide immediately into sleep.

Instead, he lingered in wakefulness long after Likari's and Olikea's breathing had settled into deep slow rhythms. He was troubled. The part of him that recalled my schooling at the Academy knew that he must act based on the needs of the situation. Strategy demanded that Kinrove's magical dance be strong. To dispense with it now would be like dismissing a third of his troops just before battle was joined. Kinrove's magic of terror and depression was a steady onslaught against Gettys, wearing the soldiers down and eating away at morale. Soldier's Boy did not undervalue it, but he dreaded the summoning and wondered uneasily when it would come. It would wreak havoc among the kin-clan and his household. That was inevitable.

He heaved a sigh. He did it for the good of his people. He was prepared to make that sacrifice, but he wondered how much of his willingness came from his drive to preserve the People and their ancestor trees and how much came from the military training of Nevare Burvelle. Would a full Speck, raised only among the People, be able to countenance such a sacrifice? Certain attitudes had infiltrated his thinking like poison in his bloodstream. He knew that what he did was a rational choice, but was it the rationality of a Gernian or a Speck?

Lisana would know.

I breathed the thought toward him. It was a distant whisper wafting against his ear. Lisana could advise him. She had enabled him to attain this position of power and authority. She had taught him all he knew of the People. She would know where that other Nevare began and he stopped.

I put his weary mind to thinking of her. I called up my most vivid memories of Lisana and focused on them until I found myself longing for her as much as he did. As he ventured toward sleep, I kept feeding his unwinding mind images and thoughts of her. My tactic worked. He drifted into a dream of her, one rich in sensory details. I joined him there and then, holding a breath I no longer controlled, I pushed us both out of his body and into a dream-walk.

I longed to go to Epiny. I also needed to speak to my sister, to know what was happening to her. I dared not try for those things.

But I could focus on Lisana and anchor myself to my memories of her and then emerge from Soldier's Boy's dreams into hers.

I do not think she was sleeping. I doubt that she had need of sleep. But I joined her in a place where she was not Tree Woman, bound always to her tree and to her eternal vigilance in watching over the spirit bridge. She was recalling autumn. She sat on a hillside and looked down across a valley filled with trees. Through a hazy fall morning, she studied their changing foliage. A wind drifted through, trailing a train of dancing leaves in its wake.

"How many autumns have you seen?" I asked her as I sat down beside her.

She replied without looking at me. "I stopped counting long ago. This one was one of my favorites. That little birch down there had just become old enough to strike a yellow note among all the red from the alders."

"She makes both colors brighter," I said.

It pleased me to see a smile touch the corners of her mouth. She turned to me, and her eyes widened. "You are marked as one of the People now."

That surprised me. I looked down at my arms and bared legs. She was right. I wore the dappling that Soldier's Boy had pricked into his skin. I wanted to say something about that, but instead I said, "I've missed you so. You cannot imagine how I've missed you. Not just your knowledge and your guidance. Your presence. Your touch." I took her hand. It was small and plump in contrast to mine. I leaned close to breathe the fragrance of her hair. A few moments before, it had been streaked with gray. Now it was a rich brown with only a few threads of silver in it. She closed her eyes and leaned closer to me, shivering as my breath touched her.

"How can you say I can't imagine how you've missed me?" she murmured. "You move in the living world. You have the comfort of other people, the companionship of other women. I, I have only my memories. But now you are here. I do not know how you have managed to come to me, and I do not wish to waste whatever time we have in wondering. Oh, Soldier's Boy. Just for a time, be here with me. Let me touch you and hold you. I fear it will be the last time."

I did not hesitate to put my arms around her and draw her near. Lisana was the one place where my sentiments coincided exactly with Soldier's Boy's. I no longer cared what had first brought us together. I didn't care that I could not recall as my own the memories of how we had come to love each other. It was good and simple and true to embrace her. This love I felt for her required no effort on my part. I kissed her pliant mouth and then buried my face in her hair, feeling as if I were finally home.

I had primed Soldier's Boy to let me escape to her, and I had. Somehow I had brought shreds of his awareness with me. If he knew I was present, he did not struggle against me. Perhaps he thought he merely dreamed of his beloved. I know that the smell and taste and warmth of her drowned the question I had been so desperate to ask her. I was here with her, and now was the only time that mattered.

We were both large people. This was no frantic and athletic coupling. Between two such as we, lovemaking was a stately and regal dance, a slow process of give-and-take. Neither of us was coy nor were we shy. The size of our bodies did not permit those types of hesitation. We accommodated each other without awkwardness, and if flesh was sometimes a barrier, it was erotic as well. It forced us to move slowly; every contact was well considered. Her thighs were thick and soft as I pressed myself against her. The bounty of her breasts was a soft cushion between us. Each guided the other to what was most pleasurable, and I enjoyed Lisana's arousal as fully as my own. In those moments, I could recall in flashes that she had been his teacher in these matters, and he had delighted in learning his lessons well. As I held her and loved her, I could glory in the soft wealth of her skin. Her fingers walked the dappling on my skin, and in her touch, I rejoiced that I had marked myself as one of her own kind.

All wonders must have an end. A drift of leaves had been our bed. Now we lay sprawled among them. Lisana's eyes were closed but the smile on her face told me she was not even close to sleep. She was savoring our enjoyment of each other, and the touch of the weakened autumn sun and even the teasing wind that now chased a shiver across her. I laughed to see her shudder like a tickled cat and she opened her eyes. She sighed and lifted my hand to her lips, to kiss my palm again. With my hand still against her lips, she said softly, "I had a fancy the other day. Would you like to hear it?"

"Of course."

"My trunk has fallen, you know. But I rise again as a sapling from the trunk."

"I know that. Oh, my love, I am so sorry that I—"

"Hush. Enough of that. It has been said enough already. Listen. The tip of the tree that once was me thrust into the earth when I fell. And now I have felt a stirring there. A second tree will rise from the nursery that my trunk has become. I can feel it growing there, connected to me. Me and yet not me."

"Just as I am," I said. I already knew the direction of her thought and liked it.

"When you die," she said carefully, without malice, for death did not mean to her or to Soldier's Boy what it might have meant to a Gernian.

I seized the words from her. "When I die, I will be brought to that tree. I will see that it is so, Lisana. That tree, and no other. And we shall always be together. Oh, would that it would happen soon."

"Oh, not too soon," she chided me. "You have the task of your magic to complete. Now that you are one, surely you will succeed. But if you died before you complete it—" She paused and her smile faltered a little at the dread thought that followed it. "If you die before the intruders are driven away and the Vale of the Ancestor Trees secured against them, then I fear that our reunion will be short-lived." She paused, and then sighed, knowing she was letting the concerns of the world intrude on our brief time together.

"I have felt the changes," she said. "Felt them, but no one has come to tell me what is happening. Kinrove's power has faded, I think. When his dance stopped, it was like the sudden cessation of a great wind. I had almost forgotten what it was like when only peace filled our valley. For a time, a very short time, I drank it in as one drinks cool water after drought. I told myself it meant that you had solved the riddle of your magic and knew what you would do with your power. I dared to savor the peace that returned to the valley of our ancestors. But it was not for long."

"The dance started again," I responded.

"Did it?" She looked surprised. "I have not felt it here if it did. No. There were disturbances of another sort." She looked down at the hand I still clasped and sighed again. "They are tough, those Jhernians, like plants that when chopped and mangled still send down roots and push up leaves again. Two days after Kinrove's dance failed, I felt them at the edges of the forest. The next day, they were hunting there. Two days after that, they had mustered their slaves and put them to work, despite the snow on the ground. The poor creatures are near naked as frogs in the cold. I suppose their work warms them. Already, they have undone some of the barrier your magic raised against them."

"Not my doing, for the most part," I said, and again I felt it was Soldier's Boy speaking through me. I let him. I was hearing what I most wished to know. I didn't like what I was learning, but it was what I needed to know. In the next moment, I liked it even less. "Nevare spent the magic we had so painstakingly gathered. All the magic I had harvested from the Spindle, gone in three short breaths. I still cannot believe it."

She was quiet for a time. Then she concurred with, "Neither can I. Oh, Soldier's Boy, are we any closer to a solution? Is your task nearly done?"

He let go of her soft hand and made angry fists of his hands. "That is precisely the problem, Lisana. All that I must do for the magic, I did. Everything that it asked me to do, I accomplished. I gave the rock. I stopped the Spindle. I kept and left the book. All these things I have done, yet the magic has not worked. I do not know any more what it wants of me. Only those three things were clear to me, and I have *done* them. When I do my tasks and the magic does nothing, what am I to do?"

For a long time, there was silence between them. They reclined together in the loose leaves, and her touch against him was sweet, but it could not free him from his torment. Finally she asked in a soft, low voice, "What will you do?"

He had picked up a red leaf and been considering it. Now he crushed it in his hand and let the pieces fall. "I had thought to gather a great deal of magic, and use it to unite all of the People under one Great One. I had thought that then I would move against the Gernians in a way they would understand. I went to their schools. I know how the Landsingers drove the Gernians from their territory and claimed it back from them. What has worked once, I thought, might well work again. Let them see us as a mighty people with weapons they cannot copy or prevail against."

"A mighty people?"

He rubbed his face with both hands. "Do you remember the story you told me of the children and the bear? The bear wished to have the fish the children had caught. They knew if they ran, the bear would chase them down."

"So they spread their cloak between them, to make themselves appear as if they were a single creature larger than the bear. And they shouted and threw stones and ran at the bear. And he fled."

"Exactly," Soldier's Boy told her. "If we can perhaps appear to be a greater force than we are, if we can confront them with a size and a power they don't expect, then perhaps they will turn and run."

"That would take time. For years, Kinrove has tried to gather the People into a single unit. With all of his magic, he could not."

"And I do not have time. This young Great One, Dasie, has forced my hand. She is the one who destroyed Kinrove's dance, in the name of freeing our own people. Lisana, she brought iron among the People, used iron against a Great One to get her way. She has threatened me with iron if I try to oppose her. All I can do is take my plan and try to make her a part of it. She is the one, the 'queen' that the intruders will see opposing them. And I have told her that we must allow Kinrove to restore his dance. Without it, we have no hope of success in our attack against the intruders."

She had been watching his face as he spoke, and now her eyes were wide with alarm. "You will attack them?"

"Yes." He spoke the word in a harsh voice that made it plain it was not his desire but that he would do it. "As soon as we are ready. Kinrove is going to make a summons to restore his dance. I do not know how swiftly the dance magic will be restored. But it must work against the Gernians for some time before we attack; men do not fight well when their morale is damaged."

She turned her head, looking at him, but I felt she was actually looking for me in his eyes. She confirmed it when she spoke. "This is not something you learned from me, Soldier's Boy. This comes from Nevare, and the school in the west. Almost I wish you had not taken him into you."

He gave a harsh laugh. "Yes. It does. We will turn their own tactics against them."

She looked stricken. "How can you defeat the enemy when you have become the enemy? Soldier's Boy, this is not our way. And it is not the magic's way. You cannot say the magic prompts you to do this."

He looked at her, and then away. I could feel something building in him. His voice was hard when he spoke. "No. I've told you. It isn't the magic's way. It's my way. It's what I am forced to do when I have done all the magic has commanded me, and none of it has worked. Many a night have I lain awake, thinking and thinking, until my brain pounds inside my skull. If the magic will not tell me what it wants, it must be because I already know what I must do. Why, then, did the magic choose me? Because it knew I would go to that school and learn these things, and that I could then turn their own teachings against them."

"What will you do?" she asked him in a voice full of dread.

He shifted away from her. Some part of him was shamed. "Whatever I must," he replied in a determined voice.

"Tell me," she demanded.

"You will not like it."

"*You* do not like it! I can feel that. But you will do it. And if you can do it, then you can tell me what it is you plan to do."

Now he sat up, pulling his body away from hers. I suddenly knew that was a fair measure of how distasteful he found the task he had planned. He could not speak of it while cradling the body of the woman he loved. "I will attack them, just as they have attacked so many others."

"Without warning?"

"They have had years of warning. They have not heeded it. Besides, my force is not so great that I can afford to give them warning. Alarmed, they could stand against us, perhaps even best us. So, yes, we will attack them without warning."

"Where?" she demanded. She was determined to hear the worst of it. "Will you attack them while they are working on their road? Will you attack the slaves, poor creatures with no weapons and scarcely a thread to their backs?"

He turned away from her and looked across the valley. "No," he said, and all life was gone from his voice. It held only death. "We will attack the town and the fort. At night. When they are sleeping in their beds." He turned back to her before she could ask her next question. "All of them. Any of them we can kill. I do not have a large enough force that I can begin by being merciful."

A very long silence passed. "And when will you do this?" she asked at last.

"As soon as we are ready," he replied coldly. "I hope that will be before the end of winter. Dark and cold can be our allies."

"She will still be heavy with child. Or perhaps recovering from birth, with a newborn at her breast."

Soldier's Boy grew so still at her words that his stillness held me as well. Slowly, slowly it came to me that Lisana spoke of Epiny. I tried to reckon the time backward and could not. Was she a mother already?

Soldier's Boy answered a question that Lisana had not asked. "I cannot care about such things. He did not care about such things among my people, when he had the upper hand."

"Are you sure of that?"

"Look at what he did to you!" Soldier's Boy exclaimed with long-banked anger.

"He didn't kill me," she pointed out quietly.

"He nearly did."

"But he didn't. And he tried to stop the cutting of the ancestor trees."

"He was feeble at it."

"But he tried."

"That isn't enough."

"And he brings you to me now, when you could not come by yourself."

"What?"

She cocked her head at him. "You did not know this? You do not feel him, holding you here? I thought you had made your truce with each other. But for Nevare reaching toward me, we could not touch now."

"I—he is here? He spies on us! He spies on my plans!"

He made a swipe at my presence, and for an instant, all was silence and blackness.

"No!" I cried out voicelessly and fought back. I fought back with a savagery far beyond any physical confrontation I had ever been in. It is impossible to convey how much I abhorred the idea of being boxed once more. "I would rather be dead. I would rather not exist. I would rather we both ceased to exist!" I clung to his awareness, refusing to let him shed me. He tried to pull his consciousness free of me. I responded by turning abruptly away from Lisana and sealing him off from her. Suddenly, he was sitting up in his bed, staring wildly into darkness, bereft of her.

"No!" he shouted in his turn, rousing feeders. Beside him, Olikea sat up in alarm. "Nevare? What is it? Are you ill?"

"No. Leave me alone! All of you! Leave me alone!" Olikea's gentle touch was the last thing he wanted, and he could not bear the concerned scrutiny of the feeders who had rushed to his side.

"Shall I light lamps?"

"Is he hungry?"

"Does he have a fever?"

"A nightmare. Perhaps it was just a nightmare?"

I suddenly glimpsed just how little privacy was left to him in his wonderful life as a Great Man. Intruding hands touched his face and neck, seeking for signs of fever or chill. Lamps were already being lit. I took advantage of their distracting him and made more secure my grip on his awareness. "You cannot banish me," I told him. "I will not let you. And while you fight me and try to box me, I promise you, I will not let you see Lisana at all. I will keep her from you. This was my body and I will not be pushed out of it. You and I will come to terms now."

"Leave me alone!" he bellowed again, and I was not sure if he spoke to his clustering feeders or to me. They fell back from him in dismay. Olikea seemed affronted, but she turned her temper on the others.

"Get back from him. Leave him alone. All he did was to shout in his sleep. Let him go back to sleep and stop bothering him!" She literally slapped at hands until the confused and still-sleepy feeders moved away from him and back to their pallets. He was relieved until Olikea put comforting arms around him. "Let's just go back to sleep," she suggested.

Her warm embrace felt completely wrong. He shrugged free of it. "No. You sleep. I need to sit up and think for a time. Alone." He swung his feet over the side of the bed. I was still firmly attached to his awareness and thus knew how out of character this was for a Great One. He rose from his bed and walked to the hearth. To the feeder there, he said brusquely but not unkindly, "Go to sleep. I will tend the fire for a time."

The poor confused man rose, not sure if he had displeased the Great One somehow. Obediently, he retreated to an empty pallet at the far end of the room. Soldier's Boy pushed his big chair closer to the hearth and then sat down in it. Olikea lay on her side in the bed, staring at him. He looked into the flames.

"What do you want?" He didn't speak the words aloud, only to me.

"Not to be crushed." That was only the barest tip of what I wanted, but we had to start there.

He scratched his head as if he could reach inside and tear me out. It felt foreign to me; my hair had grown long, longer than I'd ever worn it. "I want to see Lisana," he countered.

"We might find an agreement there. But only if I am allowed to visit Epiny, too."

"No. You would warn her of my plans."

"Of course I would! Your plans are evil."

"No more evil than the road," he retorted.

"The road is evil," I agreed, surprising myself. I think it shocked him. He was silent for a moment. "I tried to stop the road," I pointed out to him.

"Perhaps. But you failed."

"That doesn't mean that slaughter is the only option left to you."

"Tell me another one, then."

"Talk. Negotiate."

"You tried that already. Until there is a slaughter, no one will seriously negotiate with us."

When I could not think of an immediate response, he pushed his advantage. "You know it's true. It's the only thing that will work."

"There has to be another way."

"Tell me what it is, and I'll try it. Your feeble negotiations didn't work. Kinrove's dance held them at bay but it only buys us time. The magic hasn't worked. What else am I to do, Nevare? Let the road come through? Let the ancestor trees fall, including Lisana's? Let the Gernians destroy everything that we are? Would you like that? To see Olikea working as a whore, to see Likari a beggar addicted to tobacco?"

"No. That's not what I want."

He took a long, deep breath. "Well. At least there seems to be a few things we agree on."

"And many that we do not."

He did not respond to that. And when his silence stretched longer, I knew that he had no more idea of what would become of us than I did.

We spent the rest of that long night staring into the fire, looking for answers that were not there.

CHAPTER NINETEEN

THE SUMMONING

By dawn, I think we were resigned to what should have been obvious from the start. We were bound together. One might dominate over the other for a time, but neither of us would ever willingly surrender to the other. Our loyalties conflicted, but at least Soldier's Boy could take comfort in the fact that I did not wish to see the end of his people and their way of life.

I had no such consolation to fall back on. In this, I felt he was more my father's son than I was. He saw his plan as a military necessity, the lone remaining solution to driving the intruders away from the ancestral trees. My sole weapon to hold him back was that without me, he could not reach Lisana. That seemed a feeble weapon to me, but it was all I had. So we sat together, two men confined to one body, each possessing an ability the other desperately wanted.

He dared to try to bribe me. "Don't fight me. All I ask is that you don't try to fight me. And in return, I will see that when we negotiate the peace, it will be the Burvelle family who is named as being in charge of trade with the Specks. Eh? Think on that. It will be a rich monopoly for the family."

I was silent, insulted that he would even offer a trade for Epiny, Spink, Amzil, and the children's lives. Trying to bribe me to accommodate his treason.

He felt my fury and shame rose in him. Shame is not a good emotion for a man to feel. It makes him angry as often as it makes him sorry. Soldier's Boy was both. "I was only trying to make you see that I don't intend you to have such pain. Yaril is my little sister, too, you know. I'd like to see our family prosper."

"*I* will not found my family's fortune on the blood of our own. And have you forgotten that Epiny is my cousin? Also our family, and as close as a sister to me. And Spink is like my brother. Or does not that matter?".

I felt him harden his heart. "I will do what I must do."

"As will I," I told him stubbornly.

Silence fell between us, but he did not try to banish me.

As the thin gray light of winter poked its fingers in through the small cracks round the shuttered windows, he rose. A wakeful feeder started to stir, but he made an impatient gesture at the woman and she lay back on her pallet, obedient as a hound. Soldier's Boy could walk quietly for such a massive man. He found an immense wrap, large as a blanket, draped it around his shoulders, and went outside to meet the day.

There had been snow and wind in the night, but the storm seemed to have blown itself away and the day was warming. The snow would not last. A light breeze still stirred the higher branches of the trees outside Lisana's lodge. Drops of water fell in sudden disturbed spatters when the wind gusted. In the distance, a crow cawed and another answered him.

To my gaze, the area outside the lodge had changed. Soldier's Boy gave it no attention, but I disliked it mightily. The placid dignity of the forest was gone. Winter had visited. A thin crust of icy snow clung to the tops of the low-growing bushes and frosted the moss in the untrodden areas. It lay only where it had drifted down between the higher branches, making an uneven pattern on the forest floor, a negative template of the canopy overhead. But amid that loveliness, paths had been worn through the moss and ferns, and branches broken back to permit easy passage down the trail to the stream. To either side of Lisana's lodge other less sturdy lodges had been built. The newer shelters looked raw amid the ancient forest. As always happens near human habitation, the litter of occupation was in evidence here. The smell of wood smoke and cooking was in the air. Soldier's Boy walked a short distance to an offal pit behind the lodges, relieved himself, and then made his way to the stream. Overhead, a squirrel scolded and then another. He paused and looked up to see what was disturbing them.

Something landed in the higher branches of the trees. Something heavy, for it disturbed a lot of raindrops, and as they fell, they disturbed others below them, resulting in a cascade of droplets to the forest floor. Soldier's Boy stared up, trying to make out what it was. With a sinking heart, I was sure I already knew.

"Orandula." I spoke quietly in the back of his mind. "The old death god. The god of balances."

He had craned back his neck to peer up into the treetops. I saw a brief flash of black and white plumage through the branches. Another shower of drops fell as whatever it was shifted position. Soldier's Boy dodged the falling water.

"Why is the god of death also the god of balances?"

"I don't know why he's the god of anything," I replied sourly. "Don't talk to him."

"I don't intend to."

The god dropped abruptly from the trees. Wings wide, he landed heavily near the stream bank. He waddled toward the moving water, only a bird, and dipped his head on his long snaky neck to drink. Soldier's Boy turned and walked back toward Lisana's lodge. My heart misgave me.

I was not quite to the door of the lodge when the summoning came. I don't know what I had expected it to be. I didn't think it would be what it was, a simple impulse to stand a few moments longer in the early light of a winter day. The wind stirred the trees, a bird called, and the loosened raindrops pattered down. In response, I stepped sideways, hopped, turned, and came back to the path. It felt wonderful.

I heard something else then, something that was and was not a part of the ordinary sounds of the forest. It was a deep, soft rhythm. I could not perceive the source of it, but I found myself stepping easily to its beat. As its tempo increased, so did my pleasure in it. I had forgotten what a joy it was to dance. Or perhaps I had never before felt the joy of dancing. It didn't matter. Had I thought my body large and ungainly? A foolish notion. None of that mattered. There was a dance inside me, making itself known to me. It was a dance that was made for me, or perhaps I had been made for the dance. It was a dance that I wanted to dance forever, to the end of my life.

Around me, other dancers were emerging from the lodges. I scarcely noticed them. I was scarcely aware that I shared a body with Soldier's Boy. Did he move the feet or did I? It did not matter. I was caught up in my dance, and how fine it was to be dancing on such a wonderful morning. I swayed, I turned, and I had taken a dozen steps down the path when I heard an agonized call from behind me.

"No! No! Do not give in to it. Refuse the dance! Do not go to Kinrove's dance. Refuse. Still your body, plant your feet on the earth. Do not enter the dance!"

Her words were an icy shower down my back. Soldier's Boy jerked and twitched and then, by a great effort of will, broke free of the dance. He did as she had told him. He planted my feet on the earth and willed my body to stillness. It was more difficult than it sounds. The dance shimmered around me. It told me that I danced even when I did not. My breath was the dance, my beating heart was the dance, the morning wind was the dance, even the stray raindrops that tapped down on my face were the dance. The summoning spoke so sweetly; it was all I needed, it said, all I had ever wanted to do. Had not I longed for a simpler life, a life free of worries and tasks? All I had to do was come, come to the dance.

I do not know how Soldier's Boy resisted. I could not. I wanted to dance, but he leaned forward, over my belly, his hands on my thighs, and stared at my feet, commanding them to be still. I heard Olikea still shouting. Someone rushed past me, capering in wild joy. Another went less willingly, shouting angrily, but dancing away all the same. Distantly I was aware of the croaker bird cawing. It was an avian laughter, and as the bird flew off, it faded into the distance until it sounded like a man chortling. Or choking.

For most of that morning, the dance tugged at me. I had never guessed that the summoning was so insistent or that it lasted so long. Some who had held firm against it at first gave way to it later in the morning, and went cavorting down the path. Olikea continued to shout her warning at intervals. Soldier's Boy spared her a glance once, to see that she had actually lashed herself to a tree and clung to it as she shouted.

I had known summer days on the prairie when the chirring of insects was a constant, morn to night, so that after a time one could not hear them. Then, abruptly, they cease, and one remembers what silence truly is.

It was like that when the summoning stopped. For a long moment, not just my ears, but my lungs and belly felt abruptly empty. Soldier's Boy staggered where he stood, and groaned as my legs tingled and burned from my long inactivity. He straightened up. His head spun for a few long moments, and I feared that he would fall. He took deep steadying breaths and suddenly the world was solid again. I knew that he was completely back to himself when the first hunger pang assailed me. It was nearly noon, and Soldier's Boy had neither eaten nor drunk since the night before. "Olikea!" he called, desperate for his feeder.

She didn't answer. Soldier's Boy looked around me, more cognizant now. Several of his feeders sprawled on the earth where they had fallen. Resisting the summons had taken all their strength. Olikea, still bound to the tree, sagged against her bonds, weeping. She gripped the trunk of the tree as a child would cling to its mother. "No," she was sobbing. "No, no, no. Not again. Not again!"

Soldier's Boy went to her as quickly as he could manage. It was startling to me to find out how weak he could feel after a single morning's fast. Obviously my body had changed in many ways under Soldier's Boy's ownership. His hands were gentle as he set them on her shoulders, kinder far than he had been the night before. "It's all right, Olikea. I'm here. I didn't give in to the dance."

She let go of the tree only to clasp her hands over her mouth. She rocked back and forth in agony. "Likari!" she managed to say at last. "Likari has gone! I tried to catch him but he tore himself free of me and danced away. And I, I could not unfasten the knots. A great bird followed him, squawking and cawing, as if it, too, must answer the summons. Oh, Likari, Likari, why did not I bind you last night? I did not think the summons would come so soon. Always, I have heard that the feeders were not called. I thought we were safe. Oh, Likari, I thought you were safe! Being a feeder is supposed to make one safe from the summons to dance!"

Soldier's Boy was struck dumb with horror, as was I. A terrible hollowing began inside us, a dawning of loss that emptied us both and then filled that gap with guilt. Likari, my little feeder, snatched away from me by the very summons Soldier's Boy had urged. And the bird that had followed him? Orandula, the god of balances, keeping his promise or his threat. Was he taking Likari's life or his death to pay my debt? The result was the same, whichever he called it. The boy was gone from us. What a fool Soldier's Boy had been!

Dasie had warned him. Even without Dasie, Olikea's story of her mother's snatching should have been enough to make him see the danger. He had not only permitted Kinrove to send this summoning against his own kin group, he had encouraged, no, demanded it. He looked around at the other feeders who were only now rising from the ground. Soldier's Boy knew them by name. Four were gone: Eldi, Hurstan, Nofore, and Ebt. How many others had been stolen from our kin-clan? How many others mourned as Olikea mourned now? As he mourned now?

Olikea had collapsed against her bonds. She had used a long wrap to tie herself, something that she had snatched up as she left the lodge that morning. It was woven of very soft yarn, and she had pulled and strained against it until the knot had become a single solid ball of fiber. Soldier's Boy could not get it undone any more than she could.

"Someone bring a knife!" he shouted over my shoulder, unreasonably angered that no one had already done so. He tried to care that the other feeders were probably as disoriented and perhaps devastated as we were. He couldn't. Likari was gone and it was his own fault. "I'll follow him. I'll bring him back," Soldier's Boy promised her limp form. Olikea had sagged down as far as the ties permitted her to, and now was staring off into the distance, her face slack. "Olikea. Listen to me. I'll go after him, I'll bring him back. It will be all right. By tonight, he'll be back at the hearth with us."

Sempayli came and with a bronze blade sawed through the stubborn fabric. Soldier's Boy was glad to see this feeder remained to him. When the fabric parted, Olikea's weight carried her down to sprawl on the ground. She didn't move. "Carry her back into the lodge," he commanded Sempayli, and the man scooped her up as if she weighed nothing. Soldier's Boy followed them in and watched as Sempayli put her on my bed. "Sempayli, food and water," he commanded his man tersely and then sat down beside Olikea's still form.

"Olikea. Did you hear what I said?"

Only her mouth moved. It was as if the rest of her face were dead. "You can't bring him back. He went to the dance. He ran to it, he wanted to go. You can't get him back. He'll dance himself to death before the winter is out. Didn't you see his face, didn't you see the magic burning inside him like a torch? It will consume him from within. Likari. Likari."

Soldier's Boy said the stupid words, the same ones I would have said in his place. "But I didn't think you even cared for him that much."

She suddenly became even more still. I thought for a moment that his words had killed her. Then her face hardened. She pushed against the bed, sitting up. "What good is it to love anything?" she asked me harshly. "It just goes away."

He stared at her. Soldier's Boy was as thunderstruck as I was. Always, I had thought her cold toward her son. We had shared the knowledge that her fondness was only an attraction to the power of a Great Man. She'd seemed a heartless woman, one Soldier's Boy could deal with only by being as detached as she was. Now she was revealed as broken; she had been broken for a long time. The brokenness was what had made her prickly and harsh.

Soldier's Boy stood up and spoke sharply to his other feeders. "Bring me food to eat now. And warm clothes and sturdy boots. I'm going after Likari."

None of them moved. Their eyes shifted, each to another, but no one spoke or sprang to their tasks. "What is it?" Soldier's Boy demanded sharply.

Sempayli was stirring a pot over the fire. Even he did not turn at Soldier's Boy's command.

"They know it is useless. Just as I do. You say you are one of us, you have even marked yourself as one of us, but on these deep things you still think like a Jhernian. You still talk like a Jhernian."

It was the last thing Soldier's Boy wanted to hear right now. I felt the rage rise in him that Olikea could insult him so. Then, with admirable control, he forced the rage down and in a controlled voice asked, "Then tell me clearly what it is that I don't understand."

"He won't want to come back."

"I'll talk to him."

"He won't hear you. You were there, when Dasie came to Kinrove's encampment. Why do you think she came with warriors and cold iron? Don't you understand that until she broke Kinrove's dance, none of the dancers would have wanted to leave? Even after she had broken it and the dancers had come to their senses, even then some preferred to stay. Didn't you feel the entrancement of the dance? If I had not shouted to you, if you had given in to it, you would still feel the dance running through you."

"But I did hear you shout. And when you shouted, I knew that in my heart, I didn't want to go."

"And that means that the magic was not summoning you to the dance, but only inviting you. And so you could say no. But Likari was summoned. He went because he had to, and so he wanted to go, because once the dance had touched him, he could think of nothing else. Don't you think that others have tried to keep those they loved from the dance? They have run after them, and carried them back and tied them. It did no good. Still they danced, and they heard nothing from their lovers or their children, and they saw nothing and they would not eat and they would not sleep until they were released to go to the dance."

Tears had started fresh down her cheeks before she was half-way through her speech. They continued to run as she spoke, and her voice hoarsened. On her last words, her throat choked her to stillness. She stood, silent and empty. Even the tears slowed and then ceased, as if nothing were left inside her.

"I will go to Kinrove and tell him he must release Likari to me."

"I thought you might feel that way."

Soldier's Boy knew who was there before he turned. He had felt the unpleasant tingle of iron against my senses. I knew an iron bearer must be somewhere close, perhaps just outside Lisana's lodge. Dasie stood in the doorway, a dour look on her face. Yet just for an instant, I thought I glimpsed a gleam of satisfaction in her eyes. Rage rose in Soldier's Boy, and again he forced it down. He tried for a reasonable tone. "I did not expect that Kinrove would call my feeders with his summoning."

She raised her eyebrows. "I, too, am surprised at that. But perhaps we should not be. You have not given him many reasons to love you. Perhaps he considered it a sort of justice, to take from you what you had not expected to lose in this gamble."

"Gamble?"

"Our war against the intruders." She came into the lodge and advanced to my chair by the hearth. With a grunt of satisfaction, she ensconced herself, uninvited. Her feeders remained standing at the door. Outside, her iron bearer waited. Had she expected Soldier's Boy to be angry enough that she needed a guard?

"I want the boy back." Soldier's Boy spoke bluntly.

Dasie laughed. It wasn't a cruel laugh; rather, it was the laugh of someone who sees a child finally realize the consequences of his own foolishness. "Don't you think we all wanted those we loved back? Well, at least you have the power to get him back."

"You mean, if I go to Kinrove, he'll give him up?"

"Oh, I very much doubt that." She motioned irritably at my feeders, and, with the exception of Olikea, it was as if they wakened from a spell. They sprang into motion, adding wood to the fire and beginning the preparation of food. She settled more comfortably in my chair. "As I said, you've given him no reason to love you. Perhaps taking something you cared about from you brought him a special satisfaction. I think perhaps you know that he has no children. Seeing you enjoy that young boy as if he were your own—well. Perhaps he thought you deserved to feel the same lack that he does."

"You knew he would call Likari."

She cocked her head at me. "I suspected he would try. I had no idea if the boy would be vulnerable or not."

"You chose not to warn me." Soldier's Boy stated it flatly and waited for her response.

"That is correct." My feeders brought her a platter of food. She looked it over consideringly and picked up a slice of smoked fish. A similar platter was conveyed to me. Soldier's Boy ignored it, awaiting her response. It finally came, after she had licked her fingers.

"I thought perhaps you should have a higher stake in stopping the dance. And in driving the intruders from our territory."

"You don't trust me," Soldier's Boy said bluntly. "Likari is a hostage. If I don't do as you say, you'll see that he dies."

She ate another slice of the fish with evident relish. "Now there's a Jhernian concept. A hostage. Yes, you could see it that way. But it isn't that you must do what I say. Only that you must succeed in doing what you said you'd do. What you have always been meant to do. If you succeed in driving the intruders away, Kinrove's dance will no longer be needed. The boy will come back to you. But if you do not—" She picked at the fish, and then took a handful of nuts instead. She seemed to feel no need to finish her sentence.

It had been a hard morning. Soldier's Boy was hungry and the food at my elbow smelled wonderful. He hated that he could even think of eating at a moment like this, and yet my body clamored at him relentlessly. He refused to look at the platter but could not stop smelling the tempting aromas. The magic nagged to be fed. Soldier's Boy saw Dasie's gaze move from my face to the platter and back again. She knew. She knew how he resisted the food and it amused her.

This time, when Soldier's Boy's wrath rose, he did not contain it. "Leave," he commanded her. "Leave now." A sudden cold wind whirled past the lodge and swept in through the open door.

Dasie looked startled. One of the feeders gave a low cry of fear. I felt the sudden depletion of magic from my body but Soldier's Boy appeared not to care. The wind grew stronger, colder.

Anger and fear mingled in Dasie's face. Great Ones did not usually threaten one another with magic so openly. "I have my iron bearer!" she warned him.

"Yes," he agreed. "You do. And who is thinking like a Gernian now, Dasie?" The sweep of wind came inside the lodge, tugging at her garments. "Leave now!" he told her again. The feeders had retreated to the back of the lodge. Dasie's attendants glanced about uncomfortably. Her iron bearer entered abruptly, carrying his sword as if it were a gun. It was obvious that he judged its power to be in its touch rather than its edge. He advanced on me, his face grim with determination. Soldier's Boy set his teeth and spent more magic. Despite the iron, the wind still blew, but it cost him dearly.

"We will leave!" Dasie declared abruptly. "I have no reason to remain here." She rose with a grunt and strode toward the door. Her iron bearer moved hastily out of her path, putting a safe distance between his weapon and his Great One. Dasie swept out of Lisana's lodge and her feeders flowed after her. The wind seemed to follow her, pushing her along. After she was gone, one of my feeders scuttled to the threshold and closed the door behind her. We were plunged into dimness and silence. It felt breathless.

For a moment, the food still beckoned. Angrily he refused to heed it. How could the magic be so selfish? His heart had a hole torn in it. Likari was gone. Olikea was, I realized, in a state similar to battle shock. Walking wounded, I thought. She gave the appearance of functioning, but was not.

With an almost physical wrench, I felt Soldier's Boy wrest my attention to him. "I want to think like a Gernian right now." His thought to me was harsh. "Make me see clearly. What must I do right now?"

I didn't need to pause to think. The training of years slid into place like a bolt sliding home in its socket. I hastily rummaged his memories of the last few weeks, orienting myself to his situation. Grudgingly, he allowed this. I was a bit surprised to find that, as a military man, I approved of most of what he had done. As a Gernian, it horrified me.

He'd organized his troops just as if they were a cavalla force. He'd established a rudimentary chain of command. He'd made an attempt at teaching basic drill, but had to give it up. His "troops" could not understand the use of it and simply did not cooperate. They had no tradition of military obedience, and little concept of a graduated hierarchy, and he'd had no time to establish one. He'd had to be content with training them to change locations swiftly when he ordered it. Hardest for them to learn was that they themselves did not decide how to place themselves; they had to wait for his commands. It had not been easy. His troops had flocked mostly to Dasie's call and came from all the kin-clans. They were supposedly three hundred strong. The reality was that they came and went at their own whim. He'd had as few as one hundred turn out when he called. It was a great weakness and would be disastrous if he attempted an attack on Gettys. But I didn't intend to support him in that. My own fear was closer to home.

"You need to consolidate your own force," I told him. "You thought your common enemy was the Gernians. Perhaps it is, but neither Kinrove nor Dasie are truly on your side. They both use you, and each has what amounts to a personal guard, a component of your general force that is absolutely true to them. They will care nothing if you are destroyed in the process of serving them. They may even think it to their benefit if you are.

"The majority of the troops you have been training come from Dasie's kin-clan. In any sort of a pinch, they will look to her for leadership and also to protect her. There are few warriors that belong to you. Even those from Olikea's kin-clan do not feel a strong loyalty to you; some may still regard you as an outsider, for you have done little to change that perception. You need at least a small body of men who are yours first. You have very little time to establish it. Sempayli seems to put you first. Tell him to stop being one of your feeders and become your lieutenant."

"But—"

"Quiet. Let me finish." I had no time for his doubts or objections. His flaw seemed clear to me. "You've been thinking like a soldier, or at best a sergeant. You have to become the general, not a lackey for those others. Once you seize command of the full force, neither Dasie nor Kinrove will know how to take it back from you. Taking the loyalty of the troops and making them obey you are necessities if you are to survive and win Likari back."

He raised a wall of obstinacy between us, then just as swiftly dropped it. "What do you suggest?" he asked stiffly, making it clear that all choices remained with him. Good. He'd have to build on that to develop the honest arrogance of full command.

"I suggest that you look to your own kin-clan first. Care for them, and they'll care for you. Send Sempayli to the main village to find out who has been summoned. Get a tally of who has been lost to them. Send someone to Firada, to tell her Likari is gone. Ask her to come and comfort her sister. Send word to their father, Kilikurra. He will want to know his grandson has been summoned. Let your concern be known to your kin-clan. Announce your loss of Likari and let them know that you, too, grieve. Shared loss will bond them to you."

I felt heartless to exploit tragedy this way. When had I become so shallow? It was, I suddenly thought, a tactic my father would have used. I felt Soldier's Boy seize my suggestion and run off with it. My sole thought had been to guard his back and Olikea's against the machinations of Dasie and Kinrove. He leapt forward with it and I suddenly realized my deadly error.

"I will let them know that I suffer alongside them. But I must not let that blossom into resentment toward Kinrove. We will sorrow together, but when it starts to fester into hatred for Kinrove's magic, I will point that hatred toward the intruders instead. I will say to my warriors, as well as my kin-clan, that there is only one way to have our loved ones returned to us, only one path to resuming our lives of peace and safety. To go back to the days when

Kinrove's dance was not needed, we must muster every man who can stand as a warrior, and together fall upon Gettys and annihilate it!"

"No!" I bellowed the word, furious at myself as well as at him, but he suppressed my anger to a sigh. He spoke fiercely at me, arguing over and against my thoughts, trying to mute me with his own desperate logic.

"Care you nothing for the people who took you in when your own tried to kill you and you had to flee? Why do you think you owe the Gernians anything at all? Do you not fear for what will certainly befall Lisana's tree? I know you recognized the need to protect our ancestor trees. You even went to Colonel Haren to try to persuade him to stop the road. Have you forgotten his arrogance and disrespect for you? I know it is hard for you, Nevare. In some ways, it is hard for me. But you cannot go back and be a Gernian. Even if I ceded the body to you and you returned to Gettys, they would kill you. Why not let go of your foolish loyalty to a folk who spurned you? Let us live where we are loved. But to do so, we must protect the ones who do accept us and care for us. The People must rise up against the intruders and drive them all out. There is no other way. Many will die, but better that many die and the conflict is finally ended than for the deaths and fighting to linger for generations. I hate what we must do, but there is no other path to peace. I know you want as few to die as possible. My way wins that for both of us. And so you must help me."

"No." My refusal was dull and deadened. I could refuse to help him, but I could not stop him.

"I need you, Nevare. Don't fail the People. You know our war is righteous. Think of Olikea, deprived first of her mother and now of her son. That is the doing of the intruders. Shall we let it happen, over and over, generation after generation? We have to stop it."

"That was Kinrove's doing."

"The intruders created Kinrove. Without their depredations, the magic would not have needed him. It all goes back to the intruders. There is only one way to end all of this. We tried to drive them away with the dance. They would not go. So now we must kill them."

"Epiny," I said quietly. "Spink. Sem. Kara. Baby Dia. Ebrooks. Kesey. Tiber." I pushed my emotions at him. My thought was a whispered plea as I added, "Amzil. What about Amzil? I feel for her what you feel for Lisana. Can you be numb to my feelings for her? Despite all, she said she loved me. Would you wish death on her and her children?"

"Olikea!" he countered. "Likari." And balancing lives on a scale, as if he were Orandula himself, he said, "We both love Lisana. And she loves us. If the intruders are not stopped, we lose her forever, and we lose forever itself."

I knew what he meant by losing forever. If the road were not stopped, the Valley of the Ancestor Trees would be destroyed. There would be no tree for him when this body died, and hence no second life with Lisana.

"The price is too high," I said quietly.

"It is," he agreed. "No matter which side pays it, the price is too high. But there is no bargaining with fate. Deaths must be paid to buy us peace. Balance it, Nevare. A quick massacre, followed by generations of peace, or the continued erosion of years of gradual killing, the complete destruction of a people and their ancestral wisdom. How can it be difficult to choose? Our attack will be like a surgery, a severing of diseased flesh so that the healthy part can go on living. It is what we must do."

Then he turned away from me. It was not silencing me so much as it was him refusing to allow himself to hear. There was no point to my speaking. Instead, I was a silent witness to all he did that day. My father would have been proud of him. He was efficient and relentless. The only emotions he allowed to show were the ones that were useful to his cause.

He took my suggestions. In the days that followed, I watched him as he silently implemented his plan. He conferred that day with Sempayli, treating him more like a lieutenant and less like a feeder. At first the young man seemed confused by the change, but before their review of the troops was over, he had begun to offer bits of advice and suggestions. He knew the warriors better

than Soldier's Boy did, and before the day was done, he quietly offered to help sort them into those who truly wished to annihilate
the intruders and those who merely hoped to win glory and perhaps plunder. Soldier's Boy consented to that, and further charged
him to select a dozen men to be his personal guard, based solely
on skills with weaponry rather than on which kin-clan they
belonged to. He also listened to Sempayli when the young man
suggested that the troops would respond better to being treated
as if they were hunting parties rather than troops marching in
formation. I was uncertain of the wisdom of that, for it would
create many individual leaders rather than a chain of command,
but Soldier's Boy didn't consult with me on that and I no longer
cared to offer him my thoughts on anything. He might be a traitor but I was not.

When he needed information from me, I refused him, but it
was a useless show. I had little success at keeping my barriers raised
against him. He could not absorb me, but he raided my memories
as he wished for information and military tactics and knowledge.
I gained some knowledge of his forces. They were not impressive,
but I knew they were not to be dismissed, either. They would
not fight us as Gernians fought, nor as the Plainsmen had. As the
days passed, Sempayli's suggestions bore fruit. It was tedious to
have a variety of leaders reporting directly to Soldier's Boy, but he
endured it, and began to set small competitions among them, ones
that built endurance or emphasized stealth or marksmanship.

I was surprised to discover he had a small mounted force. I
had seen the horses that Dasie had used the night she had taken
Kinrove down. Now my suspicions were confirmed. They were
cavalla animals, some bartered for but most stolen. Some of them
were old animals and none of them were in the best condition.
The tack they had was very well worn and often in poor repair.
Keeping horses was not a Speck tradition, and the forest did not
offer good grazing, especially in winter. Soldier's Boy took it
upon himself to intervene in their care and grooming. That was
when I discovered to my shock that Clove was among them.
Evidently the day I'd turned him loose in the forest, he had not
found his way home. The huge beast knew me immediately and

came to Soldier's Boy for comfort. I was glad he gave it, ordering that all the horses be moved to the coarse meadows near the beaches where they could actually graze rather than being forced to browse on whatever they could reach. When he announced that he would take Clove for his own mount, the current owner offered no resistance. I suspected that very few of the mounted Specks enjoyed their new vocations; the dense forest and often steep paths were not conducive to breeding horsemen. Soldier's Boy wanted to begin some mounted drills, but the open space required simply didn't exist near Lisana's lodge. Finding proper grazing was difficult enough; the salt marshes gave them grass, but only of the coarsest sort. With reluctance, he had to give up his hope of a mounted force that could spearhead a swift attack.

As I had suggested, he showed special attention to those warriors who had come from Olikea's kin-clan, taking time to meet separately with each one of them and to ask gravely if any of their family or dear ones had been summoned to Kinrove's dance. Every one of them, of course, had lost someone to the magic. Soldier's Boy made that pain the mirror of his own, and spoke earnestly to them of how their only hope of regaining their lost kin was to give their utmost to drive the intruders from our territories. He urged them, too, to recruit others from among our kin-clan, brothers and cousins and uncles, in the hope of winning our struggle and being reunited with all our lost kin in peace and joy. He rallied his troops with stirring speeches in which he reminded them of all the wrongs the Gernians had done them, and promised them that they would right those wrongs. Over and over, he reminded them that if they fought well in the upcoming battle, they would drive away the Gernians, save their ancestral trees, and put an end to the need for Kinrove's dance. Every one of them would be a hero to his people. His efforts at making the struggle against the Gernians even more personal succeeded. The force drawn from our kin-clan doubled and then tripled in less than a week.

Such a drawing off could not escape Jodoli's notice. "How do I smooth his feathers?" Soldier's Boy asked of me late one evening as the rest of the lodge slumbered around us. I tried to hold myself aloof from his questions, but at such times, when we were alone in his mind, I felt like a prisoner tormented during questioning. I could not escape him, and if I would not surrender what he wanted, he would resort to picking through my memories. He concentrated most heavily on what my father had taught me. That wrung the most guilt and pain from me, for it seemed a double defection that I betrayed my father as well as my own people when I used my father's hard-won knowledge of strategy and tactics against them.

"How do I win Jodoli over to me?" he asked me again. Olikea slept heavy and warm against me. Her sorrow had left her limp and exhausted. She moved once, making a small sound like a baby's half sob, and was still. She smelled of tears. He sighed heavily. "I don't like to do this to you." I felt him begin to plumb our shared past, drilling through my memories in search of advice that might apply. I gave in.

"You have two options," I told him. "Either you make your cause his. Or you make it appear to him that you have come over to share his concerns. Either one will work, if you do it well."

I could feel him thinking that through. Threads of a plan started to weave together in his mind. I almost felt him smile. "And if I did it well enough, would that be how I win you over, too?"

"I will never be a traitor to my people," I told him fervently.

"Perhaps all I need to do is show you which people are truly your own," he replied mildly. "Perhaps if I think long enough and in enough detail, I will get you to face what the Gernians did to you. How your fiancée mocked you and your father disowned you. How no one wished to let you serve your king. How your 'own people' decided not just to hang you, but to slice you to quivering meat before they ended your days. And then I might remind you of who took you in and fed you and cared for you. I might ask you which women treated you as a man, and which people respected you and the magic you held. I might ask you—"

"I could remind you that Spink and Epiny risked all to rescue me. And that Amzil was willing to sacrifice herself however she must to help me get past the guards."

"She was willing to do that, but not to lie with you," he pointed out snidely.

"Olikea was willing to lie with you, but not love you," I retorted.

"What sort of a man, what sort of a soldier, cares so much about being loved and so little for duty to a people loyal to him?"

I had no answer to his words. They struck strangely deep in me. "Leave me alone," I retorted savagely.

"As you wish," he conceded and did.

When he did not need my advice, he ignored me. At those times, I felt as if I were coming loose from time as well as space. I seemed not to sleep but from time to time to lose awareness of myself as a separate entity. I felt like a tiny piece of driftwood spinning slowly in a backwater of his mind. The currents moved me but I had no influence on them. His words about which people were truly my own ate at me like acid; I felt that my core self grew smaller whenever I considered them. Buel Hitch's words from long ago came back to haunt me. Why was it a virtue to remain loyal to a people simply because I had been born into their midst? Why could I not simply turn my back on the Gernians as they had turned against me, and become a Speck with my whole heart? At such times, I think that only my small circle of kin and friends at Gettys kept me Gernian.

As from a distance, I watched Soldier's Boy court Olikea's kin-clan, trying to gain their acceptance and trust. And when the time came, he did not invite Jodoli to his lodge, but instead sought him out on the kin-clan's own grounds. Olikea's and Firada's father quickly welcomed him in. Kilikurra had been the first Speck to speak to me, and I think he felt a measure of honor in having been the first to recognize a Great One come among them. He was a man of middle years, with black lips, mismatched eyes, and streaky gray hair. I now thought of how he had lost the mother of his daughters to Kinrove's dance, and saw his fresh grief at the loss of his grandson. He and Soldier's Boy spoke long and quietly together, and Soldier's Boy made him an ally in his drive to regain the boy. It was heartbreaking how easily the man was won over by Soldier's Boy's promises of doing all he could to get Likari back.

Soldier's Boy did not try to conceal the grief he felt at the boy's absence and his concern for his well-being. I don't think that even he could detect the line between what he actually felt and how useful it was in swaying the Specks to his cause.

Yet others of Olikea's kin-clan were not as swift to welcome Soldier's Boy wholeheartedly. I suspect that Jodoli did not encourage the people of his kin-clan to trust the interloper. Soldier's Boy's presence had greatly modified the attitude of the extended family group toward Jodoli. Both he and Firada had been relieved when Soldier's Boy had taken up residence in Lisana's old lodge, well away from the village where they traditionally wintered. They had been happy to characterize him as a Great One with no attached kin-clan, a sort of renegade mage. Jodoli had begun to solidify his standing with the kin-clan, and now here came Soldier's Boy, threatening it once more.

What could have been a confrontation was defused when Soldier's Boy instead sought Jodoli's advice on the summoning, sharing his concern for Likari. At first Soldier's Boy only asked questions and listened solemnly to every answer, even when Jodoli tediously overtrod ground well known to both of them. Firada had a soft spot for her nephew, and as the evening passed into night, the consultation changed into a family discussion. Jodoli's home was twice the size of Lisana's old lodge and lush with the acquisitions of a man who had been a Great One for years. These comforts Soldier's Boy openly admired, stroking Jodoli's pride. Yet when the night deepened about the lodge and we all drew closer to the hearth, the great lodge seemed a small place where the dancing firelight illumined a circle of faces wearied by sorrow. The feeders had been sent off to their homes. Only this "family" remained, the two women and their father, and Jodoli and Soldier's Boy.

I should not have been surprised to discover that Jodoli was as fond of the boy as anyone was, and as shocked and offended that Kinrove had let the summoning take a feeder. It was a painful discussion for all involved, as Soldier's Boy asked difficult questions about how long the boy might be expected to dance. He bluntly asked how long other youths called to the dance had lived, and the answer chilled us all. Two seasons. If Likari were not freed from the dance by summer, he would almost certainly die of it.

"Two seasons in which to save him. That isn't much time," Soldier's Boy said anxiously.

"Two seasons to save him from death," Firada corrected him. "Two seasons only if you are content to bring him home crippled and broken. The dance is arduous and unrelenting, Nevare. It breaks bodies, for the magic cares little for what it demands of our flesh. In two seasons, Likari will look like a little old man. His body will be stunted, for he will not grow properly on that regimen. And his mind will have been consumed by the magic. This we have seen in those Dasie freed from the dance. The adults who were returned have regained some of their connections to home and family and kin-clan. But the younger ones were completely seduced by the dance. I have heard of at least five rescued dancers who have since decided to return. They do not know what else to do with their lives. Of those who have remained, they are very young in mind; they have not grown in knowledge or manners since they were taken. They know nothing but the dance and the infusion of purpose that the magic put in them. Likari, I think, will be more susceptible to that than most. If we wait two seasons to try to take him back, well. By then it would be more of a kindness not to, to let him spend out his life there."

Olikea had been strangely quiet. She blinked then, freeing tears that rolled down her cheeks. She did not breathe harshly or gulp. These flowing tears that spilled silently were a frequent phenomenon now, as if she wept deep inside and only her tears reached the surface. She still tended me, but she was most often silent. She appeared lost and childlike, as if she had been transported back to the days when her mother had vanished. I realized then that the view she had given me of Speck family life had been skewed to her own perspective. She had kept Likari at arm's length all his life, fearing that she might lose him. Yet when she did lose him, even that distance had not been enough to protect her.

Soldier's Boy reached out and put his hand on her shoulder. Although I knew his heart remained with Lisana, he and Olikea remained occasional lovers and she always shared his bed. Offering him that physical release was a part of her being his feeder; she did not expect romance or passion beyond the physical sort. Since Likari had been lost, it seemed to me that they coupled more often, as if seeking a comfort they could not quite find. Perhaps she tried for another child to replace the one she had lost. Perhaps he touched her so gently only because he wished to strengthen his bond with her and hence her kin-clan. In any case, I envied them what they had, the uncomplicated physical enjoyment of each other. Sometimes I shamed myself by pretending it was Amzil that my hands caressed, Amzil's mouth reaching eagerly for mine. It was a sour pretense that only left me feeling more desolately lonely than ever. At all times, there remained a bristly affection between them, and the shared loss of Likari had only strengthened it. She slept against his belly rather than his back these days, and when she cried out in her sleep, he often held her. Now he immediately reassured her.

"It will not be two seasons, Olikea. I hope it will not be much more than two days. This I have decided. Tonight we send word to Kinrove and Dasie. I will take the force that we have, and we will attack Gettys. We will make the cold and the snows our allies."

He looked around at their disbelieving faces and smiled grimly. "Fire will be our primary weapon. This is the plan. I will take our forces back to the western side of the mountains. We will go prepared to endure the cold and snows, but only for a short time. We will quick-walk down to Gettys in the darkness of the deepest cold of the night. Some will hide in the town around the fort. Others will help me dispatch the sentry on the gate. Quietly. Then we will enter. I will make maps of the key places to set the fires. At my signal, the town fires will be set, also. As soon as the archers outside the walls see the flames rise, they will let fly with their arrows, to start fires on the upper walls and watchtowers where the soldiers cannot easily douse them. I only wish that we had more than a dozen of the basket arrows.

"It will be crucial that we free the prison laborers. They have no love for their wardens and their release will add to the confusion. With luck, they may turn and attack those who have treated them so cruelly. We will set many fires, too many for them to fight. When the soldiers flee the flames into the street, we will have a chance to kill many of them while they are panicked and unarmed. That state will not last long, but while it does, we will take advantage of it.

"When they begin to rally, we will fall back. As we move through the town, we will kill any in our path. We will quick-walk our retreat, vanishing into the night. We will wait, giving them time to battle the fires and exhaust themselves. Then, when they think the crisis is over, we will quick-walk again into their midst, to kill again. If we have time, we will set more fires."

He fell silent. No one spoke, staring at him.

"If once is not enough, we will return three days later. We must be prepared to keep a guard on the road to the west. No courier must ride out to report what is happening. Gettys must simply disappear. After we have killed all of them, every structure there must be burned completely to the ground. Completely. When the supply wagons come next spring, they must find nothing there, not a wall, not a bone. Nothing."

He said it as calmly as my father would speak of clearing a field of stones or of doing the autumn slaughter. Those around him nodded, heartened by his speech, as if there were no human deaths involved at all.

Jodoli spoke hesitantly. "But what of your previous proposal? That we would negotiate with them, perhaps with a treaty that appealed to their greed?"

"Later," he said coldly. "I have decided that will come later. When they decide to try to rebuild Gettys. Then will be the time to confront them. For now, the plan is simply to kill. And when Gettys is destroyed, Kinrove will have no further need for his dancers. They will be free."

Olikea took a breath and spoke hesitantly. "Can you truly do it so quickly? Can you bring Likari back to us?"

I felt the doubt that he dared not bare to them. Aloud, he spoke with confidence. "I can. I will."

I feared that he was right.

CHAPTER TWENTY

BATTLE PLANS

It was dark in the mountain passage, and cold. Images of the passing terrain blinked before me like pages in a book, turned before my eyes could focus on the print. Only torches lit our way as we quick-walked. Ropes of ice twined and coiled down the stone walls. Horses' breath stood out in plumes of steam. The Speck warriors, unnaturally bundled in furs and wool against the cold, walked awkwardly on the slick ground. The waterway that had gurgled to one side of the passage the last time I had traversed this pass was frozen solid.

The sounds of our passage came in pieces. Creak of leather and clop of hooves and resounding echoes were stuttered with silence. Murmurs of complaint from the men and the occasional harsh laugh or curse. The distant crash of a falling icicle, big as a man. Soldier's Boy's army was on the march toward Gettys and slaughter.

He had kept his word to Olikea. Scarcely three days had passed since they had gathered around the fire to discuss Likari's fate. The events of the following days had occurred so swiftly that whenever I thought of it my mind spun. Jodoli and Soldier's Boy had called a meeting with Kinrove and Dasie. Both of the other Great Ones had been startled by their demands for immediate action. The Specks, I discovered, dreaded cold, and both Kinrove and Dasie argued against the wisdom of sending their warriors forth to fight their first battle in such an alien environment. But Soldier's Boy had prevailed, pointing out truthfully that if they struck now, the deep cold of winter would do half their work for them. He spoke earnestly of burning the supply houses and barracks and as many homes and stores as would catch fire. In detail, he explained how the intruders' food supplies would perish, along with the tools and the men who could use them. Destroy the ability of the Gettys folk to rebuild, and they must either flee back down the King's Road into the barren winter weather and impassable snows or stay where they were, to freeze and starve. Either way, the cold would make an end of them, decreasing the work for the warriors.

Convincing them to attack immediately was only half the battle. Demanding that all four of the Great Ones should be involved in the battle shocked the rest of them. He set out his plans succinctly. Jodoli and Kinrove would go no farther than the mountain pass. Their key contribution would be spending magic to quick-walk the entire force from the rainy side of the mountains westward through the draw and then swiftly down to the low-lying hills that surrounded Gettys. He needed them for that task. Moving at a normal pace, his forces would quickly be both discouraged and thinned by the inhospitable weather. I knew his hidden thought. If any of his soldiers considered deserting along the way, they would be faced with a long, cold journey home, unaugmented by the magical speed of a quick-walk.

Once the force had reached the western side of the mountains, Soldier's Boy had planned that he and Dasie would command the battle itself. They would go on horseback, mounted for a better view of the action and to allow both of them to keep up with their troops. Dasie's fire magic skills would be required, as would his knowledge of the layout of the town and the fort. Soldier's Boy had decided that his horse soldiers were too small a force to deploy as cavalla. Instead, the horses would carry supplies and perhaps the mounted riders would serve as messengers to coordinate the troops during the battle.

The Specks had no experience with the sort of warfare that involved coordinated troop movements and warriors obeying a single commander. Every step of it had to be explained. Soldier's Boy had talked and talked and talked. Kinrove did not wish to be involved in quick-walking the troops. He wished to stay with his dancers. Soldier's Boy insisted on it. "Our warriors are not accustomed to the cold. I think they can sustain a brief journey through it, and a night of fighting, but beyond that, the cold will eat at their stamina. If the cavalla troops at Gettys rally against us, we will be fighting seasoned soldiers who are tolerant of those conditions. If I must take the troops through the snow for days before we even close with the enemy, they will lose heart before they even fire an arrow." Looking from Jodoli to Kinrove, he said, "And you know that I do not have the strength to quick-walk such a force on my own. Dasie and I will require your help if we are to deliver a force capable of an attack on Gettys."

He was willing to admit that they had strength he needed, knowing that such an admission would all but force them to help him, simply to prove their own strengths. He did not admit to them that he relished the idea of seeing the Great Men in discomfort. But I lived in him, behind his eyes, and I knew. They had both bested him in magic. Now he would show them what he was best at, and force them to be present at his victory. Soldier's Boy wanted both to see, if not the battle, our warriors as they returned from it. He would have them witness the difficulty and the dangers of fighting a real war. He did not feel they grasped the reality of that, and for a reason he could not explain even to himself, he felt that they needed to.

I wondered if Soldier's Boy himself did. I wondered if I did. I had never seen battle. I'd read of it, been schooled to it, heard tales of the blood and smoke all my life. Yet here I was, riding mutely along to my first engagement, leading troops against the very country that had created me. The knowledge of that crazed me, if I dwelt on it. I held myself back from thinking of it, and focused my thoughts only on what I knew I might be able to save. I did not think I could stop the attack or the massacre that would follow. I might be able to preserve a few of the people I loved.

I tried to be small and forgotten in Soldier Boy's mind. I uttered no sound of rebuke or dismay as I witnessed him marshaling his troops. They were armed, not with guns, for the iron of the barrels and actions would disrupt our magic, but with bows, spears, pikes, and, in plentiful supply, with pitch torches. His four chosen archers carried the fire-arrows and their loads. Dasie was good at the calling of fire. She would be the one to kindle the flames when the time was right. And Soldier's Boy was to be in the thick of it, leading his troops right into Gettys and directing his cowardly attack against the sleeping foe.

And so I rode with him those last horrid days, watching him plot and plan against my people. My people. His traitorous words had found fertile soil in me and were, despite my resolve, sending down bitter roots. "My people" had disowned me and attempted to kill me. "My people" had not been able to see past the changes the Speck plague had wrought in me to realize I was the same Nevare I had always been. "My people" had no respect for the Specks who had taken me in, no interest in learning why they so vigorously defended their forest, and no intention of letting the Specks preserve their way of life. When I dwelt on those things, it was hard for me to say why I remained so fiercely loyal to a people who had no connection at all to me. Yet when those traitorous doubts came to me, all I had to do was focus my thoughts on Spink and Epiny and the woman and children they had sheltered for me, and my determination to undermine Soldier's Boy's plans came roaring back to life.

But now, as the blinking images of the narrow defile became darker as the mountains leaned closer to one another overhead, I knew my time was trickling away. When they reached the western mouth of the pass, the plan was to camp for one night, to allow both warriors and mages to rest. Then on the morrow the mages would quick-walk the entire force down to the forest of the ancients. From there, after the brief day ended and the vise of cold night clenched, we would attack Gettys and the sleeping population.

Tonight would be my last chance to try to warn Epiny and Spink.

Riding along inside Soldier's Boy on such an extended quick-walk gave me the same queasy, headachy sensation of riding in a jolting wagon all day. Jodoli and Kinrove imposed the magic on us, so I had no sensation of knowing when each stop or each flow would begin. I'm only along for the ride, I told myself and huddled small inside Soldier's Boy.

I'd had one small triumph in my ongoing battle with him. I hadn't let him make contact with Lisana. He missed her as if the heart had been torn from his chest. I'd tried to bargain with him once. "Dream-walk me to Epiny one night, and the following night, I'll take you to Lisana."

"I should dream-walk you to the enemy, so you can reveal our plans? No."

"Then you shall not see or speak to Lisana," I told him coldly. And despite how he had squeezed and poked at me, I had retained my resolve. My memories might be his to rifle and sift, but my ability to reach Lisana remained firmly in my control. And he foolishly believed, since I had sought that bargain, that dream-walking to Epiny still belonged solely to him.

I watched the glimpses of our journey flicker past. Torches had been kindled, more for the sake of calming the horses and warriors than because we needed them. We relied on Jodoli's and Kinrove's memories of this passage, memories they reinforced by drawing on the magic. Each brief glimpse was like a framed painting in some peculiar gallery. Here the walls of the divide sparkled silver and black with ice and stone. In the next, my attention was directed to some carvings of trees and faces that some long-ago travelers had etched into the walls of the pass.

We did not ride. We led the horses, and long before our day's journey was over, my feet were sore and my back ached. The other Great Ones had chosen to be transported in litters; Soldier's Boy's pride had not allowed him that option. It had been months since I had demanded exertion of my body. Soldier's Boy had allowed the underlying muscle I had cultivated with my endless grave digging to lapse. I knew he would deeply regret that tomorrow when he had to mount Clove. Although I would share his pain, I privately rejoiced that it would distract him from the business of command. I had not warned him of this. It was a tiny advantage I could offer to the Gernian cavalla. They would never know of it, but even that small thing might make a crucial difference when the time came.

Time, I had come to know, is a tricky thing. Although we traveled much more swiftly when we were quick-walked through the pass, I was still aware of each stage of the journey, and hence at the end I felt as weary as if I had miraculously walked the whole distance in a single day. As indeed, I had.

That weariness was a sentiment shared by many. Firewood was scavenged and Dasie moved among us, bringing the fires to life for us. Although Kinrove and Jodoli had gorged themselves the previous day, the effort of quick-walking the force had depleted their reserves. They kept their feeders busy preparing and serving to them the food the horses had carried. Most of the Specks had never traveled through deep cold, let alone camped in it. Olikea made no complaint, a clear sign of how deeply she was mired in her sadness. We made our night's shelter in the covered part of the pass. Shallow snow had blown into the mouth of the cavernlike entry. Some tried to sweep it away with evergreen boughs, while others used the boughs to make beds that would lift their bodies slightly off the frozen ground. Soldier's Boy had counseled them to bring woolen blankets and furs, so most were provided for, but even so, they would pass a cold night.

For all of the Great Ones, there were thick mounds of evergreen boughs overlaid with furs and warm blankets. Quantities of food had been transported, both for the warriors and the mages. As the evening deepened and the cold crept closer, the fires were fed until they became bonfires and the food a feast. There were drawbacks to this; the icy ground around the bonfires thawed and became wet. The bundled Specks in their fur-lined cloaks and deep hoods overheated and then, as they disrobed, chilled themselves. There was drink, too, brought along to ward off the cold, and all the more potent at the end of the long day's travel. None of the Great Ones kept the warriors from indulging. All this I watched silently and knowingly, and listened in, as the Great Ones finalized their plans for tomorrow night's attack.

It was late before the last of them slept. Soldier's Boy went to his bed weary from both travel and talk, and anxious for the morrow. Olikea curled around his back. Weariness soon claimed her. He closed his eyes and composed himself but sleep would not come. He went to battle a virgin to war, and yet he felt that, of the Great Ones, he had the clearest idea of what they would face on the morrow. He agonized over it. Would he acquit himself well or would he take his warriors into useless deaths? Whatever would come, he wanted to face it and have it be over. I had seen their plans and recognized that much of what he had chosen to do was exactly what I would have selected, were I ruthlessly bent on annihilating an enemy that had not yielded to any other tactics. I watched him, a darker shade of myself, the product of my father's and the Academy's teachings, and yes, of the hatred that such teachings had roused in the Specks. I had to marvel in horror at what happened when such a system was turned back on itself.

Then, deliberately, I began to consider every aspect of what might go bad for him tomorrow. I thought long and in detail of the men who had chilled their muscles, and of the strong drink that had been consumed. I thought of the depth of snow that awaited them, the trails that must be broken. Quick-walk was quick-walk; it could speed up how we traversed terrain but could not eliminate the challenges of it. I dwelt on his inexperienced horsemen and the poor quality of their tack. Dasie's mount was a cart horse, chosen solely because he could carry her weight; her mount had little experience as a saddle horse and she had even less experience as a rider. I imagined for him all of the mishaps that could arise from that combination. Into this equation, I factored his ignorance of the command of the fort now. He was counting on the sentries to be slack and the night guard but half awake.

I deliberately fed his fears and kept him from sleep long after the others had subsided into snoring. And then, when his frazzled mind had worn itself out with snapping at possible disasters, I withdrew. He sank swiftly toward sleep and I did all I could to make his rest as deep as possible. I soothed and calmed him from the edges of his thoughts, and as soon as I felt him sink deeper than the level of dreams, I acted.

Tapping into his magic was the most delicate part. He and the other Great Ones had spent the last two days fortifying their reserves, eating only the foods most conducive to their tasks. Soldier's Boy, I knew, was jealously aware that he had still not regained the size he had enjoyed before I had expended all his magic in my futile attack on the road, but in this last bout of eating, he had surpassed Jodoli. His height and bone structure gave him a clear advantage over Dasie at any time; her body simply could not carry the weight that his could. Kinrove had rapidly regained his size, the result of a dedicated team of experienced feeders. Nonetheless, Kinrove and Jodoli had insisted that their reserves would be taxed by the transporting of the army as well as its safe retrieval. They had warned Dasie and Soldier's Boy to hoard strength lest part of that task fall on them as well.

Like a tiny tick, I sucked off the magic until I felt my awareness was saturated, then bloated with the stuff. I withdrew from Soldier's Boy's awareness as far as I could and then sent a needle-sharp thought questing for Epiny.

I could not find her.

For a heart-stopping moment, I wondered if she were dead. She had not seemed in the best of health when last I saw her, dragged down by both her pregnancy and the sorrow and anxiety she felt over me. Gettys was a rough and primitive place for a genteelly raised woman to give birth to her first child. I had been glad to know that Amzil would be there at her side, but although Amzil had attended other births, she was not a doctor or a midwife. I tried to count back and decide where Epiny would be in her pregnancy, but time had slid about so much for me recently that I could not decide if she would still be pregnant or a new mother by now.

I gave way to the impulse of my heart and reached for Amzil. I found her just as effortlessly as I had the first time I'd dream-walked to her. This time I was wiser. I approached her more slowly and gently. "Amzil. Amzil, can you hear me? It's Nevare."

I knew she was there, but some sort of murkiness obscured her. I reached desperately through it. "Amzil? Amzil, please! Hear me. Hear my warning." But beyond the fog that cloaked her mind, I encountered only the same wall she'd shown me last time. She'd shut me out of her dreams, resolved to go on living without me. I could not blame her; she'd learned too well to rely on her own strength. I could not get through the defenses that kept her strong. Epiny, then. I would have to find Epiny if they were to be warned.

I mustered my stolen magic and reached out more strongly for my cousin. There was a long moment of doubt, of empty, endless reaching and then a startled, "Oh!" from somewhere in the other world.

"Epiny? Epiny, please be there, please hear me. I have only a short time, and the warning I have for you is dire."

"Nevare?" Her voice was faint, yet thick as syrup. She did not sleep and dream, but neither did she feel awake to me. I saw nothing from her eyes, sensed little of her surroundings. She was warm. That was all I could tell.

"Epiny. Are you all right? Are you ill?"

"Nevare. I'm sorry. I couldn't name the baby after you. She's a girl. A girl can't be Nevare."

"No. Of course not. Is she well? Are you well?" The baby was not what I wished to speak about, but I hoped that as Epiny spoke of her, my sense of Epiny would come clearer. It didn't work as well as I had hoped. I felt a tiny warm body under Epiny's hand. The baby was bundled close to her.

"She's so sweet. And quiet. She doesn't cry much. We named her Solina. Do you think that's a pretty name?"

"Solina is a lovely name. Epiny. I know you are tired, but listen to me. Great danger is coming. The Specks are massing for an attack. Late tomorrow night, they will descend on the fort, with fire and arrows. They hope to destroy the fort and the town with fire, but also to kill as many people as they can. You must warn everyone to be on their guard."

"I have so much to tell you," she replied dreamily. "It's lovely to know that you are still alive. Lovely. We wondered how you were doing. Oh, I had that one dream of you, of course, but that was months ago. When the fear stopped, that was so nice. I wondered, did Nevare do that? Then I wondered if it meant you were dead." She took a deep breath and sighed it out again. Thick tendrils of mist seemed to rise with her sigh. The warmth and comfort of where she was billowed around us and threatened to engulf me. I resisted it with difficulty.

"Epiny, what's wrong with you? Did you hear anything I told you? An attack is coming and you must warn everyone." She made no response and I spoke more sharply. "Epiny! What ails you?"

"Laudanum." She sighed. "Nevare, I know it's not good for me. But it's lovely. For a while, the fear went away. And the sadness. It was like waking from a dream. I got up one morning and wondered, why have I let this house be such a dreary space? And I started scrubbing and dusting, and then I was humming at my work. And Amzil came in. She said I was making my nest. Such a lovely notion. And she helped me clean and make my room brighter and prepare a place for the baby."

"I'm glad she was there. I'm glad the baby is fine. Epiny, the attack will come like this. The Specks will slip into Gettys Town very late at night. Some will stay in the town, to fire buildings there. Others will disable the sentries and come into the fort. They are targeting key structures to burn, the warehouses, the barracks, the mess hall, the headquarters, and especially the prison for the workers. But they plan to burn as many homes as they can, also. You will be in danger, you and your baby. And Amzil and the children and Spink. After the first attack, things will die down. The Specks will seem to retreat. But it's a trick. They'll wait until everyone is out and fighting the fires, and then they'll come back."

"I can't worry. That's the beauty of it, Nevare. I know I should worry, but I just can't. It feels nice not to worry, Nevare. So nice." She made a tiny effort, curling her fingers to tug her blankets closer. "Nevare. In autumn, when the fear stopped and I thought you were dead, I sent your book to my father. To put with your father's books. I tied a string around it and added a note, to say it should not be opened for fifty years. To protect everyone you wrote about."

"What?" I was horrified. Then, with an immense effort, I pushed my own concern aside. I tried to speak gently but firmly to her. "Epiny, you need to wake up now. You need to warn Spink and the rest of the household. You need to pack whatever you might need in case you must flee. Have you warm clothes and food you can take?"

She sighed and shifted in her dreamless state. "Amzil's little one is sick. She mustn't go outside. I hope the baby doesn't catch it. She's such a good baby, such a good little sleeper."

"Epiny." I spoke more slowly now, trying not to despair. "Is Spink nearby?"

"He's sleeping in the other room. He made a bed there, so I could have Solina here by me. He's so thoughtful." I felt her smile. "We had post. Such good fortune, to have a delivery come through in the winter. Good news from Spink's people. The water cure. That doctor, that one from the Academy? He believed my letter and he went himself to Bitter Springs to take some of the water back to Old Thares. He stopped one outbreak of plague with some of it. And made some of the cadets at the Academy better, just like the water made Spink better. So. Now everyone is going to Bitter Springs to bathe and take the cure, and other people are buying water to take home with them. It has made their fortune, Nevare. Spink and I are so happy for them."

Even drugged with laudanum, there was no stopping Epiny once she started talking. I broke in before she could start rambling again. "Call Spink, Epiny. Tell him what I told you."

"Told me."

"About the Specks and the attack."

"He's sleeping now. He's so tired. I told him to try the laudanum, but he said no. He thinks it's good for me to get this rest. He thinks it's good for the baby that I'm so calm now."

"Epiny, I have to go now." My supply of magic was dwindling. "You have to remember this dream. You have to tell Spink to warn everyone."

"Are you going to come and see the baby soon?"

"You have to warn Spink. Warn everyone. It's urgent!"

"Urgent," she repeated listlessly, and then I felt her rally a bit. "Father was so angry, Nevare. About the book."

Shame choked me and I could make no reply. Yet at the same time, a most peculiar sensation came over me, a sense of the completion of a great circle. I had *known* that this would happen. I'd always known it, from the time I first set pen to the paper that my uncle had sent me in my beautiful soldier-son journal. I had always known that somehow it would go back to him, and that the consequences of what I had written there would grind my future into powder. It was a strange feeling to realize that from the beginning, I had been documenting my disgrace for all to know. It was almost a relief, now that it was done and over. Epiny was still speaking in her dreamy singsong way.

"He told my mother she had no right, that it was his name she was risking. She said the Queen would never know, would never bother to find it out. She said a fortune was at stake, and he should not let his dignity cripple him. Hadn't he brought you into our home? Hadn't he married me off to a common soldier, like an innkeeper's daughter? Father was so wroth. He will speak to your father. He said. He said . . ." Her voice trailed away and her touch turned to moonlight on my hands, and then a cloud covered even that. She was barely there.

"Epiny." I sighed, and let go of our feeble contact.

I hovered, a mote in Soldier's Boy's awareness, a sort of Gernian conscience that he paid no heed to. I wanted to agonize over my soldier-son journal. I hated all I had written there, hated myself for being so stupid as to write it. Too late. What was shame to me now, a dead man, a Speck, a renegade mage against my own people? Too late to think of my good name. I had no name. What I did have was a tiny remnant of my stolen magic. Epiny had been my best hope. We'd been joined by the magic before and I had been certain I could walk into her dreams. If she hadn't given in to the dark depression of the creeping magic, if she hadn't taken the Gettys Tonic of laudanum and rum, I could have been certain of my warning being heeded. But she had. The magic had outwitted me again.

I thought I had strength enough for one more try. I would reach for Spink. I had never dream-walked to him, but I knew him well. He might dismiss Epiny's words as a strange dream; if I touched him, mind to mind, he would know it was real. I knew he would have a hard time convincing the upper echelons of the military command at Gettys to heed his warning as it was; better not to have Epiny saying that the warning was based on her dream.

I summoned all I could recall of Spink, every facet of him, from the boyish and enthusiastic cadet he had been at the Academy to the weary and harassed lieutenant and husband he had become at Gettys. I reached hard for the moments of contact that we had shared in that otherworld we had walked when the Speck fever had taken us both. Back then, he had been more willing than I to accept the reality of that episode. I only hoped that if I could reach him, he would still be as open-minded.

Dream-walking to Spink was not like traversing terrain. I felt I was a needle plunged endlessly through folded bolts of fabric, trying to find a single thread. Trying to make this new contact was more draining than reaching Epiny had been. Epiny had always been more open to magic than the rest of us. But I found Spink, and with every bit of my remaining strength, I forced myself into his dream. It was a dreary place. He dreamed of digging a hole in stony earth. He was in the hole and had to throw the shovelfuls of rocky soil up over his head. Half the time, earth and gravel cascaded back down on him. He was in the bottom of the hole, trying to get his shovel point under a large stone, and then suddenly I was there with him. He didn't flinch or start. Dreams adjust quickly to intruders. I found a shovel in my hands. Spink looked up, wiped gritty sweat from his face, and said, "You dug your hole and I dug mine. And here we are, stuck in what we've made of our lives."

"Spink. Put your shovel aside and listen to me. We are in your dream, but what I'm going to say to you is real."

I took a risk in telling him that we were in his dream. He looked at me, and I saw his eyes focus, and in the same instant, the dream around us began to disintegrate, watercolors lifting away from a painted card. I seized him by the shoulder and believed him there as hard as I could. I gripped his bony shoulders, felt the rocky soil under my feet, deliberately smelled the smells of soil and sweat. Spink stabilized but continued to gawk at me.

"Little time," I said, even as I felt the magic running out. "Epiny had a dream, too. Make her tell you. Specks will attack Gettys late tomorrow night and try to burn everything. Spink, don't forget this, don't doubt it." I was gripping his shoulders as tightly as I could, as if to make the contact more real. Inspired, I suddenly seized his hand and forced it to his face. I pressed hard, driving his nails into his cheek and tore down, scratching him. "The warning is real, real as pain. Take action. Extra guards, a night patrol, guns primed and ready, iron shot—"

I didn't know at what point my pilfered magic ran out. I only knew that the Spink I was speaking to was suddenly emptiness. I blinked and he was gone and I was back inside Soldier's Boy. He was sleeping heavily now, in the same deep, desperate sleep I'd sometimes taken when I dove after rest that had eluded me for most of the night. I thought it over and then pressed softly against his awareness, telling him how safe he was and that all was well. With every particle of my being, I willed him to sleep long and late.

In that, I was successful. By the time he awoke, half of the short winter day was spent. He opened his eyes to grayness and cold. It took him a few moments to realize where he was, and then he sat up with a shout. Not far away, Jodoli slept on. Some of the men were up and moving about, but most of the wakeful ones were huddled about the fires, talking quietly. At his shout, all heads turned to him, and some of the warriors stood up.

"Why was not I awakened!" he bellowed. The anger that filled him was more fueled than disarmed by the knowledge that it was unjust. "This force should have been on its feet, armed and ready to march, hours ago. This delay puts all our plans at risk!"

Jodoli was sitting up, rubbing his eyes. Firada was already in motion, gesturing at his feeders to hurry faster as they hastily dished up the warmed food and brought him hot tea poured from a steaming kettle. There was every indication that Jodoli's feeders had been awake for quite some time, in order to have all things ready when the Great One awakened. He turned and saw that even Olikea, morose as she had been, was awake and dressed.

"Why did no one awaken me?" he demanded again, and I cringed for him at how childish he sounded. I think he sensed my disdain for him. He thrust his legs out from under the blankets and gestured angrily for his clothing to be brought to him. He was suddenly realizing how far he had wandered from the soldier's path, and how telling that might be today. Impatiently he tugged his garments from his feeders' grasps and put them on, grunting as he did so. He had to hold his breath to jerk his fur-lined boots up over his calves but he did so, and then stood. "We eat, we pack, and then we march. We have to be at the forest's edge at the road's end by dark. There, we will have to wait until full dark before we go into the town to attack. So eat and drink well now, and see that your water skins are filled. This will be the last hot meal you get before we join battle. Take a little food with you, but only what you can eat while moving. Get ready!"

I was pleased that they were getting off to such an uneven start, but tried to keep my satisfaction small and hidden. Even as I watched the cold and sometimes sullen warriors go about their preparation, I wondered how much of her dream Epiny would remember through a mind clouded with laudanum and hoped that Spink would heed the urgency of my message. I would have no way of knowing if my desperate warning had worked until the forces joined battle. Until then, I tried to keep the gnawing of my doubts to myself, even as I fed Soldier's Boy uncertainty about the readiness of his troops. Over and over, I summoned up strong memories of how quickly the Academy cadets had fallen out before dawn each morning. I recalled for him the times when, as a boy, I'd watched the reinforcements for the eastern strongholds riding or marching past my father's holdings. The men, even at the end of a long day's march, had kept their lines straight and their heads up. He watched his warriors gather in straggling groups about their recently appointed leaders. There was no uniformity in how they were outfitted or supplied, no precision in how they gathered, and very little evidence of military discipline at all. All those elements were essential to a battle campaign as I knew of them, and they lacked them all. Their only strong asset was one that made my blood run cold. There was hatred and vengeance gleaming on every face, and the will not just to kill but to slaughter was evident in the harsh promises and cold wagers they placed with their fellows. There would be many deaths tonight. My mind wandered to the old god Orandula, and then as quickly I jerked my thoughts away from him. I did not want my attention to summon him, did not want him to construe the coming slaughter as an offer or bargain with him.

Yet as Soldier's Boy's ragtag force formed up to be quick-walked by the Great Ones down to the forest edge, I could not help but see the hand of the balancer in all of this. Could hatred and determination be a counterweight to organization and experience? I suddenly understood something about the old god of death and why he was also the god of balances. One could always make two things balance by moving the fulcrum. I had the sudden uneasy notion that I was the fulcrum that had been moved.

Soldier's Boy bid Olikea farewell. All of the feeders except Dasie's guards would remain here with Kinrove and Jodoli. From now on, the warriors under the leadership of Dasie and Soldier's Boy would go on alone. Again, the few horses we had were led rather than ridden. I had never seen Dasie mounted on her cart horse. It pleased me to think she would be a poor equestrian.

The late morning and fading light of the short afternoon passed in the flickering landscapes of quick-walk. The snow was deep in the places where it had sifted down through the trees, and the cold was enough to crack the lips and stiffen faces. More than a few of our warriors expressed discomfort and then dismay as the march went on. I think some of them would have turned back, but the advantage of the quick-walk meant that they must remain with us, or face several lonely days of hiking back to our encampment. Those who might have otherwise deserted stayed with us, but gracelessly.

For the first time since Dasie had entered our lives, she was without her iron bearer. Kinrove and Jodoli had refused to even attempt to quick-walk anyone carrying iron, saying that even to have that metal nearby disrupted their magic severely. I do not know if she feared Soldier's Boy might seize the opportunity for revenge or not. Like Soldier's Boy, she had left her new feeders behind, but her two original feeders, attired now as warriors, walked to either side of her. The bronze swords they carried looked every bit as deadly as iron, and the men who carried them appeared confident and competent, for they needed to worry only about their swordsmanship, not about any accidental discomfort or injury to their Great One. Behind her, a warrior led the hulking horse she would ride into battle. For now, he functioned as a pack beast, laden with pitch torches.

Today both Soldier's Boy and Dasie toiled through a day of walking that was a trial in itself for heavy folk who had grown unaccustomed to exerting themselves. The problem for Soldier's Boy was not the cold, but the heat his own body generated from the exercise. He wanted to avoid sweating, for well he knew how quickly his body would chill once they had stopped moving, but there was little he could do about it. Again, I experienced that sensation of lurching and halting along as the magic shoved us. It was not pleasant, but I enjoyed knowing that Soldier's Boy shared my discomfort.

Night came swiftly. The last bit of our journey we made in darkness. It was unnerving to be magically moved forward through a landscape that became, with every few steps, darker and colder. When we reached the forest of the ancestor trees that bordered on the end of the King's Road, our unnatural journey abruptly halted. In the dark and the cold, the men and the dozen or so horses suddenly milled, speaking in low voices as they located one another in the dark. Dasie had planned well. She unloaded torches, and as her magic woke each one to flame, they were passed around.

The giant trees around us were heavily burdened with snow, but had effectively blocked most of it from reaching the forest floor. There were drifts in a few places, but for the most part, it was less than ankle deep. Fallen branches were gathered, and in a short time, a score of scattered campfires leapt and crackled in the darkness. The light made monsters of the passing shadows and the updraft of heat stirred the branches overhead, prompting a few to drip or suddenly spring free of a heavy load of snow, showering the soldiers below. Soldier's Boy moved purposefully from fire to fire, talking to the men he had put in charge of his troops. Some were effective as sergeants; they'd taken charge of their troops and seen that they'd drunk from their water and eaten sparingly of their supplies. Others were more like bully boys, proud of being chosen to lead but, in their pride, pushing and harrying their warriors rather than truly leading. He should have let them choose their own leaders, I thought to myself. It would have been more in keeping with their Speck traditions. Then I was surprised that I could see how his overlayering of Gernian military tradition did not fit their culture but he could not. I wondered again at how much both of us had blended.

After he had made his circuit, he came back to his own fireside. The warriors from his kin-clan were there. He wasted a few long moments wishing that he had begun to cultivate them earlier and truly make them his own. He smiled at them and asked if they had any concerns, but could scarcely focus on their responses. In a few hours, his life might depend on them, and he barely knew them or any of the men in his command. He was no better, I let him know, than the distant officers I'd served under at Gettys. I was merciless as I gouged at his self-confidence and his ability to command. As I did so, I wondered if he had done the same to me during my long days as my father's slave and prisoner. Had he been part of my inability to tear myself free and find a new life for myself? Even the idea that such was a possibility fanned my wrath to flames. I felt no compunction at all as I undermined his self-worth with every doubt I could imagine, with every recrimination from the past that I could unearth. I reminded him, over and over, that he'd been lazy and neglected his strength and fitness, that he'd wasted opportunities to win his men's loyalty, to teach them discipline, to make them understand the necessity of drill and swift obedience.

He glanced once up the hillside toward Lisana's tree. I knew how badly he longed to climb the steep snowy slope, so that for even a moment he could rest his brow against her tree and let

her know that he loved and missed her still. But I daunted him
with a reminder of how cold and arduous such a climb would
be, and finished it with the idea that if he hadn't slept in like a
lazy pig, perhaps there would have been enough time for him to
attempt it. But now it was out of the question. He'd barely have
enough time to ready his half-trained troops for their suicide
mission.

I knew the instant I pushed him too hard. He recognized my
influence and suddenly I was at arm's length from him. I found
out something else then. He did not banish me as he had before because he did not want to expend that much strength and
attention on me. I could not contain my joy to find that it had
cost him to hold me in that limbo, cost him more than he dared
spend on me now.

Night deepened around us, and with it came the cold, an
absence rather than a presence. All drew closer to the small fires
that did little more than taunt winter. They dared not build them
big enough to cast out any real heat or light. As it was, Soldier's
Boy scowled at them, hoping that no errant hunter or night wan-
derer would see them and report them.

Never had an evening stretched so long. When the time to
venture toward the town finally came, Soldier's Boy ordered that
Clove be brought to him. The lack of a mounting block made
climbing up on the patient horse's back an undignified and
lengthy process. Dasie did little better with her horse. Clove at
least was accustomed to bearing a heavy rider. Once I was up,
he shuddered his coat as if settling himself and then stood quiet.
Dasie's cart horse mount disliked the fuss and noise of the warriors who helped their Great One up on her horse's back. Once
Dasie was up, the mare sidled and then, as Dasie gathered her
reins too tightly, backed up nearly into one of the groups huddling around a fire. Soldier's Boy had to ride to her aid, and then
waste precious moments in giving her a lesson in basic horse-
manship. Although he had not planned it that way, he decided
that he would ride at the front of his warriors, with her just
behind him and flanked by two of the warriors who were more
experienced with horses.

He rode Clove through the camp, savoring the height and command that the big horse gave him at the same time he cringed from the aches and strain that riding was awakening in his softened body. He spoke to his sergeants, making sure that they had checked their men's supplies. The torches were the most critical to his plan, and each man carried three. Some of the warriors would carry fire pots, clay pots lined with sand that held coals. If Dasie's magic could not prevail against the iron present in the town and fort, the torches would be kindled from the fire pots. He'd allowed each warrior to select his own choice of weapon. Some carried short swords, others bows with full quivers on their backs, some had spears or long knives, and a very few carried only slings. He formed them up in two columns, spaced his horses out among them, and then rode back to the head of his forces. From here to Gettys, they would travel on their own feet. Both Kinrove and Jodoli had told him that their strength for the quick-walk had been taxed to its limits, canceling his original plans to appear suddenly just outside the town. They could not move the force magically toward a place so saturated with iron. Soldier's Boy wished it were otherwise, that they could simply appear in the vicinity of the fort and likewise vanish again. Yet he knew he would have to work with the limitations set on him. The night was fully black around them when he finally lifted his hand and said, in a low voice, "Forward!"

The word was passed back, and like a feeble caterpillar, the two columns began to move unevenly. He led them on, to the very edge of the forest, and there he paused briefly. The clearing and beyond it the road were coated with smooth snow. There was a bit of light from a quarter moon and the myriad stars in the black winter night. The white ribbon of road seemed to gather the light to itself and then offer it up to the sky again. There was, as Jodoli had predicted, little sign of the effects of my desperate magic. Most of it had been repaired already. But that was actually all right. They'd cleared the road before the snows fell. It made Soldier's Boy's path plain. He would lead his men down the very road that had threatened to destroy them, and when they reached Gettys, they would turn that death and destruction back on those who had brought it.

He kneed Clove and the big horse stepped out easily from the sheltering trees. He negotiated the uneven earth of the clearing under its blanket of smoothing snow and then reached the road itself. The unbroken snow and crust was knee-high on the big horse. With a sinking heart, Soldier's Boy realized that he'd have to break trail for Dasie and her guard and for all the troops that followed him. He steeled his will, sat his horse well, and urged him forward into the night.

CHAPTER TWENTY-ONE

MASSACRE

Isuffered agonies of suspense on that long trek to town. Encumbered with heavy garments and forcing their way through unbroken snow, Soldier's Boy's troops trailed in a long ant-line behind us. Gernian foot soldiers, I thought with wry pride, would have made little of this march, but for the Speck warriors, it was a new sort of experience, one that they did not relish. The dark of night, the resistance of the deep snow, and the oppressive cold were cooling their battle ardor.

I caught Soldier's Boy wondering if his entire force would stay with him during this last leg of their journey, and then deciding it was better not to think of it. The men who had come with him this far had come for their own reasons; some for vengeance against the Gernians, some to put an end to Gettys and halt Kinrove's dance, and some, doubtless, because they were young men and this all seemed like a marvelous adventure when they first heard of it. If some chose to turn back now, there was little he could do about it. They were all volunteers, and the Speck had no mechanisms to force a man to say he would do something for a month or a season, let alone a year. I surmised again that Soldier's Boy was trying to impose a Gernian template on the Specks, one that was ill-suited to their culture. I think he caught a whiff of that thought.

"It is necessary," he thought gruffly. "To fight a heartless and evil foe, we must take on some of their strategy. We must bring to Gettys a form of warfare that they recognize. Any who escape us tonight and manage to survive their flight must carry a tale of the Specks at bloody ruthless war against all Gernians. It is what must be. I do not relish it. But I will finish it."

I made no response. I was trying desperately not to think too much about the town or the fort or Epiny and Spink. I tried to suspend my anxiety over whether or not Spink would react to my warning. Soldier's Boy must not suspect that Gettys had been warned. If I dwelt on my fears or my hopes, he might decide to pry into my thoughts. I no longer knew how much I could conceal from him when he was determined.

Clove moved with confidence, even eagerness, through the cold and dark. Perhaps the beast remembered where he was and was dreaming of a warm stable and a nice feed of oats and hay. We pushed on; our columns straggled out behind us in a display that reminded me more of a prisoner coffle than a military force on the march. The cold was so deep that the snow was dry and fluffy and sometimes squeaked as we strode through it. When we came to the more traveled section of the road where sporadic wagon and horse traffic had packed the snow, we moved more quickly.

When Gettys came in view, the warriors rallied a bit. I heard muffled boasts and the callous laughter of young men who look forward to killing. Even this late at night, a few yellow lights shone in the town that huddled outside the walls of the fort. It was still and silent, a town deeply asleep, and my heart sank in me. My warning had not been heeded. I saw no extra sentries on top of the walls, no torches burning nor sign of any activity that would indicate that the fort was any more alert than usual. Soldier's Boy's plan would succeed. He would slaughter them in their sleep.

He gathered briefly with Dasie and his chosen sergeants, to refresh their minds on the plan. It was all about silence and stealth and organization. Dasie would take the town, while Soldier's Boy would endeavor to get his force inside the fort. The warriors were organized in pairs, each with an objective to find and burn. Dasie touched again the torches the warriors carried and the archers' fire-arrows, binding them to her magic; when the time came, her magic would kindle each one. Her ability with fire-magic was strong; she believed that despite the iron in Gettys, her magic would be strong enough to kindle the flames. The fire archers each had specific targets; Soldier's Boy wanted the upper levels of the watchtowers to catch fire. His other warriors would set alight buildings at the ground level before employing their chosen weapons against all who fled the fires. The plan was that all the torches would light simultaneously, kindling fires in so many places that the soldiers could not hope to control them all. If Dasie's magic failed, they would fall back on the fire pots that some of the warriors carried. Such a tactic would not enable the simultaneous firing of buildings that Soldier's Boy hoped for, but he believed it would still suffice.

Soldier's Boy reminded all of them yet again that they would rendezvous at the end of the King's Road. When all were as prepared and eager as Soldier's Boy could make them, he nodded to them and wished them well, and then his forces parted. Dasie's group would spread out and filter into the town from all sides. Houses, inns, brothels, warehouses, and stores were their targets.

Soldier's Boy would go ahead of his warriors to eliminate the sentry at the gate. Once that way was cleared, his forces would flow in and spread out, torches ready to fire the buildings and weapons ready to kill anyone who emerged into the dark and cold. He himself would fire the stables; once his warriors saw the stables alight, they were to kindle their targets and then converge toward him.

Even before we reached the outlying buildings of Gettys Town, Dasie and her followers had vanished, melting into the night. Soldier's Boy halted and whispered his final commands. His followers merged into the shadows. Very shortly, he rode on, apparently alone, a traveler on a big horse bundled against the night's cold. The streets were empty around us as we passed. He had waited until it was so late that even the taverns were closed for the night, their lanterns long guttered out. Clove's big hooves barely sounded on the deserted and snowy streets. I felt like a ghost, returned to the scene of my murder, as we thudded slowly past the crossroads. The cold of the night was as nothing compared to the cold I felt in my heart as I passed that place.

"Which is why I don't understand why you think you owe them anything. This is where they killed you, or would have if the magic of the People hadn't saved you. And yet you still see yourself as one of them. I would think that your thirst for revenge would be the most savage of all."

I had no answer to that, so I remained still and small. Why didn't I hate these people? Perhaps because I knew them too well. I knew what sort of fears had formed that mob, and I knew the forces that could turn a decent man into an animal. Should a man be judged forever based on what he did on one overwrought night? Was a man the good soldier he had been for fifteen years, or the mindless participant in a murder that he had been for only an hour?

I turned my mind from such useless thoughts. Perhaps, I thought, I was as spineless and unmanly as Soldier's Boy and my father thought me. Perhaps all the anger and vengeance had gone into Soldier's Boy, leaving me with only a weary and jaded understanding of the people who had tried to kill me.

I knew that a substantial force of warriors followed us, yet even aware of them, I heard no sound. If there was one thing that the Specks excelled at, it was stealth.

Soldier's Boy rode up to the sentry post outside the gate. In the cold, still night, the torch burned steadily in a sconce beside his sentry box. I wondered if the sentry was dozing inside his shelter, huddling close to the small potbellied stove. I could smell the tiny drift of wood smoke and the iron of that stove tingled against Soldier Boy's skin like the beginning of a sunburn. There was a stir in the shadows within the sentry box and the guard emerged, his long gun held across his chest. "Halt and identify yourself!" he called. The dark and the cold engulfed his words and made his challenge almost too small to matter.

Soldier's Boy pulled Clove in and sat on the big horse, looking down at the man. He smiled. The sentry stared up at my face,
looked down at my horse and then up again. When he tipped his
face up to stare at me again, it was whiter with more than cold and
his mouth hung open. "By the good god!" he rasped out hoarsely,
and then caught his breath sharply.

It was all simultaneous. I recognized the man. He recognized
my face. He was the fellow who had held Amzil's arms pinned
back behind her while another soldier tore her dress open to
expose her body. He'd been there the night they'd killed me, and
now he looked up at me, sitting on the horse he'd recognized, too,
and thought he was seeing a ghost. Terror had frozen him more
than the cold. "I'm sorry, I'm sorry," he babbled hopelessly.

And as he gawked up at me, Soldier's Boy leaned down, seized
the top of the man's hood in one hand and with the other casually
drew his copper knife across the fellow's exposed throat. It happened so quickly that Clove wasn't even spooked. He nudged the
big horse back into motion, and as we rode on, the sentry fell into
the road behind us, spasming and croaking softly as blood blackened the packed snow. Like following shadows, Speck warriors
suddenly appeared and ghosted through the gate behind us. A
moment later, not one of them was visible. They had immediately
fanned out within the fort, each with a specific target to torch.

Soldier's Boy rode on. He slid his knife, oiled with blood, back
into his sheath just as smoothly as he'd drawn it. He rode on, but
I felt I was still back there, leaning down from Clove's broad back
and pulling the knife smoothly across the exposed flesh. The man's
dying words echoed in my ears. "I'm sorry, I'm sorry." Had he been
truly sorry for what he had done, or was he only feeling the emotion I'd pressed on him the night he had tried to help kill me? It
shocked me that I could wonder that. One of my fellow soldiers
from my own regiment lay sprawled in his own blood behind me.

"I didn't do that," I said, and then, as if I were praying, "I didn't
do that. I didn't do that."

"No," Soldier's Boy agreed, whispering to the night. "But you
wanted to. Consider that one a gift. A little bit of your manhood
back."

The coldness of his words struck me. They mingled with the physical memory of drawing the sharp, cold blade across the man's throat, the slight tugging resistance of his flesh as it parted, the wideness of his eyes rolled up to the night stars as he died. In that moment, I recognized how much both Soldier's Boy and I hated who we were. We'd been split in such a way that neither of us had what was needed to be the person each of us longed to be. My ruthlessness had been parted from my empathy. Each of us was only part of a man. Yet the only way for me to become a complete person was for me to stop existing and merge myself with him. Merge myself with a renegade who had just killed one of his fellow soldiers with no more compunction than I'd have about gutting a fish. Become one with the enemy.

I was trapped in a nightmare, powerless to prevent what he was doing. The familiar streets of Gettys were quiet, deserted in the night. He made his way to the headquarters building. He did not slink; there was nothing furtive about him. He rode down the center of the street as if he were a king returned to claim his rightful crown. I recognized the sense of it. If anyone had been wakeful and had peered out a window at the sound of hoofbeats, he would have seen only a single cloaked and hooded rider moving slowly down the street. Nothing to fear in that. At the corner of the infirmary, Soldier's Boy dismounted and led Clove around to the back.

Gettys was not like the cities of the west. There, Gernians had built with stone and mortar. Here on the eastern frontier, we had built almost entirely from wood. Soldier's Boy, like every one of his warriors, carried three pitch torches bundled inside his coat. He took them out now and arranged all three against the dry boards at the base of the building. He cupped his hands over them, closed his eyes, and summoned the magic. For a short time, he was aware of the nails hammered into the building. Then he took a deep breath, focused his hatred on the torches, and called the magic. What I had never been able to do, he accomplished easily. A torch leapt into flame. He crouched over it, sheltering it from possible drafts with his hands and body. The first torch kindled the other two. The cold had dried the planks of the building. The united flames licked against the rough planks and peeling paint. Once the torches had heated them enough, the planks began to burn. Flames licked slowly up the side of the building. He wedged one pitch torch between two planks so that its stubborn flame would continue to feed the fire and stayed until he saw the flames crawling up the back of the building. Then he rose, and carrying his other two torches, hurried down the alley, leading Clove, until he came to the stables and the big heap of waste straw outside it.

He thrust a torch into it, and it kindled almost immediately. In no time, smoke was rising from it, and then suddenly, flames shot up, carrying sparks and bits of floating burning straw up into the night sky. The light and the heat from the burning straw were immediate. I saw the stable wall begin to steam and then to smoke.

The light of that fire was his signal to Dasie as well as to his followers. As soon as she saw that he had succeeded in striking one fire, she sent forth the magic that kindled the other torches. I felt the magic go out from her. Although I could not see it, I knew that all over Gettys Town and within the fort, torches suddenly burned. Soldier's Boy still carried one flaming torch. Heedless now of who might see him, he led Clove right up to a cart between two buildings and used it as a mounting block to get on Clove. Torch held high, he rode toward a nearby barracks. As he went, other torch-bearing Specks drifted in from alleys and byways to join him. Their fantastic shadows danced ahead of them along the sides of the buildings. Sempayli, grinning, came running from the darkness to walk by his stirrup. "And now we shall see their blood run," he told Soldier's Boy confidently. He carried a bow.

Clove's heavy hooves on the packed snow and the thud-whisper of his fur-booted followers were almost the only sound. Occasionally one of the torches crackled and spit. No one spoke and they moved as softly as only Specks could. Yet again, there was no furtiveness about this torch-bearing mob.

Soldier's Boy reined Clove in and spoke to his men. He divided them into three units, and sent two of them off to two other barracks farther down the main street. He moved purposefully toward the nearest barracks. I recognized which one. Captain Thayer's troops would be sleeping inside. I felt queasy. Was this more of Soldier's Boy's vengeance on my behalf, that this barracks would be his personal target?

I heard a distant scream, and then a woman shouting, "Fire! Fire! Wake up, wake up! Fire!" Somewhere in the town, flames suddenly climbed the side of the building and rose, casting a ruddy light. The stables, full of stored hay, suddenly roared and the roof seemed to literally burst off the building. In a matter of seconds, smoke was rolling like a flood through the streets, while bits of burning straw floated up into the cold night sky. Chances were good that as they settled, they would kindle other fires, adding to the confusion.

Where was Spink? Why hadn't he warned anyone? Did he and Epiny and Amzil and the children all sleep on? Would they awaken before smoke crept in to choke them? Would the townsfolk who had chosen to drug themselves with Gettys Tonic awaken at all, or burn as they slept?

"You've done enough!" I shouted at Soldier's Boy as he advanced on the barracks.

One back corner of it was alight, and as I watched the door was flung open. A single soldier, hopping and skipping as he tried to pull his trousers on, emerged. He was shouting, "Fire! Fire! Wake up! Get out! Fire!"

"Just take your warriors and leave. You set the fort alight in so many places, they won't be able to fight all the fires. Gettys will burn. Give some of them a chance to escape. Don't you want them to flee alive, to carry word of the Speck attack?"

"They must carry word of a Speck *war* against them, not of a random fire that spread and burned the town down. We are lancing a boil here. Grit your teeth and be silent while I do what must be done!"

Sempayli had already lifted his bow. The arrow was trained on the door. There was a small sound like torn paper, and the hopping soldier went down on the snowy ground, clutching at an arrow shaft in his chest. He saw us then and, to his credit, tried to shout a warning. It came out as a gargled spray of blood, speckling his chin and the snow around him with black dots. Two other half-dressed soldiers burst out of the door. They too went down, feathered with arrows and blocking the door behind them.

There were two doors to the barracks. Soldier's Boy's warriors had surrounded both of them. The building was burning well now, kindled in at least three places. I heard a terrible shriek from the other door as a man escaped the fire to die under a sword. The flames were leaping up into the night. From inside, I heard shouts and the thunder of overturned furniture and coughing. There were only two windows in the barracks. One burst outward in a shatter of glass as a chair was flung through it. The man who tried to follow the chair was shot with an arrow through the throat and fell back inside. Shouts of consternation greeted this, but another man immediately launched himself through the window. He fell dying in the snow as one of Sempayli's arrows took him.

I do not know how many soldiers were sleeping in the barracks that night. Perhaps some died of the smoke. But every one that emerged from the doors or the window was killed before he got two steps. It was slaughter, not battle, for the dazed and smoke-blinded soldiers scarcely seemed to comprehend what was happening. In their struggle to escape the flames and engulfing smoke, they understood too late that a second foe, just as deadly, awaited them outside. Bodies piled up outside as cries for help and shrieks of burning men came from within.

I could not look away. I could not control the eyes. I wanted desperately to cut myself off from Soldier's Boy, to retreat to where I could not experience this in any way. Under Soldier's Boy, Clove shifted and fought for his head. He didn't like the flames, the smoke, the cries, and the blood. But like me he was forced to stand and witness. Soldier's Boy reined him in hard and held him. The torment for both of us continued.

In that endless time, two things slowly transformed me. As I watched the men die so ignominiously, half-clothed, blinded by smoke and dazed by shock, they suddenly became my fellows, my regiment. Whatever they had done to me, they had done with their own rude sense of judgment. It had not been just, and I knew that, but they had not. My regiment had not been the mob that cornered me and tried to murder me. Looking back, I knew that only a dozen men had willingly partaken of that madness. The others had been reluctant witnesses or shocked bystanders. I would not judge my regiment by the base actions of a few during a time of fear and anger.

I now understood what they had become when the mob spirit had taken them because I now saw how I myself behaved. Bereft of empathy or sympathy, Soldier's Boy mirrored for me what any man might become when hate and purpose ruled him. What I had become, for all purposes. He was me; folly to deny that. He was doing what I might have done, were I ever in a position that I hated someone so badly that I completely lost sight of his humanity.

A stray memory rose in me. I had been about fourteen the summer that an odd combination of weather had led to a suddenly burgeoning population of rats. They'd infested the barns and the corn bins, and when they had begun to appear even in the house kitchen, my father had had enough. He sent for the Rat Man, so called because he claimed that he and his pack of terriers could rid any holding of rats in a matter of days. When the Rat Man arrived, my elder brother and I had followed him and his seething pack of terriers to the barns. He ordered my father's grooms to remove every bit of stock from the area. Then "Get your feet up off the floor!" the Rat Man had warned us, and my brother and I had perched on one of the mangers. "Kill them all, boys!" the Rat Man had shouted, and his dogs had dispersed instantly. They'd raced to every corner of the barn, and nose to the walls, had run along them smooth as water, digging at every hole, yelping excitedly and snapping at one another in their competition. The Rat Man had been as active as his terriers as he darted about eliminating obstacles for the dogs. With a hay fork, he lifted the edge of a loose board. The dogs had raced in to seize the boiling rats he had exposed. Snatch, snap, and fling! Each rat was seized, shaken violently, and then flung aside for the next. Rat bodies flew and fell all around us as the Rat Man exposed hidey-hole after hidey-hole to his dogs.

And how we had laughed, my brother and I! Laughed until we nearly lost our perches and fell into the chaos. The Rat Man danced a wild jig when a rat tried to run up his legs. One of his dogs snatched it up by the head, a second grabbed the hindquarters, and a third seized the middle and tore it into pieces, sending a wild spray of blood into my brother's face. He had wiped his sleeve across his face, and we had laughed until we nearly choked. Rats, rats, and more rats, dying in a frenzy of yips and squeaks and squirting blood. Rats that fled, and hid, and bared their yellow teeth when cornered.

What fun.

And Soldier's Boy's face was set in the same hard grin that it had worn on the long-ago day. He was exterminating vermin that had overrun his territory, and he felt nothing for them as they fell and died.

The fire gave a sudden roar, and then the entire roof erupted into flames. Shingles and pieces of burning rafter began to fall inside the building and the anguished screams grew louder. Then, with a sudden crack, the roof gave way and collapsed inside. It was over. The night darkened around us as the fire that had blazed overhead like a beacon suddenly folded in on itself. Soldier's Boy gave his head a shake as if he were just waking. He looked around for his next target. More rats were hiding and must be rooted out.

Throughout the fort and town, other cries were heard: men shouting hoarsely for help, shrieks of death and despair. The flames had a voice of their own, hissing and crackling. Uneven light and wild leaping shadow populated the town. The screams of trapped horses still came from the inferno that had been the stable. The air thickened with smoke and blowing ash and floating sparks. I heard gunfire from the direction of the prison barracks, and wondered what was happening there. When it became obvious that no one else remained alive inside the barracks, Soldier's Boy lifted his hand over his head. "Come!" he shouted. "Follow me!"

He nudged Clove and the big horse was glad to move away from the fire. I prayed that we were leaving, that the Specks' lust for blood had been satisfied. Instead, Soldier's Boy led us deeper into the fort. In the dark and the smoke I could scarcely tell where we were, but it soon became apparent that he was guiding us toward the sound of gunfire. The flames and the smoke combined to turn the night to a murky red sunset around us. We passed a dark alley. A young man, or perhaps a soldier's son, clad only in a nightshirt, raced out of it. A Speck warrior was right behind him. He speared the boy, and then pinned him to the ground with his weapon as a sharp kick to the boy's head ended his struggles. Soldier's Boy didn't even pause. He led his warriors on. From the corner of his eye, I saw the warrior jerk his spear from the boy's body and fall in with us.

It penetrated my awareness that I was no longer hearing random shots, but organized volleys of fire. A surge of hope lifted me. Someone had rallied and imposed order on at least some of the troops. The same thought seemed to occur to Soldier's Boy. Scowling, he shouted for Sempayli, and then ordered him to find the other warriors and bring them to join him. His lieutenant nodded curtly and ran off into the smoke and darkness. Soldier's Boy rode on toward the prison.

Soldier's Boy's plan had been to simultaneously set fire to the prison while freeing the prisoners to add to the chaos. I think I recognized what had happened before he did. The freed prisoners, confronted with the marauding Specks, had not fled but had seized whatever they could find to use as weapons and attacked their liberators. Perhaps they had not perceived the Specks were deliberately freeing them, or perhaps they had simply chosen to side with their countrymen when faced with savages with unknown intentions. In either case, the Specks had not been prepared for the prisoners to turn on them with such fury.

The section of the fort that housed the prisoners had been constructed in such a way that the watchtower overlooked both the prisoners' compound and the outer wall. I would later hear that some of the prisoners had doused the fires set near the watchtower while others had fought hand to hand with the Specks to hold the warriors back. Their valiant action had enabled their guards to organize themselves and retreat to the upper level of the watchtower. Flames leapt upon the roof of the tower; at least one of his fire-arrows had found its target. But the forces that held the watchtower were undeterred by the fire above them. From that vantage, their long guns were having a deadly effect upon the Specks. The open space around the watchtower was littered with bodies, many of them Speck. As we approached, it was obvious to me that the prisoners and their guards had joined forces, for gunfire came now from the lower level of the watchtower as well. As long as the defenders' ammunition held out, the Specks had no hopes of taking the watchtower.

I knew that. Therefore Soldier's Boy knew it also.

His Speck warriors did not seem to comprehend it. Even as we came onto the scene, a handful more brave than sensible rushed into the open, bows drawn, to launch their arrows at the high tower windows. Coming into the open was the only way for them to bring their weapons into effective range, yet the soldiers in the tower had only been waiting for them to do so. I heard the distant shout of "Fire!" and the bark of the long guns. Every one of the Specks went down. Four lay shuddering; only one crawled back toward the sheltering shadows. Another gun cracked and he, too, lay still. Soldier's Boy's whole body twitched as if the shot had entered him.

I had a moment of icy realization. If there was one good man in that tower, one sharpshooter, I was at the edge of his range. I could die at any moment now. Terror clawed at me from the inside as if I had swallowed a small beast with sharp claws. Still, I did not hesitate. I clenched myself around my fear and did not let it show. I did not warn him, but only breathed a prayer. *Good god, let it happen now. Let this be over.* I was sure that if Soldier's Boy fell to a bullet, his followers would scatter.

The long guns in the tower flashed again; strangely, I do not recall that I heard them. Between the muzzle flash and the blows of the iron balls, I knew a thousand regrets for my life's end, said a hundred farewells. To my left, a warrior crumpled, howling and clutching at his shattered knee. To my right, a man dropped without a sound. Before me, like a tiny hailstorm, the impact of bullets kicked up spurts of packed snow and ice. Was I hit? I waited for pain.

Soldier's Boy did not. He jerked Clove's big head around and kneed him at the same time. "Fall back!" I heard him shout, in Gernian, and then he cursed in the same language before crying, "Run! Get back—stay out of the open and the light! Get back!"

The fool had never thought to teach them how to retreat in
an orderly fashion. In his arrogance, he'd never imagined that he'd
need for them to know that. Now his careless order and his own
apparent flight from the battle woke their fears, and the men who
fled to follow him did so heedlessly. I heard another volley fired
and screams behind me. Some of his warriors had not heeded his
warning to stay out of the open in their haste to follow him away
from danger.

At almost the same instant, I heard a sound that had never
been sweeter in my ears. A trumpet sang, a call to arms. And
miraculously, in the distance, from outside the fort, I heard another
horn answer it, and then the heart-leaping sound as the same
faraway instrument sounded a charge. Hope, all but dead in me a
few minutes before, suddenly surged back to life. The first trumpet
sounded again, within the fort, and it seemed much closer now.
From the watchtower, I heard a resounding cheer. Then, a volley
of bullets peppered the ground near us. A few, perhaps charged
with an extra bit of powder or simply by luck, penetrated the
shadows that hid us and found random targets. Three warriors
howled in pain, and one abruptly fell, still.

"Follow me!" Soldier's Boy shouted, and urged Clove into a
trot. His warriors needed no urging. They ran alongside him. The
leaping flames and the thick smoke that had been his allies earlier
now seemed his enemy. He turned down one street, only to have
a burning building suddenly sway and then collapse across his path
in a searing whoosh of hot air and sparks. It was too much even
for steady Clove. He half reared and whinnied in distress. Soldier's
Boy came shamefully close to falling off him before he mastered
him and turned him aside from the wreckage. But now his warriors were in front of him in the darkness, blocking his path and
milling in confusion. He had to force Clove through them, shouting, "Give way, give way!"

The trumpet sounded again while he was pushing his way
through his own warriors. It was closer still. The fort seemed a
labyrinth of buildings and streets to him, one made more confusing in that some of the streets that had been clear were now
blocked with burning debris. He cursed and I sensed his rising

dismay. Once he broke clear of his followers, he called back to them, "We need to make for the gate. We must not be corralled inside the fort!" He pushed Clove into a trot again and once more his warriors fell in behind him. I could sense him seething with fury and impotence that he had no way of summoning his scattered force to him, no way to reach all of his warriors and tell them that he wanted them outside the walls of the fort rather than within.

We retreated through a nightmare. The fires had spread, just as he had planned. The streets were thick with smoke and fallen burning debris littered the road. There were bodies as well, mostly Gernian but some Speck, and once I glimpsed a mother holding a baby and clutching an older girl by the hand. When she saw us turn down the street toward her, she silently fled, pulling her child behind her. They ran down a narrow alley. When we passed it, they were out of sight, and no one gave chase to them. Soldier's Boy was as intent now on getting his warriors out of the fort as he had been originally on getting into it.

Clove was equally willing to depart from this hellish place. My placid old mount fought his bit and jigged ponderously, longing to break from his heavy trot to a lope. Soldier's Boy held him in, shouting to his warriors to keep up with him. He could have fled and left them there; I will give him that. He did not desert his men. It was not his fault that he had passed a crossroads when, from the shadows on his left, small-arms fire burst out, dropping the men immediately behind him. Clove, startled, leapt forward, while those who had seen the men in front of them fall fled backward, shouting. Soldier's Boy hauled hard on Clove's reins, turning the big horse and then kicking him after his fleeing warriors. He was fortunate that the hidden soldiers were recharging their weapons. Clove jigged and shied over the bodies in front of him before he left them behind and caught up with Soldier's Boy's force.

"Stay close to me! We must go a different way, to another gate," he shouted to them. He glanced up at the sky, hoping to take his bearings from the stars. The rising smoke banished that hope. At the next intersection, he turned, randomly I suspect, and led his warriors on. This section of the town was mostly intact; these were the simpler homes and the less important buildings that had escaped his fires. I prayed that any folk in them would stay within and hidden, and that Soldier's Boy would be too intent on fleeing to do them any harm. The light from the fires several streets away danced eerily in the windowpanes of the crouching houses. Either their occupants had fled or they huddled, lightless and silent, inside them. We saw no one, and no one barred our way.

The air grew clearer but the darkness deeper. Surrounded by fires earlier, no one had thought to bring a torch. Soldier Boy cursed his own stupidity and then, with a deep grunt of effort, summoned the magic. Light emanated from him. Probably I alone knew what it cost him to work such a charm in a settlement so thick with iron. Even the nails in the boards of the buildings we passed seemed to snag and tear at our magic as we hastened by them. The illumination he gave off enabled his followers to trail us, but did not light the way for him. I thought to myself that it made him an excellent target for anyone who might see him, but kept that thought small and to myself.

Another turn, and suddenly the gate was before us. It was open, and torches flanked it, beckoning us. I wondered that the sentries had not roused to the fires and trumpets. Perhaps they had, for I saw no sign of them. Freedom and escape beckoned us through the open mouth of the gate. It was the north gate, the most seldom used gate of the fort, the gate that we joked led to "nowhere." Outside it, only a thin layer of town lay between us and the wastelands beyond. The north side of the fort was the least sheltered from the prevailing winds. Blown snow was always deepest there and the howl of the wind always the strongest. Only the poorest hovels were built on the north side of the fort, the homes of the widows and orphans of dead prisoners for the most part. Their huts were dark and unfired. The unimportance and uselessness of that population had saved them from the Specks' attention. Shadow and concealment beckoned in the crooked streets. Relief bloomed in Soldier's Boy heart. "To me!" he commanded his drained band, and kicked up Clove's flagging trot.

Soldier's Boy cleared the gate and a moment later, his warriors mobbed around him. They were clear of the fort's confining walls. He glanced about himself, getting his bearings. He caught a tiny flash of light, a reflection of smoke-filtered moonlight on someone's buckle. Years of Sergeant Duril's drilling me paid off for him. He flung himself sideways off his horse, putting Clove's bulk between him and the ambush, quenching his light as he fell. Muzzle-flash, the crack of explosion, and angry bees whizzing over him. Clove screamed as a projectile tore out a chunk of his neck. A wall of smoke rose up from the weapons and wafted up to join the smoke of the burning buildings. A stench of rotten eggs floated with it.

Behind him, warriors screamed. They had not seen that flash of buckle, had not dropped down to the earth to avoid the deadly hail. Instead it had cut through them, a scythe through standing grain. The warriors who remained standing were those who had been saved by the bodies of the men in front of them. On the ground in the dark, men squirmed and thrashed. Off to our right, I heard a familiar voice say, "First rank, recharge. Second rank, forward."

Spink's voice might have been reciting in a classroom, so devoid was it of emotion. Hadn't he seen me? Had he failed to recognize me? Would I fall to the command of my best friend? I devoutly hoped so. Time had frozen in its tracks.

"Ready—"

"Scatter!" Soldier's Boy bellowed to his troops. "Return to the rendezvous!" Those that could, did. He did not watch them go. Rather, with a display of strength and agility that was amply assisted by a surge of magic, he flung himself at Clove and swarmed up into the saddle again.

"Aim—"

He reined the big horse around, directly toward the ranked shooters, and kicked him hard. Startled, Clove surged forward. Before Spink could give the order to fire, we crashed into his front line. The firing line gave way before us, men leaping out of the way, some guns going off randomly. In the light of muzzle-flash, I had one glimpse of Spink's horrified face. He stared up at me, eyes huge and betrayed. In the noise of the gunfire, I saw his mouth shape one heartbroken word: *Nevare!* He'd tracked me with his pistol. The muzzle of it was pointed dead at my chest. All he had to do was pull the trigger.

He did not.

And then Soldier's Boy was through their lines and galloping down the dark side street. Even if he had wanted to, I don't think he could have reined Clove in. The big horse had never been battle trained, and this night had been one long series of horrors for him. Given the chance to flee into the dark, he took it. Soldier's Boy could only hope that the warriors who could retreat had done so. For those who lay dead or dying, he could do nothing. The thought of his wounded came to his mind, and too late, he wondered how they would be treated if captured. I answered that for him.

"Have you fired the houses of families? Will they find women and children with arrows in them or the marks of the sword upon them? If they do, they will be treated as we treat anyone who slaughters women and children."

I think at that moment he wished to die just as much as I did.

CHAPTER TWENTY-TWO

RETREAT

As we fled through the dark streets, Soldier's Boy listened for the sound of pursuit. There was none, though we heard scattered gunshots behind us. "They are killing those you left behind," I told him brutally, even though I was not sure that was so. "They are shooting the wounded where they lie." Spink would not have allowed such a brutality, if it came to him to give the command, but in times of battle, men follow first the commands of their own hearts, and sometimes their officers are too late to rein them in.

A winter dawn, gray and bleak, was seeping across the eastern sky. Smoke curtained it, but soon the light would break through. Time for all Specks to be gone, if the attack had gone as planned. Soldier's Boy had been delayed too long in the maze of the fort. His men would not have the cover of night to help them retreat. Neither would he. Clove had his head, the bit clamped in his teeth, and the big horse cared nothing for secrecy, only escape. He left the last of the scattered huts behind and galloped on over the wastelands. When he came to the end of the packed snow

trail, Soldier's Boy was finally able to pull him in. Clove pranced
a few more steps, then abruptly halted, blowing and snorting. A
long black streak of blood marked Clove's sweaty neck. There
was dried blood along his flank, too, an injury that Soldier's Boy
hadn't noticed before. Heart thumping, lungs gasping, Soldier's
Boy looked back the way he had come and tried to think of his
next move.

The red light of the flames was reflected in the smoke overhead, giving an odd orange cast to the day and to Gettys in
particular. With the dawn came a wind. Ash and cinders rode it.
Soldier's Boy rubbed his sooty face, blinked, coughed, and turned
Clove's head toward the foothills. The big horse was tired now.
Soldier's Boy had to kick him to get him to move uphill through
the unbroken snow. It offered them the closest cover. In the fur-
rows and scrub brush of the foothills, Soldier's Boy could become
invisible while he worked his way back to the rendezvous. He
was operating mindlessly now, not thinking of honor or victory
or even defeat, but only the very practical question of how to live
through the next ten minutes.

At the first substantial rise of ground, he pulled Clove in and
looked back. Smoke was still climbing in tall columns from blackened ruins, and in half a dozen places flames still leapt strongly.
The watchtower that overlooked the prison was burning well.
High overhead, murders of crows coasted in on the wind. Above
them and unmistakable even at that distance were the wide wings
of the endlessly circling croaker birds. Always, the sounds of battle
and the smoke of destruction brought such scavengers. They
would not care if they feasted on Speck or Gernian or seared
horsemeat. They'd all feed well on this disaster. He bared his teeth
at them, full of hate, and then looked down again on the burning
fort and town.

From his vantage, he could see that he had dealt both fort and
town a significant blow, but it was not the complete destruction
that he had yearned for. Folk would still find shelter there, and the
walls of the fort, though scorched in many places and smoldering in one, were still intact. The cavalla troops stationed at Gettys
would regroup and find themselves more fired by the night's attack

than daunted by it. He had failed. Failed badly. As he watched, a small band of mounted men, regimental colors aloft, came into view riding a circuit around the outskirts of the town. Prudently, he urged Clove over the hilltop and out of sight. He felt a coward as he fled alone. Where were his warriors? He'd disdained them a few days before, thinking they were not the troops he deserved to lead. Perhaps the truth was that they were exactly the sort of soldiers he had deserved, as green as he was, and as incapable at planning for all contingencies. He hadn't led disciplined troops into battle. He'd led a raiding party. And if he was any judge at all of the Gernians, they'd mount a retaliatory force before the fires were even out. Time to get himself and whatever of his warriors he could find to safety.

He set his teeth. He'd abandoned his troops. Not willingly, but he'd done it. He scoffed at his own stupidity now. He'd thought he'd dash in, deal a resounding blow, vanish, and then come back to mop up. Instead, here he was, alone, and each of his warriors alone as well. All he could hope was that they would remember to return to the rendezvous point. When they got there, he would be waiting for them. That was the best he could do for anyone right now.

The day grew lighter as he pushed Clove through the untrodden snow in the shallow vales between the hillsides in a wandering path toward the rendezvous point. He hoped that his warriors would have the good sense to stay out of sight as they worked their own way back toward the forest of the ancestor trees. He tried not to think of them, on foot, in weather they were not accustomed to, weary, hungry, cold, and perhaps injured. He forced himself to ignore his own raging hunger and weariness and the cold that found every gap in his clothing. He would face it all when he had to. For now, getting to the rendezvous alive was his sole focus.

Twice his meandering course brought him closer to the road than he liked. At intervals, he heard angry horns blaring out to one another. The Gernian troops were up, mounted, and hunting for Speck stragglers. He tried to cheer himself by thinking of how adept the Specks were at blending into the forest, but I pointed out to him that what worked in summer did not in winter. Bushes were skeletons, bare of obscuring leaves now. Men left tracks in snow.

Midmorning was gone by the time Soldier's Boy reached the place where they had all camped the night before. At first he was heartened to see that others had arrived there first. He recognized the horse that Dasie had ridden and a number of her warriors. He gritted his teeth to think that she had probably succeeded where he had failed; the town fires had burned well, and she seemed to have withdrawn her troops in good order. She sat on a fallen log, her wide back to him, in front of a small fire. He smelled cooking food and, despite his rumbling stomach, scowled at that; there should be no fires just now, nothing that might give a hint as to where they waited.

All such considerations were driven from his mind when one of Dasie's feeders saw him. The man gave a cry of relief and leapt up from where he had crouched beside his Great One's feet. He ran through the snow toward Soldier's Boy and the beseeching hands he lifted to him were red to the elbow with fresh blood. He was crying out his words even before he reached Soldier Boy's stirrup.

"I cannot stop her bleeding, Great One, and she says her magic is gone. They have shot her with iron! Quick, come quick, you must take it out and heal her!"

Such faith they had in him, and all of it misplaced. The warrior tried to take hold of Clove's bridle with his bloody hands. The big horse had had enough. He threw back his immense head and even managed to rear slightly. Soldier's Boy had already loosened one foot from the stirrup preparing to dismount. When Clove came down, he came off his horse, awkwardly. Miraculously, he stayed on his feet and didn't twist his knee, but he staggered sideways in the snow before he stood. He brushed off the efforts of Dasie's guard to support him. "Where is she shot?" he demanded curtly. "Show me."

His heart had left his body in despair. He knew next to nothing of how to doctor a gunshot wound, but for now he could not show it. He followed the man to Dasie's side. A simmering kettle of porridge sent up a wave of steam and aroma. He turned his face toward it, his eyes half closing of their own accord. He longed for it, his body gone mindless with hunger. The guard could see it. "Great One, see to her, please. While you do, I will prepare food for you."

He should have told them to put out the fire immediately. Instead, he nodded numbly and turned toward Dasie. She didn't look good. She gave him no greeting, but hunched round-shouldered on her log seat, her hands clasped over her belly. Her other feeder was on his knees before her in the snow, his warrior's sword discarded. As Soldier's Boy approached, the young man looked up at him, barely controlled panic in his eyes. With both hands, he held a dripping red cloth against Dasie's lower leg. "I think the bone is broken," he said, and his voice shook. "Can you heal her?"

No. "Let me look at it."

Dasie still didn't make a sound as Soldier's Boy got down awkwardly on his knees before her. Her face was white, whiter than the cold would make it. All around her foot, the snow had been melted away by bright red blood. "Get me some rope, a string, a tie, a leather thong, anything I can bind around her leg. And bring a small stick, too," he commanded her other feeder. To the boy who held the bandage, he said, "Keep it firm. Put pressure on it."

"But that hurts her! Because it's right on the break of the bone."

"We have to keep her from bleeding to death. Hold it firm," Soldier's Boy commanded him. He saw the boy's hands tighten, but gingerly, as if he gripped an egg. Not enough to stem the flow of blood. Irritably, he reached down to set his own hands over the feeder's and push the grip tighter. Instead, reflexively, his hands jerked back from her injury. Iron. There was iron in there and it burned against his magic. He could only imagine the agony for Dasie, yet she sat silent and impassive. He had to admire her courage.

He looked up into her face. Her eyes stared straight ahead. "Dasie?" he said softly.

Her feeder shook his head. "She has had to leave us, to escape the pain. If we cause her too great a pain, it will pull her back. For now, she is in stillness."

Soldier's Boy nodded curtly. He did not entirely understand but decided that didn't matter. The other feeder brought him, finally, a long strip of woven fabric and a stick. Dasie gave a small shudder and moan when he first touched her leg. He placed his tourniquet above her knee, and turned the stick. He watched, sickened, as the fabric bit deeper and deeper into her fleshy thigh. "Take away your hands. Has the bleeding stopped?" he asked the feeder who knelt beside him.

Slowly the man took away the cloth he held and then peeled off another sodden wrapping under it. The wound still oozed blood, but not as it had. Soldier's Boy felt he could not kneel there another moment. "Clean it well and wrap it fresh. One of you will have to hold the stick as you do. Wait a little while, then loosen the stick and see if the bleeding has stopped. If it bleeds again, tighten the stick. The most important thing now is to keep her from bleeding to death."

They looked aghast at him. The one holding the tourniquet spoke first. "Can't you heal her with magic? She can heal all sorts of hurts with magic. Cannot you?"

"Not while there is iron in there. I cannot so much as put my hands to her wound. We need to get her back to the pass and then home, to where skilled healers can remove the bullet."

Both her feeders looked frightened. "But . . . can you quick-walk her to the pass if she has iron in her? How will we get her there?"

"I will try my best. If I cannot quick-walk her there, we will use the horses to get her there as quickly as we can. More than that, I cannot do."

Both feeders stared at him, one with his mouth hanging open in shocked disappointment. He had betrayed their trust, the looks said. It was not the first time someone had looked at him that way today. He pushed the memory of Spink's face away and then tried to stand. He didn't think he could until he felt someone take his arm and help him to his feet. He turned to see Sempayli.

"I am glad to see you reached here safely, Great One. I brought the others as best I could."

And then he had to turn his head and see the men who had gathered round them as he tried to help Dasie. These were the men he had left to fend for themselves. They stood staring at him. Soot, smoke, and in a few cases, blood obscured their speckled faces. They wore the same expressions that weary soldiers always wore, no matter whose side they fought on, no matter if they had tasted victory or been drenched in defeat. They were cold, they were tired, they were hungry, and they had seen things that no man should have looked on, done things that no man should have to do. He had expected to see anger and disappointment in their faces as well, and the bitterness of defeat, but if they felt it, it did not show there. They were new to war-making. It was possible they did not know whether to consider it a victory or a defeat.

It came to him then that they had accepted his right to ride off and leave them to fend for themselves. He was a Great One, full of power, and he made his own rules. These were not Gernian soldiers, trained to have certain expectations of their leaders. There was no contract of command between him and these men. They had expected of him only what he had taught them to expect. He had told them, over and over, that they must obey him, that they must not run away from battle. But he had never told them that if things went against them, he would not desert them.

And so they had not expected that of him. It was not a Speck value. It was a Gernian value. And still it scalded him that he had not lived up to that value and that expectation.

"Perhaps, beneath it all, you are still more Gernian than you know. And unfit to command these warriors." I pushed my words to the forefront of his mind.

"Be silent!" His hatred of me, of the Gernian part of him, buffeted me so strongly that I felt I spun in nothingness. It was all I could do to keep a firm grip on my sense of self.

When I gained access to the world again, time had passed. Darkness was around me. Soldier's Boy quick-walked us through snowy forest. Behind us, Clove dragged a makeshift travois. One of Dasie's feeder-guards led him. The other carried a torch beside it. Through Soldier's Boy's eyes, I peered around me into the darkness. We moved with a very small force, perhaps no more than a dozen men. Had his losses been that heavy? I thought I had seen more men than that by Dasie's campfire, but perhaps— Even as my spirits rose, Soldier's Boy dashed them. "You have been absent for days, fool. I quick-walked our force back to the pass. Then Jodoli helped me quick-walk a healer back to Dasie. The healer was able to get the iron out of her leg. Now we take her to where she can find warmth and food and rest."

Something in his voice spilled his secret to me. "She's still going to die. Her wound is poisoned."

He struck me again, but not as hard. In the weakness of his blow, even as I spun in darkness, I read that he was cold, very hungry, and that his magic had been drained. More quietly than a spider, I righted myself and then pawed through his memories of his last few miserable days.

He had failed everyone. Nearly a third of his small force had been killed or captured. I'd been right about the troops. They'd tracked down and shot all the stragglers they could find. It had been sheer luck that they hadn't discovered Dasie. When he had quick-walked the remains of his army to the pass, Kinrove's first words to him had been, "But where are the others?" Soldier's Boy had not even been able to answer. They had read it in his face.

Jodoli's words had laid bare a great fear. "So we have failed. And now that they know of our war against them, they will turn their guns on us at every sight of us. We will not even be able to use the Dust Dance against them. We had only one chance to succeed, one chance to surprise and destroy them. It is gone. They will always be waiting for us now, and always with iron. The hatred and anger of the Plain-skins will never end now, not until they have hunted us to the ends of the earth."

Soldier's Boy had stood before him, his mouth filled with ashes. He could not deny even one of Jodoli's statements.

Kinrove had smiled. There was sadness in his smile but also satisfaction. "You and Dasie were so certain that you knew a better way than my dance. What have you done to us? How many more dancers must I take now from the People to try to keep our ancestor trees safe?" He had looked at Jodoli then, and spoken only to him, dismissing Soldier's Boy as a mage without wisdom. "I must leave you here, Jodoli, to bring our warriors home as well as you can. For I must go quickly now to my dancers, to add what strength I can to their work, and to prepare another summons to add dancers to my ranks. The fury of the intruders will give them some shield from my magic. If I do not block and quail them now, they will break through my barriers and ravage the ancestor trees simply to spite us. And they may hunt those who remain on the wrong side of the mountains, even to following our tracks here to our secret pass. I must go, and see if I can undo a little of the damage these two impetuous youngsters have done to the People."

And, as simply as that, Kinrove had resumed his mantle of power and authority. The Greatest of the Great had turned and left them, quick-walking himself and a few of his key people away. In a moment, they had vanished, some taken in midtask. Jodoli hadn't looked at Soldier's Boy. Firada had come to stand at his shoulder, her eyes hard, as her Great One said, "I have much work to do here. Choose the healer you wish and I'll help you quick-walk him back to Dasie. I will do what I can for the people here. But beyond that, I will have no extra strength to help you." He turned his back on Soldier's Boy and walked away.

Just as Soldier's Boy thought that nothing could plunge him more deeply into despair, Olikea spoke from behind him. "So. We have failed. And I have lost my son forever to Kinrove's dance." He did not turn to face her. I felt his shoulders sag beneath the burden of her words. She came closer to him and he waited for her fury. But after a time, she touched his shoulder lightly and offered in a deadened voice, "I will make food for you. Before you have to go back."

One word. "We." Despite the sadness in her voice, despite her obvious resignation to his failure, she had said "we." It was the tiniest speck of comfort he could imagine, but it was the only bit of comfort he had been offered. Tears stung his eyes. It woke a deeper shame in him, and added a more personal price to his failure. Despite his hunger, cold, weariness, and despair, it woke a spark of determination in him. He felt a resolve form in himself. If he failed in all other things, he would not fail in this.

I do not know if Soldier's Boy was aware of me rummaging through his memories or if the moment came back to him on its own. "I will do what I must," he said softly. He spoke as a man who fastens his courage to an idea, determined he will follow it through. "What are you planning?" I asked him, but he didn't see fit to answer me. Instead, head down to the cold wind, he walked on. The dark forest rippled past us in the stuttering pace of his quick-walk. I could feel the magic gush from him with every step he took, like blood leaping from a nicked artery. He did not have much reserve left. I think he heard my thought.

"I'll get us there," he said doggedly. One of his men glanced back at his muttered comment, but said nothing.

Night was deep when we reached the pass. The camp we had made in the first sheltered section was nearly deserted. A fire burned to welcome us, and Olikea had been keeping soup hot over it. The moment we arrived, a dozen of Dasie's feeders and guards converged on her. They had their own fire burning, and a bed of pine boughs and furs awaiting her, along with all sorts of savory foods. Soldier's Boy watched them bear her away and felt rebuked by how they snatched her away from his stewardship. Obviously, they felt he had failed her; now that they had her back, they wanted nothing to do with him.

He bowed his head and turned to his own fire and Olikea who waited for him. She had built a pallet of boughs and blankets for him, not as elaborate as that prepared for Dasie, but more than adequate. She helped him to remove some of his outer garments and offered him soft warm slippers in place of the ice-crusted boots she pulled from his feet. She had warmed water for him to wash his face and hands, and a soft cloth for him to dry them. That such simple comforts could bring so great a relief! Silently, her face grave, she motioned him to sit down while she served the food. He was surprised to see both Jodoli and Firada seated there as well. "I thought you would have gone home," he said brusquely to them.

Jodoli's response was grave. "I thought you might need help to quick-walk Dasie and her feeders home. The last time I saw you, you seemed very tired."

He was. Too tired to hold on to his anger. He sighed in resignation. "In truth, I would welcome your help," he said simply.

Jodoli said, "In the morning, then." And for a time, there were few other words as Olikea served all of them the soup she had kept warm for him. It was a good soup, thick and rich with meat and mushrooms. With every sip of it, Soldier's Boy felt warmth and strength returning to his body. He glanced over at Dasie's larger fire. Her feeders still clustered around her, bees tending their queen. Despite having her restored to them, they made a low hum that was anxious rather than comforted.

Dasie had scarcely spoken a word to him since they had met after the battle. Her feeders had told him several times that she had retreated to another place to avoid the pain of her injury. But even the removal of the iron from her leg had not summoned her back. He had seen the injury. The ball had hit the bone, shattering it, and then wedged amid the broken pieces. The healer who had removed it had taken out the iron, picked out small bone fragments, cleaned it, and bound the wound closed. The healer had not approved of Soldier's Boy's tourniquet, but had been glad to see that Dasie reacted when he pricked her toes.

"Now that the iron is out, she will begin to heal herself," one of her guards had declared confidently. Soldier's Boy was not so sure of that. He thought that her retreat into herself might not be solely because of her wound. The injury to her spirit might be more severe than that to her leg. He had heard tales of young soldiers who never recovered fully from their first sight of battle. From the little her guards had told him, their firing of the town and slaughtering of the residents as they fled had been "successful," if that was a word to apply to such a task. Dasie had been active and enthusiastic in the setting of the fires, and had herself slain an innkeeper and his three grown sons when they had tumbled from their beds and come outside in their nightshirts to fight the flames.

But the guard had also spoken of a woman who threw an infant from an upstairs window in an effort to save her before she, nightgown in flames, leapt to her death. The guard had chased down two little boys who held hands as they fled barefoot through the streets. He had spoken with relish of his task, reliving that brief satiation of his hatred, and Soldier's Boy had agreed with him that he had done exactly what had needed to be done. But he wondered now if Dasie had truly understood what her task would be and what she would witness when she had ridden down on Gettys. Specks were not by nature or culture a folk of violent confrontations. Even within their own villages and kin-clans, blows seldom settled arguments. He wondered if his plan had pushed her beyond her will to save her people. I felt little sympathy for her. She had looked on what her hatred had prompted. Good. Let her realize it.

"There was no other solution," Soldier's Boy said to me. "The Gernians forced us to it. We had tried everything else we could think of to make them go away or at least respect our territory. We had to do it."

"But it did not go as well as you had planned," Jodoli replied, thinking the words were intended for him. "This we have learned from the other warriors. They said that as they looked back, the town and the fort were still burning, but not in a way that would take it all to ash. So what will you do? Will you still wait for a time, and then surprise them again?"

Soldier's Boy shook his head, a Gernian gesture. He suddenly realized that and stopped. "We will not surprise them again. We had but one opportunity to slip in among them and take them unawares. I've spent that, and not bought much with it. If we tried it again, we would find marksmen on the walls and a lookout in the tower. We would be slaughtered before we could even get close to them."

"So," Jodoli asked him after a long moment had passed. "What is our next move, then?"

Soldier's Boy noticed the "our" and almost smiled. He could not decide whether to be offended or pleased. "Our" plan? Jodoli had not taken himself into any danger and had contributed little to the planning. But if he was willing to be seen as part of Soldier's Boy's plans, he should probably accept him as an ally. He bent his head over his bowl of soup and silently ate for a time instead of answering. I could feel the food enter his system, feel it replenishing his magic. Slowly he forced his thoughts back to their task. "What is our next move to destroy the intruders?" he asked at last.

"Yes."

"I don't know. The magic does not make it clear to me." The others looked shocked that he would admit it. I felt only a satisfaction, cold and hard. I hadn't known either what this magic was supposed to make me do. That Soldier's Boy had finally and bluntly admitted his ignorance as well meant that, just perhaps, it was all some great mistake. All the Specks had been pinning such high hopes on him for so long, and perhaps they were all wrong. Perhaps the magic itself was wrong. Jodoli said the same old horrible words.

"But I have seen it, in my dreams. You are the one the magic has chosen. There was something you were to do that would drive the intruders away and save the People."

Soldier's Boy set the empty soup dish on the icy ground beside him. He was suddenly very tired. Tired and sick of this life that he had been thrust into. He spoke simply, plainly. "There were small tasks the magic gave me. I've done every one of them. I allowed the magic to look through my eyes. I gave a signal to the Dust Dancers who were sent to the city. I wrote copiously in a book, and when I left the intruders, I abandoned that book. I carried a stone, and when the time felt right, I passed the stone on. All simple, even stupid tasks. None of them made any difference. And twice now, I've done things not as the magic directed me but as I best thought would serve the People. Once, when I burned every bit of magic that I had to help the forest devour the King's Road. And again, when I led every warrior I could muster against Gettys. Yet all I have done at the magic's bidding and all I have done at my own bidding have come to naught. I have no more ideas. I think the task that all believe is mine is beyond me. So, instead, I will choose one that I think I can do and devote myself to that."

I am not sure that Olikea was even listening to him. There was something dead about her, as empty as Dasie's eyes. She'd given up on life and was going through the motions. She reached to take his empty bowl and refill it. Instead, he caught her hand. He held it, not as a man holds the hand of a woman he loves but as an elder brother might hold his little sister's hand to assure her that he meant his words. "I'm going to bring Likari home to Olikea." He glanced up at her face and changed his words. "I'm going to bring Likari home to us. If that is the only thing I can accomplish with my life and my magic, then I will do it. This is not a task the magic has given to me, but one I choose."

Both of the women maintained a weighted silence, but I saw tears rise in Firada's eyes. She leaned over to take her sister's other hand. Jodoli seemed completely unaware of the importance of his offer to them. "And how will you do that?" he demanded harshly. "Kinrove has summoned him as a dancer and he has gone. We have told you. You cannot simply bring him back to us. He would not stay. He might not even know us." He looked disgusted as he leaned back from the fire and the food. "Nevare, you speak too often of what you will do with your power, always thinking you know more than the magic. You and Dasie, so sure you could destroy Gettys, even if it was something the magic had not bade you do! And now, you will steal Likari back for us somehow. It is a cruel hope that you dangle before these women. The magic took Likari. How can you use the magic against itself, to take him back? Can a knife cut itself, a fire burn itself? NO! Will you ever learn that when you set yourself above or against the magic, you are wrong? That you are doomed to fail?" He shook his head and said in a lower voice, "Kinrove and I were fools, to allow ourselves to be coerced into helping you. We should have fought you with every means we had. Neither of us will make that mistake again. Whatever foolish idea you are harboring, do not seek to include me or my feeder."

The rebuke was the harshest I had ever heard Jodoli speak. Soldier's Boy smarted under the sharp words. He seethed with anger and indignation, but could not think of a reply. "I will not need your help," he finally responded, but his words sounded childish, even to himself. His pride was pricked. What I felt most strongly was his determination to do something, anything, that would prove his worth to his followers. I wondered if he would try to pit himself against Kinrove. If he had Dasie's backing, he might break the dance once more. It would be a stupid thing to do, was my opinion. They'd stirred up Gettys like a boy poking a stick into a hornets' nest. Kinrove's dance would be the only thing holding the Gernians back from tracking the Specks into the forest and annihilating them. Stopping Kinrove's dance now would be a suicidal gesture for all the Specks.

As he and Jodoli glared at one another, a sudden howl rose from the group gathered around Dasie and her fire. It crested in shrieks of disbelief and pain. The sound paralyzed all of them for a moment, and then both Firada and Olikea leapt to their feet and ran to the other fire. Soldier's Boy rose more slowly, looking toward the ululating feeders.

"What is it?" Soldier's Boy demanded with dread.

"She's dead," Jodoli said flatly. "Dead in winter, worse luck for her. We will have to act swiftly."

"I don't understand." Those were the words he spoke, but echoing within him were other words. *Jodoli was right. It's all my fault. I failed her, too.* Independent of his weariness, a separate blackness rose at the edges of his vision; he feared he would faint. The harder he tried to improve things, the worse they became. Dasie had been a heroine to her kin-clan, and beyond. She had freed the dancers from Kinrove and then gone forth to fight for her people. For her to die now, before she could even return to them with the small triumph of the raid, would devastate her folk. Unbidden, a cowardly thought crept coldly through him. It could turn all the Specks against him. Then where could he go? To whom would he turn for shelter and sustenance?

Jodoli was not answering that, but another concern. "Winter is the worst time for a Great One to die. Her body will have to be borne back to the Valley of the Ancestor Trees. The trees are mostly dormant at this time of year; it will be hard for her chosen tree to take her in. It will be much more difficult to join her to her tree. Some of her may be lost."

"Lost?" he echoed unwillingly.

"We will have to move quickly. The sooner she reaches her tree, the better. If there is still warmth in her body, that is best of all. I pray that when my time comes, I will die when my tree already embraces me and my kin-clan stands around me singing. Dasie must go to her tree almost alone, in winter with only a few to sing to her. Oh, this is not a good omen."

Jodoli did not even go to the other fire to see if his assumptions were correct. Instead he did something that Soldier's Boy had never seen him do before: attempt to dress himself, fastening his own cloak and hood that was still chilled and damp from his day's journey. Before Soldier's Boy could reach for his own garb, several of Dasie's feeders converged on them. Soldier's Boy felt he was almost wrestled into his clothing and boots. Olikea came to help them. All of the feeders were weeping as they worked; it did not make them gentler. Never had I seen Specks move so quickly and in such a concerted way. By the time Soldier's Boy was ready, Dasie's bundled body had already been reloaded onto the travois. When Soldier's Boy sought to speak to Jodoli about what would happen next, the Great One sternly shushed him. "Do not distract her with words. Say nothing to draw her attention to us. Whatever anger you feel for me, set it aside. This is not our time. It is hers. Keep silent, and learn how a Great One goes to her tree."

And so, in the cold and the dark of night, they left the scant shelter of the stony roofed pass and headed once more down to the forest of the ancestor trees. Jodoli led the way. The horse pulled the travois with Dasie's body. Her two weary feeders who had stayed with her accompanied her again, along with those of her guards and feeders who had been in the cavernous pass. And Soldier's Boy came last of all.

Jodoli set the pace for the quick-walk and Soldier's Boy held it. Together they conveyed the funeral party through the night. It was not an easy task for Soldier's Boy. This was his fifth quick-walk of this route in but a handful of days. I could sense that it was more difficult because they had to move Dasie's dead body with them, but could not understand why it was harder to do that any more than I could grasp why it was possible to lead a horse on a quick-walk but far more difficult to ride one. Soldier's Boy was tired, discouraged, and full of sorrow. He was grateful that Jodoli minded the magic of the quick-walk and that all he had to do was help maintain it. His legs seemed made of lead and his back hurt horribly. He kept feeling tiny sharp twinges to either side of his spine. Callously, I pictured for him a suspension bridge with the cables snapping due to overload.

"Leave me alone," he retorted miserably.

After that, I rode silently.

The short winter day had lightened when we finally reached the valley of the ancestor trees. The day was cold, but not nearly as cold as it had been the night of our attack on the fort. There was a high breeze stirring the tops of the trees. Loosened snow fell in cascades and clumps, but for the most part the air was still under the interlaced canopy of branches, both needled and bare. Once we reached the edge of the valley, Jodoli stopped the quick-walk. Dasie's feeders took over leading the way and we all trudged in a long chilled procession behind them. No one spoke. There were occasional birdcalls and the crunch of our footsteps on the icy snow and the sounds of Clove dragging the travois. Other than that, the others kept silent and Soldier's Boy copied them. That battering of his inner thoughts was so loud that he could scarcely have paid any attention to conversation even if he had found the will to say something. Dasie's feeders moved purposefully through the forest, and he followed.

They came at last to a section of the forest where the canopy was thinner. Several of the older trees were scarred by fire. Between two huge burned-out stumps, a smaller kaembra tree stood. Long ago, lightning had killed and burned two of the great kaembra trees, leaving a hole in the canopy overhead that had permitted enough sunlight to encourage this young tree to sprout between the trunks. A couple of other young trees grew closer to the edge of the clearing. The bark of Dasie's tree was smooth and gray-green, its trunk only the diameter of a hogshead. A young tree, by Speck standards. Snow had settled deeply around it. Jodoli stood by Dasie's body as her feeders and guards went to work moving snow. They used their hands and feet, scooping and kicking away the loose white stuff until the frosted layer of fallen leaves and moss that was the forest floor was exposed. Only when a ten-foot-diameter circle had been cleared at the tree's base did they return to the travois for Dasie's body.

Jodoli stepped aside and again Soldier's Boy copied him. Dasie's feeders worked with efficiency that was still respectful. With a sharp knife, one man cut her clothing from the nape of her neck to the small of her back. Several of her guards stepped forward to help drag her limp weight from the travois to the selected tree. Just before they set her with her back to the tree, one of her feeders ran his knife from the back of her head down her spine to the divide of her buttocks. The slash exposed meat but no blood flowed. With chill efficiency, the man opened the slash wider. Then, as they placed her against the tree, he worked to snug the open wound as firmly as he could against the tree's bark. Jodoli spoke very softly. "Sometimes, in winter, when the trees sleep deeply, the touch of blood against the bark will waken them. So we hope for Dasie."

They were binding her against the tree now, strapping her firmly in place with long strips of leather. Her legs were out-stretched before her, and her arms tucked close to her body. One feeder secured her legs at the knees and ankles to keep them from spraddling while another finished tying her at throat and brow. When they were finished, they stepped back and waited in silence.

And waited.

There was a subtle tension building in that stillness. I was not sure what they were waiting for, but sensed the gravity of the moment. After an appreciable time had passed, one of her guard stepped forward. He met the eyes of her chief feeder and then offered his bared forearm and, in his other hand, a knife. "Perhaps fresh warm blood would awake—" he began, but in that moment, her other feeder gave a low and welcoming cry.

"There!" he exclaimed in relief. We all stared at Dasie's body and I saw nothing at all. But a moment later, the corner of Dasie's mouth twitched. I was not certain I had really seen it, but then her head subtly shifted.

Beside me, Jodoli breathed a sigh of relief. "The tree has wel-comed her," he proclaimed, and there was a flutter of movement among her feeders as they exchanged looks. Tears began to flow again, but they were like the tears shed when a difficult birth still yields a viable child. Anguish gives way to joy, and then to peace. Her feeders went quickly to work again. They shrouded her from head to toe in a woven blanket. This they doused with water from the waterskins and then shaped it to her body. "It will freeze that way," Jodoli explained, "and seal her against the tree, so that scavengers do not carry off what rightfully belongs to the tree. This has gone better than I expected. I would have liked to see a livelier joining to the tree, but this is enough. Dasie has her tree."

Her feeders and guards were busy again, now using the snow they had scraped away from around the tree to bury the wrapped body. Jodoli withdrew some little distance and Soldier's Boy did likewise, but did not follow the Great Man. Instead, he walked to the clearing's edge. He stared out into the pillared dimness of the forest canopied by the intersecting branches of the kaembra trees overhead. The day seemed darker when he turned his back to the little clearing, and the forest more mysterious. Almost he fancied he heard a soft voice calling him.

"Nevare. Neva-are." A man's voice. Soldier's Boy turned his head rapidly from side to side, scanning the forest. He saw no one.

And then more clearly, "Never, you old sonovabitch, aren't you going to say hello?"

Buel Hitch. His mocking tone was unmistakable.

Soldier's Boy turned his head slowly to regard the tree next to him. It was a young kaembra, approximately the same age as the one that Dasie had just joined. Heart thumping, he took one step closer to it. He trod on something under the snow and stepped back hastily. It had not been a branch. Bone. A leg bone.

"It was a big honor they done me. Not a Great One nor a Speck. But her kin-clan knew I had served the magic as well as I could, and so they brought me here and gave me a tree. I never got to thank you, Nevare. So I'll do it now. Thanks for keeping your word, even after you found out how I betrayed you. Thanks for letting the Specks take my body out of that wooden box and bring me here."

"Buel." Soldier's Boy spoke the name aloud with me. I do not know which half of me was more shocked, the Speck or the

Gernian, that my friend and my betrayer lived on here. Soldier's Boy pulled the heavy mitten from his hand, and set the bare flesh of his palm to the tree's bark.

"Careful!" Buel warned me, standing as clearly before me as if his bones still wore flesh. "It's a young tree and I've only been here a few months. The tree's pretty deep asleep, but if it starts to wake hungry, it'll go for you, just like a snake after a rat. So. Well, look at you. Now who's gone native, old son? Specks and all."

Soldier's Boy spoke to him. "I'm not who you think I am."

Buel grinned. He didn't look quite as I remembered him. He was taller, more muscled, and his hair was combed. I suddenly realized that I was seeing his own idealized version of himself. That was a breathtaking insight into Lisana. I might have startled Soldier's Boy by sharing that thought, except that what Buel said next shocked me even more. He shook his head and the ghost's grin grew wider.

"Oh, no, old son. Now you're exactly who I think you are. Maybe even more so." He cocked his head and then craned it down to look into my eyes, smiling all the while. And I suddenly knew that he saw me, as I was now, but that all that time, he'd been seeing Soldier's Boy as well. He shook his head in sympathy. "Well, you're still in a fix and no mistake, my friend. Maybe a worse fix than when last I saw you, though that's hard to believe. You forgave me, didn't you? Don't you?" His smile had faded to an earnest look.

I was at a loss. Had I forgiven him? How could I? He'd killed a woman and made it look as if I had done it. He'd spread the whispers that had turned public feeling against me to the point where a mob had tried to murder me. He'd done it under the duress of the magic. Yet even knowing that—

Soldier's Boy answered for both of us. "I understand you. Sometimes, when you understand a man that deeply, forgiveness becomes a moot point. You did what you were supposed to do, Buel Hitch. You did the magic's bidding."

Buel continued to stare at us. No. At me. Waiting. I spoke within Soldier's Boy. "I don't have to forgive Buel Hitch. He wasn't who betrayed me. The magic did that."

I felt Soldier's Boy scowl and knew he had heard me. When Buel grinned again, I knew he had, too. "No matter who did it, Nevare, I'm sorry it happened. But I can't be sorry for what it bought me. This."

"You enjoy being a tree?" Behind me, the others were finishing their task. Dasie's body was encased in the freezing blanket and covered now with a shroud of snow. Her feeders were caressing the snow as if they were smoothing a delicate coverlet over a sleeping child.

"Being a tree." He smiled. "I suppose that's one way of seeing it." He sighed then, not the sigh of a man who is discouraged but rather as a man sighs with satisfaction at the completeness of his life.

"Nevare!" Jodoli called him. Soldier's Boy turned to look at him, and the Great Man gestured. The others were gathering in a circle about Dasie and her tree. He was expected to join them.

As he walked away, Buel spoke after us, his words intended for me. He was not yet strong in his tree. His voice faded as we moved away from him, but the words he spoke reached me still.

"It's worth it, Nevare. No matter what it takes from you. No matter what you have to give up. No matter what you have to do. It's worth it. Relax into it, old son. Give way to the magic. You won't be sorry. I promise."

Soldier's Boy gave a short nod. I held myself still and stubborn inside him. *No.*

He turned away from the tree and the huddle of snow that still, now that he looked at it, echoed the shape of a man's seated body trussed to the tree's trunk. The others were gathering around Dasie's tree where a similar but much larger mound of snow marked her "grave." Soldier's Boy went over to them. As he plodded through the snow, Jodoli joined him. He spoke as if their quarrel had never been, or as if he had dismissed it as insignificant. "It is good that the tree took her in. She chose the tree years ago, when first she knew she would be a Great One, and has visited it yearly, giving it offerings of her blood to awaken it to her and claim it. Still, in very cold weather, it has sometimes happened that a tree does not accept the Great One's body. Then there is little that anyone can do."

"What happens now?"

"Now we will sing a farewell to her. Our songs will remind her of who she was, so that as she is taken into the tree, her memories remain strong. Of course, it should be her entire kin-clan here to sing her into her tree, rather than just two of her feeders and a handful of her guard. But we are here. Nevare, we would be very wise to honor her with very long songs, as long as we can sing, of everything that we know about her. Do you understand?"

"I think I do." He meant it would be politically wise. "I will watch you and then I will do my best."

"Very well. Let us join them."

It was as unlike a Gernian burial as I could imagine. We formed a circle around the tree and held hands. This required baring our hands to the cold, as the skin-to-skin contact was deemed very important. A few moments after we had joined hands, I understood why. I could feel the magic flowing through the circle of linked hands with the same sensation of moving current as if we all held on to a pipe with water flowing through it, through us.

Her feeders began the songs, as was their right. It was not a song so much as a chant; it had no melody and it did not rhyme. The first man recounted everything he could recall of her, from the moment he had first met her to his days of being her feeder right up to her death. He chanted until his voice gave out and then on until he could barely croak out the words. When he finally could say no more, his fellow feeder took up the tale, again recounting how he had met Dasie and on through all the days and ways he had served her. He avoided repetition of events that the first feeder had covered. Even so, before her feeders were finished the brief day was ending.

But the cover of night brought no respite. The chant went on, passed from guard to guard to guard, with each fondling his memories of Dasie and trying to recall for the dead woman how she had looked and spoken, what she had eaten or worn, how she had laughed at a humorous event or mourned a sad one. Not all the memories were kind. Some spoke of her when she was a small girl and prone to cruelty to smaller children. Others spoke of her temper as a grown woman. Some wept as they spoke of

Dasie and losing her, but as often they laughed or shouted as they recalled memories of her. One spoke in detail of her activities on the day of the battle. I cringed as he spoke of the deaths they had witnessed, and of those she had killed with her own hand. But the guard spared us no detail. All, all must be spoken to preserve it in the dead woman's memory.

I learned far more of Dasie's life than I had ever known before. When the telling finally reached Jodoli, Soldier's Boy was already racking his brain for what he could add. Jodoli spoke of how he had met her when she was a Great One, and told in detail of the night when she had freed the dancers from Kinrove. He spoke of meals they had shared and gifts they had exchanged as Great Ones of the People. He drew his material out by adding details.

Soldier's Boy's feet and legs felt swollen, and he ached with cold. Only the magic flowing from hand to hand to hand made the experience tolerable at all. He felt his energy feed it but felt also how it drew strength from every person and circulated it back to him.

It was full dark when Jodoli finally fell silent. Cold had crept and flowed to surround them; Soldier's Boy felt it was cracking the skin of his face. The hair inside his nostrils had grown stiff and prickly and he could barely feel his feet at all. Worse, he felt that there was nothing left for him to say, yet Jodoli had warned him that he must at least attempt to speak at length of Dasie.

It seemed they had left him little enough to speak of, and yet he acquitted himself well. He spoke of when he had first seen her at Kinrove's encampment, and what she had said and how she had looked to him. He spoke of her freeing the dancers from Kinrove's dance, and when he sensed how her guards and feeders loved to hear of her as a hero, he embroidered that moment. He also spoke of how she had hated him on first sight and threatened him, and this, I suddenly knew, was news to many of those gathered there. But as others had done before him, he did not skip or soften any details, not of that first encounter nor even when he was telling of how little sympathy she had shown when Likari had been summoned to be a dancer. He spoke of how they had prepared for the battle, and the moments before they had each parted to their assigned tasks and then how he had seen her, injured and staring, when they met again. He spoke of leaving her with her loyal feeders while he went to fetch a healer, and also of quick-walking her back to the pass where she had died.

And when he came to the end of his telling, the darkness was deep around all of us. Tiny sparkling stars showed overhead in the opening in the forest canopy, and an errant night wind blew snow against our faces. As he fell silent, the greater silence of the forest all around us swallowed us up and held us inside it. The magic still circled through our clasped hands but it could no longer distract Soldier's Boy from his discomfort. His back and legs were stiff and sore, he was cold, and he was hungry. Worse, he knew that a long quick-walk awaited him before he could hope that any of those discomforts would be alleviated. But the others still stood in silence, holding hands, and so he kept company with them. He sensed they were all waiting but had no idea for what.

Everyone took a step closer to the tree and he lurched forward with them. And another, and another, until they were huddled close to the trunk of the tree and Dasie's snow-shrouded body. The magic suddenly coursed more strongly through their clasped hands, pulling them close, binding them into one. Darkness vanished, to be replaced with a peculiar light; everyone there glowed with it, and the living trees of the forest were vertical columns of soft light. Every living thing gave off its own measure of it. He felt Dasie, felt her strongly centered in the tree. She was there, every bit of her, every moment of her life, every memory they had shared with her. She was newborn there, laughing with the growing awareness of this new life. Complete and at peace, she dimly gave thanks to us as she vanished into the satisfaction of her joining with her tree.

But there was more. Soldier's Boy felt everyone there through the clasp of their hands, felt the life in the trees that surrounded them, and even the slow surge of the great earth life beneath his feet. It warmed him and filled him, and eased the sense of loss he had felt. For the time that it lasted, he was one with the forest of the ancestor trees, one with the Specks, one with the People. Tears stung his eyes. He did belong here. These were his people, and when his time came, his tree would be here waiting for him. It would be the second sapling that had grown from Lisana's fallen trunk. There he would take root among this wisdom and shared life. As if his thought had summoned her, he felt a thread of Lisana in her connectedness to the greater whole, distant in the crowd, glowing with her own special light. He yearned toward her, but a different voice spoke to me.

"You see what I mean, old son? It's worth it. This is what I can feel, all the time now."

Soldier's Boy paid no heed to Buel Hitch's disembodied voice. Instead, he stretched and reached for Lisana and she toward him. For a long moment, their awarenesses brushed against each other, mingled, and then, like ember logs that fall apart from one another as the fire consumes them, crashed into separateness again. We all stood once more in icy darkness in a black forest. The distant stars could neither light nor warm us, and a cold wind was sweeping through the trees overhead, dusting us with secondhand snow.

"Her tree has taken her. It is time for us to go and leave her to it," Jodoli announced.

And we did.

CHAPTER TWENTY-THREE

TIDINGS

When we finally reached Lisana's old lodge, Soldier's Boy ate like a starved dog. He spoke not a word to the feeders who had awaited him there, keeping the food ready and the lodge fire burning. He left Olikea to deal with them, went to bed and slept for most of a day. He woke late in the night, got up to piss and drink some water, and then went right back to bed. The second time he awoke, it was daylight and his feeders were astir. They spoke softly to one another as they worked. He thought it might be late afternoon. He lay as still as a fox that has gone to earth and hopes to escape the hounds. He kept his eyes closed and listened to the sounds of the lodge around him, but gave no sign to anyone that he was awake. Every muscle and joint in his body ached. His back was a column of pain.

He did not move at all and breathed as slowly as if he were still sleeping. The bed was warm. His belly was still digesting. He turned his face into the pillow, his special pillow. It was stuffed with down but also contained sachets of cedar bark, dried forest flowers, and leaves. It smelled, I suddenly realized, like Lisana.

He lay in her bed, in her lodge, breathing the fragrances that reminded him of her. He was trying to pretend that the sounds he heard were made by her as she moved about the lodge.

"Pretend as much as you like," I said derisively. "She is gone, dead for all these many years. And you cannot reach her."

My words shredded his dream of her. He could not regain it. He still did not move.

"Did Dasie's death teach you nothing?" he thought at me. "When I die, they will take me to a tree. I will become one with the forest of ancients. And once again, Lisana and I will walk side by side."

I laughed at him. "After all the ways you have failed, do you think the Specks will still honor you with a tree? You are a fool. You are as big a failure to your people as I was to mine. Look at the wreckage strewn behind you. Dasie is dead. Of the handsome young warriors who bravely followed you off to battle, a third did not return. And many of those who did come back are injured and demoralized. Likari has been taken for the dance and Olikea has lost her spirit. Kinrove sees you as his enemy, Jodoli as his incompetent rival for power. The fort at Gettys still stands and you have raised the hatred of the Gernians against the Specks to a boiling point. You have not only failed to improve things, you have made them worse. Next spring, when we return to the forests on the other side of the mountains, there will be no fur traders, but only soldiers waiting to kill you. No trade goods, Soldier's Boy. No honey, no bright beads, no woven fabric. No tobacco. None for the People to smoke, and none for them to carry to the Trading Place. The long guns will point at the Specks, and all they will trade you are iron bullets for your lives."

"Silence!" he hissed and struck at me. I made myself small and avoided the blow. I was getting better at dodging his attacks. Like a mosquito, I buzzed and sang in his ears, only to vanish when he angrily slapped the side of his head.

From my silent concealment, I watched in satisfaction. I had shredded his dream of Lisana and left him only cold reality to consider. I'd seeded his thoughts with all his failures. His stillness became a morose silence. For the first time since the raid on

Gettys, he had stillness and time to think. He could no longer hide from his musings. Time and silence gave him nothing else to think about.

He reviewed the night of the battle over and over. He considered what he had done wrong, the situations he had failed to plan for, the instructions he had not given to his troops. Whenever I could impinge on his thoughts, I pushed my own memories at him: the sentry falling, his throat sliced. The wounded Specks squirming and crying out on the snowy earth after the ambush, and how he had ridden away. The soldiers who had died as they tried to escape the flaming barracks, slaughtered like cattle in a chute. I slid my thought across his like a knife blade across skin. "It was a cowardly way to kill soldiers. They had no chance to fight at all."

He shouldered my thoughts aside. His tone was mocking as he said, "Do you still think war is a game, with rules and limits? No. War is killing the enemy. It wasn't about a 'fair fight' or any of your strange ideas of honor and glory. Honor and glory! War is blood and death. It was about killing as many Gernians as we could and losing as few of our own as we could. It was about destroying a nest of vermin. Don't try to make me feel guilty over exterminating the intruders. If you want to saw on my nerves, think instead about how I failed my troops. Chide me for what I should have done to save the warriors of the People. Rebuke me that the walls of Gettys still stand, not that fewer long guns would peer over the palisade at us."

I kept silent. He would not bait me into discussing his failures. I could taunt him over what he had done and what he had neglected, but that would only be instructing him in how to improve the next time. I ignored him and sank into my own retreat. It was abhorrent to think that this ruthless butcher was actually a part of me—the dominant part right now. I did not want to acknowledge my attachment to him at all. I retreated into my own darkness, to mull over the things that "I" had done that horrified me still. The murdered sentry, the slaughtered troops—The worst, I think, was recalling Spink's face in that moment of recognition. What must he think of me? And if he had known me, had others?

It ate at me that I could know nothing of the aftermath of our attack on the fort.

Had Amzil and her children survived? Had Epiny and her babe? And if they had survived the fires and the attacking Specks, then what was their life now? Cold and starvation?

My thoughts turned over and over to the night I had dream-walked to Epiny. I worried that she was taking the laudanum, and tried to make sense of her rambling confessions to me that night. She had sent my soldier-son journal to my uncle, but it had fallen into my aunt's hands and she had done something with it that related to the Queen, something that threatened the reputation of the Burvelle name. I put that unsettling thought together with the idea that it had been Soldier's Boy prompting me to write so much in that journal, far beyond the diary that a soldier's son would be expected to pen. He believed he had been obeying the dictates of the magic when he did so. If that were true, what did it mean to me? Had I written more in there than I knew? How could my journal and what it contained be a part of the magic's plan to drive the Gernians away from the Speck lands? The rock he had mentioned was almost certainly the one I had given to Caulder. How could that matter to the magic? I could make no sense of that and there was no one I could ask. Soldier's Boy himself did not know why the magic had prompted him to write so much, nor why it was imperative that he leave the journal behind when he fled to the mountains. There was no one I could ask.

Save, perhaps, Lisana.

"Lisana." Soldier's Boy spoke the name aloud, and I wondered if he were aware of my thoughts or if his had touched me. Now that I put my attention on him, I realized he was again pining like a schoolboy for her. Thoughts of her were what held him immobile in his bed and kept him from wanting to interact with the others. He simply wanted to be still and think of her. He thought that she alone could offer him the comfort and understanding he craved. To all others, he must stand firm as a Great One, even when he felt he had failed them in every way. Only with her could he be honest about his confusion and fear. I felt him reach for her then, a magical groping that went in a futile circle and came back to himself. He could not find her; could not touch her, sense her; could not dream-walk to her. That ability had stayed with me. "The magic gave you Lisana. And what did I get?" he asked bitterly.

"Apparently, the ability to kill people and feel absolutely nothing. Or to witness a death, such as Dasie's, and be unmoved by it."

Something, I felt something there, something he hid before he responded to me. "Oh. So you will mourn Dasie, too, will you? She knew her risks. She had no love for us, and all but laughed when Likari was summoned to the dance. But I forget. You do not have the spine to hate your enemies. So do not let that stop you. Mourn her, and mourn the men who were glad to murder you when they had the chance to do so as a cowardly mob. Is there anyone you do not weep for, Nevare? Will you sigh over the rabbit that is simmering in the pot right now?" A pause and then, "Truly, you should have been your father's priest son. Or better yet, his daughter, always wailing and snuffling her nose in a handkerchief."

"I sigh for Likari," I said quietly and viciously. "Likari, whom you condemned to death by dancing. Dancing takes a bit longer than slitting a man's throat, but I'm sure it works just as well in the long run."

He struck me then and I felt it. "I hate you. I hate that you were ever a part of me."

I set my will and endured his blow. I think it shocked him that I could. "The hatred is mutual," I informed him coldly.

A sudden coldness flowed through him, a hatred so strong that it nearly froze me. "While you live in me I will never enjoy any part of my life. I see that now. Always you will be there, sniping and criticizing me. Always there will be a weak Gernian conscience whining at me." He paused and announced, "I will find a way to kill you."

"You can try," I retorted, my anger masking my fear. "It seems to be what you always attempt. Kill anything that opposes you. Kill anyone who makes you think. So kill me if you can. I suspect that if you destroy me, you will destroy your last link with Lisana.

And that, I think, would only be just. She is not like you, Soldier's Boy. She has a heart. She should not have to associate with a conscienceless murderer like you."

"No worse than you, Nevare Burvelle. Or will you deny that you tried to kill, not just me but also Lisana? You even believed you had succeeded. But you had not. And now it is my time."

I waited, expecting a blow or some final words from him. Instead, I received nothing. Some time passed. He stirred in his bed and instantly his feeders surrounded him. No Gernian cavalla officer, no matter how high his rank, would have allowed underlings to tend him as assiduously as Soldier's Boy's feeders did. They flocked around him, offering him food, drink, clothing to wear, and slipping shoes on his feet. They tended him as if he were the King of Gernia, and he accepted it as his due. I wondered that he could stand being cosseted so.

"Are you a man or a great doll?" I asked him snidely, but received no response. Often when he did not directly reply to me, I could sense his reaction to my barbs, but this time there was nothing. I realized I could not pick up any trace of what he was thinking. He ignored me absolutely as he resumed his morning routine. He washed, he ate, and Sempayli came in to report to him. The man had a low, soft voice. I had to strain to hear what he was saying. He seemed to be giving a solid military report of who had returned and in what condition and how the raid had unfolded for those not immediately under Soldier's Boy's commands. Soldier's Boy took it all in, but I could sense nothing of his feelings let alone his responses. I felt as if my ears were packed full of wool.

Soldier's Boy rose and followed his lieutenant out of the lodge. Some of his troops had assembled for his review. Close to four hundred warriors had followed him on his raid. He had lost nearly a third of them, and only fifty or so now awaited him. These were the men who had been most loyal to him and were now most disillusioned. A dozen or so bore injuries of varying severity. They looked at him and their eyes were full of confusion. I watched him try to rally their spirits. I wondered why he bothered. "You will not lead those troops into battle again," I sneered at him, but as

before, I felt no response to my jibe. It became harder and harder
to hear the words addressed to Soldier's Boy and near impossible
to hear anything of what he said in response. He was cutting me
off from him, I now knew. It was strange to realize that he had
been allowing me to break in on his thoughts.

And now he was not. What did that bode for me?

As the day passed, I became more and more isolated from
him. I could look out through his eyes, and hear, in a muffled way,
what he heard and even what he responded. I was aware of what
he did with his body, how he ate and drank, what he did, but he
had separated me from himself. My sense of taste and smell faded,
just as my hearing had. Even touch seemed muted and distant. It
was not the absolute emptiness that I'd once been marooned in,
but an even stranger place where what I thought had no impact
on my life at all.

My life. I wondered if I could even call it that anymore. It
was more like being trapped inside the body of a marionette, and
unable to anticipate what string would next be pulled. With every
passing day, the world outside his body became less accessible to
me. Daily he spoke to people—Sempayli, his warriors, his feeders,
and Olikea. I heard his words and could make out their responses,
but sensed nothing of what he felt. My emotions were so often
at odds with his. I was truly a man living in a stranger's body.
Where I would have wished to comfort Olikea when she silently
wept at night, he made no move toward her. When I thought he
should have rebuked a member of his household or praised one
of his warriors, he just as often did something entirely different.
My disconnection from his thoughts became a sort of madness
for me, excruciating in a very different way from my time in the
emptiness. It was like reading a book in which the words and
sentences almost made sense, but not quite. I could not predict
what he would do next.

In the times when he slept and I did not, I thought often
of Gettys and the raid. I tried not to imagine what must have
followed; the warehouses of food had been put to the torch, as
had many of the dwelling places. I tried not to think of families
without adequate food or shelter in the deep cold of winter.

Sometimes I thought about Spink and wondered if he had ignored my warning, or if he had reacted to it in a way I didn't
understand. Obviously, he'd been outside the walls of the fort that
night. Had he heeded my warning and removed his family from
the fort? I tried to imagine where I would have hidden Epiny and
Amzil and the children if I knew a Speck attack was imminent. I
was actually pleased when I could not decide; a secret a man does
not know is one he cannot betray.

The remaining days of winter trickled by. Soldier's Boy regained his girth. Olikea remained a cipher to me, her movements
listless and her face nearly expressionless. She still went about the
tasks of being his feeder, but I saw little of her old spirit. She did
not speak of Likari; had she given up all hope of recovering him?
She seemed indifferent to everything in life; even when she accommodated Soldier's Boy's need for sex, she seemed uninterested
in her own pleasure. I wondered what emotions and thoughts he
had at such times, but those, too, were hidden from me. She was
neither cruel nor contemptuous toward him. It seemed as if every
intense emotion had vanished from her, leaving a woman gray as
the overcast sky.

Soldier's Boy's status with the People had dwindled, but he
remained a Great One. His feeders did not desert him: that would
have been unthinkable for a Speck. It did seem to me that they
had to work harder to provide for him. The kin-clan had turned
the sunshine of their attention back onto Jodoli, and he was the
one who benefited from their hunting and gathering. There was
no want in Soldier's Boy's lodge, but there was not the sumptuous
plenty of days past. If he noticed it, he gave no sign of it to any
of his feeders.

For a time, his warriors continued to seek him out. They gathered outside his lodge to smoke and talk, and then go off to hunt
and fish together. I could not decide if habit brought them, or if
they somehow hoped that something more would come of their
failed effort. Each morning, he went out to greet them but every
day fewer of them came. He had nothing to offer them. His promises of victory had been empty. The intruders remained at Gettys,
the ancestor trees were still in danger, and Kinrove's dancers were

still prisoners of the magic. None of the rewards he had offered them in exchange for all their hard work had been fulfilled. After a time, they no longer bothered to wait for him, but met up with their comrades and dispersed to the day's hunting and gathering. No one spoke any more of driving the Gernians away by force of arms. His army was no more.

I made efforts to be neither idle nor passive. Any number of times, I tried to see if I could slip away from him to dream-walk. I never managed to. He was rebuilding his cache of magic, and he guarded it so jealously that I could find no way to tap into it and siphon off what I needed for that magic. I constantly watched for some vulnerability, but as day after day trickled away, my hopes receded. I felt I was an animal trapped and forgotten in a cage that grew ever smaller. Soldier's Boy often sat and stared into the hearth fire, brooding. I wondered if he planned a return to power or merely dwelt on his failure and frustration. To me, Soldier's Boy seemed like a man without a purpose.

As spring ventured closer, the Specks began to prepare for their annual migration. Food was prepared and packed for the journey, while the lodges were put in good order and all the winter equipment and garments were carefully stored away. I heard more talk about what the summer would bring, and especially I heard more discussions about whether there would be any trade at all with the intruders. The trading or lack of it seemed to bother the People more than the concept of danger or vengeance from the Gernians. Even without knowing Soldier's Boy's thoughts, I was forced to confront yet again just how different the People were from the Gernians in how they thought. These two cultures, I decided, would never find common ground. Perhaps Dasie would eventually be proven right; the war would end only when one side had destroyed the other.

The night before our migration was to begin was a busy one for everyone except Soldier's Boy. He was a center of stillness as he sat in his cushioned chair and watched all his feeders busy around him. Olikea supervised the tidying of the lodge. She determined which cooking pots would travel with us and which would be stored, how much food we would take and who would carry what. She immersed herself so completely in her task that she seemed almost her old self. Then, one of the women asked her about storing Likari's things.

The boy had not owned much. The cedar chest for his possessions was not a large one. His garments were as he had left them, tossed in, rumpled, crumpled, dirtied still from the last time he had worn them. Most of them showed the wear and tear that any boy of his years would put on clothing. Doubtless by now he had outgrown most of them, I thought. Then I wondered if he was growing, or if the constant dancing had stunted him as I'd heard it would. He had also, not toys, but the tools of a boy learning to be a man. I watched with Soldier's Boy as Olikea took them, one at a time, from the chest. A knife. A fire-starting kit in a worn pouch, one that Olikea had passed down to him. A net for fish. The sharp crystal that Soldier's Boy had used to cut himself to mark himself as a Speck. That was wrapped carefully in a soft square of doeskin. The last item Olikea exhumed was my sling. I didn't recall giving it to him, and yet there it was, among the litter of things in his chest. Olikea picked up a pair of worn shoes, and suddenly clutched them to her chest and broke down in loud sobs. She rocked the old shoes as if they were a baby, clutching them to her chest and calling, "Likari, Likari!" in a voice that penetrated past any muffling.

Soldier's Boy had not been helping with the packing. Instead, he had been sitting on a chair next to her, idly watching her work. I thought he would put his arms around her or that he would at least say something. Instead, he rose ponderously and walked away from her. At the door of Lisana's lodge, he hesitated, then strode out into the mild spring night. When a feeder sprang to her feet and would have followed after him, he curtly waved her back. For the first time in weeks, he left the lodge alone.

The area around the lodge had become a tiny village. Hearth light leaked out into the night from shuttered windows and doors left open to the fresh air. He walked past the smaller dwellings where his feeders and some of his warriors lived. The mossy trail down to the water had become a well-trodden path. Where there had been brush and brambles the first day that he and Likari found the lodge, there now was open space under the immense trees. Dry branches and fallen wood had been gathered for the fire long ago, and new paths crisscrossed each other as he made his way down to the stream. Even that was changed. A rough bridge had been built over it. He crossed it and walked on, following the stream downcurrent.

I had no sense of where he was going, and when we came to a place where the stream widened, he sat down on a rock. I thought perhaps he was taking a rest; he had walked farther than he had in some days. For a time, he sat in silence. Around us, the forest evening breathed out its spring breath. The brush willow along the stream's edge had the beginning of catkins. The water in the stream was running fast and cold from snowmelt in the mountains, gurgling over stones. After he had sat for a time in silence, tiny frogs resumed creaking and cheeping to the night. Soldier's Boy listened to their chorus.

Abruptly he spoke to me in his mind. "I must go to Lisana. I must see her, touch her, talk to her. I must."

His words reached me but he still kept his emotions walled off from me. I replied with caution. "But you can't. Unless I take you to her."

He looked down, staring at the rocks in the streambed that were blurred by the water's swift flow. "That's true. So what is your price?"

I was shocked that he would bargain so baldly, and distrustful of it. "What are you offering?"

"I don't have time to barter with you over this." Anger scorched the words. "Name what you want and I'll likely give it to you. I need to speak with Lisana."

"I need to speak with Epiny. And Yaril."

He scratched the back of his scalp. His hair had grown out long over the winter. Olikea had begun to pull it back into plaits for him. The forest folk had few looking glasses, and as Soldier's Boy was groomed by his feeders, he seldom looked in one. I was grateful. I suspected I looked even more ridiculous than I had.

"Very well," at last he said tightly. "I don't see what harm you can do to me by talking with them. Of course, I don't see what good you can do for yourself, either. But it's what you've asked for.

Take me to Lisana. Now. And while I speak to her, I wish to be alone." Grudgingly, he added, "I will provide you the magic you need to dream-walk to your cousin and sister." That suited me far better than anything I could have devised. Distracted by Lisana, he would not be able to spy on my conversations. Of course, the reverse was also true, and I was sure he had deliberately chosen to make it so. "Lisana, then," I agreed readily. "Right now?"

"We cannot go sooner," he said, and closed his eyes.

I approached closer to him and his magic. Wariness warned me that this might be some trick on his part to destroy me. To use the magic he willingly offered me, I would have to make myself accessible to him in the same way he was open to me. I weighed the risk and suddenly found I didn't care. If he destroyed me, at least it would be over. I still believed he would not risk losing his link to Lisana by killing me. Briefly I thought of how ruthless he was, and then decided I would have to take the chance. This might be my last opportunity to converse with my cousin and be sure that she had survived our raid on Gettys.

I thought it would be difficult. Instead, it was like reaching out to clasp hands. I knew that Lisana had been waiting for this. She literally pulled me into her, and for a long moment, I lingered in the warm embrace of her mind. It was healing.

For that moment, there was no conversation, no questions or answers, nothing that even resembled thought. All that existed was acceptance and love. It was how I had imagined my mother felt about me when I was a baby, though in retrospect, I had always wondered if she had. That was the most joyous thing about our joining. I could feel what Lisana felt about me; all the doubts that lovers must have were banished in that meeting. No deceptions were possible in that intimacy. She loved me far better than I loved myself. And I reciprocated it.

I think I might have lingered forever in that healing balm, except that Soldier's Boy suddenly pushed me aside. "Go to what you wish to do and leave me here for a time," he said brusquely. "My magic will serve you."

"You are still separated, still not one?" she asked us with dismay.

"He will not join me," Soldier's Boy replied sullenly.

I heard Lisana's soft rebuke. "And in your heart, you do not wish him to. You hold him as far from you as he does you. Are you jealous even of yourself? Do you think I could love you and not love all of you?"

I smiled to hear that, even as it amazed me. Trust the heart of a woman to be large enough to encompass two such disparate people and make them one. I felt his magic push me away from her, but not before she was aware of my thought. I felt her warmth follow me as she enfolded Soldier's Boy in her embrace.

Freed, I arrowed through something that was neither space nor time, traveling across something that was not distance. Unerring, Soldier's Boy's push sent me to my cousin Epiny. I found her sitting in a rocker by a fire. She was neither asleep nor awake as she rocked but wearily insensate after a difficult day. She had always thought babies were sweet little cherubs who slept and ate and slept again. She smiled at her childhood memories of her own little sister. The moment Purissa even gurgled in a discontented way, she'd been whisked away by her nurse, her wails vanishing with her when the nursery door was shut firmly behind them. She'd always imagined that her nurse quickly discovered what discontented the child and solved it and that Purissa went back to being a placid and contented infant. Solina seemed placid and contented only when being held by her mother. Held and rocked, endlessly rocked. From elsewhere in the cottage, I heard a child's voice uplifted in querulous complaint, and Amzil's irritable hushing. Dia was unhappy about something. The babe in Epiny's arms squirmed and wailed a thin protest in sympathy.

Epiny sighed and tears started under her eyelids. She was tired, so very tired, and her head hurt. Spink had stopped taking the Gettys Tonic and forbidden it to everyone in his household. Amzil had nearly left over it; if she'd had anywhere else to go, she would have. The whole household had been miserable since Spink had decreed it, and he had been so unreasonable. He wouldn't allow it in the door, not a drop, not even to soothe the children when they had nightmares.

"But you know, he's right, Epiny." I inserted myself into her meandering trail of thoughts.

"But being right doesn't get him far. When he was right about the dangers of a Speck attack, it only brought him blame for not shouting more loudly and taking more action."

"What did Spink do that night?"

She sighed. The baby on her breast was not quieting but only wailing in an endlessly hopeless way. With the toe of one foot, she started the rocker moving again. "He said he'd dreamed of you that morning, and asked me if I had. I thought I might have, but I couldn't remember details. Only that you were very agitated and kept saying that I had to warn everyone. So he tried telling people that he had a bad premonition and that we must all be extra wary that night. But of course everyone just laughed at him. The Specks go away in winter; everyone knows that. But he made Amzil and me take the children, some bedding, and some food and go spend the night in a little stone cottage outside the gates. The cottage was abandoned years ago, and it was so cold and he forbade us to have any fire or light at all. We ended up huddled together like mice under a doormat. He told his men, soldiers accustomed to working in supply, and announced that he was having a night drill, and that all must turn out for it armed and uniformed for the cold. And he took them outside the fort, too, and made them march a patrol around the town outside the fort. He thought that when the attack came, it would be noisy, with guns firing and men shouting. He never even knew that the Specks were inside the fort until the fires blazed up. He was riding back toward the fort when— Nevare? You are here? Really here with me?"

"Yes, Epiny. I've dream-walked to you. I wanted to be sure you had all weathered the attack intact."

"Small thanks to you!" she said with sudden deep bitterness. "Nevare, Spink saw you that night! He says that you looked right at him, eye to eye. He had been on the point of firing, and then when he saw your face, he could not!" A shiver of outrage ran over her. "Some have faulted him for that, calling him coward or traitor! Yet none of them faced up to you, either. How dare they speak so about him, how dare they! And how could you have put him in such a position, Nevare!"

"Epiny, you know how I am bound! I did all I could, to come and warn you both. It was as much as I could do!" The accusing tone of her words tore me. How could she believe I had done that of my own will? "Even now, I am held! My time to speak with you is short."

"I know. I do know. But still, it is a heavy thing for him to bear, for there is no possible way he could explain it. Others saw you, Nevare. Or what they said was your ghost, come back as a Speck. The heaviest losses were taken by the men who were in the mob that night when you fled Gettys; only five now survive who witnessed your death. Rumor mutters about the town. Some say your ghost led the attack to take vengeance on the town. The barracks where the men were massacred as they tried to escape? Those soldiers were under Captain Thayer's command. You remember who he was, don't you? Carsina's husband? The monster that was going to let his men rape and murder Amzil, simply as a way of tormenting you before they beat you to death! Now, whenever he sees Amzil on the street, or even little Kara sent out on an errand, he glowers and stares like a madman! He rules his own troops like a despot. I fear him, Nevare. I fear that he will stop at nothing to feel he has avenged himself. He says that Amzil is worse than a whore and he will prove it. Oh, how could you take vengeance, and then leave us here to bear the brunt of the ill will you woke?"

The agitation of her thoughts rose and with it the tempo of her rocking. Little Solina had not ceased wailing the whole time and now, sensing her mother's upset, cried even harder.

"Epiny, please! I took no vengeance! That was not me. No matter what they had done to me, they were still the King's soldiers, the men of my own regiment. I would not slaughter them like that. I cannot describe what it was like for me. I witnessed how they were murdered, with no chance to defend themselves. I would not massacre our soldiers like that, the innocent alongside the guilty. I would not choose to see anyone die like that! Surely you know me that well."

"I thought I did," she said in a low voice. "Hush, child, hush. Please hush!" The cries of her baby were jarring to her, agitating her in a way almost beyond my understanding. I knew she was not asleep, but in the light trance of a medium.

"Be calm, Epiny. Be calm for your child's sake, and for me. Stay with me. Stay." I breathed calmness at her. "Think of a good time. Think of—" I scrabbled through my knowledge of her, trying desperately to find a calm and happy memory for her. Nothing came to mind. Everywhere Epiny was, turmoil seemed to follow her. "Think of that first evening when we played Towsers on the floor of the drawing room in your father's home. The first night you spent any time with Spink. Think about that; hold to the good memories."

A wave of sadness washed through her, dulling her agitation. Her rocking slowed. "Will I ever live in such a house, so comfortably, again?" she asked me plaintively. "Will I ever be free of counting each slice of bread, of having to say to my household, 'That is enough now, you've had your share, no matter what your belly says'? Oh, hush, baby, please hush. Sleep for a little while. Please let me rest."

"Are things so difficult now?"

"Difficult? 'Difficult' is a word that only applies where there is hope. Nevare, we are starving. Unless the lands warm soon and the fear ceases to keep our men from hunting, we will all die. Yesterday, Amzil went walking outside the fort and came back with some wild greens for us. Oh, they tasted so wonderful, but there were not much of them. Gettys is shattered, Nevare." She gave a small, bitter laugh. "We missed our cemetery soldier after that attack. No one had thought to do as you had done, and dig extra graves for the winter or stockpile lumber for coffins. Folk used to say you were morbid, waiting for us to die. After the fires, there were huge arguments over whether it was more important to build coffins for the dead or use whatever wood we could salvage to keep warm. The ground was too frozen to dig graves; the bodies had to be stored. I've heard it said there is a wall of coffins out at the cemetery now; the thaws have softened the ground somewhat, but fear and discouragement boil out of the forest there like a poisonous spring. It is hard to get anyone to work there and harder still to find someone who works hard enough to get anything done."

I thought of Kesey and Ebrooks and pitied them both. I was sure that particular duty had fallen on them.

"We are in a bad way for any sort of supplies. The Speck seemed to know exactly where to strike; they burned the warehouses, and the barns and the stables, and so many homes! Those who stayed have had to crowd in together as best they might. Many others chose to flee when the fear came back. They could not tolerate it, not even with the Gettys Tonic. Not just families, but soldiers deserted by the dozen. I've no idea what became of them; I expect a lot of them simply lay down in the cold and snow and died."

"Epiny, Epiny, I am so sorry." As I listened to her thoughts wander, it seemed very unlike the usual meandering of her previous prattling. There was nothing fun or gossipy about her words; it was a recounting of an endless circle of despair. I could not think what else to ask her. Did I want to know the details of how badly Gettys was damaged? No, I decided. Belatedly, I wished she had not told me where Spink had hidden them, for whatever was in my mind might be ferreted out by Soldier's Boy.

"The despair and the fear are the worst part, Nevare. They come down thicker than ever before. Even the children talk of death and dying as an escape from it. There had been problems with suicide among the forced workers, as I'm sure you know, but not like it is now. Every day, they find prisoners who have hanged themselves. Some of the guards laugh and say it is for the best as we can scarcely feed them, but my heart goes out to them. I have less sympathy for the murderers and rapists who leave in such a way, but some of those fellows were little more than boys when they were sent east, and some for no more than stealing a silk pocket handkerchief!

"I fear I will die here, Nevare. I will tell you true, what I dare not say to Spink. I fear I will die by my own hand!" She took a shuddering breath. If I'd had a heart of my own, it would have stood still with horror. She lifted a slow hand to pat her baby's back. Little Solina's wails were subsiding, more from weariness than because she was comforted. "She is what holds me here," Epiny said in a soft whisper. "I no longer live for any joy I find in life, or for love of my husband. I live only because I know if I killed myself, her misery would be even deeper than it is. Poor little bird. I can tell when the sorrow and discouragement wash through her. Sometimes I find her in her crib, staring at the wall not even crying. That isn't natural for a baby, Nevare. I wonder that she can feel such things and still live. She does not eat well or sleep soundly. No wonder so many babies born at Gettys die before their first year is past. They have no will to live." Her voice faded away. What followed was a shamed whisper. "Last night I asked Spink to desert. I told him that as soon as the roads were less muddy, we could all run away. Anywhere would do. There could not be a worse place to live; there could not be a worse life for us than this one."

"What did he say?" The words dragged out of me unwillingly. I was stunned by her words. More shocking still was my tiny hope that Spink would do as she had suggested.

"Nothing," she said sorrowfully. "Nothing at all. He had just come home for the evening meal. Not that there was enough food to call it a meal. He did not even eat his share of it. He just put his coat on and went out again. I think he went to join the work crews. They went out for the first time yesterday. They no longer care if they are hungry or cold. The prisoners were rousted to go out, but they did not need to be forced. Half our soldiers marched out there with them. I don't know what is going on, Nevare. But Spink didn't come home last night, and I don't know if he will ever come back. Neither Amzil nor I dared to go out to look for him. Gettys has become a dangerous place for a woman or a child alone on the streets. All is darkness here, even in brightest daylight. I believe that I will die here, one way or another. I have come to understand Amzil's fear; the worst would be to lie dying and know that your baby was alive and helpless. That would be the worst."

A wordless horror rose in me. "Epiny. Do not do anything desperate. Please. Just—just live on. A day at a time, a night at a time. Things will get better."

I had no basis for telling her that things would get better. I feared, as she did, that things could only get worse for her and for everyone at Gettys. Still, I lied bravely. "The supply wagons always start to run again in spring. They are probably already on their way. Hold out a little while longer. Have faith in Spink and believe in yourself. You are brave and strong, the bravest and strongest woman I've ever met. Don't give up now."

Her thought was strained as if she forced herself to form it. "I've told you, Nevare. I cannot give up. Not while Solina lives and needs me."

"And she will live. She will. And so will you." I hesitated and then plunged on. "As soon as the roads dry out, Epiny, as soon as they are passable, you must take your horse and cart and go back to Old Thares. If you tell Spink what you've told me, he'll understand. Leave Gettys. Go to your father. Take refuge there until the regiment is moved to a better assignment."

"Flee like the coward I am," she said in a low voice. "Go back to live at ease on my father's wealth, listening to my mother tell me what a fool I was to marry a new noble's son. Live with her denigrating Solina. No, Nevare. Dying would be easier than that. But I shall do neither. I pledged my life to Spink when we wed, and here I shall stay, and do the best I can."

"But you urged him to flee."

"And that was wrong. And if—when he comes back, I will tell him I know it was wrong, and beg his pardon. No. I will stay here with him, come what may." She sighed heavily.

The babe on her breast was finally asleep, but she scarcely dared move for fear of awakening her again. Her breathing deepened and our connection became less tenuous. Instead of merely feeling the sensations she felt, the rocking chair, her aching back, the warmth of the small fire, her hunger, and the weight of the baby against her, I found myself holding both her hands and looking at her. The aspect that she presented to me was very young and plain; she saw herself, I suspected, as childish and powerless to change her situation. Her lips were chapped and her hair fuzzing out of her braids. I gripped her hands firmly and tried to put my heart in my words. "Epiny, you are brave and strong. When you share that with Spink, who is brave and strong himself, you anchor each other. Don't give up. You are right. I was wrong to tell you to flee to your father. Whatever becomes of you, you must face it together."

She looked deep into my eyes. "I will stay here. To the end, whatever it may be, I will stay here. I ask only this of you, Nevare. Dream-walk to my father. Tell him of what has befallen us. Then come back to me, to tell me that he has said he will send help to us. Please, Nevare. Can you do that?"

"I don't know." Her request staggered me. Did I know my uncle well enough to attempt such a thing? It had always been easy to dream-walk to Epiny. Her abilities as a medium left her sleeping mind open to my intrusions. My close bond with my sister Yaril had let me contact her, but I wasn't sure how much she believed her "dreams" of me. My uncle? I respected him, yes, and loved him for all he had done for me. But to enter his sleeping mind and speak to him? "I'll try," I said, though my heart misgave me. I doubted that I had much time, and I had desperately wished to see Yaril, to know if she was all right. It was a hellish choice; to use my time trying to reach my uncle and then return to Epiny to give her some hope, or to find out how my younger sister was faring as she faced an arranged marriage in a household run by my deranged father. "I'll try. I'll try right now," I told her, and let go of her hands.

Find my uncle. Find Sefert Burvelle, Lord Burvelle of the West. He was the heir son of the old line of my family, the holder of the family mansion and the estates in and near Old Thares. My father had been the second son, his soldier-brother. When my father had served his king well in the wars with the Plainsmen, the King had elevated him to the status of a lord with a small grant of land, making him one of his "new nobles." That had not suited my uncle's wife. Lady Daraleen Burvelle felt that one Lord and one Lady Burvelle were quite enough, and that my father had moved above his proper position in life. That had prompted her starchy welcome of me when I came to attend the Cavalla Academy in Old Thares. She blamed me because her daughter Epiny had met and fallen in love with another "new noble" son and a poor one at that. When Epiny had scandalized her by running off with Spink, that had been the final straw. Although my uncle still thought warmly of me, my aunt regarded me as the one who had ruined her chances to engineer a well-placed match for Epiny at court.

I tried to push my dislike of my aunt aside. It was clouding my memories of my uncle. I did not want to focus on her so much that I accidentally wandered into her dream. I tried to find quiet within my soul, to ignore the nagging sense that my time to dream-walk was ticking away, and to focus instead on my memories of my uncle. I summoned up the sensory memories that linked me to him: the smell of his tobacco, the taste of his brandy, the warmth and casual comfort of his study in Old Thares. I focused on the warm clasp of his hand on mine whenever he greeted me, and the sound of his voice as he said my name.

"Well, there you are, Nevare. And how have you been? Will you join me in a game of Towsers?"

I had to smile, knowing how much he detested the inane game that Epiny and his younger daughter Purissa so often trapped him into playing. In his dream, his daughters were in the room with him, cards in hand, but the moment I entered his dream, they faded into shadows in the background. They went on playing, slapping down their cards and leaping up to shout wildly when they'd made a point, but the actions and the sounds of their voices became distant and muffled.

"Uncle, I've little time. I'm visiting your dreams to tell you that things are desperate in Gettys. The fort has been attacked by the Specks. Their food stores are nearly depleted and their morale is devastated. Epiny and Spink are doing their best; they have a baby now, a little girl, Solina. But hunger presses them, and the spring rains bring cold and hardship. I know the roads are bad. But Epiny has asked me to reach you this way. I want to tell her that you are sending help to her. Even if it will be weeks before it reaches her, to know that help is on the way will lend her strength. Truly, times are desperate in Gettys."

"Will you have a glass of wine with me, Nevare?" My uncle was smiling at me. Our contact was more tenuous than I'd thought. In the morning, he might remember he'd dreamed of me, or he might recall nothing at all. I suddenly recalled something Epiny had said to me.

"Sir, my journal. My soldier-son journal. Epiny sent it to you. If you've read it, you'll know about this kind of magic. Dream-walking. I'm really here, in your dream, talking to you of real things. Epiny needs your help. Please, Uncle Sefert!"

"That damnable book! I am deeply disappointed in my wife, Nevare, deeply disappointed. Has she no idea how this could smear the Burvelle name? Epiny said not to read it, and I am a man of honor! But my wife made no such promise, and she has been full of folderol and foolish mysticism for too long. She will bare my nephew's derangement, for such it must be! Poor Nevare! Keft was too hard on the boy, too hard, as he now admits to me in his letters. But what am I to do? He drove his son from under his roof, and only the good god knows what became of him. I do not think he should ally himself with the Stiet name, let alone engage his daughter to a boy who is himself a disowned soldier son of a soldier son who was never truly a soldier! What is the advantage in that? I've told him he should send little Yaril to me. I would see her safely into a good match. But I fear his mind is no longer sound; my brother's handwriting looks more like a random trick-ling of ink, and his words wander more than his lines do! Curse the Specks and their dirty plague; I fear it has been the undoing of the Burvelles!"

I'd unsettled him. I suddenly became aware that his back was cold. At the same moment, he felt the draft. He left me, surfac-ing from sleep just enough to pull his blankets back into place. I waited in a limbo of grayness, hoping, but although he slept, he did not dream. "Lord Burvelle!" I cried into the nothingness. "Hear me! Your daughter needs you. She is hungry and cold and oppressed with sadness. Send help to her. Please, say you'll send her help!"

There was no response. A sudden and dangerous idea came to me. Recklessly, I acted on it. The clinging scent of her heavy perfume. The clicking of her heavily ringed hand against her wine goblet at a dinner table. The cold stare of her icy eyes. "Lady Burvelle. Daraleen Burvelle!"

I tumbled into her dream as if a trapdoor had opened under me. Instantly, I wished to be away from it. I had not thought a woman of her years and position would be prone to such salacious fancies. She was entangled with not one virile young man, but two, and from her panting, was fully occupied with the sensations their efforts were waking. I was horrified, scandalized, and embarrassed. "Lady Burvelle! You daughter Epiny is in dire circumstances and has need of your aid! The Specks have raided Gettys and near destroyed it. Do whatever you must to send her help." I barked out the words. My message jolted her from her dream and once more plunged me into a gray netherworld.

I wondered how much time was left to me. My first impulse was to return to Epiny, but I had no good news to give her. I doubted that either her father or mother would heed the messages I had delivered.

It came to me that I might still see Yaril that night and possibly fulfill Epiny's charge to me as well. I fled to my sister and found her effortlessly. The dream I slipped into made no sense to me at all. Yaril was pinning fish to the wall of the parlor, rather like the way she had once collected butterflies. But the fish were alive, slippery and thrashing, so it was a messy and futile undertaking. No sooner had the drawing tacks been put through their tails and fins than they wriggled free of them and fell to the floor. Yet Yaril seemed obsessed with finishing her task.

Even before I spoke, she was aware of me. "Nevare, hold this one, please. I think if you held him, I could pin him down properly and he wouldn't come loose again."

"Why are you doing this?" I asked her in some amusement. Her activity had distracted me completely from the desperation of my visit.

She looked at me as if I were daft. "Well, if I don't, they'll all be on the floor and underfoot all the time. What else should I do? Hold his tail flat to the wall. That's it! There!" She pushed another drawing tack into the fish's tail and then stepped back to admire the effect.

"Yaril," I said quietly as she began to choose another fish from the floor. "Do you know that you're asleep and dreaming this?"

"How would you know?" she asked me in a tolerant fashion. "Oh, look, let's have that handsome bluegill next."

"I would know because I'm using Speck magic to visit you in your dreams. Because I have something important to tell you, and many things to ask you."

"Ask away, so long as you hold the fish for me. Here. Mind, now! He's a slippery one."

"I'd rather tell first," I said as I took the flapping fish from her hands. I tried to keep my voice calm and my tone light. I didn't want to startle her out of her dream. "The first thing is that you must remember this dream in the morning, and you must believe that you dreamed true."

"Oh, I always remember my dreams. You should know that. Don't you remember how Papa sent me from the breakfast table for talking about my dreams, and you came afterward to comfort me? And to bring me a cold pastry to eat."

"I do remember that. Good. So you will remember what I tell you. It's important. I have bad news but you must take it calmly. Otherwise, you'll waken yourself and we won't have any time to talk."

"Oh, drat! That's my last tack, and I need two more."

"Here are some more." I reached into my pocket, wished for tacks to be there, and drew out a handful of them. "You pin him while I talk. Yaril, it's about our cousin Epiny. She's at Gettys with her husband, Spink."

"I haven't heard from her in ages! I expect I shan't until the post riders can get through the snow again. They say it was deep this year in the foothills." She made a little sound of effort as she pushed the tacks through the tail and into the wall. I tried not to focus on it. If I thought too much about my dainty little sister tacking living creatures to the walls of the drawing room, it would bother me, and I was sure she'd be aware of it. Aware enough to perhaps awaken herself. She stooped to pick up another fish from the floor.

"Yes, the snow was very deep. It has blocked the roads between Gettys and the west. That is why I need you to send a letter to our uncle Sefert in Old Thares. Or perhaps ask our father to intervene directly, if you think you can persuade him to do so.

It has been a hard winter in Gettys, and both Epiny and Spink are in dire circumstances." I took a deep, slow breath, willing calmness toward her. "The citadel at Gettys was attacked by the Specks, Yaril. They came by night, with fire and arrows and swords. Much of Gettys was burned, and many soldiers killed. Epiny and Spink and their infant came through unscathed, but in the days since then, the cold and the lack of food have been a great hardship."

She was staring at me. The fish slowly waved its tail. "Cannot they simply cut firewood and stay warm that way?"

"It is difficult for them to go into the forest. A magic spell makes them fear to go there."

"Wait. You say they have a baby now?"

"Yes. And that makes it even more difficult for them."

She nodded slowly, the fish in her hands forgotten. "What should I do?"

Patience, I counseled myself. Patience. "Write to Uncle Sefert. Say that you've had word of the Speck attack and their harsh conditions. You don't have to say how you know. Just tell him that he must urge that food and other supplies be immediately sent to Gettys. Even if he has to make such arrangements himself, it must be done. And if you think our father will act on it, recommend to him that he immediately send off whatever supplies he can."

"Father is not well." The fish in her hands stopped wriggling. It became a rag doll and she held it to her cheek now, seeming to take comfort from it. "Things are strange here, Nevare. You should come home and help me. I don't know what to do!"

I sensed her rising emotion. In the dream, I opened my arms and she fled into them. I held her tightly. I was a tall, strong young cadet, golden-haired and fit. That was the Nevare she needed now, and she made me take that form; she wanted me to be the hero who would come to rescue her.

"My dear, I will do what I can." I did not say that it would be nothing. "What is your situation?"

"Father is ... changed. He is healthier in body, though still he walks with a stick. He ... sometimes he seems to know that Mother and Rosse and Elisi are dead. But sometimes he asks questions about them, or speaks as if he has just seen them. I am a coward, Nevare. I don't contradict him. I let him be. He speaks of you, too, with pride. He says you have gone for a soldier, and soon will come home covered in glory. That is what he always says of you, 'covered in glory.' It is comforting to hear him speak well of you. I don't remind him that he sent you away in disgrace. It is easier, so."

"Covered in glory," I repeated softly. My father's dream for me. My dream for myself, not so long ago. For a moment, my mind wandered. The old dreams stung now but still I touched them and longed after them.

"Nevare," Yaril said, speaking against my chest. "You are really here, aren't you?"

"It's magic, Yaril. I'm here in your dream, and as real as I can be in a dream. My body is far from you, but my heart is here."

"Oh, Nevare." She held tighter to me. "Stay here. Stay here and help me, even if you must be a ghost who only comes into my dreams at night. I am so alone and adrift. And Caulder's uncle frightens me."

My heart sank. Of all my betrayals of my own people, this was bitterest and most shameful to me. My little sister was threatened, and I could do nothing. Coward that I was, I wanted to know no more. I forced the words out woodenly. "What does he do, Yaril, that frightens you?"

"He is so strange, Nevare. He and Caulder have stayed so long here, far past the length of a proper visit. I fear for my reputation among the neighbors, for all know that Father is not the man he used to be, and I can claim no proper chaperone in this household of men. Caulder feels it keenly and is humiliated. Over and over he has urged his uncle to leave. He has found some courage, he says, and wishes to go back to his father and demand that his father be the one to make an offer for my hand. He had a great quarrel with his uncle over this. His uncle was most cruel, reminding Caulder that his father had disowned him, and saying a great many things to put Caulder in his own debt. He says that he is as Caulder's father now, and has made the offer, and he sees nothing improper in staying so long as guests in the home that Caulder will eventually inherit."

These were words that stuck in me like a knife. Caulder Stiet would inherit the estates of the Burvelles of the East. Their firstborn son would be Lord Burvelle of the East, if my father petitioned the King to make it so. But he would be a Stiet by his blood. For a moment, anger seethed in me. My father could have elevated me to be his heir son, if he had chosen to do so. Many desperate nobles had petitioned the priests to move a soldier son up to the status of heir. But before my anger could turn to greater bitterness, Yaril's words caught me again.

"I overheard other words he said. He told Caulder not to be a fool, that they must not leave until he had deciphered the map you sent them. Time and again, he has asked a hundred questions, of me, of the hired men, of virtually anyone who can speak, asking about a ridgeline or a dried-up watercourse. He studies and studies the map you sent him, but will not allow anyone else to see it to interpret it for him. He is obsessed with finding the place where you picked up the rock you gave Caulder. I have shown him all the other rocks you had gathered—you thought they had been thrown out, didn't you, but I saved them. I thought they were quite interesting, but he pronounced them all just rubbish and pebbles and took no interest in them."

I recalled the map I had sent him. I had dashed it off in a matter of moments, from memory, giving little thought to accuracy or even scale. At the time I had thought to do nothing more than send him a token map in order to put an end to his nagging correspondence. "Sergeant Duril could look at the map and recognize the area I drew. Tell him to show it to Duril."

"The sergeant has offered, several times, to look at it for him, but Caulder's uncle always declines. Sergeant Duril has become quite frustrated with the man, for he says he has made him waste time riding aimlessly about when he should have been tending to the concerns of the estate."

"Duril's a good man. Keep him by you, Yaril, as close as you can. And if at any time you feel you are in danger from anyone, go to Duril and tell him."

I had no warning. Even if I had, perhaps I could not have chosen better words to end on. With a sudden tug, I felt my awareness pulled loose from Yaril's. Soldier's Boy was calling me back. "Not yet!" I shouted at him. "It's not fair! I'm not finished."

A most peculiar thing happened. Suddenly my father, eyes empty, was sitting up in his bed, his hands clutching mine. "Nevare? Nevare? Where are you, boy, where are you? Do you need my help? Son, where are you?"

He was a glimpse of a nightmare to me. He was pale and aged, and the magic had eaten holes in him, like a piece of fruit spoiled by worms. I could see, in this dimension, how it had attacked him, body and heart and mind. He'd caught it from me, I suddenly knew. It had infected me, and I'd passed it on to him. And just like Buel Hitch, it had reduced him to doing its will.

"Father!" I shouted at him. "Be strong. Protect Yaril!"

Then I was torn loose again.

As sudden as blinking, I was back in Soldier's Boy's body. This time, the wall he had held between us was gone. I was once more a party to his thoughts and emotions. It was like being plunged into a hurricane. Anger, despair, humiliation, and defeat battered him and thus me. The strength of his emotions was such that it was some time before I became aware of my physical surroundings.

Night was full around us and chill. Dew had settled on his skin. Those cold drops contrasted harshly with the hot tears that flowed down his face. He curled forward over his belly and put his face in his hands and wept like a scolded child. I thought he had seen what the magic had done to my father, and felt as horrified by it as I had. There was a strange comfort for me in that he wept. If I'd had the body under my control, I'd have done the same. "It wasn't really him, doing that to me," I told myself hesitantly. "The magic had to tear all support away from me, to make me come to where it wanted me to be. I don't have to blame him. I don't have to hate him."

"I knew that!" Soldier's Boy spoke disdainfully. "I never hated him or blamed him. I could see that much clearly; I'm surprised that you could not."

"Then what is it?" I asked at last, unwillingly. The harshness of whatever assailed him made me pity him; I felt sorry for myself in a way I never had before. No man should be as pitifully miserable as he was. He did not immediately answer me. His sorrow choked him. A very long time seemed to pass. The wind blew in the branches overhead. In the distance, I heard someone call into the night, "Great One, where are you?" Someone called something else in reply. Soldier's Boy made no response. His harsh breathing filled my ears as he got his sobs under control. I waited.

After a time, he sat up slowly. "We've failed her," he said quietly. "Yesterday the workers came again to the road's end. They have begun to clear away the winter debris and repair the last of the damage you did. Soon enough, the axes and saws will begin to bite their way through the ancient forest. The workers are no longer drugged. You know the best way to combat fear, Nevare? With hatred. I woke hatred in the intruders, and their hatred of us is now stronger than Kinrove's fear spell. They will chew through the trees like worker ants. They will cut our forest and drive straight into the mountains and beyond. They are resolved to find us, and when they do, they intend to kill us all."

"Just as you intended to do to them," I reminded him.

"Yes." He took a deep breath and sat up, squaring his shoulders. "Yes."

CHAPTER TWENTY-FOUR

RESOLUTIONS

It was dark and Soldier's Boy felt stiff from sitting on the cold rock by the stream. It took him some time to lever himself to his feet, and then he groaned as he straightened his back. He kneaded the earth with his feet as if he were a cat, trying to limber up his reluctant body. He walked for a short way, seeing the trees only as blacker pillars in a less dense darkness. We could see where the village was; a dim glow came from the lighted windows on the hillside above us, but it was not sufficient to light the path. Blundering haplessly, he soaked his feet twice before he found the bridge and crossed the stream.

At the bottom of the hill, he suddenly felt overwhelmed by dark, cold, and sorrow. He remembered his feeders calling for him earlier, and wished he had responded. He wanted to call for someone to come with a lantern and guide him home, and then despised himself for even thinking of it. He forced himself to trudge up the hill. In the dark, he could not find the trodden path. Twice he stumbled, and once he went to his knees. He staggered back to his feet, his teeth clenched on his silence.

One of his feeders suddenly appeared on the brow of the rise with a torch. "Great One! Is that you?" Before he could respond, the feeder shouted out, "I see him! He's here! Come quickly!"

In moments they surrounded him. One carried a torch. Two others took him by the arms and tried to help him along. He shook them off. "I do not need assistance. I'd prefer to be alone."

"Yes, Great One," they responded, and stepped back from him. But the man with the torch walked before him, lighting his way, and the other two followed him, ready at any moment to spring to his aid if he needed them.

Once in the lodge, he perceived that in his absence no one had gone to bed. Instead, a hot sweet drink was simmering by the hearth beside a platter of fried dough drizzled with honey. No one asked if he was hungry or thirsty. It was their assumption. The moment he sat down by the fire, someone whisked his shoes off his feet and replaced them with dry, warm socks. A blanket, warmed by the fire, was draped around his shoulders. He realized then he was shuddering with cold and gripped it gratefully around himself. Olikea poured the warm drink into a mug and put it carefully into his hands. Her words were not as caring as her actions.

"The night before we begin to travel, I have a hundred tasks to organize and you walk off into the darkness and lose yourself. If you cannot be helpful, at least do not be a hindrance!" Her eyes were still red and swollen from her earlier weeping. Her voice was hoarse with it, but none of her pain showed in her tone. It was purely the waspishness of a woman irritated beyond her limits. No one but Olikea would have dared speak to him like that. The other feeders had grown accustomed to how bold she was with him. And he almost welcomed her anger following her weeks of lassitude.

"I'm cold," he said, as if somehow that excused him. "And hungry. Just bring me food."

I do not think he intended to sound so harsh. Perhaps if he had known how close she was to breaking, he would have chosen his words differently. But spoken, there was no calling the words back. Olikea seemed to swell with her anger like an affronted cat, and then her own words burst from her in a torrent.

"*You* are cold? *You* are hungry? And what of my son, whose delight it was to serve you? Do you think he is warm right now, and comfortable and well fed? But unlike you, who make the choice to wander off into the night and chill yourself, Likari dances because he must."

She paused for breath. Soldier's Boy was silent. He continued to stare straight ahead, the warm blanket around his shoulders, the hot mug in his hands. I sensed something building in him, but Olikea perhaps thought that he ignored her.

"You have forgotten him!" she suddenly shrieked. "You said you would get him back. You said you would do something, that you would destroy all of Gettys so that Kinrove would give my son back to his kin-clan. He served you as well as a boy of his years could! He spoke of you with pride—no! He spoke of you with *love*! And you were the one who said that the dance must start again to protect the ancestor trees. You knew it was our turn for the dancers to be wrenched from our homes and families. But you didn't care. Because we are not really your kin-clan, are we? We are just the people who feed you and clothe you and see to all your needs. You do not care what we suffer! You do not lie awake at night and think of Likari's poor little feet, dancing, dancing, always dancing! You do not wonder if he is cold but so enspelled that he does not know how his skin chaps and his lips split and bleed. You do not wonder if he is thin, if he coughs when he rests. You do not wonder how he is treated during his brief rest periods." She sank down onto her haunches and rocked herself back and forth as she continued to fling accusations at him, her hands over her eyes.

"Now you will eat and drink and everyone will tend you and you will sleep well tonight, while the rest of us work to make ready for tomorrow's departure. But what of Likari? Do you know what he must do? He must dance, dance, dance, all the way back to the western side of the mountains. Nor does he sleep warm and comfortable tonight to prepare for the journey. The dancers of Kinrove dance, on and on and on. Dancing themselves to death. Just as my mother did."

Still, Soldier's Boy made no response. He did not move toward her or even look at her directly. Instead, he stared past her, as if looking at someone else. From the corner of his eye, I saw her look at him. Something seemed to go out of her. Anger had perhaps sustained her. But anger is a passion that is hard to maintain when the object of one's anger is immune to it. She spoke in a low voice, bitterly. "Go on, drink. Eat. Then sleep. All will be done for you, who do nothing for us. Tomorrow we must rise and begin the journey."

He seemed for the moment to obey her. He lifted the mug to his mouth and drained it dry. Then, heedless of its fate, he let it fall to the floor. He ignored the food that was offered to him as one of his other feeders hastily picked up the fallen cup. Instead, he stood, letting the blanket fall to the floor. Without a word, he turned away from them all. He walked to the bed, lay down on it, and pulled the covers up over himself. He closed his eyes and was still. I was probably the only one who knew that although he retreated deeply into himself, he did not sleep.

There was a stillness to Soldier's Boy that spoke of something dead or dying. I could not bear to consider it too deeply. Just as isolated as he was, I listened instead to the quiet bustle within the lodge. Olikea had spoken truly. Searching for him had interrupted the work of the feeders, and now they toiled into the night, making all ready for the morning's journey. Everything that would not be taken with them was carefully cleaned and packed for the summer's storage. Cedar shavings were tucked in among winter blankets and furs before they were packed away in cedar chests. Pots were scrubbed and hung on hooks, dishes were put away, and all food was carefully packed up for the journey. Tomorrow they would break their fasts with a simple meal before beginning the long walk back to their summer grounds. There would be no quick-walking tomorrow. Magic such as that was used only in necessity. Tomorrow all the People would begin their journeys that would converge on their hidden passage through the mountains and back to the west side of the mountains.

Within an hour, the last of the chores were done. The other feeders retired, some to their own lodges, doubtless to finish their own preparations there, and three to pallets at the end of the lodge. Olikea came, by habit I think, to Soldier's Boy's bed. She sat down on the edge of it and bent down to loosen her shoes. Then she stood up and dragged her woolen shift off over her head. She moved silently and wearily. When she lifted the edge of the blankets and got into the bed, she took exaggerated care that no part of her body should so much as brush against his. She faced away from me, and from her breathing, I knew she was no closer to sleep than Soldier's Boy was. I hoped with the strength of a prayer that one of them would have the sense to touch the other. I believed that was all it would take to break down the barrier rising between them. They did not have to be in love or even to be lovers tonight. I believed that if one so much as reached out to the other, they could have found each other and recognized the other's misery and loneliness. There would have been some comfort, I think, in that. Instead, Olikea stared unsleeping into the darkened lodge, and Soldier's Boy, just as restive, remained perfectly still, staring into the darkness inside his own eyelids. And I, I was the trapped witness to how pain could make two people incapable of giving each other even the smallest measure of comfort. As much as I disliked Soldier's Boy and distrusted Olikea, that night I pitied both of them. Life had not dealt fairly with any of us.

No one rose early. Everyone had worked too late the night before. But eventually the others began to stir. Olikea rose before Soldier's Boy moved and began the final packing up while other feeders came and went, preparing food and drink for Soldier's Boy's breakfast and laying out his clothing for the day. I was aware of all this from behind his closed eyelids. The feeders chatted of inconsequential things, reminded one another to close the trunks tightly, and sent someone to be sure that there would be both firewood and kindling waiting by the door when they returned in the autumn. They nudged one another along, apparently eager to leave soon in the hopes of catching up with the rest of the kin-clan so that they might travel through the pass as a group. Someone said that Kinrove and his feeders, clan, and dancers had already departed ten days ago. Someone else grumbled that Kinrove and his dancers would have emptied the fish traps and eaten the best of whatever grew along the route.

And Olikea came to wake Soldier's Boy. "It is time to be up! We must feed you and get you dressed, and pack or store all the bedding before we go. Here is a cup of hot tea for you. Are you waking up?"

She spoke in an absolutely neutral voice. If I had not witnessed their quarrel the night before, I would have believed that all was amicable, even affectionate, between them. The unsleeping Soldier's Boy opened his eyes and slowly sat up in bed. As he took the cup of steaming tea from Olikea, I saw several of the feeders exchange relieved glances. The storm was over. All would be well again. He drank from the cup and then held it, idly watching the steam rise.

"We must be on our way soon," Olikea reminded him.

"So you must," he agreed. He looked over at Sempayli. "You should leave now. I wish you to take my horse and not wait for us. See that he gets grazing along the way, and when you reach our place on the other side of the mountains, find him a sunny area with good grass for him to eat. The winter has been hard on him."

"You wish me to leave right away?" The man looked puzzled.

"I do."

"Very well." Obviously, there was no quibbling with a Great Man. He rose and walked out of the lodge, pausing only to hoist his personal pack to his shoulder.

When he was out of sight, Olikea gave a small sigh. "Well. I had thought the horse could carry some of our things. But we shall manage. It is time for you to get out of your bed, so we can finish storing the bedding and be on our way. We are already late leaving."

He pursed his lips, the Speck signal for denial. "No. I won't be going with you."

One of his feeders sighed aloud. Olikea looked at him for a moment in disbelief. Then, as if humoring a child, she said, "We will talk about it as we walk. But we must have your blankets to pack or store."

"I mean it," he said mildly. There was no anger in his voice, only a terrible tiredness and resignation. "I am not going with the People. It is as you said last night. I am useless to you, only a burden.

I can think of no way to save Likari. All night long I have pondered it, and still there is no answer. Kinrove maintains his magical barrier around his encampment; I cannot pass it without his consent. He wields more magic than I do; I cannot turn magic against him. I cannot even get close enough to him to try to kill him. I cannot duplicate what Dasie did; Kinrove will never be caught in such a way again. My quest to end the need for the dance failed; no, worse than failed, it made even the dance ineffective. I have failed all of you. I have failed the magic. I have failed Lisana. You would be wisest to go quickly now, leaving me here, and make haste to catch up with our kin-clan. Tell Jodoli that I commend you to his care. Follow him across the mountains to the summer grounds."

Olikea narrowed her eyes at him. "You sent Sempayli away first so he wouldn't argue with you, didn't you?" Soldier's Boy gave her a small smile. Olikea responded with an exasperated sigh. She spoke bitterly. "Enough of this sulkiness. We cannot leave you and we should be on our way."

But even as she spoke, one of the feeders glanced at the others, and then quietly slipped out of the door. After a moment, a second one followed her. Soldier's Boy glanced after them and then back at Olikea. "I'm not going. You should leave."

She had been holding her laden pack. Now she flung it down angrily. "And what are you going to do if I leave you here? You know I can't do that!"

"You can and you should. Leave now." He spoke to the sole remaining feeder. The man seemed relieved to receive such a direct command. He nodded gravely and departed. Soldier's Boy swung his gaze to Olikea. "You, too. Go."

She stood silent for a time. Her arms hung limply at her sides. Her eyes wandered over his still face, seeking entry to his thoughts. Finally she just asked him in a quiet, dull voice, "Why? Why are you doing this now? Why are you doing this to me? If I leave without you, they will say I have abandoned my Great One and shamed my kin-clan."

He spoke simply. "Tell them I am not a Great One. Tell them that the intruder half of me always held me back from what I should have been. All I have tried to do has ended in half failure. I stopped the Spindle of the Plainspeople, but I could not cast it down. I slowed the intrusion into the forest, but the intruder half of me told the Gernians how to get around Kinrove's magic. Yes. That is true!" he replied to Olikea's shocked expression. "When I lived among the intruders, I was the one who said to them, 'Drug your senses in order to dull them and resist the fear.' It is my fault that they were able to begin cutting our ancestor trees again. Every other Great One I have spoken to assures me that I am supposed to be the one who can turn the intruders back. But even when I have done what the magic told me to do, it had no effect. I can only assume that something my Gernian half did canceled my magic. Even my raid on their settlement was only half a success, and my failure to drive them out has spurred them to greater hatred of us than ever. Do you see what I am telling you, Olikea? I am not a Great One who can help the People. I am flawed, like an intruder's gun that explodes in your hands. When I seek to help the People, I do as much harm as good. It is because of my divided nature. Yet I love the People. So, to serve them, I must cast myself out from them. You must go to your summer lands. I do not know what will befall the People there, not this year or in the years to come. But I do know that my presence can only make it worse. And so I remove myself."

"And what of Likari?" she burst out when he paused for breath. "What of your promise to save him? I believed you! Not once, but several times you said you would find a way to save him. What about that promise?"

He looked down and spoke reluctantly but clearly. "I must break it. Not because I want to, but because I do not know how to keep it."

For a long moment she was silent. Then an expression of disgust formed on her face. "Oh, yes," she said bitterly. "Now I believe you. It is not the way of the People to break promises, but for the intruders, it is their constant custom." She pursed her lips and then expelled air loudly in an exaggerated expression of denial. "You are definitely not a Great One to say such a thing. You are right. You are not even of the People, and yes, I will leave you now. I will go to my kin-clan and tell them what you have said. They will think me foolish and faithless. But I will not care what

they think. Because now I must go and do for myself what I so
foolishly hoped and waited for you to do for me. Oh, I am a faithless and heartless mother! The very first day he was summoned, I
should have run after him, rather than having faith in your magic.
I myself will go to Kinrove. I do not know how I will get Likari
back, but I will. I will not stop trying until Likari is free again.
That is the promise I make to myself."

She stooped and picked up the pack she had dropped. As she
walked toward the door, she was slinging it over her shoulders.
By the time she reached the door she had it on and she walked
away from the lodge without another backward glance. He was
alone. He heard faint voices lifted in a query and a brief response
from Olikea. The conversation went on, but it dwindled in the
distance as they walked away from him, out of sight of Lisana's old
lodge, and out of earshot as well. He sat on the bed, his blankets
muddled around him. On the hearth fire, the forgotten kettle with
his breakfast in it muttered to itself beneath its tight lid. He heard
a squirrel chatter outside, and then the warning cry of a jay assert-
ing his territorial right. The birds would already be investigating
the quiet lodges to see what had been left behind. It was a good
indicator that no one else remained in the village.

Slowly he got out of bed. He walked to the hearth and took
the simmering kettle off it. He looked inside. An overcooked stew
of vegetables, squirrel meat, and a few greens was in the bottom.
He found a long-handled cooking spoon and ate directly from the
pot, blowing on each bite to keep from scalding himself. It was
good. Despite all else, the food was very good and he let himself enjoy it, knowing that it was the last meal that someone else
would prepare for him.

Belly full, he went back to his bed and cast himself down on
it. As if it were a great relief to be alone, he relaxed and found
sleep almost immediately. Hours passed. I was suspended inside
him, wondering what his intentions were. It was late afternoon
before he stirred again.

He finished the squirrel stew and made tea. He drank one cup
of it, then refilled his mug and carried it outside. Neither Soldier's
Boy nor I was surprised when we heard a heavy bird settle into

the branches overhead. He sipped his tea and looked around at the deserted village. After a time, the big croaker bird dropped down to the ground and regarded us with shining eyes. He waddled over to inspect a discarded rag, turned and tossed it to be sure nothing edible was there, and then preened his wing pinions. When he was finished, he turned his gaze back to me. "Well?" Orandula asked. "Did you forget to migrate?"

"Leave me alone," Soldier's Boy warned him.

"Everyone already did that," the bird-god pointed out. "I can't see that it solved anything for you."

"What do you care?" Soldier's Boy asked harshly.

"I care that debts to me be paid. You owe me. A life or a death. Remember?"

"You took Likari already," Soldier's Boy accused him.

"I took Likari? Not I. Besides, if I had taken him, then I would have 'taken' him. Not at all the same as you giving him to me to pay your debt. No, you still owe me."

"That isn't my debt," he said fiercely.

The croaker bird turned his head and regarded him strangely for a moment. Then he cawed out a harsh laugh. "Perhaps not. But as you are both encased in the same flesh, I do not see how that matters to me. And I wish to be paid."

"Then kill him and take his life as payment. Or his death, however you want to speak of it. It's all the same to me. If he were gone, perhaps I could think clearly." Soldier's Boy drank the last of his tea. "Perhaps if you killed him, I could truly be one of the People, even if I could not save them from the intruders."

"Kill him and spare you?" The bird cocked his head the other way. "An intriguing idea. But not very practical."

Soldier's Boy moved swiftly, snapping the empty mug toward the bird's head. The croaker bird dodged, but the cup still hit him, a solid jolt that dislodged a puff of feathers and won an angry squawk from the creature. He gave two hops, then lifted off into heavy flight. As he gained altitude, he cawed down, "You will both pay for that!"

"I don't care!" Soldier's Boy shouted after him. He walked purposefully back to the lodge and directly to the cedar chest where Likari's things were stored. He opened it and rummaged through them roughly until he found the sling. He took it and then left the lodge, not even bothering to shut the trunk. "Next time, I'll kill him," he vowed aloud.

"I don't think you can kill a god," I said into his mind.

"That doesn't mean it isn't worth trying," he muttered to himself.

"What did Lisana say to you?" I asked him abruptly. "What changed everything?"

"I told you. I woke the hatred of the Gernians, and their hatred is now stronger than their fear. Daily the work crews go to the road. They have almost repaired all the damage you did. They sharpen their axes already. Soon trees will be falling. In time, Lisana will fall. Even if I died tonight and they put me in a tree, we would have perhaps a year of this world's time together before we both died."

"There is no afterlife for a Speck without a tree?"

He shook his head impatiently, as if he could toss me and my foolish questions out of his mind by doing so. "There is. But not what we could share if we were both in trees." He was making his way down the path toward the stream as he spoke. It felt strange to him to be walking along in the daylight, all alone. All the People had departed, and the not-silence of the living forest had flowed back in to take their place.

I grasped what he told me without any further explanation. "Your spirit would go on, but without the sensations of a body. And Lisana would be somewhere else. What you want is to live on, where she is, with the illusion of being in that world corporally."

"I wouldn't call it an illusion. Isn't it what you would choose if you could? A tree's life to be with someone you love with all your senses?"

"I suppose I would." I considered it for a moment, and wondered if Amzil would still want to spend even an ordinary life with me. Useless to wonder. I did not even have that sort of a life to offer her. "But I sense there is more. What else did Lisana tell you?"

"What we have both known for some time. That divided as we are, you and I are useless to anyone. The magic isn't working, or at best works only halfway. When Lisana divided us so that I could stay with her and be taught, she never anticipated that we would remain divided."

"No. As I recall, she intended that I would die of the plague."

"I was to have the body and you were to become part of me," he corrected me.

"I don't see the difference. Isn't that what we are now?"

"No. You oppose me. Just as I opposed you when you sought to be fully in command." For a moment, he seemed invisible to me, caught in thoughts of his own. Then, reluctantly, he said, "We were supposed to become one. I was to absorb you, your knowledge, your attributes of character, your understanding of your people. We would have been one merged person, completely integrated. And the magic would have had access to both of us, and it would have been able to achieve its goals."

"But I killed you instead."

"You thought you did. And I resisted being absorbed by you, just as you have resisted becoming part of me. But until we are one, the magic cannot work. It moves by half measures, more destructive than if it did nothing at all. Lisana is convinced of this."

"She knows this?" It seemed to me there was a difference between being convinced and knowing.

"She knows it," he replied, but his words had taken too long in coming. I didn't believe that Tree Woman was certain of this. We had crossed the bridge. He sat down again on the same rock where we had spent so much time the night before. It was just as uncomfortable now as it had been then. A thin spring sunlight filtered down through the trees. He closed his eyes and turned his face up to it, enjoying the warmth on his face.

"You're guessing," I accused him.

He gave a harsh sigh. "Yes. I am. So? Nothing else has worked. I think we both need to give way and accept it."

"What are you proposing?"

"I'm proposing that we drop all walls. Become one. Completely." The sunlight, feeble as it was, was already making his face tingle. With a grunt and a sigh, he stood and moved into the shelter of the trees. It was chilly there, but his skin was no longer exposed to direct sunlight. He found a mossed-over log and sat down on it.

I suddenly divined what had conquered him. "Lisana wants us to be one."

"Yes." He ground his teeth together and then said, "She sent me away. She told me that until we are one, I can no longer come to her. She . . . she rebuked me harshly that I had not yet made you a part of myself."

"So I should drop my walls and let you absorb me. So that you'll be able to use the magic fully, to kill or drive my people away so yours can live in peace. So that you can be with Lisana."

"Yes." He gritted out the word. "Become part of me. Let the magic work through us as it was meant to. Accept what we are, a man of both cultures. Neither side is innocent, Nevare."

I could not argue with that.

Into my silence, he added, "Neither of *us* is innocent. In the names of our peoples, we have done great wrongs."

And that, too, was true. I sat, the spring day all around me, and considered what he proposed.

"How do we know which one of us will retain the awareness?" I asked him bluntly. Privately, I wondered if he would offer this "merging" if he was not already confident it would be him.

"How do we know it will be only one of us? Perhaps, together, we become someone else. A person who has never existed before. Or the person the boy we were would have grown to be." Idly he peeled a layer of moss from the rotting log. Beetles scattered, scuttling over the rotten wood and hiding again in the moss.

"I could become the person I was meant to be before I was sundered." I spoke thoughtfully. My father's soldier son. I'd take back the ruthlessness that Soldier's Boy had stolen from me, the capacity to steel myself to do the awful things that war required of a soldier.

He laughed aloud, amused. "Could not I say exactly the same thing? Did not I feel the same sundering when you parted from me and went back to our father's house and then off to that school? Do you think I don't feel exactly as you do? I had a childhood. I was raised a Gernian and the son of a new noble. I remember our mother's gentle words. I remember music and poetry, fine manners and dancing. I had a softer side once. Then I had an experience with Dewara that changed me profoundly. And Tree Woman took me under her guardianship. I watched someone else walk off with my body. But I never stopped being *I* and *me* to myself. I never became some other. You so obviously believe you are the legitimate owner of this body, Nevare, the only one who should determine what I do in this world. Can't you grasp that I feel just the same way?"

I was silent for a time. Then I said stiffly, "I see no resolution to this."

"Don't you? It seems obvious to me. We let down our guards and stop resisting each other. We merge. We become one."

I tried to think about it, but suddenly the answer was too clear before me. "No. I can't do it."

"Why won't you at least try it?"

"Because no matter how it came out, it is intolerable for me to think about. If we become one, and you are dominant, I cease to exist. It would be a suicide for me."

"I could say the same to you. But that might not happen. As I said, we might simply become a whole, a different person in which neither of us dominates."

"It would still be intolerable. I cannot imagine a person who had any of my ethics and could tolerate the memory of what you did at Gettys. Those acts were completely reprehensible to me. I cannot accept them as a part of *my* past. I will not."

He was silent for a time. Then he asked quietly, "What of your acts of war against the People? Your cutting of Lisana's tree? You were the one who told the intruders how to overcome Kinrove's magic and cut our ancestor trees. Was that not killing the People?"

They were trees, not people. The thought washed into my mind, but died, unuttered. It wasn't true. When the trees had fallen, the spirits within them had moved on. My actions had been just as responsible for deaths as Soldier's Boy's had. Neither one of us had bloodied our hands; we had let others do that for us. But the deaths I had caused were just as unforgivable as the slaughter of the soldiers. The lurch of heart that gave me, as the acid realization ate into my soul! And Epiny had told me that the tree cutting would soon resume, if it had not already. I realized it was the result of two half measures of magic; I had told the commander at Gettys how to drug his laborers to get around the fear magic of the forest. And then Soldier's Boy, with his bloody raid, had energized them with enough hate to make them decide to push on despite any fear or despair they felt. Together we had brought those deaths down on the People. And together we had made possible the slaughter at Gettys. If we had been one, could any of those events have happened? If Soldier's Boy had had to feel my emotions, would he have been able to commit the atrocities that he had? If we had been one, would I have been better able to stand up for myself at Gettys and demand that I be heard?

Something changed in me at that moment. I had not realized that I had still held the People apart from myself, still regarded the ancestor trees as other than what they were, bodies for spirits of the ancestors to inhabit. The remorse and sorrow I felt over their deaths vibrated through me, suddenly in tune with what Soldier's Boy felt. For that moment, we were closer to accord. For the blink of an eye, we were one. And then apart again. He let out a pent breath.

"Nevare," Soldier's Boy said to me quietly, "separately or together, we must bear the guilt and the remorse for the things we have done. Separately or together, we cannot change the past. But together, we might be able to change the future."

"But change it how?" I asked him bitterly. "Annihilate those who remain at Gettys? If I merge with you, you gain the knowledge that the magic will finally be able to work its will. But what do I gain? Only the knowledge that people I love may be slaughtered. I can see every reason why I should resist this, and none for why I should concede."

For a time, he was silent. I looked with him out of our eyes at the world around us. Nearby, the stream spoke softly, rippling over

stone, and overhead a slight morning wind stirred the treetops.
There was peace here. Peace and solitude. Perhaps the only peace
I'd ever know again was in solitude. I tried to imagine what I'd
do if Soldier's Boy and I merged, and I became the dominant one.
I'd still be trapped in this body, now marked by him as a Speck. I
couldn't go back to Gettys. Could never go back to Amzil. Would
I continue as a Speck Great One, with Olikea to attend to my
comforts by day and Lisana to visit by night? I doubted it. I'd
dismissed my feeders. With Likari lost to Kinrove's dance, Olikea
would never take me back, even if I had been able to bear the idea
of going to her with the spectre of her lost son looming between
us always. So what was there for me?

"If we became one, and you were dominant, what would
you do?"

He answered me honestly, but for all that, his words chilled
me. "Whatever the magic demanded of me. Because I think if we
were one, it would speak clearly to us, and we, or I, would know
what to do."

"No." It was the only possible decision I could make.

He sighed. "I feared that would be your answer." He stood, and
then stretched cautiously. His lower back ached. It almost always
ached now, except when a feeder was massaging it. I suspected it
was part of the price of being a Great One. An aching back. Sore,
swollen feet. Knees that complained. He took a deep breath. "I'm
sorry, Nevare. Lisana asked me to give you the chance to accede
to my request. She loves you, as you are part of me, and she did
not wish to imagine you distressed by what must be done. So. I
asked. I've done all I can. I've tried to force you to be one with
me. I've tried to silence you and absorb you. I've tried to trick
you into being part of me. All has failed. But until you join me, I
cannot do what I am meant to do. And I cannot be with Lisana."
He paused and then informed me, "You had the chance to say yes,
to join me willingly. I gave you that, as I promised Lisana I would.
You said no. You are certain that is your decision?"

"I am certain."

The thought was scarcely formed before he attacked me. Or
tried. I felt his attempt. He seized me and held me tightly. I could

not flee from his awareness of me, nor escape my awareness of him. I was held prisoner.

But it was all he could do. I spoke to him. "You can box me. You can take my senses away. You can ignore me. But you cannot destroy me. And you cannot force me to be part of you any more than I could force that on you."

For a time longer he held me. And then he threw back his head and gave a great roar of frustration. "I hate you, Nevare! Hate you, hate you, hate you! I hate all you are, and still I must make you a part of me. I must!" The last words he bellowed at the sky.

"You cannot," I said resolutely.

He began to make his way back through the forest toward the stream and the bridge that crossed it. He strode up the hill toward Lisana's lodge.

"What now?" I asked him.

He gave a small, dismissive sigh. "I do what I must do. I humiliate myself. I go to Kinrove, to strike the best bargain I am capable of making." He scratched his cheek and added thoughtfully, "And perhaps to keep a promise."

Before I could ask any more of him, he cut me off from his thoughts again. Once more I rode in the body, unknowing of his intentions, bound for a fate I could not control.

CHAPTER TWENTY-FIVE

DECISIONS

He did not hurry. I think he had sent the others on so that he could be alone to speak with me. Perhaps he had believed that there would be some great struggle between us, a confrontation of his two selves that no one should witness. Now he moved with purpose, as if treading a road he had foreseen and dreaded. He returned to the lodge and went directly to the new hiding place that Olikea had devised. In a heavy cedar storage trunk, beneath the layers of wool blankets and fur coverings that he removed and carelessly piled on the earth floor, there was a false bottom. It was not easy to get it open, for it had no obvious handle or catch. But eventually he pried it up and sat for a moment, staring at what remained of Lisana's treasure hoard. I imagined that he felt regret or reluctance, but could not be sure, for I was no longer privy to his feelings or emotions.

He spread one of the smaller blankets on the floor and loaded the treasure into the center. For some small time, he sat holding the ivory baby in his hands. With a fingertip, he traced the indistinct features of its face, the round cheeks, the closed eyes; then he returned it to the soft bag that Olikea always kept it in and added it resolutely to the pile. Once that was done, he tied up the four corners of the blanket to make it into a carry sack, tossed it over his shoulder, and left the lodge. He left the blankets scattered on the floor and the door wide open. Either he thought he'd never return, or he'd become so accustomed to having feeders pick up after him that he no longer noticed the messes he left.

The sun was already low, and soon the light would be lost to us. "You're a fool, starting a journey at this time of day," I said to him, but he paid me no heed. I doubt he even noticed the thought. For a time, he simply walked, following the well-trodden trail. I think he enjoyed the end of the spring day. Despite my trepidation, I did. There is nothing that smells quite like a forest in spring. The air was cool enough that walking was pleasant. Even for a heavy man, the first part of a walk can be a pleasant thing. But all too soon, my feet and knees began to complain, and my back reminded us that we'd spent far too much time sitting on a rock the night before. The blanket of swag on my shoulder began to seem heavy, and sweat began to trickle and chafe.

He took a deep breath, blew it out, and then with his next step began a quick-walk. It took me off guard and I did not enjoy the lurch from one place to another as he stepped. He had not fed as well that day as he was accustomed to, and soon he was using magic he had stored. I thought I sensed him grumbling to himself about that, but could not be sure. He strode quickly as well as quick-walked, so that the countryside flew past us. Night came on, and still we walked. He was very tired and his stomach roared with hunger before he saw fire ahead of us in the distance. He stopped his quick-walking then, and despite his aching back and muttering knees, forced himself to walk normally as he approached the campfires.

The trail ahead of us led uphill. To either side of it, firelight winked through the sheltering cover of the newly budded trees, like a string of glistening jewels scattered up the side of the mountain. As he approached, the cooking smells nearly made his knees buckle with hunger. Music floated on the night, drums and strings and the voices of the People upraised in shared song. Lisana's memories of the westbound migration surfaced in his mind. The younger folk had always loved the trek back to the western side of the mountains. During the firelit nights of the migrations, they moved freely among the kin-clans, discovering friends new and old, taking lovers, trading with one another and comparing the trade goods that they were carrying west. It was a time as eagerly anticipated as the social season in Old Thares. The best storytellers of all the People would be performing, and there would be singing and shared food and shared blankets. A good time. Up ahead, someone gave a sudden whoop. Perhaps it was a storyteller ending a rendition of a favorite, for his cry was echoed with laughter and applause. If I had been a Speck child, I would have been racing up the trail to see what wonderful event was going on.

That thought brought Likari sharply to my mind. A moment later, Soldier's Boy sighed and then paused on his upward trek. I wondered if the same thought had occurred to him. But his pause was momentary. He was soon laboring along, the calves of his legs screaming with the extra effort and stomach growling at the smells of the food.

His disappearance the night before had badly delayed the departure of his feeders, so it was no surprise that he found them around the first campfire he came to. Olikea was there with them, crouched by a pot of something simmering on the coals. At first glance, she seemed an old woman from the droop of her face and her untidy hair. She still wore a winter robe against the chill of the spring night, but it was a simple work robe, unlike the spring finery that some of the other women had donned. Grief had aged her. She was not the wild and flirtatious creature that had seduced me only a year ago. I thought of that, and marveled at all the changes that had been packed into such a short time.

While I pondered such things, Soldier's Boy walked unannounced into the circle of their firelight. One of the other feeders noticed him first and gave a small squeak of surprise. Olikea started at the sight of him. She immediately put her gaze back on her cooking and said sourly, "So, here you are. You've come to your senses, then." Her tone was not welcoming, but I thought I had detected a brief expression of relief on her face when she saw him.

"I suppose I have." He lowered the sack of treasure to the ground beside him. At the sound of it, she looked back at him with a frown.

"What have you brought?"

"Lisana's treasure."

"But . . . but—" Her dismay and displeasure were equally evident. "Surely you can't mean to trade them to the intruders! They will never give you what they are worth. And there are things there that you should never trade away, things of such value that—"

"I know." His words cut her off. His tone was almost gentle as he said, "I don't intend to trade them to the Gernians. I don't think the Gernians will be doing any trade with us at all this year. If we are wise, we will stay deep in the forest and well hidden from them and their bullets. No. I'm taking these not to the Gernians but to Kinrove."

"Kinrove?" She said the name with loathing, but a queer hope gleamed from her eyes. "Why?"

"I intend to strike a bargain with him."

"To get Likari back?"

"That will be part of the bargain I hope to make."

She had returned to her crouch over the cooking fire. Now she looked up at me, ladle in hand. I do not know how to describe the progression of emotions across her face. She looked down again, blinking very rapidly. She did not try to blot the tears. When she looked up at me again, they were running freely down her cheeks. Her voice was hoarse as she said matter-of-factly, "You need food. And rest. Look at you, hiking about in your night robe and slippers. This is what befalls a Great One with no feeder! They have no sense at all. Make yourself a seat and I will bring you food."

Here, under the night sky, it was easy to speak to the magic. At Soldier's Boy's request, moss and earth rose into comfortable hummocks for him and for his feeders. The others came to him swiftly, relieved to have their lives put back into a routine. It had escaped him that he'd traipsed off still clad in his night garments. Not even I had noticed the discrepancy. A woman came, bearing oil, and rubbed his abused feet and calves. Someone else brought him warmed washwater, and then combed his hair back from his face and plaited it so it would be out of his way while he ate. Almost as soon as that was done, Olikea placed a large bowl of food in front of him. It was a thick soup of beach-peas and dried fish, and two dark, hard rolls of the travel bread they had been baking all week. It was simple and hearty, and I wished there had been a hogshead full of it rather than just the generous bowl. Soldier's Boy ate without speaking, feeling the food revive him, and Olikea didn't disturb him with questions.

Afterward, the magic fashioned a couch for them to share. The other feeders had kept a distance, either out of respect or because they sensed that peace would be most quickly restored if the Great One and his chief feeder had time for quiet conversation. Olikea and Soldier's Boy lay down together, under a blanket of fox furs. Olikea prudently put the sack of treasure at her feet where no one could disturb it without waking her.

Up the trail, at the various kin-clan camps alongside it, the sounds of merrymaking went on unabated. This first night of the migration was always a time for gatherings and renewal of friendships. It seemed strange to me that they were so undaunted by what probably awaited them on the other side of the mountains. The best that they could hope for was a summer of remaining hidden in the forests there, hunting and fishing, but seldom venturing forth to trade or have any congress with Gettys. Then it came to me that such a season might be far closer to their old traditions than one of trading and visits. If only the two groups could agree to remain mutually isolated, there might have evolved a sort of peace. But I feared that very soon the actual cutting of the ancestral trees would resume, and then the Specks would feel they had no choice except to retaliate. I wondered what form that retaliation would take while I listened to their songs and music in the spring night. It was hard to reconcile the drumbeats and lifted voices in the night with my memories of flames and the screams of dying men. How could humanity range so effortlessly from the sublime to the savage and back again?

Olikea pressed herself against him, not in a seductive way but as one who seeks both warmth and comfort. He put his arms around her and pulled her close. Her hair smelled of the wood smoke. He rested his chin on the top of her head and felt a twinge of desire, but the ache in his back and legs overpowered it. That made him feel like an old man. She spoke into his chest. I crept closer, eavesdropping once more on his emotions and thoughts.

"When we reach our summer grounds and you go to visit Kinrove, what then?" she asked him.

"No," he said quietly.

"No?" she asked him, confused.

"I will not wait until we reach the summer grounds. Tomorrow, when we rise, we will eat well. And then you and I will depart, to quick-walk to Kinrove. I will not wait any longer. You saw the beginning of all this. You should see the end."

"But—"

"Shh. We should sleep while we can. And I cannot bear to think any longer on what I must do." He closed his eyes then, and wearied by more than his long day's walk, he sank swiftly into sleep. I remained aware behind his closed eyelids. I felt Olikea's deep and heartfelt sigh, and how she relaxed into his arms. She, too, slept, but I remained aware for hours longer, listening to the sounds of the People in the night.

I think the following spring morning was the sweetest of my life. Dappling sunlight through the trees, birdcalls, the smells of the forest as the sun gently warmed it, the deliciousness of being warm while the rest of the world was still chill; nothing in my memory can compete with it. For one long, luscious moment, I simply existed, unaware of the strife and troubles that still waited to be resolved. I was like an animal awakening to the glory of spring.

Then I tried to stretch and could not, and recalled all too abruptly that I was still a prisoner in my own body. Soldier's Boy awakened and then Olikea stirred in his arms. She slipped quickly from beneath the blankets and busied herself around the campsite while he stole a few more precious moments of dozing with his body warm and his face touched by the fresh day. At the smell of cooking food, he stirred quickly enough, his stomach's roaring more demanding than the reveille bugles at the academy had ever been. Olikea had made a porridge and liberally sprinkled it with dried berries. She brought him a bowlful, with a spiral of honey drizzled over the top. He ate it with a carved wooden spoon and washed it down with a mug of hot tea. While he was eating, his feeders laid out proper clothing for him, for the Specks would go clothed until they emerged on the other side of the mountains into the warmer days of spring there.

Olikea knelt before him to lace his feet and legs into soft knee boots after he had donned the supple doeskin trousers and simple woolen tunic she brought him. As soon as his boots were tied, he rose and lifted the sack of treasure to his shoulder. "Let's go," he told her.

"First, I must clean and repack our cooking vessels and the fox-skin robe we slept under last night. It will not take long."

"Leave them."

"What?"

"I said, leave them. I do not think we will have need of them again. I intend to quick-walk the entire day, to overtake Kinrove and to speak with him this night."

"But—" She glanced about at their campsite, at the other feeders, the dirty pots and the rumpled bedding.

He gave way before her confusion. "Take only what you think you must have. The other feeders will bring the rest."

I sensed that he didn't care what she brought or didn't bring. There was finality to this decision, one that bespoke a swift end to all things. He did not expect to need anything she had brought with her, and he himself carried only Lisana's treasure. Did he intend to kill himself? That was the first thing that came to my mind, but I could not imagine why or how he would make such a decision. How would that benefit Likari? Or, once he had obtained the boy's release with the treasure, did he foresee that as the only possible end for us? I toyed with the idea, and found it vaguely attractive, and then all the more frightening because it was no longer as unthinkable as it once would have been.

Olikea packed swiftly and sensibly, taking a blanket, food, and bare necessities. I sensed her eagerness to be on her way to her son. The other feeders accepted the Great One's decision. Their equanimity in the face of his changeable actions reflected the status a mage had in the society of the People. The magic powered his decisions, and they were never to be questioned. They simply portioned out the goods that Olikea had been carrying among themselves and bade us farewell.

With little more ado, Soldier's Boy took her hand and they began their quick-walk. He not only poured his magic generously into the quick-walk but also physically stepped along as swiftly as he was able. I was disconcerted at the level of effort he put into this; by midmorning, I was very aware of the physical strain on him, as well as the depletion of his magic. Olikea spoke of her concern at such a pace, her words fading and then recovering as they moved swiftly past the other kin-clans on their migration. "You will exhaust yourself. Should not you save some of your magic for confronting Kinrove?"

"I will have enough. Treasure and magic are not the only way to sway Kinrove." He paused. Then, "I have something else he wants," he added enigmatically.

By afternoon's end, we had traversed the cavernous pass and emerged on the other side. It was pleasant to come out into a warmer place, one where the evening light lingered on the land. Spring seemed stronger here. The tiny leaves on the deciduous trees glistened in various shades of green. The challenges and replies of the birds seemed to fill the air around us.

When Soldier's Boy paused, I thought surely he would say that was enough journeying for the day. Instead, he caught his breath for a few moments and then asked, "Where does Kinrove's kin-clan spend the summer? Where is his dance located?"

"He will be about a day's journey from here, to the southwest. He has summered there every summer for many years, at a place that offers space, water, and food for his dancers."

"Can you describe the path there for me?"

"Yes," she began, and then suddenly shook her head. "But no. Not well enough for you to quick-walk there. No!" she repeated more emphatically at his look. "All know the dangers of a quick-walk when the path is not well known to the Great One. There are tales of two Great Ones who have simply vanished forever attempting such a feat. Unless you have your mentor's memories to guide us, it is hopeless. We will need to walk the rest of the way there. It will be all right, Nevare. It is only one more night."

I heard in her voice that even one more night seemed too many to her, but also her determination that Soldier's Boy would not risk himself pushing on in ignorance. His own determination was as strong. "Very well. But we will continue walking in that direction, then. Southwest, you said?"

"Yes. But first we will go downhill for a ways. Then we will see a trail that goes in that direction. It will not be hard to find. His dancers have traveled with him and they will have trampled the path fresh quite recently. Come. Walk. But at a sensible pace. Remember, I am still your feeder and still have the care of you."

Although they no longer quick-walked, she kept hold of his hand. When he would have hastened the pace, she held him back to a steady walk. As she had predicted, it was very easy to see where Kinrove's dancers had gone. When they diverged on a trail to the south, Olikea and Soldier's Boy followed them. She dropped his hand once, to leave the path and harvest several large clumps of mushrooms by the wayside. When she returned, she walked even more slowly. Even so, by the time the light was fading, his back ached abominably and his feet were very sore. He realized he was limping, and when they came to a small stream that crossed the path, he did not object when Olikea announced, "We will spend the night here."

A hummock of earth shaped itself into a receptive chair for him. Olikea set to work immediately making a cook fire. He sat down and almost immediately realized he was far more tired than he had thought. Only the smell of the cooking food kept him awake. She glanced up at him once, to ask with a wry smile, "Are you glad now that I did not come away with nothing at all? We would be eating raw mushrooms tonight and little else."

"You were wise," he conceded, and for the first time in weeks I saw a genuine smile light her face.

The meal she made was simple, but it was hot and good. They ate together from the cooking pot, and had only fresh cold water to drink. The meal did not fill him, but then, no meal really ever had. It was enough to subdue the pangs of hunger. By the time they had finished eating, all light had fled the sky and the dark of night surrounded them. She fed the fire enough fuel to leave the flames dancing companionably, and then came to the couch he summoned from the forest floor. As she slipped under the blanket beside him, he felt a stir of arousal at her nearness. Before he could so much as touch her, she pressed herself against him.

She made love to him that night with the same uninhibited passion she had shown when first she had seduced me. They were alone, and with a common purpose, and perhaps that was all that was needed to make it seem, for that night, as if they loved each other. By the time she was finished with him, his weariness and aching joints had been replaced with a clean tiredness. She lay with her head on his chest and he stroked her long damp hair. Neither of them spoke; perhaps they were finally wise enough to know when words could only spoil something.

The dawn light through the young leaves overhead woke them. Olikea stirred the fire from the ashes and used the last of the food she had brought to make a hearty breakfast. She had saved the mushrooms she'd picked the day before and fed them to him now, and Soldier's Boy felt their rejuvenating effect gratefully. They did not completely drive the ache from his back or the weariness from his legs, but he was able to rise without groaning. Olikea quenched their small fire with water from the stream and they journeyed on, the treasure bag slung over his shoulder.

By noon, they could hear the drumming and sometimes the occasional whoop or drawn-out, plaintive calls from Kinrove's dancers. The magic, one of weariness and sorrow directed toward the Gernians, was like a cooking smell carried on the summer wind. "We draw near," Soldier's Boy said with relief, but Olikea shook her head. "Sound carries here, as does magic. I have heard that Kinrove chose the location for his dance carefully, so that the forest and the vales would amplify both the dance and the magic. We still have some way to travel, but we shall be there before evening."

As the long afternoon progressed, the sounds and the presence of the magic grew stronger. If Soldier's Boy allowed himself, he could taste the fear and the discouragement that wafted out from the dance. The sound became a constant that buffeted his senses. Although the magic was not directed at them, approaching it was still like wading up a strongly flowing stream. It drew strength from Soldier's Boy. Olikea set her face into an expression of grim determination and marched on. The music created something that was the opposite of a quick-walk; it seemed to take forever to toil up the slight rise in the trail to where a couple of Kinrove's men stood a lackadaisical watch beside the trail. Half a dozen people stood idly by, perhaps awaiting their turn to pass.

Their sentry duty seemed ridiculous to me at first. Why guard the most obvious trail into Kinrove's summer encampment? It would have been child's play to circle wide of the two idle guards and simply approach his stronghold through the forest. But as we drew closer, Soldier's Boy's leg muscles became more and more reluctant to work. By the time we actually reached the guards, he felt as if he had waded there through tar. It came to me that the whole of his encampment was encircled by this magical palisade, just as it had been at the Trading Place; the guards were not guarding so much as serving as the keys to entry. Only at that location could anyone approach one of Kinrove's guards and request to be allowed in.

As we drew slowly closer, I could see that those who sat or stood awaiting admittance had evidently been there for some time. They crouched or stood, their eyes on the guards, reminding me of dogs begging at table. Off to one side of the trail, a banked campfire smoldered. Around it were blanket rolls and a scatter of possessions. I divined that it was a pathetic siege of sorts. I wondered how long they had been waiting.

As we toiled up the path, one guard caught sight of us and immediately jabbed at the other. Both stood abruptly, lifting bows and training arrows onto us as we came. One stood taller, craning to see us, and then said something to the other guard. The first one puffed out his lips, the Speck equivalent of shaking his head. They stared at us as we advanced, their faces stony. "Will they let us pass?" Olikea asked in a whisper.

"They will. But this time, it is my turn to ask you to be silent while I strike the bargain."

She gave him a doubtful look but acceded.

They stopped a dozen steps short of the guards, not because the men had made any threat toward them, but simply because they encountered a barrier. Abruptly, weariness and aches flooded Soldier's Boy's body and he found himself questioning his reasons for coming here. What would he accomplish? Had he no faith in Kinrove, the greatest of the great? He looked at Olikea. Her face wore a similar bewilderment. She gave him a questioning glance. I deduced it before either of them did. I spoke loudly in Soldier's Boy's mind. "Step back. Two steps back will probably put you out of the barrier's range."

I do not know if he heard me or if he started to leave. But once he had retreated two steps from the guards, he suddenly shook his head and wheeled round again. He caught Olikea by the shoulder and kept her from going any farther. He focused his attention on the guards. "I want to see Kinrove," he declared. "Send him word that Soldier's Boy, Nevare, is here and wishes to speak with him. Tell him it is of the greatest importance."

They did not even look at one another. "You are not to be admitted. This Kinrove has made clear to us." The guard who had spoken added, "Know this, Great One. Kinrove's magic will slow you or anything you might launch at us. But it has no effect on our arrows. They will fly as swift and true as ever."

"I bring him gifts," Soldier's Boy said, as if no warning or threat had ever been made. Without any ceremony, he lowered his treasure sling to the ground. He untied the knots, and unfolded the blanket, baring the contents to their view. They tried to step forward to see it but were constrained, I think, by the same barrier that kept us out. They craned their necks, and their eyes grew wide as he began to sort through the jumbled treasures. Other supplicants ventured closer, their mouths hanging ajar at the wealth so casually transported in the old blanket. When he came to the bagged figurine, he hesitated, and then offered it to Olikea instead. "You, perhaps, will know best what to do with this," he said.

She accepted it from him, and something changed in her face. Her face held that suppressed gleam of satisfaction that Epiny used to show just before she leapt to her feet to proclaim she had won a game of Towsers. She didn't open the sack, but she cradled it in both hands. She smiled at the guardians. "Do not tell Kinrove that I wish to see him. Instead, tell Galea that Olikea, Nevare's feeder, stands before you and holds her heart's dearest desire in the palms of her hands. And if she can but get Kinrove to admit us, only to speak to him, then it shall be hers. Forever."

Her eyes flickered to mine as she said that final word, as if fearing she offered something beyond what Soldier's Boy would permit. But he only gave a curt nod. Then he slowly crossed his arms on his chest and waited. Olikea continued to cup the blanketed image in her hands.

They stood, an emperor's ransom on a blanket at their feet, and a treasure of unknown value cradled in her hands, and waited. Neither one stared down at the fabulous wealth strewn across the blanket. Neither spoke or moved.

The guards exchanged glances, and then leaned close to each other for a whispered consultation. They agreed on something. One of them went to a sack hanging on a nearby tree. From it, he extracted a horn and blew three sharp blasts on it. The noise was still hanging in the air as the other explained to us, "That will let them know to send a runner to us. When he arrives, he will bear our message back to Kinrove."

"Thank you," Soldier's Boy replied. Without even a small smile, he added, "In return for your swift action, I think that each of you should choose your own gift from us, from the largesse that we bring. It seems only fair."

He stepped back and then knelt down heavily to spread the treasure more temptingly across the blanket. It was an unprecedented action for a Great One even to notice guards in such a way. They were stunned and instantly avaricious, jostling each other to have the best view of what was presented, all the while glancing at each other to see if one's fellow was staring at the choicest bit that was offered. They were still leaning as far forward as they could against the magic barrier when the runner arrived. He was full of curiosity and drew as near as he could to view what they were ogling. The guards had scarcely a moment for him. "Go to Kinrove and tell him that Soldier's Boy–Nevare wishes to be allowed through the barrier to speak with him. And tell Galea also that Olikea, Nevare's feeder, is with him, and has a gift for her."

"Her dearest heart's desire," Olikea corrected him, holding the draped charm up again.

"Go swiftly, and return quickly with his reply, and from this treasure, you will have your choice of reward," Soldier's Boy announced.

I think it had the opposite of the desired effect, for immediately the runner surged forward, vying with the two guards for the best view. One of the guards told him jealously, "But we are to choose first, before you!"

"But which of us?" the other asked in sudden worry.

"I will decide that," Soldier's Boy announced. "Once the message has returned that I am to be allowed past the barrier."

"Go!" one of the guards told the runner crossly. "The message will never be delivered while you stand here gawking."

The runner made an annoyed sound, but then turned and sped away as swiftly as he had come. The two guards eyed each other for a moment, then went back to lustfully ogling the treasure. Someone tugged at the light cloak Soldier's Boy was wearing. He turned to see that one of the other waiters had crept closer. "When they let you in, will you ask that I can come with you?" she boldly asked. Her brave words were a strange contrast to her dark-ringed eyes and skeletal form. She was a woman of middle years, unkempt, with the smudges from her cooking blending with the specks on her face.

He didn't answer her directly. "Whom are you seeking to free?" he asked her.

"My son. Dasie freed him once, and I was so full of joy when he came home. But after three days of sleeping and eating, he became full of restlessness. He said he could still hear the drums. He could not lie still at night, but twitched and jerked in his sleep. Sometimes he would be talking to me and then suddenly he would stop and stare into the distance. He could not remember how to hunt. Whatever he began, he left half finished. Then one morning he was gone from my lodge. I know he is back with the dancers. It isn't fair. Dasie freed him. He should have stayed longer at home and tried harder." Her tears were falling, flowing in run-nels down her face, as if constant weeping had eroded her flesh.

He looked aside from her and spoke quietly. "I do not know if I can even get myself and my feeder past Kinrove's guards. And it is very important that I speak with him. I cannot get you in. But I can tell you that if I am successful, your son will no longer dance. And that is the best I can do."

His words had become softer as he spoke. The woman turned away wordlessly. I do not think she was disappointed; I think she had known most of the answer before she had asked. But Olikea had her own question. "If you succeed, her son will no longer dance? What do you mean? I thought we were going to get Likari back."

"Likari is part of my goal. But I have a larger ambition."

"And what is that?" she asked, her voice cooling. I could almost read her thoughts. That the first time, he and his raid on Gettys had done nothing toward getting her son back. She did not want him to have any greater plan now, only to focus solely on getting Likari back.

He took a breath but before he could reply, he was distracted by the sounds of heavy wings beating overhead. A croaker bird's descending flight is nothing like an owl's. The creature did not alight in the branches overhead so much as use one to break his fall as he came down. The branch bobbed under his weight, and for a time, he kept his wide wings out, balancing himself until he had dug his claws firmly into his perch. When he was settled, he folded his wings in and spent a few moments fussily settling his pinions. Only when he was finished did he stretch his long ugly neck out and turn his head sideways so that one eye pointed straight down at me. He opened his beak, and to me it appeared that he silently laughed.

"Has something died nearby?" Olikea wondered aloud. "What brings a carrion bird here?"

Orandula laughed aloud then, raucous caws in succession that split through the endless drumbeat of Kinrove's dance. Soldier's Boy refused to look at him any longer, but transferred his gaze to the guards staring at his treasure.

"Who chooses first?" one of the guards demanded of him.

"Don't ask him! He cannot choose at all!" the croaker bird called down. The words were perfectly clear to me and Soldier's Boy scowled at them, but Olikea didn't appear to notice that the bird had spoken.

"Who chooses first?" the guard asked again. I think that his question annoyed Soldier's Boy, for he abruptly replied, "He does!" and pointed to the other fellow.

The first guard was unperturbed. "Well, let me know what you choose, so I can decide which I want," he told his partner.

"I'm thinking!" the other man replied testily.

"Let me know what you choose, so I can decide which I want!" the bird echoed him overhead. He followed his words with his sinister cawing laughter. I heard Soldier's Boy grind his teeth.

Then the runner appeared around the bend in the trail. He ran fleetly and was grinning as if he bore rare good news. He came to a halt and said to the guards, "You may admit them. Kinrove is ready to receive them. He will open the barrier, but only to those two!" He raised his voice to convey those final tidings. The other supplicants had drawn near to hear the runner's words. They muttered and milled, but did not look likely to make any attempts to breach the defenses.

"How will we know when we may pass?" Olikea wondered aloud, but before her words were finished, she knew. From repelling us, the force suddenly pressed us forward. Soldier's Boy stopped to gather his swag, then caught Olikea by the hand and led her through with him. Above our heads, the carrion bird suddenly cackled loudly and, with noisily flapping wings, followed us.

"You said I could choose first!" the one guard reminded Soldier's Boy.

"So I did," he replied, and once more lowered the blanket. The two guards were not slow to claim their prizes. The runner, who had had less time to gawk at the riches, took longer, but eventually settled on a heavy silver medallion of a running deer on a silver chain. He looped it around his neck immediately and seemed very pleased with it.

"Follow me," he invited us, and added, "Kinrove will quick-walk us now."

The promised quick-walk began with a sickening lurch, and proceeded at a speed I'd never known before. In three steps, we stood in Kinrove's summer encampment. The noise of the endless drumming and the seemingly random blatting of the horns were well-nigh unbearable here. The circle of dancers was smaller than it had been the first time we saw it. It still wove through a village of tents established around a larger pavilion. That surprised me; I had seen few tents at our kin-clan's summer settlement. But there were many ways in which his village seemed more permanent: the dancers had trodden a trail of bare packed earth through the tents; neatly stacked firewood in a rick waited next to a stone oven near a well-tended cook fire on a stone-based hearth; fish was smoking nearby over another fire, and a platform of poles held ready caches of smoked meats and fish.

Kinrove's tent was on a raised dais; it was the same pavilion I had seen before, simply moved to this location. Four men stood watch outside it and they were armed with bows, not spears or swords. They had watched our quick-walk approach, and I perceived what an advantage this had given them over us. Kinrove had learned. I did not think that anyone would ever again be able to surprise him in his stronghold.

A waiting man looked us over, then nodded grimly and held the tent flap open for us to enter. Two of the guards followed us, nocked arrows at the ready. I heard again the flapping rush of wings. There was a thud as the croaker bird landed on top of Kinrove's pavilion. Soldier's Boy gritted his teeth but did not grant him a glance.

Within the tent was an almost familiar scene. Kinrove, fat as ever, nearly overflowed his cushioned chair. Tables of prepared food awaited his attention, while feeders came and went from them. Galea, his first and most favored feeder, stood just behind him, her hands on his shoulders. They both kept silent as we approached, but the woman did not take her eyes off Olikea's bundle. Her breathing seemed to quicken as we approached Kinrove. When we were still a good distance from him, he lifted his hand,

and "Stand there!" the guard escorting us commanded us. At the same moment, Kinrove's magic wrapped us and held us where we were. "Put down what you are carrying."

"They are gifts for Kinrove. I only ask that he hear me out, and he can keep every item that is there," Soldier's Boy replied. Before the guard could reply, he rested the blanket on the earth and then opened it wide. With a grunt, he went down on one knee and then two. He began to arrange the jewelry and treasure on the blanket, looking down at it as he did so. "All of this once belonged to Lisana, my mentor. The value of what is here is beyond reckoning. All of this, I offer to Kinrove."

"In exchange for what?" the Great Man demanded skeptically.

"If you will only listen to what I propose. That is all."

Olikea took a sudden gasp of air, and then spoke. "And for my son. For Likari. Give him back to us, free of the dance, and all of this is yours. And the Ivory Babe, the greatest fertility charm ever known among the Specks!" She drew the cover off the image as she spoke and then held it aloft, cradling it as carefully as if it were a real child. "Give me back my son, Galea and Kinrove, and I will give you this, that you can have a son of your own."

Galea's hands tightened on Kinrove's shoulders. She leaned down to whisper in his ear, and the mage scowled in annoyance, but listened. He took a deep breath and puffed it out through his lips. But then he said grudgingly, "Kandaia. Go to the dance. Watch for the boy Likari, and when he passes, touch his shoulder and say to him, 'Kinrove bids you stop and follow me.'"

Olikea gave a cry of joy and clutched at Soldier's Boy's arm. "I will tend you as no Great One has ever been tended before. You can speak to me as you wish, use me as you wish, and ever I will still be in your debt."

"Hush," he said to her, firmly but without harshness. His eyes had not left Kinrove's face. With Olikea's help, he rose to his feet and then said quietly, "Greatest of the Great Ones, will you hear what I have to say? I give these treasures and I speak these words at Lisana's bidding. She has given a task to me. It is beyond me. And so I come to ask a boon of you."

"What is this?" Olikea asked in a small, breathless voice.

"What I told you," Soldier's Boy replied calmly. "My larger ambition."

A strange expression wandered over her face. It took me a moment to identify it, and then to my shock I knew it: jealousy. "You came here to do her task, not mine," she said bitterly.

He turned to her, took her hand, and met her eyes. "I will not speak another word until Likari is given to you." He turned his gaze to Kinrove. "Given to you, whole and freed of the dance. That is the price of the fertility child. Give back Olikea's child. Make a child of your own, and someday I hope you will look down into his face and imagine what it would be if a cruel and endless dance stole him from you."

A flush of anger passed over Kinrove's face, and I thought to myself that this was not the time to bait the Great Man. Soldier's Boy had run his head into the noose. Should Kinrove decide to tell his guards to kill us he could easily keep everything we had brought and suffer no loss at all. But Soldier's Boy either did not realize this or did not care. He turned his gaze back on Olikea and smiled down on her. I could not recall that he had ever before done so. "At least to you I will manage to keep my word. One promise kept in my whole life."

She opened her mouth to say something but Kandaia had returned, her hand on the shoulder of a skinny lad. For a second I could not recognize Likari. He had gone through a growth spurt. He was taller but thin, thinner than I had ever seen him. His skin and his hair were sweaty and dust clung to him. He stared about the inside of the tent, his eyes dazed and unblinking. Olikea gave a cry. She strained toward the boy, but Galea cried out, "The charm! First the charm, then your son!" I had never heard such ruthless need in a woman's voice. Kinrove lifted his hand, and Olikea jerked to a halt.

She turned back to confront her tormentors. "Take it!" she shouted furiously. "Take it!" She lifted her arm and would have lobbed the statuette at Galea's head, but Soldier's Boy deftly caught it.

He set a steadying hand to her shoulder. "I have what you want. Send someone to take it from my hand. And let her go to our son."

A small gesture from Kinrove's hand freed Olikea and she went to Likari in a stumbling run. When she reached him, she fell to her knees and threw her arms around him. He looked dazedly past her, his mouth slightly ajar as he breathed. Soldier's Boy swung his gaze back to Kinrove. "Free him from the dance," he said in a low, commanding voice. A feeder had approached him and stood waiting to receive the fertility charm. Another stood gawking at the spread of treasure on the opened blanket.

"He has made his own pact with the magic. I can do nothing about it."

Soldier's Boy held the fertility charm in both hands. I felt his magic gathering. "Do you think I cannot shatter this image with my hands? Free him, Kinrove. Release him from your damage, and we will see what 'pact of his own' binds him to the magic."

"Please! Please! Do whatever he says, if only I can have the charm!" Galea added her own plea to his words.

Kinrove puffed his lips out, an expression of both denial and disgust, but he also gave an abrupt nod toward Likari. The boy collapsed into Olikea's arms. He closed his eyes and went limp. Olikea scooped him up. His thin legs dangled over her arms as, without asking any permission, she carried him to one of Kinrove's soaking tubs. With her hand, she laved water over his face, wiping the dirt away with her sleeve. Then she carried him to a fire and sat down, holding him in her arms near the comforting warmth. She looked up at Soldier's Boy. "He sleeps so heavily."

"It is what he needs now," Soldier's Boy told her. He held out the statue and allowed the waiting feeder to take it. The other server knelt and reverently gathered up the corners of the blanket. The man bearing the charm was only a few steps away when Galea rushed forward from her place behind Kinrove's chair. She did not snatch it from him. Instead, she made a cradle of her arms and he gently deposited the wrapped charm there. As she took it, her entire body seemed to receive it. Her shoulders curled in, her head bowed over it possessively. She looked down at the small carved baby in her arms and smiled as tenderly as if the infant were real. Then, as if she were in a dream, she carried the charm out of Kinrove's pavilion without a backward glance at any of us. When the tent flap fell behind her, Kinrove spoke.

"All of you should leave now," the Great Man said in a harsh voice.

Soldier's Boy turned toward him incredulously. "You said you would listen to my request. Will you break your word in front of all your feeders?"

"I do not trust you," Kinrove said blackly. "Shall I keep my word to one whose word I cannot trust?" One of his fluid hand gestures dismissed the other feeder with the blanket full of loot. So much for buying Kinrove's favor. He would take the bribe but not be dazzled by it.

"Nor do I trust you, but you are whom I must deal with. And you must deal with me. Today we must do what we both know is our only solution. I have seen it, Lisana has seen it, and when first I came here, you spoke of it to me. I have tried to do it on my own, and failed. Great Kinrove, I come to join your dance. To dance, as you called it, the dance that has never been danced before. You must use your magic to rejoin the halves of me. When Nevare and Soldier's Boy are one again, then the magic will be able to use all our resources to fulfill itself. Our sundering is what has blocked our success. Put me back to what I was, Kinrove, and I will let the magic use me."

Kinrove looked at him for a long, silent time. I was still and small inside him, sick with dread. I had not foreseen this. Why had not I foreseen this? He'd asked me voluntarily to rejoin him. When I'd refused, I'd thought I'd frustrated his plan. Now I saw that he had been giving me a final chance to be a party to what would happen to us. "Don't do this, Soldier's Boy!" I cried to him. "Let us walk away from here and talk some more. There must be another way."

"There is not another way, because Nevare fears and fights to remain separate from me." Soldier's Boy spoke the words aloud, to Kinrove as well as to me. "I, too, dread what must be done. I do not think that of my will I can do it; it is like staring into the sun without blinking, or putting a burning brand into a wound that must be cauterized, to let this intruder, this Gernian become part of my soul. I know what must be done, but just as I could not sunder my halves, so I cannot rejoin them. Lisana has told me that you are the only living mage who can help us. So I have come to you to offer gifts and seek your help."

Kinrove's upper lip curled in scorn, briefly baring his teeth. For that instant, he looked like a snarling dog. "Now you come, asking this? Now? After my dance is but a shadow of itself, after so many of our warriors died in your ill-planned raid? After you have wakened the hatred and wariness of the intruders against us? Now you ask this of me, when all of my strength, every hour of the day, is barely enough to hold the intruders back from the ancient ones? No longer can I send sadness and discouragement rolling into their den. All of my focus must be only on defending our ancestors. And even so, it is not enough! Daily they press against me, daily they make small inroads. But you ask me to divert my strength and focus it on you, to reunite what Lisana foolishly halved!"

Soldier's Boy had listened to Kinrove's rant with a bowed head until he spoke disparagingly of Lisana. Now he lifted his gaze and our eyes locked with Kinrove's. "The fault lies not with Lisana!" he thundered. "Had she not split me, how could the plague have been spread to the very heart of the soldiers' nest? Had she not split me, would not you even now be watching your back lest the Kidona send magic against you while you are defending against the intruders? It is not her fault that her success has been incomplete. Instead, it is as you accuse me. The first time I stood before you, I should have asked you to make me into a whole again. If I had, so many things that have gone wrong would never have come to pass!" Here he spared a glance for Likari, still sleeping in Olikea's arms. Olikea's entire focus was on her son, however. I do not think she even heard what Soldier's Boy was saying.

"I cannot go back to that day, and do what was wise. None of us, no matter how much magic we hold, can do that. So. Because I have waited, will you now wait? And in a season or a year, will we look back and mourn that we did not do now what we should have done?"

Kinrove's scowl had only deepened. "It is so easy for you to say, 'do this now.' You think not at all of how much magic it must cost me, let alone the time and the preparations that must be made. Do you think I will wave my hand and it will be done?"

Actually, Soldier's Boy had believed just that. Or so it seemed to me from the sinking disappointment that flooded through him. He took a deep breath. "What does this require then, Greatest of the Great Ones?"

Soldier's Boy's apparent humility and outright flattery seemed to placate Kinrove. He leaned back in his chair. He tapped his lips with his steepled fingers and for a few moments seemed lost in thought. Then, as if even such a sedentary activity demanded it, he gestured to a feeder to bring him food. Almost as an afterthought, he added, "And bring a seat for Soldier's Boy, and food and drink."

Feeders and their assistants sprang into action, serving not only Soldier's Boy but also hurrying to supply Olikea with a comfortable bench and offering her food and drink as well. A large chair was toted out to me, draped with soft blankets and cushions. No sooner was Soldier's Boy seated in it than a table was placed before him. A ewer of water and one of sweet wine, two glasses, a tray of sticky little balls of sweet meat and grain, a bowl of thick soup and two freshly baked loaves were set out before me. At the sight and smell of the food, Soldier's Boy's ability to think fled. He felt his hands start to shake and his throat squeezed tight with hunger. Yet, for one long moment, he sat still. When he realized that he was waiting for Olikea to serve him, to fill his glass and arrange the dishes and suggest to him which he should taste first, he shook his head and then all but dived into his food.

He had eaten at Kinrove's table before. Even so, the exquisite tastes and textures nearly overpowered him. In each dish were ingredients designed to nourish a Great One's magic, and as he ate, he became more aware of the intricate web of magics that emanated from Kinrove. The Great Man had not exaggerated the effort he was expending. He was the center of the dance that protected the ancient trees, but he also controlled the magic that surrounded his summer encampment with a strong boundary. He held a magical shield between himself and Soldier's Boy, one that at a flick of his finger could become deadly. There were other, smaller magics at work, including the ones he worked to deaden the small pains of his abused body, and others that Soldier's Boy could not quite trace. As he watched Kinrove eat, he perceived that every movement of the Great Man's body served two purposes. His gracefulness was not something that Soldier's Boy had imagined. Every movement he made, every gesture of his hand, how he lifted his glass or turned his head, all of them meant—something.

Kinrove put down his glass. He didn't smile at Soldier's Boy, but there was a sort of acceptance in his face now. "You start to see, don't you? It is how the magic has always spoken to me. I have said it before, but few understand. I am the dance; it is me and I am a part of it. And when I summon the dancers and they come, they join me and become a part of me. I dance, Soldier's Boy. Not, perhaps, in as lively a fashion as I did when I first became a Great Man. But since the magic woke in me, there is not a movement that I have made that was not a part of my dance."

Kinrove gestured at a server to fill his glass again. As she stepped forward, the Great Man shifted his own posture slightly, in a way that echoed and yet opposed the feeder's movement. For the moments that she poured his wine, she was his unwitting dance partner. As she stepped away, his hand moved toward the glass. For a fleeting second, Soldier's Boy could see the invisible lines of force that Kinrove's dance created. It all made perfect sense, for that instant. And then the comprehension faded from his mind, and though he could see how gracefully Kinrove lifted his cup and drank from it, he could no longer perceive the magic.

"You will have to be prepared," Kinrove announced, as if he were continuing a conversation. "There are, of course, foods that will raise your awareness. But the preparation is more than a matter of merely eating what is put before you. You will dance until you become the dance. It will be strenuous, and you have never in your life trained for such a thing. You may not be capable of what the dance demands of you in order to make the magic work."

Soldier's Boy was offended. He slapped a hand to his ample chest. "This body has marched for hours at a time, ridden a horse for days over many miles of different terrain. This body has dug a hundred graves, and it—"

"Still has never endured the rigors of a dancer. But it will have to. Do you understand that you may not survive this dance?"

"I must survive, to be made one. I must survive so that the magic can work through me, to drive the intruders away. What, will you kill me with your magic to be rid of me, and then tell everyone that it was my own fault?"

Kinrove was silent for a moment. His face assumed grave lines, and that, too, Soldier's Boy fleetingly glimpsed, was a part of his endless dance. "You can either let go of your resistance now, or you can dance it away," he observed mildly. "I suggest that, if you can, you banish your distrust and accept what I tell you. The magic is like a river when it carries you to the dance. Be you mud or be you stone, still it will flow, and it will cut its way through whatever resistance you put before it. It will be easier for you if you clear the resistance from yourself rather than make the magic slice through it."

"Let me worry about controlling my resistance to your magic," Soldier's Boy replied stiffly. "Whatever must be done to make me ready, then let us do it."

"My magic?" Kinrove asked almost condescendingly. "That you name it 'your magic' when you speak to me rather than 'the magic' shows that you will resist it. Very well. There is no way I can help you with that. Perhaps by the time you are ready to let the dance have you, you will have heard my counsel."

Kinrove turned his attention away from Soldier's Boy. He summoned, not one, but three of his feeders. As his hand flowed through the triple beckoning gesture, Soldier's Boy again had a tiny image of Kinrove drawing strings of magic toward him, like an arcane puppeteer. The feeders approached him and waited.

"We will need a quantity of the food that we make each day for the dancers. But it will need to be made of a greater strength. There must be much sweetness in it, and twice as much hallera bark. The root of the wild raspberry must be dug, and the youngest parts of it ground and added. Prepare also a large roast of meat, and water soured with the leaves of the atra bush. I will have other dishes that you will need to prepare, but that will be enough for now. One other task you must do for me. Use bear grease and the tallow of a doe, and strong mint and crimsberry leaves and willow tips. Make a rub for Soldier's Boy, and a very hot bath. We must loosen his joints and muscles. Prepare wraps, too, for binding his feet and legs to protect them, and a wide wrap for his belly, to support it. All these things, make ready by the evening. Go now to do these things. And send a feeder to his table, to help him fill himself with whatever he desires."

The command for food had been welcomed, but the mentions of the bath and the wraps sounded more ominous. "Don't do this," I whispered to him. "Stop it now. Take Olikea and Likari and go. You can't trust Kinrove. Neither of us have any idea of what will become of us if he tries to reunite us as one. Leave now."

"Lisana said this was our only path," he said aloud. "In her wisdom, I trust. I will do as she suggested. I give myself over into your hands." He seemed to have difficulty speaking that last sentence. He glanced over at Olikea. He cleared his throat. "I am accustomed to the ministrations of my own feeder. Might I ask that she be given help in caring for our son, so that she can assist me in preparing myself?"

At her name, Olikea lifted her head. Her gaze went from her deeply sleeping boy to Soldier's Boy and back again. Plainly she was torn. But when she spoke aloud, there was no indecisiveness in her voice. "You should not need to ask this, Nevare. No one has the right to separate a Great One from his preferred feeder. And no one has any right to keep feeders from ministering to their Great One."

She stooped and then stood up. Likari's limp body dangled in her arms. His head lolled back and his legs, longer and thinner than I recalled them, swung as she walked toward me, carrying her boy. When she reached me, she did not set him down before me, but gave him over into my arms. Soldier's Boy's arms curved, lifting Likari to hold him close against his chest. "Likari was Nevare's feeder when your dance stole him from us," Olikea said loudly. "When he awakens, if he is himself, he will once more wish to serve him. And I will allow no one to take that honor from him."

CHAPTER TWENTY-SIX

THE DANCE

One of Kinrove's senior feeders gave over her tent for our use. It was hard to become accustomed to the place. It smelled like someone else's home, and I knew that Soldier's Boy felt awkward being there. Olikea did not. She had entered and gestured to the man carrying Likari to put him down on the bed. She had covered the boy warmly against the cooling evening, and then directed the man to move the tent owner's furnishings aside to make room for the large chair that had followed me from Kinrove's pavilion. The tent had seemed roomy before the chair was brought in.

Kinrove had given way to Olikea's indignation with no argument. He had put one of his feeders in charge of us for the time being, saying that he also had to make preparations for the magic he would work. Kinrove's feeder had made the arrangements for a tent for us, and had received Kinrove's instructions as to what had to be done to prepare me. I had overheard enough of it to be alarmed. Soldier's Boy did not appear to share my anxiety. He settled himself in the chair and then sat looking over at Likari.

The boy slept on. His color seemed better than it had, but he still had not awakened long enough even to speak to them. I felt Soldier's Boy concern for the boy's mind.

"He is so thin," Olikea said worriedly. She had settled next to Likari on the pallet. Through his blanket, she stroked his back. "I can feel every knob of his spine. And look at his hair, how coarse and dry it is. Like a sick animal's pelt."

"From now on, he will only get better," Soldier's Boy told her. I wondered if he believed it. Silence settled for a short time between them.

"You spent all of Lisana's treasure to get us here, and to get Likari back."

"I do not judge it a bad bargain," Soldier's Boy replied easily.

"You called him 'our son' when you spoke of him."

"I did. So I wish him to be known. The son of Olikea and Soldier's Boy."

A long silence followed those words. I would have given much to know what Olikea was thinking. Either Soldier's Boy thought he knew or felt no driving need to know. Her next words were another question. "What is Kinrove going to do to you? Why do you wish him to do it?"

He spoke as if it were a simple thing. "Two men live in this body. One is a Gernian, raised to be a soldier. One is of the People, taught by Lisana to be a mage. Sometimes one controls this flesh, sometimes the other. For when the magic spoke to Lisana and said I was to serve it, she divided me, so that I could learn the ways of both peoples. It seemed wise to her. It seems wise to me now. But the magic can only work through me if I become one once more. A single entity, made of both Gernian and the People."

"I understand," she said slowly. And then, looking at me more piercingly, she repeated, "Yes. I do understand. For I have known both of you, haven't I? How will Kinrove do this thing?"

"He expresses his magic in dance. Perhaps he will have to dance for me, or perhaps his dancers will have to. Maybe *I* will have to dance."

"I think that is likely." She was thoughtful and silent for a time, smoothing Likari's hair as she sat beside him. Then she asked,

"When you are one, will you still want me to be your feeder?" More hesitantly she asked, "Will you still call Likari 'our son'?"

"I don't know." He sounded reluctant to consider it.

She fixed her eyes on the sleeping boy. "I know that you have always loved Lisana. I know that I have sometimes been only—"

Her words were interrupted by an odd noise. Something heavy fell onto the roof. Soldier's Boy looked up as something scrabbled wildly against the leather tent's side, clambering awkwardly back up it until it achieved a perch at the top. A moment later, I heard the croaker bird give three satisfied caws. The god of balances and of death sat on the peak of our tent.

"Likari—does he sleep still?" Soldier's Boy demanded anxiously.

Olikea heard the anxiety in his voice. She leaned down close to the boy's face. "He does. He breathes."

Abruptly the door of the tent was flipped open and two servers entered carrying a laden table. There was a single large bowl on it, the size of a punch bowl, holding a chowderlike substance. The aroma that rose from it was both delicious and repellent, as if someone had prepared a succulent dish and then attempted to conceal a strong medicine in it. The two men carrying it positioned the table carefully on the uneven floor and left. Soldier's Boy breathed a sigh of relief as the tent door fell into place, but an instant later, it was lifted again, and more feeders entered. One carried a large ewer of water and a cup. Others brought various food dishes—breads, new greens, fish, and fowl—that they set down near the vat of chowder.

This parade of food was followed by the feeder whom Kinrove had put in charge of us. She was a buxom, comely young woman, with long gleaming black hair and her face patterned with tiny specks like a scattering of fine seed. Her name was Wurta, and as she introduced herself she seemed very pleased to have been given such an important task. She almost ignored Soldier's Boy, speaking directly to Olikea, feeder to feeder.

"I have been given instructions that I must pass on to you," she announced. At her words, Olikea rose, reluctantly leaving Likari, and came to stand beside my chair. The seed-speckled feeder spoke briskly, almost officiously, as she stepped up to the table and stirred the vat of creamy-brown chowder, releasing clouds of steam trapped beneath its thick surface. "This, all of this, he must eat. We have done our best to give it a pleasant flavor, but the roots that feed this magic have their own strong taste. It may be hard for him to stomach. Kinrove has had us flavor his water to give him some respite from it. These other foods are for you to feed him sparingly. Do not let him fill his belly with them; most of what he eats must be this soup, and Kinrove judges that he must eat it all."

Wurta was interrupted by a loud snuffing noise. Likari, eyes still closed, had lifted his head from the bedding and was sniffing after the steam rising from the chowder pot. His face had a blank, infantile look, or perhaps more like that of a still-blind puppy mindlessly seeking the scent of food. Olikea looked at him with a gaze full of horror.

"Oh, no, he must have none of this," Wurta said quickly as her eyes followed the direction of his snuffling. "I will have something else brought for him right away. And some washwater? Yes."

She hastened away to fulfill those errands while Soldier's Boy leaned forward and hesitantly lifted the ladle from the pot. He touched it to his lips, and then took a mouthful. It did not taste awful. He swallowed it and waited, anticipating a bitter aftertaste. Nothing. No, there was something, a perfumy tang. Not unpleasant, but not something I would ever associate with food. It rather reminded me of the food served to us at the Academy. There was a lot of it, but none of it tasted so delicious as to make one long for more.

Likari stopped his sniffing and suddenly sagged back onto the bed. If the sound of his muffled snores were an indication, he had fallen into a new depth of sleep. Olikea looked relieved. She turned her attention back to Soldier's Boy. "Perhaps you should begin eating while it is still warm and fresh," she suggested. So saying, she came and ladled up a bowlful of the stuff and set it before him.

Soldier's Boy ate it. He ate the next three bowls of it as well. It was warm and not unpleasant, though the perfume began to be annoying. Olikea, watchful as ever, offered him a bit of the fish and some bread. It cleared his palate of the soup, and when he was finished she served him up another bowlful of the stuff and he attacked it manfully.

About a third of the way through the cauldron Wurta shepherded in a team of feeders with a large pot of aromatic salve, food for Likari, and a washtub and several pots of warmed water. She smoothly suggested that Olikea wake her son, wash him, and then feed him. While she was doing that, Wurta proposed that Soldier's Boy would accompany them to where he could be treated with the salve that Kinrove had had them prepare. Olikea looked doubtful at this, but Soldier's Boy put her mind at ease. "I am well able to speak for myself in how I am cared for. But I do not wish to entrust Likari to anyone else but you. Take care of him. I am sure I will be back soon."

"I should be taking care of you. I am your feeder," she said, but her voice held no conviction and her eyes kept moving toward her son.

"So is Likari. Tend to him for now. If I require you, I can send for you."

"As you wish," she said with relief, and even before Soldier's Boy had left the tent, she had moved to Likari's side.

Soldier's Boy followed Wurta and her assistants. They took him to a steam hut. It was small and tightly built of branches plastered over with earth. Inside, a big copper kettle boiled over a fire pit. All of them stripped before entering the hut, and once they were inside, with the door shut tight behind them, the heat and steam were close to unbearable. "First," Wurta told him, "we must open your skin, so that the salve can soak into you."

This involved him sitting in a chair while heavy cloths were dipped in the boiling water. The feeders allowed them to cool enough so that they could wring them out, and then immediately began to wrap him in them. They were not scalding, but hot enough to be unpleasant. Soldier's Boy gritted his teeth and endured the treatment. When they removed the cloth, his skin was a bright scarlet by the firelight. His specks showed dark against the redness. The feeders went to work quickly, rubbing the salve into his flesh.

As quickly as they covered his skin with the slippery stuff, they wrapped him afresh with the hot steaming cloths. Between the heat and the minty pungency of the salve, he felt giddy. The meal he had just eaten coiled and squirmed in his belly. He began to fervently wish that Olikea were there, to protect him from Kinrove's feeders.

I agreed with him. "They will kill you with this treatment," I warned him. "Listen to your heart beating. You can scarcely breathe for the steam and the stink. Tell them to let you go; they'll have to listen to you. You're a Great One. You have what you came for; Likari is restored to you. You should leave and take him and Olikea back to the kin-clan. Let us find another way to solve our problem."

It was getting hard for him to breathe. The air was hot and the pungent aroma of the salve seemed to only make it worse. Yet he said, "I will do whatever I must—"

And the words died on his lips. For the briefest moment, he breathed music, not air. It lifted him weightlessly; he felt himself rise with it, float on it, towed away from the bonds of earth and up into the air.

Just as abruptly, he was back in his flesh, and fighting, not for air, but for the music he had breathed but a moment before. "—to regain Lisana." He finished his thought in a hazy voice. He opened his arms wide, trying to bring the music back.

"Do you feel that?" Wurta asked in wonder.

Several of the others murmured awed assents.

"He will dance," Wurta said, but her tone conveyed far more than her words. "Kinrove spoke true. When he is one, he will be a river for the magic. The dance has already found him. We must hurry to be sure he consumes the rest of the food he will need."

But it was already too late.

They led Soldier's Boy from the steam hut, still swathed in the hot wraps that held the herbal unguent against his skin. As we emerged from the darkness into the forest light, he took a deep breath of the clean, cool air that greeted him. And the blood that flowed through his body turned to music. He began to dance.

The feeders cried out in alarm. Two seized his arms and tried to restrain him, shouting, "No, not yet, not yet! You are not prepared!"

Someone else shouted, "Tell Kinrove! Run, run!" and yet another one cried out, "Fetch his own feeder! He may listen to her."

When Olikea came running, I heard her voice. But Soldier's Boy did not. He was caught up in a rapture of sound and movement, far past drunkenness, deeper than unconsciousness. I shouted for him and then reached for him as one might plunge an arm into a deep, cold lake to retrieve a comrade who had fallen overboard. But I could not reach him. No part of us touched anymore, and that realization terrified me. Instead of uniting us, Kinrove's magic seemed to be separating us even more completely.

Olikea rushed to him and seized his hands. "Oh, I should not have let them take you! I should not have listened to you at all. Nevare, Nevare, stop, stop dancing. Come back to me!"

But he did not. Instead, he tried to pull her into the dance with him. He gripped her hands and dragged her along as he stepped and turned and bowed. Kinrove's feeders cried out in fear, and four of them seized her and pulled her from his grasp. Then they fought her, holding her back as she shrieked and clawed and struggled to get back to him.

"It will do you no good! He cannot hear you. If you let him seize you, he will drag and dance you to death. Remember your son, remember your boy! Stay here and care for him!"

I caught only glimpses of that struggle. Soldier's Boy's eyes were wide, but he did not look at any of the people. He saw the trees and the shifting of light through the young leaves. He saw the fluttering of a single leaf, and his shaken fingers echoed it. He felt a light movement of the breeze on his face, and he danced backward, airily wafted on it. Like many a heavy man, he had strength in his legs beyond what one might expect. His movements were graceful and controlled; the unguent seemed to have loosened and oiled his muscles. He shifted, turned and lifted his hands to the sky, mimicking the rising steamy smoke from the sweat hut. From his half-closed eyes, I caught a glimpse of Kinrove, supported by two of his feeders. Dismay sagged his features.

"It is too soon. Only half of him dances! I do not know what will happen now. Show me the kettle of food. How much did he eat?"

Olikea had sunk to her knees, still weeping and wailing. Behind her, I glimpsed a very thin Likari, a blanket clasped around his bony shoulders, trying to hurry to his mother. When the boy saw me, a thin wail escaped his mouth. Pointing and weeping, he, too, sank to his knees. My only comfort was that at the sound of his voice, Olikea had turned. She caught her breath and then crawled to her son. When he would have risen and staggered toward me, she caught him and held him in her arms. At least he was safe from Kinrove's mad dance.

I was not. The music ran in my veins like boiling water seething down a pipe. It hurt and exhilarated at the same time. For me, the sensation reminded me of being whirled around and around by my older brother when I was small. It dizzied me and I could not focus my eye on any object. There was also the same sensation of imminent disaster. When Rosse had gripped me by wrist and ankle and flown me around and around, I had always known that if he lost his grip, I'd have bruises. But I'd also known that sooner or later, my brother would tire and would attempt to land me gently. That was what had allowed me to enjoy the experience.

With Soldier's Boy's dance, there was no promise of respite. I could not find him in the densely twined music and dance. He had merged with it, become one with it rather than with me. I became even more aware of my body, or the body that had been mine. My lungs worked like bellows and my mouth was already dry. In a seizure of music, Soldier's Boy danced. He turned and spun; he made small leaps off the ground, and then bent low and swayed, a tree caught in the wind. I felt that with every step he took, he retreated from me and ventured deeper into the music's power.

I caught a spinning glimpse of Kinrove in the chair that had been brought out for him. His face was grave, but his hands moved with Soldier's Boy's dance, almost as if he were conducting it. Did he command it? There was a chilling thought. Soldier's Boy's eyes had closed to slits. I focused on the little I could see. Most of it was sky, or a brief image of tree trunks. Olikea, tears on her cheeks. One of Kinrove's feeders scratching her nose. The wall of the steam hut. Kinrove, weaving his fingers as his hands danced with me.

On and on Soldier's Boy danced, until he no longer leapt but shuffled and wove. After a time, it was a struggle to keep his head up or to lift his hands. Blood throbbed painfully in his feet and all the muscles along his spine shrieked that they had been torn loose from their anchorage. But on we danced.

I had to stop it. Whatever Kinrove had believed this dance would do, it wasn't accomplishing it. I was more separate from Soldier's Boy than ever and it was destroying the body that housed us. Breath rasped in and out and his heart thundered in his ears. Veins pulsed in his calves. I stopped trying to see out of the eyes and turned my attention inward, seeking for Soldier's Boy.

His consciousness was all but gone. I could find no sign of his awareness of himself as something separate from the dancing magic. I groped deeper, following the magic and the dance that seethed through him like a river in flood, a frightening thing to behold. "Soldier's Boy!" I shouted at it, wondering where he was in that rush, or if he had already melted into it completely. I dared not touch it. I wondered if I could seize control of the body now that he no longer consciously possessed it. Perhaps, if the dance magic had stolen him completely away, I could possess my body again.

That thought gave me a surge of hope such as I had not felt for months. I readied myself, as best I could. There was so much to take control of, and I felt I must seize it all at once. My hands and arms, my shuffling feet, my bobbing head—how did anyone ever manage to control so many pieces of a living body at once? For only a second I marveled at that thought.

Then I felt a sudden red lurch of pain in my chest. Soldier's Boy staggered three steps to one side, and I thought we were falling. But he fetched up against a tree, clung there grimly for a moment, and then, as his heart steadied its thumping, he once more pushed himself free to stand upright and then to dance. It was then that I knew he would dance us to death. I spread myself out and attempted to inhabit my body once more.

It was the strangest sensation, as if I had flung myself onto the back of a galloping horse. I was there suddenly feeling the muscles move, feeling the jabs of pain from my abused feet. The body was mine, and not mine. I danced on, awkward and jolting, like a marionette whose strings have been seized by a child. I planted my feet, but my hands and arms flapped and waved. If I focused on holding them still, then my head wagged wildly and my errant feet began to slide sideways. Suddenly it was an all-out struggle between me and Soldier's Boy as to who would control it. I felt him there, not as the twin of my mind, but as the body's will. I clenched my body's teeth and curled my hands into fists and held them there. I tightened the screaming muscles all along my spine, forbidding them to twist or sway or bow. I bent my arms into my chest and embraced myself, bent my head down to my chest and held it there. With a surge of resolution, I folded my legs under me. I crashed to the earth, falling hard, but still keeping my control. I rolled myself into as tight and still of a ball as my flesh would allow. I shouted stillness into myself and then realized my mistake. No, not my breath, not my heart. I pulled breath after deep breath into my lungs and tried to calm my leaping heart as if it were a wild creature I strove to soothe.

"Be still, be still, be still," I whispered to every part of myself. And that was how they caught me.

I had no sense of becoming one with Soldier's Boy. I felt no encounter with some "other self" hidden in my flesh. Instead, I was besieged by a decade of memories and thoughts. They were mine, they were his, but they had belonged to both of us, and I had always been aware of my twin lives and experiences. I had always been me, never Soldier's Boy, never Nevare, always me. Carsina had broken his heart as much as mine, and I had longed for Lisana just as deeply as he had. I loved the forest and he wanted to make his father proud. It was me the mob had tried to murder in the streets of Gettys, and I had every right to hate them for it. Those were my trees that they were trying to cut, the wisdom of my elders, and it infuriated me that no one would listen to me.

I rose slowly from the ground. My body settled into place around me. I was home. I was complete and all I had been meant to be. I was the perfect vessel for the magic and ready now to take up my task. Oh, but it was no task, it was joy. The magic and the music of that magic coursed through every vessel in my body, prompting me to the dance. My hands floated at the ends of my arms. I lifted my head and felt the music pull me taller. I moved with grace and beauty, dignity and purpose. I danced twice round Olikea and Likari, binding my protection round them. My hands wove, shaping a life for them. Then I moved to Kinrove and stood before him, meeting his eyes as I danced my independence of him. His hands might move and weave, but they were only his part of the dance. They did not control me. I turned my back on him, snapping the gossamer threads that had bound me to his magic. I opened my arms to the forest, and beyond it, to the wide world and all it contained. I opened my heart and my eyes and my mind, and I danced away from those who had been watching me. I had a task to do.

I danced out of the world and back into it, into its truer deeper form. Place no longer bound me, nor time. Instead, I moved through the magic, called by a series of unfinished tasks.

I returned to the Dancing Spindle. It was still; I had seen to that. I had engineered that the iron blade would fall to become a wedge beneath the tip of that magic artifact. But I had not finished that task. The Spindle still stood, and it still strained against the blade that bound it. How foolish of me. The very first time I had seen it, I had wondered at it. How could such a large spindle of stone remain balanced on such a tiny point? How could it not fall? The Gernian engineer had not been able to find an answer to that riddle, but the Speck mage knew it. He could see the filaments of magic that flowed from the tip of the spindle and shot off into the spirit world I had visited with the Kidona shaman all those years ago. Dewara had known.

I danced up the many steps that spiraled up the tower. I danced on the tower's top, and with my opened eyes, I could see the magic that held the spindle, like a string on a top. It was less than a string; it was a cobweb to me. I reached toward it. For a moment, I felt a shadow of a reservation about what I was about to do. Dewara had taught me, had been my mentor. Despite all the evil he had done me, did I not owe him something for that? And what of the wind-wizards, what of the other mages of the other Plainspeople? I sighed. They would have to go back to being

individual mages, with each mastering only the power he himself could generate. The decision was made. With one hand over
my head, I leapt, and my fingers snagged and tore that thread of
magic.

The spindle fell, coming down on the tower top. Only my
dancing saved me as the tower cracked and sighed thunderously
and collapsed. I danced atop the wreckage as it fell, not falling with
it, but leaping upon it, landing and then leaping again. Down and
down we went, and when we struck the valley floor, the spindle
fell and parted into a thousand rounds of red-and-white-streaked
stone. The circles of stone bounced and rolled throughout the ancient ruins. A haze of pink dust rose to fill the valley. The spindle
was no more. Never again would the Kidona threaten either of
my peoples. That battle was over.

And I danced away from it, leaving it behind, a task completed. Lisana would no longer have to keep a watch against the
Kidona mages. She was freed from that endless task. I sensed her
and knew that I could go to her. She would greet me with joy.
But not yet. Not until all was completed.

My dancing feet carried me to Old Thares. No distance was
a barrier to the magic. I danced into my uncle Sefert's home and
into his library. My book, the book I had so carefully written,
called me. But it was not there on a shelf. Bodiless as a shadow, I
danced, up the stairs and through the halls of his home. I found it
open on my aunt's writing desk. I danced thrice around her desk
and then she came into the room and walked to the desk and
seated herself there. She looked down at the book, and I pushed
ideas into her mind. This book held everything she needed to
become a favorite with the Queen. Again, I felt the moment of
hesitation. What of my dignity? What of my family's noble name?
There were secrets in there that should never have been committed to paper.

And yet revealing them, no matter how it might hurt me,
might put an end to war between two peoples. The greater good
had to be served. With her I turned the pages and showed her the
parts she needed to read. I bent and whispered in her ears. "A few
changes. That would be all it would take to avoid scandal and win

the Queen's favor. Think of what power you could wield if you were in her highest graces. Think of the future for your daughter. A few changes. Make those words yours. Whisper them where they must be heard. That would be all that was needed."

I danced around her while she looked at the journal. Then she opened the drawer of her desk, took out good heavy paper, textured thick as cream, and her own mother-of-pearl pen. She uncapped her inkwell, dipped her pen, and began to take notes. I smiled, danced around her a final time, and then danced away.

Away from Old Thares, following the river and the King's Road. As I went, I could see how the road had changed everything. Wherever the road had gone, little trails and paths and byways had sprouted out from it and spread their roots. Cabins and cottages, hamlets and new noble holdings, bustling towns and ambitious little villages seemed to spring up wherever there was a crossroads or wherever the road kissed the river's shore. There was good in that, and there was bad, but of itself it was neither; only change. People had to live somewhere, and population pushed from one area flowed into another just as surely as water flows downhill. There was nothing evil about it; change was only change.

To make people move, I saw, they had to be pushed or pulled. The Landsingers had pushed the Gernians, and the Gernians had pushed the Plainspeople. That push from the Landsingers taking our coastal provinces had propelled the Gernians all the way to the Barrier Mountains, just as a wave of water from a stone dropped in a still pond eventually laps against the far shore. The King's Road wasn't really the problem. The road was only the spear's point that led the way. The People had tried to push back against the Gernians. But their impact hadn't been strong enough; the People could not muster a large enough push to repel the Gernians.

No. But something might *pull* them back.

I danced to the Midlands, to my father's holdings of Widevale. Evening was falling there. I danced up the graveled road to his house, and as I went, I saw changes there, too. The signs of neglect were small, but I saw them. Winter-broken limbs had not been pruned from the line of trees that edged the driveway. Potholes that should have been filled instead held rainwater. The circular drive for carriages and wagons was developing ruts. Small things now, but untended, they would only worsen. They all suggested to me that my father had still not resumed the day-to-day management of his estate, and that Yaril, although doing the best she could, would not see such tasks until they urgently demanded attention. But Sergeant Duril should; why had not he spoken to her?

I danced into the house; the neatness and order I saw there comforted me. Here, at least, Yaril was in her element and still in command. Spring fires burned brightly in each neatly swept hearth, and sweet bouquets of early anemones, tulips, and daffodils filled the vases. The breath of hyacinth was in Yaril's room; she sat at her small white desk, writing a letter. I danced as I looked over her shoulder. It was a note to Carsina, asking why she had not replied to her earlier missive and asking her if she had news of me. I breathed by her ear: "Remind her that once she loved me, that once we were to be wed. Remind her of that." I did not know why I asked her to do such a thing; her letter was to a woman months dead. The magic suggested it to me and so I did it.

I said no more to her than that. Somewhere, I felt something give way inside my body. It is hard to describe the sensation. If my body had been a house, then it would have been the sensation of a weight-bearing wall starting to crack. For a moment, I was in that body again. I felt what the dance was doing to it. Every shock of my foot against the earth was translated up through my flesh, muscle, and bone. Like rhythmic earthquakes, they shook and tore at my body, fraying tendons, tearing blood vessels that in turn leaked blood into the cavities of my flesh. The pounding of my feet against the earth might as well have been tiny hammer blows against my body. Each step of the dance did damage.

It could not be helped. The damage was part of the dance.

I put my mind back to the magic and found myself in my father's study. A fire burned in the hearth. My father sat next to it in a cushioned chair, a robe across his knees. Caulder's uncle was seated on the other side of the hearth. I had never met the man, but I knew him by his resemblance to Colonel Stiet, his brother. He fairly trembled with eagerness as he showed my father the crudely sketched map I had drawn so many months ago. Folding and much handling had not improved my rough sketch. "This," he said, tracing the ravine I had drawn. "What do you suppose he meant this to be? Do you recognize the terrain?"

My father had grown older; his hair was whitening, and veins and tendons stood out on the back of his hands. As before, I could see the ravages of the magic. But I thought I could also see some healing of the damage, like scar tissue knitting together what remained of sound flesh. My father would never be the man he had been, but he might heal, and at least be himself rather than what the magic had made of him. It need not have him if it had all of me.

Stiet did not allow my father to hold the map he was show-ing him; he kept possession of it, merely pointing at the part he wished my father to study. My father glanced at it with polite interest, then turned aside with a vague scowl. "I've told you three times, I don't know what that is. If you are so keen to know, ask Nevare. You say that he drew it."

"He did draw it! But I cannot ask your son. You sent him away. Do not you remember that you did that? You spent most of yesterday weeping over it!" Stiet flung himself back suddenly in his chair. "Oh, you are useless!" he exploded. "The smallest, simplest bit of information stands between me and a fortune. And no one has it."

Frustration vied with cruelty in the man's words. My father's face crumpled, as if he'd been dealt a blow to the stomach. His mouth worked, trembled, and then with an effort he firmed his jaw. Seeing my father weakened and uncertain and treated so abusively by a man who was taking full advantage of my family's hospitality washed away the final dregs of my anger and resent-ment toward my father. Stiet's callous mockery of him made me furious. I danced around my father, sealing him off from Stiet's cruel words. I danced strength of will and pride for him. "Tell him to leave you alone! Tell him to ask Sergeant Duril. Duril will know what my scribble meant."

My father drew himself up taller in his chair. "Ask Sergeant Duril. He knows the boy best; he's been as much a father to him as I have. He'll recognize what Nevare's scribble means."

Stiet clenched his jaw. Nervously, he refolded the map, smoothing the creases ever deeper. "But can we trust him?" he demanded of my father. "I've told you, there is a fortune at stake here. And I do not know if we can wait until he returns from Gettys. Spring grows stronger every day. At any time now, someone else may find the place we seek and claim it for his own. And all, all will be for naught. Why did you have to send the sergeant away?"

My father folded his knobby hands on his blanketed knees. His gaze seemed clearer as he stared at Stiet. "Why, to help my niece Epiny. Yaril had word from her; the winter has been quite harsh at Gettys, with skirmishes with the Speck. Duril set out with the high-wheeled cart full of supplies. He'll look into what has become of Nevare as well. Seems there's reason to believe the boy made it that far east and enlisted at the fort there. Plucky lad. Can't keep a Burvelle down for long."

"Plucky lad? You disowned him! He'd become fat as a pig. He was kicked out of the Academy, came home in disgrace, and you disowned him!" With difficulty, Stiet calmed himself. He took a breath and leaned toward my father, speaking as if with sympathy for a poor old man. "He's gone, Lord Burvelle. Your last living son is gone. It's a shame he disappointed you so, but he's gone. All your sons are gone. Your last best hope is for your daughter to marry well, stay here, and take care of you. My adopted son is a good match for her; he's from a good family. Unfortunately, I have little fortune to leave to him. But if only we could establish where the mineral sample came from, I feel it would be of interest to certain other geologists. I could provide handsomely for the boy then. And he in turn could provide for your daughter. It could do us all a good turn."

"I want to see the rock." My father spoke with sudden strength. "I want to know what is so unique about it. Let me see the rock."

"I told you before, sir. It has been misplaced. I cannot show it to you. You must take my word for it that it shows a most uncommon mix of elements. It will be of great interest to those who study geology, but likely laymen will only find it boring. Scholars of the origins of the earth will be intrigued if they can view its place of origin."

As I danced, I shook my head. The man was lying. He had no scholarly interest in that stone. There was something else about that rock, something of monetary value. I was sure of it, though I did not know enough geology to say what it might be. Then, unnervingly, my father's eyes met mine. He did not stare through me; he seemed to really see me. In response to the shaking of my head, he slowly shook his own. "No," he said, and swung his gaze to Stiet. "No. You are not telling me the full story. And even when Sergeant Duril returns, he will not help you. Not until you are honest with us. And if my son lives"—his voice grew stronger—"if my son lives, he will come home. Don't dangle that pale little boy before me like bait. He's barely out of short trousers, and my daughter has told me she does not wish to marry so young. She'll tell you so herself." He lifted his voice suddenly. "Yaril! Yaril, I want you!" And for a moment he sounded like the father I recalled from my youth rather than the man crazed by my failure at the Academy and broken by the grief of his plague losses.

I heard the sound of a chair pushed back, and then the hurrying patter of Yaril's feet down the corridor. "Never mind, never mind," Stiet was saying hastily. "Send her away; you've no need of her. Don't make yourself upset. I only asked a simple question."

"*I* need her," the old man replied testily. Again, he looked directly at me, and I would have sworn he could see me. "I need her to do the things that I cannot do. The things I no longer have the strength to do for myself." He kept his gaze on my face as he spoke, and I had the strangest sensation of an interchange between us, as if the magic I had infected him with was now returning to me. I felt more whole for it coming back to me, and I could almost see it leaving my father and allowing him to become more himself again. How much magic had I spread, and to how many people? I knew that it had touched Epiny strongly, and Spink. Carsina, it had forced to come to me after her death, to beg my forgiveness. Yaril? I'd touched Caulder with it, when I turned him back on the bridge. Who else? How many? A part of me wished to feel guilt over what I had done. Another part effortlessly recognized that it was not me, but the magic that had acted so. It would not accept or tolerate the guilt.

The dancing of my distant body intruded again in my thoughts. Kinrove knew how to express the magic only as dance, and at his bidding, at his summons, I danced. How had I expressed the magic? I suddenly wondered, and then speculated that perhaps words had been my strongest manifestation of it. The journal, the hastily sketched map, even the letters that had flown between Carsina and Yaril and Epiny and myself. I felt something in the distant physicality. Water flowing down my back. Feeders were pouring cooling water over me. I felt it trickle and flow. Somewhere, I thirsted. I did not stop dancing, but opened my mouth and someone trickled water into it. Olikea? Perhaps.

But I could not think of her now, could not think of anything except stitching up the holes in my magical tasks. All that my separate halves could not accomplish was coming together for me. It takes two hands to weave, and that was what I was doing.

When Yaril entered the room, I knew what I had to do. A furrow creased her brow and she suddenly clasped herself in an embrace. "Is there a draft in here?" she demanded, and then hurried about the room, drawing curtains and checking to be sure that the casement windows were securely closed and latched. That done, she hurried up to my father, her skirts rustling and her feet tapping on the floor. Those simple sounds, so often ignored, suddenly seemed a part of the music and I danced with her. Her words seemed a song when she said, "Here I am, Father. What did you need?"

"I need an answer!" Abruptly my father slapped his palm against his leg, as if somehow Yaril had been deceiving him and he was upbraiding her for it.

It broke my heart to see the quiver that passed through her. But she drew herself up straight and met his gaze. "An answer to what question, Father?" she asked him. Her voice was grave, without impertinence. I saw how she used her own demeanor to recall him to his.

"This man's son—his adopted son, this Caulder. Do you wish to be engaged to him?"

She glanced down but spoke strongly for all her averted gaze. "You gave me to understand that the decision was not mine to make."

"Nor is it now!" he shouted. His voice was louder, but it lacked the timbre of his old thunder. Yaril stood firm before it. "But you can have an opinion on it, can't you, and I'm asking you that opinion. What is it?"

She lifted her chin. "Do you wish me to speak it in front of Professor Stiet?"

"Would I ask you while he was sitting here if I did not?"

"Very well." The new edge in her voice rose to meet my father's old steel. "I do not know enough about him yet to completely judge his character. I have seen him only as a guest in our home, rather than as a man about his business in the world. If I must take him, then I will make the best of it. It is what women do, Father."

My father stared at her for a moment. Then he gave a cracked laugh. "And doubtless it is what your mother did with me. So there. You hear the girl, Stiet. I don't think you've got anything we want just now. I think you can keep your damned rock and your damned slip of paper and your damned 'son.' I don't think my daughter and I need any of them."

I saw something then. I saw how my father sensed and defied the magic. It writhed through him like a squirming parasite, seeking to bend him to its will. The magic did not want Professor Stiet to leave. My father lifted a bony hand and rubbed at his chest as if trying to ease an old pain. I had a glimpse of his set teeth when his lips writhed back, but he mastered it. He fought the magic, just as I had. I recalled suddenly the day I had made that map, how I had dashed it off furiously, a deliberately sloppy rendering simply to be able to say I had done it and be finished with it. That Nevare had almost instinctively defied the magic, just as my father did now. I saw him twitch again.

"Wait!" I cried the word aloud, from my body in the distance. "Leave him. Leave him be. There is another way, a better way. Let me guide the magic in this, and I swear you will have your way. But only let the old man alone."

Without hands, I reached; without fingers, I gripped. I drew the magic out of his body as if I were pulling out a snake that had tunneled into his flesh. He cried out as I did so, and clutched at his chest. I knew it gave him pain, and worried that his body would not be able to withstand the strain. But that was uncertainty; what I knew was that if I left the magic in control of him, he would either capitulate to its will or die. I suspected he would choose death.

His face was white, his lips darker than scarlet when at last the magic came free of him. With a cry, he curled forward, clutching his chest. Yaril rushed to his side, crying, "No! No, Father, you must not die. Breathe. Breathe, Father, breathe." She turned to Stiet and barked, "Do not stand there! Call the servants, send someone to fetch the doctor from the Landing."

Stiet didn't move. Cold calculations were totted up in his eyes.

"Send for the doctor!" she shrieked at him.

"I'll go myself." The voice came from the doorway. Caulder Stiet stood there. He had become bookish, to put it kindly. If I had seen him on the streets of a city, I probably would not have known him. His hair had grown out of its military cut, and he wore low shoes on his feet, gray trousers, and a white shirt with a soft gray cravat. In one hand, he held a book, his finger marking his place. He did not look a man of action and the eyes he fixed on Yaril were puppyish with affection.

"Yes! Go!" she cried. Still, he took three steps into the room, set the book down on a side table, and then turned and hurried off.

I had considered using Caulder. That glimpse of him decided me. No. Father was right. Yaril must do what he was no longer strong enough to do. The old man was looking directly at me. His lips moved. "Thank you, son. Thank you." His head sagged to one side on his neck.

The magic squirmed against me, flailing and then wrapping around my ghost fists as it sought to escape. I danced harder, caught in the magic and yet battling with it. My heart rattled in my chest like an empty wagon hitched to a runaway team. I was the magic and I fought the magic, trying to master it, trying to force it into a channel that would not destroy all of the Burvelle family. I clenched it tightly, looked at my helpless little sister as she knelt by my father's failing body, and then doubled the magic into a loop. I pressed it to my brow, imprinting it with an old memory, searing an image into it, and adding to it a message. "This is where the stone came from. But do not give this knowledge to Stiet. Use it for the good of the Burvelle family. Gift whatever it is to the King and Queen. It is the only way."

I froze my heart. "I am sorry," I said to Yaril. "Sorry to make you serve us so. But there is no one else." And then I took my coronet of magic and knowledge and crammed it onto my sister's bowed head.

At the touch of it, she flung her head back, like a horse refusing a bridle. But the magic was there, and the knowledge, and yes, my memory of telling her all that had befallen me that summer my father had given me over to the Kidona warrior Dewara. The magic brought it back to her vividly. And she knew now, as clearly as I did, how to get to the place where Dewara had built his fire and conducted me over to his spirit world. There, I believed, was the source of the rock that I had carried with me as a reminder of that encounter, the same rock that Caulder had stolen from me during my year at the Academy.

I felt the magic, felt its anger that I had torn it from its chosen course and set it into mine. I knew, in a way that defied explanation, that my path would work. It would be more convoluted, but it would serve just as well. Even the magic accepted that, but it accepted it coldly, with an angry promise of vengeance to come. And I acceded to that. I would pay, as I had paid before. But this time it would be worth the price.

Yaril had been crouched by my father. Now she sat down ungracefully, flat on the floor, her legs bent awkwardly under her. She swayed. My father's eyes, opened to slits, looked down at her. Then he leaned his head back on his chair. He took a deeper breath and sighed it out, as if a heavy harness had been taken from him. His eyes traveled to meet mine. His pale lips parted; it could have been a smile. "Lord Burvelle," he sighed. He reached out a shaking hand and set it on my sister's fair head. "Protect her," he murmured. He leaned back and closed his eyes.

"He's dead," Stiet said.

"No." My father drew a deep, slow breath. "I'm not." He breathed again, more raggedly.

With difficulty, he shifted until he was looking down at Yaril. She still sat on the floor, dazed. She was very pale, save for a bright spot of blood on her lower lip where she had bitten herself. She lifted her hands to her head and pressed them to her skull, as if holding her head together.

"Are you quite all right, my dear?" he asked her.

"I—I am." Her eyes were clearing. Stiet held out a hand to her. Instead, she planted her own hands on the floor, pushed herself to her feet, and then swayed toward my father's chair. She caught hold of the back of it, stood up, and set her hands on his shoulders. She leaned to say quietly by his ear, "I think that everything will be fine now for both of us. I know what I need to do."

And with her words, suddenly the magic was finished with me. I watched the nimbus that had been playing about Yaril's head suddenly fade, leaving only the necessary knowledge behind. It was over. I'd done all the magic wished me to do. I'd served its purpose and it was done with me. I danced still, but more slowly.

I lifted my head and turned my vision to the east. I could still feel my body, dancing its plodding dance, but it seemed very far away from me. I wondered if I could get back to it before it failed completely. I knew there was an important thing to do, but suddenly it seemed an onerous task, one at the very edges of my ability. I turned back to the room. Some time must have passed. There was a doctor there, fussing about my father, mixing a foaming powder into some water for him. Professor Stiet was gone, but Caulder was there now, very red in the cheeks from his recent exertion, and looking at my father with what seemed like genuine concern. Yaril sat in a chair to one side of my father, and a housemaid was just setting down a tray with a teapot and several cups on it. To me, Yaril looked more physically worn than my father. I felt my distant body tug at me faintly, a failing puppet trying to call its strings back to it. I went to my father.

"Good-bye," I said. He did not look at me or give me any sign of response. I bent down and kissed his brow, as he had occasionally done when I was a little lad going off to bed. "Good-bye, Lord Burvelle. I hope you keep your title for many years to come."

My body pulled at me more strongly now. I ignored it to go to Yaril, to bow and dance a final time with her. "Farewell, little sister. Be strong. I've given you the key. You must deduce how to turn it and unlock what is there in a way that will benefit the family. I leave it in your very capable hands." I bent again and kissed her on the top of her head. She smelled of flowers.

Then I surrendered to the pulling of the magic. It drew me out of the house and down the long King's Road. It was a quickwalk of the spirit. I knew the long road, recognized the growing towns and was startled by the mushrooming farms and homes along the way. Time rushed with us, it seemed, as it swept me along at a heady pace. The magic pulled me back into evening, but when I recognized Sergeant Duril camped alongside his high-wheeled cart, I dragged my feet to a halt. He was sleeping already, in a cramped bed made upon his cart's load, with his long gun ready under his hand. His hobbled team shifted and one horse lifted his head and whickered softly as I drew near. The sergeant's hat had slipped away; he was nearly bald now. I thought of trying to find my way into his dreams and decided not to. As soft as a breeze, I danced once around his cart. Then I put my hand over his. "No matter what they tell you, try not to think badly of me," I asked of him. "I remembered all you taught me. It took me a long way, Sergeant. You did your task well."

He didn't twitch. But it was not for him that I said my farewell, but for myself. I knew that. And the pulling string of magic tugged me again and I was off, down a long stretch of moonlit road, past Dead Town, and Amzil's old house swayed to one side from last year's snowload, and on until I saw the lights and smelled the smoke of Gettys. Again I slowed my pace. It was hard to do. The failing magic pulled at me like a hook in my chest.

My body was using up the last of its resources. I needed to get there while it still lived, but even more, I needed to see the faces of those I loved. I found their house and I danced up to their door. Silent as a wraith, I flowed through plank walls and into a room where Spink and Epiny shared a bed, their child nestled between them. Epiny looked almost corpselike, her face waxy with dark circles under her eyes. Spink's hair looked dried and brittle, like a starved dog's fur. Even the baby looked thin; her little cheeks were flat rather than fat. "Don't give up," I begged them. "Help is coming. Sergeant Duril is on his way here." I dragged my fading fingertips across their sleeping faces, softening the lines there, but I lacked the strength to break into Epiny's dreams.

The pull of the fading magic was pain now. Somewhere, my abused heart was flopping unevenly in my chest. Still, I stayed for a last indulgence. I dared myself to find the woman who once had saved me. My lips brushed Amzil's bony cheek; she slept huddled with her children in the same bed, and all their faces were as thin as when first I had met them. "Farewell," I breathed at her, softer than a whisper. "Know you were loved." I tried to believe I had not failed them as I was swept away from them yet again.

Then, in the blink of an eye, I was back in the wreckage of my body. It was full dark, but a blazing fire lit the night. I still danced, but no sane person would have known it for a dance. I stood upright, my hands shaking loosely at the end of my arms. I could no longer feel those hands or the purpling fingers that hung from them. I leaned forward, unable to straighten myself. Below, I could see the shuffling of my feet. They were bare and bloody where they were not blackened. A thought came to me. My overburdened and abused heart could no longer pump my blood to my extremities. Experimentally, I tried to lift one foot. I could do it, if I lifted from the hip. I managed a lurching step forward. Then another. And another. I could only step with my left foot. The right I had to drag behind me.

"What is he doing?" someone cried out. The voice had the sound of a shout but the shape of a whisper to me.

"Let him go." Kinrove's voice I recognized. "Follow him, but do not interfere. It is his time and he knows it."

I wanted to tell him I knew nothing. But there was no strength for that. The only thing I must give strength to now, I knew, was to this shuffling, dragging walk. Something pulled at me, something stronger than the magic of Kinrove's dance. Something that was mine. After what seemed a very long time, I reached the edge of the circle of firelight. "Follow him!" Kinrove commanded again. Someone came to stand at my side with a torch. I was grateful.

The person was small and weeping. Someone else came to join him. Olikea and Likari. They stood at my side and held the torches that lit my way. My vision was fading, but I followed some other sight. I could not see far enough ahead to know for sure where I was going, but I was certain I was supposed to go there. A step and a drag, a step and a drag. I followed a path for a long way, but when it no longer went in the direction I must go, I left it. A step and a drag, a step and a drag.

As the last hours of the night dissipated, my shuffle grew slower, my step ever smaller, and the drag of my other foot ever heavier. The ground began to rise. At some point, I went to my knees and then my hands and knees. I crawled on. More than once, I heard them call for fresh torches, and torches were brought, for them to kindle from the stubs, but they never left my side. Their weeping died away to hoarse breathing. By the time I was dragging myself on my belly, they were silent. "The torch is nearly gone," I heard Likari say and, "No matter," Olikea replied. "The sun is rising. And he cannot see anymore anyway."

She was right.

I knew the place by the smell, and the angle of the dawn's light, and the familiarity of the terrain. I felt Lisana watching me as I drew nearer. I had no strength to speak to her, but she called to me. "I cannot help you with this, Nevare. This you finish on your own. And it must be finished."

I crawled past her broken stump. It was hard. Her fallen branches littered the ground all along her old trunk. I did not think I could drag my bulk past their tangle, but I did. And then I had to drag my body up, up to where the small tree sprouted at the end of the fallen trunk.

"It's too small!" someone objected.

"Let him choose. Don't argue with him." That was Kinrove's voice.

I dragged myself the last bit of distance and reached out to seize the sapling. I fell facedown, my hand clinging tight to its bark. That was all it took. My decision was clear to all of them. Kinrove spoke again.

"He has chosen his tree. Bind him to it!"

CHAPTER TWENTY-SEVEN

THE TREE

I had chosen a tree that was much younger than one a Great One would usually choose. Worse, it was not one that was rooted directly into the earth, but instead was a surviving offshoot of Lisana's fallen trunk. I gripped it as tightly as I could. It had been less than two full years since I had felled Lisana's tree. Kaembra trees grew with unnatural swiftness, but even so, this tree was spindly compared to what a Great One would ordinarily have chosen. I heard the feeders debating my wisdom with one another. One of them even had the temerity to suggest that they move me. I knew an instant of absolute terror as I felt their hands close on my wrists and ankles.

"Do not tamper with what a Great Man has chosen. Let him have his will." Kinrove's voice was full of authority. In a softer, more pensive tone, he added, "The magic lets us have so little will when we are men in this world; let him have what he can of it now."

As they tugged, hauled, and pushed me into position, I was a sentient spark in a hulk of dead meat. Pain was gone; too much pain had assaulted me. I was no longer capable of feeling it. Instead, I had a profound sense of wrongness, of so many things broken in my body that it could never be repaired, not by a healer, not by time, not even by my applying the magic to myself. My body had become foreign territory. Organs inside felt torn as the feeders moved me. I could no longer move my fingers or my feet; I had a vague recollection of them swelling, but it was a physical rather than a mental memory. I stopped trying to inventory all that was wrong; this body could no longer function, and soon I would be leaving it.

I wondered if Dasie had hovered like this, a spark of awareness inside a carcass. As they had done with her, they centered my spine on the tree's slender trunk and then bound me there. They put my legs straight out in front of me, though it felt an unnatural posture to assume. They wrapped them at knee and ankle, and then bound my chest, my neck, and my head to my tree. I felt them stand back to look at their work and wait.

I could no longer see. I could hear, but it was difficult to focus on the words. I was aware that Olikea urged Likari to the place of honor. He spoke first, as my primary feeder. It was hard to listen to him, and not just because my ears were ringing with death. His voice seemed older, as if his months of dancing had made him grow up, but not in the normal way. The memories he had of me seemed both childishly idyllic and humorously callow. He detailed how he had come into my service, how he had brought me food and guarded me in the caverns during my fever. He spoke of how we had fished together and how I had shared food with him. He spoke of how much warmth I gave off when he slept against my back, but also of the foul stench of my breaking wind at night, something he'd never made me aware of.

Olikea was the next to speak. Perhaps she had taken time to organize her thoughts on my pathetically slow journey to this place. She had put all her memories and images of me in chronological order. For the first time, I heard of how she had watched me, from the very first day of my arrival at the graveyard. She spoke of how she had educated me in the foods that would feed my magic, and took great pride in speaking of how she had taught me the ways in which a Great One should make love. She regretted she had never been able to catch a child from me. As I listened to her words, I thought that we had shared a child. Then I was suddenly aware of Lisana. She crept through our shared roots to reach me, her flowing thoughts finally touching mine with no barriers. She eyed Olikea, and perhaps there was a touch of jealousy in her words.

"I was never able to bear a child either. She has my sympathy. But sometimes I think, 'You have one son. Why are you so greedy?'"

"I'm glad she has her son again. I hope she will keep him."

"She will." Lisana was slowly coming closer to me. Now I could see her. She appeared to me as a young woman, plump and healthy. She walked barefoot along the mossy trunk of her fallen tree, balancing carefully as she approached me. She was smiling, but the curve of her lips was the least of it. Her joy made her glow. She moved toward me so diffidently, her words so casual. I understood her attitude. We were moving toward a crescendo of joy. No words, no greeting could describe it. Even to try to do so would mar it. I tried to open my arms to her, but could not move. Oh, yes. They had bound me to the tree.

"Soon," she said comfortingly. "Soon." Almost unwillingly she added, "There will be some pain. But fix your mind on the thought that, no matter how bad it is, it does not last. But we will. Our trees are young. And I can feel the magic, flowing like a wild river, no longer dammed."

"I did it, then?"

I could hear the voices of others, speaking of me, of what they had known of me. Olikea's voice was gone; it was Kinrove who chanted now. I paid little attention to his words. I cared for nothing they might say, while Lisana, she who knew me best, stood before me, waiting. I felt a shiver up my back when I thought of the pain to come and then reined my thoughts away from it. Anticipating pain was like enduring it twice. Why not anticipate pleasure instead?

Lisana's smile widened. "Could not you tell that you'd done it? I could feel it, even at this distance. I think all of us who have served the magic knew; it was like a fresh wind blowing in the evening after a long hot day. Change is coming."

"Then you are safe. And all will be well."

Her smile became more tenuous. "It is to be hoped. And in the meanwhile, we shall have what we shall have."

A second chill down my spine. "To be hoped?"

"It is as you have seen. Magic is not a single event, a snap of the fingers. It is not a matter of 'do this and that will always happen.' It is a cascade of actions, teetering on coincidences and luck, rattling to a conclusion that always astonishes us all. Yet there is a linked chain that goes back. When one follows it, if one is cynical, one says, 'Oh, that was not magic at all, but merely happenstance.'" She smiled. "But to those who hold the magic, the truth is plain. Magic happens."

"But you said, 'to be hoped.' Does that mean it isn't certain?" The tingle down my spine became an itch and then something even more unpleasant. *Don't think about it.* Don't imagine the tiny rootlets growing suddenly against the sweaty skin of my back. Don't imagine them spreading, probing, seeking for the easiest place to penetrate. A scratch, a bruise. It wasn't an itch anymore. It stung. It would pass, it would end, soon, but I suddenly feared that this was only the beginning.

Time runs differently when pain counts out the slow seconds.

"Look at me, Nevare. Don't focus on it."

"To be hoped?" I demanded again, trying to distract myself.

"Those cascading events take time. The Gernians will not go away instantly. Their anger still seethes, and their axes still swing."

"No."

"Yes. Some will fall. How many, we cannot know. It is all a part of the slow working of the magic, Nevare. All a part of—"

The pain began. What had come before was not even discomfort compared to this. I felt the jabbing of dozens, no, hundreds of roots. They were greedy and seeking. They shot into me, ran up alongside my spine like a new system of nerves, ricocheted down the bones of my arms and legs. I felt my limbs twitch and flail, and heard the happy cries of those who witnessed the tree taking me. Inside me, like spilling acid, the roots flung out a network.

I was dead. I no longer breathed, my heart did not beat. Roots were spilling into my bowels and spreading, rasping through the meat of my body. I was dead. I should not be feeling this. I should not be aware of the ball of roots that boiled into the cavity of my mouth. Someone was shouting at me. "It does not last forever!" she cried. I wanted to scream back that this *was* forever, that this pain was all I could now remember, that a dozen forevers had passed since it began.

It was changing now, that was true. I was going into the tree, as much as the tree was coming into me. It did not feel any gentler. It felt as if the nerves that had once webbed through my hands and feet were now being forced throughout the stiffness of the tree. Little ripped bits of me were being torn away from their old places and forced into new and foreign locations. In the most fitting of reversals, I felt I was being torn down into a sort of lumber and rebuilt as a tree.

"Let go of your old body," Lisana was urging me. I wanted to tell her that I didn't know how but I no longer knew how to speak to her. I was starting to feel new sensations but I was not sure how to interpret any of them. Was that wind? Sunlight? Was that the comforting grip of soil upon my roots? Or was it sandpaper against my flesh, light shining in my eyes, a terrible shrilling in my ears? This body didn't fit my senses or my senses didn't fit this body. It was all a mistake, a terrible mistake. I wanted it to stop, wanted to simply be dead, but there was nowhere I could turn for help.

The changes went on, and on, and on. For what seemed like a very long time, it was hard to think. It is always hard to form cogent thoughts when in severe pain, but that small voice that seems to keep babbling in the mind when the larger, controllable voice falls silent, even that one was absent. Thoughts happened in bits and made no sense even when put together, like scattered pieces of a book's torn pages.

My awareness was being fused with the tree's life. Leaves turning toward the sun. Roots taking up water. Leaf buds slowly unfurling. Very gradually, I began to be aware of this new body's senses and needs. It had a different sort of awareness of the world. Light and temperature and moisture were suddenly far more significant to me. For a fixed creature, these things matter so much more than to something that is mobile and can seek out what it needs. I became aware that to live I had to harvest all resources within my reach. With the nutrients from my old body, I could grow taller, produce more leaves. I could capture more of the sunlight streaming down from above, and I could shade the ground beneath me to make it harder for competitors to sprout. I wanted next to nothing growing beneath my reaching branches. The leaves I dropped there were my nutrients, to rot and nourish my own roots. I wished to benefit from all the moisture that fell within the range of my reaching roots, not share it with competitive life. It was only when I found myself thinking that in many ways a tree was not so different from a man that I realized I was using my mind again.

"Nevare? Are you there now?"

Her voice reached me in a new way. It came from the wind rustling her leaves, and more intimately, from the fallen trunk that we shared. I reached for her and found her. It was like clasping hands, and then it was far more than that.

"You're finally here. All of you. All the way here."

"Yes. I am." It was so easy to be completely aware of her. I had not known, before, that we had been shouting to one another across such a distance. Now when she spoke, her thoughts blossomed effortlessly in my mind. She had been the one reaching out to me, manifesting in a human shape that I could recognize in order to reach me. I had seen and comprehended only the tiniest fraction of what she truly was. Now I saw all of her. Lisana as tree was as lovely and seductive as Lisana as woman, and she was both. She was such a being, such a glorious life. I had never seen a person in such full spectrum. It was the difference between seeing a garden by torchlight and then beholding it in all its color and detail on a sunny day.

"Look at yourself," she commanded me, pleased with the unspoken flow of compliments I had directed at her. "Just look at what you are becoming."

My little tree had already put the harvested nutrients from my body to work. New twigs had formed, fresh leaves budding on them, and the leaves I'd had were a deeper green and larger. I stretched them toward the light and wind, marveling that I could do so. I felt the sun kiss my leaves, enjoyed the light wind that stirred them, felt even the weight as a large bird alighted in my branches. I felt him shift his weight, felt the lick-lick of his strong beak as he whetted it against my branch. Then he spoke.

"Hello, Nevare. I've come to collect a debt."

It was the voice of a god, trickling through me like cold blood mingling with warm. Orandula, the Old God. God of balances, god of death. He was a darkness there in my branch, his claws digging into my bark, his body hiding my leaves from the sunlight. A wave of foreboding shivered through me.

And yet, what could he do to me now?

"What can't I do to you now?" he replied to my unspoken thought. "Over and over, I've given you the chance to make the choice. Pay for what you took. You can give me a death or give me a life. I even offered to let you give me the boy. But over and over, you've refused the opportunity to make things right with me."

"I think it's too late for you to threaten me," I replied sanguinely. "I'm already dead."

"Are you?" He hopped closer to my trunk. I could almost feel him cock his head and stare at me. He pecked at my branch. It made my leaves shiver. "Do you feel dead?"

"I—" I didn't feel dead. I felt more alive than I had in a long time. For a few brief moments, I'd felt free, entering a new existence.

"Whatever you are. Do not take him from me." This came as a low-voiced plea from Lisana. "We have been through so much, sacrificed so much. Surely the magic cannot demand more of us than what we have done."

"Magic?" He shifted the grip of his black bird-feet on my branch. "I care nothing for magic. I do care for debts. I do not forget them."

"What do you want from us?" Lisana demanded of him.

"Only what I'm owed. And I'll even give you, one last time, the choice. Choose now, Nevare Burvelle. Choose what you give me. Or I'll take what I please."

"What does he mean, a life or a death?" she cried to me.

"I don't know. I think he finds it funny to play with the words. Gernians speak of him as an old god, one most of them have set aside. Few worship him anymore. When he is worshipped, he is the god of death. But also of balances."

"It makes great sense," Orandula interrupted. "How can one be the god of death without also being a god of life? It isn't as if they are two separate things. One is the discontinuation of the other, don't you see? Whenever one stops, the other begins." He shifted on my branch. "They balance."

"So if he asks you for your life, then you are giving it to him and choosing death?" Lisana spoke only to me.

"So I've supposed. I don't really know and he won't explain."

The god laughed. "Explaining would take all the fun out of it. Besides, even if I explained, you still wouldn't understand."

Lisana was beginning to be frightened. We had just thought that we were finally safe. "What if you offer him your death? What happens then?"

"I don't know."

"Can't you just ask him?" Lisana sounded amazed that I would not have done so long ago.

"I don't think he would answer that question. I think he finds it amusing to demand a price of me when I do not know what I am agreeing to give him."

With a sigh like wind through new leaves, she brushed past me to confront him. "If he offers you his death, what do you take?"

"Why, his death, of course."

"So you would kill his tree, then?"

I felt him shift his weight and suddenly I could see him. It was a different way of seeing. I knew the shape of him and how he blocked the light from my leaves. He'd cocked his head at Lisana's tree. "No. Of course I wouldn't kill him. That would be giving him death rather than taking death from him." The bird puffed his feathers with a shiver, then settled them and began grooming them again. "I'm not going to wait much longer," he warned us.

"Tell him to take your death," Lisana said decisively.

"How can you be sure?"

"The only other option is offering him your life. We know how that would end. He says you must decide quickly, before he does. So. We have two choices. One we know is bad. Take the other. It may also be bad, but at least there is a chance it is good."

"Not with this bird," I said sourly.

Orandula cawed out a loud laugh. "So. What do you choose?"

I steeled myself. "Orandula. Let it be finished between us. Take my death, to pay for what I took from you."

"Very good," he said approvingly. "Very good indeed."

He spread his wings and leapt from my branch. Before he touched the ground, he was flapping heavily. Slowly he gained altitude. When he was so high I could scarcely feel his shadow as it passed over my leaves, he cawed again. Once, twice, three times.

"Is he gone?" Lisana asked me.

"I don't know."

In the distance, I suddenly heard answering caws. They came from far away, but when they were repeated a few moments later, they seemed much closer. Lisana held tightly to our shared awareness, as if she were gripping my hand. "He called other birds," she said.

"I've seen croakers do that, when they find something dead. They call the rest of their flock to share it."

"Something dead?"

"My old body, I suppose." I could sense it down there. It was a weight on the trunk of Lisana's tree. My roots were firmly in it. Some nutrients had leaked out of it like water from a leaky skin. No matter. They would go into the soil at the base of the fallen trunk. Eventually I would have them. The thought gave me pause. "How long has it been?" I asked Lisana.

"What?"

"How long has that body down there been dead?"

She was unconcerned. "I didn't keep track. It seemed to take a long time for you to come into your tree, longer than it took me. But that all happened so very long ago."

I reached for her and effortlessly felt our communion, sear-
ingly sweet, true and ever fresh. I had never imagined such a
connection. She laughed low, delighted at my gladness. I sensed
something else. If I extended my awareness further, I could sense
all the other kaembra trees that held the ancestral wisdom of the
Specks. It was a community in a sense I'd never imagined it. I
could find Buel Hitch if I wished, just by thinking of him. I could
also, I suddenly discovered, feel the fear and injury of the kaembra
trees closest to the end of the King's Road. I pulled back from
their misery and despair. It was a dark edge to what had been,
until now, the purest pleasure to explore.

The croaker birds seemed to have come from varying dis-
tances. They were not graceful birds when they had to land on the
ground. They spread their wings wide as they descended, but still
seemed to land with a thud and a bounce. They were as ungracious as they were ungraceful. They waddled immediately to the
feast. I felt, distantly, the first snapping beak that caught and tore a
piece of flesh from my corpse. I regretted the loss; whatever they
took removed nutrients that my tree could have consumed. The
twinge I felt was reminiscent of pain without being as sharp. I
sensed the damage to the discarded body. A second and third bird
landed and hastened to the feed. Although there was plenty of
space and lots of carrion to consume, they squawked and flapped
at one another, jockeying for position. In between slapping one
another with their wings, their heads would dart in, wicked beaks
held wide, to close on flesh and worry loose strips of it.

Another bird dropped from the sky, and then three more, landing like fruit falling from a tree. They cawed and shrilled challenges
at the ones that were already feasting. They slapped less with their
wings now, seeming intent on ripping as much meat free as they
could and gulping it down before their fellows could intervene.

"That must have been what he meant, when he said he would
take your death," Lisana said regretfully. "Your body would have given
much nourishment to your little tree. I am sorry to see it go."

"I regret it," I said, thinking of the usefulness of the body
rather than any sentimental attachment to it. "But if that is all he
wants of me, then he is welcome to it."

An especially large croaker bird had climbed onto my corpse. He feasted busily, tearing strip after strip of softening skin and fat from the soft meat of my belly. He shook a particularly juicy scrap, tossed it up and gulped it down, and then wiped his beak on my chest. Sunlight glinted off the brightness of the eye that he turned up to me.

"Ah, but we are only beginning. This is not your death. This is just what was left over. We shall tidy a good part of it away before I claim your death from you."

Lisana shivered. "We do not need to watch this. Our deal has been struck and we owe you nothing more. Come, Nevare."

As easily as that, she took me away from that slaughterhouse scene. "There is a trick to walking in the forest," she told me as we put our backs to our trees and strolled away. "We can go wherever we have roots. And as you become stronger, you can even venture away from them, so long as you maintain contact with the forest itself. So many of the kaembra trees still share roots that we can go anywhere they grow."

"Share roots?"

"The young trees sprout up from the root system of the older ones, for the most part. Others, like the ones at the edge of your cemetery, grow from a fallen branch."

"I see." And I grasped that in some ways, they were all one organism. The thought was a little unsettling, so I set it aside. We strolled on. I became aware of how much Lisana was helping me to "see" and "feel." I was not as adept at simulating a human body as Lisana was. It took time for me to master making my feet touch the earth and being aware of the change from sunlight to shadow on my skin. I worked at it, refusing to be distracted by what I could still feel; the croaker birds were busily dismantling my old body.

I reminded myself that there was no pain. It was rather like skin peeling from sunburn or scratching a scab away. I was aware of the birds taking away pieces of me, but it did not hurt, except for an occasional twinge, as if they had reached the edge of dead flesh and were peeling into living skin. I flinched when it stung, and Lisana turned to me with concern in her face. "What was that?"

"You felt it?"

"Of course. We are connected." She frowned thoughtfully.

"I'm dead, aren't I?"

She wet her lips, considering. "*You* are not dead, of course. But that body should be. You should not be able to feel pain—"

I lost the rest of her sentence as a slash of red heat went up my back. It felt like I imagined the lick of a whip would feel, and like a whip weal, it continued to sting after the initial burn. I caught my breath. "What is that?"

"I don't know." She seized my hand and held it tightly in both of hers.

Another scalding stripe of pain struck me, this time across my belly. "He's doing something to me."

"So I fear," she said. Her eyes had grown very large. "Nevare. Stay with me. You want to stay with me, don't you?"

"Of course I do. What do you mean?"

"As before." She let go of my hand with one of hers. She reached up and with her free hand, gathered a large handful of hair on the top of my head. She gripped it firmly, almost painfully, so that it strained against my scalp.

"What are you doing?" I asked her, fearing that I already knew.

"I do not know how he could do it. But if he tries . . . if he tears your body from this place, just as Dewara once did, then I will still keep your soul. Or as much of it as I can."

"You would divide me again?"

"I hope not. I hope that all of you will stay." Tears had begun in her eyes. She put her free arm around me and pressed the soft flesh of her body against mine. "Hold tight to me," she pleaded. "Hold very tight. Don't let him take you away."

"I won't." I put my arms around her. I kissed her. "I'm staying with you," I promised. Our mouths were so close I felt her breath against my lips. I felt her tears cling to my cheeks. Another streak of pain raced down my back. I cried out, but held tight to Lisana. Another stripe, this one right next to the first. And another.

They came in a methodical flogging now, one after another, each agony laid down next to the previous one. I could not control my response to it. The body I had imagined for myself in Lisana's world had a bloody ruin for a back. The blood streamed down my legs, and I trembled with the pain, but held on to her. There was nothing else I could do, no way to defend myself from the greedy flesh-stripping birds that attacked me in another world.

It went on for a very long time. When Lisana could no longer hold on to my body because of the damage it had sustained, when I had sunk to my knees, moaning with pain, still she stood by me, weeping and gripping grimly the handful of hair on the top of my head.

The first time I had ever met her, when we had come together as adversaries, I as Dewara's champion and she as the guardian of the dream bridge, she had seized me in the same way. And when I fell into the abyss, she had kept that grip, and jerked out of me a core of my person. She had kept that piece and it had grown to be Soldier's Son. But what would happen to me this time, neither of us knew. I did not even know if I would be torn from her world. Perhaps, when Orandula was through with his torment of me, he would let me go, and I could heal and be with her.

A grimmer thought came to my pain-encrusted mind. Perhaps the torment would never end. Perhaps this was what the Old God meant by taking my death from me. That even after my life was over, I would know no peace. It seemed too cruel a fate to contemplate; could anyone, even a god, do such a thing?

For the first time since the torment began, Orandula spoke to me. "Of course I could. But that is not what we agreed upon. You told me I could take your death. And I will."

"Please! Mercy," I begged.

"But I am not the god of mercy. I am the god of balances."

"By the good god, please stop!" I begged him.

"I do not know this good god. Truth to tell, I sometimes think he is whatever god is giving you what you think you want. And thus perhaps all of us take turns being your good god."

"Then be the good god to me now," I begged. All I could feel was pain. Sunlight on my leaves was gone, Lisana holding my hand was gone, even her grip on my hair had vanished. There remained only me and the eternal punishment of this god. "God of balances, balance this, this justice you claim from me with the mercy I beg."

Another searing stripe of pain. Was this the flogging I'd escaped in that other life? Did this pain now balance the pain I hadn't had then? It was a senseless question.

Orandula seemed detached from what he did to me. "Balance justice with mercy? But surely justice can be balanced only with injustice." Words tumbled and bumped in my head. If mercy was not justice, was it an injustice when mercy was given?

Beaks were rummaging in my guts, snapping and snipping, pulling out bits of this and that, tugging them away.

"Please." In all the world, there was only Orandula left to speak with. "Please, make it be over."

I had not known I was going to beg for that. But there it was, the words were out of my mouth.

"Very well," the god replied. And I knew darkness.

CHAPTER TWENTY-EIGHT

EMERGENCE

Darkness. Absolute darkness. But not peace. My body was bathed in pain. The skin of my face, my arms and legs, my back and belly, all stung as if badly burned. That was it. As thoughts re-formed in my head, I realized what had happened. I'd been sunburned. Dewara had left my body exposed to the sun and I was burned all over. I remembered it now. Soon I would open my eyes, and find myself back in my bed, at home. My mother would be weeping by my bedside while my father kept watch.

I was going back to the beginning of it all. Back to where I could choose differently, live my life over. I would not make the mistakes I'd made before. I'd be strong and more aggressive. My father would be proud of me. I'd be an officer in the King's Cavalla. My mother and siblings would not die of a plague that I'd let loose upon Gernia. The old god had taken me back to where it had all begun, to when Dewara had sent me to do battle against Tree Woman and I had failed. Had that been a death? Was that the death the old god had taken?

"You are not even remotely correct," Orandula observed. There was amusement in his voice. Overhead, I heard the shifting of a heavy body in a tree's branches. Then it lifted off with a flapping of wings that faded almost immediately. I listened intently. He was gone. Where was I?

I could see nothing, but I could hear. The ringing silence resolved itself into night insects singing their endless songs. Cautiously, I explored my other senses. I smelled and tasted blood. Pain hummed all around me, but I had specific pains, too. I'd bitten my tongue badly. My head pounded. My innards felt wrong, as if my guts had settled into a new and strange arrangement. I sorted out my agonies and knew that I was sitting upright. I tried to move, to shift even my leg, and cried out at the fresh pain it woke. I went back to stillness.

The darkness was an overcast night. It passed very slowly, and it was some time before I realized that the blackness was nothing more terrifying and dreadful than night. The coming of the dim dawn as sunlight flickered down through the canopy of the forest brought its own terror, however. I could see, and what I saw sickened me.

I sat where the Specks had left me. The beaks of the carrion birds that had torn the flesh from my body had shredded my bindings as well. I was naked. Shreds of rotting flesh surrounded and enthroned me. My decomposed body was a slimy scum on the earth around me. Pale roots networked through it. But that was not what horrified me.

What remained of my body was a monstrous thing. The layer of skin that covered me was so thin that I could see through it. As the light grew stronger, what I could see became ever more horrifying. Red muscle, white tendons, dark veins. Knobs of bone and gristle showing through in my hands. My breath came and went in short, trembling bursts. I wondered for an instant what my face looked like and then was glad I could not know.

As the sun grew stronger, it brought light and color into the world. My body became even more hideous. I turned my eyes away from it and looked around me. There was Lisana's tree, lush and healthy. And when I turned my eyes up, my own tree towered over me, twice the size it had been when last I saw it. I was grateful for its thick leafy shade, for I feared what the sun could do to my nearly skinless body. The surface of my body stung all over like a skinned knee.

I moved cautiously, lifting my hands, not wanting to look at them but looking all the same. After a time, I stood. My bare feet protested. They barely had skin, let alone calluses to protect them. I was very careful as I picked my way through the fallen branches and other forest debris to reach Lisana's tree. I stood looking up at it. "Lisana?" I asked softly.

There was no response. But it was more profound than that. I sensed nothing that could have responded. I set both my hands to the trunk of her tree. I didn't like the sensation. The skin on my palms and fingers was new and thin. I pressed my tender hands against the roughness of her bark and feared I would tear what little skin I had. Nevertheless, I put my brow to her bark as well. "Lisana?" I called aloud. "Lisana, please, reach for me. I cannot feel you."

But there was nothing. I stood a long time, hoping there would be something. I would have welcomed it even if her tree had tried to root into my flesh. But there was not even that.

When I glanced back at my tree, I could see that its roots were rapidly diminishing the leftovers of what I had been. But from that tree I sensed nothing, no awareness, no kinship, nothing at all.

No magic.

I don't know how long I would have stayed there if thirst had not begun to assail me. I knew my way to the nearest stream, and I went there, carefully descending from Lisana's ridge, taking each step as if I were made of cobwebs and glass. My breath shivered in and out of me. When I reached the water, I had to kneel down and cup it into my hands. It was cold and wet, a painful shock to my barely cloaked nerves. I felt the coldness of it running down inside me, even into my belly. I drank a lot of water, and then sat shivering. I'd looked at my hands when I drank from them. The memory made me shudder.

By midday, I was thinking more clearly, but only because I had pushed aside every part of my experience that refused to make sense. I'd evaluated where I was and what I had. My situation was desperate. I was naked, hungry, and vulnerable to everything from a thorn to an insect bite. I needed help. I could think of only one place and one person who would offer it. I stood up and left the stream.

I stumbled through the forest, moving with exaggerated caution lest I tear my new skin. Everything seemed too difficult. My legs were wobbly and sometimes I staggered unpredictably. Once, when I nearly fell and had to catch myself against a tree trunk, I ripped the thin skin on my palm. The sudden pain tore a shriek from me, and fresh blood ran from the cut, trickling down my wrist. In the distance, almost in response to my shriek, I heard birds caw raucously, as if laughing at me. I was so weakened and befuddled by all that I had been through that the sound brought tears to my eyes, and soon they were running down my cheeks as I tottered on through the forest. The salt tears stung my new skin.

It was luck and chance that took me where I wished to go. It was evening when I finally stumbled into the summer encampment of Olikea's kin-clan. I was hungry, but worse, I was cold. My body had no defense at all and even the mild spring night seemed heartlessly chill to me. The burning campfires and the smell of cooking food drew me like a candle draws a moth. Limping and weeping afresh, I hurried as quickly as I was able toward their light and warmth.

Life in all its wonderful chaos filled that glen. People were cooking food together, and eating, or sitting around the fires, leaning on one another as they talked and laughed. As I approached, one group took up a song, and on the other side of the camp, a second group responded, with much laughter, with their own ribald version of it. The music and the sparks from the cook fires rose together into the night sky. On the side of the dell, above the others, a larger cook fire burned, and Jodoli reclined on the elevated couch he had summoned from the forest floor. Firada was standing at his side, offering him roasted meat from a skewer. I skirted the other groups and made directly for them. I needed help, and I did not think they would turn me away. Firada would know where her sister was, and surely they would send a runner for her. Olikea and Likari would come to tend me and all would be well again.

As I wound my way through the encampment, no one spoke to me. Occasionally a head turned abruptly in my direction and then slowly away. They ignored me, pretending not to see me. My mind worked slowly through it. They would have heard the news from Olikea that I had died, and my present form scarcely matched how they would recall me. Still, it seemed odd to me that no one issued challenge or gave greeting to a stranger walking into the encampment. I had no strength to wonder about it, let alone rebuke anyone for rudeness.

As I drew nearer to Firada's fire, I realized that the woman sitting with her back to me was Olikea. She looked very different. She had lost some of the plumpness she had gained as my feeder, and her proud head was bowed now, a guest at her sister's fireside rather than a woman presiding over her own hearth. Likari was there as well. He reclined on his side, his head cushioned on his arms. I was pleased to see that the boy had regained some flesh. As I watched, he sat up and tossed a bone into the fire and then lay down again.

"Olikea!" I called to her, and was astonished at the weakness of my voice. I tried to clear my throat and could not; my mouth was dry, and even the walk up the slight hill was taxing my lungs. "Olikea!" I called again. She did not even turn her head.

"Likari!" I cried, hoping his younger ears would be keener. I saw him shift his position on the ground. No one else in the whole encampment so much as turned toward me. I gathered all my strength for a final effort. "Likari!" I called, and the boy sat up slowly and looked all around. His gaze passed right over me.

"Did you hear that?" I heard him ask his mother.

"What?"

"Someone called my name."

"I heard nothing but the singing. How can they be so merry, so soon after his death?"

"To them, it is not soon," Firada replied without rancor. "A moon has waxed and waned since he walked among us. And they were not close to him. He kept himself a stranger to us, even when he lived among us and took feeders from our kin-clan. He came suddenly and left as suddenly. I know you are grieving still, sister, but you cannot expect everyone to share your sorrow. He is gone. And if Kinrove is right, he achieved his goal, and the magic is now unfettered. All will be well for the People."

"They celebrate his triumph, not his death," Jodoli added gravely. "I think it is as good a way to respect a man as weeping for him."

His words warmed my heart. I had drawn closer to their fireside. I stood directly behind Olikea as I said jovially, "Except that the man is not dead. Not just yet. Though if I don't eat soon, I may be!"

Olikea didn't jump or shriek as I had expected she might. She continued to stare gloomily into the fire. There was no reaction from Firada, either. Jodoli gave me a brief, disapproving glance and then looked again at the fire. Only Likari stiffened at my words. He sat up and looked around again. "I thought I heard—" he began, but Jodoli cut in with, "It was nothing, boy. Just the crackling of the fire."

At that moment, Likari's questing glance met mine. I grinned at him. He let out a yell of absolute terror and leapt to his feet. Jodoli's hand shot out and caught him by the shoulder. "Look at me!" he commanded the boy.

"But, but—"

"Look at me!" he repeated more sternly. And when the boy obeyed, Jodoli held his gaze and spoke sternly. "It is bad luck to look at a ghost. And worse luck for the ghost if you speak to him. He is just a strong memory, Likari. Great Ones have very intense memories. Do not look at it or try to speak to it. We must let it go so that he can become what he is meant to be."

"A ghost? Where?" Firada demanded, looking right at me. Olikea, too, turned around and swung her gaze right past me.

"There is nothing there. A Great One goes into his tree, Likari. Nevare will not walk as a ghost. He left nothing unfinished." He patted the boy reassuringly on the shoulder as he released him.

"I thought I saw . . . something."

"It didn't even look like Nevare, Likari. Don't dwell on it, or try to see it again."

"A Great One should not have a ghost," Olikea said with great concern. "Unless . . . could the tree have refused him?"

"You said you saw the roots enter him. You said that he moved with them as you sang him his memories."

"I did. They did!"

"Then all should be well. If you wish, tomorrow I will visit his tree and speak to him, to be sure he has been well received. He should be at home there by now."

"If you would, please," Olikea said gratefully.

"And I will go with you," Likari announced as he sat down again.

"As his feeder, that is your right," the Great Man confirmed.

I saw Likari start to roll his eyes toward me. Jodoli raised an eyebrow at him. Likari lowered his head.

"I'm not a ghost!" I said incredulously. "Is this a joke? Have I offended all of you in some way? I don't understand! I'm hungry. I need help!"

I stepped closer into their circle. None of them reacted. Likari might have hunched his shoulders a little tighter. I reached toward the skewer of meat that Jodoli held. It had been a bird; I seized the wing and tore it free. If he felt or saw me take it, his face did not show it. I devoured the salty, greasy meat, chewed the gristle off the end of the bone and threw that tiny piece into the fire. The flames spat as they tasted it.

By the fire, Firada spoke to Olikea as if nothing were out of the ordinary. "So. What will you do now?"

"What I have always done. I'll live."

Firada shook her head. "It was wrong of Kinrove to keep all that treasure. He should have given at least some of it back to you. You tended Nevare well. Now, except for the lodge and what it holds, you are right back to where you were."

Her sister sounded sympathetic but Olikea still bristled. "Perhaps the lodge holds more than you know. Perhaps it was not *all* of Lisana's treasure that he threw at Kinrove's feet."

Firada lifted one eyebrow. "Truly?"

Olikea smiled small. "I said *perhaps*."

Firada made a small sound in her throat. "You have always known how to take care of yourself."

"I've had to," Olikea said.

There was a skin of water on the ground beside Jodoli's couch. I picked it up and drank, but spat it out as hastily. The taste was familiar; the water was flavored with a bark that Olikea had often mixed with my water. It was an herb that amplified the magic. But now it made my gorge rise. I had no sooner dropped the skin than Jodoli picked it up. He drank thirstily, and then returned to tearing meat from the skewered bird.

"Olikea," I begged suddenly. "Please. Please help me."

She stretched out on the moss beside Likari and closed her eyes. A tear trickled down her cheek. I groaned and turned away from her.

I left their fireside and walked down the hill. A woman had set aside a stack of hearth cakes to cool. I took three from the top of the stack and ate them. No one noticed me.

I grew bolder in my efforts to make someone acknowledge me, and also to satisfy my needs. I took a man's cup that he had just filled with hot soup and set aside to cool, drank it, and set it down in a different place. He merely scowled over his forgetfulness.

My hunger sated, I returned to Jodoli's fire, in time to see Likari and Olikea settling for the night. The night was mild. Olikea spread out a blanket for both of them to share between the roots of a tree. They settled quickly and soon fell asleep. Olikea's pack was nearby. Shamelessly, I ransacked it. When I saw that she had my winter cloak among her possessions, I boldly took it from her pack, shook it out, and put it on. It was too big for me. I lapped it around my body twice. My shoes were there, too. I put them on. They fell off. I dug into her pack again and found her knife and sewing tools. I crudely tightened the soft leather shoes to fit my feet and put them on. I cannot express the comfort of them; it was as if my body had forgotten how to keep itself warm.

After I was warm and had a full belly, sleep suddenly demanded to be indulged. Habit made me look for a place beside Olikea. But she had wedged herself and Likari into the space between two tree roots, the better to trap their own warmth. There was no room for me there. I found a place near them, lay down, then sat up and moved several small branches. My body seemed very mindful of being poked and prodded. I looked at the ground and recalled how the magic would answer me and prompt the forest into providing a soft bed for me. I could recall that I had done it, but could not remember how I had even begun to do such a thing. There was not even the smallest trace of magic left in my body.

I looked up at the sky through the forest canopy and thought about that. My magic was gone. The fat that had housed the magic was gone. I was no longer a fat man. Was I dead? Was I a ghost now? Orandula had said he would take my death from me, and apparently he had, but what sort of a life had he exiled me to?

I wished I were more comfortable, but the sleepiness that was welling up through my body insisted that I was absolutely fine. As it sank its hooks into me and dragged me under, I had a fleeting moment to wonder who and what I was now. Would a ghost have been hungry and cold? Could a ghost possibly be this sleepy? I toyed with the idea that I was asleep already and that all of this was a dream. I think I fell asleep wondering exactly at what point my real life had ended and this dream begun.

I woke with the dawn to the sound of people stirring in the camp. I rolled over, pulled my cover more tightly around me, and went back to sleep.

I awoke the second time to stronger light and the sensation of being too warm, very hungry, and badly needing to empty my bladder. I flung back the cloak from my face and stretched. Then, as my life came rushing back to fill my mind, I sat up, thinking that today I was better, stronger, and that life would resume making sense to me.

All around me, people were living their lives. Two women were crouched down as a toddler negotiated her first steps from one to the other. An older woman was grinding some dried roots into flour. A boy was working a rabbit skin between his fingers to soften it. As I walked through the camp, it was as it had been in the twilight. No one acknowledged me.

I found the waste pit beyond the edge of the camp, relieved myself, and walked back, feeling even more self-assured. Surely ghosts did not piss. And my body had begun to look more normal. My skin, so close to being transparent the day before, had begun to appear more opaque. My hands and feet were still unnaturally sensitive, and the entire surface of my body was still generally painful, as if I'd been sunburned. But it didn't hurt as much as it had the day before, and from that I took heart. I noted with interest that the skin on my arms was a uniform color; my specks were gone. That seemed as great a change to me as my greatly reduced girth. For a moment, I pictured myself as torn from my old body, leaving behind a casing of fat and skin, emerging naked from behind a wall of fat. I shuddered at the image and pushed it away.

I had been fat and now I wasn't. I thought of how I had once longed for that change and how important it had seemed. Now it seemed a foolish thing for me to care about. What did it matter, what did it change? I was still myself. So what did I care about, if not the shape of my body? Where was my life? I prodded at my emotions. Amzil came to mind immediately. I cared about her. I wanted her to be safe and well. And Epiny and Spink. And their baby.

It was so strange. As I thought of them, they suddenly gained importance in my mind, as if I'd forgotten about them completely and only now their significance was coming back to me. What else, I wondered, had I lost? What had been left behind in that old body? What of it would I recover?

I wandered through the camp, watching people who would not acknowledge me. I helped myself to breakfast from various cooking pots in the camp. One woman looked straight at me as I ate from her pot. I was pleased when I found Kilikurra. Olikea and Firada's father sat by his fire, braiding sinew into a fine line, probably for a snare. He had been the first Speck I'd ever spoken to; we had not had many dealings together, but he had treated me well. I touched him gently on the shoulder. He turned his head, but his mismatched eyes looked right through me. "Please, Kilikurra. You were the first to befriend me. I desperately need a friend now." Even when I spoke to him, he gave no indication of hearing me.

I sat down next to him by his fire. "I don't understand," I told him. "Was I so terrible as a Great Man? I know I led the warriors to defeat. But I thought I paid for that when I went to Kinrove and gave myself over to him. I danced his dance, and the magic now flows free. Everyone has told me that. So why am I an outcast here? What do you want from me?"

He gripped one end of the braided line in his teeth as he wove the sinew together into a tight cord. His black lips were pulled back from his white teeth in a grimace. He abruptly finished the length of cord, knotted it off, and set it down.

"Kilikurra. Please. Speak to me."

He tossed another stick of wood on his fire, waking sparks and smoke. He ran his sinew cord through his fingers and nodded, well pleased with his own work.

I rubbed my eyes, winced at the touch of my hands on my thin skin, and then pressed my temples gently. My head had not stopped throbbing since I had left my tree. I pushed my hair back from my face, mildly surprised to find I still had hair, and then flinched as my fingers encountered the scabbed-over wound. My heart leapt in terror and then began thumping wildly. With both hands, I carefully explored the injury on the top of my head. It was almost perfectly circular. I recalled how Lisana had gripped me by the hair and held on so tightly while Orandula peeled my flesh away.

She had held me like that once before, when first I had met her as guardian of the spirit bridge. She had defeated me, seized me by the hair, and then ripped half my soul out of my body. I did not doubt for an instant that she had done so again. She had kept all of me that she could hold on to. How much was that? What part of me had she judged worthy of being her lover and companion? Tears stung my eyes. My beloved had chosen, not me, but only parts of me. That was far more bitter than if she had rejected me entirely and chosen another man in my stead. And I, the rejected bits of a man, the unloved parts, was now a ghost. What had she taken, and what was left to me? Was this why I felt so disconnected and vague? What had she done to me? Was I condemned to wander the rest of my years like this, unseen and unknown?

Fear and frustration overwhelmed me, but that is no excuse for what I did next. I leapt to my feet, bellowing my outrage and betrayal. I rampaged through the settlement. I knocked one man to the ground, overturned a cooking pot of stew, snatched up folded bedding and strewed it about. That got a reaction, but not the one I had hoped for. There were cries of dismay and fright, but no one tried to stop me. They looked at the havoc that I wrought but paid no attention to me. I stood in the center of the camp and shouted, "I'm here! I'm not a ghost. I'm not dead!"

"Be calm! Be calm! All of you, bring every bit of salt that you have to me. I shall need it all!"

The words came from Jodoli. He stood at the edge of the camp. He was panting, as if he'd just been running, but I suspected that he had just returned from quick-walking to my tree and back. Olikea and Likari were with him, as was Firada. Firada ran to their fire and snatched up her bag of cooking salt. Olikea seemed paralyzed; she stood and stared all around her. Only Likari looked at me. His heart was in his eyes.

"Likari!" My heart leapt with joy. Even if only one person would acknowledge me, that meant I was real. I started toward him. "If you are all right, then it has been worth it all."

I opened my arms to him. I nearly reached him, but Firada was there first. Jodoli seized the bag of salt from her and took a big handful. As I stared at him in consternation, he sprinkled a circle of salt onto the ground around the boy. When he closed the circle, Likari looked up at Jodoli in surprise. "He's gone!"

"He was never really here. That was a shadow, Likari, not Nevare. You saw his tree? That is where he is now. It prospers. It has taken him in, very swiftly, and grows well and strong. I spoke to him at his tree. He is well and very happy. So we should be happy for him. Let him go now, lad. Thinking of him and missing him will only call to his shadow. And that is bad luck for all. Let him go."

A series of emotions flitted over Likari's face. I watched him, hoping against hope, but resignation was what finally triumphed. He spoke softly. "When I touched his tree, I thought I could feel him there."

Jodoli nodded indulgently. "Perhaps you could. The magic permeated you when you danced for Kinrove. Perhaps it has left an awareness in you. That would be a great gift. Let it comfort you. But do not encourage the shadow by seeing it or speaking to it."

Olikea stepped up and put her arm around her boy. "We loved him, and now we let him go. He would not want you to spend your days mourning him, Likari. He called you his son. He would want you to live your life, not dwell in the past."

She spoke so sincerely. I wanted to be the selfless person she described, but I also wanted, desperately, to know that I was still real to someone. "Likari!" I bellowed, but he did not even glance my way.

Jodoli had taken the bag of salt from Firada. Other Specks were hastening to him, bringing their own cooking salt. Many of them glanced fearfully about, while others kept their eyes desperately on the ground in front of them, for fear they might see me. Jodoli held up Firada's sack of salt. "Make a little hole in each salt bag. Like this." He took out his knife and demonstrated, then pinched the hole shut with his fingers. "Then follow me. I will walk a circle around the camp. Each of you will take turns to let the salt trickle in the path behind me. Come. The sooner we seal ourselves off from his shadow, the sooner it will disperse. Don't be afraid. He cannot hurt you." Jodoli glanced at me and said more loudly, "I do not believe he would want to hurt any of you. He is simply confused and lost. He should go back to his tree, and find peace there."

I held my ground, glaring at him. He turned his back on me and walked ponderously to the edge of the camp, and then beyond it.

They made a strange parade. Jodoli walked slowly and every person in the kin-clan followed him. At the end of the line came Firada, patiently dribbling a fine line of salt from her sack. When it was emptied, another woman took her place.

Jodoli walked a generous circle. Within it, he included the waste pit and the pool where they drew their cooking and drinking water. I crossed the camp and walked beside him. I tried to speak reasonably. "Jodoli, whatever I did to break your rules, I'm sorry. But I'm not a ghost. I'm here. You can see me. Likari can see me. I think you're using your magic to keep the others from seeing me. Or something. Can you just cast me out like this, after all I've given up for the magic? I did what it made me do, and I accomplished my task. And now you will turn me out?"

He did not look at me. I reached to seize his arm, but could not. I suspected that he had protected himself and was shielding himself with the magic. I turned away from him and stalked back to his campfire. I picked up the folded blankets and threw them onto the flames, quenching them. "Can a ghost do this?" I demanded of him. I emptied one of Firada's supply bags, dumping out smoked meat and dried roots. I picked up a slab of smoked venison and bit into it. It was tough but the flavor was good. Between bites, I shouted at him, "A ghost is eating your food, Jodoli!"

He did not even glance my way. His slow parade continued. I sat down comfortably on his mossy couch and finished eating the meat I had taken. There was a skin of forest wine there. I took it up and drank from it, and then spat out what I had taken. Firada had doctored it with herbs to build his magic. It tasted vile to me. I dumped it out onto the stack of smoldering blankets.

I felt childish and vindictive, yet oddly justified in my destruction. I knew he could see me. Why wouldn't he talk to me and explain what was going on? All I wanted was to understand what had happened to me.

I looked up to find Jodoli leading his people back into the camp. I sat by his hearth, waiting for him to return and see what I had done. Instead, he went to another fire. The people gathered fearfully around him. I felt a surprisingly strong pang of envy as he called on his magic and the earth rose beneath his feet, elevating him above his listeners.

"Do not fear," he told them. "There is but one more step to drive the ghost from our midst." He turned to Firada. She reached into her pouch and handed him a double handful of leaves. "These were taken from his own tree. He cannot resist them."

With those words, he cast the leaves into the nearby fire. After a moment, white smoke began to rise. I'd had enough. I stood up and walked toward them. I would seize him by the throat if need be, but he would recognize me.

Instead, I walked out of the kin-clan's campsite. I had no change of heart, no second thoughts about attacking Jodoli to make him recognize me. If anything, my anger and frustration only rose stronger. I roared and I would have sworn that I charged toward him.

But abruptly I was at the edge of the campsite. I spun about, incredulous, and saw Jodoli carefully laying down a line of salt that completely closed the circle around the campsite. After he finished, he stood up with a sigh. He looked directly at me, but refused to meet my eyes. Olikea stood beside him. I think she looked for me, but her gaze went past me into the forest.

"Shadows are not even ghosts. They are just the pieces of a man who cannot accept his life is over. It should go back where it belongs. And once it finds that no one here will pay attention to it, it will."

"This is where I belong now," I told him, and strode back toward the village.

But the strangest thing happened. When I reached the line of salt, I could not cross it. I would step forward, only to find I had stepped backward. It was simple salt, harvested from the sea, yet I could not step past it. Shouting and storming, I circled the encampment, refusing to believe that I could not cross a line of salt. But I simply couldn't.

I spent the rest of that day futilely circling the camp, and that night, I slept rolled in my cloak, staring at the unwelcoming fires. When I awoke the next day, I was hungry and thirsty. The kin-clan was already stirring. I could smell food cooking and hear people talking. After a time, I saw a party of hunters preparing to leave camp. They slung their quivers over their shoulders and each one checked his bow. As they did so, I saw Jodoli come over to speak to them. I watched as he gave each of them a small bag to hang about his neck. And into each sack, Firada poured a measure of salt.

I was a fool. I waited until all three of them were outside the circle of salt and then charged down on them. I would prove that although Jodoli's magic might keep me out of the camp, a little bag of salt could not stop me from making them notice me. I intended to knock at least one of them over. Instead, impossibly, I missed all three and went sprawling to the ground. They didn't notice me. I shrieked curses at them as they strode unconcernedly away.

I sat on the ground, wrapped in my cloak, and stared after them. I looked up to see Jodoli watching me. "I'm not a ghost!" I shouted at him. "I'm not a shadow."

I heard a sound I had come to dread. Heavy wings flapping. Orandula alit first in a treetop and then hopped down heavily, branch to branch, until he perched on one well out of my reach, but clearly visible to me. He settled his feathers, preened his wing pinions, and then asked me sociably, "How are you doing?"

"Oh, just wonderfully," I snarled at him. "You took my death. But my people won't believe I'm alive. Jodoli has used his magic to ban me from the camp and to keep me from contacting the People. The only clothing I have is a cloak and some shoes that are too big for me. I've no food, no tools, no weapons. Is this the life you gave back to me?"

He cocked his head at me and the wattles around his beak jiggled horribly. "I didn't give you a life, man. I took your death. And even that didn't go quite as I had planned."

"What do you mean?"

"Well, I'm surprised that you need to ask. Obviously, you're dead here. You show all the signs of it; no one can see you, can't cross a line of salt—I thought you would have understood that by now."

"But I have a body! I get hungry, I eat, I can move things! So how can I be dead?"

"Well, you're not. Not completely. As I told you, things didn't go exactly as I expected them to. It often happens when gods squabble over something. Neither one wins completely."

I pulled my cloak more closely around myself. Despite the growing warmth of the spring day, I felt a chill. "Gods fought over me?"

He began diligently preening his other wing. "Part of you remained dead in this world. Part of you didn't. I feel a bit sheepish about that. I like things to balance, you know. And right now you are still a bit out of balance. I feel responsible. I want to correct that."

I didn't want him to "correct" me any more than he had. Doggedly, I tried my question another way. "Is Lisana, is Tree Woman, a goddess? Did she fight for me?"

He tucked his bill into his breast and considered me. I wondered if he would answer. But finally he said, "Hardly a goddess. She fought for you, of course. And I suppose that in some ways she is connected to Forest, and Forest might as well be a god with all the power Forest has. But, no, Lisana is not a goddess."

He shook his feathers again and opened his wings.

"Then who—?" I began, but he interrupted.

"I, however, am a god and therefore feel no obligation to answer a mortal's questions. I will be considering how best to balance what remains unbalanced. I like to leave things tidy. Hence my affinity for carrion birds, don't you know?"

He jumped off the branch and plummeted toward the ground. His wide wings beat frantically, and with a lurch, the falling glide turned into flight.

"Wait!" I shouted after him. "I still don't understand! What is to become of me?"

Three raucous caws were my only response. He banked sharply to avoid a thicket, saw an opening in the canopy, and suddenly beat his wings harder, climbing toward it. An instant later, he had vanished.

I stood up slowly. For a short time I stood staring at the kin-clan's encampment. There, people were going about their lives. I could see Olikea sewing something. She lifted it up, shook it out, and held it toward Likari. I recognized the fabric. It was from one of my robes. Evidently she was remaking it into something Likari could wear. The boy was already running naked in the spring sunshine, playing some sort of jumping game with the other children of the kin-clan. I hoped she would make it large, so he didn't outgrow it before winter returned and he could use it.

I wanted to offer some sort of farewell. I thought about that for a time, and then turned away silently and walked into the forest.

CHAPTER TWENTY-NINE

DEAD MAN'S QUEST

I thought I walked aimlessly. I crossed a stream and drank there, but it did little for my hunger. There were probably fish in the stream, and I thought of trying to tickle a few. But I would have had to eat them raw; I was not yet that hungry. It was too early in the year for berries, but I found a few greens I recognized growing there and picked and ate them. I recalled that once Soldier's Boy had eaten vast quantities of the water-grass that grew along the bank. I sampled it. Even the youngest, most tender shoots seemed unbearably bitter. Another food that belonged only to the Speck Great Ones.

I left the stream and walked on, staying in the shade under the trees. The touch of sunlight on my thin skin was still uncomfortable and when I touched my hand lightly to the top of my skull I found it was still sore there. The skin was thicker over my muscles and bones today than it had been yesterday. It was not as gruesome to look at myself as it had been. So, I was healing rapidly, but not in the miraculously quick way in which the magic had healed me. It seemed obvious to me that I had a physical body, and it moved, so I could not be dead. Yet, if I was alive, who was I? What was I?

Jodoli had told me to go back to my tree. Coincidence or an unconscious intention led me back to Lisana's ridge overlooking the Valley of Ancestor Trees. I stood for a time looking down on it before the silence intruded on my brooding thoughts. I squinted, peering at the King's Road in the distance. All was silent there. No. Not silent. Merely bereft of the sounds that men always bring to the forest. Neither shouts nor axes rang, no wheels ground along over a rough roadbed, no shovels bit into the forest turf. Birds sang and swooped through the afternoon light. I could hear the wind blowing lightly through the trees. The leaves whispered softly to one another, but the voice of mankind had been muted.

Curiosity picked at me. Then I wondered what day of the week it was. The thought rattled oddly in my brain. It had been so long since I'd thought of days fitting on a calendar and having names. But if today was a Gernian Sixday that would explain the quiet. Not even the prisoners were made to work on the Sixday. I turned away from the Vale of the Ancient Ones and made myself walk toward Lisana and my tree.

I felt a strange antipathy to both of them. In the end, it seemed that Soldier's Boy had stolen all that he wanted from me, and managed to keep it and Lisana, too. I felt spurned by Lisana. I had loved her, I thought, just as truly as Soldier's Boy. But in the end, she had taken part of me, and left this part to wander. Could she have done that to me if she loved me? Or was the *me* who walked the earth now the parts that she had found unlovable, even useless? I opened my hands and looked down on them. How could I ever even know what she had chosen to hold fast to? Those parts of me were gone now, lost to a self I'd never know.

I thought of all the things I'd always imagined I lacked during my years at the Academy and afterward: courage under duress and the aggression needed to seize control of leadership and wield it.

I'd seen other men fueled by anger or ambition, but had never glimpsed those fires in myself. Soldier's Boy possessed a ruthlessness that had horrified me. I recalled the sentry's warm blood running over my hands and guiltily, reflexively, wiped them on my cloak. Had he taken those things with him when he left?

Oh, useless to wonder what I had or didn't have in me. This self was what I had left. Could I make anything of it?

I walked past my tree with its sodden pile of rotting flesh at the base of it. It hardly even stank anymore. A few flies buzzed, but I had no desire to walk closer or poke at the maggots rendering my former body down into compost. A vengeful man, I thought, would have girdled the bark around the tree. I had no knife or tool to cut it, but even more, I had no will to do it. Such vengeance would bring me no joy.

I did walk up to Lisana's tree. Like my tree, hers had taken on new life with spring. It was noticeably larger, with glossy green leaves, and the flush of moving sap in the new tips of her branches. Gingerly, I reached out and put my palm to the bark of her trunk. I waited. It felt like a tree. Nothing more. No surge of connection. A memory stung me suddenly and I snatched my palm away from her bark. But no questing roots sought to suck the nutrients from my body. The tree was probably fully occupied with the rich soil and the warm sun of the spring day.

"Lisana?" I said aloud. I don't know what sort of response I hoped for. Silence was what I received. I followed the fallen trunk her tree had sprung from back to where a wide strip of bark and wood still attached it to her old stump. Soot still blackened one side of the trunk, but the ashes and burned wood of Epiny's fire had been cloaked over by spring grass. I looked down at the fallen trunk of her tree, to where she and my other self reached welcoming arms up to the day's light.

I sighed. "You both got what you wanted. I don't suppose it matters to either of you that you left me wandering this world as a ghost." A light breeze moved through the treetops, and when it reached the two trees, their leaves rippled in the sunlight. The leaves were deep green, glossy with health. Their trees were beautiful. I felt a moment of hate-edged envy. Then it passed. "For what it's worth to you, I wish you well. I hope you live for centuries. I hope the memories of my family live with you."

Tears stung my eyes. Foolish tears. The trees had no reason to hear me or heed me. They were alive and growing. I was more like Lisana's old stump. I looked at the weathered and rusted cavalla blade still wedged there in her wood. Idly I took hold of the sword's hilt and gave a sharp tug. It didn't come free, but the corroded blade snapped off. I looked at the hilt and the few inches of pitted and broken blade attached to it. Well, now I had a weapon, of sorts. Peculiarly appropriate. Half of a rusted sword for half of a ruined man.

I was using its rusty edge to saw a strip from the edge of my cloak, to make a crude sword belt, when I suddenly realized that I was holding and using iron with no ill effects on me at all. I shouldn't have been surprised, but I was. I thought about it briefly, decided I had no idea what that meant, and went back to my crude tailoring. After I had a strip for the belt, I abandoned all caution and attacked my cloak, cutting the fabric into a smaller rectangle and making a hole for my head. I ended up with a sort of tunic, open at both sides but belted, and with a second sash to hold my rusty sword. My "new clothes" were more suitable for the warming spring day. I rolled up what was left of my cloak and took it with me as I left Lisana's ridge. I made no farewell. I decided I was no longer the sort of man who talked to trees.

It remained to be seen what type of man I was.

Evening was falling by the time I neared the construction camp at the end of the road. Frogs were creaking in the dammed-up stream by the road's edge, and mosquitoes hummed in my ears. As I scrambled up onto the partially completed roadbed, I squinted through the dimness at what I saw. It was all wrong.

Long runners from ground-crawling blackcap berries had ventured up and onto the sun-warmed roadbed. No traffic had trampled them flat. Grass sprouted in the wagon ruts. It was short, new grass, but it should not have been growing there at all if work was continuing on the road. As I walked toward the darkened equipment sheds, everything rang wrong against my senses. I glimpsed no night watchman's lantern. The smells were wrong;

there was no scent of smoke from burning slash piles or cook fires. The manure I accidentally stepped in was old and hard. Everything spoke of a project abandoned weeks if not months ago.

Yet when last I had looked down on that valley with Lisana, I had seen smoke and heard the sounds of men working. How much time had passed since I had "died"? And what had made the Gernians abandon work on the King's Road? Had Kinrove discovered a new and potent dance to keep them at bay? But if he still poured discouragement and fear down from the mountains, why didn't I feel it? I sensed there was no magic left in me; I should not have had any immunity to his danced magic.

I turned and looked up toward the darkening mountains. I could recall breaking a Gettys Sweat. It took an act of will for me to open my senses and try to feel what might be flowing down toward me. But even after I had attempted to be aware of whatever magic Kinrove might be using, I felt nothing. It was a pleasant summer day in the forest. No fear and despair flowed, and yet the work on the King's Road had ceased. So. The magic I had done had worked. But what sort of a magic had it been?

I imagined a Gettys full of people killed in their sleep, and shuddered. No. Certainly I would have felt such a deadly magic if I had been part of it. Wouldn't I? Had my dance driven them all away? Was I the last Gernian left in the foothills of the Barrier Mountains?

Night had deepened around me. The frogs still peeped, and occasionally the deeper bellow of a bullfrog sounded. The mosquitoes and gnats had found me as well, and my open-sided attire left me very vulnerable to them. I slung what remained of my cloak around my head and shoulders and advanced cautiously on the buildings.

Things had changed a great deal since the last time I had visited. The charred remains of the buildings that Epiny had blasted had been completely removed. In the fading light, I crept up on one of the replacement structures. The creaking of the frogs and the constant chirring of the insects abruptly ceased when I coughed. That was enough to finally convince me that no one was about. I entered the structure. There was no door to open; all the buildings here were temporary ones, thrown up to give the workers minimal comfort during construction and to protect the tools from the worst of the weather. Most were little more than two rough walls and a roof overhead. This one was empty. Even in the fading light, I could see that.

There should have been harness racks and tools lining the walls, but they were bare, with only pegs and an occasional worn strap still tangled on a hook. There was a central hearth where men could get warm on a cold day or put water to boil for tea or coffee. The ashes in it had gone to cold damp clinkers; it hadn't been used in a long time.

It was the same in the next shed I visited. There were no wagons or scrapers, no working equipment of any kind. What had been abandoned was the broken stuff, tools so worn they weren't worth hauling away. I was moving more boldly now, fearless of watchmen, looking only for what I might scavenge to give myself an easier night.

Behind a broken lantern, I found a box with three sulfur matches still in it. There was a bit of oil and a few inches of wick left in the lantern. In a very short time, I had a small fire going. A brand from it offered me an unsteady light for my exploration. I saw no sign of recent human visits. Precious little that was of any use had been left behind. Yet even garbage and broken objects can seem like a treasure to a man who has absolutely no resources. Thus I found a water flask that would work if I didn't fill it more than half full, and a pair of dirty trousers, torn out at both knees, but definitely better than no trousers at all. A scrap of leather harness made me a belt to hold them up.

I found nothing to eat, but that didn't surprise me. The prisoners were given little food, so scraps were unlikely, and even if there had been anything, birds and mice would have cleaned it up by now. I spent the evening turning more of the discarded leather harness into a sling, and then curled up around my hunger next to my small fire.

I awoke to light and birdsong. I lay still, curled on my side, looking at the ashed-over coals of my fire. I tried to think what I should do next. For so long, I'd wanted to see Epiny and Spink.

I longed to know what news they had from back west. They'd be able to tell me what had happened here, if the King's Road had been abandoned or merely delayed. I thought of Amzil and a small flame leapt up in my heart. Carefully, I shielded myself from it. Best not even to hope in that area. As deserted as this place was, did I hope to find better at Gettys? It might be no more than a ghost town. Best to take things very slowly. I tried to tell myself that was being practical, not cowardly.

Slowly I sat up, and for the first time let myself notice how different that movement felt. No heaving myself upright. I was as lean as when I'd been a cadet. Leaner, actually. I think the little tree had claimed every scrap of fat from me that it could.

I poked up the coals and then fed the small fire, banked it for later, and then looked critically at my hands. They still hurt from the small amount of work I'd done yesterday, but the skin was unmistakably thicker than it had been. The backs of my arms looked an almost normal color, and hair had begun to sprout on them again. I tried to think about the process I'd been through. What had Orandula done to me, that I'd emerged from my old body like an insect breaking out of a cocoon? But thinking about it only made me queasy. I told myself I was wasting the precious dawn hour and went out with my new sling to hunt. But my luck was poor, and I had to settle for two small fish instead. I roasted them on a stick over the coals. Afterward, my belly still rumbling, I washed my face and hands in the same stream where I'd caught my fish and considered my situation.

Ghost I might be, but my body told me I still had to eat. I had virtually no tools for surviving on my own. I'd been banned with salt from returning to the Specks: Gettys was my only logical choice. If it was deserted, I'd be able to scavenge. And if people were still here, I'd be able to see those I cared about. Even if I could not speak to them, I could listen in and discover how they were doing. Gettys, occupied or deserted, offered me my best chance to survive. So Gettys it was.

I made the decision. I struck out down the road for Gettys. It was a fine day. I was not as bothered by the sun as I had been the day before; I almost enjoyed its warmth. As I walked, I tried to refrain from wondering what I'd discover, but it was an impossible task. I entertained every possible scenario. Gettys would be deserted, a ghost town for this lone ghost to inhabit. The houses would be empty. No. The streets would be littered with the bodies of the dead. Perhaps Gettys would be a plague town, full of the sick and dying, finally destroyed by Speck plague. Or Gettys would be flourishing, but for some reason, all interest in building the road would be gone. In every case, I could not imagine what would happen next.

Noon came and went, and I hadn't seen anyone on the road. Of course, no one had any reason to be there unless they intended to continue building it. For all intents and purposes, it led nowhere, except to a king's frustrated ambition. When I reached the place where a wagon track diverged from the road and headed up to the cemetery, I halted. I was hungry and thirsty. My old cabin was in the cemetery. When I'd fled, I'd left a sword there, and other possessions. If they were still there, they were still mine. And I'd never had more need of them than now.

I trudged up the hill. I thought there were faint but recent wagon tracks, but it was hard to tell. The hoofprints were more distinct. A number of mounted riders had definitely been here very recently. When I crested the rise and saw the familiar rows of graves and the little cabin beyond them, I felt a wave of almost nostalgia. Despite the macabre surrounds of a cemetery, this place had been my home, and returning to it felt very strange indeed. As I drew closer, I listened for sounds of human habitation, but heard nothing. A faint trickle of pale smoke, a ripple in the air, rose from the chimney. If the caretaker was not home now, chances were that he would return shortly. I'd be wise to be cautious.

The place was more neglected than it had been when I'd tended the cemetery. The grass was longer on the graves, and the pathways not maintained. As I approached the little cabin that had been mine, I noticed that a window shutter hung loose and weeds had sprung up all around the entry. Yet a pair of very muddy boots outside the door gave notice that the place was not abandoned.

I ghosted up to the window and tried to peer in, but the shutter was not that loose. All I could see was darkness. Well, it was time to find out. I stopped outside the door, took my courage in both hands, and knocked.

There was no response. Was there no one home? Or could no one hear the knocking of a ghost's hand? Desperately, I banged on the door again. "Hello?" I shouted. My voice came out as a rusty creak.

I heard movement from inside the cabin, perhaps the thud of a man's feet hitting the floor. I knocked again. In the interval between my knocking and the door opening, I had time to think how peculiar I must look. My hair hung lank around my ears. I was unshaven and dressed raggedly in the makeshift cloak and discarded trousers. I looked like a wild man, a creature out of a tale. I'd shock whoever opened the door. But only if he could see me. Recklessly, I banged on the wood again.

"I'm coming!" The voice sounded annoyed.

I stepped back from the doorstep and waited.

Kesey dragged the door of the cabin open. He looked as if he had just wakened. He had on a gray woolen shirt that was only half tucked into his hastily donned trousers. He hadn't shaved in at least a couple of days. He stared out in consternation and my heart sank. Then, as he looked me up and down, "What are you?" he demanded, and my heart leapt.

"I'm so glad you can see me!" I exclaimed.

"Well, course I can see you. I just don't understand what I'm looking at!"

"I meant, I mean, it's so good to see a friendly face." I halted my words before I accidentally called him by name. There was no recognition in his eyes, and yet it was so good to see someone familiar that I couldn't stop grinning. I think my smile unnerved him as much as my strange garb. He stepped back, stared up at me with his mouth hanging open, and then demanded, "What are you? What do you want?"

I replied with the first lie that popped into my head. "I've been lost in the forest and living rough for months. Please, I'm so hungry. Can you spare me anything to eat?"

He looked me up and down, and then stared at my skin shoes. "Trapper, eh?" he guessed. "Come in. I don't have a lot, and what

I got, well, you may regret asking for a share of it, but I'm willing to give it to you. My da taught me to never turn a hungry man away, cuz you never know when you'll be hungry yourself. So the good god says. Come in, then."

I followed him hesitantly. My tidy cabin had become a boar's den. Dirty cups and glasses crowded the table and the smell of tobacco smoke was thick. He shut the door behind me, closing out the bright day and plunging us into dimness and the smell of stale beer. Clothing hung from the bedpost and the hooks on the wall; none of it looked clean. The smell of old food predominated. Despite my hunger, my appetite died. Kesey stood looking at me and scratching his chest through his shirt. What remained of his hair stood up in tufts. He yawned widely and gave himself a shake.

"Sorry to have wakened you," I told him.

"Aw, I should have been up hours ago. But the fellows came out for cards last night; just about the only place we can play anymore is in the graveyard! They brought a jug, and stayed late, and well, it's hard to roust out of bed when there's no reason to roust out of bed. Know what I mean?"

I nodded. Cards with the fellows. Gettys wasn't dead then. I tried to control my madman's grin. He had crouched down to the hearth and was poking up the few remaining coals. He scratched the back of his head. "I got some coffee we can warm up. And there's some corn dodgers left in the pan. That's all I have out here. Usually, I eat in town, but the cook don't make corn dodgers. I learned how to make them from my ma. Toasted, they're not bad. Substantial, you know. Filling stuff."

"Sounds good to me," I said.

"Sit down, then, and I'll warm them up. So you been lost, huh?"

My two chairs remained. Habit made me sit in the big one. It was very roomy now, despite the jacket and the grubby dungarees that hung from its back and arms. Kesey was building up the fire with bits of kindling. Once the flames set the wood to crackling, he put a blackened coffeepot over them. Rising, he went to the food shelf and took down a pan covered by a stained cloth. In the pan were cornmeal dumplings that had been fried in lard. "I can toast 'em, or you can have them as they are." He offered the pan to me, and I took two. They were greasy, heavy, and unappetizing. I took a bite, reminded myself that it was food and my stomach was empty.

"So you're not from around here?"

Chewing the dumpling was an exercise and swallowing it an act of will. "No. I got all turned around in the forest. It was only by luck that I struck the King's Road. When I saw it through the trees, I thought sure there would be a work crew who could help me. But it was still as death out there. What happened?" I took another bite of the corn dodger. No. Familiarity didn't improve it. But it felt good to have food inside me.

"King decided to pull the work crews off. He's got more important things for them to do." Before I could ask what, he said, "So you said you're a trapper?"

Actually, he had said it, but the lie worked as well as any other. I filled my mouth with half a corn dodger and nodded.

"Yeah?" He looked skeptical. "What happened to all your gear, then? How'd you get lost from your trapline?"

I swallowed the greasy bread and hastily backtracked. "Well, I thought I was going to be a trapper. Thought I knew more than anyone else about it. I did a lot of trapping, back west in the Midlands. But it's getting real settled there, and I'd always heard the best furs came out of the Barrier Mountains. So I thought I'd go take some. Everyone warned me, but, well, I thought I had to try. The fear wasn't too bad when I went in there. You know, I thought I could take it, get some good furs when no one else could. But then the fear come down, and—well, I didn't think I was going to stay sane, let alone live. I got all turned around, lost everything I had, and I just couldn't find my way out."

Now he was nodding sagely. "Oh, yes. I think we've all known what that feels like. But lately, it's slacked off. For a while there, it was gone, then it come back worse than ever, and now it's gone again. Likely that's why you could come to your senses." He sighed. "I still don't trust it to stay gone. I don't go any deeper into that forest than I have to. I get my firewood along the edge of it. But I don't walk under the trees. No, sir."

"I expect you're wise. Wish I'd kept the same rules. So why did the King give up on his road?"

Kesey grinned, enjoying being the bearer of big news. "You ain't heard nothing about doings in the Midlands?"

"Who would tell me? The trees?"

He laughed. "Big gold strike back east. And I mean big. Some fool daughter of a noble family sent the Queen a bunch of rocks, saying she thought she'd find them interesting. Well, she surely did! King claimed it all for the Crown, but that don't stop some folks, you know what I mean. They swarmed the place. The King pulled the prison workers back from the roadwork to put them to digging for gold instead of chopping trees, and pulled most of the troops back to keep the prisoners busy at what they were supposed to do and keep other folk from doing what they aren't supposed to do. It's huge, my friend. Fellow told me that the newspaper says there's a whole city sprung up near the diggings, in just a couple of weeks!" He sat back in my chair and laughed at me. "I can't believe you ain't heard nothing. Bet you're the only man in Gernia who hasn't."

"Probably so," I agreed. My mind was whirling. I put the last piece of corn dodger into my mouth and chewed thought-fully, then followed it with a mouthful of the very black coffee. Gold. So that had been Professor Stiet's game. When Dewara had dragged me home, I'd carried off an ore sample with me. Caulder had stolen it, then I'd given it to him, he had shown his uncle after his father disowned him and his uncle had adopted him, his uncle had recognized what it was, and now my little sister had started a gold rush by sending more ore samples to the Queen. I tried to sort out all the threads. Was this magic, this complicated chain of happenstance? Had that been what the magic intended all along, that I start a gold rush to drain the Gernians away from the Specks' territory? I had a hazy remembrance of thinking that the flow of population responded more to pulling than to push-ing. I hadn't shoved Gernia away from the Speck territories. I'd pulled it back toward the Midlands by appealing to its greed. King Troven would not have hesitated. A gold mine in the hand was worth several prospective roads to a seacoast he'd never seen.

"Shock, isn't it? Gold. You can bet that the Landsingers are singing a different tune now. I heard they want to do a lot of trade with us, and are offering some pretty favorable terms. I heard some of our nobles are saying, 'Hold out for them returning our coastal provinces to us.' Wonder if they'll cave that far."

I was still trying to put it all together. "So what's that done to Gettys?"

"Well, hard to say if it's done us good or bad, but it's about what you'd expect. There ain't much of Gettys left to tell about. When word about gold got here, most all the townsfolk who could pull up and go, went. Then the orders came to bring the prisoners back as a workforce. That took the prisoners out of Gettys, and a'course their guards went with them, plus some of the regiment to escort them. My regiment was already at low strength from disease, death, and desertion. But now we aren't even a regiment. The commander and most of the high-ranking officers packed up and went west when their orders come through. Only two companies left here now, just a token force to keep the place from falling down, and our highest-ranked officer is a captain. It's like they went off and forgot some of us here. Told us to 'hold the fort.' Didn't tell us how."

"So . . ." I said, and wondered what to ask next. Would Spink and Epiny and Amzil and the children have gone west with the others? "But you're still here?"

"Guess I been soldiering too long." He took a bite of the corn dodger in his hand. With a finger, he poked it to the back of his mouth before chewing it, and I recalled that he'd always had problems with his teeth. He made noises as he ate now, trying to move the food around to where he had teeth to chew it. When he spoke, his words were muffled with food. "Obeying orders went past being a habit with me a long time ago. It's in my bones now. Me and most of the old dogs, we stayed. Sit. Stay. Guard. That's us. Played havoc with our chain of command when so many officers went back west. There's some kind of new law, some priest thing back west about nobles and their sons. Evidently a lot of them noblemen lost their eldest sons in that plague bout they had, and they didn't like it too much. Some of our officers that were born soldier sons heard they might get jumped up to heirs if some new rule gets approved. Sounds unnatural to me. A man should be what he's born to be and not complain. But it's going to mean a lot of changes if men that were supposed to be officers suddenly have to go back west and be their fathers' heirs. 'Course, there's a few we wish would leave! That fellow in charge now, I don't think he could lead a troop of new recruits into a whorehouse, if we still had a whorehouse, but we're stuck with him. Captain Thayer isn't what you'd call beloved by his troops. But we'll still obey old stick-up-his-arse, because he's got the shiny bits on his uniform that says we should."

"Captain Thayer's the commander now?" Nausea roiled through me.

"You know Thayer?"

"No, no. I meant, *Captain* Thayer is running the whole regiment?"

"Well, I told you, the most of the regiment left. Only a couple of companies left now. And they didn't have much choice as to who to leave in charge. He was ranker than most, as the saying goes, so he got it. They'll probably jump him up in rank to make it appropriate when they get around to it. I just hope that when they do, he doesn't think that means he has to get even more straitlaced than he is now."

"Pretty narrow-minded, is he?" He was the same old Kesey as ever. It only took a few words of encouragement to keep him talking.

He filled his cup again with a mixture of black coffee and grounds. "You don't know the half of it," he grumbled. "Goes on about the good god every time he talks to us. Ran the whores out of town; sent them off when the prisoners left. No one could figure that out. They were all honest whores, for the most part. But Captain Thayer says now that women are most often a man's downfall. Had a man flogged for sneaking round to see another soldier's wife, and told the first soldier he should have kep' his wife at home and busy so she didn't put wrong thoughts in a man's head. Wife and hubby both spent a cozy day in the stocks."

"The stocks? I didn't even know we had stocks! That's harsh! Sounds like he's wound pretty tight." I was puzzled. That didn't seem like the sort of man who would have wooed and won Carsina.

"Oh, he's a big one fer telling us all about our sins and how they brought misfortune down on all of us. And he says that public shame is the best remedy for private sins. So we got stocks now, and a flogging post, near the old gallows. He hasn't used them that much—hasn't had to. Makes a man's blood run cold just to walk by them. Captain says lust and whores and women of bad repute are the worst things that can befall a soldier, and he intends to keep us all safe. Well, I'll tell you, we'd all like to be a bit less safe."

"I imagine so," I said quietly. I wondered how Epiny liked Captain Thayer as a commander. The streets of the fort might be a bit safer for the women of Gettys, but I suspected his ideas of keeping women busy at home weren't too popular with her. I tried not to grin at the thought. Epiny had not escaped from being under my aunt's thumb to knuckling to her husband's commander, I'd wager.

I suddenly knew that I had to see her and Spink today, and that the risks of doing so didn't matter. I was instantly ready to go, and then I thought of Amzil, and felt an icicle of indecision up my spine. I cared for her. Why did that make me more reluctant to go and see her? I glanced down at myself and realized the obvious answer. "I need to get some proper clothing," I said to myself, and then realized I'd spoken aloud.

"That's very true," Kesey agreed with a grin. "If it weren't for the way you're dressed, I'd a never believed your story. I would have thought you were a deserter, maybe; you got a soldier's way of walking and sitting."

"Me?" I made a show of laughing to hide the little burst of pride I felt. "No. Not me. But I knew a family in the fort . . . well, I didn't exactly know them. My cousin knew them and said that if I got out this way, I should look them up. But I don't suppose I should show up on their doorstep looking like this."

"No, I don't think so," Kesey agreed with a grin. He'd always been a good-hearted fellow. I was counting on that now, and he didn't fail me. "I don't think anything I got here would fit you much better than what you got on. But if you want, I could take a note to your cousin's friends, and maybe they could see their way clear to help you out."

"I would be forever in your debt," I replied fervently.

When Kesey heard that Lieutenant Kester was my cousin's friend, he nodded affably and said, "He's one of the few officers we have that acts like an officer anymore. Why, he had a private supply wagon that come in way ahead of the military ones, and you know what he done? Shared it all, even though it didn't go far, and him with a house full of children, his own child and the Dead Town whore's brats."

It cut me still to hear Amzil called that name, and it was all I could do to hold my tongue.

"Have you paper and a pen I could use?" I asked him a bit curtly, and he looked hurt for an instant before admitting that he wasn't much of a reader or a writer, so had nothing like that. After a bit of a search, he reluctantly came up with one of my old newspapers. "Belonged to a friend of mine. I'm not much for reading, but I've sort of been saving it."

I persuaded him to give me one sheet of it, and scratched out a crude message over the print with the burnt end of a stick. There was little room to be elegant or subtle. I printed out, "I'm back, alive. I need clothes. Follow Kesey, and I'll explain all later."

I signed it *N.B.* and entrusted it to Kesey, then watched him ride away on his broom-tailed horse.

After he was out of sight, I found myself at a loss for what to do with myself. I took a brief stroll through the cemetery that I had tended so faithfully. There was a new trench grave there, so recent that the grass hadn't covered it yet. I frowned at that, for plague outbreaks usually happened in the heat of summer. Then I saw that there was actually a marker, copied from the ones I had made, made of wood with the letters burned into it. Here were buried the victims of the massacre I'd led but a few months ago. The ground would have been too hard and frozen to permit grave-digging at the time they'd died. It gave me a sharp pang to think of the bodies stored frozen in the shed until spring had softened the ground enough to bury them. Doubtless that had been a horrid task for whoever had had to perform it. Probably

Kesey and Ebrooks, I realized. I turned abruptly away from the grave of the men, women, and children I had killed and started back toward my cabin.

Curiosity made me pause and look back to where my hedge of kaembra trees had once stood. Fool that I'd been, I'd hoped to keep the Specks out of the graveyard with a barrier of trees and stone. The trees had been cut down and the sections of trunk buried along with the plague victims they'd ensnared, but I saw that the stumps had sprouted again from the roots. I tried to decide what I felt about that sight, but could not. I recalled only too well my disgust as the trees had sent their roots questing into the plague bodies, but now that I understood more fully what it was to have a tree, I felt sad that they had been cut down and the bodies buried. Would it have been so bad for those people, I wondered, to live on as trees? Could they have spoken to us as the other kaembra trees spoke to the Specks? I shook my head at myself and turned back to the cabin. That world was not mine anymore. The forest would never speak to me again.

I sat briefly in my chair, staring at Kesey's dying fire, and then could not stand the squalor anymore. I went to the spring for a bucket of water and set it to heat. I told myself that when Kesey returned, I'd tell him that I had done it as a repayment for the good deeds he'd done for me. But the honest truth was that it pained me to see that my formerly tidy little residence had become such a sty.

So I scraped and washed the dishes and pots, and then swept a substantial heap of mud and dirt out of the door. In the process of putting the dishes back in the cupboard, I came across what remained of my possessions. Kesey had kept everything that I'd left there. My clothing had been carefully folded. Even my worn-out shoes were there. I shook out one of the shirts and then put it on. It hung loose all around me, and for a moment I marveled that it had ever fit me. I wondered why Kesey had not offered me the use of these clothes, and then was oddly touched that he had not. I refolded the shirt and restored it to its place. He'd kept my things, I realized, as a sort of remembrance of me.

Trying to change clothes had shown me how dirty I was. I heated water, washed, and even shaved using Kesey's razor.

Looking into his mirror was a revelation. I was pale as a mush-room, and the skin on my face was overly sensitive. I nicked myself twice and bled profusely both times. But the real shock was the shape of my face. I had cheekbones and a defined chin. My eyes had emerged from the pillows of fat that had narrowed them. I looked like Cadet Nevare Burvelle. I looked like Carsina's fiancé. I touched my face with my hand. I looked like my father and Rosse, I realized. But mostly like my father.

Restlessness made me leave the cabin. I felt I could not sit still and wait. I put my rags back on and went out to Kesey's woodpile. I chopped some kindling for him, until the uncallused skin on my hands protested this rough usage. I put what I had chopped in a tidy stack by his door and wondered how much time had passed. Would he ever return? Would Spink come with him right away or would he think it some sort of bizarre prank? The minutes of the day dripped by slowly.

I paced. I walked out to my old vegetable garden to find it a patch of weeds. Nothing useful there. Using the rusty sabre hilt with its bit of blade and one of the table knives, I successfully repaired the shutter so that it hung straight again. I paced some more. My old sabre still hung on the wall of the cabin. I took it down, hefted it, and tried a few lunges. It still wasn't much of a weapon. It was notched and rust had eaten at it. But it was still a sword. At first it felt foreign in my hand, but after a few feints and then a solid touch on the door it felt like the grip of an old friend's hand. I grinned foolishly.

After what felt like several days, I heard the sounds of some-one approaching. But it wasn't a lone horse, or even two horses. It sounded like a cart. I hastily put the sword back where it had been and walked to where I could look down the track that wound up the hill.

Kesey was riding his horse. Behind him, drawn by an old nag, Epiny was driving the most ramshackle two-wheeled cart I'd ever seen. Moreover, she was driving it one-handed. On the seat next to her was a large basket and her other hand rested inside it. In the basket, a baby was kicking and fussing.

CHAPTER THIRTY

REUNION

The world stood breathless around me as that cart slowly came up the hill. I had time to absorb every detail. Epiny wore a proper hat, but it had been donned hastily, unless it was the fashion now to wear it nearly sliding off one side of her head. Her hair had come unbundled and half spilled down her back. One of the wheels on the cart was wobbling so badly that I immediately resolved she could not go back to Gettys in that conveyance until we had secured it. But mostly I just stared at Epiny's face.

As she drew nearer, I could see high spots of bright color on her cheeks. She was thin, but not as thin as the last time I'd glimpsed her in my dream. I could see her mouth moving as she spoke to the baby in her basket, and then suddenly I couldn't stand it any longer. I began to run down the hill toward her shouting, "Epiny! Epiny!"

Epiny tried to pull in the horse, but my headlong rush toward it alarmed the poor old creature. Instead of stopping, he veered to one side, taking the cart off the track and into the deep grass. There the wobbly wheels refused to go any farther, and that more than Epiny's tugging on the reins brought him to a halt. I reached the side of the cart in time to catch Epiny as she leapt from the seat into my arms. I hugged her tight and whirled her around, beyond joy at seeing her again. Her own arms went tight around my neck. Nothing had ever felt so healing as that simple expression of pure affection. Other than our kinship, Epiny had never had any reason to love me or to make the sacrifices and take the risks for me that she had. In so many ways, I'd brought pain and suffering into her life. But her honest embrace assured me that she still cared for me, despite how I'd damaged her. Her capacity for love humbled me. Kesey had reined in his mount and was watching us in consternation. Epiny, as ever, never stopped talking even as I spun her around.

"I knew you would come back! Even when I couldn't feel you anymore, I knew you weren't dead, and I told Spink so. Oh, that frightened me so, when I woke one morning and could not feel the magic at all. I tried to explain it to Spink, that I knew you'd said good-bye to us. Right away, he said I'd have to accept that you'd probably died. Have a little faith in him, I told him. No one kills a Burvelle that easily! Oh, Nevare, I am so glad to see you, to touch you, to know you are really back. Oh, now, put me down, put me down, you must meet your new little—what would she be, your second cousin? Oh, but that sounds silly, she is much too small to be anyone's second cousin, and I have already been calling you Uncle Nevare to her, so that is what you shall remain. Set me down right now! I want you to hold Solina! She's never met you yet, and listen, she's crying!"

I think those words finally brought me to my senses. I was so joyous at seeing my cousin alive and well after all the anxious days and nights away, it seemed intolerable that anyone should be crying, let alone her own precious baby. I set her down, and she staggered a few steps dizzily, laughing wildly all the while, and then caught hold of the cart's side and hauled herself up to take the baby from the basket. The child was so layered in blankets and wraps that Epiny looked as if she were opening a present. I held on to the edge of the cart and watched, enchanted.

Kesey spoke behind me. "Nevare?" He spoke the word incredulously.

Reflexively, I glanced back at him. Our eyes met and I had no lies or explanations to offer him. For a long moment, we stared at each other. Then his eyes brimmed with tears even as his grin showed all the teeth he did and did not have. "It is you. Oh, by the good god, Nevare, it *is* you. But you ain't fat no more! Still, I shoulda knowed you, even dressed in those drapes. Nevare!"

He fell on me and hugged me hard. The warmth and relief in his voice were so genuine that I could do nothing save hug him back. "Why didn't you say it was you?" he demanded huskily. "Why didn't you say it was you, 'stead of coming to the door like a beggar? Did you think I wouldn't have helped you?"

"I didn't think you would believe me. I didn't think that anyone would believe me."

"Well, I probably wouldn't have, if the Lieutenant hadn't told me so, way last spring. Everyone said that you'd been—that you'd died. But I'd had that dream, and then the Lieutenant came to ask me about it, and I suppose I got a little teary, saying I thought that dream was your way of saying good-bye and no hard feelings. Only he asked me if your sword was on the floor when I woke up, and I said, yes, it was, and that was when he told me the truth." He gave me a friendly shake and pounded me on the back for emphasis. "Only acourse it didn't sound nothing like the truth, sounded like the second wildest tale I'd ever heard. But the more I thought on it, the more it made a weird sense, and when I talked to Ebrooks about it all, he broke down and blubbered about seeing you killed, and said that he hadn't stopped them and he was so ashamed. He said he was the one who hauled your body off and buried it safe in a secret place. Only when I pushed him on it, he couldn't remember where he'd buried you. Couldn't remember where he'd got the shovel, couldn't remember digging the hole. So that was when he and I put it all together, all the bits, and decided that you hadn't done none of what you were accused of, and that you weren't dead, either. 'Course, it was all pretty strange, thinking of you having Speck magic or whatever. Being rescued by Specks with magic."

"Lieutenant Kester told you I was alive," I said stupidly. This was as stunning to me as my reappearance was to him.

"I told him to!" Epiny announced proudly. She was holding her baby against her shoulder and beaming at me as she spoke. "I told him it would be cruel to leave your two friends believing that you were dead and that they'd contributed to your death. And I reminded him how angry I was, and still am, that you left me in the dark for so long. They deserved the truth. And they've kept your secret."

"Well, it wasn't a hard secret to keep," Kesey said, finally releasing me. He dragged his cuff unashamedly across his streaming eyes. "The state you left the town in, no one wanted to even mention your name, let alone talk about how you'd died. If you wanted to shame those fellows for how they were going to do you, you sure did it. Most of them slunk around the town like whipped dogs for months. And I think it was their own guilty consciences that made them tell wild tales about seeing you come back as a Speck warrior during that sneak attack last winter! I told them I didn't believe a word of it. And, by the good god, don't I wish I could take you to town and parade you around now and say, 'See, I told you so! He couldn't a done it. He's been off living in the woods on roots and berries and getting skinny as a rail!' Why, you look like a kid, Nevare! That's what taking off all that fat done for you."

"Yes," I agreed with him. The wash of shame that flooded through me nearly sickened me. I wanted to confess to the old soldier that I had been at the "sneak attack," that I had been seen. But then I would have had to try to explain to him that it hadn't really been me, at least not the *me* that stood before him now. It all suddenly seemed too complicated. The homecoming joy that I'd felt drained away. What had I been thinking, coming back here at all? There was no way I could fit myself back into this life. There were too many contradictions, secrets, and lies.

I found myself looking bleakly at Epiny. I gave her a clenched-teeth smile, resolved that I would say nothing to her of my realization. But I think she sensed my chain of thought, for she held her baby out to me and said, "Hold her. Look at her. Isn't she beautiful? Everything does work itself out, Nevare, if we just give it enough time. Don't be in too big of a rush to give up. All will come well in time."

I gingerly accepted the armful of baby and looked down into her face, and in truth she struck me as an absolutely ordinary baby, one without much hair. She was so bundled up against the mild spring day that all I could see was her face and her hands. "Hello, there," I said.

Solina looked at me, her brown eyes very wide. Then her lower lip quivered, and suddenly she began to wail. Her tiny fists flailed at the air.

"Take her back, take her back! I don't know what to do!" I said in a panic, and held her out to Epiny, who received her with a laugh.

"It's only because she doesn't know you yet and your voice is so deep. Give her time. Once she gets to know you, I'll teach you how to comfort her when she cries. After that, you can hold her as much as you like. I promise!" The last two words she spoke to the baby in such a reassuring voice that the child gave a final hiccup and quieted with a sigh.

I rather thought that I'd already held Solina as much as I'd like to, but I was wise enough not to say that aloud. "She's absolutely amazing," I said truthfully. "I'm sure her father agrees with me. But where is Spink? Is he coming?"

"He wasn't home when Trooper Kesey arrived, but once I'd read the message, I knew I had to come right away. Captain Thayer had called Spink in to discuss something or other. The man can't seem to let each officer do his own job. He's always oversupervising everyone or demanding that all the officers convene so he can lecture them. So I couldn't very well run and fetch him, but I've left a note for him on the table. I left Kara watching the smaller children while her mother did the shopping. She's very good with them, and Sem has become quite responsible, too, for his age. And Amzil will be back home soon, so it should be all right. I didn't say anything about you to the children; I wanted to be sure of you before I told them you had returned. Oh, Nevare, they are going to be so happy! That book you gave them? I've read it to them until it's falling apart. And you would be so pleased to hear how well Kara has her letters and numbers, and even Sem is picking them up! He competes with his sister in everything. You'll be so proud of that boy when you see him! Amzil and I cut down old uniforms to make proper trousers and jackets for him; now don't think we've dressed him like a little trooper. That would be awful! I remember how horrid that was for Caulder Stiet, always dressed like a little man long before he was one. But he just loves to be dressed like Spink. And Amzil's skills at sewing and tailoring never cease to amaze me. I've told her she should try to open a little dress shop; there isn't one in Gettys, you know. She says the other women wouldn't do business with her. I told her that once one or two started, and the others saw her work, they'd have to come to her or risk being seen as dowdy. I just know she could succeed at it if only we had the money to get her started. And Kara is so quick to learn! She's already sewn her first sampler. Wait until you—"

I set two fingers gently to Epiny's lips. "Let's go the rest of the way up the hill and go inside, shall we? Perhaps Kesey has some coffee we could share while we talk. There is so much I want to hear."

And so many decisions for me to make.

Epiny walked up the hill beside me while Kesey drove the cart and his saddle horse trailed behind. Epiny snorted with exasperation at the top of the hill when I insisted on examining the wheels and axles of the cart. I sent them ahead of me into the cabin, asking Kesey to put on some fresh coffee for all of us. I think they both knew that what I was actually doing was taking a moment to think. When at last I entered, Epiny was enthroned in my big old chair. Little Solina was propped in her lap, looking all around with very wide eyes. The aroma of fresh coffee had already begun to fill the small room.

"You can probably drive it safely back, as long as you go slowly and someone accompanies you in case of mishaps. I don't want you and the baby stranded on the road next to a broken-down cart."

"But of course you'll come with me! I don't even know why we've stopped to have coffee. Not that it isn't pleasant to be invited in, Trooper Kesey. But of course you will come home with me, Nevare. That's why I borrowed the cart. I thought that you would ride—"

"Epiny," I interrupted. "Nothing is decided. Do you forget that I'm a man convicted of murder, among other crimes?"

"But no one will recognize you! Kesey didn't, and he knew you far better than most and—"

"And in any case, how could I go back to Gettys dressed like this, let alone to an officer's house? What would people think of you, bringing a man dressed like a savage into your home?"

"Oh, it could be managed, Nevare! You worry too much about what other people would think! You are too cautious! You need simply to come back to town and take your life back. How long must Amzil wait for you?"

"Amzil? The Dead Town whore?" Kesey put in incredulously. "She's sweet on Nevare?" He'd taken the steaming pot of coffee off the fire. As he set it down on the table, he said, "Looks like you done a lot of tidying up while I was gone."

"Amzil is not and never was a whore," Epiny said indignantly as I simultaneously said, "I just thought it was the least I could do after you helped a complete stranger."

"And it sure needed doing; I'm no housekeeper, I know that. And pardon if I spoke out of turn, ma'am, or said something wrong. It's only what I've always heard about her. And the good god knows she's got a brand-new reputation in Gettys since last winter. She stares at the troopers like she could bring the wrath of the old gods down on them with a snap of her fingers. And makes them sharp little remarks all the time. Hasn't won her any friends."

"If you knew what she went through—" Epiny began.

I cut through her stream of words with the truth. "The night everyone thought I was murdered by that mob? Amzil was there. Some of the men were going to rape her because she was my friend. To hurt me by making me watch, and afterward, to kill her in front of me. And the Captain wasn't going to do a thing to stop them. It was ugly, Kesey. I managed to protect her, but it's not a thing a woman could forget. Or forgive."

"I heard somewhat of that," he said shortly. "The regiment isn't what it was, once. Men get ground down for so long, some of them just go bad. Cavalla used to be a notch better than common soldiers, but, well . . . It's not like anyone is proud of that night, Nevare, least of all Captain Thayer. There was a Sixday service, not long ago, when he talked all about how wrong a man can be when he trusts a woman. Says even the sweetest woman in the world can be a deceiver and a temptress, and when men believe them, they can be led to commit the worst of crimes. He said he knew that no woman could be trusted, not even your own wife. Everyone knew he was talking about that night. Shocked every one of us there—well, not me, 'cause I ain't been to Sixday services in a long time, but to them that was—when he broke down and sobbed about it. Cut him to the bone, I guess, that she'd lied to him. Though he never said about what. Then he said it was a lesson to us all to live upright lives and not trust our hearts to anyone but the good god. And—" Kesey suddenly looked uncomfortable. "He said something 'bout how it was lucky you'd committed other crimes that made you deserve your fate." He abruptly stopped speaking.

"Really lucky," I said sourly. "Otherwise he and his men would have murdered an innocent man."

Kesey just looked at me.

"Kesey, I *am* an innocent man. Innocent of that, anyway. I didn't do any of the things I was accused of. Not one."

He nodded gravely and put three cups on the table. Two were tin but one was of thick crockery. He poured the steaming coffee slowly, trying not to stir the grounds from the bottom, and spoke without looking up at me. "That's what the Lieutenant told me, when he come up here about my dream. And Ebrooks and me, we talked it over, and even before then we thought it was damned peculiar— Oh, pardon my language, ma'am."

"Damned peculiar," Epiny agreed wryly, making Kesey blush. She took up her crockery mug of hot coffee and sipped at it gingerly. As she put it down on the table, she asked me matter-of-factly, "So what will you do? I think you stand a fair chance of clearing yourself if you came back and decided to do so."

"Oh, Epiny, it's so much more complicated than that. You know it is. A fair chance of clearing myself means there's also a fair chance I'll dance at the end of the rope, unless they flog me to death first. Even if I clear myself in Gettys, how do I explain to anyone how I slipped away from that mob: do you think that anyone would think me innocent if I told them I'd done it with Speck magic?"

"They wouldn't like it at all," Kesey chimed in. "Soldiers don't like to think anyone can fool them, and Nevare fooled them all. And let them live with a lot of guilt for a long time, to boot. And most of them still figure that Nevare, uh, you know, with the Captain's dead wife. Some of the fellows speculate that if she lied, maybe she was a temptress, too, and—"

"Kesey!" I said sharply.

The old soldier abruptly closed his mouth and nodded. "Right," he said. He picked up his tin cup of coffee, wincing a bit, for the coffee had warmed the metal. "I'm thinking that perhaps you'd like to speak to Miz Kester in private. And seeing as how you're her cousin and all, if I heard that right, ain't a thing improper about that. So I might take this cup of coffee and go outside and sit for a bit."

"Oh, we mustn't drive you out of your own home," Epiny decided firmly. "Nevare and I can sit outside." And so saying, she rose. With her baby in one arm, she took my arm with her free hand and guided us out of the door. I barely had time to get my cup of coffee. She seemed content to let her own remain on the table.

The day seemed bright after the dimness of the cabin. We walked over to the cart and she sat down on its open tail. The horse shifted doubtfully in his harness. "Well," she said, and then, as if it were the most important thing, she observed, "That was the most dreadful coffee I've ever tasted. How can you drink it?"

"I've been hungry enough lately to eat or drink anything that's offered to me." I took a mouthful. She was right about the coffee, but I swallowed it anyway and tried to keep my face under control.

She laughed sympathetically. "My poor cousin. When you come home with me tonight, I'll do my best to remedy that. Between Amzil and me, we put some fair meals on the table. We are not as hungry as we have been, thank the good god. The supply wagons have come through at last, so there is plenty of plain food, bread and porridge and such. And the little gardens behind the houses have started to give up a bit of fresh vegetable now and then. But for a time there, I was certainly hungry enough to eat whatever was offered to me. Oh, I've chattered like a squirrel long enough. Tell me how you come to be here? What happened to you? How was that you and not you, that horrible night—"

I shook my head. "I'll tell it all when both you and Spink can hear it." In truth, I wanted to put off that reckoning a little while. Surely my cousin would no longer look at me so fondly once she had heard of my part in the raid. "Instead, you must finish telling me what has been going on here. You were starving?"

She nodded. Her eyes grew larger and her face paled. "The Speck raid destroyed all the food stored in the warehouses. People were left with only what they'd had in their homes, and the men in the barracks had even less. They salvaged what meat they could from the horses that had died in the fires, and tore apart the burned wreckage looking for anything, half a sack of flour or a scorched bag of grain. Anything. A few people had chickens that they were wintering over, but with their feed gone or eaten by people, there was no sense in holding back. So we ate all the chickens, what milk goats there were, the hogs—it was terrible, Nevare. It was like we were eating our hopes for the future. There is still hardly any livestock left in town, and half our troops are afoot. Those last weeks, there was next to nothing. I soaked out a molasses keg and then gave the children warmed molasses water. We had no hope at all."

Despite the gravity of the tale, I had to grin. "And then Sergeant Duril arrived," I filled in.

She cocked her head, a trifle surprised perhaps. "That he did. To save the day. I don't know how that old man got through; the sides of his cart were muddy and his horses were next to dead. Oh, it was like a blessing from heaven to see that cartload of goods: flour, sugar, beans, peas, molasses, oil—everything we'd been longing for. I felt as rich as a queen when he knocked on my door and said, 'Miz Epiny Kester? Your family has sent you some help!'

"But it wasn't five minutes before every woman in town was standing in the street outside my house, staring at that food. Some of their little children were weeping and begging for a taste, and some were too starved to even do that. And Spink came out and sent them all home to get bowls and cups, so we could measure out shares for all, as far as it would go. I can't tell you how I hated him, for all of half a moment! There we were, with our own little baby down to skin and bones, and he was giving our food away! But I knew he was right. How would I ever have faced any of them, if I had kept plenty of food for my own and let their children go empty?"

"Not to mention that they might have turned on you and simply taken it all, if shares hadn't been freely offered."

Epiny sighed. "Nevare, I never cease to be amazed at the darkness of your thoughts! How can you bear to think such evil things about people?"

"I think my life experience has had something to do with it."

"Oh, such a sour outlook! But that isn't what happened at all. We shared what we had, and just as we were down to thinking of making soup from the flour sack, the supply wagons came."

A worry came to me. "What did you tell Duril when he was here? About me, I mean."

She looked at me sadly. "Nevare, what do you think I told him? What did I owe a good man like that, who has risked all for us? I told him the truth."

I lowered my eyes before her disapproval.

"Why did you think I would do anything else?" She scolded me. "He told me that he knew something of what had happened to you already, and that he was with you the night you confronted Dewara. He may not be an educated man, Nevare, and perhaps being a sergeant was the highest he ever rose in his life, but he has a lot of wisdom and common sense. It wasn't easy for him to hear. But at the end of it, he nodded, and said he hoped you were still alive and might come home to give some comfort to your father. But even if you never came back, he said, 'I won't never think badly of him. I did my task the best I could, taught him all I knew about soldiering. If he sticks to that, he shouldn't do too badly.'"

I had to ask the next question. "Did you tell him about the raid on Gettys? Does he know about my part in it?"

"Nevare, *I* don't fully understand your part in it, so I could scarcely tell him. I was so drugged with laudanum, I can barely remember that night. I think I'm glad of that. You've said it wasn't really you. I believe that. Why shouldn't I believe that?"

I looked at my feet. "Perhaps because I've deceived you before."

"Yes, you have," she freely admitted. "And it still rankles. But I think we need to move past it, at least for today. You've had a very hard time, Nevare, but now you are home. And perhaps you have had nothing but bad news and hard times and sad tidings for too long. So. Let me share some good news with you." Her smile suddenly widened. "Have you any idea how your family's fortune has changed of late?"

"I've a hint of it. There was a gold strike near my father's holdings."

"Yes, but it's so much more than that. I had a letter from your sister just a few days ago. Would you like to read it yourself, or shall I just tell you?"

"Do you have it with you?" I longed to touch paper my sister had touched, to see words written in her hand.

"I'm afraid I was a bit more flustered than that when I packed up my baby and ran out of my house! If I'd been thinking, I'd have brought it and a picnic basket! Do you want to wait until you finally visit my home?"

She was baiting me again. I shook my head with a smile and said, "Just tell me how Yaril fares."

"Well, your sister has been absolutely brilliant for one so young. She said there was a day in your father's study when he was not feeling well. And when she went to him, she herself nearly fainted. But as she fell, she saw you standing over her. She said that you showed her a place and told her that was where an important rock came from. As soon as Sergeant Duril returned, she made him take her out riding. From what she says, it was quite a trip, requiring them to camp overnight twice! But she found the place and it was the Sergeant who recognized the rocks for what they were: gold ore. I've no idea how he knew that's what it was, but he did. And she was clever enough to know that it wasn't on your father's holdings, and that if she told others about it, there would be no gain to your family, just a wild rush of greedy people trying to get what they could. So they spoke not a word to anyone. She sent the samples to the Queen quietly, suggesting that as all the lands there are the Crown's, the monarchs would wish to know the value of what was there before unscrupulous men began to secretly mine it or they unknowingly gave it away in a land grant." She grinned at me. "You'll never guess who her courier was."

I knew. I'd told Yaril she could trust him. "Sergeant Duril," I said confidently.

She laughed delightedly. "No. You are not even close. Though the sergeant is a dear, dear man, and if ever I needed a trusty courier or a tutor for my son or someone to look after my holdings, I would definitely consider him a good choice."

"Who, then?" I demanded impatiently.

She picked up her baby, kissed the little girl with a flourish, and then announced to me, "Caulder Stiet. There. What do you think of that?"

For a moment my mouth hung open. Then I replied darkly, "I fear she has played right into his hands."

"Then you would be mistaken," Epiny told me snippily. "For it was a conspiracy between the two of them, to get the samples to the Queen without letting Caulder's uncle know that they had obtained them."

"What?"

"Yaril saw it as a chance for them to build something, for themselves, perhaps together, perhaps not. They are both, she wrote, tired of being pawns in their elders' games. Caulder is quite certain he wishes to marry her, but she has honestly told him that she is uncertain and does not wish to be married for many years yet. Still, they are friends enough to conspire. She and Caulder feigned a monstrous quarrel, with shrieking and broken crockery! You know, from the way she writes of it, I think she enjoyed it! She mentions she smashed enough cups from the old china that her father will have to let her buy a whole new set now."

"That sounds like Yaril," I admitted with reluctant admiration. I knew those cups. She had always hated the dogwood-blossom pattern.

"Well, it was enough of a to-do that your father finally ordered both of them to leave his house. And so of course, off they went, back to Old Thares, with Caulder taking the rocks in his baggage. He had quite a time getting them to Her Majesty, but he prevailed, and guess what? For service to the Crown, the Crown has issued another grant of land to your father, more than doubling his holdings, and adjacent land to Caulder Stiet himself, to be held in trust for him by his father, his real father, until Caulder reaches his majority. It's almost like the Crown forcing him to take Caulder back as his son. No title for Caulder, more's the pity, but he will at least join the landed gentry when he comes of age."

"How nice for him," I said dryly. The news of my father's holdings increasing was good news, for it made Yaril an even more desirable bride. She would have better choices than Caulder Stiet, I hoped. The idea of the Stiet family having a holding adjacent to Widevale appealed to me far less.

"Oh, you sound so sour and old, Nevare! But let me finish." The baby fussed again and she spent a moment hushing her. "The gold strike, once the King announced it, has completely changed Widevale. Yaril wrote pages and pages about it. The King has sent in his engineers and they have designed and built housing for the workers, and they are setting up the mining and the refining and all of those things right in the area of the find. In time, there will be a large town there, if not a city. And Burvelle's Landing is the closest river port, and the nearest inn and shops and all of that! So it has absolutely boomed with population. Yaril writes that it has tripled in size, and of course the taxes and landing fees from the Landing all go into your father's coffers, so the family wealth is suddenly quite spectacular. In fact, your part of the family is so wealthy that even my beloved mother suddenly finds her husband's brother quite respectable and worthy of a visit. When Yaril wrote, my father had arrived and had just spent the day with your father, and Yaril said your father was up and walking about with a cane and almost acting like his old self. He planned to take his brother out on horseback the next day to look over the new land grant, and he hadn't been on a horse for months! And Yaril and my sister, Purissa, find each other's company very agreeable! Yaril is very excited that my mother has even hinted at taking her back to Old Thares for a season, so that she may be properly presented to society. I suspect that my mother will attempt to find her a better marriage offer than Caulder Stiet, but somehow I think that your little sister is more than capable of dealing with Lady Burvelle. I suspect that, if anything, Yaril *will* make a better match, but it will be someone of her own choosing. So what could be better?"

Her mention of her mother triggered another concern of mine. I tried not to sound accusing as I said, "You sent my soldier-son journal to your father, didn't you?"

She paused, then faced me squarely. "I did. It seemed wisest to me then. I didn't think Yaril was old enough to deal with the very frank things you'd written in it." Here, despite all her aplomb, she flushed slightly. "And I feared that your father might destroy it. I believed there was too much valuable information in it to allow that to happen to it. So I sent it to my father, with a request that he leave it sealed. He is an honorable man, Nevare. I knew that he would respect my wishes, and I never, ever thought that my mother, of all people, would be interested in a soldier-son's journal. I'm so sorry."

"I have only a hazy idea of why you *should* be sorry," I said gently. "But I'd like to know what became of it after she read it." Whatever had become of it, I told myself that it was all my own fault for creating such a betraying diary. The magic had made me do it, I thought fiercely, trying to free myself from guilt on that score. And abruptly I realized the other half of that truth. "Let us understand one thing, Epiny," I told her. "The magic was what spurred me to write that journal in such a way. It acted on me to create it, and it also acted on me to leave it behind when I fled. I suspect that you, too, were but its instrument when you sent it to Old Thares to fall into your mother's hands. Whatever she has done with it is what the magic wished her to do. The magic is a powerful force, like a river. We can build our levees and dams, but when the river grows strong with rain and snowmelt, it breaks all the man-made barriers aside and flows in its rightful bed. And that is what it has done to us, and that odd current has carried it to your mother's hands."

I took a deep breath and tried to sound calm as I asked, "Do you know what she has done with it?"

She bit her lip. The baby snuggled against her seemed to sense her mother's sudden worry, for she gave a squeaky cry and then was still again. "I know she wanted to take it to the Queen. My father was furious at the suggestion. I do not think he would read it after I asked him not to, but he would know something of what was in it. My mother would see to that. And he, he would not be pleased, Nevare, by the things she would surely tell him. He said that she did not seem to understand that anything she did that brought shame on the Burvelles of the East would reflect just as badly on our branch of the family. He says she is so accustomed to thinking of herself as superior to his family that she does not perceive that we would be painted with the same brush!"

Her voice had been rising and rising as her anger increased. Now little Solina stirred, lifted her head, and began to wail stridently. "Hush, dear, hush. Mama isn't angry with you." She gave me an apologetic sideways glance. "She is getting hungry. Soon I will have to feed her."

"Must you start back to town then?" I asked stupidly.

For a long instant, she just stared at me and then I said, "Oh. Well, I'm certain that Kesey would be happy to offer you the privacy of his cabin for that."

I gave her my hand to help her down from the cart. As we walked to the cabin, she said, "Sometimes I try to imagine my mother taking care of me as I take care of Solina. It's hard. There were always maids and nannies and wet nurses when I was small. But I cannot imagine her carrying me and birthing me and not loving me as I love Solina. So sometimes I speak ill of her, but even when I do, I know that I love her. Isn't that peculiar, Nevare? She is vain and arrogant, and well, more clever than intelligent. She does things I don't admire at all. And still I love her. Do you think I'm weak or foolish?"

My mouth twisted in a smile. "Do you think I'm weak or foolish for still loving my father?"

"Not at all." She smiled sadly. "It is so strange, Nevare. Yaril writes that your father now speaks as if he deliberately sent you off to be a soldier, and that soon you will come home 'covered in glory.' She says that there are just parts of the past that he doesn't accept anymore. He no longer asks for your mother or the other children. But he persists in believing that you will be his noble soldier son and gain renown." She sighed. "He is not unlike my mother in that regard. Did you know she has forgiven me for marrying Spink? She even sent me a letter."

"She did? Epiny, that's wonderful!"

She smiled wryly. "It was full of questions about the success of Lady Kester's water business and the baths that are to be built there. She wanted to know if there would be special accommodations 'for family.'"

She laughed aloud at the thought of her proud mother claiming Lady Kester as "family" and then, at my puzzled expression, exclaimed, "Oh, I haven't had time to tell you about that, have I? Dr. Amicas took seriously what we told him. He made a long trek to Bitter Springs and took back casks of the water to study. No one knows why, but it does seem to prevent or lessen plague outbreaks. And as Spink and I can both attest, it does wonders for the survivors. He tested it first on the Academy cadets, the ones who had suffered ill health since the plague outbreak. When they showed signs of recovery, he ordered more water be sent, and recalled many of the cadets who had been sent home as invalids. The recoveries have been amazing."

I thought of Trist and the others and looked at her wordlessly.

"What are you thinking?" she asked me, worried by my silence.

I sighed. "I'm happy for those who will now recover and regain their lives. But I have to confess, I'm thinking about fellows who won't. Nate, for instance. Trent and Caleb. Oron."

"Think, too, of those who won't die because of it," she counseled me solemnly. Then she grinned rather impishly and added, "And you might say that you rejoice in the change in the Kester family fortune. The demand for the water is incredible; people are using it as a tonic for all sorts of ills now, and several very wealthy families have made the trek to visit the spring itself and bathe in it. Lady Kester has hired workmen to build a spa there, with separate baths for ladies and gentlemen, and a hotel. Oh, it will be rustic at first, but the letter from Spink's sister says that will be part of the charm. She complains that they never have enough bottles for the water, and that they must find a new supplier for them. And she also says that, thanks to the water, she has an offer for her hand. You may know him? He's a friend of Spink's. Rory Hart, soldier son of Lord and Lady Hart of Roundhills?"

"Rory? From the Academy? But he never got sick from the plague at all."

"Perhaps not, but his younger brothers did. And his mother took them to Bitter Springs, where they recovered, and she met Spink's family and pronounced them delightful. She says that Spink's sister Gera is exactly the practical sort of girl that Rory needs to settle him down and keep him in order."

"I don't know who to feel sorry for, Rory or Gera," I said, and Epiny cuffed me lightly.

"Neither one. Spink says he actually thinks they will be well suited to each other, when they meet."

I shook my head, unwilling to imagine a girl who could settle Rory down and keep him in order. I wondered if she carried a club with her at all times. To Epiny I said, "It is almost frightening how fast everything seems to have changed. The world has gone on without me while I was away. I wonder how I will find a place in it again." At that moment, it did not seem impossible that I should do just that.

"You are as much at fault as anyone for these changes. Without you, how many of them would have come about?" She halted, then added reassuringly, "And some parts of the world have not changed that much. Some parts still wait for you." She smiled teasingly.

I quickly changed the subject. "You have told me all about my family and your parents and Spink's family, but not mentioned a word about Spink and yourself. From what Kesey tells me, the regiment has been divided, and only a company of it remains here. What does Spink think of that?"

Her smile faded a bit, but determination came into her eyes. "It is not the best post he might have. He knew that when he accepted the commission. But Spink says we will make the best of it. With the depletion of officers here in Gettys, he sees an opportunity to rise in the ranks. There are rumors that we will soon receive new troops to bring us up to strength. Or that perhaps the rest of the regiment will be called back to the Midlands and some other regiment replace us here. It's uncertain right now. Spink says that the King has much on his mind, with the gold discovery and a new treaty with the Landsingers. There has not been a formal decision to abandon the road, though Spink thinks that is what it will come to. Spink has told me that this is the lot of a soldier, regardless of his rank. Often he simply has to remain where he is and await new commands." She gave a small sigh. "I confess, I would love to be almost anywhere else but here. Even without the magic soaking us with fear or despair, Gettys is a gloomy, primitive place. Sometimes it is hard to read the letters that come; it does seem as if everyone else's lives have gone on, but I am trapped here, with the same work and worries, day after day."

"The lot of a cavalla wife," I said quietly.

"Yes," she replied briskly. She took a breath and squared her shoulders. "And that is what I took upon myself when I married Spink. I know that. And I intend to make the best of it."

She hesitated at the door to the cabin, and then turned to me, blushing prettily. "Would you—that is, could you ask Kesey to join you outside so that I could be alone with my baby for a time?"

"Of course," I assured her.

Kesey surprised me by quickly deducing that Epiny needed to be alone to nurse her child. I didn't have to spell it out for him, and he even made the excuse that we needed to fetch more water as I'd emptied the cask with all my "scrubbing round." We each took a bucket as we left the cabin.

"So," Kesey asked me curiously. "What are you going to do? You going to go into town with the Lieutenant's wife?"

"Not now. Not like this." I gestured down at my bizarre garb.

Kesey sniffed thoughtfully. "Your old stuff is still around, but it's not going to fit you. One of my shirts might fit you. But not the trousers. Funny. You're a lot taller than I thought. You seemed shorter when you were fat."

"Taller and younger. Not a bad trade," I said, and we both laughed. Then a silence fell between us, a silence filled with nothing to say and too much to say.

"Thank you," I said at last.

"For a shirt? No need to thank me. It probably won't even be all that clean."

"No, thank you for everything. For thinking well of me when most people didn't. For being willing to make me a part of the regiment."

He made another deprecatory noise. "Wonder if we even are a regiment anymore, the way we're getting spread out."

"It's like you told me before, Kesey. When things are down for a regiment is when the real soldiers hold their heads up and try harder."

"Does that mean you're going to come back to soldiering? Clear your name and put your uniform back on?"

"I'd like to," I said, and my own words surprised me.

"Well then, I think—" he began, but at the same moment, we both turned toward the road that wound up the hill to the cemetery. A horse was coming, ridden hard, the rider low on his back, urging more speed out of him. We both recognized the rider at the same time. "I think Lieutenant Kester is mighty glad to hear that you're back!" Kesey observed with a grin.

I had to smile, too, and then I went to meet Spink. I watched him come, an excellent rider on a mediocre mount. He was small and slight as ever, still looking more boy than man. When he drew in his horse just a few feet away from me, I was surprised. "A moustache? Epiny didn't warn me to expect a moustache." It looked good on him, but I wasn't about to concede that to him without some mocking first.

He did not smile at my jest. He took a breath. "Nevare. I am so glad to see you." He drew in another deep breath. "Amzil has been arrested. For murder."

CHAPTER THIRTY-ONE

LIVES IN THE BALANCE

There, I thought to myself in some strange corner of my mind. There it is. The tragedy that denies all the good news I've heard today. The magic takes a final slap at me, for bending it to my will. Or the balancing point for Orandula, damn him! He threatened to bring my life into balance.

Then Spink was off his horse. He embraced me roughly, saying, "Sorry, brother. That's a terrible way to greet you after you've been gone so long and endured so much. But the news had been burning a hole in me every second of the ride from town." He glanced around us. "Where's Epiny?"

"She's in the cabin, feeding the baby." My voice shook. I felt I couldn't get a breath. My fault. Somehow it was all my fault. If I hadn't used the magic to grow the garden for her, if I hadn't supplied her so well with meat before I left her . . . If I hadn't cared about her, and wanted to stay with her when the magic wanted me to move on . . . But I'd done all the damn magic asked of me; it had won and had its way with my life. Why did she and I have to be punished by it now?

Spink took off his gloves and wiped sweat and dust from his face. "I won't interrupt Solina's feeding with this sort of news. It will keep for a few minutes longer. So you're back?" He forced gladness into his voice. He stepped back and looked me up and down. "You look like yourself again, like the Nevare from the Academy days. What happened? How are you here? And what are you wearing?"

"A cut-up cloak. It was all I had. Spink, it's a long story, and I'd rather hear yours first. How can Amzil be charged with murder?"

"They say she killed a man in Dead Town, and hid his body. It's probably why she came to Gettys, to hide from her crime."

I knew it was, but I kept silent on that. "Who accused her?" I asked.

"The murdered man's wife. She had evidently taken to whoring for the soldiers after her husband was murdered. Since Captain Thayer drove the other whores out of Gettys, a lot of the fellows have been making the trip to Dead Town to see her. Somehow the Captain got wind of her trade with the troops, and sent men out there to arrest her. Captain Thayer's determined there will be no whores in Gettys, and I suppose he's decided to extend that to Dead Town, though that seems to me like a big stretch of his authority. He told the patrol to bring the woman and any troopers visiting her back to Gettys. The patrol returned today with their prisoners. That was why Thayer called out the other officers today. He wanted us to witness their summary punishment."

He paused and drew breath, then glanced at Kesey. "Trooper, do you have any water? My throat is as dry as the road."

Kesey shook his head. "Only in the cabin where your missus is. Unless you want to walk back to the spring. Or I could go fetch you some." He glanced down at the bucket in his hand.

"Would you? I'd appreciate it."

Kesey hurried off with his bucket. Spink and I walked the rest of the way up the hill. There was water in the animal trough, and he let his horse have some. We walked over to the cart and he sat down on the tail of it.

"So what happened?" I demanded impatiently.

Spink shook his head in disgust. "Thayer decided to flog all three of them, the woman as well as the two men. He gave us a long lecture about how we had failed as officers if our men could behave in such a beastly fashion. Thayer has been . . . strange since that night, the night you left town. And recently he's become even stranger. From hints he has dropped, in his lectures and his Sixday sermons, I think he knows now that Carsina lied to him, that really you had been her fiancé. I think it is devouring him, from the inside. In his own mind, he'd made a saint out of Carsina. He justified everything about that night on the basis of her innocence. And when he found out she had deceived him and lied about you, I think it swung him in a different direction. The man hates to look at me now. When I report to him, he stares at the wall. He's so full of guilt about what he did that he now tries to be perfect every moment.

"I wouldn't talk like this about a fellow officer in front of Kesey, but I just don't think the Captain is right in his mind anymore. I think it is why he was left behind here with the rest of the dregs. At one time, he could have been a good officer, but now." Spink shook his head. "At a time when the fear and despair that once overwhelmed us are gone, he seems intent on crushing the spirit out of the men. He has been organized. I'll give him that. The few men that are left, he drives. The maintenance of the fort and buildings are far better than they were, yet such tasks feel like busywork to the men. They mutter that there is little reason to rebuild barracks that will remain empty, or repair streets that carry hardly any traffic. He gives them no praise or pride in doing their work, only lectures on how it is a soldier's duty to obey and not question."

I broke into his long explanation with a question. "The dregs? What do you mean, the dregs left behind?"

He gave a small sigh. "Anyone with any connections left here with the rest of the regiment when they rode out. They left behind, well, the undesirable elements. The men who were lazy, troublesome, or stupid. The ones in poor health. The old soldiers. The scouts because they know this area, and everyone knows you can't really bring a scout back to civilization. The officers who don't behave like officers."

He halted, folded his lips. My eyes searched his as I asked the horrible question. "Why you, then?"

He gave the tiniest of shrugs and then admitted, "Epiny's forthrightness does not always endear her to people. Some find it irritating. Some officers feel it reflects badly on a lieutenant if he cannot or will not control his wife. Colonel Haren used to refer to her as a thorn in his flesh, more than once, when we were speaking. More often, he simply didn't speak to me any more than he could help it."

"Oh, good god, Spink. That's so unfair."

A smile twisted his mouth. "It is what it is. I married her because she was what I wanted with all my heart. I'm in this regiment because it was what was offered to me. I don't confuse the one kind of commitment with the other. But"—and he sighed more deeply—"I know that Captain Thayer finds her behavior reprehensible. He has spoken to me privately about her twice now."

"He'd never have survived being married to Carsina for long, then—" I stopped, wondering if I profaned the dead.

But Spink barked a short laugh. "From what little I knew of her, you are right. If she had lived, he'd be a different man. Good god, we all would, wouldn't we? But she didn't. And here we are. Her death and her deception of him have soured the man.

"He denies himself anything that might be remotely sinful or even pleasurable. Well, that's his own business, but now he's taken it beyond himself, trying to restrict the men and telling the officers how we ought to live to provide a 'good example' to the troops. Driving the whores out of town was extreme enough, but now he's suggesting things like unaccompanied women should stay off the streets in the evenings and on Sixday. He wants to make attendance at the Sixday services mandatory for everyone who lives inside the fort, and to forbid the troops from going to the town businesses on Sixday."

"I'll wager that Epiny doesn't agree to that."

"At first, when he was tightening the rules on the men's behavior, she thought she finally had a commander listening to her concerns about women's safety on the streets. He's only become this extreme in the last few weeks, Nevare. I don't think anyone realizes he means for us to live like this forever.

"He called in all the officers today, to witness him dispensing his justice. The men took their stripes—fifteen each. It just about made me sick to watch. When he got to the woman, some of us objected. I was one of them. The men were soldiers and subject to his rules, I told him, but the woman wasn't. Thayer wasn't listening to us, but then the woman said it wasn't her fault she was a whore, it was the only way she could make a living after her husband was murdered by Amzil."

He gave me a sideways glance, but I still said nothing. He went on. "That made Captain Thayer sit up and take notice. Amzil has never tried to avoid him since that night; I'd almost say she goes out of her way to put herself in front of him. She addresses him every chance she gets: 'Are you having a good day, Captain Thayer? Pleasant weather, isn't it, Captain Thayer?' She's a mirror of his guilt, a living and very present reminder of a night when he was neither an officer nor a gentleman. And this widow gave him the perfect reason to be rid of her. He immediately sent two men out to look for Amzil and to bring her to confront her accuser. Everyone knows that she works for me, so they went first to my house. Thank the good god that the Captain had allowed me to go with them; I had told him I didn't want strange men barging into my house and alarming my delicate wife."

He paused and we exchanged a look. I suspected the men would have been more alarmed than Epiny. "Amzil wasn't there, but Epiny's note was. I scooped it up before anyone else saw it. I called in a neighbor's housekeeper, one of Epiny's whistle brigade, to keep an eye on the children for me. We were headed back to headquarters when we encountered Amzil, coming back from market. The men arrested her and took her immediately to Captain Thayer." His words halted and I knew he didn't wish to elaborate.

"And then you came here?"

"No! I longed to, but knew that I could not leave Amzil to face him alone." He looked aside from me. "I did what I could to protect her, Nevare, but she didn't make it easy. I came with those men, almost like I was leading them to her." Then his eyes came up to meet mine. "I tried to tell her to be calm. She wouldn't listen to me. I gave her what protection I could. It wasn't enough."

I suddenly felt cold and my ears rang. "What do you mean?" I asked faintly.

"She fought them. They had to drag her. She was kicking and fighting and spitting, screaming to everyone on the street that Thayer was finally going to kill her and rape her like he'd threatened to do. I've never seen a woman act like that; it was more like watching a cornered wildcat. Fear, but plenty of hatred, too. As soon as they had her in the Captain's office, the woman accused her. 'She's the one, she killed my husband, and buried him in one of the old buildings in Dead Town. I know she done it, 'cause I sent him out to beg some food of her, when she had plenty and we had nothing. And she killed him and run off. Took me weeks to find his grave. My poor, dear husband. All he wanted was food.' And the widow broke down in tears."

"Did Amzil deny it?"

"She wouldn't say a word. And that other woman sat there, rocking and crying and moaning from time to time, and the Captain started questioning Amzil. 'Did you do it? Did you kill this woman's husband?' And instead of answering him, she started firing questions back at him: 'Did you strike an unarmed man while others held him for you? Did you keep silent when troops under your command said they would rape me in front of the man I loved? Did you yourself suggest that you would rape me after I was dead, as vengeance on the man you intended to murder?' For every question he asked her, she asked him a worse one. I think she knew she was facing death and was determined to cut him as deep as she could on the way. In front of every officer in his command, she accused him of those things."

I couldn't find breath to ask him what had happened. His repetition of her words "in front of the man I loved" had burned into me like acid.

"The Captain was roused into a fury. He said to her, 'Tell me the truth, or I'll have it flogged out of you.' Then she challenged him. 'You don't need a whip. By the good god, if you tell the truth, I vow I will. And if you won't, then you have no right to question me.' And it just got cold silent in that room. Everyone looking at him, because most of them knew that what she said about him was true. And then he blurted out, 'You are right. I will tell the truth and have it be over. I did those things. The deceit of a woman made me do those things. I am guilty.' And once he'd said it, Amzil looked him straight in the eye and said, 'I killed that man because he was going to kill me and my children and take our food.'"

"So she told the truth. It was self-defense."

"I don't doubt that. I don't think anyone could doubt it. But it wasn't enough to save her. Nevare, Captain Thayer has sentenced her to hang tomorrow. And he has sentenced himself to receive fifty lashes for conduct unbecoming an officer. He was so calm when he announced it, like he welcomed the opportunity. He spoke like he was giving an address, saying that he was going to accept the responsibility for failing his men and leading them into evil that night. He said that the good god had already punished many of them, that the Speck raid was the good god cleansing evil from our midst. And he said he would finish what the good god had begun, with an act of atonement for his role in the evil."

"That wasn't the good god. That was the Specks, plain and simple." I swallowed and then forced the truth from my lips. "That was me. Soldier's Boy me."

Spink made no response to my words. As the silence stretched, I finally found my voice. "I was there that night."

Spink stared off into the distance. His voice was tight when he said, "I know. I saw you."

"I know that you didn't kill me, when you could have."

"I—" he began, and then stopped again.

"My other self, my Speck self. He planned the raid. He targeted Thayer's men. That was the first barracks we went to. I couldn't stop him, Spink, or I would have."

"You—he butchered them. Like animals in a slaughterhouse chute. They were found in a heap near the charred ruins. They never had a chance."

"I know. I was there. But I swear, Spink, it wasn't me. I'll swear by anything you like. I could not have done it." I gave a strangled laugh. "He took all my hatred and lust for vengeance. And he seems to have kept it. Even now, I cannot rouse the hatred I should feel for Thayer. All I can think is that he was caught up by all of it, just as I was. Tortured and twisted by the magic. Made to do its will."

Spink swallowed. "Perhaps I hate him enough for both of us. I liked him, when I first got here. He was a good officer."

"I don't doubt that," I said quietly.

"What are we going to do about Amzil?"

"I don't know. Do you really think Thayer would hang a woman? Would the other officers stand by while he did that?"

Before Spink could reply, Kesey returned with a dripping bucket of cold water. Spink drank deeply and thanked him. Then Epiny emerged from the cabin. Her smile blossomed at the sight of Spink and me sitting together. As she came toward us, carrying her sleeping baby and making motions that we should keep quiet, she looked more beautiful than I had ever seen her. She was thin, and her hair was still in a shambles from the cart ride. Her dress was not stylish and it was dusty from the trip. But her face glowed with love and satisfaction, and it broke my heart that Spink's news was going to destroy that for her as well.

She had gone only a few steps before she read trouble in Spink's face. Her smile faded as she hurried up to him. "What is it? Are the children all right?"

"Kesey, I'll need to borrow that shirt, if I may," I said to him. I think he was just as glad to withdraw as I was while Spink recounted the disaster to Epiny.

By the time I emerged from the cabin wearing a shirt that wouldn't button around my neck and a pair of trousers that were too short for me, tears were running down Epiny's face. She leaned on Spink, not sobbing but silently weeping. Spink held his daughter and patted his wife's shoulder. I put my old clothes and my nondescript sword into the back of the cart. I turned to Kesey.

"I have to go back to town with them. Kesey, I'll never be able to repay you for what you've done for me today. But that won't stop me from trying."

"Oh, I didn't do anything big for you, Nevare. Just what a man does for his fellow soldier." He cocked his head at me. "You going to try to clear your name? I'd sure like that. You could come back and take your cabin and your job back; you're much better at it than I am. I actually miss living in the barracks; you believe that?"

"Oh, I believe it." I shook his hand, then clapped him on the shoulder. "I don't know what I'm going to do, Kesey. But thanks."

"Well, whatever you decide to do, let me know this time, will you? A man should know where his friends are."

"Indeed. A man should know where his friends are."

"And, Nevare. I heard what the Lieutenant said, and I'm sorry that the Dead—that that woman is in trouble. I hope you can get to the bottom of it and get it straightened out. Sorry I called her that name, earlier. I didn't know."

I nodded, unable to think of what I could say to that, and I bade him farewell. I climbed into the back of the cart. Spink had tied his horse to it and was going to drive while Epiny shared the seat with him, the basket full of baby between them. I folded my tattered "clothes" into a cushion to sit on and rode in the back. The ride back to Gettys was long and uncomfortable. The cart rattled and jounced, the dust from the horse's hooves quickly coated us, and we had to raise our voices to be heard. Even so, both of them demanded to hear the tale of all that had befallen me since that night I had left Gettys.

It was a long tale to tell, both painful and shameful at some points, but I had decided that these two, at least, deserved the full truth. Epiny, for a wonder, was silent through most of it, only breaking in when I spoke of the times when I had dream-walked to her. The night that I had tried to warn her about the raid, she had been thick with laudanum, she said. She credited Spink for pulling her back from that brink.

"There are many in the town not so fortunate. The Specks have stopped their magical onslaught against us, but many households still take the Gettys Tonic. It is a difficult thing to stop doing, but it is so sad to see little children sitting listless on the steps of their homes instead of playing in the gardens."

Spink was quiet for a long time after I spoke of what I saw that night. I spared myself nothing, from the slitting of the sentry's throat to my passive witnessing of the slaughter of the men at the barracks. When I spoke of seeing Spink and his men that night, he only nodded grimly. I feared he was having a difficult time understanding that all that I had done had not been of my own will, yet I could not blame him. I could scarcely forgive myself; why should I expect that he could do any better at it?

Still, they listened enraptured as I told of the days that followed, of Dasie's death and Olikea's sorrow, and when I told of Soldier's Boy's decision to do whatever he must to bring Likari home, both Spink and Epiny nodded as if there could not have been any other decision.

"It must have been hard to leave that little boy behind when you came back to us," Epiny said sadly.

"It was and it wasn't. I was not given a choice about leaving." And before Epiny could tangle me with a dozen questions, I launched into the final part of my tale. When I reached the point of saying farewell to her and Spink, she nodded and said, "I recall that, but not as you saying farewell. It was like a door closing. Well, more like a window. Do you remember what I told you, so long ago in Old Thares? That once the medium at the séance had opened me to that world, I felt I could never completely close myself off from it." She glanced sideways at Spink. "Now I can. I cannot tell you what a relief it is, Spink. No one whispering behind me when I'm trying to knead a loaf of bread, no one tugging at my mind when I'm rocking Solina to sleep."

Spink let go of the reins with one hand and reached to touch his wife's hand. "For the first time, I have begun to feel that I actually have her all to myself, occasionally. When she isn't dealing with Solina or the other children, of course."

"But it was frightening, because while that window was open, I felt closer to you, Nevare. Not as if I could reach you, but that I knew you were there somewhere. When it closed, I felt shut off. And I feared you were dead."

"Well, I was," I said, more lightly than I felt. I suddenly sighed, surprising myself. "I am dead to the Specks. Dead to Olikea and to Likari."

By the time I finished my telling of how I'd been devoured by a tree, kidnapped by a god, and driven away from a village as a ghost, we had reached the outskirts of Gettys Town. I think that only when I saw that very ordinary place did I realize how fantastic a journey I'd actually made. Yet for everything I'd experienced, I felt no sense of homecoming or relief. My heart sank in despair. I had no brilliant plan for rescuing Amzil. I myself was a condemned man, and the closer we came to the houses and buildings, the lower I sank in the cart's bed.

"I don't think you need to worry," Spink said quietly to me. "I only knew you because I recalled how you looked at the Academy. You've changed so much that I doubt anyone here will recognize you as Nevare from the graveyard unless you tell them that is who you are and give them a chance to study your face."

Nonetheless, I felt nervous as our cart rattled through the town and up to the gate. I was horrified at the destruction we passed. A number of the town buildings were still burned-out husks that stank in the spring air. Others still showed plain signs of scorching or damage recently repaired. I craned my head back to look up at the watchtower over the prison's corner of the fort. The scorch marks were plain, and the fire-arrow had triumphed. The uppermost part of the structure was a skeleton of blackened timbers.

My heart was thundering in my chest when Spink drew in the horse by the sentry box. The sentry saluted him smartly and Spink returned it. I looked away from him. The memory of my knife across another sentry's throat, the soft tugging as the sharp blade cut through arteries and flesh, the warm spill of blood across my fingers; I could almost smell the blood running. I felt queasy. The sentry scarcely gave me a glance. He saluted Spink and nodded courteously at Epiny. Spink stirred the reins and suddenly we were inside.

Here the damage was far worse than in the town outside the walls. Soldier's Boy had been far more thorough than Dasie. Almost every building showed some sign of damage, but they showed it in the form of new or mismatched lumber against the old. A number of damaged buildings had been torn down and the salvaged lumber used to repair those that still stood. There were empty lots, carefully raked and tidied of debris. We went past the corner where the storage barn and stables had been. Hammers were ringing and saws growling as a crew of a dozen soldiers put up the framework of the new structures. The smell of fresh-cut wood was sharp in the air. Had Amzil's fate not been weighing on my heart, it would have been a cheering sight to see so many men busily engaged in the construction.

But at the next turn, I caught sight of the building where I'd been a prisoner. Its stone foundation remained, but one end of the upper structure consisted only of scorched uprights and a few charred rafters. As we passed it, I caught a glimpse down the alley where I had escaped that night. Rubble still cluttered the ground where I'd broken out. A tree had sprouted in the mound of earth and broken stone and mortar. The building looked deserted. So Amzil was not being held there. Where was she?

I started to ask Spink when a shadow swept over all of us. I ducked like a small prey animal and then looked up in deepening dismay. A croaker bird made a lazy circle over the fort and then glided in to alight on the top rafter of the building. He landed awkwardly, teetered for an instant, and then got his balance. He settled his feathers around him and then, looking down, stretched out his neck toward me and gave three hoarse caws.

"You've taken my death from me. What more do you want of me, old god?" I asked in a small, shaking voice.

"It's only a bird, Nevare," Epiny said reassuringly, but the tremor in her voice was not a comfort to me.

"I wish I could go back to a life where a bird was just a bird, always," Spink observed quietly. The baby began to cry and Epiny took the basket onto her lap and held it close.

"Oh, worst luck," Spink said quietly.

I turned my head, baffled as to what he meant. Coming from a side street was a cavalla scout mounted on the finest horse I'd seen since I reached Gettys. It was a bay with a glossy black mane and tail and white stockings on its ramrod legs. I stared at the animal in admiration, feeling a pang for the loss of not only Sirlofty but even stolid Clove. When I glanced up at the rider, our eyes met. Scout Tiber stared at me for a moment; then his lips parted in a spare smile.

"Burvelle!" he called out in a friendly way. "It's been a while since I've seen you." As he spoke, the bird on the rafter cawed again, a mocking shadow of his words.

I lifted my hand in faint greeting. Tiber had a moustache now. Like every scout I'd ever known, he was both in and out of uniform. He wore his hat at a rakish angle and his jacket was open at the throat, showing a bright yellow scarf. A silver earring dangled from one ear. He was fit and clear of eye and I suddenly knew that being a scout did not much disagree with him. I could have been glad for him, if only he hadn't recognized me.

"The only man in town who'd recognize you on sight," Spink whispered with a groan.

"You know him?" Epiny demanded.

"Only from the Academy. I never spoke to him here," I said as quietly.

Tiber had stirred his mount to a trot and brought him alongside our rattling cart. "Good afternoon, Lieutenant Kester. Ma'am." He greeted them both respectfully. When he doffed his hat to Epiny, I saw that his hair was nearly as long as mine. My tongue clove to the top of my dry mouth.

"Lieutenant Tiber. Lovely day." Spink's response was noncommittal.

"Isn't it?" Tiber swung his glance to me. He smiled. "So, Cadet Burvelle, you've come east to see Gettys, have you? Only, surely it's not 'cadet' anymore?"

I found my tongue. "No, sir. I'm afraid not."

Epiny suddenly spoke for both of us. "My cousin unfortunately had to leave the Academy. For health reasons, after the plague outbreak. He's come to stay with us for a time, to see if we can't mend his constitution enough to allow him to enlist."

"Enlist?" Tiber shot me a puzzled glance.

"Purchase a commission, dear," Spink corrected her desperately in a strangled but fond voice. "Enlisting would mean that your cousin sought to be a common soldier. As a new noble's

soldier son, he would purchase a commission and enter as a lieutenant, as I did."

"Oh, yes, I'm so bad with words!" Epiny gave a false giggle so
unlike her that I expected the sky to crack.

"Ah, yes. I heard that the plague had done in many of the fellows at the Academy. Glad to see you survived. But you do look a
bit pale, Burvelle," Tiber observed socially. "When you feel up to
it, look me up. I'll be glad to show you a bit of the countryside.
You were earmarked to be a scout, once, weren't you?"

"It was suggested to me," I said faintly, wondering how he
knew.

"Well, you might come to like it. And I'm confident that
some of Lieutenant Kester's Bitter Springs water will put you
right. Seems to revive plague survivors in an amazing fashion."

"Oh, it's worse than just lingering plague symptoms," Epiny
suddenly declared. "On his way here to visit us, he was attacked.
Evil road robbers hit him on the head and stole everything he had
with him. Luckily one of our troopers found him and helped us
reunite with him today."

"That so, ma'am? Well, I'd heard we'd had a few bad sorts
working the road west. I'll have to keep an eye open for them.
Hope you recover quickly, Burvelle, and I hope you find Gettys
to your liking. I'll look forward to chatting with you. Pleasant day
to you all."

"Pleasant day," I replied numbly.

And Tiber stirred his horse to a faster trot and passed us.

"Why did you say all that?" I demanded of Epiny.

"Because it was perfect! It explains why you're poorly dressed.
And it makes it seem more feasible that you've just arrived from
the west. And thus you cannot possibly be the convicted Nevare
Burv whose name so unfortunately resembles your own." She
looked to me, her face alight with hope. "Nevare, the scout is the
key. Lieutenant Tiber is the door back into resuming your own
life. The letters from Yaril say that your father has forgotten his
quarrel with you. Go back to him, as you are now, and say you've
found a regiment you wish to join. He'll buy you a commission,
or Yaril will find a way to do so. You could be here, living near us,

rising through the ranks with Spink. Oh, Nevare, it would be a whole different life for us if you could be part of it!"

I was silent for a time, marveling at her. Then, "Do you think it would work?" I asked Spink.

"It will either work or trip us up completely."

I thought for a moment. "I won't give up Amzil," I said flatly.

"Of course not!" Epiny immediately replied. "Nor will we."

I was silent the brief distance to their home. When Spink drew the cart to a halt, I was almost disbelieving. The row of houses reminded me of the cottages my father had set up in his vain attempt to settle the Bejawi. I could see that when the row of houses had been built, they'd been well designed. But in the years since, under the onslaught of the Speck magic, they'd deteriorated. Recent work could not erase the years of neglect. Porches sagged, paint was peeling off every structure, chimney stones had tumbled off a few, and without exception the little yards in front of each house were patches of weed, rock, and dust. Two wooden boxes full of earth flanked the entry to Spink's home, with some sort of plant pushing its way up through the soil. It was the only promise of change. Epiny flushed a bit as I stared and she said inanely, "Amzil and I have been discussing making new curtains, when the dry-goods store gets new stock." She leaned closer to me and said, smiling, "Your sister actually sent us some lovely fabric, along with the food supplies. But we used it for dresses for the little girls."

Then the door was flung open and the three children boiled out. "Missus, missus!" Kara shouted frantically. "Mum is very late! She still isn't back from the market! We should go look for her."

"Oh, my darlings, I know, I know. She's been delayed. I've come home to take care of you until she gets here. Everything will be all right!"

Kara looked half a head taller than when I'd last seen her. Her dress astonished me. It was blue with a pattern of flowers, and she had a tidy little pinafore over it. Sem was dressed, as Epiny had warned me, in a suit made from cast-off uniforms. Dia, scarcely more than a baby when last I saw her, was dressed as primly as her older sister. Her blue pinafore with white ruffles matched Kara's.

Their faces were washed, their hair combed, and my heart broke when Sem looked up at Spink and said soulfully, "Thank the good god you've come home now, sir! I tole the girls you and the missus would come back and find out why Mum's so late."

"Epiny, Spink, may the good god bless you forever for what you've done for them," I said quietly, and it was perhaps the most fervent prayer I'd said in my life. To see the children groomed and healthy, to see Sem standing tall like a brave little man, concerned about his sisters: could I have asked anything more of them? Tears stung my eyes. I found myself wishing that I presented a better aspect to the children as I climbed from the back of the cart. They stared at me as they would at a stranger, and quickly dismissed my presence as they clustered around Epiny, clutching at her skirts and asking, "Where's Mummy? Will she be home soon?"

"I'll be sure that she comes home very soon, my dearests," Epiny blithely lied. And then I realized she was not lying at all; it was what she fully intended to do.

A tall, homely woman appeared suddenly in the doorway, wiping her hands on her apron. A bright brass whistle hung on a fine chain around her neck.

"Thank you, Rasalle!" Epiny exclaimed at the sight of her. "I'm so glad you could watch the children for me."

"Well, it's no more than I owe you, all the times you've helped me, ma'am. I'm going to hurry along home now. My missus will want me to start the dinner for her. Unless you still need some help here?" Rasalle eyed me curiously.

"Oh, I beg your pardon! So much has happened to me today that I've completely forgotten my manners. This is my cousin, Mr. Burvelle, come for a visit while he recuperates from some health problems. And just fancy, on the last leg of his journey, he was waylaid by highwaymen! His horse, his baggage, everything he owns was lost to them!"

"Oh, the good god's mercy on us all! Such a thing to befall you! So pleased to meet you, Mr. Burvelle, and I'm so glad that you still managed to arrive safely. I'm so disappointed that I must hurry along. Well, ma'am, you take care. It never seems to rain but that it pours on you! Your housemaid—" She halted her tongue, looked at the children, and said, "Delayed, and houseguests, all on the same day! Call me if you need any assistance! I'm sure my missus would be glad to let me help you."

"Oh, I shall, never fear, I shall! In fact, as you can see, Mr. Burvelle's own garments were stolen from him as well. But I think he is of a size with poor Lieutenant Gerry. If your mistress would not mind, could some clothing be loaned, perhaps?"

"Likely she would, ma'am. You know she's resolved to make the trip west, back home. She was looking through his things today, saying that there was no sense packing a dead man's clothes."

Epiny gave me a glance and said quietly, "Lieutenant Gerry was unfortunately killed in a raid this last winter."

"I'm very sorry," I said so sincerely that the maid stared at me. I stood, mute and frozen, not hearing the rest of their conversation.

The woman hurried away and Epiny swept us all into the house. Spink had gone to put up the horses, and she told the children to hurry off to the kitchen, and she would come to give them some bread and broth soon. No sooner were we alone than she exclaimed, "Oh, it couldn't be better. Rasalle is the biggest gossip in Gettys. Soon enough everyone will know that my cousin has come to visit."

I cared little enough for that. "I have to find out where they're holding Amzil. From what I've heard of Thayer, the man is unbalanced. Even if all his men oppose the idea, he'll still try to hang her."

"Hush!" Epiny told me sharply and rolled her eyes toward the kitchen. "Don't say anything like that where the children can hear. They don't know that their mother has been arrested. They're calm now, but I won't have them frightened." She took a shuddering breath and admitted, "I'm frightened enough for all of us."

CHAPTER THIRTY-TWO

DECISIONS AND CONSEQUENCES

As evening fell, I buttoned the collar of my borrowed shirt and then slipped on the jacket. Everything smelled of cedar. The jacket was blue, but it was cut identically to a uniform jacket. It felt strange to do up the shining brass buttons, as if I'd been transported back to my cadet days. I wondered briefly about the man who had worn this, and what he had thought about the last time he'd buttoned it up. Then I asked the good god to be welcoming to him, took a breath, and let it go.

I looked in Epiny's mirror with the scrolled gilt frame and tried to smile. It looked more like a sneer. Here I was, dressed in a dead man's clothes, possibly those of a man I had helped to kill, about to step into the biggest charade I'd ever played in my life. I'd be impersonating Nevare Burvelle, soldier son of Lord Burvelle of the East, come to present my respects to Captain Thayer. I realized I was holding my breath and slowly let it out. My chest still felt just as tight. I knew I must be mad, going along with Epiny's harebrained scheme. The only advantage I could see to her plan was it was the only one we had.

Epiny had tucked a sleeping Solina into her bed, and then prepared and served a much-needed meal to the rest of us. But Spink didn't join us. He'd gone out to inquire discreetly about Amzil's location and situation. Before he'd gone, he'd told Epiny that he hoped that Captain Thayer had come to his senses and realized that he did not have any authority over either of the two women. Several of his officers had raised that objection earlier, but Thayer had ignored it, insisting that if their transgressions involved his soldiers in any way, then he had the authority to punish them. He'd also insisted that Amzil's "confession" made any trial unnecessary and a waste of time. The sooner she was hanged, the better, and he'd settled on dawn the next day as an appropriate time for an execution. He'd been merciful to the other woman. She would spend two days in the public stocks, and then be banished from the town.

"What?" I'd asked Spink. "He'll humiliate her and then just turn her out of the town, with no horse, no supplies, nothing, to walk alone back to Dead Town? That could be a death sentence for her."

"I tried protesting. He wouldn't hear me. When I spoke out anyway, saying that my housemaid had obviously acted in defense of her life and the lives of her children, he threatened to have me disciplined for speaking out of turn. I don't think it's a question of him doing what he thinks is just, Nevare. I think he just wants to be rid of Amzil, and he doesn't want to have to think too much about what he is doing or why."

From what Spink said, I doubted that any verbal argument would sway Thayer in his determination to have Amzil hanged. Nonetheless, I stubbornly clung to the tiny spark of hope that he'd offered me. Someone might say something to him to wake him from his blind vengeance. No, not vengeance, I decided. Erasure. He would expunge from his life the woman that could accuse him. He'd have himself flogged and kill the final witness. Then I recalled how Spink had defied him that night, and I felt cold trickle down my spine. Would Spink be his next target?

Epiny, the children, and I consumed a simple meal of broth and bread spread with the drippings from last night's rabbit dinner that was also the source of today's broth. Despite my earlier hunger, it was hard for me to swallow as I looked at the three small faces around the table and dreaded what the future might hold for them. The children were reserved with me, but Kara peppered Epiny with questions about her mother, to which Epiny could reply only that she was certain that Mummy would be home as soon as she could, and in the meantime, Kara should eat her meal with her very best manners. In that regard, I was surprised to see how far they had progressed from a time when the best they knew was to squat around a hearth and eat with their hands. Even little Dia sat propped on a chair and managed her spoon quite well.

After the meal, Dia had been put down for a nap, while Epiny set both Kara and Sem to a lesson from one of her old primers. The two children diligently bent their heads over the book while Epiny and I retreated to the other end of the room to talk softly.

"They certainly absorb a lot of your time, don't they?" I observed, expecting her to say that this day had been unusual.

"Small children are a full-time task for any woman. They are missing their mother badly just now, and being the best little lambs they know how to be because of it. When Amzil is here, Kara is quite obstreperous, full of questions. And Sem is of an age where he is quite weary of the house, and longs to be out in the street with the other boys at all hours of the day. Many of the other boys just seem to run wild here. I have spoken twice to the commander, telling him that a regimental school for the youngsters would not be amiss at all, but he balks at the idea of mixing officers' children with those of enlisted men, let alone the townsfolk. I've insisted to him that it's the only efficient way to do it, but he will not even hear me out. The man is a cretin."

I thought of asking her if she realized that her behavior to his superiors would definitely affect Spink's chance for advancement, but bit my tongue. Spink had said he was content with his willful wife; I would not interfere. I suspected it would have been a waste of my breath anyway. Instead, I said, "I admire what you've done with them. But I also envy you and Spink. I'm a stranger to them, but they've given their hearts to you."

"All of that will change after you and Amzil are married," she decided blithely. "I think you'll make a very good father to them. Sem still speaks of you, from time to time, as 'the man who used to hunt meat for us.' That's not a bad image for a son to have of his father."

"You assume so much," I said shakily.

"Do I?" she asked, and smiled at me fondly. "I've mastermined one prison escape before, and it went almost according to plan. There is only one bit I haven't decided yet. Should she flee or hide?"

"What?" I was completely taken aback.

"Should Amzil flee or hide? If it's flee, then we need to steal a horse. I've been thinking that the animal that scout was riding today looked healthy and fleet."

"Epiny, you can't be considering—"

"Oh, we both know nothing else will work. It's fine for Spink to speak of the Captain coming to his senses, but I don't think that man has any senses to come to. Once Spink returns, we shall know where she is held, and we can lay our plans."

I was saved from having to reply to that by Sem coming with the primer, saying that he was ready to have his lesson heard. He battled his way manfully through eight letters, and then Kara read to us about the boy who could see the bee in the tree. I suppose I was too fulsome in my applause, for she rebuked me with a "Truly, sir, it's not that difficult. I could teach you to read, if you'd like."

That jolted a laugh from me, despite my heavy heart. Then Epiny rebuked both of us, Kara for being cheeky and me for laughing at bad manners. I straightened my face and managed to keep a grave expression as I asked little Kara if the missus had taught her to play Towsers yet, whereupon Epiny astonished both children by playfully slapping my hand and forbidding me to say another word about that game.

Yet all the while I was enjoying the children and rejoicing in the home they had found here, my heart was aching and my throat clenched over the fate of their mother. When the door closed behind

Spink as he entered, we both jumped, and Epiny's voice was too bright as she asked him if he had found what had been misplaced.

"Yes, I did," he replied stiffly. "But it's quite wedged where it has been dropped. I'm afraid it will take more than saying please to get it freed."

Kara looked up hopefully. "Sir, I've got little hands. Often my mother says that I can get things that no one else can reach, like the time that the button fell through that crack in the wainscoting. Whatever it is, I'd be glad to reach it for you, if I could."

"I know you would, darling," he replied. "But I'm afraid it will have to wait for a time. Have you saved me anything to eat?"

"Of course we have. Give me a minute, and I'll have it on the table for you," she replied in a housewifely little voice, and trotted off to the kitchen, with Sem at her heels loudly insisting that he could help.

Epiny pounced on Spink. "Where is she?"

"The same block of cells where they held Nevare."

"But that building is half burned!"

"Only the upper part. The lower cells remained intact. So they've put her in one of the punishment cells down there."

"Punishment cell?"

"A very small room, with no windows, not even in the door. And quite stoutly built, I'm afraid."

"And the guard on it?" I asked.

Spink looked ill. "Two men from that night in the street. Two men with every interest in seeing her hang so she can never speak the truth against them again. I'm sure Captain Thayer chose them deliberately."

"Two men I'd have no compunction about killing," I said, and was surprised at how calm and certain I was.

Spink went pale. "What are you talking about?" he asked, aghast.

Epiny answered. "We've been planning her escape. The only real question we have left is, should she flee or should she hide? I've been thinking that the best solution is to make it appear that she has fled, but when they give chase, they'll only find a riderless horse. So they'll think she jumped off the horse and fled into the forest. But actually we'll hide her somewhere here in Gettys, and spirit her out after they've given up looking for her. We think that that scout's horse looked good and fast. Do you know where he stables the beast?"

"Not 'we,'" I said firmly. "Epiny has been making these extravagant plans. I have no ambition of stealing Tiber's horse." I sighed. "But I'll be the first to admit that I haven't come up with anything better."

Spink looked only mildly relieved. "Fleeing or hiding, such plans are of no use until we find a way to get her out of there. I stopped on the way home and spoke quietly to two other officers. Neither of them were enthusiastic about trying a civilian, let alone executing one, and both are horrified at the thought of hanging a woman. As for the Captain having himself flogged, well, it's insane."

"Then they'll stand by us if we go to Captain Thayer tonight and—"

"They won't stand by us. They won't confront Thayer. A man capable of hanging a woman and flogging himself is certainly capable of punishing any underling who questions his authority. No. But they'd certainly be greatly relieved if something happened so that the woman didn't hang."

Epiny smiled. "So, for example, if she vanished from her cell, no one would search for her very diligently."

"Epiny." Spink looked at her levelly. "It's very complicated. Everyone knows how Amzil feels about her children. They know she wouldn't leave town without them."

"She might. For a short time, because she knows they are safe with us."

"Epiny, we'd still have to get her out of the cell."

"We have some explosives left from the last time!" Epiny exclaimed brightly.

"No. Blowing up the cell wall with black powder would most likely kill the occupant," Spink pointed out. "Those cells are tightly built with thick stone walls, not wood. Any explosion we set off that was powerful enough to break the wall would definitely harm Amzil. Nevare was very fortunate that you and Amzil blew up the wrong prison wall the last time. No. No explosions."

"Well, that's no good, then." She thought for a moment. "What is the door made of? If we get rid of the guards, can we force it?"

I spoke up. "I doubt it. My door was of very thick wood, reinforced with metal strapping and a heavy lock." I hesitated, then added, "It didn't look as if the place where I broke out of my cell had been repaired very well. I might be able to break a hole in the wall with a pry bar and a sledge. But it wouldn't be a quiet operation. And I might find myself back in my old cell, with the door still locked, and Amzil locked in another cell."

Blithely ignoring this, Epiny was relentless. "Who would have the keys?"

"Captain Thayer, most likely."

"Then we have to get them somehow. Spink, we'll have to invent a reason for you to visit him tonight and—"

"Not a chance of that." Spink sighed. "I went there before I came home, determined to make the man see some sort of reason. I couldn't get past the sergeant on the desk. The man tried to be polite, but finally admitted that he'd been given a direct order not to admit me on any grounds."

"Then I'll go," Epiny said decisively.

"That would be useless, and you know it," Spink told her firmly. "His sergeant has had orders to refuse you admission for weeks."

"I could raise enough of a fuss in that outer office that he'd have to come out."

"No, my dear. I won't risk you. The good god knows what Thayer would decide was a just punishment for a shrew in his office. Possibly the stocks."

Kara came to the door of the parlor. "Sir, your meal is on the table. I wouldn't interrupt, but we wouldn't want it to get cold, would we?"

"No, we wouldn't," Spink replied so meekly to her motherly tone that Epiny had to smile. Spink rose. "Come with me, both of you, and have a cup of tea. Our discussion might have to wait for a time, but—"

"I'll go," I said suddenly. They both looked at me, confused.

"What could be more natural? I've come all this way to see if I'd like a career with this regiment. If we can make me present-able, it would only be natural that I'd immediately call on the commanding officer. In fact, it's only courteous. And unless he has completely lost touch with reality, he can't politely turn me away."

"And?" Spink asked.

"And once I'm inside, with the door shut, I'll do whatever I must to get the keys. And after that, whatever I must to have her out of there."

Spink looked aghast. Epiny replied only, "There, you see? Flee or hide. I told you that was what had to be decided imme-diately."

"I am not stealing a horse," Spink announced and then, as Epiny opened her mouth to speak, he said more loudly, "And neither are you. Or Nevare. Come, now. Let's have a cup of tea together. And let us remember that the children are listening."

And indeed, as we entered the dining room where Kara had laboriously set out Spink's food, Kara observed severely, "Stealing is wrong."

All the adults exchanged glances, wondering how much else she had overheard, but as she did not seem overly distressed, we let the topic go. Epiny went to the kitchen with Kara, promising to return soon with a pot of hot tea and cups for the rest of us.

As soon as she left the room, I leaned across the table to Spink and asked him, "Do we have a chance, do you think?"

He looked tired. "Impossible to say. How would you get the key? By stealth or deceit? Violence? Even if you get them, how do we overcome her guards? Do they go down quietly or flee shouting for help? Are we willing to kill them to have her free? How quickly can we get Amzil out of there? And, as Epiny keeps coming back to, does she flee or do we hide her? If she is miss-ing, they are certain to search here first. And if the children are still here, well, then I think they will know she has not gone far. Irregardless of her other reputations, she is known in town as a fierce mother."

My mind had leapt ahead. "If the children are gone, they will accuse you of helping her escape."

"Or of not preventing her from doing so. To Captain Thayer, it will be one and the same thing."

"So. You are saying that perhaps we can do it, if you are willing to sacrifice your career. For if she hides, they'll know all they have to do is wait. And if she flees, with or without the children, you'll be implicated."

He nodded.

"Do you think Epiny understands what she is asking of you?"

He gave me a long, slow look. "And what are you asking of me if I don't act, Nevare? To live as a coward? To witness an innocent woman shamefully executed, and then raise her children, looking into their faces every day? Sooner or later, they will know what became of their mother. Sooner, if I know Kara. I suspect she already knows more than she is letting on to us or the other children. Eventually, they'd all know I stood by and did nothing while their mother was executed for defending them." He glanced aside and gave a short, contemptuous sigh for my quibbling. "What's a lost career compared to that?"

I spoke after a long silence. "Spink, I'm so sorry."

"You didn't do it, Nevare."

"I wouldn't be so sure of that," I muttered, just as Epiny reentered with the teapot and cups. She poured for us and sat down, but then had to leap up when the baby awoke and cried. A moment later, Dia entered, looking wide-awake but tousle-headed after her nap. Spink put her up at the table and gave her a cup of weak tea with sugar in it. Kara and Sem came to join us. When Epiny returned and I looked around at the table crowded with children, the full hopelessness of the situation descended on me. The afternoon was already waning. Could I spirit three children out of the town, hide them in a safe place, and return to break Amzil out of jail and escape with her and the children before dawn? And afterward, could we remain free?

I considered taking them to Kesey and begging him to watch over them. I shook my head. No. I couldn't involve him, and if we had to flee from there, there was no place to go. I looked across the table at Spink. His grave face echoed my own thoughts. It was impossible. Yet it was what must be done. To succeed, I'd have to get Amzil out of her cell and escape from the town with her and all three of her children. And it would have to be done in such a way that Epiny and Spink did not seem to be involved. I took a breath and spoke through the prattle of the children at the table. "I don't think I'll be able to stay long. Tonight, after I visit two old friends, I'll probably be leaving." I looked at Epiny, and when I had her attention, I let my eyes wander over the children. Then I looked back at her. "I'd like to get the earliest possible start. Would you pack the essentials for me?"

She looked at the three children that were not her own, and yet were. Her eyes suddenly brightened with tears. "Yes," she said quietly. "I suppose the sooner that is done, the better."

The afternoon passed in a strange display of false normalcy. Spink had to return to his duties and feign disinterest in the fate of his housemaid, and even annoyance at the thought of being left with the care of her children. Epiny, on pretense of gathering mending and washing for "spring cleaning," was going through the children's clothing and bedding. I went out to look once more at the rickety cart and the ancient horse. I did what little I could to tighten the wheels and gave the old beast a feed of oats. As I did so, I tried frantically to make some real plans, but knew there were too many variables.

The day both dragged and sped by me. The children's questions about their mother multiplied and increased in frequency. Epiny's promises of "soon she'll be back" began to wear thin for them. Dia became fretful, but Sem was angry and Kara downright suspicious. My efforts to make firm plans with Epiny were frustrating, for every time I sought a quiet moment with her, it seemed a little head was popping in, demanding attention or asking yet another question.

Epiny put Kara to kneading bread dough and entrusted Sem with a knife to cut up potatoes for the evening repast. While they were thus busy, we hastily loaded the wagon with the children's things, some clothing for Amzil, and a supply of food. Epiny kept adding things. A cooking pot and a kettle. Cups and plates. When she started to take their few toys and books from the shelves, I stopped her. "We're going to have to travel light."

"For a child, these are essentials," she said, but sighed and put some of the items back. We carried them out to the cart and loaded them. Over all, I tossed a blanket, and could only pray that no one would give it a second glance.

Epiny left me with the children while she hurried off to "visit" one of her whistle brigade who lived close to the edge of Gettys. In a town like Gettys, she knew the news of Amzil's hanging would have flown far and wide. To Agna, she would confide that she wished Amzil's children to be as far from the gallows as possible when their mother met her fate tomorrow. Epiny would ask if she would take them in for the night.

While she was off doing that, I was left in charge of the children, including Solina. The baby was supposed to take another nap while Epiny was gone. Instead, she woke the moment the door closed and began to cry lustily. I was pathetically grateful when a gingerly check of her napkin revealed that it was still clean and dry. I picked the babe up, put her on my shoulder and walked about the room as I had seen Epiny do. The three children had gathered to witness my incompetence. Solina's wails only grew louder.

"You're supposed to bounce her a little while you walk," Sem offered helpfully.

"No!" Kara said disdainfully. "That's what women do. He's supposed to sit in the rocker and rocker her and sing her a song."

As neither the walking nor the bouncing had helped, this seemed a good idea. Once I was seated with Solina, they all gathered round me so closely that I feared I would rock on small toes. "Rock her!" Sem commanded me impatiently.

"And sing her a nursery song," Kara added imperiously. Obviously they had gauged Epiny's attitude toward me and based their own upon it. And so I laboriously rocked and sang the nursery songs that I knew. Dia made so bold as to climb up on my lap and join the baby. When I had worked through my nursery songs, and Solina had quieted but not fallen asleep, Kara asked me thoughtfully, "Do you know any counting songs?"

"Oh, one or two," I admitted, and her theory proved correct, for before we had counted backward from the ten little lambs for the second time, the baby was sleeping. It was tricky to get Dia off my lap and then stand without waking Solina, and trickier still to put her back in her little bed without waking her. I shooed the other children out of the room. Sem and Dia had readily scampered off down the hall, but Kara waited for me. As I shut the door of the room, she reached up in the dimness and took my hand. She looked up at me, her small face pale in the darkened corridor.

"You're him, aren't you? The man that gave us food that winter."

"Kara, I—"

"I know it's you, so don't lie. You sang the same songs before. Don't you remember? And I heard the Lieutenant call you Nevare. And Mum said you would come back someday. Maybe." She didn't give me a chance to confirm or deny her words. She took a sharp breath. "And my mother's in trouble, isn't she? That's why she hasn't come home."

"She's in a little bit of trouble. But we think that it will be sorted out soon and—"

"Because there's a plan." She interrupted me. "If my mother is ever in trouble, there's a plan. She made it and she told it to me." Her head came up and she added gravely, "I'm in charge of it. I have to remember it."

She kept my hand in a small firm grip and led me to the little room that they all shared. She knelt beside the bedstead to pull up the loosened floorboard. The "plan" proved to be a small sack of coins hidden there. In with the coins was a simple silver ring with a rose engraved on it. "I'm to give this bag to the missus and ask her to keep taking care of us. She's to have it all, except the ring. She has to keep that safe in case Sem ever wants to grow up and marry a girl, so he'll have a ring to give her. It was our grandma's."

"That's a good plan," I told her. "But I hope we won't need it. I'm going to try to get your mother out of trouble. Then we'll come for you. If the missus can arrange it, you and Dia and Sem will be in a house at the edge of town. Your mum and I will come there, load you in the cart, and go. But you can't tell Sem or Dia about the plan yet. You have to keep it secret and remember it, and help them to be good until I come for you tonight. Can you do that?"

"Of course. But where is our mother? And where have you been and why were you gone so long?"

"Those are all questions that I'm going to have to answer later, Kara. For now, you'll have to trust me."

At that, she looked at me doubtfully, but finally nodded gravely.

When Epiny returned, she was not pleased to discover how much Kara knew. "That's a big burden to put on very small shoulders," she scolded me.

"You're the one who keeps telling me not to lie to people," I replied, and she sighed in exasperation.

There was no time for us to have doubts about it. Epiny loaded the children into the cart and took them off to her friend's house. By the time she returned, on foot, Solina had awakened. Epiny took the baby from me and bowed her head over her child. "It struck me as I was leaving them there that I might never see them again. I wanted to say good-bye, but could not, for fear of alarming them or making Agna wonder what was going on. It was so hard to leave them there. Kara was so calm about all of it, but Sem demanded to know why they had to stay there for the night. Dia was busy looking at Agna's two goats. I don't think she even noticed I'd gone."

I took my cousin in my arms and held her and her child close for a moment. "It won't be the last time you'll see them, I promise. I'll get Amzil out of her cell, and she and the children and I will get cleanly away. And when we can, I'll send word to you. And someday you'll see all of us again."

There was a knock at the door and I let her go. It was the neighbor's housemaid, Rasalle, with Lieutenant Gerry's carefully bundled clothing. Our time to hesitate was over. All was as ready as we could make it. I retreated to Spink's room to dress for my charade.

CHAPTER THIRTY-THREE

FACE-TO-FACE

I can't just stay here while he goes," Epiny protested to Spink. Her husband had just come in the door, and she had practically run to him to try to sway him from my cruel order.

"What are you talking about?"

I stepped around the corner into the hall, tugging at my collar. Had clothing always been this uncomfortable? Spink's second pair of boots were, despite his small size, a bit too large on me. The old workaday sword belt that held my mediocre weapon looked out of place with my fine new clothes, but I refused to set out completely unarmed. I'd have given a great deal to have Sergeant Duril's little "pepper pot" gun. Epiny had Spink's back to the door and was looking at him with rebuke. I rescued him.

"Epiny, it's not up to Spink. It's my decision. You're not going." To Spink I said, "I've told her that she must stay here while I call on the Captain. One way or another, I'll have that key. One way or another, I'll have Amzil tonight. The children and the cart are already waiting for us on the edge of town. If I must do violence, I don't want either of you involved." I rounded on Epiny and spoke as severely as I could to her. "If you go, you'll only rouse suspicion. I know it's hard. But what you must do right now is stay here and wait."

She turned to Spink. "Couldn't we go to the prison and be there, in case he needs our help?"

"And take Solina and put her in danger? Or risk alerting the guards that we are up to something? No, dear. Hard as it is, you will both have to stay here and keep the candles lit and preserve the illusion that you are enjoying a quiet supper together."

"I can't do it!" Epiny wailed, even as Spink looked at me aghast and said, "Surely you don't mean for me to stay here like a tethered dog while you face all the danger?"

"I do mean it. And, Epiny, you will. For Solina's sake. And, quite bluntly, for the sake of Spink's career. It cannot look like he had anything to do with this. It's bad enough that it will be known that your cousin was involved. But I think you can make me out to be extremely eccentric or the black sheep of the family. Or simply say you have no idea why I did it."

"But what if you need help?" Spink asked me.

"Look. I've thought it through carefully. If I fail, if I cannot free Amzil, and we are, well, captured. Or killed. Or captured and then killed. Well, you must be here and intact. So that the children have something familiar to come back to. All you have to do is talk to Kara and you will know that was Amzil's plan; evidently she always feared this would catch up with her. And now it has."

My voice faltered on those final words. "But, Nevare, see here—" Spink began.

I lifted a hand. "No. Stop. It is time for you to stop being a part of my disaster. It's time you had a little peace, a bit of content-ment, some time to enjoy your child without the hardships I've brought on you. I did all this, don't you see? I wrote it out in my journal, you read it, and you know what I mean. My misfortune opened Epiny up to the magic. It nearly dragged both of you to your deaths last time we battled it. I bent the magic to my own ends when I made the ground give up food for Amzil. And now it will have its revenge on me. It is as implacable as Orandula. And I can't let you be caught up into this scales-balancing. Stay clear.

Stay safe so that I can do what I must with a clear mind, not worrying about Solina's future as an orphan."

Epiny gasped at my last words and clutched her babe closer. I looked at Spink. "I saw you command, that night when I rode against you. I saw you made some of your line hold fire, and not step forward until the first volley had flown. Very well. Tonight you hold your fire and wait. I am the first volley. If we all go out into the battle together, when we fall, there will be no one left to catch the children's lives for them. Stand at my back, Spink, so I can go out without fear."

His mouth worked and he suddenly looked much younger. He got very pink around the eyes, and then he put his arm around his wife's shoulders and held her. "Good luck, Nevare. And good-bye."

"Nevare!" Epiny cried, but I knew I could not stay any longer. I hunched my shoulders and stepped out into the twilight. As I strode away from their humble little house, I clapped my borrowed hat on my head and breathed a fervent prayer to the good god to look after them. Then I hardened my heart and refused to think on them any more that night.

I strode down quiet streets lit only by the lamplight that seeped out from houses. Far too many of them were dark and abandoned. Even when I reached the main street of the fort and turned, an eerie quiet prevailed. There were no longer that many soldiers to be out and about in the evening, and Captain Thayer's strict rules had reduced even that number. He disapproved of drunkenness, gambling, and even rowdy songs and lively dances. With the town outside the fort reduced in population, there were few places for the soldiers to go, and little to do once they got there. No wonder Kesey's graveyard card parties had become so popular.

The cooling night air was settling the dew. The moisture woke the odors of burned timber and abandoned buildings. As I drew closer to the jail where I had been held, I debated with myself, and then decided that a bit of reconnoitering might not be a bad idea. I walked past it and then approached it again from the alley. I walked as quietly as I could through the coarse grass and the uneven debris there.

The uppermost floor had been burned away to timbers and rafters. The ground floor was mostly intact, but no lights showed through the broken panes of the windows. That left the foundation level, the cells built mostly belowground. The fire would not have bothered them. I halted and stood still, listening, but no sound came to me. The walls, I recalled, were thick blocks of stone mortared together. If Amzil wept, ranted, or screamed, I could not hear her. My heart stood still at that thought, and squeezed at the idea of her in a tiny, lightless room, waiting to die in the morning. I drew in a silent shuddering breath.

I nearly tripped over a broken piece of stone, and in the darkness, I walked right into a tree branch. I caught myself against the building before I fell and froze there, hoping I had not made too much noise. My eyes were adjusting to the dark and I suddenly knew where I was. The rubble that had tripped me had come from the escape hole that Lisana's roots had torn in the side of my cell. Daring to hope, I knelt in the darkness, but the wall had been roughly but effectively mended with stone and mortar. I'd find no easy entry there. On the ground, I could still feel the lumpy cascade of root that had torn the walls apart.

Then, with a strange shiver, I touched the trunk of the tree that had sprung up from it. In the darkness, I stood up, feeling the bark, then pinching a glossy leaf. The aroma from it was unmistakable. A kaembra tree was growing from the roots Lisana had sent to free me. Strange thoughts rushed through me. I felt that somehow I closed a circle. Touching this tree, I touched Lisana, I touched Soldier's Boy, and beyond them, the ancestor trees in the distant vale. Even, I thought to myself, Buel Hitch. But more than that, I suddenly thought. Touching this tree, I touched both forest and Forest. I touched a life left behind, and just for a moment, I yearned for it.

Then, "Good-bye," I told them all. "Chances are, I won't free Amzil. Chances are, I'm condemning myself to death tonight. But it's nice to think that you'll go on together, even if I don't. So I forgive you for taking what you could get of each other, even if it left me on the outside. I even forgive you, Soldier's Boy. Farewell."

I heard something then, a soft shifting in the darkness. I froze. I waited. I breathed quietly, counting my indrawn breaths.

Nothing. There was no more sound, and I judged that I'd heard a cat, or more likely a rat creeping down the alley. Silent as a shadow myself, I completed my circuit of the building. Very gently, I tried the door at the end. Locked. But I recalled there was another one. I went around the side to it and down a short flight of stone steps. Well did I recall trying to negotiate those steps with painfully tight shackles around my ankles. I went down them and tried the door handle. It, too, was locked. Captain Thayer's sentries would be inside, guarding her cell.

Well, then, it was time to get the keys.

I walked quiet as a ghost as I left the vicinity of the jail, and then, as I neared the headquarters building, I lifted my head and put a bit of the soldier into my stride. I knew from Spink that Captain Thayer had left the house he had shared with Carsina and taken over the commander's quarters. Those rooms I knew from my days of reporting directly to Colonel Haren.

I was surprised to find a lamp burning in the office, and when I entered, a grizzled sergeant sitting at the desk. He looked both bored and alert, as only old soldiers know how to do, and did not startle in the slightest when I came in. His gaze took in my civilian clothes but he gave me the benefit of the doubt. "Sir?" he addressed me.

"Good evening, Sergeant. I've come to call on Captain Thayer. I'd present you with my card, but I'm afraid that bandits robbed me of everything I owned on my way here." I let enough displeasure creep into my voice to suggest that perhaps I blamed him or Captain Thayer for that. In truth, one of the duties of the regiment was to keep the King's Highway free of brigands, so if it had happened, I would have been justified in my displeasure.

The Sergeant stiffened slightly. "I'm sorry to hear that, sir. And I'm sure Captain Thayer will want to hear of your experience. However, it's a bit late for this sort of call. Perhaps you—"

"Had I not been set upon, beaten, and robbed, I assure you I would have arrived much earlier and would have had the leisure to observe all the courtesies of such a call. As it is, I'd like to see the Captain this evening. Tonight, and now would be preferable."

It was too easy to slip back into that arrogance of the noble-man born, and even easier to take it the two steps into insufferable spoiled prig. I gave my head a slight toss and preened my hair back from my face as I had sometimes seen Trist do in our cadet days. I saw a cold flicker of disdain in the back of the Sergeant's eyes. He knew now that I would not leave until the Captain himself had sent me away, and he was resigned to it. He came to his feet and politely asked, "What name shall I give the Captain when he asks who is calling?"

"Rosse Burvelle." I had not known I was going to steal my dead brother's name until that very moment. To this day, I cannot say why I did it. It stuck to my tongue and I would have called it back if I could. Several people had already heard me called Nevare. And yet there it was, done in that moment, and the Sergeant had already turned, tapped at the door, and then entered to the gruff command from within.

I stood for a few moments, sweating in a dead man's good coat, and then the Sergeant returned. His manner had changed. He bowed to me and wide-eyed told me please to enter right away. I thanked him and did, closing the door firmly behind me.

When those chambers had been Colonel Haren's, they had been a retreat from the primitive conditions at Gettys. They had been carpeted, tapestried, furnished from floor to ceiling, and al-ways there had been a great fire burning on the hearth that made the room seem an elegant furnace. I wondered what had become of all Colonel Haren's furnishings. Perhaps they had been shipped back west after he died, or merely packed away into some forgot-ten storage. In any case, they were gone. The room looked barren; deliberately barren.

A tiny fire burned on the hearth. There was a heavy wooden desk and a straight-backed chair, very similar to the Sergeant's. For visitors, there was a simple wooden chair facing the desk. At the other end of the room, a narrow bunk was neatly made up next to a very plain dresser. His sword belt and saber were hung neatly on a hook next to his overcoat. A stand held a tin washbasin and ewer. The doors of his wardrobe were closed. It could have been a cadet's room at the Academy. It smelled of wood polish and the candles that burned there; there was no friendly scent of tobacco, nor any sign of a bottle of sherry or brandy to welcome a guest. Discipline. Penance.

The man seated at the desk was as austere as the room. Despite the evening hour, Captain Thayer still wore his uniform, with his collar buttoned tight. His hands rested side by side on the desktop before him as if he were there to recite a lesson. Despite his sun-weathered skin, he looked pale. He licked his lips as I came in. I'd taken my hat off and now I stepped toward him, my hand held out. "Thank you for receiving me, Captain Thayer. I'm—"

Before I could introduce myself, he looked at me and said, "I know who you are. And I know why you've come, Mr. Burvelle."

My heart sank. He knew?

"You've come to inquire into the death of your brother, Nevare Burvelle. Your sister knew he was here, enlisted under a false name. I knew that eventually there would be this reckoning. And I am ready for it."

Despite his brave and honest words, his voice shook slightly. He swallowed, and when he spoke again, his voice was a bit higher. "If you wish to demand satisfaction of me, you have that right." His hands moved very slightly on the desktop, a faint scrabbling motion. "If you wish to bring formal charges against me, you have that right also. I can only tell you that when I took action that night, I believed I was acting in the name of justice. I'll admit to you, sir, that I killed your soldier-brother. But it was not without provocation. I was deceived, sir. Deceived by your brother's false name and deceived by the harlot I had taken for my wife."

He suddenly lunged for his desk drawer, jerking it open and reaching inside. I took two steps back, certain that he would pull out a pistol and kill me where I stood. Instead, his shaking hands pulled out a packet of papers bound with a piece of string. He pulled the knot, the string came undone, and they spilled across the desk. Only then did I know them. Why she had kept them, I'll never know, but I would wager that every one of them was there. All the letters I'd written to Carsina from the Academy. On the top of the pile, smudged as if it had been opened and read many times, was an envelope addressed to Carsina in my sister's hand. He coughed as if trying to clear his throat of a sob. He took another document from the drawer. I recognized the enlistment papers I'd signed when I joined the regiment. And with it, an envelope addressed in my father's hand.

"I didn't know he was a noble's soldier son." Thayer's voice was choked. "I didn't know that he and Carsina had previously been . . . together. I had no idea until I took over as commander. Haren's records were a mess. And the command had changed so often since he died, no one had put things in order. So it was up to me. First, I found the letter from your father, warning Colonel Haren that your brother might try to enlist. It was in the Colonel's private papers. I thought it a sad little document and wondered why he'd kept it. But on the back of the envelope, he'd made a note."

His hands spidered over to pick up the envelope and turn it over. My blood moved cold through my veins. I tried to take slow breaths, to stand as Rosse would have stood as this tawdry little story unfolded. Thayer swallowed loudly. The envelope fell from his nerveless fingers. He took a shuddering breath. "I could scarcely believe what I read, sir. But when I looked up the enlistment papers for Nevare Burv, there was no denying it any longer." He looked up at me and strain tightened every muscle in his face. In a strangled voice he said, "It was bad enough to know that your brother had been a noble son, a soldier son gone bad. I felt terrible that we, that he had died as he did. But worse was to come, sir. Far worse for me."

His voice faded. He looked at his desk. His hands crept across the scattered papers there. "I felt terrible, sir, but it was sorrow for what your family had endured. I tried to write to your father and could not. Simply could not. I thought perhaps it was better that he never know the fate his errant son had met. But then, in early spring, a courier came. And I could scarcely believe my eyes. For there was a letter for my Carsina, my beloved dead wife. And it came from the sister of the man who had tormented her with his attentions and then desecrated her body. I could not believe it. How could she even have known Carsina?

"Curiosity overcame me. I opened it. And what I read tore the heart out of me: it made clear the connection between the man I'd killed and the woman I'd loved. It made a lie of the love I'd had for Carsina. I'd been a fool. She'd probably been laughing at me all the time when I offered her my name. I went through her things then, and found other letters. I found an earlier letter from your sister, one that had concealed a letter for that man, a letter she trusted that my Carsina would hand to him. I knew then she had been seeing him. And beneath her night things, tied with a ribbon, as if they were a treasure, I found all these. Letter after letter from Nevare. Highly improper correspondence.

"She had lied to me. The heartless bitch. She led me to believe she was untouched and pure. But here we have the evidence of her perfidy. She was a lying, cheating slut. And because of her, I took a man's life!"

Outrage filled me. "She was nothing of the kind!" I barked. I had never imagined that I would be defending Carsina's reputation, let alone to her husband. But as I recalled her, I could not keep quiet. "She was a frightened girl, terrified that if you knew she'd been engaged to a man you despised, you'd break your word to her. She was not wise or temperate, but she was certainly not a slut. I knew her since she was a little girl, and I can vouch for that. She'd thought she'd found true love with you." I'd advanced to the edge of his desk. Now I leaned over it, hands braced on it as I forced the truth on him. Epiny was right. Some people definitely deserved to hear the truth. "Her dying words were spoken of you, with love. She asked me to go and fetch you, because you'd promised you wouldn't leave her side. Yes, I gave her my bed to lie down on. But I never touched her that night, sir. And when we were engaged, I might have stolen a kiss or two, but certainly no more than that!"

He stared at me in consternation. "But . . . your brother . . ." He leaned back in his chair, tipping his head up to lock eyes with me. I stared back, made both fearless and foolish by my anger. "No," he said, and his voice quavered. "It's you. It was you. You're Nevare Burvelle. But . . . you were . . . you were—I killed you." He rose from his desk, nearly knocking his chair over as he scrambled away from me. He held his hands, fingers crooked, out in front of him. They were shaking. "I choked you with these hands. My fingers sank into your fat throat, and you screamed for mercy, even as I imagined that Carsina had screamed. But I gave you no mercy, for you'd had no mercy on her—"

"I never hurt Carsina. And you didn't kill me," I said flatly. "That's a false memory."

"I killed you." He spoke with absolute certainty. "You pissed yourself and when I let your body fall to the street, my men cheered. I'd done what any honorable man would do. I'd avenged my wife's violation." His voice faded. He looked at his desk. His face was pale and sweat stood out on his forehead. "But then I found the letters. She'd made a fool of me. All those sweet words, all her shyness and hesitation—all to mock me." His voice dropped on those words, chopping them out. "Did you laugh at me together, when she crept off to see you? Did you enjoy your charades in the street, to make everyone think you did not know each other? Did you laugh at me when you were touching that body, kissing those lips? That harlot's lips!"

"Don't say those things about her," I warned him in a quiet, deadly voice. I defended the thoughtless, careless little girl I'd known. "She was no harlot, sir. She was alone. Childish," I said. "Frightened. Too filled with heart and not enough head. Dreaming of romance with a handsome cavalla officer. A girl forced by circumstance into a woman's role."

I doubt that he heard a word I'd said. The man was unhinged. "I killed you," he repeated, staring at me. "I remember that night so clearly. I stood like a man and took a man's vengeance. But now it's all changed to shame and dishonor. Because she lied to me. She lied to me." His eyes lit with a sudden, cruel hope. "But you did those other things, didn't you? You killed that whore, Fala. You poisoned those men. You still deserved to die!"

"No," I said quietly. I was edging slowly around the desk, moving toward him. I'd take him down quickly. I didn't want him to shout for the Sergeant. "I didn't do those things. And I didn't deserve to die."

He looked at me. His breath was coming in little shaking gasps. "How can you be here?" he asked, and his voice broke on the words, going high as a boy's. "I killed you. How can you be here, so changed from the monster you were?"

"Magic," I said flatly. I was suddenly finished arguing with him. Logic has no impact on a crazy man. I felt only disgust for a man who would blame his bad choices on his dead child-bride. I had no time to bother with him. "Magic has brought me back. And I've come for only one thing. I'll keep you from killing another innocent person. Give me the key to the jail where Amzil is held. Give me the key, and we'll both vanish from your life. You'll never have to think about us again. You can forget all about us."

His hand betrayed him. It darted toward his coat pocket, as if to protect the hidden keys from me. Then he caught himself and suddenly quiet seemed to flow over him. "No," he said softly. "No. You aren't real. This is another dream, isn't it? Another nightmare." He pointed an accusing finger at me. "The doctor said the tonic was supposed to stop these nightmares." He seemed to expect I would vanish.

"It's not a dream. I'm real." I thudded my fist against my chest. "But I'm not here to hurt anyone. All I want is the key. Why not give it to me? Why not let it all be over?"

His eyes darted around the room. I wondered if he'd even heard my words. Was he looking for escape? A weapon? If he shouted for the Sergeant, he'd probably be heard. I didn't want to deal with both of them at once. I turned abruptly and headed toward the door. He probably thought I was leaving; instead I stopped, bolted it, and then spun back to him. He hadn't moved. But his eyes got larger.

I kept my voice calm as I moved slowly toward him. "Thayer, all I want is the keys to the jail. That's all. No one else needs to know anything else about this. You can burn those letters. You can remember Carsina as she was, sweet and pretty and very in love with you. Forget the ugly lies you've grown in your mind. Go back to being the man you were."

He shook his head. Tears filled his eyes and some spilled. His voice had gone squeaky. "Someone has to be punished for this. You both made a fool of me. Someone has to pay." He looked at me and suddenly the whites showed all around his eyes. There was no rationality there. "You came back as a Speck. You were seen. You killed all those men, all my men. You made them pay with their lives for what I had done. And now you've come back to kill me."

"I don't want to kill you," I lied. "Just the keys, Thayer. That's all I want from you." I took a slow step toward him. He retreated from me, as smoothly as if he were my dance partner, moving toward the hearth rather than his hanging sword. Good. Again I advanced and he retreated.

"Someone has to be punished. Someone has to pay." He repeated the words like a prayer. He held up both hands, palms out toward me. "Did you know I'm to be flogged tomorrow? I ordered that. I'm not afraid. I know I deserve no less. Doesn't that satisfy you?"

"No. It doesn't." I couldn't conceal my disgust with the idea. "And you shouldn't do it. Flogging yourself and then hanging an innocent woman will not change anything. They're a coward's way out of admitting the wrong you did. If you want to be a man, stand up and admit what you did. Clear my name for me. Give me back my life."

For an instant, it all seemed that simple. Here was a man who could clear me, one who could reconvene a military court and clear my name. There had never been any real evidence against me. Heads were cooler now. Hope for redemption glimmered before me. He shattered it.

"No."

"Why not?" He had retreated another step. I didn't advance. I waited for an answer.

"Because . . . because everyone would laugh at me. Everyone would know how you both deceived me and cuckolded me. Everyone would know what a fool I'd been! And you—" He pointed a sudden accusing finger at me. "You killed that whore. Everyone knows it. You did wrong, and wrong must be punished. I must be punished!" He all but shouted the words and I flinched. I didn't want the Sergeant to hear an outcry and try the door.

"No, Thayer." I said it quietly. My hopes for a sane resolution died. The man had no sanity in him. Now all that mattered was freeing Amzil and getting her safely away. Abruptly, I was aware of time passing. Surely the Sergeant would soon expect the Captain to appear and dismiss him from his duties for the night. Time to put an end to this charade. I took a breath, steadied myself, and edged closer to him. I tried to keep my voice reasonable while my heart pumped hatred for the man. "You don't need to be punished. No one needs to be punished any more than they have been. You were a man drilled hollow with grief. You weren't yourself that night, when you said and did those things. And you didn't do what you think you did. You didn't kill me. You see me, don't you? I'm right here. You don't need to be punished. And I think you know that Amzil killed that fellow in self-defense, of herself and her children. She doesn't deserve to hang for it." I spoke quietly, calmingly, easing closer to him as I did so. I wanted to leap on him and throttle him, but even more than that, I reminded myself, I wanted to get the keys from him and get to Amzil's cell without him raising any sort of an alarm.

"Oh, no. She deserves to be punished, too. She's a whore. She can deny it, but she's a whore. She . . . it was her fault. I went out there once, to Dead Town. She said she wasn't a whore, but she was. She was." He was nodding to himself now. My mind was trying to take in what he had just said. My head spun with what he had just admitted. No wonder Amzil had hated him so. As if either she or I had needed more reason.

He pointed an accusing finger at me. "She was a whore. And you were a murderer. And my wife was a *slut!*" His voice rose to a near shout on the last word. Then he dropped to a hoarse whisper as he retreated toward the fireplace. "And you all made me do bad things. And all of us have to be punished now!"

"You're insane!" I said. I tried to draw my saber from its scabbard. The notched old blade hung up on the tattered leather. I jerked at it, and the scabbarded weapon came loose from the worn belt. And then he spun, snatched up the fireplace poker from its rack, and rushed at me with it raised over his head. I tried to block the descending poker, but only succeeded in softening the blow. It hit me on the collarbone, and I muffled my cry of pain. Must not alarm the Sergeant outside. The descending poker rolled off my shoulder and down. I caught hold of the end of it as it passed and rammed the handle of it into the center of Thayer's chest. He gasped with pain and his eyes bulged. I dropped my useless weapon and grappled with him. Foolishly he chose to hang on to the poker. I hugged him tight, not giving him enough room to swing it again.

His teeth were bared like an animal's and there was no human intelligence in his eyes. He snapped at my face. I jerked my head back and then slammed it forward, crashing my forehead into his. I saw stars and he managed to get another short flailing swing in with his poker. It hit my hip. I was taller than he was. Hugging him, I managed to lift him off the floor and then threw my weight against him. We slammed to the uncarpeted floor together, and I was sure we made quite a loud thud. I had to finish this quickly before the Sergeant came in. I grabbed the man by his collar, sat up on top of him, and slammed the back of his head, hard, against the edge of the hearth. For an instant, his eyes unfocused. Then his hands darted to my throat. I tucked my head down tight to my shoulders, and while he struggled for a grip, I bashed his head against the stones again.

The third time, his head smacked wetly when it hit the masonry. Suddenly he was boneless, limp beneath me. His eyeballs jiggled in their sockets. I felt queasy, but forced myself to keep my grip on his collar. I would not be tricked. His head turned to one side. He made a peculiar sound. His eyes were open, his mouth lax.

I was shaking as I climbed off him and stood up. Blood was spreading slowly from under his head. Was he dead? Had I killed him? I didn't care. I dropped hastily to one knee and rifled his pockets. The ring of keys, heavy brass ones, were exactly where I thought they would be. I took them.

I wanted to flee. I knew I must not. I stood, caught my breath, smoothed my hair, and recovered my hat from the floor. I straightened my jacket. Then I stepped to the desk. I gathered up all the love letters I'd written to Carsina, and my sister's two letters to her. I picked up my enlistment papers, and the vicious little note my father had sent. I refused to read it. I glanced in the desk drawer where he'd kept them. A medicinal smell rose from it.

There were no more papers in the drawer, only two empty bottles, a half-full one, and a large sticky spoon. Gettys Tonic. I took the letters to the fire and dropped them in, one at a time, stirring them with the poker until I was sure that every page was burning well. Then I carefully put the poker back in its stand.

I glanced at the Captain. He hadn't moved. As I stared at him, his chest lifted slightly. Still alive, then. I recovered my useless saber, shoved it fully into its sheath, wedged it inside my sword belt, and hoped it would pass a cursory inspection. Soundlessly I walked to the door and unlocked it. Then I moved back to Thayer's side. His eyes had sagged shut. I took a deep breath and dropped to my knees beside him.

"Oh, no! What's wrong! Captain Thayer, what's wrong, what's wrong!" I raised my voice even louder. "Sergeant! Sergeant, come quickly! Something terrible has happened."

No one came. I sprang up, went to the door, and jerked it open. The Sergeant was just coming back in from outside. He gave me a guilty look. He smelled of strong, cheap tobacco. I flapped my hands and babbled at him. "He said he didn't feel well. Then he gave a sort of a twitch, and his mouth started working. And he fell to the floor and started jerking! Sergeant, I've been calling you and calling you! The Captain has had some sort of fit! He's fallen and struck his head. He won't speak to me!"

As the man rushed past me to look in on his fallen commander, I shouted, "I'll get a doctor. Don't leave him alone! He might choke. Which way is the infirmary?"

"Down the street to your right! Hurry, man!" he shouted over his shoulder.

I ran out of the building, slamming the door behind me, and turned left, toward the jail. The street was mostly dark. Light leaked from some windows, and lanterns burned outside the entry to a barracks. I ran in and out of that pool of light as soundlessly as I could, wondering if my wild tale had been foolish or bought myself more time. The Sergeant would stay with the Captain for some time, assuming help was coming soon. When no one arrived, eventually he would go to the door and shout for help or perhaps run for the doctor himself. This time of night, most likely the doctor would have to be roused from his bed. It would be some time before anyone had leisure to wonder what had become of the Captain's late-night visitor. I reached the jail. I paused and caught my breath. My imagination peopled every shadow in the dimly lit street with crouched figures. Nonsense. Focus on the real danger. There would be two of them. Some element of surprise would help. I stood in the dark, calming my breathing and trying to create a story for why I was there with the keys. I couldn't think of one and time was trickling away from me.

I went silently down the stone steps. This door would open onto the cell level. My hands shook as I felt for the keyhole in the dark. There were four keys. The third one turned the mechanism with a sharp "clack." I froze, listening. Nothing. No. A voice, muffled by distance or a closed door, inside the building. A man's voice. I opened the door, eased through, and shut it behind me. I was in a stone-flagged hallway, one I remembered too well. A single lantern burned on a hook, yielding dim illumination. The cell doors that opened off it were staggered. Each had a small barred window at eye level, and a slot for a meal tray at the bottom. I went past the cell that had been mine without looking inside it. She wouldn't be here. Spink had said she was in a "punishment" cell, one without a window.

I passed six cells and came to a second door. It, too, was locked. Luck gave me the correct key the first time. I turned it in the lock, then I pressed my ear to the door. The man's voice was louder, a droning monotone. There was no window in the door. Stronger light spilled in a puddle from under it. I took a breath, unsheathed my sword, and opened the door.

Another hall, this one lit by a succession of lanterns on wall hooks.

At the end of that hall, a door was ajar. Light and the man's voice were spilling out of it. I listened a moment. Was he singing? No, reciting something, over and over. I moved stealthily closer. I was halfway down the hallway before I recognized it.

It was the same night prayer my mother had taught me. The man was repeating it over and over in a horrid, breathless way that spoke of fear beyond measure. It made the hair stand up on the back of my neck. Swift and silent as a plains cat, I padded down the hall and then peered around the edge of the door.

It took me a few moments to make sense of what I saw there. There was a small guardroom with a table and two chairs, and beyond it, a locked door. One guard sat at the table, his head slumped forward on his chest. The other sat stiffly in his chair, laced up to attention. He was the one speaking, saying his hopeless, helpless little prayer over and over. Every surface in the room, the walls, the floor, the tabletop, the guards themselves were netted over with pale white root. The only parts of the room innocent of the spreading filaments were the iron hinges and reinforcements of the door. As I watched, a network of rhizomes worked its way up over the slumped guard, as if spinning him a shroud of white lace. It sank into him as it worked, tattooing his clothing to his flesh as it dug into him as ivy digs into a stone wall. He was definitely dead.

But the other guard was as emphatically alive. His arms were bound to his sides with roots and his legs were clenched tight together with them. I wondered how they could have both been overcome so quickly and so thoroughly, and then didn't want to know if the roots could truly grow that fast. The man looking at me gave a sudden squeal and then said, "Oh, god, oh, god, oh, god!" In horror, I watched as the roots began to thread themselves into his ears. He squealed again, and then abruptly the noise stopped. The guard suddenly spoke in a very calm voice. "He says he does what you should have done before you left the town that night. And she says, she says, she says she wants all of you, she always wanted all of you, that she wept when the old god stole parts of you away. Come to the tree outside, she says, and she will gently take you in."

He spoke conversationally, in such a rational voice that I answered him the same way. "I don't want to come to you, Lisana. I want Amzil. And as much of my own life as is left to me."

The man did not speak again. He made a gargling sound and then shook his head back and forth in a sudden, vigorous negative. His mouth opened, and a wet wad of bloody root spilled from it to cascade down his chest.

And from the other side of the locked door, I heard a woman give a muffled scream.

"Amzil!" I cried, but I doubt that she heard me. In the instant of silence that followed my horrified shout, I heard a small voice behind me.

"Mummy?" Kara asked in a terrified whisper. I whirled. She stood behind me, staring in horror at the root-wrapped men. She wore only a short white nightshirt, and she was barefoot. Where had she come from?

"Get back!" I bellowed at her. "Don't let the roots touch you, Kara. Get back!" I swung my gaze back to the small room. "Get out of my way, Lisana. I don't want to hurt you, but I'm coming through!" I touched my bared sword to the stone floor. I pushed it into the room, and the tiny tender roots that webbed the floor parted and writhed back from the deadly touch of the iron. A stouter one resisted, but then parted with a snap and curled back on itself. Panting fear, I trod the narrow path my blade created. The small room seemed to stretch a mile. I reached the door and had to free my right hand to try a key. It didn't work.

"Mummy? Is she in there?"

I glanced back. Kara had returned to the doorway. I silently cursed whatever moron had let the child escape supervision. Why had she come? How had she gotten here? But there was no time to even think of that. The rootlets were webbing across the floor behind me, obscuring my path, and creeping out the door of the chamber toward the child. "Kara, get back!" I roared at her. "Stay away from this room! I'll bring your mum to you, but you must stay back!"

She gave a wail of fear and anger at my angry response. She retreated, but I feared it was only a few steps. I turned away from her and shoved the second key in the lock. It fit, but would not turn. Something tugged at my boot. I looked down to see roots creeping across the leather toe. I could feel the tiny invasions as it thrust little anchors into my boots. I ripped my boots free of it, stamped my feet angrily, and then tried the third key. It wouldn't go in. Neither would the fourth. I didn't have the key! And on the other side of the door, I could hear Amzil wailing. "I'm coming.

Amzil, I'm here, I'm coming!" I shouted through the thick wood at her, but could not tell if she heard me.

I slashed again at the creeping roots, and the smaller ones fell away as before. But some of the webbing was thicker and stronger now and it did not yield. I started through the keys again in desperation. As before, only the second one would fit the lock. I shoved and rattled it and then, inspired, pulled the key out a tiny bit and turned it again. It gave. I pulled the iron lock free of the hasp and furiously threw it on the floor behind me. It landed on the roots and they retreated from it as if I'd thrown a hot cup of water on thin ice.

I pulled at the handle of the door, but it did not budge. The roots that had flowed across the edges of the wooden planks held it fast. I screamed in fury and slashed at them with the blade. Behind me I heard Kara's voice again. "Nevare, will they kill her? Are the strings eating her?"

"Get back!" I roared at her again, and with a mighty wrench, I tore the door open.

The revealed chamber was no bigger than a cabinet, forcing the occupant to choose between standing and crouching, and it reeked of old urine and fear. Amzil screamed as the door opened. She was pressed into the corner of the tiny chamber, dancing to keep her feet free of the questing roots. Tiny wounds on her legs were bleeding and the little white roots wriggled happily as the drops of blood fell on them.

"To me!" I roared at her, as if I were rallying my troops for a charge. "Amzil! To me!"

I do not think she recognized me, but she leapt, first to my arms and then swarming up to my shoulders. She was making terrible little panting cries that changed to a shriek of horror when we both heard a little voice crying, "Mummy! Mummy, help me! Nevare, help, help!"

I tried to turn. I could not. My feet were laced to the floor and I roared in fury as the little roots penetrated the leather and bit into my flesh. I pivoted and saw little Kara, shrieking at a root that had wrapped her thin, bare leg. The pallid white tendril suddenly flushed pink. "Save her!" I yelled at Amzil, and tore the woman I loved from my back to hurl her across the small chamber. She landed on the writhing mat of roots, yelped in fear, and levitated like a cat on a hot stove. She did not appear to touch the ground as she flew across the room and out of the door to Kara. I dragged at my feet but my boots were held firm. I felt the roots as little white worms that burrowed into my flesh. I slashed at them but I had stood still too long. The roots had grown thicker. The iron scored but did not part them.

"Kara! Kara!" Amzil cried. She was dragging at her daughter, but the root only wrapped around her leg more tightly, biting into the child's meager flesh.

"Cut her free!" I roared and threw her the saber. I saw her catch it by the blade and cry out as it cut her fingers, but then she turned it, seized the hilt, and flailed at the greedy root that gripped her child as if she were whipping the floor with the blade. In my mind, I heard an exclamation of pain as the root parted.

And then I heard Soldier's Boy, speaking very clearly inside me. "She wants you. I've no idea why. I think I am better off without you. But Lisana wants you to be part of us, and so she shall have you. Come to us, Nevare."

"No!" I said, and somewhere a woman's voice echoed that word in dismay. But my own utterance had no strength. The little roots that had penetrated my boots were worming into my feet, drawing off my blood and my will. Would it be so bad? I'd be one again, whole, and with a woman I loved, a woman who loved me. We'd live a very long time. Wasn't that what I had wanted? I would have peace.

"It will all be all right," Lisana's voice said quietly. A soft lethargy had begun to creep through me. "The child will take the woman to where she must go. They'll flee together. And you'll come back to me. It will be an end to all that has divided you, an end to living a false life. You'll be where you belong. Where you have always belonged."

I lifted my eyes to Amzil. She stood half a dozen steps from the door, Kara in her arms, the sword in her hand. "Run!" she shouted at me. "Pull your feet out of your boots and run!"

"I can't. It has me." I found I could smile. "You go, Amzil. Find a better life. Kara knows where the horse and cart are. Epiny loaded it for you. Flee. Don't stop in Dead Town. They'll look for you there. Get well away from town and then hide in the forest. It's not as dangerous now! Go!"

"No!" she screamed at me. She slashed at the roots crawling toward her, and they fell back, but that was no help to me. Shrieking in frustration, she snatched up her child and ran. I watched them go, heard the slap of her feet down the stone-flagged hall and felt the little roots in my feet dig deeper. It was done. I'd salvaged what I could from my old life and now it was time to let it go. I resolved not to scream.

But an instant later, scream I did as flames engulfed the room. Amzil sent a second lantern crashing to the floor to follow the first. That one broke, the oil splashing my boots and trouser legs. The hungry flames leapt up to follow the splattered oil. "Now run, you great idiot!" Amzil yelled at me. She came into the room, through the flames, whipping the saber's blade against the floor. Roots scorched and writhed and I heard Soldier's Boy shout angrily.

Ignoring flames and wriggling roots, Amzil clashed the blade again and again on the floor, working in a circle around me and literally chopping me free of the roots that gripped me. As she worked, she kicked at roots that squirmed and crawled toward her own lightly shod feet. I lifted my feet and like a chained dog strained against the final tethers that held me. Soldier's Boy's angry roar in my mind was abruptly silenced as a wild slice of the blade severed the last root. The oil-fed flames were licking up the walls and leaping at Amzil's skirts. The burning carpet of roots made a choking smoke. Kara had come back to the door. "Come out of there!" she shrieked at us, and hurled another lantern into the flames. As it shattered, the fire roared and leapt higher. I snatched Amzil up and held her above the flames. We fled. The hall before us was dark, lit only by the dancing flames behind us. As I passed Kara, I tried to grab her by the arm. The child was faster. She swarmed up me like a little monkey and clung to her mother. I scarcely felt her added weight as I ran down the hall.

Fire fears no magic, I thought. I glanced back once. Smoke was roiling toward us. The timbers of the ceiling were starting to kindle. I opened the door, ducked through it with my burdens, and then closed it quickly behind me. We were outside now, but still mostly concealed in the stairwell that led to the lower cells. Amzil slid from my arms to stand on her own. Kara was weeping, her shoulders shaking in terror. "Hush now," I had to tell her. "We must go quietly."

The streets of Gettys seemed unnaturally dark to our fire-dazzled eyes. The door to the headquarters building was ajar and light spilled from it. We crept from the stairwell. Amzil started to go down the alley. I seized her hand and led her in the other direction. I did not want to pass the tree. We walked quickly, quietly, and turned off the main street as soon as we could. "We'll have to make our way to a gate from here," I told them. "And we'll have to go quietly and unseen."

Kara suddenly ceased her muffled sobbing. In a thick little voice, she said, "The east gate. That's where I sneaked in. He goes behind his sentry box to drink. Everyone knows that. He smells like Gettys Tonic."

The child was right.

Once we were outside the walls of the fort, we limped through the deserted streets of Gettys Town. My feet were in agony and Amzil's little better. I wanted to carry Kara, but Amzil would not let go of her daughter. As we turned toward the cottage on the outskirts of town where the other children and the cart awaited us, I asked Amzil quietly, "When did you recognize me?"

"Kara was calling you by name. But I think I knew it was you when you threw me across the room and then flung a sword at me."

"Why?"

"It was the look in your eyes. I don't know how you can be here, or even how you can be Nevare. But I'm glad."

I knew it would be a foolish time to try and kiss her, and wasn't sure how she would react if I'd tried to embrace her in front of her daughter. So we walked a while in silence before she suddenly exclaimed in annoyance. "Must I do everything?" she demanded of the night, and then seized my hand so that I had to turn to face her. She pushed in close against my chest and I held them, mother and daughter. I kissed the top of Amzil's bent head.

She smelled of lamp oil and smoke. It was a heady fragrance. She turned her face up to mine. I bent to kiss her.

Kara squirmed between us. "We have to hurry," she told us. "We have to get Sem and Dia from that mean woman."

"What mean woman?" I demanded, suddenly afraid.

"While the missus was there, she was nice. And she wasn't mean until Dia started crying and wouldn't stop and that made her baby wake up. She scolded Dia and Sem told her to leave our little sister alone. And then she called Sem a whore's son and said about . . . said about Mummy deserving what she'd get, that she was going to hang tomorrow and was in jail tonight and we'd be orphans and that if the missus had half a thought in her brainless head, she'd turn us out into the streets."

"That bitch," Amzil said with great feeling.

"Yes," agreed Kara. "So that was when I knew I had to come back for you. And I took Sem aside and told him to obey her, so I could creep out after dark. And I told him to get Dia and our things into the cart after I left. I told him to keep Dia quiet, and to move the cart farther from that woman's house."

"He's too small," I protested, but Kara calmly replied, "You'd be surprised what Sem can do when he wants to do it. He's very determined. And he's helped the missus harness the horse to the cart before."

She was right. When we reached the cottage, all the lights were out. All seemed peaceful there. If the woman knew her charges had escaped, she did not care. Kara confidently led us past the cottage, and just beyond a shambles of a barn, Sem sat on the seat of the cart, holding the reins. Little Dia was sound asleep in the bed of the wagon. Kara and Amzil wearily climbed into the back of it and joined her. I mounted the seat and sat down behind Sem. "Let's go," I told the boy.

"You want to drive?" he asked me, offering up the reins.

"Only if you think you can't handle it," I told him.

He slapped the reins on the nag's back and we rattled off into the night.

CHAPTER THIRTY-FOUR

RETROSPECTION

Sem drove until his head was nodding over the reins. When I took them from his hands, he started slightly. Then he clambered into the back of the cart and fell asleep next to his mother. Despite an uncertain road and our wobbly wheel, I drove on until dawn and beyond. As the light crept across the sky behind me, I glanced back often, fearing pursuit. By noon, when we had seen no one, I began to hope. I stopped only twice that day, to water the horse. We shared some bread as we rattled along but I insisted that we push on until it was too dark to negotiate the rutted road.

We spoke little, Amzil and I. There seemed too much to say, and most of it was not what we'd want to discuss before the children. I was pleased when she climbed up to sit on the cart seat beside me, and even more pleased when she timidly put her hand on my arm. I glanced over at her.

"I loved you the way you were," she said quietly. She still had a smudge of smoke down the side of her cheek.

I had to grin. "Well, I hope the change hasn't put you off."

She laughed. "No. But—there's so much I don't understand. I know, from what the missus—Epiny—told me that this must be, well, the way you used to be. And she's told me about the magic and all. But still—"

"I am going to tell you everything," I promised her. "Every bit of it."

Then we drove on in silence. I winced as I imagined explaining Olikea and Likari to her. Then, even though my heart sank with dread, I resolved that she would have the full truth. She'd either accept and forgive what I had done, with the understanding that Soldier's Boy had motivated much of it, or she wouldn't. But from now on, I wasn't going to live with pretense of any kind.

As we drove, Kara told the other children a highly colored tale of her adventure and how she had rescued Amzil and me. Sem mocked her; they squabbled; Amzil scolded them and then gave them some cold biscuits to keep them occupied. After that, the children gabbled to one another, and then argued over who would sit where. Amzil matter-of-factly tore up her apron to bandage Kara's leg and her own legs. Kara drove for a time when Amzil insisted on bandaging my feet as well. I'd been afraid to take the boots off to see how much damage there was. When I did, I felt queasy and it was all I could do to clench my teeth and only groan as Amzil loathingly drew the limp little pink roots out of my feet. Kara watched in horrified fascination, all the while telling Sem, "See, I told you so. You didn't believe me about that string monster, did you, but see, it stuck strings right into Nevare's feet."

"Mr. Bur," Amzil corrected her daughter and, "Burvelle, actually," I told Amzil.

She gave me a questioning look. "I'm not going to hide who I am from them," I told her.

She looked down at the rag that was the remnant of her apron. She folded it carefully. "I'm not sure if I know who you really are."

I laughed. "Neither am I. But I think we'll have plenty of time to find out."

The first night we stopped, I drove the cart carefully off the road and behind a thicket. That evening Sem and I hunted with my sling, but not successfully, for my feet were exceedingly painful. It was just as well we didn't get anything. We'd have had to eat it raw, for we didn't dare light a fire. We ate a small, cold meal and then bedded the children down in the back of the cart. The older two fell asleep almost instantly, but little Dia wailed at the dark open sky overhead and the strangeness of it all. As I listened to her thin, woeful voice rising to the distant stars, I almost wanted to join in. Amzil walked her, pacing slowly around the cart, humming, until finally exhaustion won and Dia slept. She tucked Dia in between her brother and sister and then came to stand beside me. She hugged herself in the darkness and asked me the same question I'd been pondering most of the day. "Now what do we do? Where do we go?"

"Far away from Gettys," I said, striving to sound optimistic and certain. "To a new life." Very gently I took her in my arms. She turned her face up to mine and I finally kissed her as I'd always longed to, a slow, sweet kiss with her body fitted against my own. She deepened the kiss, and I felt as if we were spinning at the center of something wonderful and deep, something I'd never truly known before this moment. Then she took her mouth from mine and leaned her head against my chest.

"Amzil," I said, thinking I needed no other words.

But she spoke. "You've saved me. More than once. You've a right to me now, I suppose. But Nevare—" She hesitated, and that pause was ice down my back. "Nevare, I've changed since the Lieutenant and Missus Epiny took me in. I can't just get by in this life. You may not think so, after what you've seen of me, but my mother raised me to be what she was, a respectable woman. Not nobility, like you, no, nothing so grand. But respectable." Her voice was narrowing, squeezed by tears. "And that's how I want to raise my daughter. I want Kara to see herself as a woman that deserves, well, deserves to be married to the man she beds. Deserves his respect." She lifted her hand between us to rub the tears from her face. "However foolish that might seem to you." Her voice went lower, inviting me to share the bitter joke. "A murderess and a whore wanting to make her daughter think she's a respectable woman."

I took a deep and difficult breath. "We're starting a new life, Amzil. I think we should do our best to start it right." With a groan, I released her. "I want you, very badly. But I will not claim that from you as if it were a debt you had to pay. Nor do I want you to come to me unaware of who I am. I know that I love you. But you need to know who I am. It will not be easy for me to wait. But I will." I leaned forward and kissed her cheek. "And we *are* still fleeing for our lives. Tonight, we must get what sleep we can."

Although I slept little that night, my dreams were the sweetest they had ever been. And before the dawn, I rousted everyone out for another long day's travel.

On the second evening that we camped, we settled for the night in a brushy hollow away from the road's edge. Amzil wanted to boil some water and wash out our injuries, but I was not certain of the wisdom of starting a fire. "If they were looking for us, they'd have found us by now," she said irritably. "Men on horseback could have overtaken us easily. My feet hurt, and I know yours must. What good does it do us to flee if an infection kills us anyway? If they were going to catch us, they would have by now."

"It depends on how bad the fire was," I countered. "They may at first assume that you perished there. And then, when they start tearing down the charred ruins, discover that we didn't. And send a patrol to hunt us down."

She gave an impatient sigh. "We took the horse and cart. My children are not in town. Anyone who wants to know, knows that we left town. If they wanted us, they'd have us. I think fire is more important than stealth right now."

She won, but I gathered the very driest wood and kindling that I could find for her, and insisted that we keep the fire small and smokeless. Yet I was grateful when she boiled water for tea as well. There is something about a hot drink that can put heart back into a man. Just as I began to relax, a slight sound turned my head. An immense croaker bird settled heavily into a nearby tree. I stared at it, waiting, but the ugly thing only whetted its beak on a branch and looked down at us. Amzil and the children paid it no mind. Sem was begging his mother to make hearth cakes like she used to cook, and Amzil was considering our supplies to see if it were possible. I sat and stared at the bird of ill omen. I thought of Spink's words and, like him, longed to return to a life in which a bird was always only a bird.

"Good evening, Nevare."

I turned my head slowly. I'd already recognized the voice. Tiber had come up on us as quietly as a stalking panther. He stood at the edge of our camp, looking at us. Kara gave a little shriek when he spoke. Amzil froze where she was, with the pot just lifted off the fire so that she could pour more water on the tea leaves.

"Good evening, Tiber," I said in resignation.

I think he realized that Amzil was more of a threat than I was. "Evening, ma'am," he said with a respectful nod to her. He smiled disarmingly and asked, "Could I beg a cup of that tea from you? It smells very welcoming."

Amzil looked at me. I nodded slowly. Tiber approached our small fire carefully, like a stray cat moving into unfamiliar territory. He smiled at me, nodded to the children, and then hunkered down to accept the cup of tea that Amzil gingerly offered him. He seemed disinclined to speak immediately but I could not stand the suspense. I asked him directly, "What brings you out this way?"

He smiled. "Well, you know, Nevare. I'm a scout. I'm scouting."

"For what?" I knew scouts had various duties, usually defined by whom the commander was. Buel Hitch had been sent on errands to fetch smoked fish, but also to keep a watch on how many Specks were in the area and to watch for signs of highwaymen working the road. Most often, scouts kept in touch with the indigenous populations and acted as liaison with them. Buel had spoken to me of such duties. It was likely that when he'd died, Tiber had inherited them.

"Well, you'd mentioned you'd been attacked and robbed, so I thought I would ride this stretch of road and see what I could see. I'm pleased to tell you I've found no signs of robbers or thieves.

Whoever attacked you must be long gone. But that's not my only errand."

He blew on his hot mug of tea. I waited. "Gettys is in a bit of a stir. The commander is in the infirmary. The doctor says he probably had some sort of a seizure. His mind hasn't been clear since then. No one was surprised. He's seemed a bit erratic the last few months. Poor fellow's on bed rest now, and Captain Gorling has stepped up to command." He took a sip of tea and nodded to himself. "I like him. He's not as excitable as Thayer, except when his wife gets to him. He leads the men instead of driving them. The men seem relieved. The very same night the Captain fell ill, we had a bit of a fire in the old jail. Burned through some beams, and the whole building collapsed into the cells below." He glanced at me and away, glanced up at the croaker bird and then came back to me.

"But how about you?" he asked sociably. "I thought you were going to stay around Gettys for a while. I even dropped by Lieutenant Kester's house, same night we had all that excitement. I thought I'd visit and see if you might want to hear about being a scout for the regiment. We're short on scouts right now. In fact, there's only one. Me. We lost one of our best scouts last summer in the plague." He paused and looked at me carefully over the rim of his cup as he drank more tea. I said nothing.

"Fellow name of Buel Hitch," Tiber went on. "He was before your time at the Academy. You wouldn't have known him there. He was 'invited to leave' when I was just a first year, for pretty much the same reasons I was invited to go be a scout, somewhere else. The man couldn't tolerate bullies. Hitch wasn't meant to be a standard-issue officer, but he was a man's man when things got tough. Knew who his friends were. He saved me from a couple of bad mistakes when I first got to Gettys. And stories! The fellow could tell stories all day, craziest tales you ever heard, mostly about the Specks and their magic. He'd make them seem real. Too bad he's gone now. I think you'd have liked him. I know he'd have liked you."

The children had fallen silent. Dia and Kara both crept closer to their mother. Amzil put her arms around them. Sem was in the wagon, unobtrusively looking for something. When he stood up, my sling dangled from his hand and he was breathing carefully through his open mouth.

I was still and silent, the mouse frozen by the watchful cat's stare. Tiber drank off the last of his tea and set the mug down with a regretful sigh. "Well, folks, I have to be on my way. Thanks for a pleasant pause, but I've got a job to do. You watch out for those highwaymen, Burvelle. Oh, and I should warn you. When I left town, there was a rumor about some escaped criminal. Said to be dangerous. I'm supposed to be looking for her right now."

"Really?" I managed to say.

"Really." He stood up slowly. "So far, not a sign of her. But you be careful." He lifted his arms over his head, stretched, and then said, "Oh, pardon me, ma'am. Sometimes a scout just gets used to doing things his own way so much that he forgets how people expect him to behave. But that's what Hitch said he liked best about this duty. Making his own decisions." He swung his gaze slowly to Sem. "You a good shot with that thing? There's a place, just down the hill from here, where it opens out into a little meadow. Bet you could get a nice summer rabbit there. But use a smaller rock than the one you've got there. That's big enough to knock a man cold." He smiled at the boy in a friendly way, and Sem returned him a sickly grin. I thought to myself that Buel had taught Tiber well. Tiber gave the boy a slow wink and then turned to me. "Well, you take care, Nevare. Nice little family you got here."

"Thank you," I said reflexively.

"Good evening, ma'am," he said to Amzil, and doffed his hat briefly, a courtesy that surprised her. He turned and walked away as softly as he had come. Uphill of us, I heard his horse give a soft nicker. Just before he vanished into the surrounding brush, he turned back. "Funny thing, Nevare!" he called back. "I still can't stand a bully." Then he turned and walked away.

We stared after him for a time in silence. Sem hopped down off the wagon and came toward me, sling in one hand, stone in the other. "I thought—" he began quietly.

"I know. I'm glad you didn't."

"Oh, thank the good god you didn't," Amzil said fervently.

In the bush, the croaker bird suddenly rattled all its pinions. I stared at him. He cawed raucously and then cocked his head at me. "I think that balances nicely," he said. In a smirking voice he added, "And it was interesting to be the good god for a change. Farewell, Nevare." He lifted his wings wide, launched awkwardly, caught himself, and then ponderously flapped his way to a higher altitude. He circled overhead once and then flew east.

"Save your stone, Sem," Amzil advised her son. "That's a carrion bird. We don't eat them."

"He was out of my range anyway. What an ugly bird."

I'd been the only one to hear his words.

That was the last time a god ever spoke to me. And I haven't felt the touch of the magic since then. But being freed of the unnatural didn't mean that life became suddenly easy for us. In fact, the next month was very hard. The weather stayed mild, but food was short and the journey uncomfortable. When we went through Dead Town, it was late in the evening. Not a light showed anywhere. Amzil was very quiet for a time. Dia didn't seem to recognize the place. As we went past the collapse of their old cabin, Kara asked quietly, "Is this where we're going?"

"No," Amzil replied. "Anywhere but here."

And we did not stop.

I lost count of how many ways I found to keep the cart from falling apart. As time went by and we left Gettys farther and farther behind, we began to stop earlier in the evening. Sem and I hunted meat for the pot or caught fish in the river when we came to it. We did not eat well, but we didn't starve. I told Amzil my tale, in bits, as we sat by the fire in the evenings after the children were asleep. Much of it was not easy for her to hear. But she listened and she accepted it as truth. Then she told me her own tale and it was enlightening to me to hear of the young seamstress who had married the daring and handsome thief. She'd never liked her husband's trade, but he was what his father had been before him, just as the good god decreed. And they had been happy there, in their own way, in

Old Thares before the city guard caught him one night. And I felt a bit ashamed that it was hard for me to hear of her happy times. But I listened and accepted that that was who she had been.

We married in a small town named Darth. The priest was a young one who had vowed himself to a year of wandering and service. We wed in the courtyard of an inn. Amzil wore wildflowers in her hair. The proprietor of the inn was a widower and a romantic who spread a wedding meal for us and offered us two free rooms. His daughter sang for us and all the inn patrons enjoyed the festivities and wished us well. They backed up their good wishes with a wedding basket full of coins, two chickens, and a kitten. Kara observed that we now had everything we could possibly need.

And much later that night, as I was dozing with Amzil in my arms, she asked me softly, "Is this how you imagined your wedding night?"

I thought of the protracted torture of Rosse's wedding, the endless preparations and fuss, and said, "No. This is much better. This has been perfect."

And that, we both felt, truly began our lives together. We left the town as an established household, with Kara holding the kitten in her lap and the two tethered chickens clucking to themselves in one corner of the cart's bed. We went north, and without quite knowing how we decided it, ended up in a very small town named Thicket, not far from the citadel at Mendy. Unlike Gettys, Thicket's population had settled there willingly, attracted by gentle land and rich soil. The small farms looked prosperous. Thicket had lost some population to the gold rush to the Midlands, but most of the well-established folk had stayed.

The town was actually glad to see a new family arrive. Amzil quickly found work as a seamstress, and worked longer hours and brought in more money than I did. A local stockman who raised cattle to supply Mendy with meat and leather was glad to let me exchange labor for rent on a cottage. In the evenings, Sem and I walked to a nearby creek to hunt or fish. As often as not, we took Dia with us, for while Kara was old enough to help her mother with the simpler sewing, Dia was still a thread-tangler.

At night, when our candles were too dim a light for good workmanship with her needle, Amzil and I sat near our hearth and talked. In many ways, we scarcely knew each other, but I never doubted our compatibility. I played simple games with the children and tried to continue the education that Epiny had begun with them. Sem did not like his letters, but quickly saw the use of numbers. Kara read and did her sums but spent most of her time learning embroidery stitches from her mother. Beyond those basics, I told them stories from the history of Gernia, and the boy loved those, especially the ones about famous battles, the bloodier the better. The night that he rose from listening to tales to go off to bed and exclaimed, "When I am old enough, I shall be a soldier, and win fame and fortune on the battlefield," my heart suddenly smote me.

"Well, what do you expect?" Amzil asked me later as we prepared for bed. "When it is the only sort of story you tell him? You make it sound so exciting that I'll be surprised if Dia and Kara don't try to enlist as well." She said the words with humor, but I suddenly perceived a lack in my life. The tales I told the boy were the ones I had best loved when I was that age. Buel Hitch had perhaps been wrong. Soldiering might have been the only future that was ever offered to me, but that did not mean that it had not been my dream as well.

I lay awake that night after Amzil slept and considered my life. We were thriving. If Amzil continued to have as much work, we'd soon have enough saved to find a little place of our own, and then I could start to really build something. I lacked for nothing. I had a woman who loved me for who I was, and three fine children. Sem was as smart as a whip, Kara would soon be as skillful with a needle as her mother was, and Dia was everyone's sweet little despot. What more could I ask for that the good god had not already given me?

And yet, I was not as content as I should have been. There was an empty spot inside me, and I wondered at nights if it were because Soldier's Boy had taken some essential part of me or because of some shallowness in myself. I threw myself more earnestly into my work, repairing and improving the little house we rented until even the landlord commented that it didn't look like the same place.

Several times Amzil reminded me that I had promised to write to Epiny. There was no mail or courier service out of Thicket, and I had neither pen nor ink, I would remind her. But one day close to the end of summer, she abruptly declared that I had procrastinated long enough and that it was cruel of me to leave my cousin and my sister wondering what had become of us. Besides, she wished to see a larger town, and there were things she needed that the small store in Thicket didn't carry. So we loaded the children into the repaired cart, hitched up our nag, and made the trek to Mendy.

Mendy was a serious citadel, three times the size of Gettys. A prosperous little town surrounded it, a place of straight streets and tidy buildings with a bustling population. I found a letter-writer's stall without difficulty, and bought paper and ink and pen from the proprietor. I composed letters to both Epiny and Yaril, begging forgiveness both for the delay and for the brevity with which I updated them. I also asked each to write to the other with my news, in case either of my posts went astray. I paid the substantial post fee for each letter, and made sure that the owner of the shop knew I'd be returning in a month to check for a reply. "Likely it will come faster than that, young man. We've got a good service now between here and Franner's Bend, and they send out regular deliveries from there," he assured me.

That business tended to, I went to meet my family. Amzil had told me she would be visiting a large dry-goods store that we had seen, and there I found her, Dia in her arms, driving a hard bargain with the harried man behind the counter. She was buying fabric and notions, as well as a number of minor household goods we'd been unable to obtain in Thicket.

When she noticed me watching, it seemed to give her more energy for the bargaining, and shortly after that, she'd reduced the poor man to compliance. That finished, she collected Kara, who was lovingly surveying a display of sugarplums, and declared she was ready to go.

"Where's Sem?" I asked her.

"Oh, he saw the sentries changing, and nothing would do but he had to stand and gawk at them. No doubt he's still there."

I took the heavy basket she carried on one arm and she claimed the other. Dia filled her other arm and Kara trailed after us as we walked to the cart. "Do you know, there are only two dressmakers in this town, and one is so expensive that only the wives of the officers can afford her services?" Amzil told me in a hushed voice. "I visited the other's shop, and while he sews a fine seam, he doesn't really have an eye for how he puts his dresses together at all. Fancy a yellow dress, with red cuffs and collar! And that's what he had in the window. Nevare, if we saved a bit more and moved here, and if Kara practiced her embroidery stitches a bit more, we could do quite well here. Quite well indeed."

I scarcely heard her. A mounted troop of cavalla came up the street behind us, returning to the citadel from some mission. I turned to watch them come. The men had weathered faces, and their uniforms were dusty, but they rode as cavalla should, and their proud horses, however weary they might be, held up their heads and trotted in ranks as they came. Their colors floated over them, a small banner held aloft only by the wind of their passage. I watched them pass, a boy's imagined future come to life. A young lieutenant led them, and just behind him came his sergeant, a husky man with long drooping moustaches and a permanent squint. At the end of their line, with them and yet apart, came a scout. With a lurch of my heart, I recognized him. More than a decade of years had been added to his face since I'd seen him stand up for himself and his daughter at Franner's Bend. As he passed, he glanced my way. I suppose I was staring, for he gave me a nod and touched his hat to Amzil before he rode past, following the troops. I felt as if hooks dragged at my heart as I watched them go by. There, but for strange luck and stranger fortune, went I.

"Look at Sem," Amzil said softly. I followed her gaze to the boy who stood, awestruck, by the side of the road. His face shone as he looked up at the passing troops and his mouth was ajar. I saw the last rank of horsemen grinning at the small boy's worship.

The trooper closest to him snapped him a salute as he passed and Sem gave a wiggle of joy. "He looks just like you," Amzil added, startling me from my reverie.

"Who? That trooper?"

"No. Sem. Staring with his heart in his eyes." She gave a small sigh. "You'll have to temper the tales you tell him, Nevare. Or somehow make him understand that only a soldier's son can become a soldier."

"That's not always true," I replied, thinking of Sergeant Duril. "One of the best soldiers I ever knew was really the son of a cobbler."

"You're the son of a soldier," Amzil said quietly.

"And now I'm a hired hand for a cattleman," I said without rancor.

"But you shouldn't be," she said.

I made a sound of dismissal and gave a shrug. Her grip tightened on my arm as we walked. "Do you think I never heard Epiny and Spink talk about you, and how much you dreamed of a career? They often spoke of what it would be like if you could come back, clear your name, and serve alongside Spink. I don't think they could imagine you doing anything else except being a cavalla officer."

"That's gone," I said.

"Why? Why couldn't you enlist here? Use your real name; you've never signed up with it before. I don't think you'd be a common soldier for long. You might not be an officer, at first, but even if you never rose to the rank you were born to, you'd still be what you'd dreamed of being."

"Amzil—"

"Don't you think I know how important that is?"

"I'll think about it," I said quietly. And truthfully, for I knew I could not help but think about it. We collected Sem and headed back to Thicket. The ride home was quiet, the children asleep in the cart bed while I was caught in my own thoughts.

Two nights later, at dinner, Amzil abruptly asked me, "What holds you back from doing it?"

"Fear," I said shortly.

We both noticed the children listening to us, and let the conversation die. But later that night, as we nestled together, Amzil asked without preamble, "Fear of what?"

I sighed. "When my father first disowned me, he was very angry. And very thorough. He sent out letters to the commanders of various forts, letting them know he had taken his name away from me."

"You still managed to enlist at Gettys."

"Oh, yes. He left me that, telling them that if they could give me any sort of a life as an enlisted soldier, he would countenance that. Even so, I had to use a different name. He'd forbidden me his." I sighed again. "Amzil, I don't want to go back to living under that shadow. I don't want to enlist as someone's failed, disowned son."

She was quiet for so long that I thought she had fallen asleep. Then she said, "You're already living as someone's failed, disowned son." She softened the words by putting her arms around me. "You should stop doing that," she said quietly. And then she kissed me, and for a time I failed at nothing.

When the month had passed, I returned to Mendy to see if I had any replies to my letters. Amzil rode along, tight-lipped and fairly quivering with excitement. In her lap, she carried two paper-wrapped dresses she had sewn. She intended to show them to the dressmakers in Mendy, to see if one of them might take her into his shop as an assistant. Kara and Sem each clutched two precious pennies they might spend. Dia held hers in a tiny cloth bag Kara had sewn for her. I left them to their errands and went to the letter-writer's shop.

He charged me threepence for holding my post for me, and I thought it an outrageous sum until he reached under his counter and brought out the stack of envelopes he had carefully tied up with string. "You're a popular man," he observed, and I dazedly agreed with him. I left his shop. Across the street, there was an open-air booth where a man was selling sweet tea and brown cakes. Feeling guiltily self-indulgent, I handed over one of Amzil's hard-earned coins for a cup of tea and a cake with raisins in it. Then, my courage bolstered, I went through my stack of post.

There were five fat envelopes from Epiny and two from Yaril. One of the ones from Yaril had been sent from Old Thares.

I felt a strange sense of trepidation as I turned them over in my hands. Did I want to open these things, open the door and admit the Nevare I'd been? For a moment, I considered tearing them up and tossing them to the wind. I could walk away from that Nevare just as I'd walked away from Soldier's Boy. Amzil and I had begun something new together. Did I want to risk unsettling that? Then I decided that I already had, when I'd sent my first two letters. I sighed, carefully arranged my post by the date it had been sent, and opened the first one.

It was from Epiny, and she went on for seven closely written pages about how she had worried about me, and the conditions of chaos at Gettys on the night that we had fled and in the days since then. Tiber had indeed called on them that evening, and made her so nervous that she had scarcely been able to eat a bite of the meal she prepared. As the scout had told me, the fort was now under the command of Captain Gorling and had returned to a modicum of military stability. She and Spink were delighted to hear that Amzil and I were safe and doing well. They missed the children dreadfully, and was I keeping up with lessons for Kara and Sem? She went on for two pages about what I should be teaching them before saying she'd had several delightful letters from my sister, who had tremendously enjoyed her visit to Old Thares and was getting along famously with Epiny's mother and sister. She closed with an admonition that I should write back immediately to let her know how we were doing, and in detail. I smiled and set it aside.

The second letter was from Yaril. She first assaulted me for leaving her in ignorance so long, and then begged me to forgive her for responding with such a short note. She was packing to go to Old Thares with Aunt Daraleen and Cousin Purissa. Uncle Sefert would be staying on at Widevale for an extended visit. He seemed to feel his presence could help his brother and that the holdings there needed a man in charge for a time, with all the new developments going on due to the gold discovery. (She trusted that Cousin Epiny had informed me of those and she wouldn't bore me with the dull details.) Father did seem much better when Uncle Sefert was with him. Uncle Sefert suspected he had suffered a stroke that had affected his mind, but hoped that company, the conversation of his brother, and a gentle resumption of a complete life might restore him. Uncle Sefert had commended her for choosing Sergeant Duril as her overseer and promised to keep him in that capacity. Oh, and Uncle Sefert said he would be writing to me very soon, and Sergeant Duril was overjoyed to hear of my survival and Aunt Daraleen sent her very best wishes to me as well. And that was all she had time to write as she was to leave for Old Thares on the morrow and wasn't half packed yet, and she wanted to take a goodly selection of her frocks, even if Aunt Daraleen thought them a bit provincial and wanted her to buy all new ones as soon as she reached Old Thares.

I both smiled and frowned to hear Yaril sound so giddy and girlish again. I had left her with heavy responsibilities. Belatedly I thought we should have brought our uncle into our difficulties months ago. I was glad that Yaril could have some time free of worries and that my father was in good care.

With a smile, I opened Epiny's next letter. She missed me. Spink missed me. They both missed the children horribly. Solina missed Kara. Why had not I written back yet? Was all well? Gettys was in a state of flux again. It looked as if they would all be shifted back to Franner's Bend to rejoin the rest of the regiment. She did not bother to tell me which regiment would be coming in to replace them. Instead, she was bubbling with the idea that Spink was very likely going to become a captain much sooner than they had expected. After several delays, the new rules of male succession had been approved by the Council of Lords and sanctioned by the priesthood of the good god. For a change, a church decision made sense to her. Now younger sons could be legitimately moved up to be heirs, for if the good god did know all, then he undoubtedly knew which heir sons would die young and had, in his wisdom, decreed that noble soldier sons could also serve as heirs. It would not affect Spink, of course, for which they were both grateful. He loved his elder brother far too much to wish to take his place. But it had affected a number of the officers in the regiment, and some of the older officers would be leaving the military to go home and assume the duty of being heirs. Spink had told her it greatly increased the chance that he would be promoted when the regiment was reunited, and oh, wasn't the prospect of Franner's Bend exciting? She'd be able to visit Yaril from time to time and get to know her properly. She, too, scolded me for not writing back more quickly.

The next letter was from Yaril. She wrote that she had hoped to hear from me by now. Her next sentence apologized for what was undoubtedly going to seem to me like a transgression on my dignity. She assured me that Aunt Daraleen had first come up with the idea, and that she and Purissa had merely gone along with it. At first it had seemed to Yaril no more than a prank, but she hoped that I would agree that the ends justified the means.

Aunt Daraleen had become a medium, and was currently the Queen's favorite mystic advisor. The spirit of a Speck wisewoman spoke through Daraleen, telling the Queen many great secrets of their spirit world, and revealing to the Queen why the King's Road had failed. Through Lady Burvelle, the secrets of the Speck ancestor trees were revealed to the Queen, as well as the spiritually enlightening properties of certain herbs and mushrooms and rich dishes. The Speck wisewoman revealed to the Queen the epic love story of how she had fallen in love with a noble soldier son, seduced him from his duty, and endeavored to have him join her forever in tree love.

My ears burned red as I realized how much of my private life Yaril had become privy to, and that my sexual escapades with Olikea and Lisana were Daraleen's fodder with which to titillate the Queen and her court ladies. No one at court knew the true identity of the "dashing young soldier," but that was small consolation to me. Yaril and Purissa greatly enjoyed their supporting roles as they tended to the moaning and twitching Lady Burvelle when she fell into her trances. Aunt Daraleen had hired an ambitious and very handsome young man as her secretary. He attended on her daily, writing up her revelations as chapbooks. Each was published, chapter by lurid chapter. The printers could scarcely keep up with the demand. I could read between the lines that my uncle was horrified and humiliated by his wife's dramatics, yet Daraleen finally had everything she had longed for. She was the Queen's favorite and a woman of great power now in Old Thares. Not only was it likely that Purissa would become engaged to the Crown Prince, but that Yaril might choose whomever she wished for a husband from among both old and new nobility.

I worked my way hastily through the remaining letters. Epiny had heard of her mother's charlatanism and was both horrified at her antics and pleased that the King's Road would progress no farther and that the sacred trees were now under the Queen's own protection. Every other sentence seemed to be an apology to me that the secrets I'd entrusted to her and Spink were now the stuff of popular literature. Over and over, she assured me that the identity of the "mysterious young nobleman" was safe, and that there would be no tarnish on the Burvelle name.

Yet her letter was laced with good news as well. The Queen had proclaimed that all kaembra trees were sacred. No more would ever be cut. The Queen herself was planning to visit the "holy grove of the mystical ancients" the next summer, to see if she and her "medium" could not make direct contact with the natural spirits of the great trees. I shuddered. How gullible could the woman be? Yet at the same time, the Queen seemed very shrewd to me, for she had also decreed that to protect the Specks and their otherworldly wisdom, the Crown would now monopolize the tobacco and fur trade with the Specks and that traders who wished to deal with them must purchase a license.

I slid the last letter back into its envelope and leaned back in my chair. I contemplated the busy little town around me. A man hawking fresh bread passed me with his musical cant. A courier galloped past him and pulled his horse up sharply in front of the letter-writer's shop, sending a plume of dust drifting. A wagon laden with a cage of squawking chickens went by in the other direction. So much life in motion, so many minor occurrences and coincidences, all intersecting in a strange and wonderful web.

I bundled my letters and stared down the dusty street, thinking that the trees of the Specks were now safe. I wondered if this was what the magic had intended all along. Had I trodden that harsh road, tripping from circumstance to coincidence to near death to serve this very end? My words had gone from my aunt's prying eyes to the Queen's ear. Lisana's tree would not fall. She and Soldier's Boy would know a tree's life of time together. I had given a rock to an annoying boy, and triggered a gold rush and the burgeoning fortune of my family.

And here I sat, the conduit for vast changes in the world, and what did I have to show for it? I smiled sourly at the vagaries of fortune, and then gave myself a shake. Why, I had it all. My freedom. A woman who loved me. A home of my own making. I stood and stretched. Across the street, the letter-writer came out of his storefront and pointed at me. His eyes were very wide. The dusty courier said something to him and he nodded vigorously. Then he led the courier across the street to me. As I stood up, the letter-writer bowed to me. "An important man, I should have said. I should have known. Yes, sir, this is him, Lord Nevare Burvelle. I can vouch for him. I've received many posts for him."

The courier gave me an insouciant grin, as unimpressed as most couriers seemed to be with their missions. "Pleased to meet you, sir. I've a packet for you, one to be delivered directly into your hands." With a bow, he offered me a large fat envelope made of calfskin. It had been laced shut, and the tied laces were secured with a large blob of hard red wax. I looked at the sigil pressed into it. A spond tree. It had been so long since I had looked upon my family crest that I felt a strange rush of emotion. Whatever was within this packet, it came from my father. The world rocked around me.

"Sir? Sir?" I looked up, vaguely surprised to see the courier was still standing there. I felt as if a week had passed. "Sir, I was told that there might be a reply."

"Not . . . not immediately," I told him weakly.

He nodded, satisfied. "That's as well. My beast and I could use a day or two of rest and food. When you want to find us, he'll know where we are, and waiting solely upon your commission." He tipped his head toward the letter-writer and grinned again. He turned his back on me and sauntered away to where his horse waited. At a glance from me, the letter-writer retreated and I was left alone with my packet.

The label had been addressed in what looked like my uncle's hand. I instantly feared the worst; my father had died, and this was my notification. It took some little time before I had the courage to break the hard wax and unlace the cords. The calfskin unfolded, revealing a stack of papers. On the top was a thick ivory sheet of my father's stationery. In a shaky hand, he had written in overly large letters, "Son. Please come home." The signature at the bottom of the message was unintelligible. I lifted the page and stared at it for a long time before I could set it aside.

Beneath it, again on my father's stationery, was a letter dated less than ten days ago. "*My dear nephew Nevare,*" the letter began in my uncle Sefert's firm, clear strokes.

> *Please forgive me that it has taken me so long to communicate with you. I have delayed the sending of this letter until I was certain, both of the situation here and of your own circumstances.*
>
> *Before Yaril departed for Old Thares, she confided much to me. I have also been the reluctant and unwilling receiver of a great deal of information from your journal, via my prying wife's tattling tongue. I must apologize to you again for her breach of what I regarded as a sacred confidence. And I fear I must also rebuke you, for not taking me into your confidence long ago. As strange as your experience has been and as harsh as your father's treatment of you was, did it never occur to you to present the matter to me, especially since it seems so tangled with my own daughter's life? But we will save that discussion for another time, for a late evening with good tobacco and old brandy, when all of us will find it much easier to forgive the others' transgressions.*
>
> *I have been very concerned with my brother's health and state of mind. You must know that your father's health is failing him. As his elder brother, I find it painful to see the younger sibling that I expected to outlive me in such a state of decline. I have had three doctors in to see him, but they have offered me little hope. My own treatments of him with Bitter Springs water showed some promise, until his most recent stroke three days ago. My lad, I fear that he will never be the man he was and that soon he will no longer be capable of running his own affairs. Your Sergeant Duril has proven*

to be very capable as an overseer, but you cannot leave the family fortunes in the hands of a hired man and your young sister for too long. So, it is time you ended your wild adventure and came home. Not only your family duty demands this of you, but also the laws of your king.

By now, I am sure you will have heard of the recent rulings on the uniformity of succession by birth order, a clarification by the priests of the good god's scriptures about the foresight of the good god. I am also sure you must realize your new position. You are expected, of course, to serve as your father's soldier son during his lifetime, but you are also expected to stand ready to assume your duties as his heir son upon his death or whenever he becomes incapable of managing his own affairs. I fear that that hour may soon be upon you. As the closest male offspring in our family's line of descent, you in time will also inherit my title and estates. But not for some time yet, your fond uncle is selfish enough to hope. I will also tell you plainly that when that time comes, I hope you will find it in your heart to provide well for your aunt. As difficult a woman as she has sometimes been, she is still the mother of my children and I would wish her respected as such.

In that regard, both Epiny and Yaril have informed me that there is a woman in your life. When I dared to ask if she was of good family and capable of being a loyal wife to you, I received a sermon from Epiny, several pages long, about the right of a man or woman to choose a lifelong mate without regard to such silly things as parental approval. I suppose I must be content that your choice has met with your cousin's discerning approval. According to Epiny, you have chosen well indeed and I will look forward to meeting this illustrious person who apparently can meet any need of yours that Epiny can foresee you ever having.

Enclosed you will find sufficient letters of credit and cash for you and your family to make the journey back to us. Epiny has insisted to me that it is only right that a commission be purchased for you, and has made a very strong case for you to join Spink's regiment, pointing out that as it is currently stationed at Franner's Bend, you could frequently be at home and near your father. Your father has expressed to me his fond hopes that you will, instead,

*wish to serve your king under the standard of his old regiment. And
I have indulged myself by writing to Epiny a three-page sermon in
which I have waxed eloquent about the right of a young man to
choose the regiment that he wishes to join.*

*As you can see, we have much to discuss. I will look forward to
receiving your response via the courier I have dispatched to Mendy.*

With great fondness,

Your uncle,

Lord Sefert Burvelle of the West

I sat for some time in stunned silence. I looked into the
packet and found, as my uncle had promised, a letter of credit for
a substantial amount, and beneath it, cash carefully packaged in an
oilcloth bundle. I hefted it in my hand without opening it. I did
not need to. I knew it contained more money than I'd ever held
in my life. With shaking hands, I returned it to the calfskin folder.
I put the letters back in as well, in the exact order they'd arrived,
as if I were carefully restoring a grave I'd disturbed. My heart had
begun to thunder in my ears. It was only when I tried to lace
the packet shut again and could not that I realized how badly my
hands were trembling.

I checked my pockets to see if I had enough coins to buy a
second cup of tea. Barely, and for a moment I chided myself for
being a spendthrift. Then I laughed aloud, called the serving girl
over and asked her to bring me another cup of tea. I glanced up to
see Amzil and the children trudging down the street toward me.
I hastily amended the order, telling her to bring a pot of tea and
half a dozen of the brown rolls with raisins.

Amzil swept up to me in a flurry of skirts and chattering children. Her smile was brimming with good news. She plopped Dia
into my lap, and as she sat down, she said with satisfaction, "Our
troubles are over. He was very impressed with my work, and said
I could start as an assistant at his shop within the week! At twice
the rate I've been making in Thicket! Now tell me, Nevare, could
there be better news than that?"

"Perhaps there could, my dear," I told her. "Just perhaps."